Climates of Our Birth

Stuart James Whitley

A Novel

Climates of Our Birth

Watson & Dwyer Publishing • Winnipeg

Printed in Canada by Hignell Printing Ltd.

Published with the generous assistance of the Canada Council and the Manitoba Arts Council.

Canadian Cataloguing in Publication Data

Whitley, Stuart James, 1947-

Climates of our birth

ISBN 0-920486-76-2

1. Red River Settlement - Fiction. I. Title

PS8595.H47C5 1994   C813'.54   C94-920057-3
PR9199.3.W44C5 1994

*For Christie, as this book is
'mixed with thy spirit',
to borrow Byron's splendid idiom*

But that which keepeth us apart is not
Distance, nor depth of wave, nor space of earth,
But the distraction of a various lot,
As various as the climates of our birth.

Lord Byron, (1819)
"Stanzas to the Po"

One

i

On the outskirts of the village of Rackwick on the island of Hoy, steep sandstone cliffs thrust like a hermit's fist against the relentless surge of the grey North Atlantic. Their grassy, treeless summit is usually shrouded in fog; 'witch's breath', the locals call it, for the Orkney Islands are a cold and wet archipelago, without the cheer of much sunshine. Now and then, after testing the limits of human patience, the weather lifts, and a magnificent view is possible far out to sea toward the shadow that is the northern coast of Scotland. On such a day, one might track the progress of the inter-island packet, which plied regularly during good weather between Stromness and Thurso, the rugged Scottish fishing port on the edge of the Pentland Firth.

Few ships call at the exposed and dangerous port in Rackwick, for the shoreline is palisaded with steep red reefs, one of which, known as the 'old man of Hoy', towers four hundred and fifty feet above the churning water. There is a rugged beauty to these coastal cliffs which arrests the eye. There is, too, a forbidding mood to the landscape and its inhospitable reaches. The islands and their ramparted sandstone outriders huddle against the convergence of the Atlantic, Norwegian and North seas. The waters are seldom calm, and sometimes fierce storms cut off shipping not only from the Scottish mainland, but from the fifty-six austere outcrops themselves. The effect of near-constant gale-force winds on the islands' topography is harsh; animals and men huddle in the lee of their stone shelters—some of which have been continuously occupied for more than four thousand years. Yet, when the sun shines and the winds are fair, the sullen side to the islands' temperament seems very far away.

It was to these cliff tops on a bright spring day in early May, 1836, that Ephraim Blude brought Victoria Towrie in his father's pony cart.

Ephraim's father supplemented his meagre crofter's existence by the extraction of reddle in a pit at the rear of his property. This red-coloured substance, no more than simple iron oxide suspended in clay, occurred by some geographic anomaly in this tiny quarry which the Blude family had worked for several generations. Many of the villagers believed that the family name was evoked from their persistently red-stained hands, marked as if with blood. In truth, however, more than the hands of father and sons were tinted with the dye, for clothing, household and field implements were discoloured with it. The substance was used chiefly for the marking of sheep which were in great numbers in these latitudes; and it was required by carpenters and shipwrights for use in chalklines. Though this industry generated a small additional income, the Blude family was not much better off than their neighbours, in that their ramshackle holding was easily the poorest on Hoy.

Almost eighteen, Ephraim anxiously contemplated his prospects. Unlike his four brothers, he was not resigned to the life of poverty and hard labour that his father and most of those about had known. His resentment fuelled his desire to get off the island, to escape the drudgery of his existence and the unending routine. Above all, he hated the red dust which permeated his person and possessions, and even now stained the hem of Victoria's dress, as she clung grimly to the lurching cart. Still, he knew he was not without assets. He was taller than most of the compact, powerfully built Orcadians. He was handsome, possessed of clear blue eyes and a thick thatch of copper-coloured hair, borne to him of some distant Norwegian ancestor—for Norway had occupied these islands between 865 and 1468. Years of heavy toil were reflected in a lean, well-muscled figure which as yet showed none of the ruin which continuous exertion had registered upon his father. He knew from the ragged piece of mirror he kept in the tumble-down hut by the quarry that he had a pleasing appearance. He monitored it carefully.

Ephraim had not gone unnoticed by the local maids; a fact not lost to him. In spite of the ridicule inspired by the family's red-stained clothing and hands, girls were intensely drawn by his brooding good looks. They would fall in love with his dreams of escape from the island and beautiful life in faraway lands. He found the conquest of such women contemptibly easy. In their arms, his rough clothing and blemished hands were of no consequence; he was a dreamer, and dreams permit even beggars to fly. The power of dreams can lift the thoughts of others, and on such wings he carried the hearts of young women, and stole their virtue along the way. But like most dreamers, Ephraim never saw the foreground. He believed his appeal lay only in his physical presence, and he was determined to exploit that quality as a means to immediate fulfillment. It was this attraction for the fairer sex which his neighbours resented, for the reddleman's family was a butt of popular jest, as indeed was their family before them.

Ephraim glanced at Victoria. Of the girls he had known, she had held out the longest against his importunings. Distant and aloof, she was by that reason alone intriguing, but she was physically bewitching as well. Even in her poor clothes she had a radiance which set her apart from the others. She had fair skin, and light-blue, wide-set eyes. Her nose was aquiline, somewhat overlarge, and her lips were always parted, as if she were about to speak. A mannerism which drew him to her was the way in which she toyed with an errant lock of gossamer blonde hair over her temple, when she was concentrating. The overall effect of this woman was magical, he thought. He was captivated by her, and he sought union with her with urgent but as yet unfulfilled insistence.

He did not heed the inner strength this woman seemed to possess; he took it merely to be a stubborn, frustrating desire to hold onto her maidenhood. He was determined, however, not to be trapped by any crofter's daughter, as so many lads of his acquaintance had been. He was so wary, that in the act of pleasuring he would withdraw at the moment before climax, to anguished cries of frustration and disappointment from his partners. He would lay his seed when the proper time came and not be snared into taking a wife before it suited him to choose. His father had been foolish enough to sire him by a woman whose pleasuring obscured the obvious fact that she was a tyrant in all matters, not merely those of the bed.

Nevertheless, for all his caution, Ephraim Blude had become entranced to the point of obsession with Victoria Towrie. She not only shared his dreams, she added colour and dimension to them. Unlike him, she loved reading almost to the exclusion of all else. The Romantic poets were her favourite reading; the passages which thrilled her, she copied out in a tight, well-formed hand. She was enthralled by their extreme assertion of self, their intensity, their imagination. Byron and Keats were particularly fascinating, for their lives were even more stirring than their writing. She read to Ephraim often, even though he did not comprehend all the words. But poetry has the capacity to speak directly to the heart, and above else Ephraim was a man of passion. The words and cadence were stirring. It thrilled him; more, it aroused him to listen to her voice exult in language so mysterious and grand:

> *Bold Lover, never, never canst thou kiss,*
> *Though winning near the goal—yet, do not grieve;*
> *She cannot fade, though thou hast not thy bliss,*
> *For ever wilt thou love, and she be fair!*

Books gave Victoria a vantage point, a secret hiding place from which to view the passing world. She thought of herself as a watcher at the wall; no, more appropriately a gatekeeper, for she was very careful about whom she permitted inside. Victoria read all manner of texts and in consequence knew much about distant places. Ephraim eagerly wove these threads into his lofty schemes for the future, and she saw herself very much a part of those plans. Even as they shared the intimacy of dreams, however, his relationship with her was one of utility and his need for union with her was no more than that.

Once at the crest, the cliff tops ramble on in terrace, outcrop and scree, dropping suddenly and precipitously to the seas below. As the narrow trail levelled off, Victoria sat forward, watching: 'After this mound…here,' she said, pointing a slender white finger. Ephraim steered the shaggy little pony off to the side in the lee of an immense shelving of sandstone. Close in behind, accessible only on foot, there was a broad shelf, open to the sea, carpeted with heather and bracken and the wild tufted grasses native to this archipelago. Twenty paces or so away was the sudden, unbroken drop to the ocean floor, more than three hundred and fifty feet below. In fluttering cries, nesting birds attended to their newly hatched offspring. The salt air carried up from the neap-tide beach was a tonic to the lungs. All around, gorse bushes were bursting into fragrant yellow blooms, an impudent contrast to the frail scattered crocus. This protected space in the sun was Victoria's private place; it had been a refuge from the world since she was a little girl.

There are places defined by memory and circumstance to which the heart is always drawn: this was such a place for Victoria. On clear days, she came up here to read and think, and to watch the ships as they sailed to exotic ports of call. It was more than an hour's walk from town, but she felt safe here; it was hers. She had never let anyone enter before Ephraim.

Ephraim leapt from the trap, and lifted Victoria down. He felt the warmth of her waist, and her loose breasts swung against the upper sides of his palms. He brought her to him, and kissed her eagerly. She pulled away after a moment and laughed, her eyes crinkling. She took the bundle she had been holding in her lap and sat down on the heather near the rock face. Unwrapping the bunting with spare, efficient movements, she spread it out before her. There were slabs of thick brown bread and slices of yellow, sweating cheese. With her, and cradled more gently than a gathering of fresh eggs, was a bundle of her treasured poetry, copied down on cheap, heavy paper, and wrapped in a length of faded ribbon.

Ephraim hobbled the pony, and lifted a costrel of ale down from the cart. Walking back to the hidden place, he squatted down awkwardly beside Victoria, his face brushing her hair as he did so. He felt as if he were experiencing desire for the first time, so keen was his longing for her. But she seemed utterly unaware as she busied herself portioning the victuals she had brought. Bemused, he watched this small pageantry. There was a vast difference between the economies of table-setting as practised by his mother, and the feminine ritual being played out before him. She lightly slapped his hand away from the cheese slices in mock admonition for his impatience. They laughed together, the sound ringing like the pealing of small bells carried on the breeze from a secret place of worship.

They ate and drank and looked out over the firth. She recited bits of verse as the moment suited her: 'Behold,' she said, 'redd'ning Phoebus lifts his golden fire! The birds in vain their amorous descent join!' Ephraim smiled; the words were stimulating, and his admiration for her grew. He had never met anyone who could quote written works from memory, let alone use the passages in appropriate circumstances. He would love to have such a faculty, he thought, but a woman had more time for the learning of it, and a man was more suited to the listening. He settled back comfortably, and listened to her musical voice drift over him, palpable as a kiss.

It was one of those rare days in the Orkneys—still cool, but clear and sunny. Here in the shelter of the sandstone bluff the reflected glory of the sun made them warm to the point of discomfort. Ephraim drew off his stuff shirt and, leaning back on one elbow, looked out to sea. The island packet, a fore 'n aft coaster, was hull down on the horizon; it prompted him to speak again of life beyond the rim of their present world. The reverie those thoughts inspired filled him with well-being, enhanced by the ale, the warmth, the privacy of this place, and the closeness of Victoria Towrie, surely the most desirable woman God had seen fit to put on these islands. He stretched his head back and sighed inwardly, aroused.

He studied her covertly. She was lying close to him, eyes almost closed, lips slightly drawn over her teeth in that familiar gesture of imminent speech. She had loosened her bodice, and from where he lay, he could see her breasts rising and falling with each slow breath. The claw in his guts clenched to the point where it made him feel almost sick, and he rolled to her side, drawing his knee up, and her skirts with it. She felt his hands roam over her, and she was distantly reminded of her father. Again she felt her body's resistance. 'Don't hurt me,' she said in a small voice.

He kissed her deeply and she yielded wetly to him, opening her mouth. He could taste the ale on her tongue, and a groan of urgency passed from him into her throat. He took her hands, and guided them firmly beneath his breeches. She gasped as her hands closed about him; the thickness and the hardness of him startled her. Though she was yielding to this intoxication, her inexperience in such things compelled her to speak. 'Oh, what shall I do with you?'

'Put me somewhere warm,' he muttered through clenched teeth, and they began to move together, clothing urgently pulled aside. She winced at a sudden, fleeting, pricking sensation, then opened her eyes widely at this new fervency she was experiencing, the fullness of him, the need to lift herself to meet his thrusting. She reached both hands to touch his face as his arms stiffened, and his slack expression betrayed his abandonment.

'Yes,' she said simply, as he surged above her.

His thin cry of completion was lost among the shrieks and calls of the gulls and petrels as they wheeled and soared above the cliffs, oblivious to the timeless ritual below.

ii

Victoria knew something was seriously wrong with her. Her monthly blood had not come, and now this: before the sun was up, she was vomiting in spasms into the tin chamber pot under her bed. She was grateful that her retching had not wakened her mother, for she was a bitter and maundering old woman. Her father was long dead. The son of a fisherman, he had lost his own father to one of the many sudden North Atlantic gales. Six years old, he had been staying at a cousin's house, and they had lain awake listening to the men in the other room talk about the horror of discovering the body of a drowned man, or what was left of it after the crabs and other scavengers had been at it. They had alternated between grim chortles, superstitious beliefs, and fearful reminders of their own mortality. He promised himself then that he would never set foot in a boat for any reason, and true to his fear, he lived on a poor holding near the edge of the village for forty-seven years. He had gone out one evening to bring the family's only cow in from a sudden fierce storm which had buffeted even some of the flagstones from the roof of their house. The beast stood between simple poverty and abject ruin, and this slim margin was worth venturing out for even on such a foul night. The cow was tethered in a pasture as steep as the pitch on a doryman's roof, and as the tempest increased in fury, both man and cow were blown off the cliffs to the roiling blackness below.

When she had been told of it, Victoria became hysterical with laughter. It struck her as hilarious that her father and the cow had been blown away. Her mother had wanted Victoria to fetch the beast; at six years of age, it was her responsibility. But the gusts were so strong that Victoria could not walk upright. No child was abroad that afternoon. Though her father hated to go out at dusk, he elected to go over his wife's objections. When Victoria laughed nervously at the ludicrous image, her mother beat her without mercy in front of the men who had found the remains of the cow and a single glove in the knotted tether. The compounded humiliation was too much for Mrs Towrie, and she laid into Victoria with a vengeance which had its roots in her late husband's cowardice and abuse. The men dragged her off Victoria, but their relationship for the following years was civil, and only that. Her mother's anger toward her husband was undiminishing over time, assigning blame even for the fact of his own death. Why did he persist, when the weather was so bad? Why did he leave us destitute and alone? How could he have been so selfish and stupid?

What was the profit as against loss of life, her mother would keen over and over again. Victoria silently disagreed, thinking that all risk had to do with the belief in oneself, and that one might just as well be capsized at sea, as be waylaid in pursuit of a cow. In either case the gain was to be considered only; fear of loss could only paralyze the will. Her father's death had condemned them to the most meagre existence, with much hard work and little to show. Her life was centered about the small pig sty upon which the family fortunes depended, and the books she devoured when the teacher allowed her to stay late after school. Her circumstances kept her from making friends easily, for she was vaguely ashamed of the fact that she had no father, that she was a keeper of swine, and that she was so very poor. She also suspected that others knew about her, that her relationship with her father was whispered about, and made the subject of reproachful gossip.

Victoria retreated into herself, creating a rich world in her imagination. She felt one day she would leave the island, and live the life she believed she was created for, if only the opportunity presented itself. She was surprised and pleased when Ephraim began to pay attention to her, but for some time put him off, believing him not to be seriously interested. Unlike the other young men of the village who had taken notice of her comeliness, he was not to be deterred by her shy ways or her many excuses to avoid him. Slowly, he had won her trust and her affection with small bunches of wild flowers, or a pretty shell from one of the tidal pools, or even on one occasion, a tiny rabbit he had trapped up at the quarry. Its fur was almost entirely crimson from the reddle on his hands, and her red rabbit became for the moment a symbol of magical possibilities. When he gently placed it in her hands, his own closed around hers, and she saw the longing in his eyes.

By the middle of June, Victoria could not bear the feel of rough cloth against her nipples. Her breasts were heavy, and she knew past all denial that she was with child. She considered that a life with Ephraim Blude would not be unwelcome, though it meant in all probability that her life would not change much. Some of the girls she knew ended up needing to get married in a hurry. That fate wasn't so much a matter for worry as the distant restlessness she had come to see in him. They had lain together four times since that first encounter, and had seen each other almost every day; though for the better part of this past month, Ephraim had been hard at work between the quarry and weeding his small crop, and was too tired at day's end, he said, to see her. More, she realized that not once had he said anything of his feelings for her. She knew well enough of his reputation as fickle, even scornful of those he had bedded. Nevertheless, she decided to tell him of her condition before tongues got to wagging. She could not visit shame upon her mother's household in addition to her other burdens.

Her nausea having passed, she drew on a coarse woollen shawl against the rain, and set off for the Blude house. She hoped to catch him before he left for the fields. Day was just beginning to show in the lightening of the grey eastern sky. The rainfall, light but steady, did not let up for the hour she had walked. She tramped along the muddy, rutted roadway, each sodden step slapping forlornly. A sense of foreboding invaded her, chilling her as surely as the rivulets of water which had penetrated her thick shawl, and had begun to trickle down her back and chest. She quickened her pace.

With not more than a mile to go to the Blude dwelling, she noticed a horse-drawn cart appear in the distance, moving toward her. The driver was in a hurry; she could see the plumes of spray as the two wheels bounced over the puddled roadway. As it drew closer, Victoria realized with relief mixed with anxiety that it was Ephraim. He stood up in the trap and, leaning back, reined in the pony. The cart clattered and splashed to a stop beside her. She looked up, bedraggled in her soaking shawl clutched at the throat, and he, still standing, looked down at her with surprise openly showing on his face. She had never come to him at his dwelling before.

'Well, what in the name of merciful Jesus are you doing here—in this weather, at this hour?'

'I must see you,' she began, 'I have news...' she trailed off, not knowing how to deal with the subject. She had been turning over in her mind the various introductions she might employ, but his sudden appearance had thrown her off, and her thinking now was uncertain. This was not the best of circumstances to be discussing such an important matter. He seemed to be impatient, and his expression was distant—a look she had seen several times before.

'News!' he expostulated. 'News! Listen to this, will you; this very hour, the new steamboat—the *Sovereign*—will put into Rackwick on its way to Stromness. On board is a recruiting agent for the Hudson's Bay Company. He's looking to sign up strong young men for inland service. This is the wilds of North America I'm talking about!' His excitement distorted his speech in exaggerated tones. 'There's a bonus of twenty shillings, six pence for signing up and free passage to Hudson's Bay. Can you imagine the pure adventure of it? It's been close to two years since recruiters have been here with such a generous offer!'

'To tell it truthfully now, I've been thinking about this for quite a long time.' He was breathless; his eyes gleamed as she saw his dreams assume a shape he could take hold of. 'This place is west of the Canadas—far west—and there's some places that have never even been seen by a white man!' His voice was shrill as he broke into a loud laugh. 'Can you picture me on the northwest frontier—a trader and explorer? Better yet, king of the forest with my robes of fur?'

She tried to interrupt; she was confused by these mad references, for never had he mentioned the fur trade. Ephraim's dreams were in the towns and cities of Europe. She felt a sudden swell of anger. 'Ephraim,' she said sharply, 'I must...'

His head jerked down to her, a frown creasing his forehead in an expression of puzzlement, as if she had suddenly materialized on the roadside for the sole purpose of impeding his journey.

'...must tell you my news. I am carrying your child.' The words tumbled out in a sudden rush. She looked at him intently, hopefully, anxiously; her emotions became telescoped and flew across her resolve like scudding clouds. Her heart pounded at her ribs, and she was sure Ephraim could see the growing dread she felt at the infelicitous way things were going. He did not say anything. The rain pattered gently for several moments before he spoke. 'Are you sure...'

She broke in, cutting him off in her apprehension. 'Oh yes, of course, I...'

'…it's mine?' he finished grimly.

She stepped back in astonishment at the slur. She blinked at the image of him suddenly gone out of focus in the drizzle. She fought the tears which welled up suddenly.

He looked at her sternly. 'Look here. Carry on to the house; there's none at work today for the weather, and they'll look after you. You need to dry off and warm yourself a bit. We can talk about this, ah, when I return.' There was no time to reply. With a cry to the pony, he was off. Victoria saw that he did not look back.

It was true that she would be looked after. Ephraim's brothers had only met Victoria two or three times, but her easy, if somewhat shy grace with them had the boys completely infatuated. They would welcome her, and attend to her until Ephraim returned with the cart. Her heart bursting, she trudged the final mile to the Blude cottage. Stunned by Ephraim's reaction to her condition, she felt a sense of betrayal alternating with confusion. As she walked, she went over and over the brief conversation until it started to disintegrate, in the same way that a much-worked piece of cloth begins to come apart, its fibres no longer holding any semblance of pattern.

Three days passed before Victoria finally came to accept that Ephraim was gone. Everyone knew that he had departed with the recruiting agent on the short run to Stromness. Usually the agent did not visit the outports, so local gossip was enriched by this small event. Late in the day that she had last seen him, Ephraim's youngest brother Mathew had walked her back to Rackwick. There by the quay, they had found the Blude pony still in harness. Though the rain had stopped, the wretched animal was shivering, and Victoria wondered why Ephraim had left it unattended. Mathew took the bridle in hand, and led the pony back the way they had come. He spoke to it softly, as one might to an errant child. As he turned up the narrow main street, he turned and waved forlornly to Victoria. She watched as the red-splotched cart clattered out of sight. It seemed obvious to her that Ephraim had left the island, but the irrational denial in her kept all manner of possibilities flickering alive.

Victoria returned to the squat stone building which had served as the Towrie home for more than two hundred years. Her mother's querulous interrogation as to her whereabouts grated sharply, and Victoria was uncustomarily short with her. Her mind tumbled and staggered. In the span of a single day, she thought, she had gone from a cocoon of fancy to a state of disgrace. As she climbed the stairs to the sleeping loft, her mother's cavilling over her absence faded. She knew from the poster she had seen at the quay, that the Hudson's Bay ship *Prince Rupert* sailed from Stromness before dawn the next morning. The Orkneys were the last watering and supply stop before the three-month voyage across the North Atlantic to the great Bay of North America. The *Sovereign*, on the other hand, would be back in two days, this time passing through Stromness on its way back to Thurso. Perhaps Ephraim would be aboard, for he had said they would talk upon his return. She decided she could wait until then to make decisions. For a long time she lay on her pallet, hands clasped behind her head, watching the setting sun stream through the tiny window, staining the worn muslin curtains the colour of a reddleman's smock.

Three days, then, after Ephraim's departure, Victoria returned at midday to the docks. The steamer was already being made fast to the stone bollards as she paused at the ramp. Somewhat elevated where she stood, she could see the gangplank being set in place, and the small knot of passengers waiting to disembark. Ephraim was not among them, and her disappointment was keen. A grey morning indeed, she thought, though the sun was trying to push through the thin cloud cover. She waited, however, until everyone was ashore and it was clear the ship was being readied for departure that afternoon. As she turned from her vigil, the poster on the wall of the low stone warehouse caught her eye. She had looked at it the same day Ephraim left, and she was certain that this was the lure which had caught Ephraim's imagination. She moved close and read it again.

Plenty of other young Orkneymen had succumbed to the temptations of the fur trade. Local gossip had it that more than three-quarters of the Company's servants were drawn from the islands. But Ephraim had never expressed any interest in exchanging one barren location for another. She held down the corner of the flapping poster. It announced the arrival of the Company's recruiting agent, Master Douglas Binscairth, who would be signing up boatmen, clerks, and 'other servants of the Company of Adventurers of England trading into Hudson's Bay and environs'. At a salary of sixteen pounds a year for five years, with commissions and signing bonus, fully found, Victoria could well understand the appeal of the Canadian North. Compared with the meagre prospects for such an income anywhere in the Orkneys, Victoria wondered why there was a man left at all.

She noted the date of the departure of the *Prince Rupert*, 1 June 1836—two days ago. The departure of the next Bay ship, the *Esquimaux*, was set for 15 June 1836. For a long time she stared thoughtfully at the tattered document as it whipped and rattled in front of her.

'If only I had been born a man,' she sighed out loud. I should go too, was her thought. Her reflection telegraphed sudden inspiration. Well, why couldn't I follow him? That was it; she would go after Ephraim. As surely as they had shared their dreams on the clifftops of Hoy, so too would they find that sweet intimacy again, in the wilderness of what was known as Rupert's Land. She smacked her hands together at this new possibility. Exulting, she began to focus her thoughts upon how it was to be accomplished.

iii

Throughout those short, dreary days, Victoria was obsessed with her plans and readying herself for her flight after Ephraim. Paying for passage, even if a single woman travelling alone on a Company ship was a possibility, was just not an option. The Towrie household was not one where much cash was available, and what there was of it, was well tucked away by her mother. No woman would be acceptable to the Company recruiters, so she resolved to seek enlistment as a man. There simply was no other choice.

When she had the opportunity, she took down her father's shirt and trousers from the trunk stored in the rafters. These she rolled into a bundle around a pair of heavy boots. The parcel was secured with a thick leather belt, then replaced in the trunk, ready for quick access. She was determined to withhold the money from the sale of the two yearling pigs at the fortnightly market, which was to be held the day before she was to leave for Stromness. The new steamer service was proving to be far more reliable than the ancient ketch-rigged packet which still operated. With its powerful paddlewheels, it was able to leave the treacherous harbour at Rackwick independent of wind and tide, and this predictability was essential to her plans.

She was resolved to be on board the *Sovereign* so as to connect with the *Esquimaux* the following morning. It was a plan with no margin should any of many variables change, especially the weather which could go from fair to foul in a trice, and remain so for weeks. She decided that this voyage lay in God's hands, as she had no other sponsor to protect or advise her, and so she committed herself to this trip with the hope of success, if it were His will. She would return the money withheld from her mother by post once she had received the signing bonus. Victoria's entire existence revolved around these plans; she became totally self-absorbed, to the frustration of her mother. Without these plans, and her vision of reuniting with Ephraim, the desperation of inevitable shame and ridicule, as well as the absence of any hope of a future for her son (for a son she was certain it was), threatened to choke all hope from her. The intensity of this dream both attracted and diminished doubts, the same way moths were drawn to and perished in flames.

'Aye, a fool's errand, maybe,' she said aloud, out at the sty, where she would often address the snuffling coarse-haired pigs as if they were reluctant students, 'but the risk be worth it, do you not agree?' She comforted her mind with the self-reassurance of all those poised to leap for a distant goal: the effort is everything; the try is all. Fear of failure is a coward's laziness. And so her father's influence drove her in a way he could never have known even if he had not gone to a watery grave.

Her father was a distant ghost for her. Tightly repressed vignettes of her childhood would come filtering back at the oddest moments: the way the small bed would groan when his weight was added to it, his hands on her private places, pushing and hurting, his whispered affections—'I love you, my precious! Oh, sweetness, how wonderful you are!'—And so on. The sounds of her mother snivelling somewhere distantly, while he crushed Victoria to him in his writhing urgency, played like a half-heard tune in her head. And his final shuddering gasp, leaving a wet, sticky, foul-smelling mess on her hip or bottom, still nauseated her, even now. Yet she felt a welter of emotions for him. She loved him and she loathed him in a way she was unable to comprehend, so she simply put the experience away, as one might place a book not worth reading again on a top shelf.

Perhaps things were different for him now, she thought, and she recited aloud to the anxious hogs:

Full fathom five my father lies;
Of his bones are coral made.
Those are pearls that were his eyes:
Nothing of him that doth fade
But doth suffer a sea change,
Into something rich and strange.

When the day finally arrived, Victoria was so tense, she thought her heart would fail her. She rose earlier than usual, well before sunup, and left for the weekly market in the church square. She had secreted the bundle of clothes, together with her other possessions, in a cheap canvas bag, out behind the sty. The piglets had been loaded into a small cage of woven boughs, and placed on an open-sided wheelbarrow which rumbled along on a single iron wheel. She skulked through the house, grateful that her mother was still abed, for she had become suspicious.

Victoria's behaviour had changed over the last few weeks, in spite of her best efforts to pretend all was normal. She dreaded her mother's sharp questioning, for though the woman was cursed with the most wretchedly negative view of the world, she was perceptive to the point of witchcraft.

There were witches on Hoy, her mother had told her many times. As she thought about it, Victoria hurried her step, for it was still dark, and this was the time it was said that Satan's attendants most preferred. As the iron wheel of her barrow squeaked and grated along the narrow streets, she thought about the old women in the islands who called themselves 'soothsayers', who were known to sell charms to faint-hearted sailors and would-be adventurers to the New World. Indeed, the Royal Navy for many scores of years had brought the wild-eyed crimps of the London press gangs to these islands, pausing only to take on fresh water. Shore leave was limited to the time it took to top up the scuttle-casks, and wait for the tide to turn. Anxious sailors and landsmen were quick to part with sixpence or more, for a protective witch's charm: perhaps a small pouch of ground beetle wings in spittle, or a pig's tooth. Some had sheepish expressions as they tucked their mystical ornaments into their blouses: 'Well, what's the bloody 'arm in it?'

The talisman which Victoria had sewn into the lining of her father's smock, was a lock of Ephraim's hair which she had playfully cut away that afternoon they had first lain together on the clifftops. God in Heaven, how far away that sunlit, hopeful day seemed now.

The stone pier could not be seen from the marketplace, but the belching smokestack signalled the arrival of the *Sovereign*. The vessel was still very much a novelty, and it drew dozens of onlookers to quayside. The deep-throated blasts from the whistle on the smokestack sent children scurrying, hands clapped to ears, screeching in happy terror. The machine was to Victoria the very embodiment of human ingenuity. Surely if man could build such a craft as this, to defy the very tides, then he could do anything.

The morning passed with glacial slowness. She had sold the two pigs almost immediately. She had thrown in the use of the wheelbarrow to take the animals up country, on a promise for its return by the end of the week. She spent the morning loitering about the rough stalls, chatting with those she knew, and making small purchases which she required for the voyage. When she heard a long blast from the *Sovereign* reverberate around the village, she hurried with many others down to the pier. Nearly half of the inhabitants saw her, heavy bag in hand, run up the gangplank even as shouts for its removal roared out from the ship's bos'n. She could feel many of their eyes upon her, and others casting about for her mother.

As in any small community, gossip was an important commodity. Everyone possessed the necessary currency to enjoy it; all had an eye or an ear to collect it, and a tongue to embroider it. Victoria Towrie, aloof and beautiful, had set the villagers a-tattle, for no one went anywhere without announcement and much discussion, least of all a young, unescorted woman.

After paying the fare, her cheeks burning with the attention she knew she was attracting, Victoria quickly found a place on the seaward side of the vessel, away from prying eyes. It was a spectacular day. The Orkneys have a quality of air which makes sunlight brilliant, colours sharper, and smells more pungent. As she watched the shore recede, Victoria's senses were as inundated as her emotions. The deck beneath her rolled gently, and she reached for a rail to steady herself. The village quickly receded from view and she tried to suppress her excitement. So it had begun! Good-bye to Rackwick, she thought, and she wondered why she was not more disconsolate. Every farewell contains an element of finality, of acceptance that there is no returning to the same thing. With each departure, the universe irrevocably changes in its infinite arrangements, because the very act whether borne of will or compulsion—it matters not—has created the start of something new. A refusal to acknowledge this, she thought, sowed dragon's teeth sure to yield some future misery. Even these towering cliffs, which would soon be out of view, would never be seen through these same eyes. Whenever and if ever she were to return, Victoria Towrie would not be the same person who used to live in Rackwick with an aging and disappointed mother.

She had never been to sea, even in a small boat, largely because of her father's paranoia, but in the end because she had neither need nor means. She had not known many who had gone off the island. There was a mystery associated with the most common of voyages, perhaps only to Stromness, or one of the other islands. Yet here she was on the first leg of a trip which would take her to the father of her child, to a land of which she knew little, save from her reading. She did know there were few white women there. She shuddered, even though here in the leeward side of the Sovereign, she was warm and comfortable enough. She put a hand over her stomach, and spoke aloud, 'We'll find him, Johnathan, we'll find him.'

The short trip to Stromness passed with Victoria motionless in the same seat. There were other passengers from Hoy, whom she did not want to engage in conversation. Some of them vainly tried to make eye contact, to speak to her. With a cold smile and a downward glance, she was able to avoid any intrusion. An accomplished introvert, she was to all appearances acting no differently than usual and interest soon dissipated.

The familiar coastline of sandstone battlements and reef-torn seas held her eyes, as her mind seethed with the planning of the next phase of her travels. She would take a cheap room for the night, prepare herself, and the following morning she would enlist at the last possible opportunity. This was the step which carried the greatest risk. Would the quota of recruits be filled? Would her sex be discovered? Victoria recalled what was common knowledge in the islands: the Bay ships had been calling at Stromness for over one hundred years, to take on water at Login's well. Over one-half of the men from Mainland Island had left with these ships; most had not returned. It was getting more difficult for the recruiting agents to sign up their full quotas of the quiet, hard-working islanders. With the *Esquimaux* being the last ship of the season, she felt that there would be every likelihood of a berth for her.

As to her sex, that was another thing. She hoped that her father's clothing would adequately conceal what she was. She had brought along a pair of heavy shears to cut away her long hair. Years of tending pigs and hauling them to market, gathering kelp, and searching for firewood had made her body lean and hard. She was used to heavy labour, and her calloused hands showed it. Yet there was no denying her femininity, as she recollected the effect she seemed to have on the young men she had no time for. These thoughts troubled and preoccupied her.

Disembarking at the harbour, she noticed the Hudson's Bay Company flag flying from the Company building. On the other side of the wharf, she could see the *Esquimaux* being watered and victualled. Alongside, the harbourside teemed with activity. The sight made her tremble. This close, the huge ocean-going ship was intimidating, but she had no time to dally. She needed to secure a room for the night. There were plenty of taverns and rooming houses, she had heard. A brisk trade had grown up in Stromness, catering to sailors and homesick young lubbers who had enlisted in the Company's service. Most miserable of all were the hapless ones who had been pressed into duty in the Royal Navy. This sea-going underclass of the streets of London, Plymouth and Liverpool crowded the low stone taverns and inns during the last few hours of shore leave, for a tankard or two of stout, and a firm pallet on an unmoving floor. There was never any fear of desertion in the Orkneys, for there was nowhere to hide, and few means of escaping the islands without particular knowledge of the surrounding currents and tides.

Not more than a ten-minute walk took her to a three-storey inn, with a cheap room in the garret. Curiously, the stairs to the upper level were on the outside of the building, though to reach the second floor, she had to pass the landlord's rooms. Once in, she closed the tiny door and, leaning against it, slid the wooden latch home carefully, in the manner of a conspirator. Laying out her bundle without pause, she began her transformation. With the black iron shears, she cut away her hair, trimming it close at the nape and tufted at the crown, after the fashion of a poor crofter's son. Brushing away the light golden skeins from her bodice, she paused to look into the worn mirror which was hung over the water shelf. Her eyes filled with tears as she studied the pale image gazing back at her. Her cropped hair stood out in all directions, giving her an ungainly appearance; made her nose look very big, she decided. I am cutting away a part of my soul, for I am beginning the denial of who I am.

She stripped suddenly, and stood in the drab pool created by her cast-down clothes, shivering. Cupping her breasts, she studied herself in an almost detached way. At home, this would have been unthinkable, for even lingering overly long while bathing was behaviour which her mother believed was improper, even wanton. She let her hands slide slowly along the sides of her gently swelling belly, tracing the flare of her hips, passing them around and under the fullness of her buttocks. It was this, her femininity, which was to be suppressed and contradicted, so that she could move through the world of men.

Or was it? Was it not the first woman who was responsible for the original coverings on men and women, those poor aprons of leaves? And was there no denial of sexual identity and responsibility before God, as it was written in the Book of Genesis? Was the fulfillment of the flesh only to be reserved for the Holy Sacrament of marriage?

Could disguise and subterfuge cover up what she was, or was the nature of a woman something beyond hiding? She trembled, in part because of the dank coolness of the room, but chiefly because she suspected that this latter thought was true.

Brusquely wiping her tears away with the back of her hand, she bent and drew on her father's thick underpants, then his heavy, blanket-lined trousers. Victoria felt an odd thrill, a faint titillation at the sensation of her slender, breasted form thus attired in male garb. No proper woman would dream of wearing a man's clothes. But there was something distantly erotic and forbidden about these unfamiliar garments. Even with Ephraim, she had not explored his clothing, the fasteners in intimate places, or even the order in which a man disrobed—if indeed there was a ritual to these things. Victoria always supposed there was, yet her face blushed powerfully when Ephraim moved to dress or undress, and she would turn away, or cover her eyes.

She pulled on a woollen shirt, and a coarse blue smock over that, the hems of both garments falling to the tops of her thighs. She snugged the outfit around her waist with the broad belt, which had a tarnished brass buckle the size of her hand. The thick-soled boots were heavy and awkward, and once she had laced them up, she clumped about the rough floor planks, worn smooth by the constant passage of such footgear, like a marionette in the hands of a novice puppeteer. Peering into the mirror again, she moistened her fingertip and blackened it with the lamp chimney. Working slowly, and with plenty of spittle, Victoria worked the soot into the skin of her lower face. Wiping the surplus with a piece of skirting, she stepped back to try and get an overall impression. But she had almost forgotten the finishing detail; she rummaged among the articles she had brought, and it was produced: her father's pipe. Every mature man she knew smoked tobacco.

The pipe would give her authenticity, for no woman would consider this exclusively male vice for a moment. Tamping it full of tobacco, she held a match to the bowl, and stepped back to render her appraisal. Too late the room had become shadowed, and at the same moment she shook with an explosion of coughing, as she sucked the smoke down into her lungs. Hacking and gasping, her eyes watering furiously, she spat the pipe out, sucking great drafts of air to calm herself. This was a masculine preserve into which she would have to tread carefully, for she could not fathom how anyone could find such an activity pleasurable. She threw herself down on the straw-filled ticking, drew her knees up and lay on her side. The heavy clothing was too warm to require bedclothing, so she placed both hands, in the manner of one praying, under her cheek, and contemplated the encounter with the recruiter, come dawn. There could be no thought of sleep that night, for she hoped that fatigue would line her face, further diminishing her woman's softness. She thought about Ephraim, and wondered whether he was thinking about her. Two lines she had read, written by Byron, came into her head, almost unbidden:

> *Man's love is of man's life a thing apart;*
> *'Tis woman's whole existence.*

Victoria woke with a start. There were crimson streaks in the morning sky showing through the leaded casement. 'Red sky at dawning, sailors take warning': the mariners' homily rang ominously in her mind as she chewed on her breakfast of bread, cheese and dried mutton. She reckoned it to be about half-past five in the morning. The recruiter would be at his post at six, likely getting a fire going in the little iron brazier she had seen there yesterday, for there was a chill in the early hours in these latitudes. Victoria wanted to be there at the time of his arrival, perhaps while he was tired himself and, God willing, not too alert.

She gathered up her possessions, hurried out of the room, and as she reached the street, she felt a sudden overwhelming rush of despair. Slowing to a walk, then a halt, she settled on the curb in the deserted street with a low groan. What was the use? This was hopeless, a voice seemed to be saying. Doubts, always in pursuit of the strongest and most determined minds, had caught up with her at last. Like wolves, they had stayed back and waited until the last moment, until the few remaining embers of courage lay winking and glowing. She clutched her head in fear. Was this not the most futile undertaking imaginable? Could she really expect to live and function in a man's world without detection? And this while carrying a child? Whether she would catch up with Ephraim was imponderable, for the country to which she was going was so impossibly vast.

She sat for several moments, her cheeks wet with tears, and considered her options. She quickly discarded the idea of going home. She had come too far with her plan now, and the pursuit of Ephraim was really the only avenue open to her. She must try to play the venture out. Effort was everything, she reminded herself grimly. She stood up and dried her tears gingerly, so as to preserve her make-up efforts. She blew her nose with pinched fingers, wiping them on her sleeve as she had seen her father do, and strode off to the pier in what she hoped was a masculine swagger.

The early morning sun glanced along the narrow streets in broken shafts as tattered clouds scudded before a southeast wind. In another couple of hours, the tide would turn, and the *Esquimaux* would be casting off. She hurried down to the stone quay, buffeted by the wind. It would be a rough day at sea, she thought.

Aboard ship, the deckhands swarmed to their tasks. Their boots thumped over the deck planking as they hurried to and fro under the watchful eyes of the officers. Near the aft quarter, she could see a small group of Orkneymen standing with a handful of other landsmen. Even to a novice, it was easy to set the men apart by the cut of their clothes. Most distinctive was the mariners' dress, being three-quarter trousers and canvas smocks. Near the wharf, in the Hudson's Bay Company's large warehouse the Company agent waited, although he did not expect any last-minute recruits. For the last one hundred and thirty years or so, the Company had actively sought out the strong-backed, taciturn islanders as ideal employees for the hard, dangerous business of the fur trade. In that year of eighteen and thirty-six, there were more than six hundred Bay men scattered across the northern wilds of Rupert's Land and beyond, and well over five hundred of them had been drawn from the islands.

Recruitment, for that reason, was well down from what it used to be. Master Binscairth rubbed his hands and blew into them. With fewer indentures came diminished commissions, a very grave reason to be out of sorts this chill morning. And so it was that he was closing his books, when Victoria came through the open door to his counting-room.

'I wish to enroll in the service of the Company,' said Victoria, keeping her voice as low and rough as she could contrive.

At these words Master Binscairth visibly brightened. He squinted at her, and worked his mouth as he appraised his new candidate. 'How old are ye, boy?' He hastened to lead her before she could respond. 'Ye must have fourteen years at least, under the new directives from London, or we'll not see proper service from ye.'

'I'm of my sixteenth year,' replied Victoria, 'and able enough.'

'Good, good,' the agent chuckled, slapping her on the shoulder. 'They're about to cast off, so ye've not much time to spare.' He brought out his ledger and picked up his pen. 'Ye can read an' write, of course?' It was clear he did not expect any contrary answer to these perfunctories. Victoria realized with not a little relief that she had been right to come late when the pressure of time would keep questions to a minimum.

She signed where his finger pointed, using the name Donald Blinkarn—a reclusive neighbour she barely knew. He handed her a copy of the agreement, then counted out her bonus with elaborate precision. It became quite apparent that his relationship with coinage was special. Grubby and nail-bitten, one would not ordinarily expect that such a man had wealth. Well beyond the reach of want, his miser's spirit continually contemplated the prospect of more, even in such amounts as he might embezzle from small trusteeships or shorten from some unsuspecting bumpkin. He took each gleaming shilling and half-crown from his rounded-top cashbox lined with worn green felt, stacking them in low, silver queues orderly as chessmen. Selecting each one in proper order, he counted them into Victoria's outstretched palm. The heavy clinks satisfied him, breaking his momentary spell in order for him to move on to the next denomination. Let the ship sail, and the gates of hell slam shut, for there was to be no interruption or haste brooked with the counting of the Company's money. Otherwise he would have to make good any shortfall, though he could pocket any such miscalculation, intentional or otherwise. Victoria almost cried out in her impatience, but she was well aware that this was not the time to attract attention to herself. It was her many anxious glances at the activity alongside the ship which resulted in her failure to notice that one shilling which was hers remained in the recruiter's brassbound money-chest.

At last the transaction was done. Binscairth straightened himself and a look of urgency came over his face. Now was the time to rush the lad off to the ship. But before he could open his mouth, Victoria fled from his office and ran to the tavern opposite the wharf which served as the depot for the Royal Mail. As it was just opening its doors, she rushed the yawning attendant with the thick cardboard envelope from her bag, dropped in half of the larger coins wrapped in a piece of skirting, addressed it to her mother, and raced back to the docks. She ran up the gangplank, and flashed her indenture at the mate who directed her with a gesture to the group of landsmen she had seen earlier.

She climbed up on a hogshead to catch her breath, and watched the final preparations for departure. Sitting apart, watching and recording were her favourite pastimes. All activities had common themes; all human behaviour was fascinating to her. This ship, pungent with the thick smells of tar, timber and brine thrilled her in its novelty. Overhead, a tracery of lines and cables stretched hundreds of feet in the air. Arcane shouts of command sounded, and tasks were being performed around her which had neither meaning nor observable result. She need not have hurried after all, for it was almost an hour later that the cry came to set the topsails, and shortly: 'Cast off abaft!'

Groaning and sighing, the laden ship backed and stood from the quay, fell off the wind and gybed. Bending on more sail, the *Esquimaux* gathered way, and made for the North Atlantic. I am away, thought Victoria. This has been easy. No one could care who I am. She was exhilarated. But to the south, stern-browed thunder clouds were knitting and frowning; soon the sun was gone. And upon the ship clearing the headland, the full weight of the blustering wind began to make the shrouds and rigging groan like a haunted manor. As the sky darkened, there seemed to be no sign that Victoria's luck would continue to hold.

iv

Before the space of one hour had passed, the *Esquimaux* had left Stromness but a blurred smudge on the horizon. Originally planned for the burgeoning Liverpool-New York trade, the ship was deemed too small to compete profitably as expected. She was purchased before completion by the Hudson's Bay Company, for her dimensions were ideal for the fur trade. At ninety-three feet on deck, she had a twenty-five-foot beam, with nearly fifteen feet in depth of hold. *Esquimaux* was rigged as a barque; that is, of her three masts, the two forward were square-rigged, and the mizzen mast was rigged fore 'n aft with a huge sail known as a spanker. Bluff-bowed and heavy-timbered, *Esquimaux* was built for cargo. The needs of her human freight were secondary.

Victoria's enchantment with the ship continued for the moment. Though she had seen many such craft passing the island, she had never experienced the vantage of a deckhand. The masts soared almost one hundred and sixty feet from the deck. Their webs of standing and running rigging appeared to her as complicated as a cat's cradle to a child. Though from the clifftops of Hoy, such vessels seemed to be borne along by captured clouds, she could see how weathered and patched the distressed canvas really was. Waist-high green bulwarks surrounded the unpainted decks, capped by a varnished wooden rail. At the stern, a raised deck was dominated by the ship's wheel, more than a man's height in diameter. Immediately forward of that was the binnacle, housing a large brass compass, and upon whose points the helmsman kept a casual but practised watch.

Forward of the mizzen there were two large hatches which she saw being checked for tightness; beneath them the trade goods awaited dispersal across the northern reaches of the Company's empire. Further forward yet was an improvised chicken coop, and a sty of grunting, squealing pigs who had yet to find their sea legs. They were commodities taken on in Stromness to feed the passengers and crew—fresh meat to prevent scurvy. The five dozen laying hens and four cocks flapped and fussed their unhappiness with their new accommodations. Victoria was beginning to share their concern, for the ship's motion was reaching the point where she could not remain secure without taking firm grasp of support. She marvelled at the seamen who made their way across the deck by using the rhythm of the ship. The significance of the commands which the mate barked into a shining brass trumpet continued to escape her, but the men scampered aloft, or laid to the sheets according to the direction of the moment. The movements of almost sixteen able-bodied seamen were orchestrated in a perfect, complex symphony of man and vessel.

The mate, Mister Hartley Huggins, was a short, thick man of wind-burned complexion, with a nose like a well-veined potato. His hair was thinning, but he wore a grey, spade-shaped beard to compensate. He was blessed with a resonant, stentorian voice which even in ordinary speech boomed over the bleatings of regular folk. To describe Mister Huggins as curt would be kind; his orders were transmitted in the minimum number of syllables, and he favoured the omission of all non-essential words. He was known to all who served under him as 'Heartless Huggins'. With nothing more than a shout: 'Oy! Oy!' he summoned all the passengers aft to be addressed by the captain. The group of eighteen recruits, mostly lubbers, stumbled and lurched their way to the quarter deck. Five of the others were Orcadian, and were apparently comfortable at sea, but Victoria could hear many sneering references by the crew to the floundering novices, some of whom were now violently vomiting their breakfasts into the sea. The mate kept his hooded eyes on them, and stood off to one side, near the rail. He picked at his nose vigorously, which seemed more of a preoccupation when in thought than an exercise in utility.

The mate was the captain's proxy. The rank designated the chief of operations for any seagoing vessel, and it fell to him to assign and oversee the work, supervise and discipline the crew, and ensure that proper entries were made in the ship's log. The bulk of the passage was left by the captain in the hands of this forty-one year old man, whose life for the past twenty-nine years had been spent at sea. Though he was referred to as the mate, he was never openly called by any name other than the one his rank and authority entitled him: Mister Huggins.

Captain Warwick came among the passengers at length. He was shorter by a hand's span than his mate, of slight build, and soft-spoken. Victoria had to strain to hear him, though the words were spoken carefully, in the manner of a preacher. He had a cold, and he held a soiled handkerchief to his nose frequently. Hawking the phlegm from his throat with some difficulty, he spat with the wind, and addressed his charges.

'Some of you have heard this before,' he began, 'but no matter. It bears repetition. Your main job'll be to keep clear out of the way, and let the men do their work. You'll be expected to keep your quarters clean and your small-stuffs stowed in good sea-order. There'll be tasks assigned as needed, and as your abilities permit. You're Bay men now, and this is a Bay ship. It may be that you're called out to lend a hand to run the ship; in that case,' and here he gestured without looking at the mate who was wiping his fingers on the seat of his trousers, 'the mate will divide you 'twixt starboard and larboard watch. You'll not turn out unless you hear the call for 'all hands', and then you'll take your place with your watch on deck. Now, when—' he broke off, staring at Victoria.

Victoria was slowly sagging at the knees. She was becoming seasick. The growing nausea was now impossible to ignore, and she sprawled forward on all fours, retching mightily and noisily. The sight of her half-digested breakfast of cheese, curdled bread and slivers of dried mutton made her convulse and vomit again, splattering the captain's boots. He stepped back, stamping his feet.

'A fine mess, boy,' he snarled disgustedly. 'You'll have this filth off this deck straight away. Fetch that bucket and wash your spew into the scuppers.' He turned to the others: 'If you must toss your guts, by God's oath, lay yourselves to the leeward rail, and spare the rest of us!'

'Now when that happens,' he continued as if uninterrupted, while Victoria stumbled to do as she was bid, 'you'll turn out smartly topside to your station, and wait for your instructions. From time to time you'll be shown the ropes, so if it comes to calling on you, you'll have some idea of what's expected. You'll mess with the second table; that means you'll take your food with your assigned watch after the officers.' He paused and looked over the motley group, five of whom were beginning to show advance signs of seasickness, as the acrid stench left by Victoria assailed their nostrils.

Captain Warwick continued, 'I have but one general rule for all my men. I'll have no sogering. You passengers may have idle time enough, but I'll not stand for any slovenly conduct or malingering. Try me on this score, and you'll find me a stern man indeed. Mister Huggins, if you please.'

And with this dismissal, he turned for his quarters. Two of the most ill of the group jumped for the weather rail, which was closest, ignoring the captain's earlier injunction. Adrip and bespattered, the two drew chortles from those members of the crew close by. The mate was disgusted, and told them to clean the ship and themselves, in that order.

Stopping suddenly, Captain Warwick spun around in the direction of the retching men. 'I'll have no women on this ship!' he barked. Victoria froze in horror, until she realized he was not addressing her. 'Find your sea legs and your manners, and pay attention to what you're told, or stay the hell out of my sight!' And he disappeared down the aft companionway.

Victoria caught her breath. The captain had used a reference to her sex as a mark of contempt for men who did not know any better than to throw up into the wind. It was not something she hadn't heard before, but in her present situation it alarmed her. Here she was truly alone, an imposter. If discovered, she would be relegated to a station below even the most lubberly deckhand. She shuddered, and bent to her cleaning task, mindful that the wind was freshening. Moments later the cry came to shorten sail.

Cold air from the arctic ice packs north of the track of the *Esquimaux* flowed southward to burrow under the warm frontal masses of air to the south. This caused towering black cumulo-nimbus clouds with which Victoria was well familiar. She knew, as all islanders did, that an initial breeze toward such storm clouds could be followed by a strong outflow of cold air of varying intensity. Such a storm could be capable of tremendous ferocity. It was just such a blow which had carried away her father. She hoped that the black clouds were not some sort of unhappy portent. This matter of her resolve, she thought sadly, seemed to require constant attention. She was always looking for reassurance or warning in the omens God placed before mortals to let them know He was watching.

V

The storm passed in hours, and more canvas having been bent on, the *Esquimaux* ran like a deer over the cresting swells left from the tempest's aftermath. She had settled into a consistent fifteen-degree angle of heel, which took some getting used to by most of the passengers. Their world was now circumscribed by the outer limits of the ship; it constantly moved in three dimensions rolling, pitching and yawing in a predictable sequence. The sounds at sea never abated below a certain level of rushing, churning water, groaning timbers, and always the wind-song chorus of varying intensity.

The *Esquimaux* had two principal decks. Descending from topside, the 'tween decks, the forward portion of which was the forecastle, or fo'c's'le. This was the accommodation area, split between the two watches. The after part, at the rearmost sections of the ship, was given over to the officers' cabins and the galley arrangements. Between the two, amidships, was the upper hold for fine freight and perishables, and below, running virtually the length of the ship, was the heavy freight. In the case of the *Esquimaux*, the lower hold was packed with trade goods and implements for the continuance and expansion of the fur trade.

When Victoria was shown to her quarters in the fo'c's'le, her eyes had some difficulty adjusting to the gloom. The deadlights set in the deck above were small and few in number. A single lamp hung over a large trestle table fastened to the centre of the cabin sole. A group of hands sat around it, casting dice for plugs of tobacco. The air below was close and stifling, for the single hatch could not be opened more than a crack, since one of the ship's boats had been lashed over it, blocking both light and ventilation. Weather permitting, both passengers and off-watch hands spent their leisure time topside. With sea air in her lungs, and salt beef and biscuit in her belly, Victoria returned from the mid-day meal to sling her hammock above the locker she had been assigned to stow her gear.

The simplicity of the hammock, once the task of getting one's body into its embrace had been mastered, was that it remained relatively motionless as the ship rolled about it. There was an art to the rigging of

'Neptune's sleeve', however, which had to do with a fore 'n aft arrangement, and a proper tension of the outboard grommets, as well as the head and foot stays. It was a marine tradition, and this applied to all employees on Bay ships, that new hands were given wrong instructions. The idea was that the sling would very quickly pitch its anxious freight onto the cabin sole, to hoots of merriment all round.

Victoria took the measure of her shipmates very quickly. They were a loutish lot. The servants from Orkney seemed to be a slight cut above the mariners, but that was, she thought, in large measure to do with the refining influences of church and family which the land could offer. She had seen poverty all her life, but nothing of the urban poverty which made even a twelve-year-old lad think that a life at sea was a better bargain than a future in a factory or a workhouse, or a prison for debtors. There was a hard edge to them; Victoria could see it in their faces and hear it in their petty sarcasms.

She paid careful attention to the way in which the old hands arranged their affairs, and she rigged her gear accordingly. She was immediately branded a spoilsport. The others were accepted according to the way in which they bore the japery of the crew. As each was flung from his bed, or stationed under a persistent leak, or perhaps was directed to hang his ditty bag next to the hull where the sweating timbers would drench it through, the snickers and chortles were expected to be met by even greater gestures of hilarity from the sore, sodden or mildewed victim.

Victoria thought this was all foolishness, and though she tried to keep to herself, her stand-offishness marked her for sarcastic asides and other special attentions. And so she would be jostled from her place in line at mess, or the stays on her hammock retied with slip knots. On another occasion, she found a dead rat in her boot, withdrawing her foot with a shriek of revulsion, which had most of them convulsed with laughter. Victoria felt that all this was bearable, for it served to lessen the chances of her discovery. It was a worry, though, because she never knew when to expect the next indignity, or the next unpleasantness which passed for humour among these men. They were only just a week into the voyage, and she hoped the others would get tired of tormenting her.

The mate had told them that the passage would be about 'eight or nine weeks, depending on the mood of Mister Davy Jones'. They were to arrive at the roads in Hudson's Bay, off York Factory, and depart by mid-September at the latest. There was some rumour and consequent grumbling that, if the timing wasn't right, they might well have to winter in the Bay, a prospect that the seasoned mariners deplored. The ship might easily be lost in the ice. No one was happy at the thought, and even though the mate scoffed at this possibility, it persisted in contributing to a vague mood of anxiety in the fo'c's'le. This in turn gave rise to a shortness of temper and a want of tolerance already in short supply in the highly structured society of a vessel at sea.

Sensing their mood, the mate kept the crew hard at work, and called for a song from them frequently. These shanties seemed to Victoria's mind to serve a number of purposes: the heaving of the halyards and the winding of the windlasses (which could require four, eight, or even twelve men, according to the task) required coordination of effort which the music provided. There was a competitive quality to them, and each verse could call for greater volume and commensurate effort.

The songs appeared to be good for morale. Danger was all around; a false move in the footropes overhead, out on the pitching bowsprit known to all sailors as the 'widowmaker', or even walking the saltwater-slick deck in a blow could be fatal. Many of the songs laughed at the devil waiting for carelessness. All of the songs had verses covering subjects which were close to any sailor's heart, and were a means of giving expression to innermost feelings. Victoria had joined in these tunes, as Mister Huggins, in rich baritone, set tone and topic:

'Lay to hearty, lads! Cheerily now, and with a song!'

There was to Victoria's ear one song that seemed to inspire the crew to greater exertions; there was a genuine enthusiasm to the chorus of 'Return to Hudson's Bay'.

> *For we're going back to the frozen north*
> *to the land where spunk is spunk—*
> *Not a tuckling stream of lukewarm cream,*
> *But a solid, frozen chunk!*

Still, it was hard to shake off the gloom. After the first day, the sun did not reappear except in brief intervals which would send the navigator or the captain scrambling with sextant for a sighting. For the most part, dark clouds scudded across a grey, lowering sky. The sea, bleak as gun-metal, was swept by rough winds which scarred its restless surface with cresting waves. Cursed with small accidents and minor breakages, the crew felt the ship had become an unlucky one.

For all this, they were making good time, for this weather system had been pushing the *Esquimaux* at a rapid pace since they began. The motion of the ship was a kind of truce with the waves. She rolled steadily, pitching as she left one breaker to the trough beyond. At regular intervals an odd wave would cause the vessel to yaw, and the helmsman would correct for the movement to bring her back on course. The ship sloughed and shrugged in a tedious, monotonous manner, which belied the awesome forces at work above and below.

It was the men at their toilet which troubled Victoria. On the Sabbath, assuming reasonable conditions, the men washed in seawater, if they chose, and rinsed off with a tea pail of fresh water. These were occasions when some of the men would parade their skinny white bodies lewdly before one another, and snap at each other with wet towelling. Others would rub themselves indecently, causing their maleness to stand out in a way that was both lascivious and absurd. 'Salute the one-eyed admiral, boys!' There would be contests to determine who could keep a sou'wester hung by its laces from a tumescent member, while the others gathered around to count in unison until the erection faded. 'one, cock-a-jimmy; two, cock-a-jimmy; three, cock—Hey Foster Leggit, no cheats! Get your hands away!' And the whole muster would collapse in merriment.

Victoria hated this infantile show of masculine preening, and would not watch. The only man she had ever seen partly unclad was Ephraim, and she could not reconcile that encounter with the utterly repelling way in which these men treated their sexuality. This disdain did not go unnoticed by the others. Gradually, she became aware of a latent hostility marked by an increase in sarcastic asides and open contempt for her.

One day, in the third week of the passage, as her watch was gathering their mess kits preparatory to laying aft to the galley for the afternoon meal, a small group gathered around Victoria. She was bent over her locker, rummaging about, when she was kicked from behind. She sprawled awkwardly, scraping her elbows and shins.

'Sodding idiots!' she growled. 'Why can you not leave me be?'

The snickering died away. Hector Flynne, the red-faced bully boy of the starboard watch stepped forward and raised his booted foot to the edge of Victoria's locker, rested his elbow on his elevated knee, and looked down at her, laying a finger along his nose.

'Idiots, be we all?' he sneered. 'And yer, why, yer a strange little bitch to be with the likes of us.'

Victoria felt a familiar stab of panic at this reference to her gender. Had this lout leering at her so closely found her out?

'A feller wif yer snooty ways and sogerin' attitudes needs some special attention, I'm thinkin'. Mind you,' and he sniffed at her like a dog at the tail of another, 'what yer really needs is a wash, for I'm thinkin' yer've not been out of these togs since yer boarded. D'yer think yer a gentleman, perhaps it is, what they got no room fer in th' officer's quarters?' Laughter and catcalls accompanied these remarks.

Victoria felt a welter of emotions sweep over her. Again, the feminine reference to underscore derision. It threw her off, for she still reacted to it literally, not fully understanding the scorn men held for women. When a man did not measure up, he was dismissed as an 'old woman', or a 'bitch', or worse, that harsh, dismissive word for her most intimate part: 'cunt'. Did this have something to do with the betrayal by Eve, and Adam's disgrace?

Victoria had not been unmasked, but she knew what was in store. If a man skipped bathing to the point where he was a stinking unpleasantness at table, he was given a dousing. This meant that he was taken to the scuppers, stripped, and sluiced down with buckets of sea water. He was expected to take this in good spirits, or he could expect the further humiliation of his genitals being coated with tar. This was known at sea as 'blackening the bishop', and was reserved for a special category of loathing, such as someone who had been caught masturbating. She was well aware that her inability to wash herself properly made her clothes start to smell a bit gamy, and her avoidance of any sort of public toilette was the source of critical sneers.

When this sort of hazing took place, the recipient was made to wear the bucket for a cap—and nothing else—back to the fo'c's'le. Not only would her secret be out, but she might be in for some rough handling, should this unruly bunch lay to her.

Flynne sent two hands topside for two buckets of sea water to be drawn up. 'Will yer be outta yer rags on yer own, Mister Blinkie, or shall we be helpin' yer?' he asked, grinning at her.

Victoria sat up and began to fumble with her smock lacings. She tried not to look at the companionway door, which the two who had just gone for the buckets had left ajar. She could hear it slapping open and shut. The others were joking and jostling one another, not paying her particular mind. She waited for an irregular wave; they came once in about every ten, and as each hand, including Flynne, stepped back automatically to compensate for it, she leapt to her feet and bolted for the companionway.

Delighted, the pack was after her with a howl. This was part of the sport, for the further the chase, the longer back the ignominious march would be, with the attendant raps on the upended bucket, the pinchings, the derisive remarks. Not knowing where else to go, Victoria ran for the galley. The officers were just rising from their meal when she burst in. Etiquette demanded that the second table wait their turn in the passageway outside the mess, until the cook called for them. To intrude was unthinkable. There was no offending the hierarchies and protocols of this tiny universe.

'Mister Huggins,' said the captain calmly, without looking at Victoria after her sudden entrance, 'I'll not be puked upon again.'

'Have you taken leave of your senses, boy?' snapped the mate. 'Have you—'

Victoria almost wept as she cut him off, and a choking cry came from her throat. 'I've dire need of the cook, Mister Harris, sir,' she gasped, and she bolted for the galley, behind which lay the cook's quarters.

Captain Warwick and his officers seemed mollified by this request, though many shook their heads. The cook also served as the ship's surgeon, having jury-rigged many a tourniquet, splint, and bandage over the course of his long and lonely career at sea. Victoria had given the impression of being unwell, with her flushed face and expression of distress. The officers were suspicious of the breathless group of men hard by the mess companionway, but made no comment. For the moment, until the cook called, Victoria was safe.

Meeker Harris was a man who looked much older than he actually was. The remnants of his hair were wispy fronds, white as a gull's belly, carefully woven from side to side and pasted down with some greasy concoction from his larder. He had a round, cratered nose, and a frizzy white moustache which draped over heavy jowls. Short and pudgy, he looked like a grotesque gnome, from whom the magic was long gone. Over his smock he wore an apron of salvaged sailcloth, which bore the splattered remains of at least the last several dozen meals served at sea. He had a way of rolling his eyes under his puffy lids, as if he were in a constant state of incredulity. When he spoke, he was constantly wetting his lips, then drying the corners with his thumb and middle finger. He was missing the tip of his left index finger, in consequence of some far-off confused sea and an errant cleaver blow, as well as one too many sips from his cask of rum. It was a tribute to his sense of humour as well as economy that he tossed the severed digit into the stew-pot, later announcing at table a broth 'with my special touch in it!'

Of such a man, Captain Warwick had said that his food was tolerably good, if only one put the image of the preparer out of one's mind. He had become, over the years, somewhat eccentric. His life began as a foretopman in the East India Company, but a bad fall resulted in a compound break of the right leg. Set poorly, his leg no longer gave him good balance, but as apprentice to the cook, he had learned the trade sufficiently well to keep at work. For this he was grateful, for the life of a cripple without means soon led to beggary or some fetid poorhouse. But it set him apart from whole men, he thought, and his reclusive behaviour made others think him a queer duck. Nevertheless, a ship's cook was critical to a safe passage, and enjoyed special prerogatives and jurisdictions. He need not serve in any watch, nor turn out to the call for 'all hands'. In the mess, he set the rules to which tradition required even the captain to defer.

He eyed Victoria, as if half asleep. 'What be the matter with yer? Have yer been gobblin' some of yer longshore swash?'

'No,' said Victoria, gathering her breath. 'I've a serious problem, a difficulty I need help with. I've nowhere else to turn.'

Meeker Harris, cook, surgeon and cynic, leaned back into the steadying sling rigged just forward of the stove. In a seaway, by thrusting a hip into this device, he could save both hands for the practice of his culinary arts. He studied her pensively for a moment, then wiped the corners of his mouth. Victoria thought it was a particularly sinister gesture.

'And what might yer troubles be?' he asked.

vi

Victoria said nothing for a long moment. She tried to assemble her thoughts, for she had no plan. The need to say something was obviated by the cook's sudden short direction. 'Look yer, the larb'd watch needs their horse, and they shall have their tummies' fill o' it. I shall speak to the mate about yer new apprenticeship,' and he cackled at some mysterious levity as he turned away.

After her watch had been fed their evening meal of salt beef, boiled potatoes and thick pea soup ladled over, Victoria was directed to clean the iron kettles, which appeared not to have been seriously cleaned since the Battle of Trafalgar. She had been painfully aware of the glares and sneering comments of her shipmates, but she had no idea how to respond. In point of fact, she was afraid to try, for fear of antagonizing them further. Together, they seemed to possess a single mind, like a flock of sheep, or perhaps more like a pack of wolves. There seemed to be no point or lesson in their torment of her, save for their possible resentment for her avoidance of their society.

Victoria had believed that disguising herself well, simply looking like a man, was to run the constant risk of exposure, because of the difficulty in cloaking her womanhood. Her increasingly rumpled and unwashed appearance assisted her in this subterfuge; yet her exposure, ironically, appeared imminent not because she failed to look like a man, but because she did not think like a man. Or at least, act according to how men seemed collectively to think.

And yet, as they filed out of the mess, farting and belching, slapping each other's shoulders and whinnying at some private joke, they seemed already to have forgotten her. She was still afraid to return to quarters. As she cleaned utensils, she pondered her options. The noisy clamour of the off-watch could be heard as the galley clock chimed off the first dog-watch. Soon the cold, hungry men would be barking like sea lions for their feed.

Later that same evening, Harris left Victoria alone. He had said that she should stay out of sight for the moment, and that she could rest in his quarters. She was delighted to find a proper bunk, rather than the hated hammock, and she threw herself across it. When she awoke, it was because she sensed that he had returned. Sitting up, she started when she realized he was on the opposite side of the closest mess table, seated in such a way as to be able to see her. He was no more than fifteen feet away, and he was staring intently at her; both of them were bathed in orange lamplight. He rose and walked over to her, steadying himself as a gust heeled the ship. Victoria squirmed under his gaze.

'Well, I spake the mate, and he said yer can bunk wi' me from now on. I tol' him yer'd be me new apprentice.' He snickered at this, then narrowed his eyes as he saw Victoria's uncertainty. 'I'm thinkin' yer not getting along wif yer mates. They can be a sorry lot, them. Make it right unpleasant. Yes. Yer can earn yer keep wif me; I've arranged it fer yer.' Again Victoria did not reply, but looked at him, nonplussed.

'There's something wrong with yer, boy?'

'There's naught wrong with me, Mister Harris,' replied Victoria in the lowest voice she could muster.

He grinned at her, leaning over so that his face was close to hers. His breath had a sweet, nauseating trace to it. He reached for her in a quick motion, and squeezed her breast. She yelped in pain and surprise.

'Aha! I knowed it! I knowed yer was a wench the moment yer burst in here! Yer a wench fer all that!' He was very pleased with himself, and he gave her breast another squeeze, just to reassure himself of his discovery.

'Well,' he said, 'yer little secret's safe wi' me, as long as yer lay to with a will. I want no sogerin' about, neither. There might be one or two other small favours yer'll be doing for me...' He trailed off, looking at her the way a fat man might consider pastry. There was no mistaking his meaning.

Victoria felt faint. Was there to be no escape? She was completely at this man's mercy. 'Please, sir, I'm with child; more than three months gone I am–'

'I'll have none o' yer miseries,' the cook replied, 'fer I've plenty of me own.' Saying this, he went to the galley door and secured it, then sat down at the table where he had been when she had first noticed him. The ship rolled and creaked purposefully as the lamp cast swaying shadows against the bulkheads.

Victoria looked at him helplessly, holding her hands in front of her. Harris looked at her intently, and wiped his mouth. Suddenly he spoke. 'Show me yer titties!' he rasped, swallowing hard. Her heart fell. Was she to be raped or mistreated in other unspeakable ways?

'I am with child, Mister Harris,' she repeated.

'Show me yer titties, girl, an' we'll be done wif' it. Be quick about it, fer yer've no choice in the matter.' He nodded his head, urging her on. 'Come now, be quick, or I'll turn yer back to yer friends in th' fo'c's'le. Now won't they be glad t' see yer?'

Not knowing what else to do, and praying that this appeasement would satisfy him, she slowly unbuttoned her smock. Pulling up her blouse, she felt the cool air on her breasts, and her nipples stiffened in response. Weeping silently, she closed her eyes for the shame of it, and bowed her head. Her tears were for the helplessness of her situation, the powerlessness of her sex, the inexplicable rapacity of men who would take of another, weaker person. She cried for her unborn son and her absent lover, for the coward who fathered her, and the bitter scold he married. She wept for herself; her humiliation and oppression, and the constant fear, keen and threatening as a knife to the throat. Soundlessly, the tears coursed down her face, dripping wetly over her nakedness.

Harris had moved onto his knees, placing one hand against the edge of the table, which was between them. With the other, he fumbled at the buttons of his breeeches. At his clutching and groaning, Victoria looked up, bewildered, in time to see him come gasping to the point of his release. With a whimper, his head sank down onto the back of his hand. Victoria felt an overwhelming rush of contempt. She rearranged her clothing, feeling defiled, yet grateful he had not abused her in some other, more intrusive way. She remained seated as the cook stood up, holding his pinched foreskin. He walked over to a bucket of slops and expelled his seed into it. With a rag, he mopped himself as one might wipe seagull shit from a bench before sitting. He resumed conversation matter-of-factly, as if nothing unusual had taken place.

'Yer'll berth there, abaft the pantry. Stow yer gear atop that rack a hogsheads. Yers can use me quarters t' wash. Be a help t' me, and yer'll stay here till we raise the Bay. Give me a bother, an' yer back to the fo'c's'le afore yers know it.' This was said without heat, or any expression Victoria could discern. He turned and went out of the mess.

Victoria felt relieved and despondent at once. There were no choices for her. The worry of being unmasked as a liar, a fraud, a betrayer of her sex, was compounded by her fear of the wolf-pack mentality of her shipmates. She had no doubt either that the ship's officers would show her little comfort, given her scandalous attire, her shameful condition, and by what she surely must have witnessed on wash day. No. There was naught for it but to press on, even at sufferance of Meeker Harris.

And so it was to be in the coming weeks. Victoria, whose taken name was reduced to 'Master Blinks' by the cook, and just 'Blinkie' by everyone else on the ship, became a nonentity, a mere drudge in the ship's galley. Eventually she reclaimed her gear from the fo'c's'le. Oakum had been rubbed into her clothes, and someone had left a turd in her tea pail. With this last bit of pettiness, she seemed to have faded from their consciousness. Her isolation, merciful in some ways, was a price she felt she must pay to live with men as one of them, but not able ever to be one of them. Being alone suited her anyway. She had plenty of spare time, and in all but the worst weather, she preferred to be topside, in the lee of the quarter deck, where she could watch the ceaseless mood variations of the sea, the working of the ship, and the ever-changing sky.

The demands of the cook became no greater, though he sought his release through her passive assistance every week or so. She dreaded an escalation in his attentions, but that did not seem to be happening. The second encounter was while she bathed with her meagre allotment of fresh water. Her clothing partly off, she preferred to sponge herself with a moistened rag. She was unaware of Harris's presence until his ragged gasp signalled his completion. Gradually, this became their routine, so that she could attend to her toilette, while a short distance away he could act out his voyeuristic fantasy. She became somewhat indifferent to this bizarre need of his, even pitying it. Their relationship in all other respects was tolerable, and there was no hint of his earlier cruelty, when first he had discovered her secret.

It was not the oppression of the dictator demanding perpetual submission that made life unbearable, she thought, but the tyranny of a thousand petty cruelties people inflicted upon one another. These were the levers by which advantage was secured for the moment. What made these infinitely more difficult to live with was that they were occasioned at the instance of family, friends, and colleagues as well as strangers. The only protection from such depradations was power, and in Victoria's world as it had become, this was doubly true. She knew only two kinds of power: wealth such as that possessed by landowners and merchants, and physical strength which could demand respect among men. Possessing neither, she felt irrelevant and afraid. There was a strength in her sexuality, she had once thought, but it had been demonstrated clearly that this was a card easily snatched from her hand.

Though she was mindful that her bargain with Harris had won her some measure of safety, she had no faith that her deception would remain intact. It depended wholly upon the wretched man's indulgence. Her imagination remained fired with apocalyptic fantasies involving what dreadful possibilities might befall her should she be exposed. How ironical that her salvation lay in the old cook's sexual inclinations and kitchen drudgery.

Victoria enjoyed her vigils on the deck. To avoid the attentions of the mate and his officers, she passed the time plaiting baggywrinkle. This was a form of insulation against chafe upon canvas, made by weaving unrove hemp into fat thatches, to be sewn into critical areas where sails were likely to come into contact with standing rigging. She was good at the task, for she had nimble fingers. More importantly, it was mindless work and it allowed her to think, or to enjoy relief from her galley chores.

At first she dwelled upon what she now believed to be a powerful injustice, universal in its application: freedom had something to do with manhood. Even the simple act of walking in her father's breeches put wings on her feet. She remembered the day she had trudged up to the Blude cottage, and the weight of the soaked hem of her skirts. How confining her awkward dress had been compared to what she wore now! How quickly she could move! All the convenience, and the power lay with men, she thought. To the subcaste where she belonged, the only influence she had rested in her sexuality. Herein lay the paradox: to be free to fly across oceans, she was required to construct a fiction, central to which was a denial of self. To be able to maintain the charade, she was compelled by Harris to use her sexuality. Here indeed were competing cruelties of suppression. Her goal of reunification with Ephraim kept shifting out of focus, because she could not escape the obvious conclusion that he was himself a man, perhaps not unlike any other on this ship. Could it be true? Her optimism and determination fluctuated between rage and frustration on the one hand, and her romantic quest on the other. As she sat in the fleeting sunlight, she struggled to recall a stanza from Byron which she had copied out as a girl, struck by its melancholy.

> *If I should meet thee*
> *After seeming long years,*
> *How should I greet thee?*
> *With silence and tears.*

It was here at her post, while washing shrivelled potatoes in sea water, that she saw one of the young seamen, John Pixel, fall to his death. August was well advanced, and the nights had become chill. The sun set further and further in the southwest each evening, and the ratlines and footropes often had a slick of ice in the morning. Frequently, the off watch was set to chipping the rails and rigging free of the deadly coating; not only was it treacherous underfoot, a top-heavy vessel in a seaway is a dangerous prospect no sailor wants to think about.

Pixel, or 'Pixie', as he was known (there were so many men aboard named 'John', that each one had some sort of fanciful moniker bestowed upon him by the other hands), was a sixteen-year-old who was without doubt the fastest and most daring of the upper-topmen. He was always first to the cross trees, as sure-footed and confident on the yards as a squirrel. He was a little given to small feats of daring, and he had been chastised by the mate for foolhardiness: 'One hand fer yerself, and one fer the ship!' In fact, however, his admiration and that of the crew, for the boy's courage, showed plainly.

There was a heavy swell running with the sea only a little confused from a squall just past. The ship was rolling, and the watch had just been sent aloft to bend on more canvas. The buntlines, jackstays and footropes were all stiff from the light rainfall. Victoria loved to watch the men work the canvas, responding to calls from each other and shouts from the deck far below them.

She gasped as she saw Pixel's body hurtle soundlessly to the water. No splash, and he was gone as if swallowed.

'Man o'erboarrrrd!' came several cries at once. A fresh cacophony of orders shrilled out as a red and white pennant fixed in a barrel of cork was hurled out to mark the place where Pixel had vanished. Aghast, Victoria watched the futile drill as it played out like a frenetic pantomime. A square-rigged sailing ship is no readily manageable creature, but the mate made the *Esquimaux* respond faster than Victoria would have thought possible.

'Keep her full for stays!' screamed Mister Huggins, as the helmsman struggled to keep way on the ship, all the while craning his eyes to look for his mate. 'Ready about! Lee-ohhh!' and to the anxious helmsman: 'Damn yer eyes, sir; down helm, and look to yer work!'

The wheel was spun, all sails taken aback, and with a great shuddering aloft, *Esquimaux* passed through the eye of the wind.

'Mainsail haul!' cried the mate, and the crew, all of whom were by now on deck, ran the sheets in, and hauled the main yards around.

'Let go and haul!' came the shout. The crew let go of the headsails and fore yards, and hauled them over to the new tack. Thus the search proceeded, tacking and wearing off in exhausting succession.

In mid-August, the northern seas are only one or two degrees above freezing. The life expectancy of the average man luckless enough to fall into such water is less than five minutes. Everyone knew this; yet the search for John Pixel went on for more than three hours. Men climbed into the rigging praying for a glimpse of their hapless comrade. At length, the mate called off the search, clearly reluctant: 'Now lads, ready about!' and the ship was returned to her course. The off-watch remained at the aft quarter rail until called down for mess. The death affected everyone, and there was none of the usual horseplay and foolery.

Victoria did not know whether the men were silent out of respect for their missing shipmate, or because the accident was an immediate and powerful reminder of their own mortality. Many took out charms or Bibles, and some prayed openly. The futility of attempting to cheat one's fate by prayer, enchantments, or even by being overly cautious, was no easier to dismiss simply because one acknowledged it. Victoria's father had lived most of his life according to his fears, and his fate was no less violent or wet than if he were to have lived much differently. Instead, he allowed his lack of courage to shape his existence. Better to live, even briefly as John Pixel had, with courage and a clear eye for that which one required from one's existence, than to remain huddled and frightened by the enormity of forces arrayed against happy human existence.

Pixel's death profoundly affected, even inspired Victoria. In the end, she thought, it was obvious why he did not cry out. He knew that as a fore-top man, one of the best, a watery grave was a possibility with each call to go aloft. To scream impotently would have been inconsistent with the brash young seaman's view of life, and he had accepted his fate, dying as he had lived. As one of the men observed, 'Twas a manly thing to do!' It reaffirmed Victoria's yearnings that the child she carried would be male. Only a man could be free to shape his fortune, independent of the mythologies which surrounded and ensnared women like her. A man in boots and breeches could stride the world.

vii

Well into Hudson's Bay the winds began to increase in strength. Since they were blowing steadily from the northwest, this should have been a boon to the voyage, permitting a broad reach down to the roads at York. However, these winds brought with them a light, persistent rain which quickly turned to ice on the ship's superstructure. All hands were kept busy chipping ice, and the heavy Russian storm canvas became stiff and unyielding so that the upper sails were ordered unbent and taken below. Once the yards were dropped, the sails could only be freed with an axe. Each one was lowered ponderously to the deck, reducing the weight aloft. Still it rained.

The skies became a lowering tapestry of torn smoke and flinty ash, as ragged and ruined as the complexion of a corpse. The storm had the curious effect of eliminating all colour. Detail was expressed in various shades of grey, and so the ashen face of Nature appeared to Victoria as she left her turn at the pumps, and struggled below. The wind's tortured shrieking through the rigging was muffled by the wet gasps of rain that enveloped the vessel. The men were chilled through their heavy layers of clothes topped by oilskins and sou'westers. Waves slopped up against the hull, casting over plumes of bitter salt water, some as high as the lower topsail yard, more than forty feet above the deck. There was seemingly no constancy to the gusts. 'More foul wind tonight than ye'll get from the devil's arsehole!' shouted a member of the crew to a nodding mate, as they worked their way along a safety line stretched across a wildly pitching deck.

The weather grew progressively worse. The winds increased in strength, still gusting erratically, as a weak low-pressure ridge passed to the south of them. The seas, shallowing to the southern end of Hudson's Bay, began to pile up, and the ship, short-canvassed and top-heavy with the ice on her spars, began to labour in the swells. Work aloft was now virtually impossible, so wet and slick and cold were the conditions. All hands fervently prayed for the voyage to conclude. Already they could smell the faint but lush scent of spruce boughs, as the breezes which had travelled thousands of miles over tundra and forest carried the pungent fragrance of the north down to them.

On 18 September 1836, with two men at the wheel struggling to hold a course for York, the rudder unshipped and the vessel swept broadside to the waves. Rolling in exaggerated plunges, ice-covered and wave-swept, the deck offered no man a steady footing. The captain, who had been on deck for the last two days, shouted instructions to the mate to steady the ship with a sea anchor. This device, rigged from the bow, would allow the vessel to ride with the storm, head onto the waves, under a few scraps of storm canvas set aft to weathercock the hull into the wind.

Now the officers and crew worked furiously at the construction of a new rudder. Though the ship's carpenter and those assisting him could barely see for the blowing spume—and the mad careening of the deck made matters more difficult still—they were able to rough-saw spars into planks, and shape them into a form closely resembling the rudder now lost. Victoria, taking a shift at the pumps, thought it looked more like a large stable door, and a pretty crude one at that. Yet its construction was a lesson in will overcoming impossible odds. One of the Orcadians was going to Rupert's Land in the service of the Company as a blacksmith, and he was able to fashion heavy iron pintles from the massive spare masthead fittings. This, too, was not without hazard, for the forge which had been hastily set up was knocked over twice, the second time severely burning the smith.

The rudder was hoisted over the stern, and as the gusts caught and pummelled it against the hull, the crew strained and swore as they tried to contain it. The new rudder post was reeved up through the well. Chains and guys and turning blocks leading to the helm managed to restore a degree of manoeuvrability. Victoria anxiously watched this fantastic feat of construction, and was heartened when a great cheer went up from the men as the ship responded, if somewhat sluggishly, to her new steering arrangements.

For a time the crew rested, as best they could, and ate greedily of the hot porridge which Meeker Harris had made by some miracle of culinary persistence. But the wind now noticeably increased, something which Victoria would not have believed possible. The gale roistering about the ship sounded as if the lid of hell had been pried off, and all the demons which lived in the fears of men had begun screaming at once. The tops of waves were torn off and flung with the rain almost horizontal to the seas. The noise was unbearable for Victoria, especially below, where the hull seemed to magnify the sounds. How difficult it was now to condemn her father for his fear of the sea. In her prayers, Victoria swore that, upon her deliverance from this nightmare, she would never set foot on a vessel of any kind again.

Topside, the men at the pumps moved in robotic rhythm, having been at their stations in continuous shifts for the last two days. The hull timbers were being stressed to the point where the seams were opening, and the influx had to be contained. Soon Victoria and the others would be called out to take their turn, and Victoria dreaded a return to this task. She would be tethered again to the pump by a length of rope, so that there was no chance of being swept away; but neither was there any chance of escaping the work either, until the mate called a shift change. She was so weak that she felt unable to contribute to the effort. The scene on deck was confused and chaotic enough that she was sure the man next to her was unaware that he was carrying the entire load on their side. Yet the cry to turn out at the pumps came soon enough again, and she dragged herself reluctantly to the madness on deck. At the companionway she looked at the commotion, in the midst of which were four rows of men at the pumps, their backs arching and rising opposite one another, like some ghastly parody of a medieval dance.

At the helm, meanwhile, the ship's officers were regarding worsening conditions with considerable alarm. A consensus was reached that they should no longer lie hove-to, but should try and make for the mouth of the Hayes, driving the vessel ashore, if need be. So the orders were given to bend on 'a spit o' jib', and the cable to the drogue was to be cut. When that was done, the ship fell off quickly, and a course was steered which would take her slowly at a shallow angle across the waves. No sooner had the new rudder taken the weight of the ship than a great wave thundered against the hull, covering the decks in foaming torrents as high as a man's waist. The rudder cables gave way, and the ship foundered. Again the men scrambled to repair the damage, relieved that at least the steering blade itself had not been carried away.

The *Esquimaux* had a total of six boats shipped aboard; two were locked into falls, two were lashed on board, and a longboat and lighter or barge. These vessels were needed for the transfer of freight, since the deep-drafted ships were required to anchor some five miles off the mouth of the Hayes River. These boats were made ready, in the event that the rudder failed again before the storm abated.

When the rudder gave way a second time, the *Esquimaux* rolled heavily onto her beam ends. Righting herself like a stricken fighter, the wind caught her again fully abeam, and broached her. She slid slowly back into a trough, the strain tearing away the unstayed rudder. The roiled seas rose up, yawning and snarling like starving hounds, looming open-mouthed over the starboard rail. A great cry went up to launch the boats, the frightened and desperate voices of men rising even above the sounds of a wrathful sea.

Victoria made for the boat that was closest. As she scrambled aboard, she heard a sea gull scream overhead, its thin cry a pitch higher than the howling turbulence. She looked up, startled at this incongruous sound, and the bird disappeared like a handful of thrown sand. She took this to be a hopeful omen; all other signs suggested that the *Esquimaux* was lost. About her, men were chopping at the boat's lashings, clutching at the gunwales, and bracing for the worst.

With a hissing, incoherent roar, the piled-up seas broke over the decks in a tidal rush. The ship rolled heavily, burying her rail under tumbling, chaotic, black water. The twenty-four-foot gig into which

Victoria had climbed, was carried up and away like a cork. The ship's lower yards were immersed, and the sodden main and fore course canvas held her momentarily. The following sea broke mightily against her, and there was never a chance for the *Esquimaux* to self-right. The twelve in the boat, including Victoria, were the only survivors, and they were immediately preoccupied with bailing water from the boat. Victoria bailed with her hands, and then with her woollen cap, once she realized it had somehow remained on her head. No one spoke, for each hand was required to keep the boat afloat. Anxious glances for the *Esquimaux* were in vain, for there was never a sight of her after the gig was borne away. In the space of three or four pounding heartbeats, the ship was gone. The survivors struggled with their bailing, as the mate wrestled with the tiller. So it continued until dawn.

With the new day, the rain stopped and the winds diminished. The sun spread its roseate fingers across the eastern skies, and though the air was chill, the exhausted castaways huddled together for warmth, and slept. Each two, after a time estimated by Mister Huggins, got the chance to be encircled by the others. There was no substitute for the furnace of hard work, however, and soon they were pulling at the oars, three pairs of which had been lashed to the thwarts.

They were well south of York Factory, but the western shoreline was a smudged pencil line on the distant horizon. Such was the magnitude of the disaster that no one spoke. Each pondered the miracle of his own survival, and coped as conscience permitted with the guilt of escape. Their shipmates' fate filled them with dread, and the thought of the last minutes aboard the *Esquimaux* was horrifying to contemplate. Victoria was haunted by the images her mind conjured up of the men who had been trapped below, and how their final moments had been prolonged as the ship sank, filling with water and breaking slowly apart. One of the castaways, a wizened old sailor named Benjamin Hicks, knelt in the boat and prayed his thanks, hands clasped, and face uplifted. The others bowed their heads and closed their salt-encrusted eyelids in thanksgiving for their delivery. But grief folded over them as firmly as a cerecloth.

viii

When Victoria arrived at York Factory in the late autumn, 1836, it was a settlement of some two dozen permanent buildings, dominated by the trade depot at the centre, overlooking the Bay. A daily watch was being maintained for the *Esquimaux*, for she was long overdue. The sighting of the longboat's tiny sail rigged to an oar caused a flurry of activity, with nearly all one hundred and twelve inhabitants flocking to the landing platform, and two boats being put off.

News of the disaster deeply stirred the collective emotions of the post inhabitants. Not only were the expected trade goods and personnel lost, but so were the latest instructions from London. Worst of all, coveted news from home was lost: letters that would have been pulled out and reread many times over the long winter months. By the time she was helped ashore, Victoria had no sense of the disaster at all. Her initial glimpse of the settlement and the actual landing did not register with her. She, like the others, was in a state of shock. Her hands were painfully blistered from her shift at the pumps and her turn at the oars. The land rose and fell beneath her, as her balance—which was long accustomed to the ceaseless motion of the deck—tried to compensate for the unyielding soil. All of them were afflicted with 'mariner's swagger', exacerbated by their weakened condition. The cumulative effect of all this was that Victoria became quite sick. Once in warm, dry clothing, bandaged and fed, she was shown to a bunk in one of the servant's houses. Here she threw herself down and passed into unconsciousness.

She and her surviving comrades were abed until the third day of their arrival. She awoke, disoriented, her bladder aching for relief. She looked about. The small room in which she had slept was as dingy as the fo'c's'le of the Esquimaux. The two-tier bunk was crowded against the wall; beyond the open door she saw a table and chairs facing a fire pit. Two small windows admitted light into the gloomy house of logs, heavily chinked with moss and mud. The air was close with the smell of evergreens, smoke, damp and piss. In a corner, she found a bucket which served as the chamber-pot, and she quickly availed herself of it. The building appeared to be otherwise vacant, and she was grateful for that.

Stepping outside, she shielded her eyes against the brilliant sunlight. All around her, bearded men in brightly coloured shirts, trudged by with huge bales on their backs, supported by a tumpline which passed over the forehead. The impression to Victoria was that of a suddenly disturbed anthill. The entire little colony seemed to be on the move. Down to the riverbank ran rough-hewn wooden footpaths. These extended over the mud and dried brown river grasses to the water. Here, there was a small flotilla of double-ended boats, each about forty feet long. All were rigged with a single mast and square yard. She assumed that these were the craft which would continue on to the inland posts.

She was hailed suddenly. 'You be Master Blinkarn, then?'

Victoria looked toward an approaching man and nodded uncertainly.

He was a giant of a man, well over six feet tall, with carrot-red hair and full beard. He was outfitted in a tartan tam, hide shirt, and rough, stuff trousers tucked into skin boots laced up to his knees. He held a white clay pipe in one hand, and a large blue ledger book under the other arm. Jamming the pipe into the side of his mouth, he stretched out his hand.

'McTattall,' he said simply.

He identified himself as a 'humble servant of the Company', and he expressed condolences for that which Victoria must have endured during the loss of the ship. He was a kindly man, and Victoria noticed that his eyes crinkled at the corners when he spoke. She liked him straight away, but she only half listened to what he was saying. Her preoccupation was with the intense hunger which gnawed at her innards. But she quickly forgot about breakfast as she discerned the import of his message.

'There's no time to tarry, lad, I regret to be saying,' he said, rolling his 'r's' in a heavy highland brogue. 'The brigade was waiting for the *Esquimaux* but the natives have warned of an early snow and freeze-up. With no freight now, they've taken our reserves, and they'll be off in an hour or so. You'll be with them. I regret to tell you,' he added softly, 'that we've been searching the coastline these past two days, and we've found not a trace of anyone or anything.' He lifted the front of his tam, and scratched his head. 'It's as if...' and he trailed off, thinking the better of it.

Victoria was surprised. 'But I've no clothes or instructions, and I'm not sure I'm able to travel.' She held up her bandaged hands. 'Where am I to be going?'

'You'll be a clerk's apprentice, as I believe was intended at the time of your recruitment. I've no document for this, but one of your company so advised me.' There was no objection from her, so he proceeded. 'At the moment you'll be sent to the post at Lower Fort Garry, and the Company will be assigning your posting from there. As it's so late in the season, it's my thought that you'll spend the winter there— 'bout time you had some luck. The boats'll take you there directly. And you'll have poor Tweedsmuir's kit; poor lad, he was devoured by a white bear this spring, while a-hunting. He was such a tiny fellow, he couldn't have been much more than a mouthful. Until you came along, his clothing wouldn't fit anyone else.'

He said it so matter-of-factly, that Victoria thought this was some sort of horrid jest. 'Eaten by a bear!' she exclaimed. 'Eaten by a bear?' Why, what kind of country had she come to? And what about wearing a dead man's clothes? She felt that there was something disrespectful or at least untoward about such a thing, and she expressed it so to McTattall.

'You're wearing some of them now,' he said quietly. 'You'd be well advised to take them all, lad, for there's not a great deal of choice. Bitter weather will be upon us all 'fore long, such weather as I warrant you've not experienced, even on those grim pieces of rock you call home. Such other supplies as you'll need, you'll be issued at the fort. Now get yourself back up to the mess hall for some proper tuck, then go and see the brigade leader, straight away.'

He pointed him out. 'He'll place you in one of the boats. '

She ran to do as she had been bidden, and after a morning meal of caribou and potato pancakes, with hot sweet tea, she was assigned to a boat, along with a dead stranger's tin-bound wooden trunk. There were three other survivors of the wreck, one of whom was an Orcadian, Wesley Isbister. Victoria remembered him as one of her tormentors, though he, by the look of his pale, surrendering expression, had little on his mind except the enormity of the tragedy he had narrowly survived. As the crews of the boats came down to take their places at the sweeps, they spoke in an exotic mixture of languages. She recognized the lilting dialect of the Orkneys, the French and Native tongues, and the more nasal English expressions.

And so the second phase of her journey began, with scarce time to develop her plans. She had asked in passing about Ephraim when she had been speaking with McTattall. He believed he was still at Pembina, a little more than two days' journey to the south of the lower fort. Two days! She exulted that she was so close now. Victoria longed for their meeting, and she saw it as the end of her masquerade and her misfortunes.

She was less than pleased with her treatment by the Company, however. There was no thought of convalescence. She was given the leavings of a dead man for apparel and hustled out of York within two hours of waking. Why, it appeared as if she was nothing more than a commodity: a bale of trade goods, correctly entered in the manifests, and shipped off to the interior posts as expeditiously as climate and conditions permitted. She hoped that this was not some portent of what was to come at the hands of Company officials. As cordial as McTattall was, it was just possible that his expressions of concern were nothing more than superficial. Still, a driving preoccupation with business would see no undue attention paid to her, and she supposed that was blessing enough. Her fatigue and generally unsavoury condition continued to diminish her femininity, and the oarsmen paid her no heed. They all knew what had befallen the newcomers, and to intrude on the grieving thoughts of others was a grave indiscretion none of them would consider.

Victoria had no thought that she would not be welcome, once she made her presence known to Ephraim. She was, however, troubled by her shift in perspective toward all men. The change of mind was an accretion;

an incremental subsidence of values. It was all very well to behave in a certain way while disguised, but her masquerade could not be maintained forever. Her fate was necessarily and inevitably yoked to a man, and she resented it even as she knew she must accept it. Perhaps with Ephraim, she could recapture the magic of their union on the clifftops of Hoy.

As the boats were pushed off, the twenty-foot oars dipped in unison, churning the water in the muddy shallows. The mouth of the Hayes River has a broad fetch, and the boats quickly spread out, vying for the lead position by the first bend in the river, some three miles upstream. The short, grizzled man standing in the stern, leaning against the steering sweep, called out lines from a song, and the tripmen repeated it in deep, musical voices:

> *J'ai cuelli, la belle rose,*
> *J'ai cuelli, la belle rose,*
> *Qui pendait au rosier blanc;*
> *La belle rose au rosier blanc!*
> *a belle nos'du rosier blanc !*

Victoria looked ahead, upstream. On either side, the terrain was low, treeless and inhospitable. She knew very little about this strange land, save what she had read at the parish school. One book in particular she remembered; this was the adventures of Henry Kelsey, the Hudson's Bay Company's boldest explorer, only a boy at the time of his indenture. In 1690, almost a hundred and fifty years earlier, he had set off along this very river, on the instructions of a Company goaded into exploration by critics who charged the traders of 'sleeping at the edge of a frozen sea'. Kelsey wrote in his diary with some melodrama, and a hint of awe:

> *Then up ye River, I with heavy heart*
> *Did take my way and from all English part*
> *To live amongst ye Natives of this place.*
> *If God permits me for 12 years space,*
> *The Inland Country of Good report hath been*
> *By Indians but by English not yet seen.*

Victoria recalled that somewhere at school, an excerpt of these adventures had been read to the class, which collectively shivered with fright, as Kelsey described 'a huge bear, bigger than any white bear, and neither white nor black, but silver hair'd like our English rabbit'. Victoria thought of poor Tweedsmuir, whose garments she now wore, and looked fearfully at the scrubby, implacable bush on the riverbank. Surely the land through which they now passed was unchanged since the great deluge God had wrought on a sinful world. She turned her attention to the boatmen.

Victoria's escorts were short, heavily built men. Their massive thighs and forearms bulged and rippled with the easy tensions of rowing. Each man wore his hair to the shoulders, the better to fend off sun and flies in summer. Some were clearly native; others were of mixed blood. But the Europeans were so sunburned that they looked as aboriginal as the rest. Nearly all of them wore a cap of some kind, and no two were identical. Most of the caps had some kind of adornment, such as beads, quills, coins and other such frippery as seemed inconsistent with their fierce appearance. All of the men wore moccasins, some with bead and quill work. They were quiet folk, and when they did speak, it was a low, almost guarded sort of murmur. It was the opposite, though, when it came time for a pulling song.

All but four of the thirty-five tripmen wore flannel or wool plaid shirts, red being the favourite colour. Trousers were uniformly of leather construction, or at least leggins, which were drawn up over the bare legs, and secured with a sort of garter to a belt. Those with leggins wore a breech-clout in the manner of the Indians Victoria had seen at the post. Their most prized possession was a pipe bag, which contained their pipes, tobacco and sulphur matches, the latter being dipped in wax to keep them waterproof. If these were not slung around their necks, lying upon their chests, they were safely stowed below a thwart, within easy reach.

Victoria awoke to a cool breeze on her face. She started, at first unaware of where she was. The brigade had halted at a lagoon surrounded by steep rock cliffs, perhaps twelve or fifteen feet in height. On the opposite side of this still water, just below a rushing cascade, the river churned and fussed through a narrow channel. The rapids were obviously too brisk to traverse under oar, and the men were engaged in dragging the boats one at a time by line and harness. Others in the boats fended off the rocks with stout poles. Victoria was in the fourth of seven boats, and she watched as the men strained like beasts, wobbling along the narrow, worn path around the falls. Once over the rapids, all hope of conversing was lost, for the clamouring water in the channel obscured all other sound. Nevertheless, no signal was needed, for each seemed to know what was expected.

Victoria was handed a pole, but her bandaged hands and general ineptness did not permit much in the way of its effective use. She flushed with embarrassment as she staggered and slipped, and ultimately dropped the pole into the current.

Once at the head of the fast water, a halt was called where the rock face shelved out into the river, creating a natural pier. The men sat or lay down to await the meal. Owing to their late start, this stop occurred well into the afternoon. Victoria was wet from the light spray of the falls, and she had bruised the back of her knuckles when she had made a futile grab for the errant staff. In all, she was uncomfortable and depressed by the thought that this part of the trip was as likely to be as cheerless as the first. She sat apart from the men in a natural armchair of stone. This open ledge was surrounded closely by thick, scruffy bush, fringed by brooding, skinny poplars. Shorn of their foliage, they stood naked and forlorn attendants to the pungent spruce groves. The woods formed a curtain which muffled the rapids' chatter; the silent forest precluded anything but a shout from being overheard.

The men laughed and talked quietly among themselves. Victoria was handed several strips of dried meat, and half a loaf of dense brown bread. She was directed to the water's edge to drink; indeed some of the others were already sprawled out, lapping like dogs. Victoria observed that these rough men had a peculiar modesty, extreme in the Indian oarsmen. Unlike her erstwhile companions at sea, each man went out of sight in the bush to relieve himself. There was no exposure, not even an arrangement of buttons or breech clout or any indecent comment. Soon, the group moved back to the boats, for they were apprehensive about the weather, and eager to be on.

Daydreaming, and chewing at her jerky absent-mindedly, Victoria became aware suddenly that she was one of the last to board. Jumping up, she slipped on a patch of moss, which gave way under her weight. She slid upright down the rocky embankment, waving her arms as if she were on a tightrope. Her foot caught in a crevice, and she fell awkwardly, twisting her ankle so painfully that she cried out. She groaned and clutched at her foot; tentacles of fire licked at her lower leg. It was impossible to put weight on it, and she gave up trying to walk.

Quickly, one of the voyageurs stepped to her side, and knelt in front of her, offering his shoulders to her. 'Pick-a-back!' he laughed.

Taking her arm, he loaded her as if she were no more than a small bale of trade goods. Wading out to the boat, now the last one, she was handed up and put in among the bundles with a jolt. Whimpering with the pain, she crawled to her place between the forward thwarts. A bucket of water was drawn up, and she was instructed to take off her boot and immerse her foot in its chill, the only anodyne available. It relieved the throbbing considerably, and she was grateful for their kindness, though she did not express it. In truth, she had become suspicious of men. She tried to make herself comfortable, and she found herself pondering this further change in who she was.

It had to do with trust and dependency, she supposed. She was utterly dependent upon men; at the present time, these men. All her hopes were fastened on a man whose love for her was becoming more and more uncertain as the miles between them diminished. Even her spiritual nourishment depended upon prayers offered up to a male God. Yes, of course she trusted these men, and the God which thus far had looked after her, but Victoria intuitively understood that secular and Divine grace seemed to hang on a keen appreciation of one's place. As an imposter, little could be taken for granted; as a woman, nothing could be taken so, if one were not prepared to accept the passive and subordinate roles assigned by men. She sighed. Back at home, her life was being played out in ways to which she mostly gave little thought. Only the exigencies of this dreadful passage had illustrated the inherent unfairness which seemed to lie in Nature's arbitrary assignment of sex. Perhaps with Ephraim, she hoped again, things could return to their natural alignments. There was a comfort in the thought. Warmed by this flickering of hope which retreat always initially inspires, she snuggled down in the cargo bales that smelled of musty burlap, and dozed off and on.

The steady clump and swirl of the oars had a hypnotic effect, and she remained still as a cairn. The coolness of the ambient air caressed her cheek like the gloved hand of fate. She had a natural disinclination to assert herself, to speak up in the way that men did: easily, roughly, with a leavening of humour. This quality, as well as her desire to avoid attention, relegated her to the margins of activity. She was not addressed, consulted, or respected. As a woman, she would have been shown some deference as the weaker sex, but for now she constituted another bale of freight, insignificant as a mote to the important affairs of men.

At the moment, it was a preferable condition. But she wondered with an inward shiver whether it was possible to reverse the condition. Was her only contribution going to be the life within her? Was she no more than a carrier, her own existence subordinate to all else? A shell to be discarded once the seed has germinated? Perhaps a woman had no entitlements beyond her union with a man. But then, that's why she was on this quest. Alone with her books and the hogs, her routines and her daydreams, she felt worthy and confident enough. But with her connection with Ephraim, there had been a transference of dependency to another. In his approval and his acceptance, his hunger for her and acknowledgement of her worth, she was validated. And the curse of it was, it could not be recaptured without him. Like innocence once yielded, it was gone.

The trip quickly fell into regular syncopation. The day's travel was broken into pipes, or about four miles. The oars were idled on a lake or backwater, to the ancient command, 'Allumez!' For about a quarter hour, the men smoked and chatted quietly, until the soft command, 'Alerte!' or perhaps, 'Allons!' All day the boats would move from pre-dawn until dusk. The sun was taking less time to describe its arc each day, and the brigade was impatient to get on.

The tracks at each portage were well worn after more than half a century of heavy traffic to and from the Bay. Where the water was too violent, the York boats were emptied, heaved up on log rollers in place from earlier trips, and rumbled across rock and stump in great splintery crashes to the upper reaches of the swift water. Little wonder that a York boat's bottom was good for two seasons at most.

Victoria watched the men in amazement, as she hobbled with the aid of a forked bough. Often soaking wet, they would take on their backs as many as two or three pieces, each ninety pounds or so, and scamper—the only word to describe it—after the boats. There was a pride in exhibitions of strength, speed, and agility which left Victoria and her fellow newcomers astounded. On long portages, and there were so many of these that Victoria felt as if she were walking to Fort Garry, the boats and freight were put down at well-defined spots, which some of the veterans called a pose. All of the vessels and their contents were thus relayed through the bush, and around the rapids.

Late one afternoon, as the sun was descending below the ragged screen of forest to the southwest, the brigade came upon an encampment of Indians. Their village of bark and hide lodges was clustered at the forks of a small stream which flowed into the river which the boats were ascending. Those in view, pursuing various acts of husbandry, remained motionless, their heads turning to watch the procession rowing by. No cry of welcome sounded, nor any gesture of menace. Silently, they watched. None of the others appeared to take any notice, but Victoria distinctly and unpleasantly felt like an intruder. Though they were not close enough to make out subtlety of expression, nevertheless she had seen this sort of look before in her mother. It had happened when the landlord had paid his annual visit, and had requested a dipper of water. He did not take off his filthy boots, and tramped his way into the kitchen, leaving marks across the floor; he had taken no notice, made no comment, offered no apology.

The gaze reflected fear and anger in perfect equipoise, she decided. But she did not comprehend the nature of it here. After all, these vessels were loaded with trade goods, and their life in the forest must be the easier for all that. Other than a brief glimpse of them at York, all she knew of Indians was what she had read. All chronicles were consistent in their descriptions, referring to them as children or heathen savages. She decided that their manner was evidence of their incivility, and dismissed the unease she was feeling. Striking up a fresh song, the boatmen bellowed out the chorus of 'A la Claire Fontaine',and leaned into their work. Alien sounds they yet were to these still, boreal forests, and in the cool evening air the strains lingered faintly over the water, palpable as a footprint.

It was late by the time a halt was called, the meal was done, and all turned in. Victoria lay in her musty sleeping robes, looking at the stars. Deep in the woods, a fox yapped his disappointment in the hunt, and further beyond a wolf began a mournful elegy. Others joined in, and Victoria was filled with dread at the prospect of wolves close to the camp. All the fairy tales of her childhood portrayed the wolf as the very embodiment of evil, and for a time sleep was impossible, as her imagination was fired by glinting eyes and drooling fangs closing in upon her. Huddled against the side of a boat, she at length became aware that no one else seemed concerned about the sinister howling, so she decided that this was yet another aspect which this country demanded the traveller endure. Still, she dozed fitfully, starting at each new sound.

As the moon began to set, she suddenly heard a cry that seemed to issue from the rended soul of this primitive country. A shivering, undulating wail, the like of which she had never heard before, seemed to come from the water's edge, echoing from the opposite side of the quiet water. It was followed by a quickening chorus of the same notes, in urgent variation. Then came silence. The mocking shriek repeated suddenly, mournful and haunting. Victoria was terrified, and she sat up and tugged at the man sleeping closest to her. 'What was that?' she hissed. The voyageur slept soundly, his body insistently requiring the replenishment of total repose. She yelped as a white face loomed up beside her, drawn as a phantom.

It was Wesley Isbister. 'What do yer reckon that be?' he asked her, looking around anxiously. 'It sounds as if it's from the pits o' hell!'

She shook her head. 'I don't know, but no one else seems a bother, so it's probably of no harm to us.' It comforted her that the next ululation seemed much further off.

This seemed to be of little comfort to Isbister. 'It'll be doin' us no good, yer cocking a snook at the devils in this place!' he whispered harshly. He was sorely regretting spending his signing bonus, for an inability to pay it back, plus the cost of the passage, meant indenture for the term of the promise. And from what he could see of the lives of the servants at York and these boatmen, life in this country was hard enough. The tales he had been told of the winter, now not far off, to say naught of the wreck of the *Esquimaux*, had put him in a very depressed state of mind. He squatted down beside Victoria, twisting his cloth cap in his hands.

'I'm to die in this land,' he said, the hopelessness in his voice as tangible as the thin ghost of breath which accompanied each sigh. 'Twas a wrong choice, and there's been nothin' good come of it yet.' He broke off as the tremulous lament sounded again, distantly. He was, Victoria remembered, one of those who had been deeply affected when poor John Pixel had fallen to his death, and like many, had taken the event as a sign which portended ominously for him. This was confirmed overwhelmingly in his mind by the sinking of the *Esquimaux*.

Isbister looked around with disgust at the sleeping figures, dusted with silver in the moonlight. 'They could all be eaten where they lie,' he sniffed.

Victoria sat up, and put her arms around her knees. She was strangely heartened by Isbister's dejection; she felt strong. Perhaps misery loves company, she thought, and she tried to console him. 'There is a purpose in our deliverance,' she said, 'God's will has intended us for other things, and I can assure you it's not to die in this forlorn place. You must take heart, for there's naught to be gained by a dim view of things. We must all take heart.'

What an irony, she reflected. This wretch may have been the one who soiled her clothing, or urged on bully-boy Flynne, and otherwise joined in her torment. She was sure he was, those weeks ago. Yet circumstances now placed him in need of her generosity. But for her own fear, she may have turned her back to him, as indeed she had avoided contact with all of them. Well, where was the advantage in demonstrating meaness of spirit? Revenge, she decided, was not worth the energy it consumed. When she had lain awake thinking about all the injustices done to her, as she had frequently enough, she found that the bitterness excluded all other thoughts. Left long enough, her existence could be poisoned as surely as hemlock. She had seen it in her mother.

She turned to Isbister. 'It'll be a new day dawning soon. Try and get some sleep. You can bring your bedding over here if you like, so that if we are to be devoured by the creatures of the night, well, at least we'll be consumed together.'

He whickered at this, and scuttled off. Seconds later, he threw down his robes, crawled in, and was muttering to himself when Victoria fell asleep. She was to laugh in astonishment the next day when she was told that the nightly wailing was the work of a bird, the loon-duck.

The trip to the lower fort on the Red River from York Factory took eighteen days. This was somewhat longer than usual, but the autumn water levels were low, and more time was spent on the portages. The load included a pair of heavy bronze bells, cast in Scotland, for the twin towers of the second cathedral at St Boniface; the building would be completed in mid-June of the following year on the site of the one which had burned down.

The tripmen worked hard all the way up river to the important inland post called 'Norway House', after the Norwegian axemen brought by the Company to attempt to construct a winter road to Fort Garry. Norway House was at the crossroads of northern commerce, for it was here that the brigades headed west to Edmonton House and the Mackenzie River. Or the boats could head south, toward the Red River of the North and the Forks, where the Assiniboine meets with the Red after meandering across a thousand miles of prairie. The busy settlement was just north of the vast body of water known as Lake Winnipeg. After a brief stop, where three of the boats left the brigade, the little fleet continued on.

In 1656, French traders excitedly reported to Quebec that a great sea lay to the west of Lake Superior. This sea had tides, it was said, and could be the fabulous passage to the Orient. It was named Ouinipeg, meaning 'murky', or 'foul'. Nevertheless, the search for the 'stinking water' revealed that Lake Winnipeg was merely a vast landlocked body, murky with sediment, and prone to the tide-like surges known as 'seiching'. It was on this huge lake that the tripmen had their first break in their strenuous routine. A fresh breeze was stiffening from the northwest. The tattered square sails were set, and the voyageurs enjoyed an easy run over undulating swells, southward to the Red River Settlement. As the breeze continued to pick up, and their course broadened to a reach, some of the load was moved to the windward side of the boats. Pipes were broken out, and the crews settled comfortably between the starboard thwarts. They would continue in this way until the breeze failed, or night fell.

By the end of the fourth day, the brigade reached the outlying silted shallows at the southern end of the lake. Beyond lay a broad, low-lying marsh. Here the last flocks of migratory birds were gathering, and the cacophony overwhelmed ordinary speech. The tasselled swamp grasses rippled in the cool autumn breeze. Cattails nodded and curtsied at the channel's edge, their spilled seed emptying like ragged down across the fen. Victoria could smell the rich moistness of sodden, rotting plant matter.

There was no mouth of the river as might have been supposed. Rather, a series of partings in the boggy foliage confronted the boats. These were traversed without pause, though no buoy or marker told the way, as in the top-knotted tree beacons which Victoria had seen on the shorelines of the northern lake. Here and there, the marsh parted in glistening reaches of water—false channels with not more than a few inches of water covering thick infestations of roots, underwater growth, and black, sticky mud. Rolling in all directions, to the height of a man's chest, the swamp closed about the brigade, and nothing to Victoria's eye hinted at the direction that the men should take.

At each bend, more of the avian stragglers rose clattering and whistling into the air; wheeling and fussing, the waterfowl settled behind, once the boats had passed. There were ducks, geese, gulls, and birds Victoria had never seen, in huge numbers. Along the banks, otter, mink and muskrat slithered and splashed to her amusement. The brigade's passage was surprisingly quiet in these sheltered waters. Only an occasional thunk of an oar against a thole pin broke the steady rhythms, as a weary tripman shifted position, or eased a cramped buttock. The light chop stirred by the catspaws and zephyrs slopped gently against the hulls as they slipped through the darkened water. Steadily, they picked their way south through open leads, but it confounded Victoria that they were able to pilot unerringly through this rustling, brooding maze.

There was something more here, Victoria suspected, than simply knowing the way. Rather, there was an intimacy, a oneness between this seemingly oppressive land and these men, regardless of their birthplace. It was different in some ineffable way, from her home. The Orkneys were hard enough for Orcadians to eke out a living, but harsh and utterly repelling to strangers. Even the absentee landlords who came to inspect their holdings once each year, could not wait to quit 'these bloody islands'. Severe though it was in North America, there was something seductive, fecund, and compelling about this wilderness through which they had been passing; something which drew and secured the soul. Many of the men who had taken Indian wives chose not to return to Europe, even though passage for them and their families was freely available at the end of their service. Choices most often had to do with beginnings, and for most, even though there was an initial desire to 'come home', the roots set down in this new land proved as deep and tough as prairie grass. Victoria remembered that she had thought, upon her departure from Hoy that long-ago morning on the deck of the *Sovereign*, that each farewell changes a soul forever. Perhaps destinations claim a piece of it.

This land, she decided, embraced those who lived on its terms. You could see that in the confident faces of the voyageurs, smell it in the muck-laden waters, taste it in the larded pemmican bags that sustained the men in their gruelling labours, and hear it in the distantly braying geese as they flung their faltering wedges across the evening sky. This was a place of contrasts: vast plenty on the one hand, and a grim harshness on the other. But in between, there was a sufficiently broad margin to permit a man to make his way.

The final leg of the journey passed along the river quickly. There was a continuing abundance of wildlife. Great moose feeding in the river shallows crashed away into the thick underbrush, water streaming from their flanks. Fat, round, black bears wandered sleepily in search of a last meal before escaping the coming snows, and everywhere, rabbits scattered in their bumpy gait, their coats already sporting hints of white.

Lower Fort Garry was built by the Hudson's Bay Company as a replacement for old Fort Gibralter, originally set up at the Forks by the North West Company, operating out of Montreal. The fort was renamed in 1822 after Nicholas Garry, a stubborn, forceful and domineering member of the Board of Governors of the Company. In 1826, a great flooding of the two prairie rivers lifted the old wooden battlement off its foundations and, rather than rebuild it, Governor Simpson made the sensible decision to conduct operations from higher ground some twenty miles downstream just north of the rapids at St Andrews; about a day's journey. It was a grand structure of limestone blocks, with the Big House at the centre. The banks of the river at this point were easily fifteen to twenty feet high.

As the men approached the stone fortress, bright sashes were brought out, beaded vests put on, and the crews broke out in song, as the race began for the honour of landing first:

En roulant, ma boule roulant!
En roulant, ma boule!

As a small crowd gathered on the bank, under the snapping Company flag, the men made the water roil with their oars. Victoria's craft was the second one in, and the men shipped oars as the long keel slid up the muddy shore and listed. All of those above now swarmed down to the landed craft, and a great babble of different languages filled the air. The news of the *Esquimaux* produced consternation, and Victoria could feel their eyes upon her and her fellow survivors. No matter. She was only two days away from Ephraim, and her first task would be to see the factor and explain everything to him. She would secure his help in getting to Pembina, and all would be well. She stood up uncertainly in the bow, gingerly testing her injured leg.

Teams had started to unload the bales of guns and shot, powder, traps, twine, blankets, axes and all products required 'for the continued prosecution of the fur trade', as the manifests read. Wives and family members had already begun to lead their men away from the boats, and soon Victoria was left standing alone. No one paid any attention to her; the mood of the crowd was quite self-absorbed. With considerable difficulty, she swung her feet over the side of the vessel, and dropped clumsily into the shallows. Her outstretched hands sank into the mud and she gritted her teeth with the ache in her ankle. None of her travelling companions came to her aid and she stumbled up the bank, her boots squishing in the sucking gumbo underfoot.

Never mind. She had arrived at the threshold of her quest. All that remained was to harden her resolve, gather up her courage and cross it. The resonance of her anxiety flowed not just from the encounter which she believed now to be only hours ahead of her, but from the echoes of lessons learned while sojourning in a man's domain. She had stumbled upon a disaffirming divide which cut the world into ghettoes of opportunity and denial. There was just a trace of despair in her thoughts as she felt the uneasy tug at her will; with Ephraim, she would surely find peace, wouldn't she? There was more than a hint of a truly terrifying possibility that she would never find peace again, for the knowledge of diminished opportunity clung to her like the river mud underfoot.

Grimly she recalled something she had read several times, but which now took on greater, more sinister meaning:

> *Though thy slumber may be deep,*
> *Yet thy spirit shall not sleep;*
> *There are shades that will not vanish,*
> *There are thoughts that will not banish;*
> *By a power to thee unknown,*
> *Thou canst never be alone;*
> *Thou art wrapt as with a shroud,*
> *Thou art gathered in a cloud;*
> *And forever shalt thou dwell*
> *In the spirit of this spell.*

'Donald Blinkarn,' roared the brigade leader who had come back to the top of the riverbank: 'Will ye be taking the rest of the day, or have ye a mind to go back to York?'

Shaken out of her reverie, Victoria stifled a sob, took the weight off her lame foot and called out, 'I'm all right! I'll make it yet, never mind!'

Two

i

Ephraim Blude trembled a little as he squinted down the barrel of the heavy musket. Excitement surged through him nearly out of control. Fifty yards away, a small herd of buffalo snuffled and grunted in a shallow glen split by a nearly dry creek. He sat with two other hunters in a low copse of skinny poplars, waiting for the animals to work their way toward them. His weapon rested in a fork of a sapling and, his companion having hissed his instruction to shoot, he jerked the trigger impatiently. The gun boomed in the thicket, releasing an acrid cloud of smoke. Nothing happened; the herd seemed unconcerned, and it was certain that the shot had gone wide of its mark. Ephraim cursed and reloaded. The others snickered.

'Try again, *moonias*. This time, squeeze the trigger; hold the gun as if you had a woman in yers arms!'

Ephraim flared his nostrils. He detested being referred to as a greenhorn, and he gripped the stock less firmly; this time he squeezed the trigger gently. Before the report had echoed back from the other side of the valley, the bull closest to them crashed to earth as if his legs had suddenly collapsed under him: a heart as big as a man's head had been torn apart by a tumbling, ripping, quarter-ounce lead ball. Ephraim grinned with pride, but the mixed-blood beside him snorted. 'Didn't I say to aim for the cows? Why not take the sweeter meat? Go now,' and he gestured, 'take that one.'

Once again the report resonated, and a small cow bucked and twitched, blood streaming from her nostrils as she sank to her knees. Still the other beasts took no notice of the carnage, not even when the cow stumbled and crashed heavily to earth. And so it went until the little herd was slaughtered, including the bulls, so that Ephraim could practise his shooting.

Ephraim's love affair with Rupert's Land was total and consuming. Upon his arrival at York Factory, he was posted as a labourer to Pembina, a full day's journey upriver from the Forks on the Red River. Pembina was the European version of *nepemenah*, the Cree word for summerberries— the same fruits which were mixed with dried buffalo meat and lard for the brigades. The small settlement was a staging area for the hunts against the southern herds, and was formerly known as Fort Daer. This had been built by the hapless Red River settlers the first time they had been driven out from the area north of the Forks in 1812, by the Métis servants of the North West Company. It now served as the principal meat supply depot for the Company. The crimson stains of reddle on Ephraim's hands and clothes had been traded for the carmine of bison blood.

There were three general grades of service in the Hudson's Bay Company, classifications which reflected the sharp class distinctions of the day. There was, however, possibility for upward mobility between the classes, which in the mother country was virtually impossible. This advancement depended upon intelligence, courage, ambition and, above all, patience. At the upper level of Company society was the chief factor, a full share holder with the rank of officer. Below him in status was the chief trader, or one-half share holder; and below again, the clerks. More than a decade must pass before there was any hope of advancement from the rank of clerk. The approximate equivalent of the clerk was the postmaster, who might have charge of a small post. After this came the apprentice clerks who were the young men of certain minimum schooling, and the interpreters. These latter were the old hands, well versed in the lore of the frontier and capable of conversing in the various native dialects, as well as French and English. At the initial levels of service, the labourer was the jack-of-all-trades, who was responsible for tasks not reserved to those of standing in the Company, from warehousing to counting skins. It was owing to Ephraim's poor handwriting and obvious dislike for ledgers and journals, that he was assigned to more menial work.

His principal assignment was to supervise the Métis in the unloading of the ox carts which they used to bring in tons of buffalo meat, most of it already dried under the furnace of the blazing prairie sun. Pemmican required the dried meat to be pounded between two stones, and the pulverized flesh put into a hide bag with hot lard; the ninety-pound bag was then stitched tightly across the neck. This food was frequently eaten raw, but it was favoured when boiled together with flour and water, especially if it had been flavoured with different sorts of berries.

Some years earlier, all the pemmican had been prepared out at the kill, according to the dictates of time and weather, but with the volume of traffic extending to the Arctic and Pacific oceans, the corporate appetite for meat from the plains herds had become ravenous, and Pembina saw feverish activity during the summer months. From a single hunt, more than fifteen hundred tongues might be brought in; the rest of the meat was cut up and dried, ready for packing.

In the boisterous enthusiasm for the hunt, there was no thought anywhere that the vast numbers of buffalo could be depleted or even diminished by the incursions of the hunters. In addition to the voracious demands of the Company, the engines of industry in the American east required millions of miles of industrial belting, and the tough, spongy leather from the plains bison was ideally suited to this function. As the British Empire continually expanded, the red-suited militias of Queen Victoria, who would take the throne the following year, strode the globe in boots double-soled in buffalo hide. Even leather panelling was becoming fashionable in the homes of the well-to-do, and these markets fuelled an enormous trade in skins. Still, the herds could be seen in seemingly unending numbers in the parklands and the plains west of the Red River. The relentlessness of the slaughter was as short-sighted as the buffalo itself, for with their passing, so were to pass the dreams, and indeed in some cases, the very existence of a people. But to men like Ephraim, the exhilaration of the kill was like a drug.

His first glimpse of the buffalo was mundane. It was a captive, held in a rough pen by one of the other labourers. Although the bison was notoriously unpredictable in close quarters, collectively the beasts were stupid. The ways of the herd were well known to hunters, and Ephraim eagerly sought each crumb of information that would enable him to participate in the chase. The tales about the magnitude of the herds were beyond his imagination: a herd of large animals which took four days to pass? So many beasts that the ground was torn up, shrubbery levelled, and the terrain fetid with their droppings? Such a story, when first suggested to him, made him think that he was being taken for a tenderfoot.

Other stories were related to Ephraim in the glow of the fire in the bachelors' quarters. He was told of the savagery of the Plains Sioux, and of their enduring hatred for the Cree and the Métis. They would torture, scalp and enslave captives, it was said, and to fall into their hands would be the start of a nightmare from which few were known to have awakened. And what about the great hunchbacked bear, now rarely seen, which was known by natives to stalk men as a fox creeps up on a partridge, and once having made the kill and devoured the carcass partly, hung the remains in a tree for later consumption. It was well known this creature had mystical powers.

These tales of horror fed the jokes the men were fond of playing upon newcomers. One morning, Ephraim, upon hearing low-throated snarling, awoke to find a bearskin draped across his chest, its head mounted with the skull propped open in a menacing grimace. He screamed with fright, his bladder spilling involuntarily as he sprang from his robes. A chorus of shrieking laughter met him at the door of the dormitory. The telling and re-telling of the episode provided amusement for days. Ephraim loved it, and offered creative suggestions for the torment of subsequent arrivals.

He was drawn intensely to the lifestyle and the freedom of the Métis and English-speaking Halfbreeds whose life centred around the hunt, and he was quick to adopt their manner of dress, including their penchant for ornament and glitter. He wore his dramatic red hair long, and was told many times that Sioux warriors would go to great lengths to have such a trophy dangling from a war lance. In the fiery late summer of 1836, Ephraim became as brown as his Indian and mixed-blood associates who were quite taken with him. He was one of those Europeans who wanted to be like them, to live with them, to be one of them. Gradually, in the words of the chief trader, he was 'going Indian', a phenomenon discouraged but not unknown to the Company. It was troubling for white Christians to see such behaviour, but there were some compensations. It was just as likely to make their servants unreliable as it was to render them valuable in the way of interpreters or guides.

As early as 1790, a Scotsman named George Sutherland had joined the Company, and within two years had gone to live on a bend in the South Saskatchewan River, well beyond the frontier. The journals of the time lamented that Sutherland had 'gone Indian', for he had taken a wife 'in the manner of the country', and then two more, eventually siring twenty-seven children. All had their own families, and identified more closely with their Indian neighbours, the Plains Cree, than any other group. Decent white men shook their heads.

The Cree and their allies, the Assiniboine, had a long tradition of welcome. Other than in the serious matters of sharp trading, the Cree accepted the European without guile, absent betrayal or hostility. The most worthy example of this hospitality was Ojibway Chief Peguis, who readily gave land, shelter and succour to the early settlers brought in by the earnest goodwill of Lord Selkirk. Without the generosity of the Ojibway, the colonists surely would have been starved out. And so it was that Ephraim began to spend all available time with the welcoming plainsmen, both Indian and mixed-blood.

There were over five hundred Métis at Pembina in 1836, about seventy white men, mostly Orcadians and Scots, and a population of

Indians whose numbers ebbed and flowed according to the demands of the moment. At all times there were dances, horseshoe pitches, gambling with dice, horse races and endless other pleasurable pursuits to occupy a young man's idle time. Very quickly Ephraim began to pick up basic expressions in French and Cree and the peculiar mixture of languages known as 'bungee'. By October, the senior officers decided it was necessary to make a change in Ephraim Blude's arrangements, and it was decided to send him further inland. There the Company could capitalize on his remarkable grasp of native dialects, and at the same time, perhaps, arrest his seemingly headlong dash toward dissolution.

Orders were drawn up, and on 16 October 1836, Ephraim was summoned to the desk of the chief trader, a dour and deeply religious old Scotsman named MacDonnell. He was a member of the lay clergy, and fond of sciolistic biblical references. After advising Ephraim his new posting was to be Brandon House, some three days by canoe to the west on the Assiniboine River, he cautioned Ephraim that his wild ways were habits he would be prudent to outgrow. Ephraim was deferential to authority, and he remained silent, barely nodding his head.

'If ye heart be not in this business, then the company shall be looking for refunds, and its costs be repaid,' said the sour, red-faced trader. 'I'm thinking ye be listenin' to the wrong sorts a folk; remember, the Book teaches us: "the instruction of fools is folly".'

Ephraim lowered his head in acquiescence. He did not understand the lecture, though he was aware of the disapproval. Well, he was used to that. But the reference to returning money and passage home was a little disturbing, so he offered in a meek voice, 'Well sir, I'll be tryin' that much harder at Brandon House.'

MacDonnell rolled his eyes. 'Try harder at what is the question. Be warned. We have enough savages and breeds in this country. Ye've a career ahead of ye with the Company, but perseverance and hard work is the only path to success. "He that is slothful in his work is brother to him that is a great waster." Go, and luck to ye, boy.' And he picked up his quill and began to write. So dismissed, Ephraim turned away.

ii

The original structure at Brandon House was built by Donald McKay forty-three years prior to Ephraim's reassignment. The crude foundation of earth banked between cribs of poplar boughs measured twelve feet by twenty-two. The site faced south, over a tortuous bend in the Assiniboine

River, some one hundred and thirty miles due west of the Forks. Winter was coming, and shelter was urgently required. But for now, at five in the afternoon and getting dark, he and his party would break out the rum to help fend off the deepening chill. 'Very cold weather,' he later wrote in his journal. Pouring a little into a tin cup, he reached out to christen the new trading post, to assure good luck. Before he could do so, another man stepped forward, a Glaswegian Scot named Norrie. 'Ach, no, mon! You've not a name yet for this drear place!' His burr was thick, the more so that evening after a double tot of rum.

In truth, McKay had been thinking about it. There was precious little in this land to remind him of home. Most often his thoughts were of the woman he had left behind—a slim, raven-haired slip of a girl. They had lain together in a sweet-smelling haystack on the lands belonging to Brandon Hall, a manor once occupied by the Laird of Kilmartin. A grand place it was, especially by the standards of the west coast, and following the consummation of their ardor, they lay together and wondered about the life of those who lived in such splendour. Well, why not, thought McKay, it's as fine a wee lodge as these parts have yet known. He reached out and tilted the battered tin cup toward the recently built foundation and spoke. 'To Brandon House, and to our noble Company's health and success!'

But before he could pour, Norrie snatched the cup from his hand and downed its contents in a single gulp. To McKay's protest, he responded, 'What a bloodie waste a guid grog! Wha's the harm in ma usin' it furst?' Then unbuttoning his breeches, he walked straddle-legged to the excavation, and urinated on it in an exaggerated arc.

'Let's be realistic, laddies! 'Tis a piss-poor excuse for a lodging in any case, an' when it's done, it'll be not much better!'

The small group of Cree were used to the white men and their inexplicable bad manners, but the sight of any man fouling his lodge seemed hilarious. They broke into laughter. McKay grinned broadly, too, for Norrie's irreverence had lifted the gloom. That night, near a candle in a 'skin lodge', he would record for his masters in London that 'all hands as yesterday, self laying the foundation of the House' and after chewing a calloused thumb over the right choice of words, he scribbled in a firm hand that would remain legible for more than a century. 'Baptised house Brandon House.'

When Ephraim arrived almost half a century later, the original sod and log building was gone, and a group of log and clapboard structures formed the compound. They were set up in a U configuration, across the front of which was a reinforced palisade standing about eight feet high.

Sioux raiding parties were not unknown this far north of their traditional hunting grounds, and the Cree, Assiniboine, and the Métis were their sworn enemies. Well back of the gate was a small eight-pounder, stuffed with grape shot that consisted mostly of bent nails, hammerheads and scrap wire. With each report of skirmishes out on the plains, the little field piece was unloaded and checked over, and reloaded.

Yet when Cuthbert Grant, 'Captain of all the Half Breeds in the country', and his band, having been spurred on by the Nor'Westers out of Montréal in their enmity for the white settlers, attacked Brandon House in 1816, not a shot was fired. There was not then, nor was there now, much confidence in the fortifications of the rough little bastion. After the rival fur trade companies settled their differences by amalgamation in 1821, the only dangers lay out on the plains, as the Blackfoot and Sioux became increasingly assertive about encroachments into their lands.

Nearby was a village of Assiniboine Indians. Their lodges were visible across the river. The valley at the spot chosen by McKay was sheltered from the worst of the weather, and was well wooded in poplar, maple, tamarack and spruce. It was comfortable enough, but visits by anyone other than trading parties were few. It was not long before Ephraim had taken a wife 'in the manner of the country'. He had become infatuated with a young Assiniboine woman whose name, Kwasitchewan, loosely translated, meant 'Glittering Waters'. After a frustratingly prolonged court-ship, according to the demands of the tribe, and the payment of a dowry, Ephraim took 'Glittering Waters' to live with him in his wooden tent.

She was attractive, attentive and hard-working. She did not intrude on Ephraim's love of the hunt, but saw to his needs in clothing, cooking and bed. She did not object when he named her 'Elizabeth', for when she asked its meaning, he replied simply that it was a beautiful name.

It was not long before Elizabeth became pregnant. Ephraim was mildly annoyed at this, for once it was certain, she began to sleep in a different bed, allowing no intimacies with him. It was another of their infuriating customs, he understood, and there was nothing he could do about it. The Indians of the village were a strict lot who would not take kindly to any attempts at dalliance with other young women, and the 'whisky indians' who hung around the post begging and offering to prostitute themselves for a tot of grog, repelled him.

In the summer of 1838, a son was born to this union; an eleven-pound boy who almost killed his mother during birth, with dark brown skin, and a shock of coppery red hair. Ephraim was away on a hunt at the time, and upon his return showed little interest in the child, save that the hair colour caught his attention. 'There's no doubt the little bastard's mine,' he laughed, and went off to attend to the affairs of the Company. Glittering Waters had her son named 'Enatik', or White Spruce. He was tall, and would be wise, she was sure. Though he would encounter terrible storms in his life, and would bend, she believed that he would remain firmly rooted and strong.

Ephraim would have none of it, and named the boy 'David'. Though she was expected, under threat of a beating, to use 'Elizabeth' and 'David' when around Ephraim or the other white traders, she sang to David in her own language, and always referred to him as Enatik during Ephraim's absences, which were frequent. In fact, for most of David's childhood, the greatest part of his time was spent with his mother's people. He became fluent in the languages of the plains very early. Ephraim demanded the use of the English language at home, and forbade David to speak in any other language in his presence. 'Some day, boy, you'll be a gentleman to be reckoned with, and you'll thank me, right enough.'

David was ten when he accompanied his parents on his first great buffalo hunt. Though he had become an accomplished rider in the Assiniboine camps, and in the races and games practised by the other mixed-blood boys, he was left in no doubt as to his role. He would work with his mother, first recovering the tongues of the buffalo his father brought down, and then skinning and butchering the animals. David knew all about this sort of work; it was hot, dirty, and worst of all—except for the skinning—it was women's work. David's father was now no longer an employee of the Company. He had opted not to re-enlist, or sail home with his pay. He became a hunter, a supplier of meat and robes to the Company. He was indistinguishable from any other native of the plains in dress and speech, except for the mane of red hair. The Company ledgers of the time disclose that Ephraim now spelled his last name, 'Bloode'. It was entered phonetically during some transaction by a struggling apprentice clerk, and Ephraim fancied it.

In the third week of June of 1848, David, his father, his mother and his sisters of six and four years, travelled by ox cart in a small brigade to the staging area for the hunt into the Dakota territories, the land of the Sioux. The great throngs of beasts from the northern herd were no longer close to the Red River Valley, and each year hunters were required to range further afield to find their quarry. The southern approach was preferred to the great western hunt, for the latter took the buffalo runners deep into Blackfoot territory. The fierce fighting between the Blackfoot and both the Plains Cree and the Assiniboine would not diminish until after 1869, when an enormous battle left more than seven hundred dead.

In truth, neither choice of hunting ground was particularly

attractive, but by starting in the east, a bigger group could be put together from the Red River Settlement. The larger force was necessary both for protection against the Sioux, who did not look kindly upon such trespasses, and to ensure greater efficiencies necessary in so vast an undertaking. It was a time when both the English and French-speaking mixed-bloods hunted together, bound by common need and trust imposed by the fruits of cooperation.

The meeting place this year was an open stretch of high ground along the Pembina River. Some were already calling the place 'St Joseph', even though it was no more than a cluster of seasonally occupied shacks. It was at this spot that many settlers found refuge during the occasional but persistent flooding of the Red River and its tributaries. The range nearby offered ample fodder for the stock, and room for the transient settlement which this year would number more than nine hundred strong in all. When the Bloode family arrived, most of the hunters and their entourage had assembled.

It was a spectacular sight, not only for David, who had never seen such a huge gathering, but for anyone—including the veterans of the chase. The children ran to and fro, implements jangled and carts squeaked; the neighing of horses and lowing of oxen, and the shrill cries of the huntsmen as they gathered in council or delivered orders, raised such a clattering buzz, it could be heard long before the encampment was in sight. The smudge from more than two hundred cooking fires hung over the assembly like a pall, until it drifted lazily off to the southeast.

The Bloode caravan consisted of an ox-drawn, two-wheeled, wooden cart which squeaked and shrieked on its dry axles. Any greasing of the moving parts would have attracted dust, which would have in turn seized the wheels. It was trailed by two shaggy ponies. As they squealed their way to the perimeter of the camp, Ephraim passed the driving line and switch to his wife. He sprang from the cart and, taking the tether from the rail with an impatient tug, he leapt astride a pony and rode ahead, a study in impatience and excitement.

David watched him go. His father flew like the embodiment of joy, his tangled copper hair marking his passage in the afternoon sun as he went. David felt a mixture of emotions. He did not feel close to his father. Ephraim was stern, distant and, above else, rarely at home. The nature of his father's relationship with his mother seemed to David quite different from those he saw in his mother's people. There was no closeness, little warmth. David did not see the little glances, the private looks and smiles that some men and women give one another, when they think no one is looking. He never heard the intimate *nicimos*, sweetheart, at home, and he wondered about that. Ephraim was not cruel, but if food was not prepared, clothing not mended, firewood not gathered, or any of hundreds of chores not done to his timing or liking, he would raise his voice or even cuff his wife. She never complained, but David had been sorely whipped when he had interjected as a small boy.

Some of the other horsemen rode out to meet him, whooping and shouting a welcome. Though his speech was still flavoured by a sharp Orkney twang, he was conversant in the bungee dialect, Plains Cree and the close tongue of the Assiniboine. There was an easy camaraderie between English and French mixed-bloods, though that would change toward the middle of the century. For now Ephraim represented another gun, and was welcome as a brother.

As the perimeter guards spoke with Ephraim, David could see that the camp was laid out in an enormous circle of carts similar to their own, with their shafts pointed outwards. With much gesturing, their ponies starting and balking, the outriders indicated where the Bloode family was to rest. David's mother got down and led the animal where directed, then swung into a routine of arrangements for the feeding and shelter of her family. Ephraim would not reappear now until the evening meal was ready. David's job was to collect twigs and chips to fuel the cooking fire. He sighed. Being among the latecomers, he would have to range far beyond the perimeter to find kindling. He set off for the river, thinking that his luck would be better in the ragged shrubbery lining its banks. But it was more than a mile there and back, and it was getting dark. From a distance, in the dusk, the hundreds of fires and the low murmur of the camp made the scene resemble the vast bivouac of some marauding army.

The next morning, no fires were set. David tied up the bundles of unused twigs and dry boughs and slung them under the cart. A tall peeled sapling was being raised near the centre of the camp; a pale blue flag fluttered weakly at its summit. The pole was lashed to the rail of a cart, and this signalled a half-hour to departure. There was a horizontal figure-eight design stitched in fraying white fabric on the pennant, and he was determined to ask his mother about it.

The industry of the camp now picked up perceptibly, as the horsemen who were the soldier-guides rode up and down exhorting the breaking of camp. One rider in particular had a loud, shrill voice. His long beard flew in the wind as he galloped from one side of the assembly to the other. Short, stocky, and completely dressed in beaded skins, topped by a splendid if incongruous bottle-green frock coat, he cut a dashing figure on the plains. Though his shouted commands, most of which were in French, were lost on the breeze, the sense of his orders nevertheless was understood, and the hunters and their families bent to their tasks.

At last, the cart to which the flag was affixed started forward, threading its way to the western edge of the waiting group. Singly and in small groups, as the guides waved them on, the carts fell in behind one another, their wheels staggered, left wheel to right track, in a span of eight or so, then back again. The caravan was arranged in an undulating zigzag across a broad track. This strategy prevented the carts from wearing a deep rut in the prairie soil, which could become a serious problem in the event of rain. The guides were ceaseless in their urging directions, until at last the entire brigade was on the move. A dreadful squealing and screeching was set up; David wondered that the buffalo would remain within a hundred miles of this frightful din. Still, the ears seemed to become accustomed to it, in the way that one becomes accustomed to a bad smell, or an aching back. The guides fell off into prearranged positions flanking the procession. No lagging or forking-off was permitted without permission of the master of the hunt. This was but one of many rules; for any infraction, the penalty could be severe.

A transgressor could have his saddle and bridle publicly cut up. A multiple offender could have the shirt ripped from his back and be flogged, so seriously did the community see the need for order in their quest for meat and robes. One headstrong, impatient move could easily put in jeopardy the success of the chase itself.

Twelve days passed in a uniform succession of repeated events. The guides and the soldiers, under the direction of the captains, were organized in groups of ten, after the manner of the godfathers of the plains hunt, the Sioux. Overall direction was maintained by the warden, or master of the hunt. These men ordered the daily routine according to a strict, predetermined pattern. Ephraim was one of the soldiers, and David could follow his comings and goings by his bright hair and the emerald-coloured sash he wore over his antelope smock and leggins. Each captain supplied guides and soldiers in rotation, so that each rider and mount would get a chance to rest. When the flag was lowered, the brigade knew a halt was imminent, and the guides would issue directions for an orderly stop.

It was during the stop on the twelfth night that David decided to ask about the flag.

'Mother,' he said, speaking in Assiniboine, 'Why is the flag of the brigade so made, with two circles, each running into the other?'

A woman of few words, Glittering Waters replied, 'It stands for the peoples of two bloods, who speak the French tongue in their lodges.'

'Am I not of two bloods?'

'Yes. But your father is of the white race. They are a different people, and hold different thoughts.'

David pondered this for a moment. 'I don't see much difference. They look the same; everyone speaks some of the other's language. Both English and French work for the same fur company, and both sneak to the American traders to do some business with them.'

His mother had no answer for him. He would find out soon enough that the differences between people usually emerged during times of trouble. For herself, well, a woman took the people of her man as her own; that was how she had been raised. But the few white women she had seen on the occasional trip to Red River had shown her nothing but scorn.

David felt the power of the bond for his mother—the person who had given him life, and had nurtured him. She had gone without many times so that he would flourish. She spoke so few words in any tongue, he found it hard to understand her. When his father was present, her English was so poor that she was reluctant to speak, unless he addressed her directly. She seemed to expect that David would understand her, regardless of how few words she used, and he often did. Her silence was never indifference, for their love for one another required no constant vocal reassurance. This time, however, she went on.

'The blue is the colour of the eastern traders who gave us better prices for our fur in the days of my father and his father than the pale men from the northern sea. The two circles mean the joining of the French-speaking peoples and the Cree-speaking peoples, and the existence of their offspring forever.' She gestured here with a finger drawing the lazy figure eight in the air, the sign of infinity. 'Forever!' she said emphatically again.

This was a longer speech, David thought, than he had heard from her, except in song. I wonder where that leaves me? As an English Halfbreed, he felt an affinity for no one except an old man related to his mother, whom he called 'grandfather'. He was a Métis, a French-speaking Catholic who worked for the Company building boats. David had visited with him and his family only a half dozen times or so, but he felt a strong kinship with the old man. He had worked with the Bay men since they had made the decision to trade inland in the great boats which he now helped to construct and repair. But David felt excluded in some ineffable way. It was not that there were any overt acts against the Bloode family by any of the Métis; quite the contrary. It was just that he had begun to feel the thin tendrils of comprehension for his mother's studied silences, when she was with anyone other than the people from her village. This was something he would explore with his grandfather upon their return, for the Bloodes would be wintering this year at Lower Fort Garry.

iii

The following morning, news came before sunup that the herd was within a two hours' ride. Excitement flickered its way through the camp like a prairie fire. A council of captains was struck by the master, a thick-set, heavily bearded man by the name of Ambrose Lépine. His skin was the colour of scorched leather, and his black eyes glittered as he issued his instructions in short, sharp demands. 'All must be in readiness for the run,' he said, scratching a diagram into the dry earth with the point of his knife. 'We will assemble thus and so, and no one, I repeat, no one will move on the herd until I give the signal; that will not occur until I am sure it is all clear; explain how we will proceed to your men. I want no mistakes!'

He ordered the captains to take their positions with their troops well before the sun was up, and downwind of the buffalo. The men sprang to their feet and ran to their tasks. Twenty minutes later, more than two hundred and sixty riders were arranged in a great semicircle, in their designated groups. There was not a rattle or a clink to be heard, notwithstanding the ponies' bucking and chafing, and little steps of eagerness. All the men were shod in leather moccasins. All tack was of rawhide and sinew from the beast they now drew upon. Yet the muffled shuffling and thumping charged the air with tension, and the assemblage in formation appeared grand and warlike.

David shivered. Here in the smoke-light of the day's awakening, he looked at a fearsome army in readiness for the kill. He could almost feel the single mind of this vast array of predators, and he wondered about the object of such intent. The plodding beasts had no chance, though they could in their furious flight extract their own form of vengeance. This must be the way of war. His grandfather had told him stories of war: of the ancient struggles between the plains tribes, and the great honours bestowed upon worthy young men who distinguished themselves by feats of valour. To be recognized for courage was the highest possible attainment, or so said his grandfather.

As with the hunt, there were compelling reasons for war. Territorial encroachments, vengeance for wrongs committed, or the protection of trade supplies were among tribal interests to be protected by the waging of war. This seemed sensible to David. But there were some frightful things about combat which disturbed him. The taking of scalps, for instance. David had rubbed the top of his head anxiously when he was first told of the practice. His mother's people had related that the taking of a scalp with white hair was a great honour. To accomplish such a thing, a warrior would have to fight his way into the inner circle of lodges where the women and children were protected by the old men. To reach so far into the enemy camp would necessarily mean that many warriors would have to be defeated. To David's young mind, the slaughter of old men for proof of courage was contradictory, even repelling. He did not understand this aspect of his mother's people any more than he understood his father's rejection of his own people. It was an unsteady balance that required each foot to be planted in different worlds, he decided.

Ambrose Lépine mounted last, then turned and faced his hunters. He raised his musket, and David could see that a thin strip of red worsted had been tied to the barrel. At this signal, the hunters moved off. The hunt had begun. It was a stirring cavalcade, drawing emotions which usually slept in the shadow of the soul: menace, arrogance, fear and envy. David watched them until they were nothing more than a dust cloud in the distance. He had lost sight of his father very quickly. Ephraim never looked back in any event. His son wished that, just once, his father would wave; that he would pause and look back, and show him some sign that the thread of blood between them endured. David turned and made his way back to his mother, who would be readying the cart for the trek to the kill site. There was much work to be done once there, and he was keen to ease his mother's work with the butchering.

The master of the hunt stood beside his pony, unrolled the brass and leather spyglass he carried bound to his saddle pad and for several long minutes squinted into it, for they had come upon the herd. For an hour, the pungent musk of the animals had been carried down to them on the light morning breeze. The first sight of the herd never failed to inspire awe, even in the veterans. It defied description that there could be so many of them; they stretched like a furry carpet across the horizon. Nodding and bobbing, the shaggy, humped beasts gave the impression from this distance that the earth had suddenly come alive, taking on the appearance of an amorphous, undulating, breathing being. Massive shoulders were contiguous with atrophied hindquarters, switching tails, and lowered heads, burly and pugnacious in appearance.

At this distance, the stench of their collective excrescence wafted heavily down upon the assembled hunters. Their horses, all experienced buffalo runners, were restive; their eyes rolled and they pawed and thumped the ground in excitement. The men strained to contain themselves and their mounts.

At last the order was given, and the men arranged their units in a rough semi-circle, facing the strengthening breeze. Swinging his musket in an arc on both sides of his head, the master led off with a cry which was lost in the breeze: 'En avant!'

Ephraim was in the third wave which would take up the flank of the herd as it began to wheel in the direction of the wind. His mouth was full of lead musket balls; their taste was stale and metallic at the back of his throat. The projectiles were carried so, in order that reloading on the run was made easier. The gunpowder was tumbled from the horn, the bullet spat into the muzzle, and the butt of the weapon was pounded on the pommel long enough to set the charge. Once the target was chosen, all that remained to do was to swing the muzzle over, brace it on the left forearm which held the reins of the dashing pony, and pull the trigger. All of this was performed in a tightly orchestrated sequence, while the mount leaped over obstacles, swerved to avoid hooking horn tips, and chased in enough dust to render the riders wholly unrecognizable at the end of the run.

Ephraim had done this many times by now, and he was addicted to the euphoria which came with the frenzied slaughter. But for the balls in his mouth, which he worked with spittle to keep them manageable, he would have shrieked with excitement at the leap forward to the kill. As it was, he and his fellows cantered at a steady pace, waiting for the first signs that the old cows watching the herd at its perimeter had become alarmed.

As they drew upon them, with less than a thousand yards of shimmering grass left between them, the men could see the first signs of anxiety. Sniffing and blowing, giving little jumps and scraping up the soil like dogs, the buffalo tested the air uncertainly. These animals had poor eyesight, and relied on a sharp sense of smell to alert them to danger. Lépine waved his musket for the last time, and all the hunters broke into a full gallop. The thundering of this army across the hard dry sod resonated in Ephraim's body cavity. As the first group reached the milling animals, the first faint popping sounds of musket fire reached Ephraim's ears over the clamour of the horses' hooves.

Suddenly, with a single movement, ropy little tails in the air in fright, the mighty beasts swung into motion and stampeded away from the rushing horses. The shock of so many animals in full flight clapped violently around Ephraim's being. It seemed as if the entire world had convulsed into motion. Heavy dust clogged his nostrils and lined his eyelashes; Ephraim could now see only ten paces or so in front of him.

Then he was upon them. He lowered his weapon at the fat cow just ahead. The pony drove in so close that Ephraim could see bloated ticks just behind the beast's massive shoulders. He fired, and the animal staggered; acrid smoke blew for a moment into Ephraim's face. The shot had passed through the lungs; the telltale blood streaming from the nostrils indicated that the hunter could select another target. Ephraim took a small white stone from many he had tucked into the cuff of his moccasins at the knee, and he pitched it at the fallen buffalo as he swept by. Other hunters, despite travelling several miles and killing as many as a dozen in the tumult and the confusion, were able to trace their way back to each one. This was an extraordinary talent of direction and memory, but quarrels were frequent, and had to be arbitrated by the master. Ephraim preferred to remove all doubt.

Snatching up the powder horn again, he tapped a measure of the coarse, black grains into the barrel. He spat a wet ball into the muzzle, and tamped it hard against his saddle. Once again the lithe pony charged in close to the next beast. Ephraim swung his musket down, and took aim. As he did so, the pony lunged to cross a pair of badger holes, and stumbled momentarily. Ephraim fired, but the shot was not true. He saw the projectile slash the buffalo's flank, and rip into its gut. It did not pause, or give any indication that it was hit, and Ephraim hastily repeated the loading sequence.

He fired again, and the breech exploded in his hand, carrying away three of his fingers. The painful shock caused him to gulp, and as he choked on the mouthful of shot, he realized he had shaken too much powder in the barrel. How many times had he been warned about this? Better to let the animal go than to rush the powder! In the same moment, he clutched his shattered hand without thought, and let the rein slip over the pony's lowered head.

During this time, all of which, it seemed to Ephraim, was being played out in slow motion, like some distant dream of a hunt in hell that could not be stopped, his mount tripped upon the trailing rein, yanking his head down sharply, so that it was thrown sideways, colliding against their quarry. This tormented animal, now feeling the fire in its torn belly, twisted suddenly. The horse veered by instinct, but the lowered, hooking horn gored the pony, tearing the hide across the ribs, and ripping the soft flesh of the belly in a cruel, emptying wound. The creature shrieked with an almost human cry of pain, and fell heavily. Ephraim, whom fear had fixed in a trance, was thrown forcefully to the ground.

The blow shook his breath from him. The thundering continued all around him unabated; no one had seen him go down. His pony lunged to his feet and fled, entrails flapping like obscene pennants. The herd parted momentarily and swarmed around him; the vibrating earth made his body shudder and twitch. He lay on his back, squeezing his ruined hand, and observed that, oddly, a whirlwind of dust existed, through which he could look up at the clear blue prairie sky. Sky such as you'd see on a fair day on Hoy from the clifftops where he had lain for the first time with the fair Victoria all those years ago. The sky darkened, and the weight of the herd exploded upon him, drawing shut in the span of a single heartbeat a red curtain of exquisite pain.

Three

i

The cramps in her abdomen began distantly at first, gnawing and pinching in the tentative way that chronic pain invades the body: a gradual, disconcerting awareness of a part of the body with which there has been no regular conscious association. Victoria would pause in her clerical work at her stand-up desk, and rub the small of her back, kneading the tightly rolled muscles which lay alongside her spine. By degrees, the aching became more insistent, not placated by the altering of posture, stretching, or shifting of weight. The thought that this might be her time flickered in and out like a guttering candle, but as her panic grew she became possessed of an irrational denial, and she remained in her bed all the following day.

By midday following, the pain had become generalized and had settled into more recognizable rhythms. Victoria dozed fitfully as the contractions of the powerful uterine muscles ebbed, but as the urgency of her condition reasserted itself, her eyes sprang open in fear. 'Will God help me?' she groaned through clenched teeth. Finally, she decided she must have help; sweating and frightened, she waited for the cramping to pass, so that she could roll from her bunk. The chief factor was in the counting room of the trade shed, a short distance away, and she resolved to go to him. The dread she felt had to do not only with the ordeal of birth, but also her departure from the world of men and the right to come and go as she pleased.

Alexander MacDonnell was an officious man. Short, dark and portly, he wore small, round spectacles for close work, so that he habitually tilted his head downwards, so as to peer over them. His black beard was flecked with thick slivers of grey, and his eyebrows were continuously arched, giving him a quizzical, demanding look. Other than his footwear, which were moosehide moccasins, he eschewed the clothing of the country preferring European dress. His worn collars tended toward grubbiness, however, and his rumpled suits projected the impression of a minor gentleman well down on his luck. But he ran a tight ship, as he liked to say, and expected a full day's work for a full day's pay. MacDonnell was insular, preferring the company of books and his diaries to the company of his fellows. His misanthropy made him keen in the observance of nature, but purblind in the affairs of man.

He looked up sharply as Victoria burst into his room. His shirt was unbuttoned; his tie undone. His wing collar stood out like a semaphore, and he fumbled instinctively with it. He never made an appearance unless properly attired, and this sudden entry vexed him. It was Blinkarn, that odd-looking, dirty-faced boy who never uttered a word, but who turned in good work in a neat, careful hand. He started to admonish Victoria, but was struck with the distress that distorted her face. 'What be the matter wi' ye, boy? Be ye sick, then?' The annoyance sounded in his voice.

Victoria cried out, gripping the back of a rough chair for support. 'Please help me, good sir. I'm with child, and its time has come!'

MacDonnell was nonplussed. 'Is this some poor jest? Is there no end to the tomfoolery that goes on here? Would ye draw even me into your childish fun? Get out!' he thundered, half rising from his seat. He was not a man to be trifled with, and he wanted this message to have constant reinforcement.

She slumped against the door frame, her face covered by a sheen of perspiration. Her voice was low, as she fought the mounting waves of pain. 'I am a woman,' she gasped, 'not a man. I am with child. This child is…about-to-be-born…please-help-me.' She finished this through clenched teeth.

MacDonnell looked at her, still in a near-upright stance, his face a sea of confusion. His jaw worked, and his eyebrows knitted and unfolded. After a pause, he said quietly, 'I will not be taken in by this foolish game. Be gone with ye this very moment!' And he sank to his seat again, his collar bouncing unchecked and unnoticed at his shoulder.

Victoria tore open her blouse, and lifted her undershirt. 'Look upon my bosom, sir,' she said, her face aflame at this bold immodesty. 'They are full of milk for the wee one. You cannot but assist me, for I am a woman whose time of birthing is nigh.'

MacDonnell stared at her heaving chest, his mouth forming a perfect circle. His eyelids arched to show the full ring of his bright blue eyes. Speechless, his face reflected a transparent mask of total astonishment. So complete was his stupefaction, that he would not make a record of the event, beyond a terse entry in the log that 'a child was born to an imposter, who had by various subterfuges, kept the identity of her sex from everyone at the fort.'

Victoria snapped her clothing shut, and slumped to the floor. She was vaguely aware of the frigid draft blowing through the door, left ajar by MacDonnell's hasty departure. There was a bitter taste of bile in the back of her throat, and the agonizing shuddering in her lower abdomen forced tears from her.

She lifted her head weakly before slipping away in a faint.

Regaining consciousness, she found herself between two Cree women whom she had never seen before. They were helping her to sit up in a skin lodge which was heavy with the pungent smell of sweetgrass. Her lower garments had been removed, though her feet were bound up in rabbit skins, the warm, soft fur turned inward. One of the women was singing a repetitive song in a high, though softly modulated voice. Victoria's knees ached with the effort of prolonged crouching on her heels.

She was depleted by the labour. The bite of air cooled to 28 degrees below zero was scarcely kept at bay by the small fire in the lodge. Each time the heavy, thick-haired buffalo hide on its frame was pushed aside to permit passage, the draft chilled her sweat-drenched body, naked from below her swollen breasts. Squatting against the willow frame erected at the back of the lodge, she grunted with the contractions. She felt like a martyr on a medieval instrument of torture. Her hooded tormentors were two Indian women who massaged her legs, and wiped her belly, and urged her on with low, incomprehensible sounds. In her pain, their attentions felt like abrasions.

The cramps came with pronounced intensity now, and Victoria cried out at their apex. Weakly protesting the urgings of the two women who spoke in language she could not understand but whose intent was beyond debate, she was dragged into a squatting position, and her elbows were hooked over the stout willow thwart which had been wrapped with rabbit fur.

An instinct to bear down gripped her. The two women smiled and nodded encouragement, as they squeezed and massaged Victoria's distended belly. Victoria felt her bowels suddenly empty, and the stench completed her humiliation. Her attendants seemed not to notice, and the refuse was scooped up, wrapped, and cast outside. As the covering skin was moved aside, a chill blast gripped Victoria's exposed limbs and torso and her teeth chattered. The sounds of the two women's urgings and songs rose in crescendo; all three voices were intermingled in grief and joy. Then, with a rending, swelling spasm it was over, and a small white body, covered with what seemed to be bastings of lard, was snatched up and wrapped in soft blankets made of woven strips of winter rabbit fur.

Victoria was exhausted by her ordeal, and barely comprehended what the others were doing; their tones were reverential, and they sang a low song to the little bundle, which now sounded a thin, quavering complaint. At this, one of the women pinched the sound off by holding the infant's lips shut. She eased pressure as his tiny face grew red; the infant drew a breath, but its cry was cut off again by the woman, who crooned a soft tune to him. Victoria's groggy sense of comprehension could not grasp this mix of apparent cruelty and kindness. 'What are you doing to him?' she said, struggling to lift herself from the robes where she had lain, shivering in her depletion. Reaching out with a single hand, she implored them to cease their torment of the child, before she slipped into darkness.

Victoria awoke by degrees, consciousness returning in layers like the dawn. She lay very still. She realized that she was in the factor's bed, a great, luxurious bed with a mattress filled with the down of the wild goose, and heavy, four-point trade blankets lay over her. Oh, what a grand bed, such as she had only seen! At each corner was a turned cedar post, with a round 'cannon-ball' carved at the summit. Incrementally, the full weight of her reality returned to her, though she fought the return of frightful memories of the last few months. But they stood out, like carelessly discarded bits of trash in a riverbed, drawing the eye, and striking a discordant note.

Sitting up slowly against the headboard, which was lined with black bear fur designed to deflect the chill seeping through the drafty walls, she became aware of the forms of the two women who had attended her in the birthing lodge. She felt her breasts, swollen and urgent; droplets of fluid seeped from darkened nipples. She put out her arms, about to call for the boy.

There was a thin, short cry, barely more than a half-note from the child, and Victoria watched in horror as one of the women gently pinched the boy's lips together. The baby snorted and strained, and a large bubble of snot formed under one nostril. The woman hummed gently, and as she took away her hand, the baby relaxed, breathing deeply through his mouth. The other woman, older, nodded and trilled a song to the boy.

Victoria shook her head. 'What are you doing to my child?' she demanded angrily. 'Are you trying to kill him? Give him to me!' She snatched the bundle to her, and the red-headed little boy fastened himself greedily to her breast. Neither Indian woman could speak English, though they obviously comprehended that she was angry. It was equally clear that they were perplexed and they both retired from the room, with signs that they would return.

Later, Victoria discovered that from the first hour of its existence, a native child must learn that no one was permitted, by even a single, uncontrolled cry, to raise alarm, or to give away (however inadvertently) one's position to the enemy, or destroy the chances for success during a hunt. Either of these events could determine the fate of the entire village. The bleatings of children were pinched off at birth.

Nor was this a one-sided proposition. Victoria was given to understand that a child of one was the child of all, and it was not exceptional for the two old women who had supervised the birth to carry away the child for hours, to show him off, and croon over him as if he were one of their own. This gave Victoria the much-needed rest she required to recover, but it was overshadowed by a deepening, more upsetting frustration: she was never to hear her son cry—for her or for anyone else. She took from this that the brutal country in which she was presently imprisoned by snow and ice and impossible distance, had robbed her of something else that was precious.

When she was able, Victoria held her son on her shoulder, reached for the door latch, and stepped outside. The sudden stab of cold air made her wince, and the child silently squirmed deeper into his fur-trimmed bunting bag. The snow crunched underfoot as she walked slowly toward the frozen river. At the top of the bank, where the path led down to the drifted surface of the Red River, she paused, and stood silently at the hem of Madam Winter's glistening robe. A snippet of verse from her school days came to mind.

> *From frozen climes and endless tracks of snow,*
> *From streams that northern winds forbid to flow;*
> *… the winter in a lovely dress appears.*
> *Ere yet the clouds let fall the treasur'd snow*

All around the blazing whiteness enveloped the land, rolling and smothering in starched, seamless corrugations down to the river's edge, where the gaunt oak thrust their bony fingers from an ermine cuff. The sky was as blue as she had ever seen; a deep cerulean vault in which the sun hung suspended, coruscating in each silent bank of snow. She had never, in all that she had heard about the winters in this land, imagined that there could be so much snow. One step off the packed trail would plunge her to her thighs. The snow took the landscape as its own, redefining, dominating, and muffling it completely. The freshness and cleanness of it invigorated her.

'Look, my boy,' she said. 'Could you ever imagine such snow? All is so fresh and clean under its mantle.' She thought for a moment. 'Snow,' she repeated. 'That shall be your name; Johnathan Snow. Like your namesake, you shall have a fresh new beginning. Together, you and I, we shall never look back!'

Victoria had come to a decision that, like the gestation of the new life she had brought forth, had taken time to ripen. As it took flight, she felt liberated, for she had determined to return to England on the next Bay ship. No longer would she tie her fortunes to a man—or any man, for that matter, let alone one she hardly knew. Though she had written twice to Ephraim, who was supposedly at Brandon House, or Fort Ellice, there had been no reply. She had maintained that he was a distant cousin, and at one point, someone had told her that Ephraim was 'going Indian', even having taken up with some Assiniboine squaw. At the time, this news had crushed her, for she could not see the blessing in having had such a narrow escape from such a man. When love became hate, she could not say, for it was an inexorable process. The dimensions of the betrayal were only just beginning to register, forcing aside her powerful self-denial.

It surprised then humiliated her that no woman apart from the Indian midwives had called upon her. There were some about, for she had seen them scuttling back and forth in their wraps, head down in the bitter cold. But in a more reflective mode, she knew that this was not something past understanding; she had posed as a man in a man's world, and had delivered forth a bastard son as the result of some unknown shameless union. As yet, no one had connected her inquiries and letters to Ephraim with the child. She had overheard disapproving remarks about marriages a la façon du pays, which she took to mean living 'in sin', as it was understood at home. Sunday at prayers meant a regular infusion from the pulpit of the importance of decent living, sobriety, chastity, and moral probity. Victoria felt vaguely embarrassed that her son was born in a skin lodge, rather than a proper bedroom with midwives in attendance.

She could feel, even in the six months she had been here, that the Indian women constituted a sort of sub-class in the society of Red River. This was a condition considerably improved by formal Christian marriage to white traders. Ambivalence to Indians was reflected in the fact that in February of 1837 the Council of Assiniboia, after considerable debate, decided to accept the evidence of Indians admissible in cases where traders were selling whisky and rum in return for furs. It had been well recognized that selling liquor was a short-term, though profitable activity. The fact was, however, that the effects of drink were so deleterious to the production of furs that it was eventually determined by the Company that such trade was not in their best economic interests. Even so, there was a reluctance to convict on the testimony of a Indian. Hell, the nature of a formal oath was unknown to them.

She knew she could not survive alone in this wild land; nor did she want to. She decided that her son would grow up in England, for there was no returning to the Orkneys, either. There was nothing for either of them in Hoy. So all thought became focussed on the return. Overhead, a bunting called its long trill: a single note calling forth the dry, scolding rattles of the wrens that huddled under the eaves of the outbuildings nearby. Victoria became aware of the cold creeping under her smock, and made her way back to the house, drawn by the warmth and the sanctuary of the factor's bed.

MacDonnell was in an ugly frame of mind. He made no secret of the fact that he felt Victoria's disguise was a 'fraud on all womanhood', that she had been 'living a perverse lie'. Yet there was a curiously chivalrous side to him. It was for this reason that he felt that he should give up his bed. Not a man to suffer a want of comforts gladly, his naturally cantankerous disposition became even more so. He made it plainly known to Victoria that she would be off with her 'child'—he said it as if it were the Devil's handiwork—on the very 'fust brigade to th' Bay'. Victoria nodded, for this was exactly what she had hoped for. So far there had been no mention of repayment or anything in the way of penalty. She decided not to raise the subject. Leave well enough alone.

Her former colleagues were ambivalent toward her. All regarded her with curiosity, now that she actually dressed and acted as a woman ought. But some were openly contemptuous of her, knowing what she would have seen, travelling as a man. Others, perhaps not surprisingly in this lonely land, came seeking her attentions; but she would have nothing to do with any of them. Ephraim had poisoned the well of her trust. Moreover, the difference in her freedom, now that her sex was a matter of public knowledge, was palpable. Decisions were made for her. She was removed from her clerical duties, MacDonnell fuming over this 'necessary injunction', for he felt he was already short-staffed. She could no longer wear men's trousers, for to do so would scandalize the fort. Instead, she was required to wear skirts hastily made up, which dragged in the snow and became crusted with ice, then sodden once indoors.

With the help of the Indian women, she learned to look after the boy with the limited means at hand. Johnathan seemed strong, but his daily output of waste was prodigious, and it kept her busy with cleaning up after him. She took to receiving her meals in the bedroom which became her universe, save for short walks in the snow. There was a goodly supply of the factor's books in a chest at the foot of the bed. Delighted at the discovery, she devoured their contents. MacDonnell was an eclectic reader; all manner of texts were in his possession. She read of the ancients, marvelling at their understanding. She read Pliny, discovering his insight that the source of courage, of inspiration, of force in the human being lay in the heart. 'Inside itself,' she read, 'the heart in its winding passages provides the first home of the soul and the blood. There the Intelligence resides.' She would reflect on such pithy statements, realizing that the heart's yearning depended upon its own strength, and not upon any other being or thing. True even for a foolish woman such as she had been, Victoria thought.

She read and re-read Aesop's Fables. She read to Johnathan, lying quietly in his cradle, a converted cheese box lined with furs.

'An astronomer went a-walking each night to observe the heavens. One night, as he made his way through the village, his eyes fixed upon the firmament, he tumbled into a deep well. His piteous cries brought a neighbour, who called down to him. Upon learning what had happened, the neighbour said, "Why pry into the heavens when you cannot see what is here on earth?"' She laughed with delight. 'Don't you see, my bonnie lad? All this time, I've had my eye on the heavens! Well, no longer.'

Johnathan would wave his tiny fists in response, and in this quiet way the icy clutch of winter slowly relaxed its grasp, and spring came.

ii

When the swollen Red River had swept the floes and shards of winter's remnants away, and the current had subsided to a level more adequately contained within its shallow banks, the first brigade set off for the Bay with Victoria and her son aboard. The boats were loaded to the gunwales with the trapping season's furs, neatly compacted into ninety-pound 'pieces'. It was a wild, exhilarating run to the coast, for the current was with them all the way, both channel and rapid engorged with the spring run-off. Even the passage along Lake Winnipeg was smoothed by steady, warm breezes from the southeast. With the single yard rigged, the little fleet of fourteen boats spread out, and the tripmen lounged with their pipes, or dozed among the bales of fur, as they ran before the wind. Though it was yet cool, the buds had started forth with the promise of new life. Clouds of water birds chattered and called overhead, in numbers beyond counting; ragged tapers of high-flying geese, stragglers by now, pointed the way like avian signposts. Victoria held her son tightly to her, and felt imbued with the hope reserved for all beginnings.

What awaited her in England upon her arrival, she had no way of anticipating. She simply believed that it would work itself out, that providence would yield opportunity. After all, when she had made this trip the previous year (was it really only eight months ago?) she had been determined that she would locate Ephraim. That was not to be. Surely there was a divine influence in the affairs of human beings. Perhaps it was enough to yield to ineluctable fate.

The men were very solicitous of her, attending to her every need. The journey to York Factory was uneventful, save for a vessel careening out of control, striking the steep channel walls of a narrow stretch of rapids, the blow having stove in the starboard bow. The wreck was hauled up below the rapids and unloaded. Quickly the ribs were spliced, and the distressed seams patched with canvas and tar. While the work was in progress, the other crews lounged about, until one of the men was treed by an angry black bear.

Having gone off to relieve himself, the voyageur had stumbled between the sow and her two mewling cubs. The other men quickly dispatched the animal with an axe, several holding the angry beast with tripping poles from the boat. This seemed quite a foolhardy venture to Victoria, who was frightened by the bear's menacing rushes. But it was no match for the combination of destructive human will and well-hafted English cast; it was felled with a single blow to the skull. They then scooped up the two cubs for sport. About the size of small dogs, they provided amusement for the men while they waited for the others to finish repairs to the boat. Within three hours of the accident the boat was partially reloaded and, with the balance of its freight redistributed among the other craft, they were off again.

Victoria was troubled by the orphan cubs, for it seemed that without their mother, they were doomed by the harshness of the land. Johnathan too was an orphan, so to speak, and Victoria made herself a vow that Johnathan would never be without his mother, for as long as he needed her. She turned and watched the confused cubs as they capered back and forth on the narrow strip of sand where the brigade had drawn ashore, until they were out of sight. For a time beyond that, she fancied she could hear their pathetic bawling, bewildered and despairing. She shuddered; with God's grace, she and Johnathan would soon be quit of this cruel land forever. She pulled a large trade blanket over her, and put Johnathan to her breast.

York Factory in early June was a different place from what Victoria remembered. Two or three brigades had already arrived with winter furs baled and ready for export to London. In addition, there were more

Indians than she had ever imagined, assembled in groups of lodges, according to tribe. There were perhaps three hundred people at the post, as it began its short summer season. It was cool, here by the Bay, and the mosquitoes had not yet established their dominion over all moving things, so that everyone was about. The place presented quite a gay air as Victoria's brigade arrived, voices raised in a rollicking boating song. The large red ensign with the HBC on the fly drifted overhead at the masting, and the whitewashed buildings stood out brightly against the pale blue northern sky. The chatter of voices, the bustle of activity, the pageantry of uniform, wing collar and buckskin, with all other possible variations and combinations of dress, created a pleasant confusion. Her senses were bombarded with the smells of damp muskeg, fresh-sawn spruce, baskets of netted fish, woodsmoke, and the pungent musk of men at hard labour. There was a vibrancy, she thought again, that this land inspired in the men who claimed it.

But there seemed to be considerable ambivalence about whether this was a new land with its own character, or a place where the old order would be superimposed. For a time, the land was dominant, and the newcomer was introduced to the ways of the original inhabitants. But that was coming to an end, she suspected, for even in this brief time that she had been here, she could sense the currents of change. In the florid, wind-burned faces of missionary and factor she could see the prejudgement, odium and determination that would eventually compel submission to rules of another place; a regime which would bring with it fresh cruelties in place of those abrogated.

The ship from England was delayed beyond its expected arrival in late August, but no one seemed alarmed. For Victoria, however, it was a reminder of that dreadful time last year, and she feared the worst. When a cannon sounded, calling all to the waterfront, it was clear that the *Prince Rupert*, a ship long in Company service, had merely been stalled in pack ice in the strait, a common enough event at both the opening and close of the shipping season. The vessel's arrival had the effect of an intoxicating drug in the remote settlement, and before long, many joyous hands were reaching down to help with the off-loading of the gig and longboat, which brought the ship's officers and Company officials ashore. For many hours, Victoria strolled with Johnathan along the shallow bank, watching the various small boats disgorge their freight, day following day. The types of packages ranged from bales and sacks, each with their coded labels, to implements, and furniture that included a large upright piano. A stern white woman in hooped skirts and starched collar supervised the movement of the instrument with many sharp calls and directions to treat it with care. Victoria smiled to herself as she thought of the rough journey ahead, which would probably take its toll on the piano's fine finish, even as the new world sod had already besoiled the hem of the lady's handsome dress.

Victoria had just enough time to settle in a private room in the Bachelor's Hall, when there sounded a tap at the door. Upon opening it, she was greeted by a shrivelled dwarf of a man who snatched the worn cap from his head as soon as he saw her. 'Good day, madam,' he said. Victoria took an instant dislike to him, but her manners forbade her slamming the door in his face, as sudden impulse suggested.

'What can I do for you, sir?'

'If I may,' he started, insinuating his way past her into the small room. With a quick look at the sleeping child and a sniff as if there were something contagious about it, he sat himself on a corner of the narrow bunk, closest to the miniature window, no bigger than a handkerchief. Without a further glance at her, he opened a battered ledger book on his lap, and ran a thin index finger down the columns, then suddenly at right angles. 'Ah,' he nodded, looking up at her, with his finger marking the place that had engaged his interest. 'My name is Phineas Crump, Chief Prothonotary for the Company in Rupert's Land. I've come about the matter of the ...er, outstanding account.'

Victoria could feel the anxiety welling up, stealing her breath. She looked at the open book with its ruled lines and neatly scrolled entries; at the dimple where his insistent finger pressed accusingly into the page. 'Wh-what account?' she faltered, knowing the answer. She still held the door open; though she did not want anyone to overhear this conversation, she was loath to detain this man any longer than necessary. It was obvious that he felt quite superior to her and her bastard son, for in his unctuous manner, there was a self-importance, an imperiousness that she had seen in many such men. The smaller the authority, she thought, the more abusively it is exercised.

There was not a hint of regret or apology in his demeanor. 'According to our standard form indenture, the Company paid you not only twenty-and-six, but covered the cost of passage. Failure to serve the required term requires that the entire amount be refunded with, of course, a small interest.'

'Passage!' Victoria snorted. 'A fine passage it was, too, nearly costing me my life, to say nothing of my possessions, which—by the way—contained the money advanced me at recruitment.'

'Act of God! Act of God!' said Crump, shaking his head, and fluttering his left hand dismissively. 'We can no more be held responsible for shipwreck than for snowfall or icebergs. Then there is the matter of the fraud…'

Victoria paled at this; she said nothing.

'I think we both know whereof I speak. It's nothing to me, you understand,' he said, 'but I think it'll count against you in the end.'

Victoria remained standing, looking at him, resisting the urge to fly at him and tear his accountant's eyes from his head. Why did men seem to enjoy their dominance, in all its protean forms? She sagged inwardly, for there was no competing. She assumed the proper aspect, and fetched a worried smile. 'But good sir, I have not a farthing beyond this single shilling,' she said, holding up the coin she had taken from a knot in her shawl. 'What shall be done with me?'

Crump reached out and flicked the silver from her fingers, as a frog might pluck a fly from a leaf. 'That'll be applied on account, yes. Of course, there are other options…' He trailed off.

'You'll not keep me here.' Fear swept over her.

'Oh, no, madam,' he said. 'The Company's of a mind to return you on the very next ship. They do not want to bear the cost of your brat, with all due respect.'

Victoria bridled. 'With all due respect'. How many times had she heard such an expression used between people? Invariably it meant that no respect whatsoever would accompany the exchange. 'Well, then, of what options do you speak?'

'Well,' he began, puffing out his lower lip, 'there are the agricultural gangs for women such as you. Gangmasters will advance our agents almost the entire amount owed, and you could simply work it off. Better'n debtor's prison, to be sure, especially for the little one.'

It was all Victoria could do to keep from crying out in despair. Gangs! Debtor's prison! Or a workhouse.

Crump continued, oblivious, 'I've heard women can make as much as fifteen pence a day, following the stock and breaking up dung with a fork, or the same amount ladling cow piss on the land to improve it. And all this while carting an infant around on their backs! Think of it, you'll have the debt squared away in no time.' He looked up at her, and rose himself. He was still shorter than she by almost a head, and he drew himself up, lifting his heels. 'You'll not be permitted to land until the arrangements are made, so you'd better be thinking about your responsibilities.' He tucked the ledger smugly back under his arm, examined the silver coin carefully before slipping it into his vest pocket, and marched out to the stairway.

Victoria closed the door after him, and lay down on the unyielding bunk. She had heard about the horrors of the gang system of working the land, but had always thought that this was a fate reserved for the dispossessed and the downtrodden. There were stories told of rape and abuse, of rampant disease and hardship far beyond the hoeing, weeding, stone-picking or manure-spreading that was expected all the daylight hours. The choice between workhouse and debtor's prison was the same: no future, perhaps not even a life, for Johnathan. She put both palms to her temples, and wept.

iii

Ten days later, when watering and provisioning were completed, outbound passengers were taken out in relays. Looking up at the huge hull, Victoria had a momentary surge of panic as she remembered the dying moments of the *Esquimaux*. She bolstered her courage with the thought that no one could be so unlucky as to suffer two ships wrecked underneath them. As one of only two women, Victoria was escorted out in the captain's gig, along with the downcast native wife of a retired trader from Manchester House on the north branch of the Saskatchewan River. She was a descendant of the Cree who had turned against the fort in 1793, as the result of the abuses of the Nor'Westers, and who had found the complacent Hudson's Bay men easy targets. Now she was being taken from her home by a man whose love for her would ultimately cost her her life, shunned and despairing in a strange land, whose people had no wish to know her as more than an oddity. Her dark eyes remained fixed on the smoky scrabble of buildings until night fell at the end of their first day's travel. Only then did she go below, at the urging of her husband. Victoria seldom saw her after that, but neither did she seek the woman out. The isolation Victoria now felt was far greater than that she had endured on the outbound passage. She knew that this was the result of the absence of hope—or at least the near absence. For as long as she had Johnathan, she would persist. Perhaps Byron was right: woman's love is woman's whole existence. Her love for her child now consumed her the same way in which her yearning for Ephraim had drawn her to Rupert's Land. But never had the future seemed so bleak.

There were no obligations imposed on Victoria. The *Prince of Wales* was a comfortable ship, with cabins for the officers of the Company, and steerage for the servants of lower rank. As a white woman, Victoria was given a cabin which was equipped with miniature furniture, all fixed in place. There was even a fold-down sink, deep, with a broad lip to prevent spilling, that served as a perfect crib for Johnathan. Meals were taken with the officers, who were courteous toward her, but Victoria sat somewhat apart from them, and remained aloof.

The truth was, she felt ashamed. She imagined that they talked about her when her back was turned. Surely everyone knew about her disguise as a man, travelling with men. God knows what embroidery the stories about her had accumulated. She fancied she could see leering when men smiled at her; she believed there was lechery in any interest taken in her. She took to spending long hours with her strangely silent boy, watching the sea as she had done the previous year. How she loved its manifold expressions and moods. The relationship of ship with water was one like wind and bird; the vessel moved with plunging grace over a roiled but yielding surface. Standing behind the helmsman, she could see how he instinctively moved to compensate for gust and wave, so that the compass point nearly always remained steady. Victoria decided that this was how she was to live her life: she was to decide what was valuable to her, what she wanted, and steer steadily for it. She had already decided that Johnathan was her life's purpose, and it was through Johnathan that she would live. He would have all the chances, all the opportunities that she could never have, but which she had glimpsed when she had lived as a man.

On her walks about deck, and her vigils aft near the helm, she had noticed another solitary figure. A tall, slender figure, he was about fifty, but with the step of a man much younger. Well dressed, he turned out to read on deck or simply, as she, to watch the shifting, restless ocean. He wore a dark-green broadcloth greatcoat, though when the weather was inclement he wore the fashionable Macintosh, after the waterproof garment invented shortly before by the tailor of the same name. His trousers were a pale yellow nankeen, wide-topped, and narrow at the ankle, fastened with straps under the instep. His satin waistcoat was quilted, an unusual feature, but one which made sense, given the climate. A thick velvet tie was knotted at his throat, and though he occasionally stepped out with a proper felt hat, having lost one to an errant gust, he usually elected to go about bareheaded, with the heavy collar of his greatcoat turned up against the wind. His silver hair was worn long at the neck, with thick 'mutton-chop' whiskers extending almost to the sharp cut of his jawbone.

He was a handsome man, studiously civil, but who quite apparently wished to be let alone. Victoria felt he was far above her station in any event, and put him out of her mind. But very often, they were the only two passengers about on the deck.

The lone passenger's name was Sir Alexander Archibald. He was a baronet. This curious title was established by James I, to encourage settlement of, among other places in his realm, Nova Scotia. Sir Alexander's *proavus*, great-grandfather, prudently chose not to go out to the New World, however, but supported settlement. He had a ton of soil brought home on a returning ship, and laid on the Esplanade near Edinburgh Castle, so that he, in company with his peers, could take sasine of their lands on Nova Scotia soil. This familial trait for strict but cunning observance of the law attracted Sir Alex to his calling as an advocate, though his hereditary properties outside Edinburgh afforded a small income upon which he could live comfortably.

Sir Alex had been commissioned by Nicholas Garry, then Deputy Governor of the Hudson's Bay Company, to go to Rupert's Land to look into declining profits. In 1832, fur exports were such that a dividend was declared at 20 percent. The following year saw a decline to 16 percent, and in 1834, the dividend was further reduced to 10 percent. There were plenty of theories in London; even pilferage was considered to be a possibility, though admittedly remote. John Jacob Astor's American Fur Company seemed a more likely culprit, even though the Hudson's Bay Company had exclusive jurisdiction in Rupert's Land, by a grant under Royal Charter.

In 1821, when the North West Company merged operations with those of the Hudson's Bay Company, ending a sometimes ruinous, occasionally murderous competition, Garry had been sent out to oversee the merger. As a bachelor, he was the one available committee member to be sent out from London to make the grand tour of posts from Montreal to York Factory, by canoe and York boat. Fourteen years later, he felt that another visit to Red River was necessary, and he turned to his Scottish friend, Alexander Archibald, who had just received a knighthood with the help of influential friends. His selection of Sir Alex was natural, for the two men had become close friends over the years that he had been retained to prepare or review contracts for the various undertakings of the Bay men.

The two men often shared their experiences: Garry reminisced about his tour of Canada and the posts of Rupert's Land, regaling Sir Alex with his confrontation with the Nor'Westers at Fort William. Over claret, Sir Alex explained why he had chosen to spend so much time in London, in solicitor's work when his heart pined for his beloved Scotland. His father had close connections with the Countess of Sutherland, whose husband was in the forefront of the 'Clearances', the forced removal of thousands of tenants in 1819 and afterwards, so that the land could be put to the more economical use of raising sheep. No tenant had been put off Gleneaglesham, the Archibald estates, however, and no hearth had been levelled nor a single thatch put to the torch, as in Grummore and Grumbeg, the ruins of which still stand on the banks of the Loch Naver as a grim memorial. Nevertheless, passions ran deep, and the loyalty of Sir Alex's father was seen as betrayal by some. Some of that sentiment clung to Sir Alex, for even sixteen years later the memories were raw.

Over a glass of claret, Garry had engaged his friend for the task of inspecting the principal posts. He had already planted the seed of interest in the younger man's mind, by his wondrous tales of the New World. Sir Alex had never been much for travelling, and certainly had no experience with rough living, but this prospect intrigued him. After all, he would sail to New York, travel overland to Montreal and then by canoe to the Red River Settlement. There would be no need, Garry assured him, to spend a dreadful winter in Rupert's Land, some six months of frozen hell; he would sail home from York Factory on the first returning ship. Nasty as the winters were, Garry was at great pains to reassure Sir Alex that the summers were wonderful, and 'no balmier a place could ye e'er hope to lay eyes upon, surpassing even your own bonnie Scotland!'

One morning in mid-September, Victoria awoke to a terrible sense of despair. The ship rolled steadily in a rhythm consonant with the deep breathing of the North Atlantic. She would get herself into these dreadful fits of despondency at least once each month; she knew it and tried to discount it. But here it was again, thick, dark lenses, through which all seemed futile. The tiny cabin closed in on her, and she dressed hurriedly, anxious to get out. She snatched up Johnathan, wrapped him in a thick blanket, and rushed out on deck, sucking deep breaths of damp salt air. There was a thick fog running, and visibility was not more than a stone's throw from the rail. The ship moved like a phantom through strangely hushed seas.

Victoria felt the wetness on her face from the mist, and the warmth from her tears coursing down her cheeks. She bent over the rail, shuddering as the sobs came, thinking that this time, there was no way out. An indenture to some work gang or poorhouse seemed inevitable. How could Johnathan survive when she must keep him with her at her labours? She cried out softly to the impassive waves, 'God in heaven, help me!' And she lowered her forehead to the rough, salt-pitted timber that formed the top of the rail, squeezing her child tightly against her. For a terrible moment, she thought about ending her life; the two of them could make the leap together—it would be over in a moment—and they would be reunited forever on the other side, all torment stilled.

She felt a hand, light as a bird's wing, on her shoulder. It was Sir Alex, snugly done up in his Macintosh. She could see the moisture beading on its surface, tracing rivulets across his shoulders.

'Madam?' He studied her with clear, intelligent eyes. 'Be ye in need of help? Allow me to introduce myself: Sir Alexander Archibald, at your service.'

She looked up, startled, for she thought that on such a dreary day, she would be alone. No one else was topside, except the impassive helmsman, who had eyes for naught except the ship and the gently swaying compass card gimballed in the brass binnacle in front of him. Victoria could not speak, so overcome with despair was she. Sniffling, she turned seaward, and was silent for a time. She was conscious that he had not moved, but he said nothing more, choosing to look out to sea, where the tattered remnants of fog were lifting like a curtain in a vast and ghostly playhouse. She pondered his introduction, so formal it was, and a knighthood attached. She was unsure how to respond. Did one curtsy? Or bow? How did a commoner behave? She was wary, but deferential.

'I've not the intent, sir, to be rude—' she began.

'Look,' said he, interrupting, 'see how the sun strikes a double rainbow as it chases off the morning fog! 'Tis well-known that such a sign is a harbinger of good things to come!' His voice was confident, matter-of-fact, the voice of one in authority, not used to being questioned. He handed her a handkerchief, shaken out, with heavy white stitching-work at the borders. It was a beautiful thing, ornate without being garish. She hurriedly dabbed at her eyes, started to blow her nose, then thought the better of it. She handed it back to him with mumbled thanks. Absently, he stuffed it in an outer pocket and unbuttoned the front of his Macintosh as the sun's rays began to flex their strength.

'I'm sorry, sir, it's a hard time I'm having, seeing anything in the way of good things at the moment.'

'Forgive me, good lady, but I see a very great number of good things. Look at the grandeur before ye!' and he gestured with a sweep of his arm to the surging ocean at their feet and beyond. 'If we were birds, we could not have better advantage to view Neptune's kingdom!' When she did not say anything, he turned to the small bundle she was clutching to her. 'And what of the wonder of new life, then? Can ye not take heart in the pleasure such a wee one must surely bring?'

'Oh, aye, he's a great favour to me, but it's our future that I'm...' she trailed off, blushing, for her lapse of manners in unburdening herself to this stranger. She tossed her head. 'It's nothing. A woman's momentary weakness that'll soon pass.'

Sir Alexander pursed his lips and nodded. Speaking to her as he gazed out to sea, he said, 'I beg your pardon for this imposition, but everyone on the ship knows who you are, and the difficulties you presently face.' He turned to her for a moment, as if he could feel her cheeks and ears flaming.

'But the Company which has engaged me is not without heart. You know, another young woman did the very same thing you have done—a very courageous thing, it was—in 1806, I believe it was. Her name was Isabel Gunn. My word, they still speak of her in Fenchurch Street— Company headquarters in London,' he added, in response to her puzzled glance. 'She'd enlisted as one John Fubbister, I believe it be, and her secret was discovered only after her child was born. But she had to work off the balance of her indenture at one of the posts, Albany House, yes; she stayed there until 1808 or 1809, doing domestic work. There was a terrible fuss made of it at the time.

'But I think that things are a bit different now; there's more in the way of modern thinking, and I don't believe the Company would want to compel a woman to remain in such a place against her will.'

Victoria thought about the parsimonious Mr Crump, and wondered if the Company of which Sir Alexander Archibald spoke was accurately represented by the accountant. And how humiliating that her story was the talk on everyone's lips.

'All well and good, sir, but I shouldn't wonder whether Missus Gunn had not a better time than I shall be having, even if it were to be in that bleak land we've just left. I've not heard much good about work houses, labouring gangs or debtor's prisons.'

He grimaced. 'We shall be at sea for the next two months or so. There seems to be precious little to be gained by worrying about things that may never happen. Good day to you.' He raised the supple leather gloves he had taken off as the day warmed, and touched them to his forehead. His expression was a mix of concern, condescension, and rebuff. There was something else, too. Was he another predatory man? She thought not, but experience gave her nothing to go by, save the knowledge that she must protect herself, if only now for her son's sake. Johnathan stirred in her arms, and rooted sleepily for her breast. Victoria took him below.

For the next few days, Victoria saw only glimpses of Sir Alex. On one occasion their eyes met, and both looked away quickly. Victoria was annoyed with herself for allowing her curiosity to show. She wondered at his interest in her, decided for no particular reason it was malignant, and resolved to keep to herself as before.

Victoria was standing at the rail when the oceans parted not a hundred feet from the ship. A large, glossy bulk, slightly awash, appeared from beneath the surface, and with a deep hissing sound, a fine spray of water plumed about twenty feet into the air. Then another and another. Recovering from her amazement, she cried out, 'Whales, Johnathan! Whales!'

They had come upon a pod of five or six whales, sounding and blowing, and showing apparent total disregard for the presence of the ship. All hands gathered at the starboard rail to watch the beasts, and much excited chatter passed back and forth between the men. One weather-beaten old Scotsman, heading home from the fur trade for good, identified them as 'blues'. A whaler in his youth, until he had tired of the filth and stink of a whaler's life, he added, 'Aye! They're blues! five—six, maybe more. Headin' sou'-sou' east. We'll hae a bit t' tell 'ere we reach home!'

There were general comments about their size, but the wizened Scot was the authority. 'Aye! There's twa there 'tween sixty an' seventy feet. Thar ones on the near side's probably a cow an' calf. That's a gey wee spout, the yin on the left; but thon's a muckle beggar o'er there!'

Over her shoulder, she heard Sir Alex's deep voice. 'There'll be flensers, lemmers, cookers and harpoon men swarming around these creatures before the week's out, I'll warrant.'

She looked up at him, 'What do you know of whaling, sir?'

He laughed. 'Only from the business side, I'm afraid. But I do know that a floating reserve of oil such as these represent won't be let alone for very long. Do you know that one of these beasts alone may yield as much as eighty barrels of oil—that's over thirteen tons!'

Victoria knew something of whaling, for it was done by many Orkneymen. But there it was a matter of need. She had come to understand that animals were more than dinner or footwear; they represented profit. Whether fur torn from the backs of forest-dwelling creatures, or oil rendered from the flesh of enormous giants such as these now moving steadily away from the vessel, wealth lay in the appreciation of opportunity for exploitation. She turned to Sir Alex.

'It's hard to look at such beautiful creatures, and see only barrels of oil.'

He laughed again. 'To be successful in business, one must be free of sentiment. I think that's why financial affairs are the special province of men. God has arranged the plenty of beast and fish for man's consumption. Our dominion over the lower order of creatures is complete. Didn't God tell Noah that "Every moving thing that liveth shall be meat for you"?'

Victoria felt, but did not comment upon her strong feeling that she was one of his 'lower order of creatures'; perhaps all women were.

'Miss Towrie,' he leaned around toward her, 'I should be pleased if you and your son would join me in my cabin, for a supper.' It was a statement, not a request. Not a syllable hinted that there was any opportunity for refusal. No one else was around now that the whales had disappeared. She looked up at him firmly.

'Oh, aye sir. I'd be most grateful. But I won't be staying long, mind, for the little one's to be abed soon enough. Thank you.' He smiled and bowed slightly, then walked away.

And so their curious relationship began. He was old enough to be her father, she decided. He was keenly interested in her company, for he would delay her as long as it could be managed without pleading or demanding; yet there were no attempts at physical intimacy: no unnecessary touches, or clumsy innuendos which she was expecting. Slowly, her guard came down by degrees, and their talks became more frank and, perforce, more intimate.

She was well read. The rich and the titled had no monopoly on books these days. Literacy was a narrow plank to be laid across class lines. Though tentative and deferential to such a man by instinct, Victoria gave no ground in the expression of ideas inspired by her reading. It delighted her to be defeated by his lawyer's logic, or when he yielded to her passionately held beliefs.

She was vaguely aware of the other passengers and crew members whispering about them, for they were increasingly seen only in one another's company, so she was insistent for 'decency's sake', that their lunches and chats in his quarters were not unduly long. If anything, such artifices seemed to increase shipboard speculation.

Victoria was curious about his interest in her. He was titled, monied, and obviously someone of influence. Why was he so attentive to her? She was wary, waiting for the sexual overtures she thought certain to come. Yet no such hint appeared. Once, during a conversation about her disguise, he remarked that she was an 'uncommonly handsome woman'. The intensity of the comment caused her to hold her breath momentarily, but looking at him, she could perceive no menace in his cool blue eyes.

She found herself drawn to him in some ineffable way. She looked forward to their time together, though at night, at rest, she would ponder the source of her growing affection, and the nature of it. It could be that she was lonely, true, but being alone had never bothered her before. There was something about him that was reminiscent of her time with Ephraim. He was a bit of a dreamer. He too could see beyond horizons, though it was usually in economic terms. The other aspect of his personality she found engaging was that he was a listener. He had the ability to draw her out, without being judgmental, without overlaying his own evaluations and advice. It was fascinating, almost narcotic, to be empowered in simple conversation this way. She loved it; she was afraid she was beginning to love him a little. A strange, delicate affection this was, that was not physical, though he was not unattractive.

Sir Alexander was, however, not without his unyielding side. He was an intense Sabbatarian, even to the extent, 'years ago', as he once said, of requiring that potatoes to be peeled, and joints to be carved for the Sunday meal, be prepared on Saturday evening. 'I have softened considerably, as I have become older,' he said, 'but my faith remains the core of me. God's grace has permitted me to live well, and has allowed no great tragedy to befall me. I still take cold meals on a Sunday, as you know. Observance of His customs is not merely obedience; it is respect. Holding certain things in high estimation keeps us on the right path, I believe. We walk by faith, not by sight, as the Good Book says.'

He sounded faintly sermonizing to Victoria, though not unduly so. She thought the idea of observing the Sabbath so stringently seemed not what God intended, but his explanation was rational. He tended to be paternalistic. His attitude to Johnathan was cool, detached. He rarely took more than a perfunctory interest in the child, but the baby's calm, quiet manner was a continual source of comment from him. He allowed that a child such 'as your red-headed son' might change his views on the matter of children yet.

Victoria was coming to realize that in the matter of relationships there were seldom those who perfectly matched. In her small experience, she decided that it would always be a matter of taking the bad with the good, if that were bearable, and one evening, as the sun was setting in a blazing melt into the sea, they discussed this very subject.

'Tell me, Sir Alex,' she said as they stood looking out to the horizon, 'why is it a man such as you never took a wife?'

He stood at the rail, leaning with both hands; a smile crinkled the corners of his mouth. 'And what sort of man is a man such as me?'

She flushed slightly, and said hurriedly: 'Oh, I meant no slight.' She looked at him and saw the sparkle in his eye. She punched him gently on his forearm, feeling the tiny resonating tingle of intimacy in that first touch of him. 'I mean that, uh, a man such as you should have children, for there is so much you could teach them, to say nothing of the start in life you could afford them. It seems such a natural thing.'

He clamped his lips together, the half-smile gone. There was almost a tinge of sadness in his voice when he spoke. 'I have met many women during my life, yet none seemed suitable. It seems to me that what underlies a good marriage is a woman's obedience to her husband. The Epistle of Paul speaks of sound doctrine, including the need for women to love their husbands, and to be discreet, chaste, keepers at home, good and obedient to their husbands. Yet erelong I met a man's wife who was utterly obedient to him; never could I imagine such a creature as my daily partner. 'Tis a paradox, to be sure.'

Victoria hated it when he used scripture to reinforce his position. It sounded pontifical and beyond question. She thought hard about her own religious teaching. Everything in the Bible seemed to confirm the lesser station of women, which might work well if the man was good, decent, and hard-working, but what if not? She determined to give him holy text in return. 'But didn't Paul the Apostle say to the Ephesians that men should love their wives as their own bodies, and that he who loves his wife loves himself?' She hoped she had the citation correct.

He laughed. ''Tis not often that a woman debates holy text with me; you are right, as far as you go. In the same chapter, Paul exhorted, "Wives, submit yourselves unto your husbands, as unto the Lord. For the husband is the head of the wife".'

'Aye, Sir Alex, that may well be true, but the wife is the heart of the husband, as Solomon found to his sorrow.'

He nodded vigorously, smiling. 'Well said. And as long as that wife is no fool—'

She shot back, with a tone more acerbic than she might have wished. 'Surely the point is made. If either the man or the woman be a fool, the marriage is done, though it linger.'

His smile became laughter. 'What I enjoy about our little talks is that you are a woman with spirit. Well-read, intelligent. I suppose that the reason that I have never taken a wife, in truth, is that I have never met such a woman as you at my station.'

The words stung like vinegar in an open wound. She looked intently at Johnathan, who was starting to smack his lips and pucker up as he did when he was hungry. With a mumbled reference to the baby, she fled for her cabin. Later, as she sat with her son suckling at her breast, she reviewed the conversation, trying to get at why it had hurt her so much. The words he had spoken had been expressed neutrally. His acceptance of their respective classes, and of the implicit gulf that yawned between them, was as taken for granted as the air they breathed. She knew and understood this, but somehow she had harboured the feeling that matters of rank had dissolved, and that there was a relationship between them that was predicated on mutual respect and affection. Perhaps there was, but it was clear that their differing social class could not be factored out, at least by him.

Victoria looked down at her simple clothes. There had been precious little choice at Red River, and these clothes were the result of 'Christian generosity', as the Anglican priest William Cochrane coolly reminded her, when he presented them. Victoria had suspected that they were the belongings of someone who had died, for she could not imagine anyone giving good clothes away in such a desolate place. She ruefully reflected on the fact that, within the space of less than a year, the garments of three dead people had outfitted her, each for a different purpose. Her eyes moistened with the painful realization that she had been deluding herself since the return voyage had begun, and here she was, perhaps three weeks from landing, with no prospects, a small mouth to feed, and the burden of debt around her neck. These bleak contemplations hung like millstones upon her, and she felt the all too familiar pangs of despair.

She sat holding Johnathan past the point where, sated, he fell asleep. The light at the tiny porthole grew wan, and the cabin grew as gloomy as her outlook. She braced her foot against the weatherboard which kept her from rolling out of bed in a heavy sea, for the wind had freshened, heeling the *Prince* over another ten degrees or so. There came a tap at the door, sharp, the sound of an object rather than raised knuckles. In her mood, she was of no mind to receive visitors, even though she suspected it was Sir Alex. There it was, she thought. He calls me 'Victoria'; I refer to him by his title, and he has never suggested otherwise. That should have told me I was just a pastime for him, but no. I had to begin believing there was more. Well, to hell with him!

The taps came again and again, the third time insistent, clamorous. Wearily, she looked at the door, 'Come.'

He stepped through the narrow doorway, cane in hand, and stood leaning in the corner, close by the portlight. He was wearing a heavy Inverness against the breeze, and seemed to fill up the cramped space.

'Is he asleep, then?' he nodded toward the baby.

Victoria nodded in response.

'Look now,' he began, uncertainly, 'I've this notion that you're a little annoyed with me, and I'm not sure why. I feel I've been proper...'

Proper! She groaned inwardly. The man has clarity of vision in so many respects, yet sees no farther than his nose in matters of the heart. 'It's none of your concern, sir.' She was deliberate in the formalizing of her address. 'I'm most anxious about my prospects when we make our landfall—or should I say lack of prospects.' She made no effort to cloak the bitterness in her voice.

There was an uncomfortable silence. He studied the carved ivory head of his walking stick. Then he spoke. 'It's not as if I have been unmindful of your problems; I have been giving a great deal of thought to them. The truth is,' he paused, drawing himself up in the manner of a man about to make a leap across a dark void, 'I...I have become quite fond of you, and think of you as one might, uh, think of a sister. At the same time, I have no desire to interfere with your life...'

She barely heard him as he carried on. His sister! What a fool she had been! She, a destitute woman, with tales of scandal and a bastard son in tow, what could she expect? To leap into his arms and live happily ever after? What false hope! Yet the truth of it was, she did have secret yearnings that exactly that would come to pass. Perhaps there was no such thing as false hope, only hope itself. And what she was now hearing was its resurrection, slightly different, more subdued, more homely than before, but perhaps within reach this time.

'...come with me,' he was saying, 'for Gleneaglesham has plenty of room, and I've made up my mind that I shall be returning there once and for all. I'll not be living in the filth of London for another minute. If this trip has taught me anything, it's the value of clean air and simple, hearty food. And a place which still resembles the world as God made it, in all its glory. Scotland, for all its troubles, is still such a place.'

Victoria heard only half of what he was saying. Come with me? Was he asking her to be his wife? Emotions, long suppressed, roiled within her. To be plucked from the brink of disaster in this way was almost too much to bear, yet she gazed at him, uncomprehendingly, her eyes streaming with tears as she let go. In the darkened cabin, he appeared not to notice, and his voice filled with a passion she had not heard before as he spoke of his native land. Oddly, even his polished speech began to show traces of a burr.

What was he saying to her? How could he mix the course of their lives together with talk of glen and loch? What was it about men whose infatuations made them purblind to all else? She reached out her arm to him. 'Stop this moment!' she said. 'What are you saying to me; be you asking that I become wife to you?'

He broke off his encomium, and even in the gloom she could see the incredulity on his face. Then he laughed. Then he laughed again as the thought took hold, and her spirits fell like a cold stone in a well.

'Oh heavens! Did you not hear me then? I said maid, not mate! Oh heavens indeed! It's quite true I'm fond of you, perhaps more than I'm prepared to admit, but all I'm able to offer is work. Work with room and board, of course, and at a fair rate of pay naturally enough. I've no real need of more help—especially when I'm giving up my practice in London— there'll be rooms to let, and staff enough to let go as it is. But I think you and your boy will be happy with an appointment at Gleneaglesham.'

He said all this with a singular tone of voice; there was no condescension that she could discern. It was all as natural to him as if they were discussing the employee roster at one of his inland posts. He seemed genuinely perplexed at her reaction, as well as her confusion about his offer. The absurdity of it all struck her at once. Here was both deliverance and destiny. She was to commit her adult life to serving two men: one not yet grown, the other close enough to touch, yet forever out of reach. Barely hours prior, she had been tormenting herself with the possibility that Sir Alexander would somehow fall in love with her, and now it had turned out that his relationship with her was never one more than he might enjoy with a spirited governess. She laughed bitterly. 'Aye, Sir Alexander, I'll take your generous offer of employment at Gleneaglesham. Will you have me in the scullery or the still-room? Or shall I be a maid-of-all-work?'

He noticed the edge in her voice, and it puzzled him. 'That will be up to Mrs Chinney, who minds the house for me. You will not be disappointed. I am prepared to secure your appointment at fourteen pounds per annum, the very upper level awarded for such work...' He broke off, seeing the tears welling in her eyes. Taking them for a sign of gratitude, he continued.

'It's really nothing; I'm happy to do it.' She nodded as he took his leave, unaware of the profoundly altered nature of their relationship.

That night there was a storm, the only one that had overtaken them on this journey. As she lay in her berth, clutching Johnathan to her, she could feel his bewilderment at the rough motion of the ship. He clutched at her, and opened and closed his mouth repeatedly; his breathing was rapid. She found it odd he did not cry out, as most babies might. She thought him a brave little man, and took heart from his innocent example. She resigned herself to the fact that events which were shaping her life now were as implacable as the tempest which raged outside the vessel. She could no more dictate to the wind than she could alter the circumstances into which she had been born. She had tried, God knows, but she had been dragged down as inexorably as the *Esquimaux* had been drawn beneath the waves. 'Perhaps for you, my boy,' she said out loud to the greedily suckling boy, 'it will be different.'

iv

The work of a servant below stairs was manifold and unending. At Gleneaglesham House, there were more than five hundred towels, each with a tiny embroidered number, assigned to a specific function. Sir Alexander was fastidious in the requirement of such minute observances, and the head housemaid, Mrs Chinney, was determined to please her master in this regard. The house staff was regimented and arrayed each morning in the stone-floored kitchen after-room for inspection. Mrs Chinney was as severe as any sergeant-major in the review of his troops. No loose threads or ill-creased attire was permitted. This suited Victoria well enough, for she had always been careful about her dress, though she found the portly old woman a little annoying at times in the sorts of things she took exception to. On one occasion, Victoria's hair was not fastened as tightly into a bun as demanded by the old termagant, and she was sent away to restore the stray wisps of hair at her neck.

For this infraction, she was given the less desirable task of blacking the fire grates with a concoction of ivory black, treacle, oil, small beer and acid. The tasks divided between the four other maids were infinite in variety, as were the secrets to their proper execution. Polish was stripped with vinegar and replaced with a paste of turpentine and beeswax; drapes were drawn on the south side of the house minutes before the sun slanted its ruinous rays on rugs or furniture, then opened within moments of the danger passing. Cut flowers were changed before they wilted, and carried away for drying, so that their petals could be placed in bowls during the winter months to keep the air fresh. Carpets were relieved of mustiness by sweeping them with damp tea leaves, and brass or pewter fixtures were polished with sand as fine as sugar. Unused beds were stripped every week, aired and remade; the slats on Venetian blinds were unstrung, cleaned, polished and put back. Above all, the slate floors in the working areas were scrubbed and rescrubbed daily. Not a mote of dust was permitted at Gleneaglesham House, for Mrs Chinney stood watch as jealously as a cleric regards sin. Woe befell the servant in whose jurisdiction the offending streak, spatter or feculence occurred.

Johnathan thrived at Gleneaglesham. There were only two other children at the residence: one, a boy named Calvin, was the son of the water-man, whose task it was to keep the house supplied with water. The boy seemed a miniature of his father, a great hulk of a man, and quiet in disposition. The other child, slightly older, was a girl named Elsie. She was the daughter of the chief groundskeeper and his robust wife who assisted him in this task. The three children were inseparable in their early years, and Johnathan's earliest memories were of Calvin's father carrying the two boys in the empty, swaying buckets dangling from a thick wooden yoke, while Elsie capered between them, tossing bits of gravel from the carriage way.

Johnathan was curious about his own father, and had asked Victoria on many occasions about him. She had put him off, saying that he had 'gone away', and that she would explain 'when he could understand'. At the age of five, Victoria told Johnathan that his father had gone to sea with the Hudson's Bay Company, and that the ship had foundered. His father had died; that was all. Johnathan was puzzled by this, for he did not understand why this had not been told to him all along.

Sir Alexander took a special interest in Johnathan. The other two children were hurt and confused by the preferential treatment he received. Sir Alex spent more time speaking to Johnathan's mother than any of the other staff, save perhaps Mrs Chinney. It was obvious that the other employees as well as the head housemaid resented this, for Mrs Chinney felt that all communications with the master were to be directed through her.

Watching his mother with the master, Johnathan felt that there was something here that he had not been told about. His mother looked at Sir Alex with moist eyes; she seemed to lighten when he spoke to her. Yes, there was something different about the way the master spoke to his mother, as compared to the other servants. He held Johnathan on his knee, and listened with genuine pleasure as the boy recited Byron, for Victoria's love of the Romantics had, if anything, intensified over the years. She had been reading to Johnathan from the beginning of his memory, it seemed to him, delighting in the vast library at Gleneaglesham. An early image of his mother was of head bent over volume, searching for a verse after dampening her finger on her lip. At the age of five, Johnathan had already committed to memory a number of works, but his favourite, and one he related with childish theatrics, was 'The Destruction of Sennacherib'.

> *The Assyrian came down like the wolf on the fold,*
> *And his cohorts were gleaming in purple and gold;*
> *And the sheen of their spears was like stars on the sea,*
> *When the blue wave rolls nightly on deep Galilee...*

Sir Alex was charmed. 'Byron makes almost a better story than the original in the second Book of Kings!' he exclaimed. 'And the boy reads it well! I think he's destined to make a warrior of himself, yet!'

Victoria had not the slightest intention of allowing her son to become a soldier, but said nothing. She was vaguely unsettled by Johnathan's precociousness. He was aggressive, and not what one might call a warm child. He got on famously with Sir Alex, who seemed to spur the boy with manly encouragements. Although familiar with the boy, he would brook no impertinence, and any lapse of courtesy or compliance with instruction would result in a slap to the back of the head or, on rare occasion, a good hiding. Johnathan learned to keep his feelings to himself, and remained outwardly indifferent to correction. This was in sharp contrast to Calvin, whose gentleness was not well disposed to corporal punishment or slight. Tears would well up in his eyes, and he would snivel at the least chastening. And there were many in the life of a poor country boy. Elsie was moved by this, and comforted him. 'See, you must be more like Johnathan. You must shake it off, and be brave!'

At the age of six years, both boys were enrolled in grammar school, the same school where Elsie had been attending at Aberlady, some four miles from the estate at Gleneaglesham. It was a large stone structure, once an abbey, whose nuns had mysteriously been carried off by a fatal affliction which had only struck the unfortunate sisters. For years it stood vacant, slowly becoming overgrown with choking ivy, until the parish governors decided that this would be an ideal place for a grammar school. The parish imposed the modest charge of five pence per week for each child; thrupence if there was to be no instruction in writing. Though she was bright and learned quickly, Elsie hated school but she would never disclose the reason to the boys. On their first day at school, they both understood, and never again teased Elsie that 'learnin' was not fer lasses'. The schoolmaster Joachim Friar was hated and feared by his pupils.

He was a thick, balding man, with a pronounced hunchback brought on by the erosive effects of tuberculosis on the bones of his spine. His foray into pedagogy was the necessary consequence of being invalided out of the army. His pension was penurious, and no other prospects were in the offing. He, like most other teachers, was paid the niggardly sum of eleven pounds six per annum, and was forced to take on night work as a bookkeeper to make ends meet. A bitter and cruel man, physically repelling, he held the view that knowledge could only be driven into the skulls of obstinate children by brute force, as he himself had been taught by a fear-inspiring parson wielding a willow scourge.

The parson had his own form of enforcing discipline, which required the commitment to memory of the twenty-eight verses of Chapter twenty-six of the Book of Proverbs. The maximum number of strokes which could be levied for an infinite number of infractions was twenty-eight. The parson would call out the first part of the verse: 'A whip for the horse, a bridle for the ass...', as he applied the stick to an outstretched palm, and the hapless recipient would finish: '...and a rod for the fool's back!' Any forgotten lines or stumbling recitations could carry an extra stroke. Friar had taken this form of punishment for his own, and found it quite to his liking. His pupils referred to it as 'getting the twenty-sixth'.

The most often caned were the boys, but Friar would take the girls into the small study behind the general classroom, saying that it was not fit that young females be chastised before their male classmates. When it came Elsie's turn, she would refuse to talk about it afterwards and, blushing furiously, she would put the boys off. It did little good to complain of the headmaster's thrashing at home, for parents were just as likely of a mind to add a couple of cuffs in the bargain, feeling that 'yer must a done sommit a deserve it.'

The school at Aberlady was one of the few in the British Empire at that time which taught more than grammar, the classics, and a heavy dosage of Scripture. Friar's students had arithmetic, geometry and navigation in their curriculum, the fundamentals of which he had picked up during his service in India. Johnathan was entranced with sums, often working at older boys' problems, even though failure at higher levels brought the same harsh corrections from Friar.

The consumption with which Friar was afflicted made him cranky, easily irritated. Once a sergeant in the Queen's Own 10th Independent Artillery, his skills in calculating trajectory made him a valuable man with howitzer and fieldpiece. Just when he acquired his disabling condition, he wasn't certain, but the variety of pathologies and virulent infestations with which a man could be felled in the tropics made it a wonder that he returned to Scotland at all. Moreover, the non-commissioned soldier was not held in high regard. It was noted at the time of Friar's discharge that the allowance of air for a convict under close detention was one thousand cubic feet; for the enlisted man, it was four hundred cubic feet. The death rate for soldiers from consumption was five times the rate for civilians; the rate for typhoid even higher. Maintaining discipline under such conditions was accomplished by punishments of the most grotesque dimensions. Flogging was common; a sentence of two thousand lashes was not unheard of, though in 1836 the Articles of War limited a disposition to two hundred; not in sufficient time to be of assistance to Sergeant Friar's comrades, however. Friar was well equipped by experience and inclination to maintain order in his classes.

Teaching was accomplished by the 'monitorial system', a system developed some thirty years before, by which the older students assisted in the teaching of the younger. By this simple expedient, Friar was able to retire from the more onerous exertions of imparting knowledge, preferring to stalk about the classroom, birch rod in hand, looking every inch the schoolboy's nightmare. But this technique had its profit, for in the interchange between upper and lower forms, the gulf between schoolmaster and pupil was bridged to a degree.

Calvin was a favourite for Friar. The boy tended to stumble over his readings, for his own mother did not, could not spend the time with him that Johnathan's mother had always taken with her son. Moreover, Calvin had a peculiar high squeal which seemed to appeal to Friar for its deterrent value on the other children. Johnathan was a source of annoyance, for he could never get a sound from the boy. Victoria was horrified to find, one evening, that her seven-year-old son had ugly red welts on both hands, so that he could not hold his writing crayon properly. Seeking out Sir Alex, she was rebuffed.

'The schoolmaster stands in loco parentis—in the place of the parent! "He that spareth his rod hateth his son: but he that loveth him chasteneth him betimes". It is God's word. Don't worry yourself, the boy'll get over his hiding, as we all did.'

'But Sir Alex, this manner of beating seems to me excessive—'

His impatience rarely showed itself, but resort to scripture was a sure sign. '"Foolishness is bound in the heart of a child; but the rod of correction shall drive it far from him"! That boy has a stubborn streak in him, which will stand him in good stead, providing that he applies it to his studies, and not to some tomfoolery. Good night, Victoria.'

Johnathan applied himself to his schooling, as did they all, according to their ability. The threat of Friar's 'twenty-sixth' hung over them like bad weather, and they came to bear it as they accepted the long walk of four miles each way, between home and school. Only Elsie seemed to despair, as did some of the other girls. As the boys grew older, they tried to help Elsie: Johnathan in particular was very good with Bible studies, classics and mathematics. She dreaded confrontations with Friar, but was still reticent in talking about them with the others. Some of the older boys whispered about what went on, and why the girls were not caned on their hands. But fear of Friar was palpable. He was so evil, the children thought, that if they spoke their suspicions out loud, he would know it, and perhaps his wrath would be visited upon them in the forms he described to them from his experience in the Indian Army.

One morning, two days after his eighth birthday, as Johnathan was staring out the lead-paned window at a dreary Scottish winter sky over the firth of Forth, the sound of Friar's rod crashing against a desk top made him jump; indeed, all eighteen students in the room started. Johnathan was sure it was he who was the intended victim. Upon lifting his eyes carefully, he saw that it was Elsie who was being lifted tearfully by an elbow.

'Call that an "e"? Looks more like a "c"! After all this time, thy handwritten work is still a hen's scratching! Come with me. The rest of you, keep at your tasks, or there'll be more work for Master Birch!'

He took the whimpering girl into the study, and closed the heavy door behind them. In a flash, Johnathan was away from his desk, ran outside around the buttressed walls of the old building, and crouched at the narrow window that looked in on the study. This room had been at one time a shallow cellar, where preserves were put up by nuns who had first occupied the building. Above it were the quarters now occupied by Friar. Johnathan was observing from a slightly elevated vantage point, through thick, warped glass, set in rectangular leaded panes. He could not hear, but he could see the two figures. The man was seated on a stool. Thankfully, Friar's back was to him.

It gave him a start when he realized that Elsie's knickers were around her ankles. Her head was down, and she was obviously crying, for her thin shoulders were shaking. Her arms were bent at the elbows, and she had gathered her skirts up, so that her pale white buttocks were exposed. Johnathan felt both sickened and fascinated with the spectacle. Friar sat for a moment, looking at the girl. Johnathan could not see his expression, but he could imagine his glittery, dark-eyed stare, cold as the handles on a pauper's coffin.

Friar pulled the girl roughly to him and laid her across his lap. He began to slap her, slowly, his hand leaving red marks visible even to Johnathan. Elsie kicked and squirmed, and at one point Friar stopped. The words were inaudible, but the upraised index finger suggested that the girl was being threatened with more if she continued to move so. The beating continued for another four slaps, but then Friar began caressing the girl's bottom, stroking the upper parts of her thighs, and her private places between her legs. All the while, Johnathan could see that Friar was speaking, for his head was bobbing, and his neck craned to see the areas that his fingers were exploring.

Johnathan was dizzy with the melange of emotions gripping him. He was enraged at Friar's conduct. He was, he felt guiltily, intensely aroused, for he felt his cock as hard as when he manipulated it at night, when abed. He was afraid, for he had broken one of Friar's fundamental rules in leaving class without permission. But above all, he was only too aware that what he had just witnessed was wrong, dreadfully wrong, but he was bewildered by the awful prospect of doing something about it. What was a boy to do?

Abruptly, Friar stood up, and Elsie hurriedly arranged her clothes. With a fierce look, and a stern warning of some sort, the girl was pointed back to class and she fled. Friar drew out a soiled handkerchief and mopped his forehead. Then reaching down to his buttoned trousers, he flicked open the top button and, with the handkerchief, reached inside. He seemed to be squeezing and kneading, but Johnathan could not see with certainty, for once again, the schoolmaster's back was turned to him. Like a deer, Johnathan flashed back to his place and took up his Bible again just as Friar returned. Elsie's head was down, just as it always was after these sessions, her cheeks aflame for all to see. No one dared snicker. It now was clear to Johnathan why, following the disciplining of one of the girls, Friar was relatively quiet for the next couple of hours. He was no better than the old goat they kept at Gleneaglesham; when he had expended himself on one of the nannies, he lay on his side, eyes rolling and helpless, for half of an hour.

On the way home that night, Calvin was unable to contain himself. In two and a half years, no one had ever defied 'Frightful Friar' as they all called him, once well away from the schoolyard. Calvin pranced and badgered Johnathan.

'Where did you go? What did you see? Come on!'

Johnathan said nothing, but stole a glance back at Elsie who was walking several paces back of them, head down. 'I didn't see a thing,' he said, by and by. Calvin, who admired Johnathan, did not pursue it, short of warning that Johnathan 'stood to catch the twenty-sixth, should Friar ever discover he was away from his place'. Johnathan could not sleep that night, tormented as he was by the images graven in his mind from the afternoon. By cock's crow, he had decided what he must do.

Well before a quarter of eight, Johnathan arrived at school. Friar looked up, startled. He was writing out sums on a blackboard, in preparation for a test that day. He was plainly angry at the intrusion, for no entry was permitted until he rang the commencement bell. Especially on a day set for examination.

'Does your insolence know no bounds, laddie?'

'I've need of a word with you, sir.'

Seizing up his birch, Friar brought it down with a crash on the desk in front of him.

'Stand to me, you little wretch, and give me your hand!' he roared. His round face twitched with perceived affront.

Johnathan stepped forward, extending an upraised palm. Fetching back, the schoolmaster put his shoulder into it, muttering the introductory passages to the twenty-sixth chapter of Proverbs: 'As snow in summer, and as rain in harvest...' and he brought the rod in a cruel arch, whistling its message of pain. At the last moment, Johnathan snatched his hand away, surprising Friar, whose momentum carried him half around again, putting him off balance.

'...so honour is not seemly for a fool.' Johnathan completed his portion of the verse, coolly, studying Friar through narrow eyes.

Friar was flabbergasted. He had never been addressed so indifferently by a mere boy. He raised his whip over his head, rage now beginning to cloud all other judgement. Damn this impudent whelp! He would teach him a lesson he'd not soon forget. 'Stupid,' he snarled. 'That will double your strokes. Now I shall have ten verses.'

Before he could make another move, Johnathan spoke, looking up directly at him. 'You shall have nothing.' He paused. 'If you persist in your senseless beatings, I shall report to my master, Sir Alexander Archibald, that you have been misusing the children of his staff.'

Friar was speechless, arm still uplifted, the open gape of his mouth, lined with the yellow stumps of his teeth, frozen open in astonishment.

'I saw what you did with Elsie,' Johnathan continued, his voice becoming a little uneven, as he began to realize the enormity of his actions. 'I saw where you touched her, and we will go to Sir Alexander, have no doubt, sir, and he will have you flogged, even before he brings you before the autumn Assizes for judgement!'

Friar faltered. There was something new in his face: was it fear flickering at the corners of his mouth? Johnathan realized that this battle-weary, disease-ravaged old campaigner was afraid of a boy not yet nine years old. Not because of what the boy knew, but what he might do with the information. The power balance had shifted simply because the boy had somehow gotten a glimpse into the schoolmaster's weaknesses.

The two of them stood, facing each other: the man still holding his lash absurdly in the air; the boy, hands on hips, trembling in the shadow of the upraised rod. Friar's thoughts were feverish. Who would believe the boy? What would the girl—or for that matter, the other girls say? The penalties for lewdness or debauching young girls could be severe, he knew. He had been flogged only once, while in service, and that for stealing away from barracks to the fleshpots of Jabalpur, in the Central Provinces of India. He could not bear such pain again, even though the sentence of the regimental court-martial then had been merely a half-dozen stripes. Flogging was still retained for offenders in moral crimes.

Johnathan saw the hesitation in Friar, sensed the subtle rearrangement of influence. Yet his was not a position of complete strength, he knew, and the moment should not be overplayed. Whether fear or good sense was a factor in this, Johnathan could not be certain, as he later replayed the scene over and over in his mind. He repeated his implicit demand. 'You shall no longer chastise the girls in such a fashion, and stop your senseless beatings of all of us.' With that, Johnathan spun on his heel and marched as bravely as he could muster, out of the classroom. At any moment, he expected Friar to come to his senses, and erupt in a torrent of curse-laden, pain-inflicting rage. But neither footsteps nor oath followed him out.

All that day in school, the classroom was strangely quiet. Friar conducted the lessons with a minimum of speech, and for the first day any of them could remember, there were no beatings. In the lane, after classes, the children were abuzz with speculation, but Johnathan was quiet, reflective, and feigned indifference to Friar's inexplicable tolerance. Calvin was suspicious that Johnathan knew more than he was letting on, but did not press the other, for he knew better than to try Johnathan's resolve.

The following school day, a Monday, the atmosphere was the same. The children stole glances at one another and wondered.

As he was gathering with the others for dismissal, Friar's harsh voice boomed out, 'Stay behind, Master Snow; I've need of a word wi' ye!'

Johnathan fell out, wondering at this new development. He was not a little afraid of Friar. When they were alone, the school master took up his rod in both hands, turning it and examining it; this seemed to be comforting to him. Perching on a corner of his writing desk, he looked up at Johnathan, who was standing more than ten feet away in the middle of the classroom. 'I've been thinking about our wee talk of two days ago. I have concluded that I cannot be held to ransom by a small boy.' He tapped the rod menacingly in his hands. Johnathan felt some anxiety at this announcement, but kept a neutral expression.

The teacher continued. 'I'll warrant ye've seen things that ye've no right to see, and it may be ye've concluded I've taken liberties. I've not the intention of debating such matters wi' ye. Still, ye can make things difficult for me, of that I've no doubt.

'But on the other hand, if ye make yer complaint, and it's not substantiated, ye shall be the one who is flogged, make no mistake. I have made parents around here satisfied wi' their children's progress, and so I...' and here he trailed off in his speech, and looked at Johnathan silently, sliding his cane through a fist, as if he were playing a slow tune on a silent violin. Johnathan said nothing, for he was uncertain where Friar was heading.

'The lasses will be punished in the classroom in half measure as the lads. The 'twenty-sixth' remains; the pupils will learn or be chastised. That is all. Make a complaint if ye will; but remember, ye'd better bluidy well make it stick!'

Johnathan needed no careful review of his position to understand this was the best deal he could make in the circumstances. He was grateful that the old soldier was wise enough to settle the dispute without further loss to either side. Johnathan turned, and fled the classroom. The cane came down with a crash behind him. Outside, the children scattered as he flew from the steps. He was laughing nervously, and though the others had heard the smash of wood against wood, they had no idea of the reason for Johnathan's detention. Johnathan was as closed-mouthed as before. The possession of certain information meant power; its currency was easily devalued by sharing it.

As Johnathan grew, he became more intrigued with the question of who his father was. That he had 'died at sea', as his mother had told him, seemed insufficient. There was a mystery to it, which deepened as Johnathan matured. He was well aware of the persistent gossip that he was actually Sir Alexander's son, for the affection between him and Victoria was overt enough for anyone to see. And Victoria and her baby had mysteriously appeared with Sir Alex, just at the time he returned from his expedition to Rupert's Land. It was remembered, too, that Sir Alexander had red hair as a young man, before it turned prematurely to a pale grey. Johnathan's own flaming mane seemed to provide the decisive clue.

Victoria had been promoted very early on to the position of 'upstairs maid', a coveted standing at Gleneaglesham, since Sir Alex was not married, and in consequence, there were no children's beds to make or a woman to pick up after. Sir Alex was generally austere in his personal habits, and once his bed was turned down in the evening, the upstairs maid's day was at an end. This promotion had caused a small ruffle among the house staff, for such assignments were the sole jurisdiction of Mrs Chinney. Sir Alexander had taken the unusual step of interceding and requesting Victoria's new assignment. 'While scandal is too strong a word to put on it,' the cook was overheard to whisper to the laundry maid, eyebrows raised, 'this'll ne'er do!'

The result was that Victoria and Johnathan obtained quarters upstairs, in the north wing of the house. There were two very small rooms, and Jonathan slept in the one which would have been occupied by the lady's maid, had there been one. One night, as he lay awake, restless and unable to sleep, he heard the floor board immediately in front of his room squeak. It made a different sound according to whether one passed out from the servant's suite, or whether one was coming in from the narrow hallway. This was an outgoing signal, so Johnathan surmised it was his mother. The moon had gone down, so he knew it was quite late. Where was she going? Perhaps she needed help. It may well have been that she had forgotten something promised or needed for the morrow, for Victoria was a conscientious worker, and was sensitive to the master's apparent favouritism. Johnathan decided to get up to see for himself. If it were some chore she had overlooked, he could assist her with it, and then perhaps he'd be tired enough to get some sleep.

Padding to the door in his bare feet and nightshirt, he opened it. His mother was nowhere to be seen. Perhaps he had been mistaken; he turned to his mother's room. The door was slightly ajar, and dark within. He pushed against it gently and called to her. There was no answer. The drapes were drawn and, in the blackness, it was impossible to see. Groping to the foot of the iron bed, he realized that there was no one there; that the bed was still made up. His mother had not yet been abed. Puzzled, he made his way to the outer landing, which was lighted by a single lamp, its wick turned very low. Following the balcony around to the main part of the house he could see no sign of his mother. Below him, in the gloom, the big, long-case clock interrupted its heavy ticking to sound off the hourly chimes. It was two o'clock. Why would his mother be prowling around the house at such an hour?

Johnathan sat at the top of the grand staircase to think. Perhaps she had fallen asleep in the rocker next to her bed and he hadn't seen her, or perhaps her chamber pot was full, and she had gone to empty it. He returned to her room, but both these thoughts proved to be wrong. He was beginning to become alarmed, for his mother's actions made no sense. He retraced his steps back to the top of the stairs, and thought about going to see Mrs Chinney, or waking Sir Alex. No, Mrs Chinney was not about to be understanding in this case; she tended to be very curt with Victoria. Johnathan set off for Sir Alex's suite, which was rather secluded, in the west wing of the house. Pausing outside the double doors, Johnathan was unsure about waking him for a reason which seemed a little silly, now that he thought about it. Maybe his mother couldn't sleep, and had just gone for a walk. What else?

As he turned to go, he thought he heard a low moan. He was not certain, but there—he heard something again. He raised his fist to knock at the door, but something still held him back. He dropped to one knee, and peered in the keyhole. If the door was locked, then the bottom part of the hole should be clear, and so it was. Johnathan looked in on a large room, centrally dominated by a large, canopied bed. A glass lamp cast a bright glow over the room, making the fine damask curtains and bedding seem to coruscate with reflected light.

What rooted Johnathan to the spot was the sight of his naked mother, leaning over the turned mahogany rail at the foot of the bed, arms outspread and gripping, her full breasts shivering with each impact from Sir Alex. He was kneeling on the bed behind her, holding her hips as he thrust against her with great force. The smack of their flesh was audible even to Johnathan. Both their faces had the look of persons in pain, and as she shook her head, Victoria's pale golden hair came loose, and cascaded over her features, cloaking the contortions which were so upsetting to Johnathan. With a deep groan, Sir Alex collapsed over Victoria's back, and the two of them tumbled on the bed. There they lay, spent.

Johnathan was horrified. He leapt to his feet and, as quietly as he could, he raced down the hall to his own room. Sleep was now out of the question, and as dawn began its stealthy claim on the day, Johnathan heard the unmistakable muffled protest of the floorboard, as his mother passed in to her own room. He felt as confused and aroused as he had that day he had spied on Friar and his treatment of Elsie, more than a year ago. Elsie had become a young woman, and had been taken out of school to be put in service at a smaller house nearby. Johnathan often thought of her, as now, when he was aroused, and his nascent manhood lay thick and inflamed against his belly.

Each night, except Sundays, he was now aware that his mother slept with Sir Alex. Each morning in the pre-dawn, she returned to her own bed for less than an hour. This more than anything else convinced him that Sir Alex was his father. But it remained imponderable why this simple fact should be denied to him, unless it had something to do with the fact that his mother was an unmarried commoner, and did not for that reason become entitled to a claim on Sir Alex. He began to hate them both for this unfairness and hypocrisy.

In fact, his mother's condition and circumstances, her loneliness and disappointments, were well below Johnathan's childish horizon. The slow ferment of character was rather the product of his narrow vision of the world—which Victoria had unwittingly helped him shape—than it was the consequence of moderate teachings and balanced opportunity. But he was by no means alone, for all the children with whom Johnathan had any association were raised according to the belief that they were made tractable and submissive by stern correction. Still at a tender age, they were launched into careers, often at hard labour. Schooling was largely religious training and classical instruction, though under Joachim Friar's tutelage, this was somewhat expanded into more practical concerns; chief among them, for Johnathan, was geometry. His mother taught him the love of the Romantic poets, though she could not bring herself to tell him anything of her inner self.

When Johnathan was fifteen, he was the only boy still in school at that age. Three years before Calvin had been taken out to work in the fields. Though they still attended Sunday school together, it was apparent to Johnathan that the long hours of labour were slowly stilling Calvin's brain. He often dozed during sermons, and appeared to be fixed upon marrying a ploughman's daughter who seemed to have time for all the boys except Calvin. It was clear to Johnathan they were growing apart. Though the boy and he had been inseparable chums since they were children, Johnathan seemed to have little tolerance for differences these days.

What continued to grow in passion with Johnathan was the joy his mother had imbued in him for poetry, especially the Romantics, and in particular the work of George Gordon, Lord Byron. Sir Alex kept a complete and current library and Johnathan was free to read such books as he pleased, though Sir Alex was strict about the care which one was to lavish upon any written text: no dog-ears, underlining or scribbled notes in the margin. Johnathan was of quite another view. He felt that books were intimate things, objects which not only reflected the love of their creation, but the impact of those who read them. So it seemed entirely appropriate that they should be marked and noted upon, so that a reader's reflections could be captured along with the thoughts of the author.

Byron was the personification of excitement and daring for Johnathan. Even his relatives were men of extremes: his father had been an admiral, known in the fleets as 'Foul-weather Jack', for frightful storms blew up wherever he voyaged. He was a notorious libertine, who had married well on two occasions, but who had managed to spend his way through both fortunes. Even such a father as this, Johnathan would have enjoyed having, he was sure. Better than no father at all, or worse, a father who slept with his mother, but who was unmarried, and did not acknowledge him as other than the child—not his—of his serving woman.

Byron lived and died in glorious extremes. When rebellion broke out against Turkish rule in Greece, Byron became an avid supporter. In 1823, he settled in the marshy, fever-ridden town of Missolonghi, and attempted against heavy odds to put together an artillery brigade. In 1824, he became ill, and within ten days died. Just before he slipped away, he came out of his delirium for a moment, to see his friends gathered in a death watch: 'O questa e bella scena!' he exclaimed. Johnathan was entranced by the life of such a man. It was with great excitement that he saw a new volume obtained by Sir Alex for the library:

Thomas Moore's The Life, Letters and Journals of Lord Byron, published only sixteen years earlier.

For Johnathan, these letters were to shape his expectations, structure his ambitions. They fired in him the desire to see the world, to savour the richness of experience which lay beyond Gleneaglesham, and the dusty village of Aberlady. The style of Byron's writing gave his experiences a special clarity. Feelings and ironies, ideas and sensations were captured almost casually in the description of events and places.

Increasingly, Johnathan spoke to his mother of his desire to travel, to see the world. Victoria smiled inwardly, thinking of the dreams that she and Ephraim shared more than a decade ago on the clifftops of Hoy. The poetry she had read to her lover infused his imagination in the same way that his son was now inspired to adventure and romance. How very much like his father he was in some ways, down to the hard edge to him that unsettled Victoria. She related Johnathan's unfocussed ambitions to Sir Alex, who agreed that the boy should have an education, and travel as he wished. 'But these things take money, so the boy must be realistic about his options.' Victoria's heart sank when he trotted out his economic rationalizations. They were a constant reminder that her son was not his, even though he was fond of the lad in a detached sort of way. She knew the gossip that held Johnathan to be Sir Alex's bastard son, but did little to dissuade anyone from such a belief.

No, the answer to Johnathan's future, as far as the baronet was concerned, was a career in the army. Not in the non-commissioned ranks; that would be sordid. Sir Alexander assured Victoria that he would purchase a small commission for Johnathan, and attempt to use his influence to get Johnathan into the Corps of Royal Engineers. Commissions were easily obtained for the cavalry and infantry, though the initial price and that of subsequent promotion, could be high. But the artillery and engineers did not follow a practice of allowing the purchase of commissioned appointments. It took no particular skill to dash into the mouths of assembled enemy ordnance, but the engineer's art of surveying and bridge building, and the gunner's art of trajectory and measured shot required education of a highly specialized order. Johnathan was showing signs of proficiency in mathematics, geometry and cartography, which by chance was being taught by the grizzled old schoolmaster in Aberlady. There was a very good chance that Sir Alexander could secure a position for him.

Victoria was less than enthusiastic that her son join the military. But there were no options other than personal service or the hardship of the fields. Worse, her boy might gravitate to the towns where, as a man without means or position, he would be drawn to the slums. What Sir Alexander was offering was not the most she had hoped for, but it was far more than presented upon her return from the Hudson's Bay Company. Oh, how long ago and far off that seemed to her now. What a fool she had been to chase off after Ephraim, someone now she rarely thought about, until some chance foible in Johnathan reminded her of her long-ago lover.

And so it was that at the age of sixteen, in September of 1852, Johnathan was taken in Sir Alexander's four-wheel barouche to the railway station at Musselburgh, for the long trip to the Royal Military Academy at Woolwich, southeast of London. His mother accompanied them to the station, in tears most of the way. Johnathan was embarrassed by his mother's vulgar display of emotion. He had taken on much of Sir Alexander's mannerisms, and often appeared haughty and cool even to his friends, who now saw him on rare occasions.

He was surprised to see that Elsie had come to see him off. In servitude since she was fourteen, it was apparent that hard work and long hours were telling on her. She looked worn. He pecked her cheek, self-consciously; now he was almost a head taller than the older girl.

'God be with you, Johnathan,' she whispered, her eyes bright and moist. 'Come back t' see us, then.' She had come with Calvin, who characteristically had little to say. Calvin had filled out like his father, and presented a stout frame, heavily muscled.

'Yers th' only one to get outta here,' Calvin mumbled. 'Don't forget yers old friends when yers famous!' Then after a moment, 'I'll be gone myself 'fore too long.'

Sir Alex alone walked the boy to the train. As they stood beside the puffing locomotive of the Great North of England Railway, he handed the boy a brass-bound pocket watch, with a heavy brass chain. Popping open the cover, he saw that it had been inscribed: From your loving mother, Victoria. Johnathan knew that his mother could not have afforded this token, any more than she could have afforded sending him off to school, and he was grateful to the man in spite of the resentment he bore him. He stepped forward, and took Sir Alex's hand. 'Thank you sir, for everything you have done for me and mother. We are grateful.' As an afterthought, he added. 'I shall do nothing to dishonour you.'

The older man smiled. 'God speed.' Pushing a small Bible in a black leather slip case into Johnathan's hand, he continued, ' "Do all that is written herein, for then thou shalt make thy way prosperous, and thou shalt have good success." '

Johnathan smiled at the irony. 'There are many lessons in the Book of Joshua,' he said. How could this man, who lay in adulterous fornication nightly with his mother, spout scripture to him? But Sir Alexander took the reply at face value, and was greatly pleased at the boy's knowledge of biblical text. He took Johnathan's hand with both of his hands, and squeezed it warmly: 'You're the son I wish I'd had.' It was the closest show of emotion for him that Johnathan had ever seen. It made him uncomfortable. He pulled away, as his mother cried out and ran to him.

'I am so afraid I'll not see you again. Please come home to me soon!' she exclaimed. Victoria pressed a small, worn volume of Byron's poetry into his hand. 'I almost forgot! Keep this always; it will protect you as it has me!' Johnathan took the faded book and tucked it in his shirt.

She wept as her son boarded the train, pausing only momentarily to wave. 'I'll not see you again, of this I'm sure,' she said in a choking half-voice, as distant and hopeless as an orphan's prayer.

Four

i

David was not sure how he felt about his father's death. Wasn't this just as if he was off on another trip somewhere, leaving no word about when he would be back? It was like the time he had gone up to Edmonton House, and wintered over. He showed up in the spring, chatting and carrying on as if he'd been away two or three days.

His mother seemed moved. There were no expressions of the abstract in the Assiniboine dialect. It was a simple but descriptive language, and many of the expressions were linked directly to the emotions. It was the only time that he had ever seen her cry. Tiny tears rolled like birdshot down her cheeks. She made no sound, nor did she move. Wordlessly, she turned away from Lépine who, cap in hand, had informed her of the accident. She walked to the cart and crawled underneath. David did not know what to do, so he took his two bewildered sisters and followed her. He wrapped the girls in their bedrolls, and soothed their whimperings until they fell asleep. Then he hunkered down beside the wheel, and waited.

As he sat, his mind was empty of feeling. His world was being changed, he knew, in some as yet unforeseen way. Not far off, the entourage moved among the fallen buffalo like hesitant wolves, sniffing this way and that for the right kill. The hunters, still in the rapture of the chase, darted madly back and forth on their horses, calling out the identity of the animals they believed they had brought down. David watched them dully. He saw the families begin the task of skinning and butchering. The large families had the best of it. He thought of Ephraim's kills, if he had made any, getting cool and hard to skin. He thought he might go and see whether there were animals belonging to the Bloodes, but there was no sign of instruction from his mother. So he waited.

The buffalo is a large animal, often weighing as much as half a ton. To remove the skin from a fallen animal, it must be rolled on its back and maintained there, while the hide is opened from throat to groin, then along the base of the short tail to the thick woolly clump at the end. Each leg was slit from the central cut to a point above each hoof. The head was encircled, then the heavy hide was peeled back, peeling surprisingly easily from the creature, provided the carcass was still warm. Where the skinning proved reluctant, drawing the long, thin knives between hide and flesh moved the process along. After a side was stripped, the beast was wrestled over, and the skin removed altogether, placed outer side down to receive the butchered meat.

With careful economy, the reduction of the naked animal began. First came the extraction of the long sinews from the backbone and shoulders. The ribs were cut with an axe, and the limbs were severed between the joints with a sharp, two-bladed knife. Internal organs were removed; the teats and heart were considered choice, next only to the tongue. Parts of the muzzle, liver and kidneys were eaten uncooked. Often the liver was eaten on the spot. Sometimes the old people who had come along on the hunt drank the milk from nursing cows. It was back-straining labour, and all except small children joined in. David took it all in, sitting motionless, until his mother touched his shoulder. He started, then looked up at her. Her eyes were red-rimmed and underscored by dark circles. She said nothing, but together, he holding the cuff of her generous sleeve as he had done as a small boy, they walked down to the killing run, and were shown with great deference to the two animals which Ephraim had slain.

It was hot, messy work, and became more so as the sun climbed over them. The blood made David's hands slippery, and as he dug about for the liver, he realized the cow was pregnant. Deftly, he slit open the amniotic sac, and a perfectly formed buffalo calf slithered out of the remains onto the trammelled prairie. Its huge sightless eye stared mournfully at him. He was used to death, and the necessity of it; yet the death of his father crowded into his head like an autumn fog. Never in his short life had he ever given any thought to the idea of death.

But here before him was an unborn calf which had the beginnings of life, but would never know life in the way that such beasts pursued their destiny. Waiting for its chance to spring forth in the glory and fullness of being, it had died painful minutes after its mother's great heart had failed, because a hunter's bullet had filled her lungs with blood.

David decided that the spirits had simply extracted a price: his father's life for the almost one thousand buffalo which dotted the plain for three miles. One of the medicine songs his mother sang to him played in his head as he looked at the wet, still foetus.

buffalo like this the sun goes around
it has been knocked over
around four times they danced, making a dancing noise
buffalo around, four times they are stamping around
bone whistles blow! shout!

It was a song of life and death and continuity. Four was a sacred number, representing the basic directions. He hummed the song almost unknowingly, for it comforted him; his mother looked at him upon hearing the familiar tune, and their eyes met. What passes between mother and son when such moments mark the passing of childhood can not be perfectly articulated. Nor need it be. She nodded.

His father had became enraged when he heard such songs, for though in all else he accepted the Plains Indian way of life, he took pride in his Christianity, even attending mass on the trail, holding that Catholicism was better than no worship of God at all.

Glittering Waters had urged Ephraim in the early years of their relationship to seek a spirit helper if he were to live on the plains away from his own people. Without a *pawakan*, one was at great risk from all the evil spirits which were everywhere. Ephraim scoffed at the advice, urging her to abandon her 'heathen, puny beliefs', and accept the Word as it was infrequently available to them on their occasional trips to Red River.

David's mother was in all other matters obedient. However, when Ephraim was absent, she took David as an infant to a shaman in her village. She was determined that David should have a proper protector and spiritual helper. She had taken some cloth and tobacco, which she offered the old man.

Lighting his pipe, the old man prayed to manito in a loud thin voice, breaking into songs of power. Taking the mewling baby from her arms, he closed his eyes tightly, and stood still for several long minutes. David stopped whining. The shaman opened his eyes, and spoke aloud the name of David's spirit helper: Kapiwapickwac totinepiw, he-who-sits-wearing-an-iron-cap. 'He shall be called Enatik!' The child was passed around to the most elderly man in the village, who referred to him by his new name, and said, 'I hope you will kill many buffalo!'

Passing him on to the next elder, David was held up, and a further blessing was similarly invoked. 'I hope you will have a long life!' And so on, until all the elders, men first, then the women, had held forth for the child all their collective aspirations for his future, which was now theirs by common will. The crier announced the new boy by his name to the village.

David's mother had repeated this story to him several times while he was growing up. She warned him about his father's unease with matters of magic, and so he had never raised it with him.

All this passed through David's mind as he contemplated the buffalo calf. Perhaps his father should have taken the advice of Glittering Waters: to walk the woods and plains of a strange land required the protection of its gods. Perhaps his father's gods were strong only in the land of his father, and impotent here. David shook his head, and reached for the calf's tongue. As he cut it out, he thought that, like the death of this calf, one's own death is tied to events one cannot see or even anticipate. One could not be too careful in the appeasement of spiritual protectors.

That evening, as the exhausted sun slumped and flamed dramatically across the horizon, a Catholic mass was said for Ephraim Bloode, sometime Protestant. David huddled with his mother and sisters. He, like his mother, showed no outward sign of grief, but his face worked with confusion. The two girls whimpered and fussed; their mother sat still, looking straight ahead, and holding their hands. Soon it was over. Before the last bits of sod were heaped upon his meagre remains, the crowd had dispersed to their campfires.

As night drew her sleeve over the camp, small casks of rum were brought out to toast the success of the hunt. Dancing started to the accompaniment of three scratching fiddles and the sounds of many hands clapping time. Soon, singing and loud laughter rang out in all quarters of the great camp, and sentries looked in glumly, cursing their luck. Campfires sputtered and flamed with the fat of roasting steaks; everywhere the rich smell of well-done meat permeated with mouth-watering pungency. Here and there bodies moved together under the carts, some ill-concealed from view. David could hear the moans and small cries of men and women as they lay together, and it generated an odd, breathless feeling in his stomach.

His parents had moved and whimpered in such ways, he remembered, but in later years it was only when there was something to celebrate: a homecoming, a successful hunt or payday at the company depot. Sex fascinated him, but his father had caught him masturbating once, and had beaten him soundly. He had warned of a creeping form of insanity, and painted a gruesome picture of a crazy, demented creature, whose mind had rotted from self-abuse; it had made a powerful impression on David's mind, to say nothing of the worst thrashing he had ever received. Among his mother's people, physical correction was almost unheard of, and while great value was put on modesty, he knew his friends in the village experimented with their own bodies, for they would talk about it in a studied, almost detached sort of way, as if they had been scouting for duck eggs or comparing horses.

His mother had withdrawn, and some time ago had crawled under her robes with the young children. David had wandered away from the frivolity to the outer edge of the camp, and sat facing the prairie with his back against the six-foot wheel of one of the carts. An occasional sentry rode by, but otherwise nothing moved under the luminous silver face of the new moon. Overhead, the campfires of the sky people winked and glittered. David considered that if each flame had but a single family around it, then what a vast number of people there were who had passed on to this barely visible world. He wondered if, as the groupings seemed to hint, that these peoples assembled according to family and tribe, or whether traditional enemies took their hatreds and long-standing quarrels with them. When he joined them, whose people would he join? Would there be his father calling him to sit with the whites? His grandfather? Would he hunt with the Métis or would he be claimed by the 'Protestant gentlemen', as his father liked to refer to himself from time to time? He decided that he would dwell in the lodges of the Assiniboine.

There were few of his mother's people here. They preferred their own hunt, even if it took them into the lands of the Blackfoot, for the Assiniboine were a proud and courageous people. When the artist and traveller George Catlin went among them in 1832, he wrote that they were 'the finest looking, best equipped, and most beautifully costumed...the most independent and happiest race of Indians I have met with'. They were a Siouan people originally, but separated from their brothers and allied themselves with the Cree many centuries before the coming of the European. Many of them became, with their allies the Cree, what were termed 'house people', waskahikan-wiyiniwak, families who arranged their lodges around the log, sod and clapboard shacks of the traders. These people wore the clothes of the whites, and adopted many of their mannerisms. These were not the same as the whisky Indians, whose wretched dependence on drink reduced them to the status of beggars and refuse pickers. They degraded themselves before the Europeans. The women prostituted themselves, and the men would haul firewood, and carry away the slops and toilet waste of the outpost in shallow wooden buckets. This for a two-pint draft of rum which would burn the throat, make the eyes water and, in the space of one-quarter of the sun's journey, cast up all the food from the body, leaving one weak, trembling and prostrate. These people were treated with contempt, and few survived the winter. When the white man's diseases struck, these were the first to succumb. Yet each year, their ranks were replenished by craving, shivering addicts.

So who were his people? The question had become urgent because the Bloode family had lost its provider. No longer could they expect to get credit at the Company post, as they had during Ephraim's absences. He had seen the loss of pride in families among the Cree and Assiniboine, because they had no provider, though there was a system of sharing which saw that no one went hungry, at least in times of plenty.

Who were his people? David did not know. His first language was English, because his father had insisted upon it; yet he was more comfortable in his mother's tongue. He was fluent in the language of the Montréal traders, simply because there were so many of them, and his father spent a great deal of time with such men during his service with the Company. Yet the people of his father had no time for him, holding even his father in low regard. Once, when Ephraim had taken his family to the colony at Upper Fort Garry, he had entered the factor's house to transact some business. David, his mother and his sisters were all required to wait outside the walls of the fort, even though it was a cool autumn afternoon, and there was a rat's tooth of a breeze blowing from the northwest. The disdainful looks from passersby were not lost on David, nor were the snide remarks made near him, as if he could not understand spoken English.

It was with his mother's people that he was most comfortable, particularly the House People, who were at ease and accepting of all peoples, even if there was considerable intolerance of them by whites and Indians alike. Even some of the Métis were starting to think of themselves as a nation of special people. Well, as far as he was concerned, it was back to the Assiniboine village west of Brandon House. He would, as the eldest male in the household, announce his decision to his mother and sisters in the morning.

ii

Things never seem to work out exactly as planned, David thought, as the dozen carts split away from the main body four days later, and headed east. His mother had flatly ruled out a return to Brandon House. Over his protests, she had explained that they needed someone to look after them, and the wealthiest relative they had was David's grandfather. They would go with the others as far as Red River, then make their way to the Lower Fort. They would not be going empty-handed, for in addition to the two buffalo which were assigned to Ephraim, they had been given two others, and the cart was fully laden with meat and the four robes. They had the remaining two horses, as well as all of Ephraim's kit that was not lost in the chase.

David's grandfather lived in a log shack and dressed in mostly European clothing; yet wore his hair in long braids, preferred his food in the traditional way of the Assiniboine, and slept on the floor in his lodge, much as he had done as a boy on the plains. Osawask, Yellow Bear, was called 'Ozzie' by the white traders. He was part of the legacy of the Cree middlemen who dealt with the traders at the edge of the great bay of the north. With the wealth and power of such strategic status, they were able to move from the northern forests out into the parklands and the luxuriant plains beyond.

David's grandfather was a pragmatic man, one of the few Indians, like Chief Peguis, who could see the irrevocable changes which his people were undergoing. His marriage to a Métis woman seemed to him only to confirm this belief: all his children were hunters and tripmen, or married to men whose lives thus depended. His offspring were no longer at the margins of either Indian or white societies, but were part of a Métis community which pursued its own destiny. The Indians continued to believe in their own superiority over all, and the traders' journals were replete with references to their feelings of grandeur. Alexander Henry the Younger wrote: 'Let no white man be so vain as to believe that an Indian really esteems him or supposes him to be his equal. No—they despise us in their hearts.'

Osawask felt the arrogance of the white traders well enough through their exclusionary practices, and in particular from their women. He was treated sometimes as one might deal with a child. Yet he felt no antipathy toward them. He was a natural woodworker and was paid well for his work. Starting out as a helper, then apprentice to an Orkney shipwright, he learned the art of putting together the great wooden boats of the traders, and could wield an adze and chisel with confidence and skill.

David and his family were welcomed by Osawask, whose wife had died the previous winter. Glittering Waters and the two girls would be a help around the lodging, and David could assist with the work, and learn a useful trade.

David loved the smell of the freshly worked wood; it was exciting to watch the transition from standing timber to handsome watercraft. During the winter of 1847 and afterward, he would accompany the labourers on snowshoes to pine forests at the mouth of the Winnipeg River on the east side of Lake Winnipeg. Teams of 'sloopers' would fell the huge trees with ten-foot double-handed saws, and the logs would be skidded out to the lakeshore to be placed with those that had been stacked there the season before. David's job was 'lopper'; he trimmed off the small branches with a hand axe. He sat around the blazing fires at night and listened to the men from many cultures talk about the things that mattered to them. In all cases, it was the same: wealth, love, and God's approval. And though they were professed in the opposite order of importance, the degree to which each subject dominated reflected that wealth and love weighed heavily on the minds of even the most pious.

After a season or two on the shores of Lake Winnipeg, the logs, stripped of bark, were rafted and floated upstream to the lower fort. The rapids just above Fort Garry at St Andrew's was the main reason that boat building become centered there. Another season in the drying shed, and the logs were rendered into planks in the saw pit. Here two men would work the rip saw, one above, burnt and sweating in the sun, and the other below in the damp, cool hole, cursing the shower of sawdust which rained upon him with each draw of the blade. As David reached his teens, he took his turn at the sawpit, and in slooping timber; soon his stripling body began to harden with the labour.

His grandfather's work seemed tranquil by comparison. There was some resentment about the fact that an Indian was doing such work, when they were traditionally allocated menial tasks, given the prevailing view of their unreliability. Yet such was his skill that the factor had designated him as the principal builder, under the Scottish shipwright. This man's preoccupation with rum kept him away most of the time and Osawask was free to pursue his work with the same slow deliberation that marked his speech.

The building of a York boat took about thirty-six days. The keel was laid on ways established before David's grandfather came to Red River. His prized possession was a large pocket watch on a brass fob, though Osawask could not tell time and had no interest in such a foolish notion. Once the keel was laid, David would hold the ancient timepiece at one end, and his grandfather would crouch at the other, his ear against the timber. If he could hear the ticking clearly, the vessel's construction could begin. For if the noise sounded indistinctly, there was an imperfection somewhere, perhaps redwood in the heart, and the keel would have to be rejected. To retain such a keel was a false economy, for if a heavily laden boat broke its back in the rough usage it would undergo, the Company would suffer losses much greater than a length of timber.

Following the keel were the stem and stern sections, with tamarack deadwood bolted in, to which the planking was fastened. Only about ten minutes in a long steambox was required to make the wood pliable. The lower two planks were carvel-built, or laid end to end, and the top two planks were clinker-built, or overlapping. The clinkers were copper-riveted with rivets made from the hoops on the Company's sixty-six pound powder kegs. Timbers were put in and gunwales fitted. The thwarts also served as seats. David learned each step of the process, and felt the gratification of the craftsman as his creation rose under his hands.

The boat was run out of the shed, caulked with oakum, and rubbed with a mixture of boiled pitch and tar. This was rubbed smooth after being scorched with birch-bark torches. The hull was left black, except for the top two planks—really nothing more than splash guards—which were painted with rust-coloured ochre. The vessel was put into the water, filled, and left submerged for two or three days to swell the wood tight. David knew all of these steps by the following season. He had started by doing the simple tasks, such as burning the old and battered boats so that their nails and bolts could be collected for re-use. But because of the nature of boat building, there were plenty of times when he worked close to his grandfather, holding a line, or passing rivets. On such occasions, he would talk to his grandfather in their native tongue about the things which concerned him. Osawask felt it was his place to guide the boy in the absence of his father. But some of David's questions troubled him, especially the ones which revealed David's anxiety about where he belonged.

One day, during the late fall of 1850, the two were paying a seam between planks with oakum. The fibrous material came in ten-pound rolls, and David fed it into the seam, while his grandfather tamped it with a mallet and small spade. The buffalo had not come that year for those on the southern hunt, and it was a topic on everyone's lips. There were stories about the Dakota, and the problems they were having with the American traders, who were refusing them credit. Tripmen on the brigades from St Paul brought stories of isolated incidents of violence. A settler shot an Indian whom he suspected of stealing a cow. There were retaliatory incidents involving a barn being burned, chickens being stolen, and more shots being fired. It was clear that in the new territory of Minnesota at least, tensions between whites and Indians were increasing.

David asked his grandfather, 'Can we expect these troubles we hear so much of to come here?'

Osawask paused for a moment, and looked at David. 'The white man chases riches in the same way our people do. As our fathers would get one musket for fourteen prime beaver pelts, so would he resell it, after much use, maybe, for fifty beaver to our enemy the Blackfoot. In this there is no wrong.'

'But,' and here he held up his hand with the mallet, three fingers outstretched, 'there is much that is wrong between enrichment and greed. In my younger days, there were ways to punish greedy people, and to keep this evil force in check. Now…' he trailed off, momentarily, 'the old ways are crumbling before the white people's will. See, the right to be a chief was an earned prestige. A man must show his worthiness in battle and the hunt, or show qualities of charity, oration, industry and leadership. This does not suit the traders, who opened negotiations with gifts of rum and small goods. A band might have many chiefs, each with their followers, yet all might live together in a single village without quarrel.

'The traders preferred to deal with one chief, to keep the cost of gifts small, and they favoured docile trappers and discouraged warriors, so that chiefs whose abilities to put forward their followers' best position, in the most forceful manner, were not what they might have been.'

David thought for a moment. 'So these troubles come from the will of the whites to seek enrichment—excessively?'

Osawask nodded. 'There is more to it. The whites come in great numbers. Many of them chase the yellow metal they call gold. In the summer just past, gold was found far to the west, in a place whites call Cal-i-fun-ya. So many people came that much astonishment was felt by the Indians whose lands they crossed, that there could be so many. All this I have heard at the depot building. Even some of the people here along the river have run off to find gold.'

David asked 'What can I do with gold?'

'You can buy anything the traders have, and more than you can carry. You can afford many wives, and keep many horses. You need not labour at anything while you have it.'

'I think I should wish to have some of this gold,' said David, reverentially, his imagination contemplating such wealth. 'How can it be obtained?'

His grandfather chuckled. 'It can be dug from the ground, or found in rushing water—but it has never been found near here,' he added hastily. 'The easiest way to obtain it is from fools who have it already and who will pay extravagantly for what you have. But do you see the problem?'

David looked at him, puzzled.

'…you become a fool, then, in your turn.'

This was too much for David to process, and his brows furrowed as he turned again to his work, stretching one stiff leg, then another, for they both worked on their knees.

David's grandfather was keenly aware of these developments. He had often gone to listen to the great chief Peguis speak in council. When the land was free of whites, all things within the tribe's territorial claims belonged to everyone in that tribe. With the coming of the whites, and the intensifying of trade, a loosening of strict territoriality gave way to a more open access to lands. But with the settlers coming in 1812 under the sponsorship of the man named Selkirk, a more rigid system of property ownership started to come into being, and it became an increasing source of tension between peoples.

Chief Peguis complained about the insatiable white men who took but did not honour. Only nine years later he was to write in exasperation about the lands which had been stolen from him on the strength of promises. 'We have had enough of all fur companies. Please send us out rather mechanics and implements to help our families in forming settlements...' Though well-meaning responses to the Indians' complaints were uttered, the Chief was to die in 1862, depressed and impoverished, but a practising Protestant. David's grandfather compromised much of his life, as did Peguis. But unlike Peguis, he retained his Indian identity while living nearly as a white. He attended service in the chapel at the Indian settlement under the direction of Reverend Cowley, an Anglican missionary who lived there with his wife, for his masters were pleased with his piety. But he had no illusions about the white man's god, and he spoke to David often about the teachings of Indian beliefs.

There was one development of Osawask's church attendance which had an unwanted consequence for David: beside accompanying his grandfather to Sunday morning service, the Reverend Alistair Cowley decided, with no debate being allowed, that David was to attend school. He had engaged a native schoolmaster to assist in the teaching load which he and his wife initially shared. David was introduced to academic study, with the Holy Book as the sole grammar text, and a small black slate for the practice of writing and the calculation of sums.

David chafed under this new regime, but was required to attend school only half days, so that he could work with his grandfather. Many of the lessons he learned from the Bible were familiar to David, for the same sort of messages had come from his grandfather. The Reverend Cowley intoned, 'The Bible commands us to use our time wisely, "be careful how you walk, not as unwise but as wise, making the most of your time." There are many people who start out to do something, something important, perhaps, but become distracted, and never accomplish what they set out to do in the first place. These distractions are of this world: flesh, material things, pleasurable pursuits, or gold!'

David wondered whether, his cynicism notwithstanding, his grandfather had not been influenced by his weekly attendance at church. There it was again, this matter of gold. It fired his imagination, and he dreamed of possessing this magic element which would allow him to live as the rich people of the settlement lived, with their horses and carriages, fine clothes and grand abodes.

One day after class, he approached Reverend Cowley. He was a small man, with an extremely thin neck, so that his clerical collar hung like a barrel hoop, showing his bulging red goitre. He had a tight, pointy nose which made him appear like a weasel, but his eyes were kind, and the tenderness in his expression made David feel safe in approaching him.

The Reverend looked up as he realized David was standing next to his writing table. 'Yes?'

His manner was so stern that David almost bolted. 'I would like to ask a question,' he mumbled.

The good Reverend swelled with importance. Because of his sharp manner and ferret appearance, few members of his flock approached him unless they were ill. At night, relatives of his patients would creep into the church, and gently bang on the stovepipe, which led up through the ceiling to his private quarters in the attic. He was a talented man with ointments and scalpel, but his bedside wit was stiff and riddled with arcane biblical verse. 'Go on, boy,' he urged, his curiosity aroused. 'Speak!'

'I should like to know how I can obtain a little gold,' David began, then added quickly, as he saw Cowley's expression, 'Not a lot, just a little.' At thirteen years of age, David was wise in the ways of the land, but utterly naive in worldly matters. The clergyman stared at him incredulously, and was about to respond harshly, when he realized that David was serious.

'Now, why would thee be wanting gold, my son?' he asked in the intimate form, which had fallen into disuse in the common language, except in the speech of a few clergy.

'There are things I need, sir; soon I'll be wanting a home of my own. Though I have my father's guns, I shall need powder and shot. I shall need a horse and kit for the chase. As you are aware, my father is dead, and I must provide for my mother and sisters. My grandfather grows old...'

'Are ye not paid for thy work on the boats? Is this not a fit and proper calling?'

David replied that the wage for the work he did was paid to his grandfather, who in turn cared for the Bloode family. He did not, would not, expect to be paid for it. Besides, though he did not mind the labour, it was not, he felt, the calling he was meant for.

'Ye should consider the peaceful and productive life of a farmer, then,' said Cowley. 'This business of seeking gold disturbs me. In the Book of Job it is asked: "But where shall wisdom be found? and where is the place of understanding?" It is written there that it "cannot be gotten for gold", it "cannot be valued with gold", nor is it equal to gold.

'Boy, what is required at the moment is understanding, and that ye shall have in learning, and in the revelation of His Word. I hear ye speak of gold as if it were the answer to all thy problems. What trip-trop! Study, learn, keep thy counsel, then make thy decisions with His help. "A prudent man concealeth knowledge: but the heart of a fool proclaimeth foolishness"!'

The Reverend Cowley had worked himself into a small fit of self-righteousness by the end of this short sermon. He no longer spoke to David, but seemed to speak right through him. Preaching was not a vocation, but a passion with him. ' "Ruin awaits thee, should thee make gold thy hope"! That too, is from Job's scripture. It be good advice, and it would do thee well to heed it.'

David was nonplussed. Gold was obviously something which stirred powerful emotions in men. The poorer the man's condition, the stronger the reaction. He thanked Cowley, and backed out of the room. He never brought the subject up again, but he resolved that he would have some of this gold, someday, and see for himself its magical properties.

iii

There is a supernatural quality to the aftermath of a prairie thunderstorm. As the clouds pass to the east, the sun bursts upon the rolling, glistening lea with the intensity of a slap. The air has a scrubbed quality to it; a man can almost taste the freshness of it. A deep breath fills the lungs with sweet effect, the eyes close and a smile involuntarily tricks the corners of the mouth. Even the usually discordant entry of man and his machines is muted, for the infernal shrieking of the cart axles has been dampened by the deluge. All about, the infinite shadings of green take on sharper distinctions.

The storm's passing is signalled joyously by a resumption of the meadowlark's rich, three-note warble. More ominously, the surface of the wagon trail which only moments before had been as unyielding and rut-scarred as glacial rock, has become an oozing mud-slop. The glutinous 'gumbo', as it is called, clings to boot and hoof and rim like hot tar. It is here that the Red River cart comes into its own, for the six-foot, dish-shaped, narrow wheels shed the mud with each slow rotation. The oxen's splayed hooves are ideally suited to traversing such terrain; his ancestors developed their split hoof in the mist-cloaked marshes which covered these plains at a time beyond the span of memory of the first aboriginal peoples.

In the autumn of 1855, after such a cleansing rainstorm had swept the prairie, David accompanied his mother on a buffalo hunt. She wanted prime hides for winter sleeping robes, and by early November, the hide showed a slate blue when skinned, and the fur was thick. This was the principal aim of the hunt, though select portions of meat would be brought back as well. Two carts ventured out on this small undertaking. The buffalo had not been coming in their great cycles, in such vast numbers as even six or seven years prior, but there were plenty of small pockets of animals, and the hunters expected to take no more than a half-dozen beasts.

In the second cart, also drawn by a short, woolly pony, were David and his mother. Glittering Waters was now showing grey streaks in her thick hair bunched at the neck. Leading the party was an aged former Company scout, Joseph Smoking, who, it was said, had accompanied Alexander Mackenzie on his prodigious trip through the Peace River Canyon, down the rushing complex of streams to the Fraser River, then overland to the great salt sea of the Pacific. With eight others, Joseph had watched the thirty-year-old employee of the North West Company scratch his name on the face of a massive boulder, looking out to sea. This put Joseph, David reckoned, somewhere in his seventies. Yet he was as lean and tough as a winter wolf.

His wife had died two years before of a mysterious illness which had tortured her without mercy for months. Joseph said it was a sickness of the white traders, and it had been unknown before their coming. He was somehow related to David's grandfather, and he had undertaken to guide them out onto the southern plains to find buffalo.

In Joseph's cart rode David's two sisters, Victoria and Sarah. In their tenth and twelfth years, the two girls were very close. Gleeful that the rain had stopped, they jumped from the slow-moving carts and ran on ahead, picking berries, gathering late-blooming flowers, and pushing one another under their mother's narrow gaze. They had been brought along to help with the skinning and butchering, but principally because David's grandfather was getting too old to look after them. His knees were stiff from years of working in a kneeling position. David grinned as he watched the giggling girls cavort on the trail ahead. He envied their carefree life, as he was starting to feel the heavy responsibilities of manhood.

David looked ahead to Joseph, who had given the switch to Victoria, and had mounted one of the two chase ponies. He had ministered to his wife until her death, and her suffering had profoundly affected him. It had shaken his faith. He became taciturn, withdrawn. He had a talent for finding buffalo and he was efficient at their destruction. The group had brought along one of the guns which David had inherited, and Joseph's own heavy weapon. He rode a little to windward of the fine dust being stirred up by the little caravan. Every now and then he would pause, stand in the stirrups and look over the gently rolling terrain. Squinting under his wide-brimmed hat, he would sniff, his nostrils flaring, creasing his leathery features. David would strain to see what had caught his attention, or what he might be looking for. And so the party proceeded.

By the end of October, they had ranged to the head of the Stinking River. There had been plenty of sightings of small game in drab fall colours, but not a single buffalo. In late autumn, the turgid prairie stream was no more than a damp ribbon. The surrounding countryside was given some relief by the poplar, willow and scrub oak which grew along the shallow riverbank. Rolling terrain would shortly give way to vast, tawny plains; the rapidly thinning foliage had a ragged, tatterdemalion look, for winter was not far off. The songbirds which usually inhabited the parklands were long gone, leaving only twittering buntings and the occasional magpie.

There was no certainty as to the track of the migrating buffalo, especially as the cold weather approached. They generally headed in the direction of the warm southeasterly flow of air, away from the portentous cooling of the northerlies. Their coming was presaged by a deep rumbling, on a still day audible as far as twenty miles away. It was easiest to confirm by putting an ear to a badger hole. If the wind was up, a man could smell their heavy musk; Joseph sniffed the air like a hungry coyote.

Their huge, shaggy heads were lowered in a storm, and they could be counted on always to face into the wind. After a blow, they would seek out the wind-cleared ridges where the grass was exposed, but while the wind was strong, especially if snow-laden, the herd would try to find shelter in a ravine or a break in the tableland. Here they would rest, chew their cud, and wait out the weather. Sometimes, following bad weather, the collective breath of the animals would hang like a fog over the gully where they had paused. It was cool enough now that Joseph kept a vigilant watch for such sign as well.

The wooded slopes of the river were replete with deer, antelope, and small game birds. As yet, they had no need to touch their travelling supplies, for Joseph's gun brought them all they required. From time to time, he would ride off, returning within one or two hours with a small pronghorn across his saddlebags, or a brace of grouse strung from his pommel. David would watch enviously each time Joseph rode off from the plodding ponies. He would apply the goad sharply to the animal in harness, with no appreciable increase in speed.

Behind him, his mother saw and understood his impatience. Far above them, a raven kited and soared in tight, concentric circles, on wings that never seemed to move. She believed that her son's spirit longed for the freedom of that distant bird. He had not been free to do other than help with the work at the yards, for the family had four mouths to feed. Still, the old man had not much time left, and she wondered whether David would stay at boat-building, lifting his head enviously each time a brigade passed for the twice-annual convergence on the plains. It was clear he preferred the gun and saddle to the slate and text. Even now, flicking idly at the draft pony, he was happier than if he was sitting at the long, rough work table at Reverend Cowley's schoolhouse. She felt that it was fitting that he be here, on this hunt, where perhaps he might learn something from Joseph Smoking about the way of the chase, and the land itself. She knew that his grandfather was urging him to pursue his studies, and to become proficient in the use of the tools, for he could see with the clarity of a Peguis that the old ways were disappearing before the white men's influences, in the same manner the spring sun burns off the mist from a prairie pothole. But since Ephraim died, she had longed increasingly for her old life, seldom speaking other than her own language. There was a comfort about living in the past, and she tended to daydream, to linger there, becoming forgetful and distant as she wrestled and bargained with the claims of ghosts. She was not so afraid that the land would one day lure David, but that it would entice him as it had so completely seduced her husband. David, for his part, knew of his mother's anxieties and was in turn hemmed in by his own sense of guilt and fear.

He had approached his grandfather on the general subject of making decisions. How could you act with certainty and wisdom if you were trailed by suspicion and fear?

'In everything, as in the building of this boat,' the old man gestured, 'there must be balance. For each taking, there must be a giving—as here, where the keel meets the plank I am about to lay in. If I plane away too much, the plank will not marry up; too little, and it will not be fair.' He spoke using many English expressions, for the terms he had learned for the boatbuilder's art were even then a thousand years old in the English language.

'Either way, the seam will admit water, and the boat will be useless. This balance is everywhere. For every man who acts with daring and haste, there is another with caution and prudence. Both may be brave or cowardly; neither has any assurance of being safe or right.'

'It may seem harsh to judge people in this way. It is necessary to look closely, for within the heart of every coward are the seeds of courage, if they are but looked for. Each bad thing can be put right by an equal good one, but things can never be the same afterwards.

'Balance, you must seek balance in all you do, while not allowing that search to lock your hands into inaction.

'The long grass feeds the buffalo; the great beast exists to fill our needs. When we die, we return to the soil upon which the grasses feed. Do you not see the design, the balance, the great circle which is at the centre of our beliefs?'

David's expression indicated he did not. Osawask stood up and walked over to a nearly finished craft, and placed his hand on the gunwale of the forty-foot vessel. 'Look,' he said.

'To move through the water in a straight line, there must be harmony and balance in all the dimensions of this boat. Just as its gunwale moves through its arc to the stern, so must its other side be evenly matched. Failing this, the boat will be ugly and difficult to manage. It might, with such a flaw, cast its load into the water.' He paused in his slow speech, and they watched a brigade of six boats pull past them, headed upstream to Garry, as the upper fort had come to be known. Each group of oarsmen strained in unison, the muscles and tendons on their thick arms standing out clearly in the afternoon sun.

'So it is for you,' he said quietly to David. His black eyes were intense, but as was the custom of his people, he rarely met anyone's gaze; he turned over and over a small block plane in his hands. 'It matters not who you think is better than you. It matters not what I think would be best for you, or your mother, for all that. Your life must be devoted to finding your own balance. Be excessive in nothing except the desire to know yourself well. If you are afraid, try to understand the nature of the fear; it may well be that the fear will keep you safe. However, it may be that you must do that which will enable you to conquer it. No one can make these decisions for you, for it is you that will have to live—or die—by the consequences.'

All this did not help David then, or now, for that matter. He was still unsure of what he should do with his life, so for the time being he did nothing but drift with the easy currents which were taking him along. But he felt the impatient need to get on with the business of being a man, and finding his place with his people, whoever they were. His shoulders slumped, and he dozed on the swaying cart.

Two days later, though they had not seen any buffalo as yet, Joseph announced that the herd was close. That evening as they sat around the small fire, the night quiet but for the yowling chorus of coyotes in the distance, they heard the distant squeal of a cart, possibly two. It was faint at first, then the thin squeaking grew in intensity. In the cool air, the sound could have originated anywhere up to fifteen miles away or more. The little group lay in their robes; the girls were asleep already. Discordant and sporadic, the groaning made its way toward them.

Joseph suddenly stood and sniffed in his peculiar way. He narrowed his eyes, holding his chin with the crook of his index finger, thoughtful, reflective.

He stepped to one of the carts and opened the bindings on his scabbard. He slithered his hunting weapon from its casing, leaving behind the old Parker field-trade musket, and went over to his pony hobbled a short distance away. Throwing his saddle and bridle loosely over his mount, he walked quickly into the gloom, and disappeared from view.

'What's got into him?' asked David of his mother who made no reply. As far as they knew, Indians did not use carts, and it had been some years since Sioux war parties had ranged this far north. David poked at the embers under the tea pail. The squeaking, louder in the distance, had become by reason of Joseph's unexplained actions, more ominous.

Abruptly, the shrieking of the carts stopped. The sound had placed the carts, now surely two of them, somewhere to the east and south of them. Soft night sounds closed in on the little encampment again. Within seconds, Joseph stepped back into the level clearing where David and his family were bedded down between their two carts. He no longer had his gun or mount, and he began to prepare for sleep. This familiar and unconcerned routine comforted David, for it seemed to take the edge away from the moment. He lay back in his robes, hands behind his head. And yet there was an expectancy now, brought on by the prospect of company. Someone out there had approached their camp only so far by cart, and had come no further. But they must certainly have seen their campfire, small though it was.

They had not long to wait. Three men approached from the gloom beyond the campfire. They moved silently, coming up from the river through the ground fog like phantoms. David shivered. They did not hail the camp as was customary. They were all carrying uncased buffalo guns, which was unheard of where no hunt was in progress. These were inauspicious signs, and David eased out from under his robes.

Their apparent leader, a burly man with a thick bush of a beard, carried a new Sharps .50 calibre breechloading cavalry carbine, which marked them all as American hide hunters, probably out of Fort Benton, seeking winter robes. Such hides brought a premium price, even though hunting conditions were harder, including the risk of being trapped by an early winter blizzard. The fact that they were using prairie carts was unusual, for the American hide hunters favoured large, four-wheel freighting wagons which had five or six times the capacity. Still, the easily repaired, cheap and sturdy cart had clear advantages, especially for a second-string outfit, which this clearly was.

They were all dressed the same, in leathers soaked with blood and sweat; no mistake, they were hide hunters. All of them scratched for the buffalo mange, or maybe the lice that thrived in their bedrobes. They lived with vermin that could have been done away with by the simple expedient of laying their belongings out on an anthill, in the sunlight, as the Indians did routinely. The man in front was the marksman, the other two were the skinners, by the look of them. The stench they gave off was disagreeable, even by David's robust standards.

All three wore wide-brimmed hats, pulled low over their foreheads. This was another serious discourtesy. Anyone approaching a stranger's camp doffed his cap as a gesture of respect. The standard cry was: 'Watcheer!' from the English traders, 'What good cheer!', or perhaps: 'Boo-jue-me!', as the French, 'Bon jour, mes amis!' had become truncated on the frontier. Either way, no greeting was forthcoming, and a tension settled in the group like bad news.

The leader of the three stepped over to the fire, unbidden, and hunkered down. Holding the tea pail with the cuff of his coat, he slopped a steaming draft into a nearby tin cup. He gulped noisily as the liquid scorched his throat, and the other two stood near him, watching the others, and waiting their turn. The man on his haunches took an inventory of the camp. He could see the carts were empty. An old man, and an unarmed, anxious young man, both breeds, probably; an Indian woman, Cree likely, from the round, pleasing face on her, and two girls. Not much resistance here. The old man hadn't missed a puff on his pipe, nor even given them a second glance. Maybe he was crazy.

David's mother rose. She took some bannock from a pail in one of the carts, and some pemmican. Without speaking, she offered these to the strangers. One of them had discovered the remnants of the evening meal in a pan, and scooped it out with his fingers, licking and sucking at them in obvious appreciation. All three accomplished their feeding without laying down their arms. They cradled rifles awkwardly, as a child might cling to a favourite toy. Several long minutes had passed since these men had arrived, yet the scene was being played out like some bizarre pantomime. Would they leave soon, after taking their fill? David hoped so, but said nothing. It was as if the utterance of a single word would break the protective spell which held these sinister men silent and, so far, benign.

The marksman rose from his place by the fire, stretched and farted mightily, as he wiped his fingers on his trousers. David followed his every motion; he could see that his clothing was soiled with a thousand such expediencies. David's mother had cracked his hands for such conduct, for the grease broke down the garment, to say nothing of the stink. It was wasteful. He wondered if this silent bear of a man had a mother.

The bear spoke. In a rough French, for he supposed they were Métis, he said, 'Nous voulons les femmes.'

David's mother quickly stood, and addressed them in English.

'Take your pleasure with me. The others are only children.' The girls, meantime, had gathered at their mother's skirts, whimpering quietly.

The bear drew heavily through his nose and spat, ignoring her. 'One of the chickens is mine—that one, with the blue ribbon in her hair; nicely wrapped, I'd say!' He guffawed, and moved toward Victoria, who had begun to blubber with fright.

Her mother stepped between them with a single word: 'No!'

Reaching down, the hunter seized the girl by the arm, and with his left hand, he jabbed the butt of his rifle sharply into the woman's gut. With a 'whoosh', she fell back, landing hard on her bottom.

'Here,' he growled to the smallest man of the three, 'you seed the cow, we'll butcher the calves!' The other two scrambled to do his bidding, licking their chops at the prospect, and menacing the two men not to move.

Joseph had not moved, not even when both girls had begun to wail in earnest. His pipe embers glowed and ebbed as he smoked, sitting up against one of the cart shafts.

David felt the growing fear rise like a stench in his nostrils as he saw the three women in his family being dragged off to the shadows. Fear burned his belly, skewered his heart, and loosened his shit. He clutched at the dry grass beside him, for he had not moved, nor could he summon the resolve to act or even to protest. Fear rooted him where he sat, and a soft moan escaped his lips as he heard the sounds of his sisters' torment. The men's muffled curses, the sounds of rent clothing, shrieks of pain and pleas for mercy crashed upon David like blows. Whipped by the savaging of his family, and by the lash of his own impotence and fright, David wept.

Within minutes, it was over. They had taken their release in the same gluttonous way they consumed their food. Within moments of each other, they sauntered back to the carts, buttoning trousers and exchanging raw, obscene comments about their conquests. David was sickened, and felt his lips draw back from fangs of deep, irreconcilable hatred. One of the men felt his baleful stare, and lashed out at him with his rifle. David cringed, cursing himself silently for his cowardice.

They went to the carts, and dissassembled the few bundles. They took the trade musket, laughing at its antiquated design. Two of the best knives were stuffed into waistbands, and a bag of pemmican was slung over a shoulder. Chuckling and wheedling between themselves, they left the camp, unconcerned, indifferent, their weapons propped over their shoulders. The noises of contempt and greed and cruelty faded, then gave way to their residue of pain and grief. David lay very still, listening to the sobbing of his women. For twenty minutes, the tableau was unchanged, until the carts started their creaking and squealing, headed southwest.

Joseph rolled out of his robe. He rose and started for David's mother, who could be heard weeping softly. David screamed at him, 'You craven old bastard! Why didn't you do something?'

Joseph looked at him as he walked away. His expression did not change in its physical arrangement, but David thought he could see something in his eyes, as they reflected the dying firelight. What was that? Pity? Was it resignation, scorn? David was suddenly aware that he was projecting his own loss of self-esteem, and he began to shake, crying again as he did so. Joseph helped the weeping woman to her feet, and she walked, obviously in pain, to the aid of her children. Moments later, she took them down to the river. They clung to her and wailed.

David's mind staggered under the enormity of the wrong done to his family. It was cruel, vicious and criminal. Yet it had been wrought with indifference. These men had helped themselves to everything the Bloode family had with them, and used the women as mere receptacles. They had acted without restraint, turning their backs contemptuously on the men, and taken their property without concern for the owners' needs. It was as if Joseph and David did not exist. David felt shame's finger pointing at him like a scornful child, and this oppressive emotion was more unsettling than fear. Snatching up one of the discarded skinning knives, he brandished it with both hands, waving it back and forth, then dropping to his knees, he stabbed it repeatedly into the earth, crying out, 'Ah! Ah! Ah!' with each wild blow at the enemy who had stolen and raped, and who even now was stealing his pride and his manhood.

When David's mother finally got the girls settled in their robes, the three of them sat around the freshened fire. They could see the wisdom now in the hiding of their principal hunting weapon and chase pony.

'We must go on,' said David's mother. 'The girls' wounds will heal, though they will suffer long from what has happened. We must go on, for we need the robes and meat.' In the low flames, her black eyes glittered and narrowed, as if she fought to put the evil behind her. She nudged a dry bough toward the fire with her moccasined toe, and it flared up, crackling. In the sudden glare, all three faces showed worn and drawn, as each struggled with the disbelief, the shock, and the unspoken worry that the predators might return.

Joseph nodded. 'We find buffalo tomorrow. We go on.' And so they sat until the fire was a greying pile of hot ash. One by one, silently, they turned in. For David, this great wound would scar him forever. But now, it was too raw to touch, and he fought the reliving of it until sleep enfolded him with the blackness of a raven's wings.

It was not the morrow, but the following day that they found their quarry. Sign was everywhere; dried droppings, churned soil and torn vegetation, and in the distance, stragglers, diseased or lame, shambled this way and that, followed by the flitting grey shadows of hungry wolves.

The girls had not regained their former exuberance. They were sullen and withdrawn, remaining in the cart. David's mother had sharp pains below her ribs where she had been jabbed with the rifle, and she had an ugly mottled bruise under her eye, squeezing it partly shut. She kept turning to look at the girls, worried that their torn and battered bodies would not heal properly, and more anxious that their minds had been damaged, as she had seen before in cases of rape.

The loss of innocence for most people is a gradual realization rather than a single event. But for these two children, the betrayal and ugliness that lay in the underbelly of human imagination had come in a tidal wave of despair, swamping their childhood forever. For David, the event had altered his view of the world permanently. Already he could feel the suckering verdancy of hatred curling its roots around his heart. His vengeful imaginings were cold flames that flared as the unreal memories slipped their restraints and flooded his mind.

David wished he could talk to his grandfather about what had happened. He would probably repeat something he had said before—something enigmatic, such as: in all acts of cruelty there must be the will to forgive, or the wrong itself will take on a life more important than that of the wronged. As usual David would be confounded; yet it was as if his grandfather spoke to his intuition. His mind sought to comprehend the things his grandfather had said or might say, and if they seemed puzzling, David was calmed by the sense that, if understanding was presently beyond his grasp, nevertheless, it was not far off.

The musky, dung-laden stench was carried in on the breeze. This was no small pocket of beasts; this was the main herd, the great northern throng. Halting just before a low rise, they dismounted and crept up to the ridge. The sun had just cleared the horizon, and under its crimson blaze, the rolling plain shivered and rumbled with a living carpet of hooved animals. The buffalo at this time of year were sleek and fat. Their pelage was shiny-dark, the guard hairs thick and tufted. Here before them were thousands, tens of thousands, perhaps more. They could pick their animals carefully. The buzzards and ravens overhead seemed to be waiting for the killing to begin, as they hovered lazily in the red sky.

'Tomorrow,' whispered Joseph, as if a spoken word might make this herd wheel and vanish, 'we'll take our animals. Early.'

The group made its way back to the carts, and set up a camp in a narrow draw close by. The cool night air freed them from the misery of insects, but it carried the rumble of the herd, just over a mile away, so that sleep was difficult. All of them were unable to rid their minds of the awful events only two days old, and sleep was a much-needed tonic.

Joseph was up and about before the day dawned bright, clear and cool. His plan was to fetch up the carts as close to the kill site as he dared. The undressed hides might weigh in excess of a hundred pounds each, and they would be rolled, flesh side in, ready to be lifted into the two carts. There could be no dallying, for the more the slain animal was allowed to cool, the more stubborn the skinning process. This usually meant more nicks and slits through the pelt, which diminished its value as bedrobe, greatcoat, or cutter rug.

Once they had hobbled the ponies, Joseph took his gun and a length of willow which had a fork in one end. Pulling one of the old travelling robes over his shoulders, he tossed his hat to David, and made for the slight rise just ahead. He motioned to David to do the same; David eagerly snatched a worn robe, and followed.

Just at the crest, he dropped on all fours, tugging the robe over his back. Crawling slowly, this way and that, he made his way gradually to the herd; David imitated his movements. The herd appeared largely indifferent to them, though a few cows would swing their enormous heads up now and then, looking at them, and tilting a horn this way and that with a threatening toss of the head.

After a time, Joseph sat up, cross-legged, with the robe still draped like a shawl over him. Slowly, he worked the willow branch into the soil, and cradled the end of the gun barrel in its fork. Steadying his aim, Joseph squeezed off a shot, and the report slapped David's ears, making him flinch. At the rim of the herd, one of the biggest cows grunted, and slammed to earth as if her legs were made of paper. The animals nearby grumbled and lowed, their little ropy tails switching nervously. But they settled within minutes, grazing around their fallen comrade.

Joseph's weapon spoke again, and a young bull tottered a few uneven steps and stumbled ponderously, a large pink tongue lolling out of his slack jaws as he fell on his side. All told, sixteen shots brought sixteen beasts down, the number previously established. Standing quickly, he began to wave the robe about, shouting incoherent noises, dancing and jumping about like a madman suddenly seized. Alarm telegraphed through the near side of the herd, and very soon, the snorting and milling seemed to infest them all. As one, tails in the air, they whirled and ran, their flight shaking the sod beneath David's feet. It was fully fifteen minutes before the last animal was out of sight; Joseph and David kept up their antics the whole time, in the event that the blind panic of the buffalo caused them to wheel about, and thunder back down upon them. Many a careless hunter had failed to take into consideration the uncertainty of the stampede, especially when, as now, the winds were light and fluky.

Once they put their robes down, weary, Joseph signalled the carts to be brought up. This was done, and the work of skinning commenced. Joseph had chosen well, for each animal was no more than about fifteen paces from another. David much preferred this work to butchering. As it was, only the hump, tongue, liver, and a few choice cuts were taken. There was not room to take much more back, for a Red River cart was well-laden at seven or eight hundred pounds. At day's end, clouds were rolling in from the north, and the first few wisps of snow were dancing in the air. They were anxious to make a start back.

The next day, a dusting of snow covered everything. The party was off while it was still dark. Joseph fretted about the wheel tracks, for they could be seen at a very great distance, and he wanted no repetition with intruders. Toward the end of their first day returning, Joseph was more and more uneasy, though no explanation was forthcoming. The wind had shifted around to the southeast, and while this likely meant milder weather, it meant stronger winds and given the frowning skies, rain. If it came too strong, the prairie could become a sea of mud, with the melting snow. It might come to travelling only at night, and then only if the ground froze. They set no fire that night, and Joseph roamed the perimeter of the camp, sniffing and listening like a cougar abroad on the hunt. David caught glimpses of him flitting soundlessly in the moonless night, and could not rest. Looking over, he could see that his mother was awake, ears cocked. Yet neither heard anything discordant, or made any remark, comforting or otherwise.

The next day they were off again, the caterwauling of the loaded carts seeming even louder than before. Well into mid-morning, Joseph had become convinced that they were not alone, but he had seen no sign as yet. Half a dozen times, he had signalled a halt, so that he could listen for the creak of carts, or the thud of hooves. Nothing. And so they had proceeded, anxious, jumpy, and constantly looking about. Eventually, Joseph's instincts proved right.

David noticed with sudden astonishment that they had been shadowed by two Indians, Dakota-Sioux by their markings, about a quarter mile out. They did nothing menacing; they kept their distance and maintained the same pace as the tiny caravan.

Joseph rode up alongside, and hissed to the others. 'Keep a straight face,' he said sharply. 'To show fear is to invite death. These people despise cowards as beneath contempt.' As an example, he took out his pipe, and packed it. This was something he never did, for a pipe was taken at rest. This act of studied nonchalance was for the benefit of the uninvited outriders. David took his cue, and called to his sisters to join him in a song. Their faltering notes scraped out a simple boat song in a semblance of harmony. Moments later, the Indians wheeled away, disappearing below the crest of a hill.

Joseph pulled his pony close in to the carts; the alarmed faces of the four showed their distress. 'There's been trouble in the Dakota territories. They're being pushed off their lands, and some are heading west. But they have not been this far north since the time of my father. Maybe they follow the same buffalo we have just left.'

David asked, 'Will they come back? They didn't look as if they meant harm. Why would they show themselves to us?'

'They have nothing to fear from us, boy. But I do believe they will return, for those two were scouts, lightly armed and with no sleeping robes.'

'Jesu-Mary!' David cursed, remembering an oath from one of the labourers at the fort. 'We're done for!'

Joseph fixed him with a stern look, for the young girls had sensed David's fear from the tone of his voice, and had begun to whimper. David's mother spoke her concern in Assiniboine to Joseph: what were they to do?

Joseph decided that they had no choice but to continue all night, provided that the weather cleared. Mercifully, the clouds thinned, and the moon rose. A fat harvest moon it was too, that lit up the countryside with an eerie blue cast. This night they were all tired, and they alternated dozing and keeping watch, starting at each jolt of the trail. They would stop at intervals, their ears straining against the night sounds for anything sinister. Then chewing on cold jerky, they continued, Joseph picking the trail carefully, just ahead.

To the north, the aurora borealis flickered and danced, their green shades illuminating the night sky after the moon set. The south wind dropped to a whisper in their ears, and the darkness with all of its unknown horrors was kept at bay till the dawn.

Sunrise the next day was muted. Stone-grey clouds overcast the sky before the mid-morning halt. All but the two girls had been walking, as the land had begun to rise, and the ponies were labouring under the heavy loads. In the stillness, made sharper by the sudden cessation of the carts' squealing, they listened; nothing but the thrice-called shriek of a grey jay, called by some the 'whiskey-jack', sounded from a poplar-covered bluff at a bend of the river. David decided it would take no cleverness to find them, for their carts left black ruts behind, and a blind man could follow them for the din. After a hurried meal of dried meat, they trudged on.

Without warning, their progress was arrested by two warriors astride ponies. These were not the same men they had seen the day before; these two had an ornamentation of dress that proclaimed them as men of consequence in their village. They were Dakota. Both wore their hair very long, in two thick plaits, for the Dakota believed that long life was associated with forebearance to cutting hair. There was nothing to do but approach them and stop. For long minutes, the parties stared at one another. Joseph puffed on his pipe, and appeared as calm as he had the night the hide men had mauled the women. Though his mother was calm in the face of her people's ancient enemy, David felt as if he would throw up; he struggled to keep his features neutral, as Joseph had instructed.

One of the two warriors raised his leg, and slid off his horse. It was a fluid, single movement, performed without apparent effort. David had heard that the Dakota, along with their brothers to the west, the Lakota—the godfathers of the plains—were the rivals of the Blackfeet, the Plains Cree and Assiniboine; all were accomplished horsemen. These two men were regal in bearing: handsome, lean-muscled men, who were said to know nothing of fear or weakness. Though the air was cool, both were bare-chested, and covered only with a shabby blanket drawn over the shoulders, locked with a single strip of ornamented leather. They had war-whistles made of the leg bones of cranes on thongs around their necks. Their leggins were well-made, but worn, and trimmed with trade buttons and weasel tails. They were, in fact, a curious mix of menace and dilapidation. It was apparent that they were from a poor village. But David took little comfort in anything that he saw, especially the eagle tailfeathers worn by each man, for each one represented an enemy slain, and a scalp taken.

The dismounted one stepped quickly, like a cat, to Joseph's horse, seizing it by the bridle. He spoke one word, sharp and nasal, which David did not catch, but which Joseph seemed to understand, for he nodded. The other returned to his mount, and sprang to its back with the same economy of movement used in dismounting. He wheeled it around without touching the single braided rein which ran from the pony's lower jaw. It was understood they were to follow. The two Dakota rode on ahead, never looking back.

Is there something so weak and unworthy about us that they know we won't kill them? David pondered this, as he turned over wild options in his mind. What's to stop me from taking Joseph's rifle, right now, and cutting down both of them? They wouldn't even know what hit them. Why do they seem to know, as did the hide hunters, that there would be no resistance? Could they sense my cowardice? Do they believe that the old man does not care? David tormented himself with these thoughts as he walked along, one hand on the cart.

His grandfather would know what to do. 'As you act, so you are,' he would say in his deliberate, epigrammatic way. 'Control of events is an act of the will; to be governed by events is passive. A wise man knows when to act, and when to sit still. A fool will be overwhelmed by forces which he does not comprehend.'

David fretted over this advice. How do you know which course to take, especially when the mind is choked with fear?

The small Sioux encampment came into view. There were only six lodges, each structure about fifteen stripped poles, sixteen feet or so in length, over which was stretched up to twenty tanned buffalo hides. These were marked in various ways, according to the exploits and inclinations of the owner. Two poles adjusted moveable flaps which could be set to draw the smoke from the lodge. There were very few children, and most of the inhabitants were gathered at the far end of the village, down by the flats hard by a creek which flowed into the Stinking River. David realized that their group would have run into one another, for the place was the best location to ford.

The two carts squealed and creaked to a stop. In the sudden silence, the babble of the small crowd of about two dozen fluttered up to them. As they became aware of the newcomers, they turned their attention momentarily away from what had been absorbing their interest.

Over the chattering shouts and cries, came a thin, whistling scream, terminating in a pleading screech. 'Ah, where is God? O where is God Almighty?' A series of broken whimperings followed.

Beyond the group was a cart, with a large draft horse still between the shafts. Tied to one of the six-foot wheels, spread-eagled, with thongs passing around his neck and forehead, David recognized the naked, bloodied form of the shortest of the three hide men. Two flayed bodies, the whiteness of them strangely pink-tinged like skinned buffalo, lay not far off in the grass. David turned his stunned attention back to the wailing wretch on the wheel. His eyes seemed to be rolling wildly, until David realized with a cramping lurch that his eyelids had been cut away, giving him the look of a panicked horse.

He had been emasculated, and his scrotum was being brandished, stretched inside out on the fist of a nearby woman, who was rubbing it with willow bark and dried grasses. David had heard rumours of such receptacles being used for medicine purposes, and he felt his own scrotum shrivel. A young boy, not more than twelve years old, leaped to the cart and clumsily tore the scalp from the hapless hunter. No warrior would consider taking such a trophy from a snivelling, unworthy wretch as this. But it was fitting for a boy on the threshold of becoming a member in the soldier society to take his first scalp in this manner. It was done by running the point of a knife in a circle around the top of the head; with a sharp tug, the scalp pulled free. The women would stretch them on a circular frame of willow, paint the inside red, and suspend them in the lodge. Usually, no more flesh than the span of a man's hand was taken, but in this case, a ragged piece of skin and hair the size of a handkerchief was torn from the screaming man.

David's senses tried to deny this grotesque scene. His fear scalded him, for he thought they were all next. Victoria had realized who was being tortured. Calmly, deliberately, she squirmed down from the loaded cart and walked over to him. His rolling, lidless, startlingly white eyes looked down upon her, his whimpering continuing unabated. She bent down and scooped up a handful of mud. Without pausing, she flung it upon him, and spat at him. The onlookers made small cries of approval. Stiffly, she turned and marched back to the carts, where her family remained rooted in their anxiety.

Joseph took his lead from the change in mood which this bold act of Victoria's had triggered. He walked over to a pile of goods, obviously taken from the hunters' carts. He picked up his musket and the two skinning knives which had been taken several nights before. The warrior who had led them to the encampment moved quickly over to Joseph, motioning his arm in a sharp slice downward, palm extended down. 'No!'

Joseph knew some of their language and, between signs and pointing at the man on the wheel, he gave to understand that they had been robbed by these men, and their women violated. He discovered in turn that this small breakaway Dakota band had decided to resist settlement on reservations being set up by the proposed Treaty of Mendota. These people were determined to find a larger group which had left the proposed reserve along the Minnesota River, for the game was almost depleted and the young men were scornful of farming as a way of life.

While the men had been away looking for game, the hide hunters had stumbled upon their encampment, and had been wrong, fatally as it now turned out, to believe that only two old men were around to look after the women. And so they had taken what little they felt was of value, and vented their lust on a young girl who even now sat apart from the rest, her face bearing fresh self-inflicted cuts of shame. When the warriors returned, they had painted themselves with black pigment made of charcoal and rendered fat, half the face, and a heavy circle around the other eye, and red slashes across the shoulders. After a short prayer, they set off in pursuit, accompanied by the whole group. There was no difficulty in catching up with the slow-moving carts and bloody revenge was taken by the nearest relative of the wronged woman. But these were not worthy foes, and there would be no scalp dance.

For whatever reason they had been brought to the encampment, the mood now was palpably different. Indians from the group at the cart now walked about them, gesturing and pointing, speaking among themselves. As Joseph stood there holding his possessions, the man who faced him waved him off with a wide sweeping gesture. Again the intent was clear: go. Joseph wasted no time, but returned to the others, placed his musket and knives atop the hides, and led the ponies in a half circle, intending to cross the creek closer to where it flowed into the river.

David's guts were in a turmoil. He fought with but lost the urge to look back. As he glanced over to where the doomed man was still tied to the wheel and wailing, a warrior scrambled to the deck of the cart. He thrashed the startled horse and the cart rolled forward, rotating the bound man who remained fixed at head and wrists. His legs and torso began to flop obscenely with each turn of the wheel, and his dismal shrieking could be heard over the squeaking of all the carts. David turned his head quickly, a sob tearing from his throat.

Out of sight from the encampment, barely a mile along their path, David dropped off the trailing cart, for his guts were roiling. He crouched behind a naked willow bush. Etiquette of the trail required that no one look back, for there was little cover even in summer, for the private attendance to toilette.

He dropped his breeches, still overwhelmed by the experience and his deliverance. In violent spasms, he vented his surging bowels into the prairie grass. He sobbed uncontrollably, as his grandfather's words came back to him, 'Each bad act can be put right by a good one, but things can never be the same afterwards, of course.' David agonized. How could the unspeakable cruelties inflicted on the men who defiled his family obliterate what had happened? Oblivious to the foul stench of his fright and confusion, he remained squatted, clutching at the spindly willow bush. He thought it was a nasty, vile world, and not worth living in.

David remained crouched for a time. The creak of his family's carts was barely audible. Hunkered over and rocking gently on his heels, he was oblivious to the presence which loomed up behind him. Suddenly he felt a thin, stinging blow on the side of his head. Yelping in surprise and pain, his stiffened legs failed him, and he sat back into his shit. Looking up, he saw a man sitting astride a horse, large as a god from this perspective. As his vision focused following the blow, he recognized with dread the unmistakable markings of the Sioux: hand prints and hoof patterns to show bravery, having touched an enemy in battle, or success in horse raids.

Close by, a thin, unsmiling, flat-faced warrior held a notched, painted stick, as slim as his middle finger, about the length of his arm. A tiny white pebble had been set in a split at one end. This was the coup stick which had struck David. Two other men sat motionless on their mounts behind him; each had a field-dressed deer carcass draped behind the withers, and across their thighs. They were obviously a hunting party from the village David had just left, he concluded with some small relief. The man closest to him had now inexplicably spun around on his horse, so that he was facing backwards. He was laughing. 'Truly you have counted a great coup, brother! Songs will be sung in your honour! Truly you have met a worthy foe in adverse circumstances!'

The man with the coup stick was not laughing. He prompted his pony to take a step or two, leaned over David and dropped a braided line of horsehair, thin as a bowstring, over his neck. He tugged on the noose. David lurched forward, choking, and stepped out of his breeches. Stiff-legged, half-naked, and beshat, David was thus led off, a captive. The one who had been sitting backwards rotated on his horse, and fell in beside David's captor.

This man was a *heyoka*, one of those mysterious people peculiar to all the Sioux nations, who had dreamed of thunder in their fasting period during puberty. To avoid the threat of the thunder god's lightning lance, he was compelled to do things in a backward and unlikely way. This included walking on his hands, holding his bow pointed toward himself, and plunging his hands directly into the kettle to take his meal. He was expected to be the master of sarcasms and double meanings, for his most important role was to deflate the pompous, mock the arrogant, and to prick the pride which, unchecked, could ruin an otherwise good man or woman. The scoffing chuckle of the *heyoka* was reason enough to avoid too much self-importance, for his caustic witticisms bit deep, and were designed to bring gales of laughter from anyone in earshot.

The *heyoka* served another purpose: he lifted the spirits of the people in times of difficulty. He raised the hopes of those who lay dying, perhaps of wounds received in battle or, more likely now, one of the white man's dreaded diseases. He was in fact the embodiment of balance in a natural, harsh world which demanded parity and complement. And even as David watched some of his antics, and tried to catch his import, he felt some, a little, of the intense anxiety about his predicament lift.

Though he was being led back to the encampment as a prisoner, he was sure that the fate of the buffalo hunters was not his. Perhaps they would even let him go, once the mistake had been exposed. He fretted at this, as well as his nakedness. The men around him were relaxed, including his captor. They chuckled at the jokes of the *heyoka* as they progressed at a slow pace to the camp. He remembered Joseph's advice, and he resolved to behave in a brave and manly way, though he felt very much like a frightened child. He desperately wanted to call for his mother, who would surely have missed him by now. In his heart, he knew his mother would expect him to look after himself, for he was a man, expected to make his own choices and fight his own battles.

His nakedness caused him to be chilled, and he cupped his crotch for warmth. His scrotum shrank and his buttocks tightened with the breeze. The horsehair leash chafed his neck, and with one hand he eased the line from his skin. Feeling ridiculous and completely vulnerable, he strode behind his captor's horse back into the camp of the Dakota.

Those who saw the hunting party return set up a cacophony of trilling cries. The few children there were, dogs and women streamed out to greet the hunters, and to gawk at the unexpected trophy. The warrior who held David led him over to an old woman, and dropped the line into her hands. 'Yours!' He gestured with a thrust of his jaw, not meeting her eyes.

He was immediately engaged with the other men, who were pointing to the dead hide men, now drawn in a heap on the other side of the creek. The camp was in the process of breaking and packing. They drew off in council, some pointing and speaking loudly about David. There was obviously confusion about David's return in this manner.

David was acutely embarrassed about his naked and fouled condition. As he stood shivering and clutching himself, small children hooted and screeched at him, and pelted him with bits of sod and dried horse turds. David endured these small additional humiliations, flinching and dodging when he could. He was growing more and more apprehensive about his fate. Close on, the old woman was exchanging heated remarks with the other crones in the camp, punctuating her assertions of ownership with sharp tugs on the leash, causing David to stumble forward to ease the choking.

This termagant was the mother of the warrior who had led David in, as the cries of approval for a son's generosity indicated. Her name was Wakandayamani, or Spirit-that-Rattles-as-it-Walks. She had a brittle, sour cackle that passed for laughter. As she opened her mouth in glee, David noticed that her upper and lower front teeth, those that were there, jutted out at odd angles. Even in repose, one of her lower teeth protuded like the lower fang of the great black hogs brought to the settlement on the York boats.

Some thirty years before, Wakandayamani, had taken her first and last drafts of trade whisky, a cask of which had been given to her husband in return for twenty cured robes. In a blind stupor, she had walked off the edge of a steep gully, and had fallen heavily on her face upon a sun-dried stump, some six feet below. The poorly set jaw was a legacy of that event; she was fiercely against the rum and whisky traders ever since, but her husband had succumbed to alcohol, and had last been seen near Fort Sully on the Missouri, in the tattered collection of native hangers-on and beggars that huddled in the lee of the fort's palisade. Humiliated by her husband's shuffling and grovelling, she had divorced him by casting out his few belongings, and naming him Ehpeya, no-longer-mine.

She advanced upon David, who regarded her uncertainly. The men had broken their council, and the matter was clearly left to the women.

The old woman announced to the festive group of women in dry, emphatic words, 'If he be mine, then he must be properly marked!' She seized David by his arm and leg, and with surprising strength for one so aged, she flipped him over in a sudden movement, the way she might overturn a freshly killed deer. She brought David over her knee, and closed her mouth on his left buttock, and taking what flesh his skinny haunch afforded, she bit down sharply.

David squealed like a scorched pig. He clutched at his behind, and felt the sticky flow of blood. Were these people going to eat him alive?

'Faugh!' said the old woman, as she spat. 'This one is covered in shit! Were there no clean ones out there for you to bring me?' The little crowd roared in amusement as David huddled in a ball, frightened and in pain. He heard, but only partly understood the gently derisive tones of the *heyoka*: 'Old woman, if you want to get any work out of him at all, you must treat him much worse than this!'

This alarmed David even more, for he had yet to understand the sarcasm of a contrary. Moments later, he felt the heavy mustiness of an old robe thrown over him. He hastily gathered its warmth about his tormented body, and Wakandayamani led him to her lodge.

So David was taken as a slave of the Dakota. Humbled, frightened, naked and branded as he was, a people had chosen him to live among them, though not as one of them.

iv

These Sioux called themselves Dakota 'the people' from their word *hoda*, meaning 'friend'. The life into which David found himself thrust was not the cruel bondage of the slave as described in the Book of Exodus. Nor was it the horror of campfire tales told during the hunt to sharpen sentries' eyes. It was a life where his bodily needs were met, but beyond this minimum, he did not exist for the others. Even the children tired of tormenting him within a day or so, and David fell quickly into a drear routine of assisting the women, fetching fuel and water, carrying away slops and tending the horses.

These were tasks not unlike those he was used to, but there was no acknowledgement, praise, or recognition of his contribution to the welfare of the band, which a day later had joined the main body they were seeking. All of them now pursued the buffalo herd. During the intensive labour which went along with the hunt and preparation for winter, David saw others receive a nod, a smile, a welcome. By contrast, his own isolation was the more painful. Instructions were always simple, direct, and after a time, unnecessary, for he came to know what was expected of him. He had no name, but was referred to as Pahinshasha-wacekiye, or Red-hair.

His place in the lodge of the man who had taken him, Otakle, Many Kills, was at the outermost edge, by the door. He slept with his face to the inner liner of the tipi, and even in this he was set apart. He was expected to be abroad before the sun's first rays cleared the eastern hills. When he heard the women trilling the names of successful hunters, he ran out to take the game from their backs.

His work was his solace. His discipline chased the ghosts of loneliness, fear and loss which haunted his thoughts in the few moments when he flung himself into his sleeping robes, exhausted.

And so the days passed. It grew colder, and the band moved to a wintering place in a scrub-filled valley protected from the worst of the chill northerly winds. The pace of the camp slowed with the snow and the people spent more time in their lodges. Otakle lived with his mother, Wakandayamani, and his brother, Wakinyanwaste, Good Thunder, who was as unlike Otakle as it was possible to be. He and his wife, Snana, Tinkling Sounds, were both from the Kaposia Band of Madewakanton Sioux, and both had some education at the mission school, Snana having attended almost four years. Both were gentle, quiet people, who despaired of the poverty which had beset them and their band. Both could speak English and a little German. They had decided to move west with this desperate group, as a last attempt to keep to the old ways. When they spoke of giving up and moving back to the reservation at Kaposia, Otakle became angry, and would not hear of it, reminding them that all three of their children had died from mysterious diseases, leaving them only one daughter, Mahpiyatowin, Blue Sky Woman. This girl was about David's age, and as pretty as her name. She seemed shy, like her parents, and never looked at David, though he found himself stealing many long glances at her.

The other inhabitant of the tipi was an old man of uncertain relation to Wakandayamani. He was called Taopi, Wounded Man, by the others. His right side bore horrendous scars, and he walked with a painful limp, though he was never heard to complain about this or anything else. David knew that in the lodges of his mother's people, when one became too old or disabled from the hunt or any sort of endeavour requiring strength, he was taken in by a family of wealth. It was considered honourable and worthy of a man to show such generosity.

Their lodge was spacious, about eighteen feet across, with a heavy inner liner of buffalo hides, fur side facing the outer wall. The inner surface was decorated with patterns and pictographs which represented the exploits of the family and the village. Across the centre, just over six feet high, a single bough was lashed between two of the lodge poles; from this was suspended the large copper cook pot, as well as many of the talismans which kept the spirit world content.

Sometimes feasts were given, and when Otakle was the host, David was required to keep the fire fuelled and fetch such things as he was directed. Being present at some of these gatherings thus afforded him the opportunity to learn the formal customs of his captors, and to polish his understanding of their language. Since the Assiniboine spoke the Nakota dialect, David found the common sound shift easy to get on with. The telling of tales was a winter pastime, for the gods were at rest, and did not mind the vainglorious references to exploits that at other times would have invoked their reproach. In the telling of tales, and the medicine ceremonies which followed, David came to understand the Dakota heritage, and their aspirations.

The elders were responsible for the 'winter counts', which was a means of preserving Dakota history. The exploits of the village would be memorized and recorded by means of pictographs, to be handed down to subsequent generations. Events which had significance for the people, as in the case of hunts, forays against enemies, and important feasts, were recorded.

At one such feast, held in the darkest days of December when the snow lay deep against the lodge walls, Otakle dressed in his finest robes for his role as host.

He had a deer-tail roach headdress, and his winter leggins were ornamented with yellow and blue trade ribbons which passed through garlands of metal bells, arranged like small ladders on either side of his thighs down to his heavily lined moccasins. Around his neck was an otter collar, once resplendent, but now somewhat thin from wear. Its border was decorated with quill work, for his mother was adept at such ornamentation. Interspaced was a row of brass buttons from a military tunic. Such a collar was the badge of a man of influence.

Over his shoulder Otakle had slung a rope of braided sweetgrass, the smouldering end of which he held in his hand. It gave off a pungent sweet smell which filled the lodge. Worn fur bracelets of mountain-lion hide on wrist and bicep were strong medicine-helpers, as was the circlet of hawk and eagle feathers attached to the back of his neck by a thin strip of wolf skin.

Otakle gave a speech as the wind groaned and snored through the wind flaps, sending small puffs now and then back into the lodge where about sixteen men were gathered. The snow lay deep against the lodge, on the north side to a depth of six feet. This, together with the press of bodies and the small, smouldering fire, made the tipi uncomfortably warm. Most of the men were bare-chested, and the sweat glistened on Otakle's face and arms as he stood to speak:

'Friends,' he said, waiting for complete silence. He held up four fingers. 'Four nights ago I had a dream. I have thought about it at length, and I now reveal it to you. I dreamed that we had come to winter in a place we had not known before, and we joined with a village whose people welcomed us and shared with us. These were trusting people. And as the snow was so deep, and the winter's chill so great, no sentries were put out, nor were the horses watched closely, for no one believed war parties would venture out in such weather. Too, the principal chief of this village was an elder whose experience and power was very great.

'In his lodge, at the foot of his sleeping-place, was a medicine-circle of unusual force. The outer edge of this *wacipi* was marked by peeled stakes, painted red, and driven deeply into the earth. Suspended over the circle was the elder's medicine bag, in which were carefully arranged bundles of sacred objects. No one was allowed into the sacred circle, nor was anything introduced there which had no spiritual significance. Even though it took considerable space within the winter lodge, strict protocol were observed by everyone: no one could pass between it and the fire. And so the village had prospered; hunger cast not its shadow over them.

'One night, the elder was visiting another lodge in our village.' The listeners, their sweat-dampened faces inclined to the speaker, now sensed something dramatic was about to be disclosed in the story, and their attention was keen. Otakle paused for effect, then continued:

'Much feasting and celebrating was taking place between our band and theirs. The elder had three wives, who were abed, yet one had an anxiety that she could not dispel. Restless, she had turned to face the fire, which had diminished by then to a heap of glowing coals. She drew in her breath sharply, silently, as she was horrified to discover that a stranger had made his way into the lodge, and now sat huddled and shivering in the medicine circle.'

There were murmurs of concern, and expressions reflected puzzlement and disquietude over this inauspicious turn in the narrative.

'She addressed the stranger,' said Otakle, his voice compelling the mutterings to die away, 'who responded not, nor did he move. Throwing a handful of grass onto the fire, she saw in the sudden light cast by the shooting flame, that there was nothing to identify this stranger. No features could she see, no dress that could be recognized—nothing. Terrified, she leapt from her bed robes, and fled to summon the others. Outside, the night had become very dark, a wind had sprung up, and the blowing snow stung the face like sand.

'At length, the elder and those of us in his company—our chiefs and warriors—returned to confront the stranger who was still huddled in the sacred circle. In sign and in word, he was called upon to identify himself, and to explain why he had offended the medicine circle. He gave no answer; his only response was to sink lower under his poor robe of uncertain origin. Many of those present became angry at his silence, and before they could be counselled by the elders, some laid hands upon him with great force, and snatched him out of the medicine circle. He was placed with no gentleness on the floor of the lodge.

'The old man whose lodge it was expressed deep displeasure at this inhospitable behaviour, and ordered the stranger placed in his own sleeping place, the place of honour at the back of the lodge.'

Among the listeners there was clearly disagreement about the choice the old man in the dream had made, and small quarrels broke out between men with furrowed brows and anxious expressions. Otakle was pleased, for a good story teller should have this effect, and he expected the debate to become even more intense as the balance of the dream was told. Yet the fervency with which he related the story was not entirely the product of his skill as a teller of tales. The vision troubled him as well, and he looked forward to hearing the thinking of the others.

'As they placed the stranger into the warm robes of the elder, the thin robe fell away, and the stranger was seen to be a white man. His dress was strange, with many fine fastenings, and boots unsuited to travel in such bitter weather. His face was heavily whiskered, and the skin of his nose and cheeks pale with the bite of the cold.

'At once a great council took place. Many urged that the stranger be killed at once, and his head separated from his body, so that his spirit could not rest, and therefore, could do no harm. Only this measure, some felt, could appease the profaning of the sacred circle.

'Still others argued that the stranger's medicine was very powerful— more powerful, in fact, than that of the sacred circle. For had not the stranger walked into their encampment unaided? And had he not only chosen this lodge, but also had entered the magic circle itself? A pipe was smoked, and much debate passed back and forth, for the resolution of this problem was not an easy thing.

'Ultimately, it was decided to bring meat and hot soup to the stranger, which was done. His strange and quite useless clothes were replaced with warm, lined moccasins, and a proper robe placed around his shoulders to shield him from the cold. So, he fell asleep on the elder's own bed. The elder and the others returned to the feast, which now had been supplanted by intense discussion about this event. The talk went on until the false sunrise, when the elder stood up and announced his intention to retire to his lodge. This was a signal for the others to retire also, as it is for us…'

Otakle broke off, and looked around. Normally, the remark would have attracted some polite laughter, for in the extreme rituals of courtesy, it was always the youngest of those present who were expected to announce their fatigue first, so that no elder would withdraw because his failing stamina required it. None of the listeners said anything, for their attention was rapt.

'Upon his return to the lodge, the elder was shocked to find that the stranger was gone, the medicine bag was missing, and his three wives slain where they slept. Hastily stepping outside to raise a cry, he saw that the horses had been run off, making chase impossible in the mounting storm.

'Disgraced, his medicine bag gone, the old man cast off his robe, and walked off into the blizzard, stumbling and staggering in the drifts. He showed no sign that he felt the icy lash of the storm against his naked flesh, and very quickly he was lost from sight. A silent, awestruck people watched him go, this offering to the gods as generous as the betrayal of the stranger had been evil.

'This was the end of my dream.'

Otakle stopped speaking; his eyes were downcast. No one spoke for a time, and then David, who was crouched spellbound by the door, heard someone ask a question almost reverentially: 'What happened to the people?'

Otakle shook his head. 'My dream ended there. I saw no more. But I have no doubt that a hard time follows such a mistake.' And he sat down suddenly, his legs crossed under him.

David went outside with a tin pail full of bones. He threw these to the dogs who sprang from the snow snarling and snapping at each other. Behind him he could hear the controversy sparked by the telling of Otakle's apocalyptic vision. David pondered it as he watched the dogs fight each other for the scraps: the images of the dream were as dry as ashes, empty of hope. Most of the men in the lodge agreed that the vision was equal to the coming of the white man, and its desolate consequences for aboriginal people. There was anger and heat in the wrangling, and a slender stab of fear.

This was not a fear borne of cowardice, for there was no higher virtue for the Sioux than courage. It was rather a fear of events which, like the occasional disappearance of the prairie rabbit every seven years or so, or the failure of the buffalo to return, were at the outer edges of human understanding, and beyond contemplation.

The feasting was taking place at the lodge of the war society, whose responsibility it was to police the village for that moon. The village was so small that there were few societies to which the men belonged. Membership was fluid, and each society attracted according to talent or inclination. Where regimentation was demanded was during the hunt. David could see the origins of the Métis and Halfbreed society at Red River in the loose but tangible commitment to the welfare of the whole group, while fiercely maintaining individuality. It was this single-mindedness which prevented any firm conclusions about the import of Otakle's speech. Perhaps there was no resolution of what they already knew to be a deepening problem: they were out on the plains, away from the parklands of their homes because their lands had been taken away, and the game had been driven out. To remain free to pursue their lives in the manner of their forebears, the men had decided in council that they must leave.

Even the women had a large measure of personal liberty. Indeed, the lodges were female-dominated, as David well knew. There was no doubt that in all matters within her generous jurisdiction, Wakandayamani was in charge, even despotic. Women had full rights of divorce, requiring only a public declaration of non-compatibility, usually accomplished by casting her erstwhile mate's belongings from their lodge. If a man, challenging the virtue of a virgin, failed to make his case that he or others had lain with her, he was driven from the village, his property destroyed. In return, four essential virtues were expected from the Dakota woman, as the living representitive of Maka, the earth. She was required to be hospitable, fertile, faithful and hard-working.

The continuity of this life depended upon co-operation from the gods. Their appeasement required adherence to virtues and values which the people had placed above all else. These things at least were within human control: tolerance, bravery, chastity, generosity and respect. Failure here meant the invitation of disaster; the disapproval of the gods. When men were cowards, or the women unchaste, the buffalo did not come, or the winter was unduly long and harsh.

Yet, the white people had flooded the land, and with their weapons and tools, customs and beliefs, they had defied all that was orderly and decent, and still their numbers persisted, and still the buffalo seemed to dwindle in number. Even the winters of late, particularly this winter of 1856-7, were harsh, with the cold piercing and the snows deep. It was confounding. David felt their unease, and hoped it boded no ill for him.

With the following spring came enormous flocks of water birds, winging their way north. There were geese and a rich variety of ducks, the drakes resplendent in mating plumage. Swans with their flat, sharp mating calls rose in clattering clouds from the marshes swollen with the spring run-off. Cranes, herons, and smoky clouds of smaller, long-legged, narrow-billed shore birds, gulls and pigeons beyond number filled the air. From dawn until dusk, the nattering of wildfowl, pierced with sibilant mating cries, was a constant presence.

Small boys with their first bows stalked the larger birds with fire-hardened points. Buds burst forth, and wildflowers—yarrow, fireweed, and the pale yellow crocus—proliferated in the glory of the spring, and the *maga-okada*, geese-laying-eggs moon. The moist earth smelled of fecundity, and the bellies of the deer were swollen with young, ready to drop.

While out checking a set of rabbit snares near the marsh, with the sun blazing overhead, David decided to move beyond the beaver dam, and set more of the traps intended to catch small game by the neck as they crossed well-defined trails beside the water. As he walked, he became aware of the tinkling sounds of women's laughter and chatter, not far ahead of him. He drew closer, heard splashing, and realized that this was the place of their bath, where it was forbidden that men should go. He stood rooted in the narrow trail, with the forest thick at his left side, and the water visible through a thin screen of willows and marsh grass to his right. Just ahead, the river curved in front of him, and it was from there that the enchanting sounds emanated, only a few paces from view. His heart thumped with the prospect of what he might see, and he was riven with indecision. He knew that if he was found out, he would be severely beaten, perhaps in his low station, even killed, for the Dakota woman would permit none to look upon her, save he whom she had accepted as husband.

Deep within himself, David knew he was going to have a look. His delay seemed designed only to appease his conscience, and perhaps to bolster his courage. He dropped to his knees and crawled slowly, belly to earth, to the thicket which stood between him and the weir created by the beaver. With painstaking deliberateness, he eased himself to a point where he could see the women. He gasped. The pond was only about twenty feet wide, and on the other side were a half dozen women from the village, most of them naked in the shallow water, or at its edge. After a long winter, the hot sun and the cool water were a welcome balm.

David lay frozen, scarce able to breathe or blink for fear of discovery. His eyes greedily took in the scene: here a graceful young woman waded into the pool, crying out at the icy nip of the stream, her pointed breasts swaying as she shied away from the water lapping at her thighs. Beyond were two others, scrubbing each other with handfuls of wet grass, laughing and singing out their approval of the sensation. And over here! Sweet Jesus! as his father would have uttered, Mahpiyatowin stood with her back to him in the stream up to her knees, trilling a song as she scooped water to pour over herself. David's heart thumped as if it would leave his chest, and a tight claw clenched sickeningly in his guts.

As he gazed upon her slender back, his eyes fell to her waist where it flared over her hips. He felt his cock squirm and thicken beneath him. He was so close to her that he could see the goose bumps on the rounded flesh of her buttocks. With a shift of her feet, she parted her stance slightly, and David heard the sound of her urine spilling into the water. His cheeks flamed in embarrassment at this further invasion of her privacy. But he could not turn his head away while she continued to attend to her bathing.

Each time she bent over, he thought he would cry out for the longing and the want of her, the proper expression of which was surely denied to him because of his lowly stature. She was as gentle and kind as her parents, and though she never addressed David directly, he sensed in her a warmth for him, or so it seemed to his affection-starved imagination. At a shrill bird-cry, she turned to face him, and his thudding heart skipped a beat. He had never seen anything so beautiful. She shaded her eyes as she looked toward him, bending and squinting, trying to pierce the wooded gloom. Her breasts wobbled and trembled enticingly with her movements. Had she seen him? He lay still as a child's doll carved from wood, not daring to blink, but taking in every detail of this luminous creature. She looked away after a moment, called by one of the others.

He pulled aside his breechclout and grabbed at himself, feeling the urgency pulsing in his swollen cock. Within several heartbeats his release came, and David closed his eyes in relief and shame. He lay where he was until the women had retired from their bath and their chatter sounded faint as distant birdsong. He got up, arranged his clothing, and traced his steps by a longer route back to the village. Upon his return, he could not look at Mahpiyatowin, so deep was his guilt; he threw himself into his work extravagantly, like a man possessed.

The hunters in the village were restless as they examined and re-examined their equipment. Eagerly, they watched for the scouting parties who were out looking for the return of the buffalo. David was kept busy honing cutting edges: skinning, scraping, cleaving and splitting blades were now all of mild steel, but they required a constant keening. This was a tedious exercise which consisted of a circular grinding against a sharpening stone. The hunters danced for the return of the buffalo and waited.

Because the buffalo fed into the wind, their progress was certain but inconstant. Their annual migrations led them in a circular pattern, which varied according to the harshness of the winter, the effects of localized drought, or disease. The pace of the herd was dictated by the richness of the prairie grass. Sometimes the herds did not come, and this was a time of great calamity and soul-searching. Such events, though infrequent, were recalled in hushed tones, and viewed as consequences of human failing.

When word came at last that the forerunners of the great herd had been seen, singly at first, then in groups, a great cry of thanksgiving went up in the village. The scouts riding their ponies in tight little circles on the ridge to the west of the camp, signalled the sighting of the buffalo; the hunters leapt to their mounts, crying excitedly. The women trilled and sang songs of encouragement and success. The ground reverberated as the hunting party galloped off, leaving only four warriors and the old men to guard the village, their faces crestfallen and anxious. David watched the excitement passively, until Wakandayamani summoned him.

'You will come with the women. There will be much work to do when our brave hunters are done.'

David nodded. He thought now, in his second year of captivity, there was not much hope of slipping away to find his own family. He still thought of them often, but the images were becoming blurred, for reminiscing seemed to be a product of leisure, and David had little enough of that. The village was well to the south of the Sheyenne River, near the cousins of the Wahpeton Dakota, the Yanktonais. Alone, he could leave the village, as he often did in the pursuit of his chores, and even though the camp guards were unlikely to give chase unless he had stolen, the long trek through unknown enemy country was daunting. He had yet to realize that the nature of his captivity had changed; his fear held him as surely as any bond.

Five

i

The warrior's art of siegecraft reached new levels in post-medieval Europe. The attack of the fortress garrison depended upon the work of engineers who dug trenches to enable a safe approach to the fortress wall, which was undermined and collapsed by carefully positioned charges. These trenches, called *sapes* in French, originally protected artillery advances, which in turn attracted enemy fire upon the *sapeurs* who were responsible for construction. It was dangerous but necessary work, and the sappers, as the engineers came to be known in the British Army, were a hardy, resourceful lot, who well deserved the additional pay they drew.

Out of an ad hoc corps drawn as needed from the officers' ranks of the infantry, the Corps of Royal Engineers was founded in 1787, and the Royal Military Artificers was set up the same year to ensure that the standing army was adequately supplied with tradesmen. The Academy at Woolwich, known to all who passed through it as 'The Shop', was established in 1741 for the training of such military skills. There were traditions and practices well established in a profession which reached back to the classical world, and which formed much of the mysterious world which Johnathan was about to enter.

The Academy was an imposing, sprawling collection of buff-coloured limestone buildings, rambling in a loose rectangular shape across the military campus. It was set in low, rolling hills of trees, and to the east of it were vast exercise fields for the carrying out of military formations, artillery drill and the preparation of defensive earthworks. The main entrance was through a massive arched doorway, in a building flanked at each corner by three-storey square towers capped by green copper cupolae. In front was a large parade square, with the Royal Artillery School off to one side. Together with barracks and marching halls, a chapel, stables, two canteens, barns for rolling stock and various mechanics' sheds, infants' school, gymnasiums and married quarters, it was something of a self-contained small town.

On the first day of his arrival Johnathan was mustered with those others who were to form his class. After a hail of instructions, none of which Johnathan could remember, they were herded off before the regimental quartermaster sergeant for kit parade. Uniforms, tack, belting, boots, towelling, kits, cutlery, notebooks and Borrowdale graphite pencils were piled into the outstretched arms of each recruit. Staggering under the weight, the officer candidates, thirty-six in all, were led to their barracks by uniformed men who barked arcane commands at them, a condition which was to be part of their lives for the next eighteen months. Some of the young men had their own attendants, who were fixed with the responsibility of the heavier chores, and who slept on a roll-up pallet at the foot of their masters' beds. Rules strictly observed did not permit this, but wealthy patrons of the college had certain influence, and their children benefited.

The Corps of Engineers was the only branch of the military into which a commission could not be purchased. Proficiency at the essential subjects was, in theory, the only route to officer status. Passing in examinations was mandatory. Those with wealth and influence, sons of nobility or the upper classes, could expect a much easier path to a commission, though every student met the same hurdle at beginning and end of course. Johnathan and several of his classmates watched with envy their better-financed colleagues who had a wider selection of food, menservants to handle less pleasant tasks, and tutors to make up what they had difficulty comprehending in class.

At the first introductory session they were addressed by Captain Phineas Grundy, a veteran engineer who had seen campaigns with Wellington as a boy. Barely fourteen years of age, he had joined with the 28th Foot as a drummer boy, and had been at Waterloo. On the field during that battle Sir Thomas Picton had three of his men lashed for cowardice, and drummer Grundy was ordered to lay on with the cat o' nine tails, under fear of having a rattan across his own shoulders, should he shirk. One of the men was killed by enemy fire within two hours following his scourging. As Grundy retold the story in all its gory detail, he walked between the ranks, peering at each man, taking his measure. 'The point is, laddies, Her Majesty expects that you shall not retire from your duty, under fire or no. Those of you who think that the life of a sapper is one of ease, with little danger, will soon find out in the next campaign—and there's never any shortage of fighting—that there's nothing more difficult than attending to your duties under the malicious intentions of the enemy, when any sane man would seize his weapons and defend himself.'

The Commandant of the engineers' school was Sir John Burgoyne, who was later to assume command of the Engineer Corps in the Crimea when war broke out two years later. The new men were paraded before him to hear a rambling speech of welcome, delivered with great enthusiasm but little coherency, for the better part of two hours. Now seventy years of age, he was afflicted with an enlarged prostate which required him to disappear every half hour or so to relieve himself.

Everywhere Johnathan looked, the senior levels of the military were of advanced age. Wellington, the greatest hero of the age, was still in charge of the army, and during the declining years of his tenure he dawdled and snoozed his way through his workday, leaving the details of command policy to other less capable men. The great British war machine at Waterloo had been allowed to disintegrate from want of care, though Johnathan could not as yet recognize this. England was more concerned with commerce and profit; among the leadership of the mid-nineteenth century there was held the common view that grand wars were a thing of the past. However, with an Empire upon which the sun never set, England had work aplenty in the colonies, keeping unruly natives in line, putting down mutinies, and unseating petty kings and rajahs who stood in the way of profit.

But there was little time for politics or contemplation of military policy. The candidates were swept into a maelstrom of classwork, military technology, drill, obligations of command, and technical exercises. The academic syllabus included history, geography, mathematics, and the first six books of Euclid. Horsemanship, use of the sabre and lance, firearms and drill rounded out a schedule which started at five-thirty in the morning, and lasted until well after dark. A high pass rate was set in all courses, so each man was expected to work hard, study long hours, yet present well on parade. In addition there was kit to keep up and uniforms to clean; odious tasks if one didn't have a 'man' about. Occasionally the other officers would rent out the services of their 'batman' to one less fortunate, who had scholastic deadlines to meet. Such amenities were not officially allowed to the young cadets, but with rank and wealth came privilege, even in the halls of a military academy—particularly one which government expected to pay its own way.

The faculty at Woolwich, especially the Royal Sappers and Miners, and the Corps of Royal Engineers (who would be fused in 1856 into a single corps), viewed their calling as near that of spiritual commitment. Grundy in particular was such a teacher. Patient but demanding of his students, he had short time for those who owed much of their way in life to influence. On the first day of class he had called upon each man to rise and identify himself and his sponsor, according to particular circumstances. As each man rose, it became obvious to Johnathan that most of his classmates were from important families, but whose place in the order of birth made their choices of career limited to the military or the church.

As he stood up, he identified himself as Johnathan Snow; present by the good graces of Sir Alexander Archibald of Gleneaglesham.

Behind him, a delicate voice calculated to carry widely, said, 'I suppose that's literally true; yet another rich man's bastard sent off to avoid embarrassment!'

Johnathan whirled around furiously, but he could only see averted eyes, and thinly restrained smiles. Grundy called the class to attention. 'There'll be no joggering in my lectures!' He was plainly angry, and Johnathan took it to be implicit that Grundy's classes were to be attended in silence, save when called upon. Following the lecture, Grundy called Johnathan aside with a curt gesture. He stood silently while the rest of the class trooped out. Johnathan looked at him as he appeared to review his notes at the lectern.

Tall and straight, with none of the thickening of face and body that usually comes with a man entering his sixth decade, he was nearly bald on the top of his sunburned head, with great feathery grey whiskers at the sides of his face. His blue tunic with red piping was taut, and his kit was gleaming white with pipeclay. He presented a perfect image of efficiency and military bearing; Johnathan wondered why he was still only a captain.

At length Grundy turned to him and spoke. 'Many of the men in here are toffs, bright enough, but whose advancement will come easy, and at that in the preferred positions. You are a commoner, like me; a baker's son. I will leave the service one day, but the rank I bear will be no different than that which appears on my shoulders now. And it took me thirty years of service to attain it at that. But I retain this position because I am the best damned engineer they have.'

He studied Johnathan for a moment. 'I tell you this because you'll have more of the same jibes from your betters, plenty of them, before you're done. And the only response worth making is to be the best damned engineer in the group. Whether you've the sand for it, we'll soon see.

'And mark you this: lacking another major conflict somewhere, there'll be precious few commissions available, and then only to those whose families can pay. The only exception, and the only one, is if you stand at the top of the class. And all that takes is hard work and concentration! Dismissed.' And he turned away from Johnathan gathering up his notes.

Johnathan was enthusiastic about college, if less than thrilled about his new comrades. Surveying was the principal course to begin with, and it captivated him. The science had begun in Egypt, Griff had told them, and it was used to re-establish property lines following the flooding of the Nile. Then, it was identical with geometry, which still underlay the most important part of the theoretical principles. Johnathan remembered well schoolmaster Friar's lectures on geometry, for he had developed a passion for the subject, and it came easy to him. He learned about the theodolite, or transit, which measured angles on a graduated line. He studied the correct use of the compass to determine the bearing of lines with respect to the magnetic meridian, the aneroid barometer for elevation calculations (and the differential boiling temperatures of water at increasing distances above sea level, should the barometer fail). The Gunter's chain of sixty-six feet and the engineer's chain of one hundred feet, tape lines, stadia-rods and principal meridians entered his daily language. Plane, geodetic, topographic and compass surveying all formed part of a growing expertise which represented the most advanced refinement of his craft.

Throwing himself into his work, he kept to himself, and should have been happy enough. The work was not hard; there was just a lot of it, when all the other demands of life in the army were taken into consideration. But one of his classmates, Lionel Battersea, third son of the Second Earl of Crampdon, seemed determined to expose what he considered to be the 'obvious inferiority of those of lower station whose impertinent sponsors had secured positions for them'. Never mind that those falling below a certain average mark were sent away to other non-technical brigades or divisions that might have a commission for purchase—or worse, sent home.

Battersea was handsome, fair-haired, and bright. He was possessed of a searingly cruel wit, funny enough to his cronies, but biting to the recipients of it. Of an extraordinarily rich family who desired a military career for him, he had chosen the Royal Engineers as representing one of the arts of warfare which presented the least danger. And there were plenty of military artificers to draw upon for the actual heavy work. Yet there was enough academic challenge in the work to keep him interested, for he became bored easily, unless there was challenge.

When one of Battersea's friends referred to Johnathan in contemptuous tones, 'There goes the red-haired bastard!', Battersea called him up short, well within Johnathan's earshot.

'Come now! Is that any way to refer to such a man of the same uniform as we all wear proudly? Have you no manners?' And he put his arm around Johnathan's shoulders in a fulsome gesture of conciliation. Johnathan was uneasy under his touch.

'You see, out on the hunt, when the fox is at last sighted, no such vulgarities are permitted. It's Tally Ho! Of course!' The others dissolved in laughter at the old joke, and thereafter when Johnathan came near, likely as not, the cry 'Tally Ho!' would sound. By and by, this became shortened to 'Tally', which became Johnathan's nickname for the rest of his stay at 'The Shop'.

One of the disciplines at which Johnathan rapidly became proficient was fencing with the sabre. Arm on hip, Johnathan and his colleagues practised the tierce, quarte and seconde guard movements, feints and parries, all under the stern tutelage of a short, bad-tempered instructor, who had no patience for those who could not follow his sharp, staccato commands. One evening after exercises, as they sat sweating in the fencing hall, he took the podium and addressed his students:

'When crossing blades with an adversary, but before closing in combat, one must take in at a glance the intellectual and physical powers of one's rival, so as to judge of the employment he will likely make of them. Make a decision by the first few movements of his weapon. This, above all, is the first rule of engagement. Listen well.

'Is he a man of nerve, or will he be easily intimidated or confused? Observe on the instant if his guard is faulty, and what advantage may be taken of it. Discover by feints and natural parry, and by his natural attitude and aspect, whether his forte is the attack or defence.'

He looked around the room, satisfied that his students were giving him undivided attention. He was not a man to waste words.

'Will he rush in, trusting everything to strength and audacity, or will he circle warily with the caution of a seasoned warrior? It is the careful man, more so than the fool, who must be attacked with caution. While the fool strives with his heart, the more deadly foe moves with his head. Yet beware the fool who may move unexpectedly. Anticipate, and the momentum of the witling shall assist you. In mortal combat, seek to determine at the outset the natural advantage, and array your own conduct accordingly.'

As Johnathan progressed in his studies of supportive warcraft, it became apparent to him that the fencing teacher's instruction could be applied to everything learned at Woolwich. What most of the others took as technical advice, Johnathan construed as spiritual wisdom. He began to form the instincts of a warrior, the attitude of one who always seeks the advantage; the genteel opportunist.

To deal with Battersea was another matter. The man had set himself up as the leader of the class and, by the force of his personality, dictated how things should be, who took which turn at serving in the junior cadets' mess, who should ensure a good supply of port, and who would call questions for the nightly quizzes. All influence and decorum became the call of Battersea, as his mood dictated.

Johnathan watched Battersea at work. He distributed wealth and favour to a chosen few, and in this way secured their loyalty. They would lie for him, wait on him, and close ranks around him in the event of some challenge to his authority. Johnathan felt that support of this nature would soon erode should the money-pit dry up. But there seemed little chance of that happening, for the estates of his father in England as well as Ireland were vast; the income from them, fabulous. He was said to be one of the richest men in the country.

For a time, Johnathan tried to avoid any contact with Battersea. But in fencing it seemed as if, by dint of being the best two adversaries with foil and sabre, they were regularly cast against each another. Battersea was the better swordsman, having been tutored in the art since the age of ten. Addressing each other during the salute, with masks under arm, Johnathan found he was put slightly off guard by Battersea's smirking look. The man had sharp blue eyes, draped at the outer corners, and voluptuous lips, slightly parted. He missed no detail, though he gave the appearance of unconcern. Johnathan felt he was being appraised in the manner of a guinea pig being contemplated by an adder. Battersea took the position of guard almost lazily, disengaging and parrying, indicating his appel almost carelessly. It was, Johnathan was sure, nothing more than strategy to lull the opponent into a sense of over-confidence. No matter how many times they engaged, however, Battersea never changed his approach, and it occurred to Johnathan that this idle contumely was as much a part of Battersea's irritating snobbism, as it was a form of strategy. Perhaps all relationships for him were a form of combat.

It was a considerable surprise, then, to respond to a knock at the door of his quarters, and find Penforth, Battersea's man. He was an unctuous little fellow, very dark-skinned and clean-shaven, with thin hair combed back and slicked down with a strongly perfumed pomade. Not officially allowed at barracks, he nevertheless seemed always around. Johnathan's room-mate looked over his shoulder suspiciously at Penforth. 'He's not coming in here?' he warned querulously. Penforth ignored him and looked directly at Johnathan.

'Master Battersea requests the honour of your company at his quarters this evening at, say, eight?'

Johnathan was puzzled. 'Is there some particular reason? Is this about lecture notes?' Johnathan was not keen. It had been a hot day, and an even warmer night. Little air moved through the barracks, and Johnathan was splashing himself from a small tub of cool water. The little man shrugged and walked away.

'At eight, then?' he laughed, and without waiting for a reply, he scuttled off down the hall, still chuckling.

At the given hour Johnathan tapped on Battersea's door.

'It's unlocked.'

Johnathan pushed open the door. The room had much the same dimensions as his own, but being a corner space, it was somewhat larger, and had an additional window. The man obviously had the whole room to himself. It was dimly lit by a single, large candle in a red tulip-shaped glass, which gave a scarlet hue to the interior, and Johnathan's eyes had a difficult time adjusting to the gloom.

'Come in, dear Tally! Come in!' cried Battersea. The air was close and the smell, acrid and heavily sweet to the nostrils. Battersea was sitting on the floor wearing only baggy white under-drawers, his knees drawn up to his chest, taking opium from a water-pipe, which he called a hookah. It was set up against the fireplace, and blankets were hung so as to ensure that the smoke escaped up the chimney. Johnathan had only heard about opium; wasn't there a lot of it going on in the Indian Army? Smoking was against regulations, never mind smoking opium. On his unrolled mattress, Penforth sat cross-legged and quite naked. Johnathan was a little startled to see that the man had breasts; small, but quite well-formed breasts. His wonderment showed as he took a chair indicated by Battersea's outstretched palm.

'Sit down! I see you've noticed Penforth's little titties already! Nothing wrong with your eyes, then!'

He chuckled as Penforth looked at him coyly; Johnathan felt uneasy about the unspoken exchange that passed between the two men, but elected to remain as he was until he gained some idea of what this meeting was all about.

'I say,' Johnathan began, 'don't you think this is rather risky, this use of such substances? I mean...'

Battersea broke unexpectedly into song, cutting him off:

> *A big duck shat in a little duck's eye*
> *What did the little duck say?*
> *Shiiiittt!*

Penforth chimed in the last, breaking off in cackles of laughter, rolling over backwards. The man was definitely of the male gender, Johnathan could see, for he had a cock like a truncheon, but with a strangely shrivelled seed sack beneath.

'Call of the orderly sergeants, don't you know?' said Battersea. 'No sense in stating the obvious. Shit in the eye is just shit, and all that.'

Johnathan was confused. The opium had made Battersea and his bizarre associate quite intoxicated. He decided it would be best if he took his leave, and tensed as if to rise. Battersea caught the gesture, and cried out, 'No! No! You must stay until you have tried a little of the poppy seed. This comes from the best growing areas in Turkey. It cost me eight guineas a pound and you simply must try it!'

Johnathan shook his head dubiously, though he was intrigued. With some reluctance, he took the mouthpiece of the hookah and drew in a draft of the smoke, surprised at the lightness in the head it produced almost immediately.

Battersea smiled. 'You read Byron, I understand? Penforth said he saw a number of volumes in your room, and I have noticed you carrying his work about, from time to time.'

'An obsession of my mother,' replied Johnathan, as he inhaled again. 'I admit I enjoy his poetry, even though presently he seems to be out of favour.'

'The scorn of the petty, purblind, moralistic middle class falls upon a man, not for his work but for his lifestyle! Christ! A pox on those who cannot see past the current fad!' Battersea shook his head contemptuously, and reached for the pipe again. Johnathan was sweating profusely, and unbuttoned his tunic.

'Take the whole thing off! You're only forty paces from your own quarters,' said Battersea. 'I think he fell into difficulty when he married the virtuous and wealthy Annabella Milbanke, in—what—1815? Probably for her money.' Johnathan realized he was talking about Byron again, as he reached for the pipe a little more eagerly this time.

'Married her, but fucking his half-sister! No wonder his wife left him!'

Johnathan commented that he knew little of Byron's domestic life, but understood that he was eccentric.

'Eccentric!' laughed Battersea. 'Eccentric? This was a man who could not abide the sight of a woman eating. Kept loaded pistols under his pillow; that is, when he slept, for he stayed up at night, and dozed in bits during the day. He had strange rages which left him shrieking and howling like a demon, and would go on diets to control a persistent plumpness, taking nothing but soda water and dried biscuits. Eccentric? I should say. But what of it? Is a man and his work to be shat upon simply because we don't appreciate or understand how he lives?'

'What I do understand about him is that he was a symbol of human freedom!' said Johnathan. 'He gave his life in the cause of Greek independence. His death was as grand as his writing. But dying in a marshy, fever-ridden town far from home, against impossible odds for success—what was the point? Had he lived, who knows what else he could have composed?'

Johnathan peeled off his cotton shirt, which by now was soaked through with sweat. Battersea commented on his physique with approval, then responded enthusiastically. 'The man made a sacrifice for the greater good. Like his work, the larger view was more important than the immediate. The man was an embodiment of the zeitgeist, the spirit of the age!'

Johnathan nodded agreement, but added, 'I read Byron simply for its content. Is there any reason to try to understand the poet?'

'The poetry is the man,' Battersea snapped back. 'Just as what comes out of your mouth is you. How else is one judged? Remember, when viewers all round were shitting on Don Juan, which in my view was his greatest triumph, his response was, "Confess you dog! It may be bawdy, but is it not good English? It may be profligate, but is it not life? Is it not the thing?" '

'Well said,' replied Johnathan, now dreamily intoxicated. 'Don Juan is my favourite piece as well; though I can hardly reconcile the Don Juan of true life with the one of Byron's imagination, for in his work, women are the aggressors.'

'Indeed they are, my dear Tally,' said Battersea. 'All women are, never be fooled.' He closed his eyes and recited:

> *Oh sin! Oh sorrow! and oh womankind!*
> *How can you do such things and keep your fame,*
> *Unless this world, and t'other too, be blind?*

Johnathan at this point barely listened as he struggled out of his trousers which had soaked through. He sat on the floor near Penforth, who seemed in a trance. Battersea had taken up a volume, and was reading desultorily from Don Juan. 'The man had an eye for young girls, though, wouldn't you say? Listen to this.'

Aurora Raby, a young star who shone
O'er life, too sweet an image for such glass,
A lovely being, scarcely form'd or moulded,
A rose with all its sweetest leaves yet folded.

He continued to read from the more erotic passages in the epic, every now and then darting a glance at Johnathan. Penforth moved around behind Johnathan who was pulling gently at the hookah, and began to rub a faintly sweet-smelling balm over his shoulders, and down his arms and sides. The effect was astoundingly sensual, and Johnathan began to feel intensely aroused. As Penforth's fingers began to rub the oil into the intimate places beneath his undergarment, he made no protest, being conscious of the man's nipples tracing his back as he worked. He looked up as if in a dream, and one of the last things he recalled with any clarity was Battersea's pale face very close to his, whispering from among the last verses of Don Juan:

...The ghost had remarkably sweet breath.
A straggling curl show'd he had been fair-hair'd;
A red lip, with two rows of pearls beneath...

And Juan, puzzled, but still curious, thrust
His other arm forth—Wonder upon wonder!
It press'd upon a hard but glowing bust,
Which beat as if there was a warm heart under...

Johnathan put his hand against Battersea's damp chest, struggling to his knees. But Penforth kept up his insistent coaxing with his lathered fingers, and Johnathan yielded to the combination of sensations upon his person. When Penforth's fingers entered him and pressed inside him gently, he made no protest, but merely groaned as he felt something urgent building within.

Johnathan awoke with a start. The orderly sergeant had been pounding on the door for some time, it was obvious from his remarks. He was naked upon his bed, and his body felt hard used. He reeked of the oil which had seemed so intoxicating the previous evening, and his belly was streaked with what he was sure was dried semen. He prayed it was his own. As he sat up, a sharp stabbing pain tore the film from his eyes, and he cried out.

'All you all right, sir?' called the sergeant. 'Shall I tell them you'll report to the infirmary?'

'Yes!' cried Johnathan, holding his head with both hands. 'Go away!' His mouth was dry to the point of dust, and the taste in the back of his throat was the flavour of dog shit. Well. The bastard had seduced him and used him like a rag. A rage overcame Johnathan, and he sprang to his feet, then nearly toppled from the dizziness, his heart racing wildly. He sat for a moment, then decided he had to get to the bath house. He felt unclean, but once in a tub of cool water, he could think.

It was the next day when he saw Battersea again. Griff was in the middle of reviewing the algebraic principles of stadia measurements for determining distances, when Battersea walked in. He tended to be casual about class time. Griff was visibly annoyed, and remarked that, 'Should you come late once again to my class, sir, you shall come no more to it.' He turned back to his blackboard. Battersea opened his mouth as if to make some excuse but thought the better of it, and continued to his seat. Passing by Johnathan, he glanced at him with the barest trace of a smile, sat at his place, and turned his attention to the lecture.

Johnathan seethed with mixed reactions. On the one hand, he wanted to fly at Battersea, confront him and condemn him. On the other, he felt the cravings for the sensations of opiate-induced euphoria and sexual tensions brought on by the sensual insinuations of Penforth's skilful hands. These competing forces almost effectively cancelled one another out, and Johnathan was left undecided and empty. Class exercises droned on, and he was glad that Griff did not call upon him. He could not get out of his mind what he could remember of the earlier night, but he elected to say nothing to Battersea.

He had not much time to consider the matter, for the next day the entire group was taken out for practical exercise in topographical and plane surveying. Johnathan was assigned the survey of twelve square miles of rural land, which was based on a triangulation which located the positions in longitude and latitude of several pre-determined stations. Lines were then run off in various directions, marking locations of landmarks by stadia sights. Levels were run by which the contours of equal elevations were determined, so that a picture of the relief of the surface could be obtained. All of the manoeuvres were carried out on a wartime footing, so all work was done 'at the double'. The entire day was spent running and carrying equipment without the benefit of enlisted men. It was exhausting work, and Johnathan was eager to get into his tent and collapse on his cot once 'Lights Out' sounded at 10:30.

The talk around the cookfires was of the growing prospects of war with Russia. There had not been a major action by the British Army since Waterloo, and there was considerable enthusiasm for the opportunity to enter combat. War was still considered to be gloriously romantic by all those who had not been engaged at the front lines, and great public adulation was heaped upon the warrior—especially one distinguished in battle. To lead in battle was a gentleman's finest aspiration.

By 1850, Russia was looking covetously at the Ottoman Empire, particularly the Balkans. She declared herself the true protector of the Greek Church in Turkey, and under the pretext of offering protection to the Christians in the Balkans, troops were sent to occupy the provinces of Moldavia and Wallachia, and in 1853, Turkey declared war. Early reverses in battle made it appear to Great Britain and France that Russia might eventually seize the whole of the Ottoman Empire, thereby upsetting the balance of power. It appeared to European diplomats that the Turkish Sultan required propping up.

The public debate over the Czar's intentions was reflected hotly in the army. To a man, Czar Nicholas was perceived to be an enemy of freedom and liberty abroad, and the champion of serfdom and enslavement at home. The 'eastern question' became almost the exclusive issue of debate. Battersea was anxious to go to Turkey; war, he observed, was the quickest way to reach the heart of a country, and lay one's hands on the things worth having. 'I'm not talking about thievery here, just a quick path to pleasure. Turkey, I'm told, has something for everyone!' He licked his lips at the prospect, as his intimates drew close to hear what he had in mind.

To Johnathan's ear, this was yet another contradiction in the man. He could find the same joy in poetry as Johnathan; yet he had instincts of a common looter. Nevertheless, there was something to be learned from him. He seized life by the throat, and seemed indifferent to consequences. Such a man had power and influence over others. He was a man whose vanity condemned him to success.

Battersea was quick to seize the mood of the moment, and capitalize on it. Sometimes there was an immediate gain to be had; at other times, there was a larger ambition. He sensed a national belligerence toward Russia, and sponsored it at every opportunity. During servings of port in the junior officers' mess, he would loudly recall among other things that at the Great Exhibition of 1851, Prince Albert's showpiece to the world of 'Works of Industry of All Nations', only one nation had failed to deliver its exhibits to the grand Crystal Palace built for the occasion: Russia. What was there to fear from a backward country whose petty intimidations in Hungary are of the same consequence as its questionable industrial might? Other more senior officers nodded their approval, for the prospect of war had created patriotic stirrings among a military gerontocracy which had not known glory since Waterloo. They took to this eloquent young spokesman, and made him the darling of Woolwich and, later, London.

During the winter months of 1852-53, when Johnathan was working the hardest at the mastery of his profession, Britain and Russia drifted further apart on the issue of intervention in Turkey, notwithstanding diplomatic attempts to avert a confrontation. But at the gatherings where men like Battersea prevailed, there grew a steady demand that British steel put to rout the Russian alloy. That Turkey had in the previous ninety years fought with Russia in four arduous campaigns without the assistance of any western power was seemingly irrelevant. The national blood was up, and the first engagement of the Turkish fleet at Sinope on the Black Sea by the Russians, which concluded in a bloody victory for the Russians in their screw-propelled vessels, was characterized by the British press as a 'massacre'. The *Morning Chronicle* declared that: 'To stop the unprofitable contest by striking down the aggressor with a blow is as plain a duty towards humanity as it was to send succour to Sinope'. Upon reading this and other statements, Johnathan decided that Battersea could have been the author of any of them, so consistent was the tone.

One evening in July of 1853, Battersea burst excitedly into the mess. Johnathan and the others looked up with some amazement, for it was unusual to see Battersea excited about much of anything.

'Guess what, chappies,' he cried, seizing the decanter of sherry on the table. 'The candidate of highest standing will be chosen to become part of Sir John Fox Burgoyne's staff. As hostilities between Russia and the Sultan seems likely, he will be needing to get his office on a war footing. As you all will be keenly aware, that candidate will be me!'

The others did not seem impressed, though one or two could not disguise their envy. One remarked, 'But the final marks have not even been posted as yet. How can you be so sure?'

'Ha!' cried Battersea. 'It's in the bag! I've already instructed Penforth to begin packing, to be out of this dreary place. My commission will be concluded by apprenticeship, if not on the field of battle. I've come here just now to await the posting of the standings.'

But as luck would have it, both Johnathan and Battersea tied for first place. When this fact was put to Burgoyne, his staff urged him to take Battersea, who would 'fit in so much better'. But Burgoyne at the age of seventy-two, was reluctant to be told anything, and demanded that both young men be seconded to his general staff with the rank and pay of ensigns. Johnathan felt as if his fortune was being tied to the dissolute rake whose climb to the upper levels of the military establishment seemed effortless.

Far from being resentful, Battersea was delighted. 'Wonderful, dear Tally! Perhaps we'll have some fun yet in this dreary army!'

Johnathan trembled inwardly at the prospect; he had never forgotten that murky evening in Battersea's quarters. He had not said anything to Battersea either, for though he was repelled by the events in one respect, he was afraid that he would rather enjoy another such encounter. The tug of the opium had remained with him for several days, and had it not been for the exertions of the exercises, he might have gone back to Battersea. As acolyte or lover? Johnathan could not believe he was entertaining such thoughts.

The two top men in the British Army were Lord Raglan, Master-General of the Ordnance, and Sir John Fox Burgoyne, now Inspector-General of Fortifications. Raglan was seventy-five, and had only one arm, the other having been lost at Waterloo; Burgoyne was almost seventy-three. Johnathan met them upon his arrival in London. Battersea was comfortable around these men and their staff, notwithstanding his junior rank, but Johnathan felt intimidated and did not assert himself as did Battersea. Some of the general staff took this to be an affirmation of their earlier assessment, that Battersea was the better choice for such work. Nevertheless, Burgoyne, who was self-minded to the point of obstinacy, would insist on consulting with all his staff, even though it seemed to make no difference in his initial appraisal of conditions and strategy. Battersea was very quick to pick up on this, and invariably tailored his opinions to match those of the Inspector-General.

Burgoyne's study of maps and charts, as well as his own experience led him to conclude that a military base should be established near Constantinople, easily supplied from the sea, in the event of a Russian invasion through the Balkan Mountains. It was Johnathan who pointed out that the promontories around the Turkish capital would not be conducive to such a plan, and Battersea observed that the plan was still a good one, but that an easily defended base on the Gallipoli peninsula would be preferable. An allied army could be established on the narrow neck of land so as to provide a springboard from which to attack the flank of any Russian force seeking to threaten the Turkish capital. Johnathan had his misgivings about the viability of this plan. Such a force needed support far beyond the modest means of the region to sustain, but he and the others who shared this view were quieted by Burgoyne, who after all had been in Sebastopol in 1801.

Johnathan took Battersea aside, following one of the strategy sessions. 'What good does it do to simply parrot what the old man appears to have decided? Do they not want to hear what we have to say, and if not, why are we here?'

Battersea looked at him, surprised. 'The best of the class is always given the opportunity to work with the general staff. If we end up going to war—which seems inevitable—the chances for advancement are very good.'

'But what about my question? What is the point of simply adjusting your opinion to fit the prevailing one? It is dishonest, and men's lives could depend upon the proper assessment.'

Battersea snorted. 'Men's lives! Don't get sanctimonious with me. If we go to war, men's lives will be lost by the hundred score. Has the history of war we have been studying these past dozen months not taken root yet? It's all irrelevant. What in hell will we gain by sending men to die in the Crimea? Glory? The gratitude of the Mussulmans? The eternal salvation of the Greek Orthodox Christians? A few hundred yards of parched Russian soil to fight over in the next conflict?'

Johnathan objected. 'But this aggression by Nicholas is unjust! We are doing the right thing by objecting to it. This is a just fight.'

Battersea looked at him mockingly as if he had suddenly taken complete leave of his senses. 'Do you really believe such rubbish? The dreary repetitions of history are nothing if not predictable. Common to each conflict is the God-given assurance that each side is 'right'! Give over!

'Understand this: the only thing that war brings, besides death and privation, and horror beyond description, is opportunity. I couldn't care less if they think that building a floating island in the Black Sea for the purposes of staging an invasion is the best plan. For I will be with them. As long as I am not in command, and I hardly aspire to that, it matters not.

'If there is victory, I shall be there to bask in it. If there is disgrace, I shall distance myself from it, for only the top heads roll.'

Johnathan was appalled. That Battersea appeared ruthless was not surprising, but that he should be so candid about it seemed disgusting and ill-mannered. Johnathan kept his own disingenuous thoughts to himself, and he thought it unusual and suspicious that someone else should be so apparently guileless. Johnathan was cynical about the motives of men, and thought that even the apparent candour of the sort displayed by Battersea was part of a more subtle camouflage.

Subtle or not, Battersea's strength of personality and clever mind enabled him to become attached to the personal staff of Lord Cardigan, commander of the Light Brigade cavalry. Cavalry of the time was distinguished between 'light' and 'heavy', the difference chiefly being the type and size of horse and armament. James Thomas Brudenell, seventh Earl of Cardigan, was one of the most disliked soldiers in the British Army. At fifty-seven, he had trailing behind him a long list of scandals and incidents involving, for the most part, his own conceit and poor judgement. In 1832, he had purchased command of the 15th Hussars and, having lost that command by intolerable behaviour, he bought his way into the 11th Light Dragoons, with much the same result, except that his notoriety was such that he was booed in the street, and hissed at in the theatre. Finally, having steered his way through these difficulties with amazing indifference, he was given the command of the Light Brigade at the time of the opening of hostilities with Russia. This suited him well enough, except that he was placed subordinate to his brother-in-law, Lord Lucan, whom he passionately despised. He took pains to gain assurances that he had an independent command, and need answer to no one. That the aristocracy should lead, regardless of competence, was unquestioned. It was natural that Battersea would be drawn to Cardigan. What was that old saying about birds nesting safely in a fool's hair?

War was not declared until the end of March, 1854. Even so, no troops were engaged for several months, principally because of the logistics in the transport of militia, horses, ordnance and supplies at so great a distance. Malta was the staging area for the fight, but there was great difficulty in the shuttle of the invasionary force to the Dardanelles. Raglan had chosen the landing place at Varna as the point of entry, and twenty-six thousand men and sixty-six guns would be joined with the thirty thousand strong French contingent. Johnathan was to travel with them, stopping over at Malta.

Johnathan would be going to war; that much was obvious, and he wrote to his mother advising her so in one of his infrequent letters. She wrote back to him with all manner of motherly instructions, and sent two enormous parcels of Darjeeling tea. She instructed him to 'drink nothing else in strange lands other than tea'. This simple advice was to save Johnathan's life.

The departure from London was stirring, with the first Battalion of the Coldstream Guards marching to the strains of the regimental band playing 'The Girl I Left Behind Me'. Johnathan marched along the Strand behind them with a contingent of ensign sappers, feeling intensely proud and patriotic. There was a stirring quality to the martial music and the pageantry of uniform, gun and trumpet. The populace of London was mad for it; the like had not been seen for more than thirty-five years. There was still an innocence about war; for it was considered to be a thrilling enterprise, steeped in glory like a field-games picnic. Many comforts and privileges were available to officers. For them, wives were allowed to accompany expeditions. This held true for certain non-commissioned officers as well. At least one woman, married to a corporal in the Rifle Brigade, put on a uniform obtained by her husband, shouldered a new Minié rifle, and marched aboard the troopship alongside her mate, with their co-conspirators winking and smirking at the subterfuge.

Somewhere in the crowd was his mother who had come with Sir Alex to see Johnathan off, but they had missed the meeting point designated in their exchange of letters, and in the enormous throngs of people come to send off their troops, he could only hope that they would see him pass by. He was strangely relieved that they had missed each other. He felt more comfortable that they should bid farewell from a distance. Marching along, he wondered why this would be so; he had already made his leave-taking once, not two years ago. It had required no ruthless purge of sentiment. He was eager to be off then, as now. The world lay at his feet, and this invasion he had embarked upon was simply the next opportunity. In moving across horizons, a man could easily trip over sentiment. The only repository of trust can be in oneself, he thought, even though there be ten thousand trained warriors behind me.

ii

Johnathan shipped with his own company of sappers, together with the 17th Lancers and the 8th Hussars. The voyage from the Thames to Varna was wracked by bad weather, and the men and horses suffered terribly. As the vessel began to roll badly in the Bay of Biscay, the animals could not keep their footing. Those that were not in slings fell heavily against manger and stall; some were injured and others died. The cavalrymen, sick as they were, had to go into the dimly lit holds to attempt to calm the frantic beasts. The filth and urine, together with the shrieking horses and shouting men, themselves vomiting and unsteady, made for frightful conditions below decks, and Johnathan was relieved that he was not required to attend to a mount.

When the water calmed as they made for the Mediterranean, Johnathan helped with the removal of carcasses, and the swilling down of the lower decks with vinegar. More bad weather beset the vessel before landing at Varna, and several horses had to be destroyed and levered overboard. In all, twenty-six of the mounts belonging to the 17th were lost, and a dozen more had to be put down before the voyage was over. These were the best mounts available, costing hundreds of pounds. To add to the miseries of the horses, landing was not possible at Varna in a controlled way, for there were no wharves capable of accepting ocean-going craft.

The animals were winched overboard and allowed to make their own way ashore in the scorching sunshine. The better part of the day was spent in this exercise, before Johnathan could get a look at the place that Raglan had chosen as their point of entry. It was not an auspicious landing. In the light waves lapping over the beach, wild dogs tore at the bloated bodies of two pack animals. Beyond, the bleak countryside showed no relief save the tumbledown Turkish barracks where the men were eventually billeted.

Johnathan and his men were assigned the tasks of making the barracks habitable, as well as arranging for appropriate sanitation. However, in the first of what was to be many deficiencies of supply, the necessary tools had not been sent with them. Walking ahead, he was sickened by the condition of the dilapidated sheds which were to be home to the troops. As he strode about, enormous grey rats 'big as bloody house cats' leapt up and scuttled away, squeaking annoyance. At some point, livestock had been kept in the buildings, and the disagreeable odour of rotted manure permeated the interior. Johnathan quickly got a troop of grumbling privates to work, and assumed temporary authority over a platoon of cavalry, who were most unhappy at the prospect of cleaning hovels 'unfit even for their horses'; several chose to make a camp beyond the barracks.

The main street of Varna was little more than an open sewer by the short time that more than fifty thousand men and animals had left their mark. The stench seared the nostrils, and there was a terrible outbreak of fleas. Where the infantry and some of the cavalry had unwittingly elected to set up their encampment was the site of a mass grave where Russian soldiers who had died of plague during the war of 1828 were buried. Wells which Johnathan had a part in surveying produced tainted water—green in some places—and many of the men were resentful of the engineers who had in their opinion performed so incompetently. But Johnathan did not know of the gravesite; his only concern had been to keep the water sites free of the latrine trenches and offal pools, most of which became full to overflowing very quickly.

When cholera broke out, it was Johnathan who was seized by an angry group of infantrymen, carried to the harbour at a point where the filth drained into it, and cast bodily into the fouled water. Disease was linked with filth and, particularly, stench, and it was the job of the engineers to arrange for proper quarters, orderly encampments and bath houses. Though Johnathan was not the commanding officer, he was present when the soldiers' anger boiled over. Two were court-martialled for their conduct, though only one of them was convicted, and ordered detained for sixty days on bread and water in a prison ship anchored in the bay. Temperatures inside the hull easily exceeded one hundred degrees. Johnathan had a small worry that the man might not survive his sentence, but dismissed it. The men, having hands laid on him, though only for a ducking, upset him. Serves the idiot right, he thought, putting the matter out of his mind.

Still, he had to acknowledge that there was plenty to be angry about. Apart from the heat and the insects, good water was scarce, and the landscape was rapidly being despoiled by the constant quest for forage for the animals and for fuel to keep the cookfires burning. The inability of the supply corps to keep up with demand had been evident from the start of the campaign. Parliament had recently quashed a proposal to lay in a reserve of feed in anticipation of the coming winter, in the interests of fiscal restraint. The air reeked from the hundreds of carcasses lying about; it was the habit of the Turks to leave the dead beasts where they fell, and the carrion fed the legions of bold rats, and squabbling, half-wild dogs. It surprised no one when cholera struck in mid-July.

Cholera was particulary gruesome; it had been known in Europe as the 'dreaded cholera' since it had made an appearance away from its home on the Asian continent about thirty years earlier, with the increase in global trade. Though it had been most prevalent in the almshouses, grogshops and two-penny brothels, no one was safe; and it struck at both nobility and common folk. The initial symptoms were uncontrollable diarrhea and vomiting, coupled with painful cramps. The virus raced through its host from the onset of these indications, often killing within a day. The body rapidly dehydrated, so that the eyes became grotesquely sunken in their sockets, and collapsed capillaries turned the body a livid purple colour. Victims had a telltale croak as their vocal chords dried out, and their cries of agony became raspy and tortured. By the end of July, the barracks had been turned into a hospital, unimaginably foul and filled to overflowing with human misery. More than seven thousand soldiers perished, without ever having fired a shot. Those who recovered were emaciated ghosts who were utterly unfit for battle.

The causes and prevention of disease had a small part in the syllabus at Woolwich, and Johnathan had some notion that cholera was attributable to unfit drinking water. Most notably, work had been done by a physician of no other name than Johnathan Snow, who traced the common factors to those dying of the disease. Though it seemed inconclusive, the source of water appeared to be central in all cases. But for every lecturer like one Surgeon Buzzard, who spoke of his concerns regarding the role of the water supply in the matter of contamination, and the importance of drinking only boiled water, there were others who were 'miasmatics' who believed that bad odours were linked with disease, and the worst effects could be escaped by avoiding stench. Unfortunately, regardless of which theory held sway in Varna, the prevailing odour was of putrefying flesh, both man and animal. The French attempted to send a small expeditionary force north, as much to escape the conditions of camp as to obtain intelligence about the Russians, but the cholera followed them, striking down just over six hundred men in a single day.

Johnathan continued to be astounded at the reluctance to give unpopular advice, or even propose alternatives that were novel. Not having the kind of experience with the aristocracy that would assist in the subtle or oblique presentation of ideas, he was often dismissed with a glance, or cut off with a patronizing smile. He urged at all opportunities that the officers select a better place for the encampment of what remained of the army. He gathered statistics on his own initiative, and made them real for the purblind men he advised, reporting that trumpeters were so scarce that battalions were borrowing from each other so as to be able to play the last post. Supply lines were so poor and complicated that coke could not be obtained for the farriers' forges, and on the stony grounds, shoes were being lost by the horses at an alarming rate. In the harbour, scores of bloated corpses defied the stones tied to them, and floated like so much driftwood in the tide. It was nearly impossible to find a place to bury the dead which had not previously been dug over for a grave.

Johnathan was not without allies. At his level of rank and especially below, there was near universal despair; men wrote daily in their diaries of the frustration of burying their comrades, and waiting listlessly for the plague to carry them away. It was with a sense of wonderment that Johnathan and others awoke each day without the telltale signs of disease gnawing at their guts. It was with an equal sense of dread that they would see yet another man stricken, filling his trousers with putrid feces while walking in the street, or vomiting suddenly and violently in the middle of a conversation; men who were hearty and hale during the mid-day meal, could be dead before the bugler sounded 'lights out'. The mood of the men turned mutinous yet still the senior officers lingered, hampered by indecision at home, and the length of time it took to get dispatches and orders from London and Paris to the Middle East.

Johnathan lay in his tent. It was a circular structure, supported by a single eight-foot pole in the centre, and by smaller poles outside the 'knee wall' which stood about a yard high. It was designed to accommodate a half-dozen enlisted men, or four officers. Johnathan was alone on his camp-cot; only one other officer shared the space with him, a Lieutenant James Arnell Bliss, who had served as an engineer in the Indian Army, and who was out leading a party looking for forage for the horses. The tent offered scant relief from the heat, which now exceeded one hundred degrees each day. At night, it became very cold, and the dew dripped incessantly on the sleepers. When a violent rainstorm struck, water passed through the thin canvas almost without hindrance. Waterproofing was not available from the quartermaster, since it was felt 'unnecessary' back in London.

As he lay on his cot, Johnathan stared at the motionless white fabric stretched over him. The peculiar smell of hot cotton duck filled his nostrils, and he thought that if he ever were to escape Turkey, he would never want to sleep in a tent again. He considered that poor shelter had contributed almost as much as poor leadership to the desperate plight they were now in, and shelter was one of his principal responsibilities. But failure was a shared responsibility, even if the honest leader takes it upon himself. He had been unable to convince anyone with influence of the folly of remaining as they were, even with the chorus of silent entreaties from thousands of men dead, and the death rattle of thousands yet dying.

The four horsemen of the apocalypse—war, famine, pestilence and death—were revealed to him daily here at Varna. Reaching into his trunk, he pulled out the battered Bible which Sir Alex had given him and flipped it open to Revelation 6:9, and read aloud:

> *… I saw under the altar the souls of them*
> *that were slain for the word of God and the testimony*
> *which they held.*
> *And they cried with a loud voice saying,*
> *How long O Lord, Holy and True,*
> *dost thou not judge and avenge our blood*
> *on them that dwell on the earth?*

Johnathan pondered these words. If the dead were to have given their lives for any purpose, was it this? That they should be avenged? All that this meant to Johnathan was that there was no end to the misery of the human condition. It occurred to him that there was another horseman, a bold outrider who made his appearance long before his ill-omened brethren: that rider was folly. If there ever were proof required of the welcome this rider was granted, it was this sorry expedition upon which he was now engaged with so many others. The exhilaration he felt as he marched down the Strand to war seemed futile now. The cheers of men and the blown kisses of women were a distant folly.

The tent flaps were rigged so as to catch any breeze that might pass; they ruffled as Bliss stepped inside. His uniform was faded and torn. Great half moons of sweat stained his underarms, and he threw his dusty cap in a corner in disgust.

'Christ in Heaven!' he exclaimed. 'Bad enough that we could not secure much for the horses to eat, but that bastard le Marchant was taking names of men 'not in proper kit'. Why can't the idiot confine himself to the 5th Dragoon Guards? And to top it off, Cardigan has taken the Light Brigade on a march into the plateau of Yenibazar! In full dress! He has as much as has condemned them to death in this blistering heat! Have these officers taken leave of what little sense they seem to have?

'And you sit here reading the Bible! Give us a prayer, then! Perhaps that will have more effect on these bloody toffs!' He threw himself down on his cot. Johnathan lay quietly. After a moment, Bliss spoke again, the anger in his voice gone,

'Is there more of that tea?' Johnathan picked up the tea pail and handed it over. 'It's gone cold, I'm afraid.'

'Never mind,' replied Bliss. 'It's better than that green filth available at the water cask. And better than the coffee made from green beans!'

It was true. Unripe coffee beans had been shipped to troops who had no means of roasting it, nor mill to grind it. So men were driven to heating the beans on their shovels, and grinding them between two rocks. All this increased the anger level among the soldiers, who suspected that the officers were not doing without much of anything. But officers were dying at the same rate as the other men, anyone could see that. And not all officers were indifferent to the suffering of the men they commanded, often sitting with dying subordinates until the end.

At last London decided that, in concert with the French, an invasion of the Crimean peninsula would be made, with its object the Russian naval base at Sebastopol. The decision came none too soon. In addition to an appalling death rate which now topped eighty on some days, a fire had broken out which almost levelled Varna, and nearly struck the French, English and Turkish powder magazines, which inexplicably had been established very close to one another. Warehouses with precious short supplies went up: boots, clothing, salt pork and biscuits were destroyed. The fire threatened the scores of ships rafted together in the nearby harbour, before it was contained by extraordinary effort.

On 26 August 1854, Johnathan sighed with considerable relief upon hearing the news that the force was to embark for the Crimea. The loading of so many men, horses and artillery pieces was a formidable undertaking, much of which was cast upon the engineers to accomplish. The invasion meant that at last they were to engage the enemy.

Six hundred sailing ships, aided by steam tugs, and several hundred screw-ships covered the sea to the horizon. The allied armada could bring more than three thousand guns to bear once they had fetched up together. Such firepower outmatched the Russian fleet at Sebastopol. The landing location was secret, but eventually the ships put in at a narrow harbour about forty miles north of Sebastopol, called Calamata Bay. There was black humour among the men at the prospect of landing at a place known as 'Calamity Bay'. This location was selected because it was felt by the engineers at a meeting of deputies—the French commander being too ill, and Raglan unable to climb the hull of a heaving ship with only one arm—that the weakness of the Russian fortifications at Sebastopol lay to the north, away from the harbour.

Johnathan pointed out on the maps that represented the latest intelligence, that the fortress to the north of the harbour at Sebastopol, known as Fort Severnaya, had no outer galleries or sheltering earthworks that one might expect to see in a major fortification, and the way the guns were emplaced left a serious 'arc of opportunity' to the north. This would be the thrust of the allied attack, for the consensus was that whoever held Severnaya, held Sebastopol. But first the enemy was to be engaged at the escarpment overlooking the River Alma, some fifteen miles north of the city.

The Russians were so confident of their ability to drive off the invaders, weakened as they were known to be by disease, that many prominent citizens were invited to the heights outside the city to watch the battle. Men and women dressed in their finest turned out with picnic baskets, parasols and blankets. Even a grandstand had been constructed for the event. The battle opened with exchanges of artillery, which were punctuated by an enormous blast as several huts in an abandoned village were blown up in front of the allied advance. This turned out to be a disaster for the defenders, for the smoke from the explosions was so dense, it masked the activities of the invaders. When the British were able to manoeuvre a cannon along a path to heights which overlooked the fort, the fight turned in favour of the allied force, particularly when a shot from a second cannon ignited an ammunition wagon. It detonated with a spectacular burst of fire, incinerating men and horses within an area of two dozen yards about.

High on the ridges where spectators had not yet broken out their lunches, there was sudden panic as shells began to explode at closer range, and balls whizzed through the air close by like lethal wasps. A man on the grandstand shrieked as a ball, nearly spent, lodged itself in his thigh, and in the ensuing panic, the bleachers collapsed. Soldiers coming soon after, snatched up the cold chicken, bottles of wine, and pastries which had been jettisoned in the dash for safety. Total casualties by late afternoon were about two thousand allied dead, and almost six thousand Russian dead left on the field.

But it was the wounded that fired Johnathan's horror. Nearly six thousand men lay in various conditions of distress: burned, broken and bloodied, they were; some without visible injuries sat muttering and weeping. Johnathan's own commander, Brigadier-General Tylden, who led the sappers, survived a flesh wound only to die from cholera the following day. All through the night, the evening air, already thick with smoke, was rent with the horrifying cries of the wounded and dying. Unlike the cholera which consumed the body from within, and brought the voice low, the smashing fist of war created a whole new range of agonies which tore life from men's bodies with bloody tenter-hooks.

To his dismay, Johnathan realized that there were no hospital facilities, no litters or field ambulances; not even carts with which to transport the seriously wounded. Accordingly, more men perished than was necessary, and the cholera, which they had brought along in their flasks and canteens, carried off hundreds more. What madness was this which sent men to risk their lives, but made no preparation for what might befall so many of them?

In the arrangements of large timbers to make a bridge over a stream, the squad of sappers Johnathan was supervising was surprised by a bursting shell. It had struck the scaffolding, tumbling it into the fast-moving river, and the timbers collapsed on Johnathan who tried to ward them off. He was unharmed except that he had taken two large splinters into the palm of his hand. The wood penetrated so deep, and was so painful, he was unable to use his left hand, and had a companion wrap it in a piece of shirting torn from a corpse. Later at a crowded field hospital, he waited until an exhausted surgeon could attend to him. The man tottered wearily over to him and sat down. His eyes were red-rimmed and hollow; his smock was foul with blood and unidentifiable bits of residue from the night's endeavours. 'What troubles you, son?' he said.

Johnathan raised his hand, covered with the bloody rag, 'Not a wound that covers me with glory, I'm afraid,' he replied. The surgeon took his hand, and spun off the filthy rag.

'Ah. We'll have them out in a trifle. It'll hurt some, and I'm afraid I have nothing for the pain.' He rose, and returned in a moment with a pair of nickel-plated pliers. 'Hold still, and we'll be done in a wink. One, I'll need to push through, and the other, draw.' He splashed the wounds with rum, and it burned the raw flesh.

'Hang on.' He grasped the hand, and worked with his pliers. The ragged timber tore at Johnathan's palm as it was withdrawn. Johnathan remained quiet, and the surgeon expressed surprise. 'No sense, no feeling, eh?'

Johnathan looked at him, 'How can you remain a sane man in light of all you have seen here? How is it possible that death has so many faces?'

' 'Tis sad that there's nothing here today that I haven't seen before. Fighting men die in some terrible ways.' He worked at the second sliver, which was proving stubborn.

Johnathan continued with what was on his mind. His own pain was trivial to what he could see around him, and what he had seen earlier. 'How can it be worth such suffering? This is so terribly far away from home, and such a dreary place. Is the death of even one gallant man worth what we gain?'

The surgeon eyed him, with almost a twinkle in his eye. How many times had he heard this theme from the mouths of suffering boys?

'We fight for ideas, son. Not land or prisoners or even booty. The fight here is about the rights of Christians, the power and prestige of the English and French governments, and the right to insist on a balance of strengths in the world. Look beyond broken bodies and wasted lives, or you'll go mad.'

Johnathan reflected on this as the splinter came free in a spurt of blood. 'I think I am quite mad already. Who could look upon what I have seen—what we all have seen today—and be unchanged?'

The surgeon sighed. 'It's all how you choose to look at it, son. It's all how you choose to look at it.'

This surely was the core of madness: to look upon the world and not see what plainly is; rather, impose over it a reality which rationalizes, defends and above all, comforts. General or politician, rebel or criminal— all could sing the same refrain of justification.

The Allies moved the fleet from Calamata Bay because of its exposed harbour, and resettled at Balaclava, just south of Sebastopol. This was to be the staging area for the siege of the city. A flanking action was planned so as to bear down from the northern reaches, which still appeared to be the weakest part of the defences. The Russians could see the strategy in the making, and even if this were not so, the war correspondents faithfully published all the available details in the British newspapers, which were eagerly pored over in St Petersburg. The harbour at Balaclava rapidly became foul and congested, and the pretty little port town soon disappeared under the heels and wheels of the invading army, which commenced landing on 15 October 1854. A petty disruption in the crowded harbour occurred when Cardigan's private yacht, *Dryad*, arrived. Cardigan insisted on a convenient location and called for a squad of sappers to set up proper boarding arrangements. Johnathan was ordered to take command of the group, as this 'little job of wharf-building' was considered to be light duty.

The harbour was a narrow finger of water, ending in steep ground, through which a single dirt track climbed to the plateau leading on to Sebastopol. At the end of the harbour was a butchery, and the waste was allowed to fall into the water where it raised a vile stench, swarming with flies, scampering with rats and other vermin. Cardigan wanted his vessel conveniently close to the roadway, yet not so near the sewage and waste as to suffer inordinately from the miasma which clogged the far reaches of the inlet.

As Johnathan was supervising the dock-building, he noticed a familiar figure come on deck yawning and stretching mightily. It was well past ten in the morning, Johnathan noted with disgust, and squinted his eyes at the man: it was Battersea. 'Good Heavens!' he cried, the other sweating sappers looking up in some surprise. 'Battersea! Battersea!'

Battersea looked up at the sound of his name. He saw the familiar red on blue uniform of the engineers, and all at once recognized Johnathan.

'Tally! You red-haired bastard! Tally, of all people! Come aboard!'

Racing up a slim plank which wowed precariously under his weight, Johnathan leapt aboard the *Dryad* and seized Battersea by the hands: 'I never thought I'd be glad to see someone like you,' Johnathan exclaimed, 'But I am! How are you?'

Battersea squeezed Johnathan by both hands but withdrew when he felt him stiffen; he noticed the bandages and exclaimed, 'Sorry old man. Had no idea.' Johnathan shrugged it off.

'Tell me about what's been happening to you. It's been a filthy war for us so far, but we seem to be winning it, although at a dreadful cost.'

Battersea smirked and led Johnathan to a table underneath a canopy, on the upper after-deck of the yacht. 'Sit down here; it's as far away from the stink as it's possible to get, and we might have a bit of a breeze blowing in from out there.' He gestured with his thumb offshore.

'So,' said Johnathan. 'You seem to have done well.' He looked about the vessel with its brass and mahogany appointments. It reflected the considerable wealth of its owner. 'Did you come out on her? I sort of lost track of you when Burgoyne let you be seconded to Cardigan. I've heard all manner of stories about him: his imperious temper and fastidiousness with detail of dress.'

'Oh, he's a prize all right,' laughed Battersea, 'but the damndest thing is, he actually likes me. Not too many people can put up with the rubbish he deals out. I'm the longest lasting aide-de-camp he's ever had. But it has its benefits.

'We didn't make the trip out here by sea, which I understand was quite sordid. We came overland, via Paris. The old man gave a smashing party at the Café de Paris, and shortly thereafter we were received by Napoleon and the Empress at the Tuileries.

'Then we took the train to Marseilles,' he continued. 'Again, two days of parties, and from there a lovely sail over to Athens, where we took in the sights for a couple of days. Spectacular sight, the Acropolis, crowned by the Parthenon. Triumph of Pericles. You simply must see it, old chap. For professional reasons.' He looked dreamily off to sea through the thicket of ships' masts. 'Simply wonderful. Then we end up here in this frightful sewer.' He wrinkled his nose petulantly.

Johnathan smiled. He obviously hadn't been ashore to see just how vile the place had become. Battersea poured him a small glass of sherry.

'Has Cardigan reported to Lucan yet? We hear that there's a good deal of bad blood between them.'

'Well that's a bit touchy, really. *Reported?* I'd say not. You see, Cardigan thinks he's got an independent command, and so he called on Lucan as a courtesy, though God knows there was very little in the way of courtesies. Cardigan is used to living well, and always sets a fine table. Lucan lives like an enlisted man, and had fare to offer which bordered on the disgusting. Thank goodness I didn't have to eat with them.'

Johnathan thought for a moment, then said, 'It concerns me considerably that two of the most senior officers don't get along, and to top it off, the subordinate thinks he has an independent command. How will that work?'

A disbelieving expression came over Battersea's face. 'It will mean that more men will die more quickly, that's all, so that we can get on with the business of waging peace. Competent command only prolongs the conflict; isn't it obvious? Throw in a little honour, sense of duty, gallantry, and one has a formidable recipe for perfect horror.'

'I trust you keep these observations to yourself, Battersea?'

'Of course. Were you to repeat them as beliefs I hold, I would condemn you as a liar, and attribute them to you.'

Johnathan smiled thinly. 'You would lie to a fellow officer? What about ethics and chivalry?'

'Of course I would deny it. And deny it hotly. I would not throw away a career when a simple lie would cover me. Oh, perhaps if larger issues were at stake, beyond the vanity and peevishness of old military types, I might risk the truth. But only if it served some glorious purpose.'

Johnathan sighed. Battersea was consistently self-serving. Only he could justify an untruth. 'Well, be careful with such views. Even when you think you're alone, you might not be; even...'

Battersea cut him off. 'Don't say it. I trust you simply because you have no ambition. You want nothing from me, and from what I've seen, keep much to yourself. You toady to no one, and shrink from no one. I can trust you for those reasons, and also because—for those same reasons—you have no influence.'

Inwardly Johnathan cringed at these words, for they made him feel peculiar, unworthy. He braved a smile, nonetheless. 'I understand. It's not me you can't trust; it's the people I tell.'

Battersea laughed as he raised his glass. 'You won't tell anyone. But enough of this nonsense. We're quite alone here, you may say what you wish.'

Johnathan looked around, not a soul about. He looked back to the work party as they struggled with the heavy dock timbers under the climbing sun; it had started to get quite warm, and he could almost make out the murderous glances of the sappers as they glanced up to the two men sipping sherry under a bright blue awning. It was too far to hear spoken words, but Johnathan could guess what they were saying.

'So where's Penforth?' he asked casually. He thought he saw a glint in Battersea's eye. 'Oh, he disappeared in Marseilles. A little too much of a good thing, I'm afraid. This has happened before, but he always shows up, little the worse for wear.

'Cardigan didn't like him at all. When he asked me to join him as his secretary, he forbade Penforth to accompany me. Called him a greasy little Mussulman behind his back. But I insisted. Penforth is indispensable.'

Johnathan quickly changed the subject: 'But you're trained as an engineer. What a waste of education, taking on the role of an aide.'

'Education's never wasted. I may never use a transit, or drain a canal, or survey a siege trench. But I'll always use my brain; that's why Cardigan took to me. That, and the fact that no one else could stomach the pompous old bastard!' He laughed, and Johnathan joined him. Their laughter rose and fell, a slender wraith of glee in an otherwise joyless place.

The Russians moved to counter-attack the allied force, and the resulting clash was the battle of Balaclava. Balaclava had a force of three thousand Turkish warriors, one thousand marines, and the 93rd Highlanders, who repulsed the initial surprise cavalry attack thrown at the garrison by the Russians on 15 October 1854. The correspondent covering the battle wrote for *The Times* that all that stood between the garrison and the main force of the enemy was a 'thin red streak', which became the 'thin red line' in military mythology. The cavalry had the duty of supporting the Highlanders until the infantry could be brought up.

The cavalry responded with two charges, the first by the Heavy Brigade of less than a thousand men, uphill, against more than three thousand Russian cavalry, which had already driven the Turks from their position. The second, by the Light Brigade under Cardigan, was a glorious futility, and one which Cardigan, who so perfectly exemplified that expression, nearly missed.

Seven miles from the place of battle, just before dawn, Cardigan and his young aide Battersea were asleep on the yacht *Dryad*. No hint existed that the significant battle of the war in the Crimea was to begin; it was wet and cold, and wriggling down in his heap of blankets, Battersea was glad that he was warm and dry. As the morning sky paled to the colour of wet slate, a distant redoubt named by the allies 'Canrobert's Hill' showed two flags snapping in the offshore breeze, to the first of the allied pickets. This was the signal agreed upon to indicate the main advance of the enemy. The Battle of Balaclava had begun.

The Turkish force was outnumbered more than twenty to one, yet they fought stoutly. Terrible losses were suffered under the Russian cannon, with round shot falling upon the men and horses like slow-moving rubber balls. Their effect was dreadful, disembowelling men and beasts alike, smashing gun emplacements and artillery like toys. By fighting so fiercely, they had given their allies ninety minutes to bring up reinforcements. One hundred and seventy dead remained on the hill as the Russians made a final charge under fixed bayonets and slashing sabres. Those who had thrown up their arms to surrender had their limbs severed by the cossack blades, and the horror could be seen plainly by the Heavy Brigade under Lucan. Moved by the butchery, he ordered some of the heavy cavalry to cover their retreat.

Aboard the *Dryad*, Battersea heard the distant thumping of cannon fire. At first, he dismissed the sound as thunder rolling in the hills, vestiges of the system that had brought lowering skies and continuous drizzle all the previous night. But footsteps upon the deck above him, excited shouts and, above all, Cardigan's distinctive voice calling out orders, signalled to him that the fighting had started. He was dismayed when a corporal banged on his door and entered without bidding. 'Lord Cardigan wishes you to rise and accompany him to the battle. He will see you at the stable immediately. Dried fruit and biscuits shall be packed for you. Full dress if you please, sir.' And he started out, turning at the door with a barely contained thrill in his voice, 'So it has begun in earnest! Oh that we shall play our part in it, sir! Right, sir?' He ducked out and was gone, scampering up the companionway.

Battersea scratched his head and cursed. He could have used a couple of hours more sleep. Snatching up a small canteen, he decanted rum into it; it was likely to be a long day, and dried fruit and biscuits were just not enough.

Meanwhile, Johnathan had spent a miserable night with Sir Colin Campbell's 93rd Highlanders, with all the other invalids who were strong enough to move under their own power. His hand throbbed with each heartbeat, and it kept him awake. He anxiously examined the wound by lifting the stinking bandage, and drawing off the accumulated pus with a knife. He had mustered with the other invalids to support, if necessary, the Highlanders who stood as if on parade in their bearskin hats and dark green kilts. Handed a rifle with bayonet already fixed and a pouch of percussion caps, he stared at the weapon, mystified. Though he had done some training in the handling of firearms, he was an officer, and in the Engineer Corps at that, and was not expected to be proficient in marksmanship. He fingered his sabre hilt, and wondered if he would see hand-to-hand fighting.

Campbell led his force to the mouth of a small gorge that passed to Balaclava; it was at a higher elevation than the plain which was being traversed by the main force of the Russians. As the first rows of the enemy cavalry advanced close enough to make out the purple and gold of their glorious uniforms, the Turks broke ranks and fled. They paused only to loot the camp of the 93rd, though scolded sharply by a couple of soldiers' wives who were loath to leave their possessions behind. That the Turks had withstood withering fire bravely until overwhelmed was not acknowledged, for the Europeans considered them unworthy soldiers, and most of the men made no bones about their contempt for them.

The six hundred men were lined up in ranks of three, with the invalids at the rear, then ordered to lie on their stomachs. Thus disposed, they would not be readily seen by the attackers. Campbell rode slowly back and forth, first in front, then well to the rear. His voice boomed out from behind.

'Men! You must remember, there is no retreat from here! You must die where you stand!' Coldly Johnathan recalled Battersea's cynical remarks about duty and gallantry, as he lay with his face in the sparse wet grass. He ached to lift his head, but he could hear Campbell chastise those who did. 'Damn your eagerness! Hold still sir!' And then, 'Now my gallants! To your formation!'

The approaching army was startled by the spectacle of a red-jacketed wall of men suddenly risen from the soil, and slowed their mounts to a walk. Puffs of smoke showed from levelled rifles, before the roar of the Regimental Sergeant Major's, 'Fire!' accompanied the downward stroke of his sabre, and the simultaneous crash of gunfire. Horses fell, men cried out, and the front line wavered. The volley was repeated, and more bodies fell. And again, and again, and the line was repulsed, this time as artillery fire from the allies began to find its mark.

So far, Johnathan had not fired a single shot. He stood transfixed by the carnage he was witnessing just below him. It seemed unreal, a curious exhibition taking place at a distance: a cannonball decapitating a man; another screaming silently, holding his shattered throat; horses shrieking like doomed souls, and the curious hissing sound of a crush of men and mounts straining to escape the steady hail of lead and iron. It was like a dream in the half-sleep before waking. Nervous energy demanded outlet, for he was no well-drilled infantryman. He spoke aloud as he had done as a child:

> *The Assyrian came down like the wolf on the fold,*
> *And his cohorts were gleaming in purple and gold*
> *And the sheen of their spears was like stars on the sea,*
> *When the blue wave rolls nightly on deep Galilee...*

Ah, Byron described this scene from Kings as if it were doomed to be repeated for each generation, he thought. He started the next stanza, but no more than a sound was uttered before he fell silent as the man in front of him fell, collapsing like a sack dropped from a collier's cart. Quickly, he stepped forward, filling the guardsman's place, then raised his rifle, resting the forestock on his wrist just back of his damaged hand. He was conscious of his heart beating against his ribs like a wild bird. But the order to fire did not come, as the entire front ranks of the enemy had broken off and wheeled to their left, to move up the north valley to Balaclava. Johnathan lowered his weapon, and leaned upon it as the extreme tension of the moment began to ebb. The wails of injured men rose about him in a smothering din.

Cardigan clattered up to Lucan, who could barely conceal his disdain. 'You're late, sir!' And without waiting for a reply, Lucan ordered him to deploy with his brigade a quarter mile up the valley, below the command on the Sapoune Heights. From this spot, the Light Brigade could be seen arrayed in perfect dress formation, more than six hundred horsemen strong. As yet, they had been given nothing to do. Meanwhile, the Russian cavalry paused to regroup after they had been frustrated by the rifle volleys of Campbell's men.

It was at this moment that the Heavy Brigade, big men on chargers standing fifteen or sixteen hands, wearing light armour and carrying heavy sabres, charged into them, smashing the Russian line with their impact. The metallic crash dissolved into an odd buzzing noise, the sounds of hissing men and snorting horses, the grunts of the wounded and the slap and whack of blades.

The fighting was fierce, and Johnathan ran to the edge of a gully near the command post on the Sapoune Ridge to watch as the second and third lines, the 4th and 5th Dragoon Guards and the Royals in brilliant red serge threw themselves into the mass of struggling men. It was not ten minutes before cheers started to sound from the English side, though it seemed an eternity before the Russians broke and fled. No attempt was made to pursue them, and down the valley to the south, the Light Brigade were restive, agonizing over what they perceived as a missed opportunity.

Johnathan heard his name: it was Battersea. Cardigan had sent him back to the *Dryad* for a silk scarf which was a luck charm. He seldom rode without it, but in the haste of departure, had left it behind. Battersea had thought him a little irrational; Cardigan had screamed at him to fetch the scarf without delay, for until he had it, he could not, would not, lead his men.

'I say, Tally, what on this wretched earth are you doing so close to the fighting, and holding a firearm like some common dragoon! And wounded too!' Though it was cool, his mount was lathered in sweat clear down to the fetlocks; its nostrils flared pink and moist with the exertion. Taking advantage of the pause, it reached down to snatch at the poor tufts of dry grass, chomping over its bit, sides heaving.

'It's all over, my part for now, with not even a shot fired, though I was in the line of battle!' Johnathan's voice was shrill, for he was more excited by the tumultuous events than he had thought. His words came out jerkily, then in a rush.

'Well, I must be away to his Lordship!' Battersea waved the scarf over his head. 'Seems he's forgotten his knickers, and won't fight without them!' He pulled away his protesting mount, and addressed Sir Richard Airey, Quartermaster-General to Raglan: 'Whither Lord Cardigan, sir?'

Airey pointed with his gloved hand to the floor of the valley, some six hundred feet below, and looked away as Raglan, who was peering through field glasses, called out to him. Battersea was uncertain, for the slope was broken-surfaced, with loose boulders and water-torn gullies. Cardigan was visible even from such a great distance, magnificently turned out in his blue tunic with gold braid, and tight cherry-coloured breeches. 'Cherry-bums' his men were called, though this was refined to 'cherubim' when in company, or when shocked Victorian glances called for explanation. Battersea contemplated the best way to reach him.

Raglan was muttering, seemingly to himself, the stump of his arm twitched in frenetic punctuation to his angry utterances: 'Damn it! Damn it! The miserable creatures are making off with our twelve pounders! Damn it!' Acolyte of Wellington, who proudly asserted that he had never lost a gun, Raglan found the sight of the enemy disengaging and dragging off the cannon abandoned by the Turks was inconceivable. It was personal, and therefore a matter of honour. He dictated a note to Airey, announcing that the cavalry must advance at once to protect the field pieces. Airey scribbled with a stub of pencil on a scrap of paper. 'Lord Raglan wishes the cavalry to advance rapidly to the front—follow enemy to try and prevent enemy from carrying away guns…immediate.' The error which was to result in disaster was that their vantage point was not the same as that of the men on the floor of the valley; the only guns in view were those of the defenders at the end of the valley, well positioned.

Airey read this back while Johnathan and Battersea looked on, then handed it to an aide for transport to Lucan. Raglan interfered, instructing that it be given to Captain Louis Edward Nolan, recently arrived from a posting in India where he had seen no action. He had been seconded from the 15th Hussars, as something of an expert in cavalry warfare. Johnathan had seen him about, and had taken a dislike to the man, largely on account of his tireless self-promotion. A brilliant horseman, he had written extensively on the art of mounted combat, though none of his theses had as yet been put to the proof. He was of the view, which Johnathan thought preposterous, that even repeat fire massed in volleys could not be delivered sufficiently fast to inflict a serious loss on cavalry, provided that they were able to get up to charging speed. The events of that very day notwithstanding, Johnathan knew that Nolan would not change his mind. Experience had shown him that fidelity to an idea was more important in the scheme of things than was any hint of uncertainty. Exceptions could always be explained; vacillation was perceived to be weakness to the point of fatal flaw. And one such as Nolan had always to think of advancement.

Nolan allowed his enthusiasm to spill over as he snatched the paper from Airey's hand. He was astride a troop horse of the 13th Light Dragoons, and it reared back with the tension in the reins as Nolan put the spurs to its flanks. Battersea called out to him holding the scarf aloft, but Nolan thundered by him, low over the saddle, his eyes shining with excitement. With an exasperated expression, Battersea wheeled in behind him, hoping that Nolan would not lead him off a precipice.

Johnathan watched the two of them go. Both men were part of the fortuitous stew of people that come into a man's life. In direct or subtle ways, each one had the power to influence and shape one's thoughts and life patterns. Nolan may have been pompous and obstinate, but he was one hell of a horseman, flying down the shattered slope with a deft hand on the reins. Battersea was nowhere near the rider, and fell behind. He was easy to follow though, for somewhere he had shed his pelisse, and his white shirt stood out sharply in contrast to the navy blue twill of Nolan's tunic.

Nolan reached the bottom of the valley, and galloped furiously across to Lucan, his horse winded and blowing heavily. Someone called out, as Battersea heard, drawing close, 'What is it to be, Nolan? Are we to charge, then?'

Nolan's reply was caught by the light breeze and carried down to the men, who were dismounted and eating. Some were taking a smoke. 'You will see!' he cried. 'You will see!' He giggled like a schoolgirl, and the men snickered mirthlessly to one another, and rolled their eyes; a few muttered under their moustaches about 'fools in high places'.

Lucan studied the note. It was obscure, for no guns were visible from the floor of the valley, though it was known that there were artillery positions at the end of the plateau. And Nolan was not forthcoming about which guns were intended to be protected. Along both sides of the valley were more than twenty-four thousand Russian troops, and a brace of heavy cannon faced them at the end. Lucan was puzzled. 'What guns? Where and what to do?'

Nolan's horse stumbled, still heaving, as Nolan yanked the bit sharply. He waved his arm vaguely in the air to the bottom of the valley. 'There, my Lord! There is your enemy! There are your guns!' His tone was sarcastic and entirely insubordinate. Cardigan was outraged, and shouted.

'Keep a civil tongue! A civil tongue, sir! I shall have you seen to!'

But there was no debating it in Lucan's mind, for he accepted without quarrel the formalities of command. He said to Cardigan with stiff correctness, 'We are to advance, then.'

Battersea looked around incredulously. This was suicide! Those guns would be well within the range of Russian artillery and rifle fire, and as yet there was nothing in the way of reinforcements, either infantry or artillery. He rode over to Cardigan as the orders were being given. Men now came from all quarters: the butcher, a prisoner, and a man in a nightshirt and cap with a scabbardless sword. One of the Lancers, lightly wounded at Balaclava, cantered up on a stray troop horse, both rider and mount covered with blood. He had two swords confiscated from corpses, having broken his own earlier.

'I'll be damned if I'll be left behind, and so lose the fun!' he cried, provoking nervous laughter from the line. Some one called out to Battersea. 'Will you join us, sir? Will you have a slap at the Russians?'

Battersea handed the scarf to Cardigan, whose eyes were grateful as he stuffed it in his blouse. 'Well sir? This is the time to show off that fabled swordsmanship of yours. You're out of uniform, but I shall not count it against you.'

Battersea was astonished. Cardigan was not joking with him. He turned his back as he took up a position about fifteen yards in front of his brigade, clearly expecting that Battersea would fall into position in the first line. Battersea looked back at the ranks of more than six hundred men. Behind the two lines of the Light Brigade were three lines of the Heavy Brigade with their larger horses and light armament. In all, and up close, they were a pretty ratty-looking lot, for the horses were thin and hungry-looking, mangy and in want of proper grooming. Uniforms were tattered and rent, with buttons missing and epaulettes removed or fallen away. Belting and trim had not seen pipeclay for months, and the whiting had faded to grey, adding to the shabby appearance.

This was a moment that Battersea feared all his life: the thrusting of a decision where control was effectively taken away from him. His entire career was dedicated to the protection and advancement of self. To ride away was possible, but profound disgrace would follow. To fall in was folly; it probably meant death or dismemberment, but there was a chance of glory, perhaps recognition and preferment. It was a hellish election, and one which was made for him as the trumpeter sounded the advance, for the front line expanded and drew him in. At once Battersea realized that the horse he was riding was one which knew its duty, falling in automatically with the others as it had been trained to do.

Up ahead, Nolan was now feverish. Years before, at Maidstone Barracks, he had drawn such a manoeuvre on a display board for a cavalry class. He was actually about to see his theory become reality, and he was as confident as a cock. As the jingling horde trotted forward, his mount lunged ahead, and he crossed in front of the line, but behind Cardigan who rode stiffly ahead, shouting something to the men. As Nolan turned, his sword raised, the first shell landed with an earthen thud, then exploded nearby. A splinter of hot steel struck Nolan at the buttock, tearing upward and exiting at the sternum, exposing his heart. Looking down disbelievingly, his arm still raised, he let out a frightful shriek so unnerving that battle chargers near him shied and plunged. Nolan's horse turned back and bolted among the advancing cavalry, until the corpse was unseated, the first casualty of a charge he principally aided in starting. Cardigan did not look around. Battersea slacked his reins and, while his mount carried on without instruction, he took out his neckerchief, and bound his hand to the pommel of his sword.

On the heights, Johnathan was incredulously watching the events unfold. Battersea had joined them! Then suddenly, as he saw the mounted ranks continue down the valley instead of swinging right to the captured guns, he shouted in vain, 'No! Go back!'

Around him, the command staff were startled and joined in the chorus which had not the faintest chance of being heard. Others, including spectators, officers' wives, and various sightseers whose luncheons were as yet untouched, began to cry out in alarm as the mistake was revealed. Men wept as they saw the concentrated fire of the Russian infantry and artillery batteries begin to find their range. It was a dreadful mistake! How could this be happening? Turn back! Turn back!

Johnathan watched through stricken eyes. Horses were being destroyed underneath their riders. Men were decapitated or unlimbed by cannon shot. For twenty-five minutes the carnage continued, and the smoke and dust grew thick upon the battlefield. Squinting, Johnathan followed Battersea's white shirt along. They had drawn their sabres now, on Cardigan's lead. He was still in the forefront, but having trouble containing his men who seemed to want to dash ahead under the withering fire.

Then suddenly, Battersea appeared to stand up in his stirrups, his arms outstretched. Then horse and rider went down and were lost to sight. To Johnathan, it was as if he were watching theatre from a great distance. It all seemed so unreal and disconnected. The heavy cavalry pulled back but did not retreat; it looked as if they were positioning themselves to cover the return of the light cavalry. With an enormous crash, the dozen bronze cannon of the enemy fired their last salvo, tearing a savage hole in the remnants of the first line. Then the remaining cavalry were among the gunners, who broke and ran. It was difficult to see much of the action for the distance, but it was clear that skirmishing was going on, and a great many men were on foot. The despair at the command post was palpable, for the retreat was if anything worse than the charge; the Cossacks harried the returning men, most of whom were without mounts, were wounded, or were dazed from battle.

'We have lost the Light Brigade!' cried Raglan, to no one in particular.

No, thought Johnathan, five hundred men have been lost. But maybe Battersea was right after all. Perhaps it was necessary to break men's bodies on the anvil of human stupidity before such quarrels could be settled. What an irony that Battersea might be among the fallen.

iii

Of the six hundred and seventy-three men who participated in the charge down the north valley, just under two hundred returned to the allied lines. Cardigan, with the luck of the uncomprehending idiot whose actions pull worlds apart, rode down the valley and back again without so much as a scratch, taking the cheers of men for the returned survivors as plaudits for his own courage. He rode slowly, saluting this way and that with the hilt of his sword to his forehead. He was oblivious to the gestures of disdain thrown at him behind his back.

More than five hundred horses were lost, including those which had to be destroyed by the farriers' pistols. Stretcher duty was called and all available men, including most officers, picked their way among the dead and dying who were at the outer edge of the enemy fire. Others were more daring, searching for friends among the torn earth and battlefield litter. Lucan offered a personal reward to the man who could find anything of his nephew, who had not returned. Under enemy sniping all that could be returned were his watch and his sword, and his wallet of personal papers.

Threading his way among the boulders, Johnathan moved toward the location where he believed he had seen Battersea fall. He had not been among those who had returned, but it seemed impossible that a man so full of life, and so certainly in control of it, could have been taken. For hours, under spitefully humming bullets, Johnathan worked this way and that, coming around the body of a limbless horse, when suddenly, there Battersea lay.

He was lying on his chest on the rough, uneven ground, arms outstretched as Johnathan had last seen him. A sabre was knotted to his wrist with a scarf; the blade was broken off about a third of the way from the hilt. His head was turned sharply, as if he were looking over his shoulder, watching. His wide, brown eyes were open, and his mouth was quizzically formed, almost as if in a faint smile. There were no marks of injury apparent. He looked alive, almost as if he would demand, 'What took you so long?' But he was certainly dead. Johnathan crouched beside him with a sigh, brushing the light hair from his brow. Battersea was cold to the touch, and Johnathan involuntarily withdrew his hand.

As he sat beside the silent corpse, he looked into the brown eyes that gazed sightlessly into his own. Johnathan remembered reading somewhere that more than twenty years were required to bring a man from the state of a plant to a condition of maturity and reason; thirty centuries to know a little of his structure, and an eternity to know a little of his soul. But only a moment to kill him. Battersea was one of the most complex men he had ever met, and one who at once repelled and attracted him. Now he was so much carrion, and would contribute nothing more to anyone's life, any more than his death had contributed to this mad venture in the Crimea. Wasn't it Voltaire who had observed that it is forbidden to kill, which is why murderers are punished, unless they kill in large numbers and to the sound of trumpets? Johnathan shook his head as if the thought was obvious to anyone who had seen a battlefield still warm from blood. He rose to his knees to attempt the return of the body. He wasn't sure precisely why he was doing this, save that there was no other rational explanation for having come out here in the first place.

As he lifted Battersea, he recoiled at the sight of the terrible wounds in Battersea's scorched abdomen; the man's innards threatened to spill out should he jostle the body much more. Moving him in this state with rifle shot whizzing about was impossible. Battersea had no personal effects on him, and his weapon was destroyed in the fall, so Johnathan cut a thick lock of his hair away, to be shared between the man's mother, if he had one (for Johnathan had never heard him speak of her), and Penforth, should he ever appear again. He withdrew Battersea's pocketwatch from his trouser pocket by its golden chain; a glorious timepiece indeed, still working, and slipped it into his own pocket. For a fleeting moment, he felt uncomfortably like a looter, but banished the thought by an assertion of will: what possible use could a dead man have of time?

Johnathan pondered the matter of an appropriate prayer, then closing Battersea's eyelids with his thumb and forefinger, he recited aloud:

> *For the Angel of Death spread his wings on the blast,*
> *And breathed in the face of the foe as he pass'd;*
> *And the eyes of the sleepers wax'd deadly and chill,*
> *And their hearts but once heaved, and forever grew still!*
> *And there lay the steed with his nostril all wide,*
> *But through it there roll'd not the breath of his pride;*
> *And the foam of his gasping lay white on the turf,*
> *And cold as the spray of the rock-beating surf.*
>
> *And there lay the rider, distorted and pale,*
> *With the dew on his brow, and the rust on his mail:*

And the tents were all silent, the banners alone,
The lances unlifted, the trumpet unblown.

'Good night, Battersea. Sleep well,' said Johnathan without emotion, as three rounds piffed into the gravel a short distance away, scattering small stones. He unslung his pelisse, and covered Battersea's face. After piling a few flat stones over the body, Johnathan stole away carefully, for his movements had attracted attention from the Russian sharpshooters in the hills. At this distance, only fortune could ensure a hit, but Johnathan did not feel particularly lucky.

Working into the night, in falling temperatures which left a thick coat of frost the following morning, Johnathan and all able-bodied men continued to assist the influx of patients into the surgeon's bay, which by now resembled an abattoir. Blood was everywhere, and corpses and amputated limbs lay in piles like firewood. Wounds were stitched without more than a splash of rum, and cavities were probed for musket balls with shrieking, squirming men being held down by their comrades. The scene was hellish, and would remain graven in Johnathan's mind for the rest of his life.

But already, the mood was changing, though the bitterness and recriminations at such a needless loss would not entirely die away for a time. Words like 'glorious' and 'spirited', 'magnificent' and 'courageous' were being thrown about. When a truce was arranged for the exchange of prisoners, it was clear that the Russians had not been unmoved by the charge which was 'against all military law'. In his dispatches, even though Lucan despised Cardigan, he described the charge as 'very brilliant and daring'. Cardigan's own role was written in terms which suggested that his leadership in the attack was in 'the most gallant and intrepid manner'.

It was the same sort of folly, Johnathan thought, that led Napoléon to conclude that 'the finest army that ever existed' was not defeated by men, but by nature. The sea to the south, the fire in Moscow, and the ice of winter all had conspired to defeat him. It was the problems of nature that were insoluble; opponents of a universal regeneration commanded by Nature herself! How impossible to contemplate that this brilliant military strategist could delude himself into believing such a proposition. And yet, could men otherwise engage in the destruction of one another without justification and assurances that right and reason, to say nothing of God's own divine grace, were on one's side? It seemed to Johnathan that other men's lives were simple currency for those whose privilege it was to make decisions which would put their existence into the balance. And this day, that currency had been spent for nothing more than the destruction of a

Cossack battery. Were there strategic issues beyond his understanding? It must be so, or there could be no comprehension of either this battle or this war. Perhaps, as the enlisted men said, it was simply 'the way of it'. Well, he wanted very much to be on the right side of 'the way of it'.

Johnathan felt useful at stretcher duty. It eased his mind at not being part of the fighting in any meaningful way. The heavy work wiped his mind clear of the horrors around him. His left hand was not healing well, but with four men to a litter, he was able to manage the task, learning to keep his right leg in step with the inside legs of the others, so as to keep the stretcher level and the wounded man as comfortable as possible. All through the night they worked, though it became uncomfortably cold. Some of the men were taking great risks to explore the battlefield for survivors, and still others limped in as their fading energies permitted, and darkness shielded them from enemy fire.

One of the last men to stumble back to allied lines was Alexander Dunn. A great cheer sounded as some of the Hussars recognized him through the accumulated blood and filth of battle. Private Levett, also of the 11th Hussars, had been under attack by a Russian lancer, and though unhorsed and wounded, was still feebly warding off the lance strikes. Having just emptied his revolver, Dunn seized his sabre which he had jammed under his thigh, and fought off Levett's attackers. As Dunn made ready to follow his commanding officer in retreat, he noticed Sergeant-Major Bentley under attack by three cavalrymen. Standing in his stirrups, he wheeled at the enemy, flinging his empty pistol at the first man, who fled. Dunn was a tall man, standing six-foot-four and, despite official cautions, carried a sabre which was nearly six inches longer than regulations permitted. Like a madman he tore upon the Russians, cutting both of them down, enabling the Sergeant-Major to catch a passing horse and escape. These exploits, which three years later were to result in one of the first awards of the Victoria Cross for valour, were retold in camp, and his men anxiously awaited some sign of his return.

Johnathan was present as Dunn staggered in. Exhausted, he collapsed. He was quickly trundled aboard Johnathan's litter and carried to the surgeon's tent. Though he was covered with blood, and his clothing torn in a dozen places, there were no wounds of significance, and he was waved aside. Johnathan asked to be relieved of duty, volunteering to sit with the man, though it was more the matter of his own numbing fatigue that clamored for rest, or at least lighter duty.

Johnathan woke with a start. He had fallen asleep sitting against a tent pole, oblivious to the groans of suffering men, and the comings and goings of surgeons and orderlies. Dunn had reached out and touched his boot. 'Water? Do you have any?' he asked weakly through cracked lips.

Johnathan rummaged for his canteen, holding it under his arm to remove the bung, for his left hand throbbed with pain. After Dunn drank noisily, spilling down the front of his grimy tunic, he wiped his sooty face with his sleeve, and grinned at Johnathan. 'Tea?' He was an exceedingly handsome man, with dark eyes, heavily lidded. His hair was parted in the middle of his head, and broad side whiskers met a thick moustache, effectively framing a strong face. His chin was shaven, though this morning it showed a heavy stubble and considerable dirt. He reached out an dirty hand. 'Dunn, Alex, Lieutenant. 11th Regiment of Dragoons. Yours was the last face I saw before I must have fainted.' Johnathan took his hand. He had a firm grip, and a curiously flat accent to his voice.

'Snow, Johnathan. Ensign. Sapper cum stretcher bearer.' Johnathan took his hand away, noticing blood on it.

'Oh, sorry.' Dunn examined his own hand. 'Only a scratch.'

'You made quite a showing out there, I hear,' said Johnathan. 'Even Cardigan was asking about you. I think that means you'll be mentioned in dispatches.'

Dunn snorted, but said nothing. Then after a while, 'Bloody waste. Almost my whole unit cut down. Oh, my aching head; I can hardly see straight for a headache. Are you my nursemaid?'

Johnathan shook his head, grinning wryly. 'I said I'd watch you. They couldn't find anything seriously wrong with you, but as one of the extraordinary heroes of the charge, there was sufficient concern to warrant a proper vigil. But I have to confess I fell off to sleep the very moment I sat down.'

Dunn put the back of his arm over his eyes and sighed. 'What's wrong with your hand?'

Looking down, Johnathan seemed surprised to see that he was holding it gingerly with his other hand. 'Wood splinters!' He laughed dryly. 'Hurts like hellfire. But nothing too serious.' He was not convincing.

'Say,' said Dunn. 'Would you do me a very great favour?'

'Anything, so long as it takes only one hand.'

'I received this letter from home,' said Dunn, taking a soiled envelope from his tunic. 'I've been a bit superstitious about it, and haven't wanted to read it until after Balaclava. It's from my sister. I don't know, I think it'll be bad news somehow. Would you read it to me? I'd be grateful.'

Johnathan studied the sweat-and blood-stained envelope. The handwriting was elegant; sweeping letters flowed across the paper like good manners. In the upper centre, there were three thrupence stamps, yellow and orange, showing the image of a beaver, above which a British

Crown separated the words 'Canada Post'. Johnathan opened the thick, creamy envelope, and took out the folded letters. Smoothing out the folds on his knee, he read the address aloud:

'Belvedere, fifty-eight Carleton Street, Toronto, Canada West. The date is August fifteen, eighteen fifty-four. Little more than sixty days to reach this God-forsaken place from Canada! Must be some kind of record.' He looked at Dunn, who made no answer. His arm still covered his eyes. Johnathan turned back to the papers in his hands:

'Dearest Alex. We are all so worried now that war has been declared, and Prince Albert's Own Hussars will be off with you to the Crimea to do battle. We gathered the other night around Papa's big atlas, to find the Crimea, and there it was in the middle of the Black Sea, hanging down like a sore tonsil! It seems so frightfully far away. Here's what our reference library says about the place: "Along the coast abounds in beautiful mountain scenery; the valleys are luxuriant with vines and olives and mulberry plantations, while the northern slopes give large yields in cereals and fruits." It sounds like a wonderful place, were it not for the reason of your visit!

'We eagerly await the daily edition of *The Globe* (it went daily just recently; we are becoming quite the modern city!) for the latest information on the progress of the war, as well as the more detailed accounts by that man Russell in *The Times*, and the *London Gazette*. And of course the *Illustrated London News* when it's available. So far the news has not been all that comforting, what with the cholera and the putrid fever plaguing the allies. We pray for you every day, and hope this letter finds you well.

'The same mite that gave you the wanderlust must have bitten our little brother Andrew, for he has left to seek adventures of his own. He has struck out for Rupert's Land. Apparently he ran into one of the Captains of Artillery from the Royal Regiment of Foot, under the command of Lieutenant Colonel Crofton (whom you met through Papa), who went out to the Red River Colony during the Oregon crisis. The man couldn't stop talking about the beauty of the country, the opportunities, and the land for the taking. It certainly convinced Andrew.

'So he was off to see for himself, in spite of Papa's stern warnings about ferocious Indians and Catholics running wild out there. If anything, Papa's disapproval was encouragement enough. Sound familiar? If he should not amount to anything there, he'll strike out for California, though I think the gold excitement has mostly settled down. None of us was very happy to see him go, but he would not be dissuaded, and off he went. He's almost as stubborn as you. Papa said he was not to have a penny, but I caught him stuffing bills into his pocket, just as he did for you!

'Well, there is no other news, really. The papers here are full of stories about Dr John Rae, the Arctic explorer, who has come across evidence of the lost Franklin expedition. Apparently they all perished in terrible circumstances of cold, fever, and starvation, having resorted to cannibalism at the end. Isn't that simply awful? So remember, things could be worse! Ha! Ha!

'Mother is well enough, and Dorothy says to write her a note. Please write soon. Love, Your adoring sister, Jenny.'

Johnathan looked up. 'That's a nice letter, especially that bit at the end about things could be worse!'

Dunn lay still for a moment, then took his arm away from his face. It seemed to Johnathan that his eyes were moist.

'That's my crazy sister. Eighteen years of age, and pretty as a picture. If there's one thing I miss about home, it's her.'

'What of your other family? The letter seems to hint at a closeness?'

'All my father lives for is his work. He was former Receiver-General of Canada, and member of the executive and legislative councils of Upper Canada. It was my mother who taught all of us that there was a world beyond what one could see from the front porch. Though in truth, my father bought my commission and sends me a pension. I cannot protest too loudly.'

Johnathan handed back the letter. 'And your country. Do you not miss it?'

'Oh, well enough. It's a beautiful land, as much as I've seen of it. My young brother will see a lot more of it than I ever shall. It was the world I wanted to see, and under the Union Jack I shall see it—though I have to say that this particular part of the world, perhaps, I could have missed.'

Both men were silent with their own thoughts, until Johnathan spoke again. 'My patron has had some dealings with British North America, the fur trade. Hudson's Bay Company. He would often reminisce about his travels in a wild and beautiful land. Sometimes I used to think, listening to him talk, that he'd left his soul over there.'

'Well, I could see it happening,' said Dunn. 'Canada is a place that produces a longing in any expatriate. A place of almost violent beauty, and wild extremes. This is not sentimentality. A land so abundant and primitive, so magnificent in its range and contrasts, cannot help but imbue one with a sense of opportunity, promise, and fantastic possibilities. Even now it stirs me, and when my lust for peering beyond horizons is expunged, I shall go back there to make my fortune.' It was a long speech, and he seemed exhausted. Johnathan stood up, and promised to return with food. By the time he looked back from the entrance, Dunn was asleep again.

Johnathan was invalided out of the army that December. His hand had swollen to the size of a watermelon, hot to the touch, and there was talk of cutting it off. A surgeon lanced the hand in several places, and thick, foul-smelling yellow fluid spurted from it. In the hospital at Scutari, he was bedridden for two weeks with fever, and daily the matter of amputation was considered. It was only incompetence, the indifference bred by hidebound army regulations, and the machinations of the civilian Purveyor, that prevented the decision being taken. Two out of every five casualties admitted to these hospitals did not survive. Johnathan was lucky, and by January of 1855, he was recuperating in Gleneaglesham, his mother fussing at his side, and a distant Sir Alexander Archibald seemingly brooding at the rather sudden return of his upstairs maid's son.

Even more delighted to see him was Elsie, who was away from her first position and now employed at Gleneaglesham. She was a dark-haired beauty, whose pleasing form caught Johnathan's eye before he realized who she was.

'Your mother read us all your letters,' she said to him, shy, adoring.

'I'm afraid that there weren't many. Not much happened in the Crimea that was worth the telling.'

'But the newspapers have been full of the stories of courage and terrible conditions. It must have been awful for you!'

And so Johnathan settled into an easy time of recovery, and the Scottish spring was glorious in the year of 1855. Crocuses, daffodils, Belgian tulips and poppies sprang from the earth in a riot of colour around Gleneaglesham. His boyhood chum Calvin had joined the army of the Honourable East India Company, and was now serving in Bombay. He had written only two letters to his mother, Elsie reported, the last one of which was to announce his promotion to the rank of sergeant. 'Imagine,' said Elsie, 'A sergeant already!'

It was only a matter of time before he seduced Elsie, who yielded to him with a gasp somewhere between awe and triumph. She moved expertly, and he suspected that Calvin or someone had been her lover long before he was. The affair was over before very long, for Johnathan had become restive, bored; he had stood at the threshold of grand events, yet had not played a part of significance. He had received a few jibes about the nature of his wounds: attacked by a bridge, was how one wit put it. This vexed him, and he found he had little time for anyone, including Elsie, whose grief at being rejected was all the more difficult to bear patiently.

One evening, Sir Alex summoned him to the parlour to take a sherry. His ostensible reason was to review the now infamous charge of the Light Brigade, which was being constantly revisited in the press as the best possible reason for reform in military command. As they sat, Johnathan replying to his host's questions with stiffness and economy, Sir Alex asked,

'Your hand; is it well?'

Johnathan flexed his left hand, holding it at the wrist. 'Yes, well enough. It's still a little stiff; I suppose that I'll have some discomfort for a good while yet.' Looking up at Sir Alex, he said, 'I'm grateful to have a hand at all, for the decision very nearly was to take it off, as you know.'

'Ah.' Sir Alex paused. Then he spoke abruptly. 'You don't seem happy here, though your mother is of course delighted to have you back.'

This was more in the nature of a question than a statement of opinion, and it was clear that Johnathan was expected to answer. He decided to come straight to the point. 'In point of fact, no. I have seen just enough of the world to acquire a taste for more. It's just that I'm not certain where to look next.'

'Hmm. I thought as much.' He seemed to have this all planned. 'Let me tell you. I can help.' And he held up his hand to forestall the objection which he saw forming in Johnathan's mouth.

'I am a member of the East India Company's court of proprietors, solely by virtue of the nature of my investments there. They're always in need of officers in their army—particularly trained engineers with field experience—and I believe I can get you a position without difficulty.'

So this was how Calvin ended up in India; Johnathan had wondered whose doing it was. Still, Johnathan had no prospects once again, not having served anywhere near the required time for a small pension. And so again, he decided to accept the largesse of his patron, suspecting it was having to do with his mother's attentions, rather than anything else.

'I've not much in the way of field experience, sir. Laying out camp sites, designing temporary dockage, and a bit of mapping and surveying won't have them kicking down my door.'

'Never mind all that. This is India, remember, and in all likelihood you'll be snatched as a prize.'

Six

i

One day, late in the summer of 1857, David was hard at work stretching and scraping buffalo hides. In his twentieth year, he had grown lean and strong; yet his development remained stunted, for he was allowed no serious interaction with the others. Always he sat on the periphery, watching, helping, obliging, but never fully participating. The hides upon which he was expending his efforts were summer hides, thin and poor, but the buffalo were so scarce that year that nothing was wasted. Ordinarily, such hides would have been discarded, or at best cut into thongs for lashings and other fastenings.

Feeling eyes upon him, he looked up. Wakandayamani was watching him, He had not heard her approach. So many times it was this way with the old woman. She drew near soundlessly, and seemed to vanish evanescently. David looked away from her gaze in appropriate deference, and continued to drive stakes into the perimeter of the hide with a round, flat rock. It was hot, messy work. The hide was still fresh, and teemed with ticks and the mange. Wiping the sweat from his brow with a forearm, he glanced at the old woman again; her expression was unchanged. She squatted a few yards from him, but as yet had offered no word of greeting or explanation.

David had come to know that she was something of a medicine woman, a healer. He had seen her entering the lodges of the sick ones with the shamans of the village. Health, to the Dakota, as with the Assiniboine, was a matter of wholeness, of balance and completion. In the most serious cases of illness, only the medicine of a man and a woman could restore life's symmetry. The medicine women were a secretive group, operating in the shadows of the community, and with less ostentation than the men. David did not see much of their activity, nor did he understand how their cult functioned.

Still aware of her looking at him, David spoke as he worked, not raising his eyes, 'Do you wish something of me?' His tone was deferential, as always.

This was met by silence. David was uncomfortable under her gaze, and he continued to scrape for a moment before he spoke again. 'I would ask something of you.' And he darted a glance at her. Her expression seemed unchanged; David thought, however, that he saw something in her eyes that he had seen only in the children he watched over now and then: recognition.

'You have worked well for me,' she said in her thin, brittle voice.

David blurted out, 'Then why am I not acknowledged by anyone as worthy? No one will address me respectfully; I am referred to as 'red hair', or mostly, 'he-who-helps-the-old-one'. Why is this?' Astonished as he was at this outburst, perhaps the longest speech in over two years, he could feel the tears of bitterness well up in his eyes. He was ashamed, and he kept his head low so as to hide the pain. He scrubbed furiously at the fatty tissue which clung to the stretched skin.

'You are not one of us, yet you are of us,' she said quietly. 'You are not a boy, but neither are you a man. There has been no mortification,' she added.

'What does that mean?' he whispered without looking up.

'You have remained tied to your tasks; you are of the earth. Many say there is no spirituality to you, which even the most docile captive shows now and then.'

David mulled over this judgement which, by her tone, the old woman did not seem to share.

'I have seen you with the young children,' she said. David felt that, once his initial torment was over, the children accepted him in the curious, passive way of all children, and he felt free to help them in their play-hunts, and in their search for eggs, and other small quests of childhood. 'And I have seen you at work. I think it is open to you to be tested. Are you willing?'

'What does that…' he was cut off suddenly with a raised hand, and she rose to her feet. The breeze tickled strands of uncombed white hair across her face, and her snaggled tooth stuck out defiantly, giving her the appearance of mystery and worldliness. She had become inscrutable again.

'I will come for you before the morning's half-light. Be ready. You will need nothing but your breech clout. Bring no food.'

When David raised his eyes, she was gone. He went at the hide with renewed vigour, and when the scraping was done, he put away the tools and went down to the creek to bathe. Washing carefully, he tried to put out of his mind the shapeless dread he felt about the testing, and what was expected. Of the time he had passed with this village, he had never been permitted to attend any of the dances or sacred rituals involving powerful magic. He knew that young men were tested during the *wi-wanyang-wacipi*, the sun-looking-as-they-dance. Afterwards, some had been stricken with infections of terrible gashes in their chests and backs, the flesh torn and mutilated. He slept fitfully. His anxiety mounted as he traced the moon's passage across the open smoke flaps, and he began to explore possible excuses to decline.

He sat up, cross-legged, and stared at the sleeping figures around him. The old woman was not among them. He looked at the gently rounded form of Mahpiyatowin, but worried more about the coming dawn. The sight of this young woman whom he had seen in her glorious nakedness afforded none of its usual comfort. He shifted to his knees, and David Bloode began to pray. Hands clasped in front, eyes closed, he silently began to mouth the almost forgotten prayers that the Reverend Cowley had made him repeat. When he opened his eyes, the old woman was crouching at the lodge entrance, her glittering eyes bright in the gloom.

Wordlessly, she stood up, using a long staff to assist herself, and David followed, knowing that his destiny was connected, for good or ill, to this woman who had marked him with her teeth as her property. She handed him a large, flat rock; it had a red circle painted on it, surrounded by a series of dots, daubed in with the same pigment. He was then directed to pick up a buffalo skull, white and bleached by the prairie sun. He stooped to lift it, surprised at its weight, even though it was dried by several seasons in an open space.

The skull of a buffalo was sacred. It had four massive points, being the horns and the facial bone plates over the wide eye-sockets. The number four had powerful meaning; all that was, came in a sequence of four: the seasons, the winds, the phases of the moon, the stages of a man's life, the basic directions. David noticed that it had four lines painted with the same red pigment, all joined above the nasal opening, in a 'V'.

Together, they walked from the camp. They had covered several miles before the pre-dawn began to fade the canopy of stars. This was the time when the coyotes set up their tremulous chorus, and the tattered wisps of fog lent the land an unreal quality. David shivered, and not merely because he was cold. The old woman led on, walking briskly, purposefully, as if she had been following a well-defined path. Yet no marker was visible, and David was vaguely aware that they were headed in an easterly direction. His arms ached with the weight of the skull and the stone.

By and by, the old woman uttered a single word: 'Now.' And she gently dropped the medicine bag she had been carrying on the thick grass. David looked about. They were at the summit of a shallow hill, the only elevation of significance for any distance within sight. There was nothing in view but scrub prairie, with occasional bluffs of stunted oak and poplar groves. There was nothing special about the place that David could see. He turned his attention to Wakandayamani who was on her knees, opening the medicine bundle from its casing of soft elkskin. She must have had it under her blanket, he thought, for he had not noticed it until now. She took the green stake she had been carrying as a staff, its point fire-hardened, and raised it with both hands in the direction in which the sun would rise. It was slightly shorter than the span of a man's outreached hands, and about as thick as a woman's wrist.

'Take the rock, and drive this into the earth,' she instructed. 'Here,' and she pointed to the place in the soil she had chosen.

David eagerly did as he was told, for the work eased his apprehension. Progress was slow for the earth was dry and hard. His guts rumbled from want of nourishment, and the task increased his thirst.

Singing quietly to herself, the old woman took out a twisted, light thong of rawhide, about six good paces in length, and unwound one end to a distance she measured from fingertip to elbow. David tried to keep his attention fixed on the top of the stake so as to prevent his fingertips from being crushed, but his curiosity was such that he was compelled to try and follow what was happening.

Wakandayamani removed two bone pegs from the bundle, each slender, tapered, and about the length of a man's handspan. Left in the bundle was a braid of sweetgrass, still smouldering in a wrapping of green buffalo hide taken from the lower leg of the beast, and a small medicine bag made from the scrotum of a bull elk. Each item was arranged and handled carefully, respectfully.

She stayed on her knees for a time, singing quietly, her eyes closed; she swayed ever so slightly as she blew intermittently on the glowing end of the sweetgrass.

> *Wakun-tanka accept now our prayer*
> *send a helping washicun*
> *send a helping washicun*
> *let the smoke rise upward to thee*
> *it bears our prayer, Wakun*

David shifted from one leg to another, hungry, thirsty, muscles aching, and uneasy. He knew that a washicun was a spirit helper, who came only to worthy young men. He was as yet uncertain what he would be required to do out here in this vast empty space.

She rose, taking the two bone pegs in her left hand, and raised her eyes to meet his. He looked down, respectfully.

'Listen,' she commanded. 'Heed carefully what I am about to say. Let not your courage fail you. Shrink not from me; utter no sound.'

She went on without opportunity for comment. 'There are but two things that hold you to earth, from finding the place of the powerful: the first is the limits imposed upon you by your man-form. This is the physical bond to earth.

'The second is anung-ite. This is two-face; it is fear. There are things you must fear which require preparation and readiness, and the fear of a coward. This is a binding most difficult to throw off. All these things are true.'

She held up a slim steel knife, grasped by the cutting edge, in the manner of a pen. She laid the point on his chest, over the left nipple, and pushed the blade in to the depth of her smallest finger's thickness. Then she tugged it down, leaving a small slit.

David gasped and flinched, and made as if to draw back.

'Hold yourself, boy!' she hissed. 'I shall not have you yield at the cutting. Look you to the moon. Take its measure with your mind, and fetch it to meet the sun's gaze. Do this with your every thought, and you will not pay attention to me.'

David's body quivered and sweated in the cool dawn. He seized the fading crescent of the old moon with his eyes, and exhorted it to move eastward across the heavens to meet the sun. His eyes bulged as the old woman cut down again, then deftly slipped the bone skewer in the first cut, under his flesh and out the other opening in his skin. He still held the moon, and he squeezed his eyes shut to retain the image.

He screamed silently at the moon to obey his injunction, sensing, rather than feeling the other set of incisions. The skewer seemed rougher this time, for it tore the musculature as it passed through. He faced the warmth faintly spreading from the east, and opened his eyes. The image of the moon was reticulated over the spilling blush of the rising sun, and David wondered at the power of such magic.

Wakandayamani held up the light line of tightly braided rawhide. Flaking it down, she took the unravelled ends and tied two of them to the exposed ends of the bone skewers, wrapping the third thong around both knots to form a secure purchase. She repeated the lashings at the other peg, and picked up the opposite end of the line. Fashioning a loop, she dropped it over the stake which David had planted. Finally, she took the buffalo skull, blew on it four times, and set it on the top of the stake, positioned so that the first shafts of sunlight would pass through the tapered arches of its horns. She turned to face David. 'You are now, and must remain, okashka najin, being-tied-standing-up.' Then she addressed him sternly.

'Back up! Back up! To the limit of your tether!' This was a command, harsh as a father's anger. 'You must move about the stake, in the direction of the sun. Thus!' And she demonstrated a sideways jog, like French dancers he had seen at Red River. 'It will be your duty to escape these bonds,' and she placed both fists over her sagging chest, flinging them out suddenly, fingers spread: 'So!'

Taking the small medicine pouch, she approached him, opening the neck. Drawing mightily and noisily through her nose, she spat a wet sluice into the narrow bag, held open with her two thumbs. She next dipped a finger into the bag, which contained a little mixture of charcoal, yellow earth and tallow, combined with maple bast and leaves which had been roasted. The colour black represented a fresh beginning, such as the burning out of the fires of revenge. Stirring, she withdrew a blackened digit, and applied it to David's hairless chest.

There, she drew a circle, marked with four short dashes to show the sacred directions. On his forehead, she made four marks similar to those on the buffalo skull. The empty medicine bag was given to David to hold in one hand, and the thick braid of sweetgrass in the other. He stared at the tightly wound strands, the three twists representing body, mind and spirit, in almost all aboriginal cultures on the prairies.

Stretching her hands in the air eastwards, she cried out. Facing in each of the other sacred directions in turn, she called upon all of the spirit helpers of unseen powers who might find this boy worthy. Turning to David, she spoke in a low, dry voice, choked as a raven's plaint, 'Dance, boy, the wi-wanyang-wacipi, sun-looking-as-he-dances. Pray for the strength to be free, for you will need much strength. If you have courage, you will have help. If you should fail, you will remain a non-person, and if you should be killed, no one will mourn you.

'Have the courage to call to you a helping spirit, then to fly with him. Now begin!' And she lunged toward him, her white wispy hair flying about her, her mouth open with its broken, crooked teeth framing her shouted order. She pushed against him with surprising vigour.

David fell back, startled, and the thongs took hold. He felt the sickening sensation of tearing flesh, and he lost his balance. His chest on fire, he fell in a tangled heap, and blackness flooded his mind.

When consciousness came again, the sun was high, and the old

woman was nowhere in sight. He was powerfully thirsty, and the thought
of food made him feel faint. He gathered himself in a cross-legged slouch
in the high grass, and gingerly fingered the protusions in his chest. He felt
overwhelmingly captive and helpless. Walking over to the stake, he
removed the skull and flicked off the braided line. He gathered it in,
holding it up; it was deceptively fragile in appearance. He studied it, and
thought of escape. All about him, as far as the horizon, stretched the
shimmering, fecund prairie.

Overhead, a hawk cried its sharp, tearing note. David dropped the
loop back over the stake, looking around like a thief. He returned the skull
to its perch, trying to adjust its vacant gaze as Wakandayamani had done.

Almost mechanically, he backed up until the thin line raised off the
ground. He squatted unsteadily, and picked up his totems. Slowly, he
sidestepped in a circle, keeping the pressure light on the thongs pinned to
his chest. Around and around he went, trying to count his revolutions, for
the concentration required to minimize the pressure on his flesh was
great. He began to sing, to match the rhythm of his awkward jumps, a
song popular with the tripmen as they had pulled into the fort where
David and his grandfather were working. He sang for all his lungs were
worth; he howled, he shrieked the chorus to the empty plains:

> *En roulant, ma boule roulant,*
> *En roulant, ma boule.*
> *En roulant ma boule roulant,*
> *En roulant ma boule.*

He leaned back, feeling the pins tug at his skin. As the pain and
gathering exhaustion intoxicated him, he tripped and fell, the tearing
flesh causing him to cry out. He got up and staggered on, beginning to
luxuriate in the loneliness, the debasement, the pain and the utter self-
cruelty of the moment.

All afternoon David capered and swivelled about his leash. By
evening, his songs had become a mere croaking of mostly forgotten
verses. At last, utterly diminished, he collapsed and slept without
movement or dreams. He started awake at daybreak, cold, and shaking
with the chill. He chewed for a while on the sweetgrass to moisten the
inside of his mouth, then got moving to warm himself. Around and
around he cantered, stopping only once to relieve himself, a thick, acrid
stream into the tall grass. He shambled on, becoming more and more
oblivious to the pain in his chest. Another verse of a song floated into his
head, and he mouthed the words:

Seul en bois, que j'ai en de soucis
Pensant toujours à mes si chers amis
Je demandais: Helas! Sont-ils noyés?
Les Sioux les auraient-ils tués?

This song was called 'The Little Rock', and the irony of the verse, and the rock he had carried all this way, just to fashion his own torment was not lost on him. He strained at the bonds which were now part of his living flesh.

'Les Sioux les aurient-ils tués?' he screamed, tears of frustration, pain and near hysteria flowing down his cheeks. The saltiness was bitter in his parched mouth. Shuffling and chanting, he greeted the new day, the bone shards in his chest now impossibly stretching the skin and muscle tissue of his chest.

As the sun rose to its full height, David knew he could not last. He would try to make a final attempt to burst his bonds, for he felt now he could not fail. The old woman's admonition held a warning of the cost of failure; it promised much worse than his present torture. He began to run forward in the circle, the long tufted grasses now crushed into a clearly defined pathway around the silent, mocking skull. Running clockwise, as he had been directed, the tether in his right chest pulled painfully, for it was now tearing in a different direction.

Gathering speed, he swept around until he was sure he could go no faster. With a cry which came from his soul in a soaring intensity, he suddenly veered inwards toward the skull, leapt over it, and ran, his hands outstretched imploringly, with the line over his chest and under his right arm.

The line snapped taut. The full weight of his body was taken on the right fork of the line, and the flesh tore; the pain poked needles at the base of his skull. The weight of his body now against the other line, he snapped around and fell in agony. As he spiralled to earth, he looked at the sun. He saw the old woman rush at him again, reaching out her bony fingers like talons to grab him and push him. As he cried out with the pain, the woman's twisted face and flowing white hair flooded his consciousness; her fierce determination was as intense as a striking owl, whose huge, silent wings lifted him and bore him away.

Late in the day, Wakandayamani returned to the boy. She noted with satisfaction the well-trammelled circle, and hurried over to his body lying awkwardly in the deeper grass. Seeing that he was alive, she put down her water pouch and took a medicine bag to the circle created by David's passage. Entering it from the east, facing the sun, she blessed it with a scattering of tobacco and prayers of thanks.

Returning to the boy, she turned him over. She noted the tear in his right chest, but the bone pin remained in his left. Tracing the strand, she saw that it had parted at the base of the knot. She pondered the meaning of this portentous sign. Moistening David's lips, she lifted an eyelid. He moaned and opened his eyes.

She proffered the water sac, splashing the liquid in her palm, and holding it under his chin. Weakly, he turned aside, shunning the drink, as he knew he must. The old woman grinned in approval. 'For our mother earth,' she nodded, 'from whom comes all life.' And casting down the brilliant droplets, again she offered the water. Yet again David turned aside.

'For family and clan,' she agreed, spilling the precious fluid. And a third time was the water declined, as the ultimate sacrifice demanded of those who would put the life of all others before one's own. The cool wetness was so close that David was ready to lunge for it. At last, he was permitted to suck at the woman's dampened palm, allowing a trickle of sweet water to sear his parched throat. He moaned with the ecstasy which the life-sustaining elixir can produce in the nearly dead.

'Tell me of your sacred dream,' she demanded immediately.

David struggled with the shadows which clung to the edges of his consciousness. 'At the very last, I saw an owl which lifted me to the sun,' he said, in a parched, cracked voice full of wonder. 'It clutched me here.' His crossed arms touched his shoulders.

The old woman nodded. 'Hinhankaga,' she said softly. 'The owl. The helpers who were of the owl-beings, miwa'tani, had great power,' she explained. 'The headdress of owl feathers was permitted to be worn only by a powerful and important order, which originated with our cousins, the Teton Sioux, in very ancient times.' She allowed David to lick the moisture from the sweating bladder, before taking a sip.

'The purpose of this society was to encourage friendship among the people, but in particular, to serve as example, especially in deeds of valour. Only one such member of the society remains in our village.'

'Who is that?'

'The man of our lodge known as Taopi, Wounded Man. His true name is Bull Elk, He-Haka.'

'How did he receive those terrible wounds?' asked David, hungry for information about the people he had lived with, but been so distant from.

'When he was a young warrior, Taopi was severely wounded, as you have seen. These wounds also caused his limp. Many winters ago, our village was attacked by the Ojibwa, who had come to steal horses.

'In the defence of the village, whose elders and women and children were fleeing, Taopi took a position well in advance of the main body of defenders. He was wearing his battle-sash, something which is rarely seen now, and he fastened it to a stake in the ground, much as you have placed there,' she nodded in the direction of the protruding stick, with the skull still hanging from it. 'This sash is about the measure of four paces.

'This signifies that the warrior has chosen to remain at his station of battle until victory or death. It takes enormous courage.' She sighed. 'The enemy set upon him fiercely, and struck him many times until he fell. The time thus gained by the courage of Taopi, allowed our warriors to gather in strength, and fall upon our foe, driving them off. It is a measure of his power, and the power of his spirit helper, Hinhankaga, that he survived his wounds. After this, he was known as Taopi, and he is honoured among us. All these things are true.' She paused to examine his wounds, suddenly yanking the bone skewer from David's chest.

David winced, but did not cry out. It was clear an example was expected of him, and he did not want to disappoint Wakandayamani. She applied a poultice of cat tail down, chewed hoproot and tallow to the wounds, and bound them with a flap of hide and the thong which had served as David's tether.

She drummed her fingers thoughtfully against his chest, as he lay in the grass. She spoke again. 'You have shown yourself worthy. You have defeated your bonds; yet, the remaining one stayed fixed over your heart, and was not torn out by the force of your will. The binding itself failed.'

'What is the meaning of this?' David asked.

She leaned closer to him, looking at him intently, as if she would see into his soul. 'You are of mixed blood; you are of the white people, and our distant cousins, the Assiniboine, who have become our enemy. It may be that you will always be heavily influenced by the people whose blood flows more forcefully in you.' She narrowed her eyes. 'We must consider this further, but at another time. We must return to the village, and a song must be sung about your hamdepi.'

ii

David's integration as citizen into the small community was not sudden, or even, to David's eye, perceptible. After a day of convalescence, he was summoned by Wakandayamani to his old chores; Mahpiyatwin paid no more attention to him than before. He was surprised, then bitter, then disappointed about this unexpected continuance of events, though he was not entirely sure about how things were to have changed. He waited for people to start treating him differently, but nothing happened. He remained the nameless slave, and he continued with his menial tasks.

David struggled with the strain of keeping his emotions under control. There is nothing like dashed hope to weaken the resolve. Rage, jealousy, frustration and envy were the dark emotions, the expression of which was frowned upon by the Sioux, and sure to draw the sarcasms of the heyoka. David began to think actively of escape, though how this could be accomplished he did not know. It still had not occurred to him that the lesson of his ordeal was that the active will to accomplish preceded the means, and that merely wanting something rarely achieved results; waiting for the means of doing something meant a long wait indeed.

One day in the late fall, when the village re-established itself in the shelter of the headwaters of the Mouse River valley, David was returning to camp, carrying fuel. He was approached at the edge of the camp by the heyoka, walking backwards.

'It seems you are still proving your courage by carrying and fetching?' Though people had started to address him directly, David had missed the significance of this, as he did now. He bristled with anger; his face worked and reddened. This was not lost on the heyoka, who continued to bait him.

'Do you not hear the old woman sound the war whistle? Quickly. You may yet get scraps from the evening meal.' The sarcasm was heavy, biting. Yet had David looked closely, he would have seen that there was no laughter in the heyoka's eyes, nor his usual mocking smile. His barbs were nothing more than what they appeared: a provocation. David shook with anger, which made him oblivious to everything save his own vanity.

'It is said that your sacred dream was of the owl. Yet your patience is not of the miwa'tani; it is more like the ground squirrel the owl seeks at night. How is it such a mighty totem would visit one so unworthy?' He laughed mirthlessly.

David lost his temper. Lifting his bundle of dried poplar boughs, he dashed it to the ground. 'Why does my torment continue? Was my ritual not enough to satisfy you, or must I endure more?' The spit flew from his mouth as he shouted his frustration.

The heyoka shook his head and backed away, embarrassed by the outburst. 'Clearly, you are a worthy one,' he said. 'How could I have made such a mistake?'

David lost any self-control. He smashed the firewood against the ground. Then leaping upon the crumbled branches, he danced and smashed and flailed, reducing the pile to a heap of shattered twigs. Exhausted by his tantrum, he fell on all fours and groaned, his head hanging low. The laughter of the heyoka faded as he walked away in disgust.

The rage passed in moments, like a summer storm. He lifted his head. He flushed brilliantly to see Wakandayamani squatting not more than two paces from him. She had a querulous, disappointed look. He looked down again.

'So my dream quest did not help me.'

She waited several moments before answering.

'You who are of two worlds should have the power to see and understand the magic in both. Yet you seem to see nothing, and understand nothing.' She paused, as if drawing upon reserves of patience to keep her voice even.

'Everything given has with it an obligation, 'a price' as the traders say.' She used the English word, probably the first word to be comprehended by Indian peoples, and certainly the most repeated when dealing with the whites.

'If you are not worthy, you will lose what you have been given. This could happen at any time, to anyone. As each gift makes one glad, so does it increase one's burden.'

David was not surprised by any of this, for it was consistent with the teachings of his mother's people. But what was the point the old woman was trying to make? David felt stupid and irrelevant, for he still could not grasp what was expected of him.

'As your sacred dream has revealed to you,' she continued, 'the power within you and the mystical helper who stands guard will always be with you, if you are worthy. But you must constantly demonstrate that you are worthy. In your case, you have skulked around the village like a starving coyote looking for scraps. Such behaviour can only result in the loss of power, of magic, and even of life.' These last words were said in a near whisper.

A sudden zephyr rattled the dead grass and bits of twigs which were the remains of David's foolishness. He felt at his lowest ebb since his capture. He gathered himself into a position of dignity, sitting cross-legged, with his arms folded. He breathed deeply.

Keeping his eyes averted, he addressed Wakandayamani. 'Teach me, old woman,' he said in a firm voice, 'for I must begin again.'

When she uttered her next words, it was in a voice significantly changed. The tone was almost deferential, prayer-like. It seemed that she was not speaking just to him, but through him, to his inner soul.

'The first step is to hear—even for a child—it is to hear; more, to want to hear, to open the self to all that is known, and yet unknown. This means to pay close attention at every present moment of your life. It is only in such a state that you can find revelations from the spirit world, or that your encounter with the earth can be consummated. We cannot act in the past, which is accessible only in our memories; nor can we act in the unborn future. Each moment, then, becomes laden with purpose. Sometimes the purpose is clear to you, as in the teachings of the elders, who tell us how to live, and set the example. And sometimes the purpose is revealed to you, in a sign, a dream, or some event.

'If you are vigilant, if you are always open to hear, to see, to receive, you will not miss the unfolding of new and greater possibilities.' She closed her eyes, pursed her lips and nodded intently. She reached out and made a fist, then smote her chest gently.

'You must see with your heart, that each moment of the present is precious, and so you must be open to learn, to commit to the moment. If you are closed—as you have been,' she chided gently, 'you will not flourish; you will not be worthy of your spirit helper who will guide you and protect you in matters beyond your understanding. All these things are true.'

She paused in her speech, which was delivered slowly, but with strength. The afternoon breeze had turned much cooler, as the sun drifted to the eastern horizon. The taste of the first snow was already in the air. Neither person moved.

David was skeptical. 'How can this be?' he asked. 'Surely the striking of the lance is more important than the carrying of it, or the lance which misses its target? What purpose or value is there in failure?'

Her flinty gaze, off somewhere in the distance, was as patient as stone. David thought he saw a smile, but perhaps it was the wind rippling the thin strands of white hair over her grizzled face. At length, she spoke again. ·

'The seizing of the shaft, the hunt, the approach, the cast of the lance—all these moments are interrelated by purpose. Failure is mostly the want of commitment to purpose, which translates to lack of effort at some or all the steps of the endeavour. But the missed target can teach much about the next attempt—if only you consider it, and learn from it, and do not seek to put the blame elsewhere than here—' and again she touched her fist to her heart.

'Many things happen, to all appearances, by chance. Things over which we have no control, it might seem. A sudden snowstorm, a great fire in the dry-grass month, a fall in the dark,' and she gestured ruefully at her broken, crooked teeth. 'But are these things truly chance, or is there not a great design in which we can play more than just a passive role?'

David took all this in, and he recognized some of the common themes in the teachings of Reverend Cowley. His mind soared to the words of Ecclesiastes, that cynical old scribe who spoke through the flourishes of the Reverend Father in such plain language, yet in paradoxes. 'When I applied mine heart to know wisdom, and to see the business that is done upon the earth—then I beheld all the work of God.'

Now here sat this powerful, wise woman, unlocking the same secrets to understanding for him. Unlike his talks with his grandfather, however, his present needs made understanding more urgent. Conditions can motivate, focus and concentrate the mind, he decided. So why could not one do this without the press of exigent circumstances?

Was all understanding common to all people? If this was so, then what sparked the cruelties and bitterness that existed not only between peoples, but between people? He had never understood the historic enmity which existed between his captors and the Red River Métis. It was taken for granted, palpable and substantive. It was taught and nurtured on both sides. It was to be acted upon, preserved, even revered. It was used in both communities to scare children into submission; it perpetuated the hatred that prepared young men for war. Hatred, David decided, had no independent life of its own, but required the fuel of man's stupidity to keep its spark bright.

He thought to ask Wakandayamani why this was so, but her attitude had shifted ever so slightly. This time she looked directly at him. 'I can see you are thinking about the things that I have said, and this is good. You will have more questions, but as you begin to see with your heart, as I think you have begun to do, and seek the purpose in every moment, the answers will flow naturally and as surely as the geese follow their spirit guides in the spring and fall.' She was looking at a distant formation of late-starting geese as she spoke.

David nodded his head slowly as he watched the birds, their grating cries barely audible. He was beginning to comprehend why the world was called Grandmother Earth, for the Dakota held that the earth is female, from which all life springs, and hence all secrets of life's wonder. Yet the key to those secrets could be found by either men or women, and the sex of a shaman related only to duties, not power. If this were true, David thought, then I too can have this power.

When he turned from the distant, wobbling lines of geese, elated, to share his insights with Wakandayamani, she was gone.

iii

Taopi was a war prophet, in addition to being the only member of the Owl Society. Part of the mystery of this high office was the use of special tongues in which the gods were asked for guidance and protection in matters of war. Each village had such an official, whose salient characteristic was extraordinary courage. A badge of such a man, though it was by no means confined to that office, was the war sash, which Taopi had worn with great honour in the defence of his people. When mounted on horseback, the sash reached to the ground in a splendid drapery of the finest quill and beadwork. The tales of Taopi's courage served as example to all young men, and gave him a stature not exceeded by anyone. The horrible defacing scars along his rib cage, and his withered right leg were reminders of the pain and suffering he had endured, and continued to endure, in the protection and glory of his village.

Though he did not show it, Taopi had considerable pain associated with his wounds. Much of his energy was devoted to maintaining control over the small agonies which wracked his ruined body. He had come to expect it at its worst when winter approached and ebbed; and daily, several hours after eating when the stress of his condition exacerbated his ulcerated stomach. At night he gulped great mouthfuls of air as he lay sweating in his bed robes. Arising before daybreak, he would experience a severe bloated feeling, which felt like pressure on his chest. He found that his only relief was the passing of gas, and this he did in formidable volume.

With the scrupulous manners by which he was raised, and now living as he was in a lodge of many people, he would stroll out of sight of the encampment, where he would fart loudly and generously, lifting this leg and that to maximize his evacuation, and perforce his relief. The children of the village had often spied upon him, and afterward would mimic his strutting and bending and crouching, and send forth loud, rude noises from pursed lips. They were always careful not to do this near the adults, for disrespect was met with severe disapproval. Among themselves, they called this 'the-dance-of-the-bull-elk-who-farts-at-dawn'.

Like the others, Taopi took no notice of David in the early stages of his captivity. But he was shrewd, and little escaped his attention. He noticed the way David would steal glances at Mahpiyayowin. But he said nothing, for the boy worked hard and was discreet. Because Otakle was often away from the lodge in search of game, Taopi was the nominal head of household. The reality was that Wakandayamani did most of what was required to keep the lodge together. So Taopi was free to pursue his beloved craft of weapon-making, though almost all the men now used rifles in the hunt and on the battlefield. The making of weapons was prohibited now by the white men, who were increasingly confining dark-skinned to reservations of land where game was scarce.

When Wakinyanwaste, Otakle's brother announced that he and Snana, and their daughter, Mahpiyatowin, would be returning to their ancestral home along the Minnesota River, Taopi was the one who voiced the strongest objections. Wakinyanwaste argued that the buffalo were getting more scarce each year, and virtually all the warriors were occupied with the getting of meat. There was almost no surplus with which to trade for essential goods. On the other hand, the American government was paying Indians annuities in gold, and allotments of goods guaranteed in the treaties. There was a new agency for the Sisseton and Wahpeton tribes, near the mouth of the Yellow Medicine River. Almost four thousand of their cousins were now resettled there.

Otakle spat. 'Treaties! You have heard of the abuses of the agents at the Redwood Agency: the shortages of proper food, our people thin and hungry. You know of the intention of the whites to make us turn from our ways, to live by digging in the earth and planting corn. Is this the way you will live? Will you forget your own people?'

There was to be no answer to these compelling questions, for they were clearly troubling. Taopi was incensed, and while he was normally taciturn by nature, he could not help but criticize the plan.

'Listen to your brother. Life here is hard, but life on the reservation will be harder still. And do not think that you will be left alone. Remember what our brother, Chief Little Crow has said many times over. "We are only little herds of buffalo left scattered; the great herds that once covered the prairies are no more. See! The white men are like the locusts when they fly so thick that the whole sky is a snow-storm!" '

Wakinwaste listened to all counsel with patience and forebearance, summing up thus: 'I know the wisdom of the words of Little Crow. But do you not see the import of his message? It is that the whites have come in greater numbers than even the buffalo we knew. They cannot be resisted. It is time for me to make a new life for my family while the opportunity is still there for us. We have decided: we shall leave once the winter snows have melted, at the end of the eye-sickness moon, in March.'

David listened but did not participate in this debate. He was horrified that Mahpiyatowin would be leaving, and decided that he should press the case with her for remaining in the camp. That would be difficult enough, for young women never went anywhere without a chaperone, and already several young men in the village were trying to catch her attention. Still, David lived in the same lodge and this gave him an advantage. As well, since his ordeal, and the singing of the song by Wakandayamani of his encounter with the miwa'tani, it had become possible to speak directly to her, though he found it difficult to overcome the old patterns of deference and subordination. Added to this, his infatuation made him stumble over words and phrase things imperfectly, when she was around.

At last, however, they found themselves alone. She was making a courting shawl, which was to be worn by a couple when they were sitting, discussing intimate matters. This was traditionally made by an older sister, but in this case, there was no such relative for the girl who was being wooed, and Mahpiyatowin had taken on the task. She sat at the entrance to the lodge, where the light was best. David had come to retrieve the sharpening-stone, for it was now permitted that he wear a knife; formerly, he had been allowed only to carry one in his hand. She did not look up, but kept to her work.

As he rummaged about, taking more time than was necessary, anxious about how he might begin, she spoke suddenly, 'Is it your intention to court me?'

These words tumbled upon David's senses with the impact of a felled tree. He was dumbfounded. Absently, he picked up a trade axe.

'Will you strike me then?' she said wryly, as she looked at the hatchet in his hand. He followed her gaze, startled, and dropped the axe, blushing furiously. 'You take me by surprise; words fail me.'

Marriage among the Sioux was not arranged, for it was a matter of mutual choice, the woman having as much say in the matter as the man. Pleasing the family was of concern to both parties, however. Mahpiyatowin knew she was attractive to the young men of the village, and flirted with those who sought her attention. She saw here that she had the upper hand.

'You are surprised! You who are looking at me all the time! You who have seen me at my bath! Creeping upon your stomach, like the red fox waits for mice!'

This last utterance finished David, for he knew not what to say.

'It was an accident,' he stammered.

'Faugh!' she scoffed. 'Accident! Would you lie to me now as well? Is this any way for a courtship to begin?'

The woman was infuriating, David thought. But she had caught him in all his shameful little posturings, and David was contrite. He decided to address his feelings, as the old woman had counselled. 'I am ashamed of what I have done. It has not been honourable.' He paused, to collect his thoughts, for the moment was not to be wasted.

'Yes, I do wish to court you, but I have been troubled by the fact that I have no means to make a gift to your parents. Besides which, I think that they will not approve of me. I think that their minds are made up to return to the agencies.' The words tumbled out in a rush, giving away his fears.

'The problem of the gift is yours to solve,' she said simply. 'The question of their approval is silly to worry over, before you have asked it;

but I shall probably return with them if I am not married by then. Perhaps there will be a good selection of young men.'

'I wish you would not tease me in this way.'

'What, are you so frail that your heart would break?' David was silent. After a moment, she spoke again, 'But do you not long to return to the lands of your people?'

This question stirred thoughts which David had long suppressed. The truth of it was that, though he missed his family, he missed not much else. Not even the work he did on the boats. As for his people, well, who were his people? He had struggled with that question long before he had been taken by the Sioux. He said slowly,

'I have no answer to these questions, yet. I believe that I shall return to my family in the north, but I do not think that this will be soon.'

Their talk was interrupted by the return of Taopi and Wakandayamani, and so David scrambled out of the lodge, his heart bursting with the prospect of new promise.

Taopi had become increasingly obsessed with making full the circle of his life. He wished for a new robe of elkskin to be made, but from an animal which he alone had taken. This was to be his burial robe, and the mask which would cover his face in death would be of the same hide; this the thick, woolly crown below the horns. All his sons and grandsons were either dead or had retired to reservations. He no longer considered those who had opted for the life of the corn planters his people. So he set out his instructions to Otakle.

Otakle was patient with him, but he was unsure that the old man, with his crippling disability, could make the long journey to the hills where the elk wintered. Nonetheless, he paid careful attention to the old man's directions.

He was to be painted yellow, and to be holding in each hand new hoops wound with wild bergamot, an herb sought by the elk and much fancied by young men for its fragrance. He would be laid out in his new winter robe, with his false face in place. So prepared, he would be ready to enter the wanagitacanku, the galaxy known to the whites as the Milky Way.

The old man's wishes, unbeknown to him, put a great deal of pressure upon the family. One morning, after he had gone for his customary walk in the fresh snow, Otakle turned to Wakandayamani in the false light of dawn and expressed his anxiety, 'He cannot go on this hunt alone; I think he is expecting me to go with him, though he has not said as much.'

Wakandayamani reflected upon this. 'He cannot go alone; this is true. And there is so little food that all the men are required for the hunt. You are the war chief. You cannot be away for so long.'

No one said anything for a time. The air was cool in the lodge, and some distance off a dog barked. The silence seemed oppressive. Wakinyanwaste stirred, and shifted up on one elbow. 'I should go with him. Perhaps the hunt will succeed quickly, and we will bring home much meat.'

There was further discussion about this. Everyone knew, but did not express the fact that such an exhausting journey would likely kill the old man, and the weight of his body would preclude the return of any meat from the hunt, even should the chase be otherwise successful. And the body must be returned for proper preparation, for Taopi was an important man. David listened to the debate without contribution, as always. The importance of burial rituals was clear: they had the power to comfort, to give order where none seemed to be in the condition of things. While Taopi was the bravest man in the village, and had demonstrated this on occasions past number, he was nevertheless fearful that death might summon him before he was ready. In all this, David saw an opportunity to bring honour to himself and the lodge and, significantly, to the parents of Mahpiyatowin. He spoke up, choosing his words carefully,

'It is I who must accompany the old man, for it is I who can be spared from the camp.' Small exclamations of surprise, followed by approval, met this statement.

David went on, 'I am not skilled in the ways of the elk hunt, but the old man is. I am strong, and can manage the weight of the gear for two men, for I have no weapon to carry. I shall have the influence of the miwa'tani to assist me. We cannot fail.'

All present sounded their acclaim. Dances would be held to assure good results. When Taopi returned and was advised of the news, the relief and gratitude showed on his craggy face. 'It is good,' he said, urgently aware that this hunt would be his last. David noticed that Mahpiyatowin was looking at him warmly. She nodded slightly, before looking away. David's chest swelled with pride and he felt worthy and esteemed.

Through the next two days, preparations were made for the journey. Taopi's lance was sharpened, his skinning and butchering implements whetted, and his rifle, an old Spencer-Henry single-shot buffalo gun, of massive .50 calibre, was cleaned, oiled and plugged with rags to keep the snow from entering. Taopi fretted about the weather, for in the drying-rice moon, Wi-wazupi, heavy snows could fall at any time, which could delay their journey or drive the elk further away.

As it developed, a blizzard struck at the end of the second day, and raged for the following three days before it blew itself out. The people were confined to their lodges, leaving only to cleanse themselves, and to move the mounds of snow from the entranceways so as to keep them clear and ensure access to fuel. The wind howling around the cozy tipi, rattling the smoke flaps and drumming against the taut hides stretched over the upper, soot-blackened dwelling, would normally have induced sleep, a smoke, or lazy story-telling. But Taopi could not relax. Now that plans were underway, he was eager to be off. He smoked and offered up prayers for the appeasement of Taku-shkan-shkan, who lived in the North Wind.

Taopi had prepared long narrow snowshoes, with the sharply upturned points decorated with tufts of red wool and short, downy feathers for the journey. These were made from split birch frames and thwarts, with braided green rawhide strips woven into them; they were then set to dry over a slow fire. Only in this way could the journey be made to the elk pens in the Moose Mountains, well north of the Missouri River. But the strength required to move on snowshoes was much greater than on foot, and Taopi's worry showed plainly on his face. He sought the counsel of other elders, and it was determined that he would need the strongest medicine possible.

Wakandayamani was summoned to prepare the medicine hoop of the elk-dreamer, which the hunter would carry with him. Such a hoop was described in songs as a rainbow, for this was one of those ephemera which linked sky and earth, two of the four sacred elements. The hoop, in the shape of a rainbow, was made of elk hide, finished with the fur left on, intertwined with sacred herbs and trade buttons. Hung from one quadrant was a quilled loop and breath-feather, which would be wound in the hair when the quarry or its fresh track was sighted.

David had a mixture of feelings about the forthcoming hunt. For one thing, the weather had not settled, and it was notoriously unstable at this time of year. For another, he had serious doubts about the old man's stamina. If he were to die, David had some anxiety about finding his way back to the village. He had never been more than a day's march from it, no matter where it became established. But the most troublesome thoughts were those which crept into his head, unbidden, like vandals. He knew the Moose Mountains were about a five or six days walk from Brandon House. There would be plenty of opportunity to slip away from the old man, and all that was required was to head east, find the Mouse River, and then simply follow it to the Assiniboine River. In a week at most, he would be among the people of his mother.

But he was not so certain now that he wanted to return. His growing affection for the people of his lodge, and his powerful attraction to the beautiful Mahpiyatowin, tugged insistently at his will. Each night competing thoughts roiled his brain, and he could come to no clear conclusion. He decided that he would see the hunt through, and then make a decision according to what signs were available to him. He knew that this suggested a want of commitment, but the truth was that he was uncertain where his obligations lay; now above else, he wanted this hunt to succeed.

He had not long to wait. The hunt was to commence when the weather cleared; it did so with a sharp plunge in the temperature that frosted eyelashes and hung tiny icicles in the nostrils. David began to worry afresh that they were on a fool's errand. His imagination presented him with the worst possibility, upsetting his stomach, and clouding his vision. He was plagued with the gnawing doubts of anticipated failure, which promised visits from its ugly relatives, rejection and scorn.

Once the two men were off, however, things seemed better, for the constant movement pushed thought into a far corner. Taopi was exhilarated, and he loped along with a funny, swinging gait, several paces ahead. He was carrying only his lance and the medicine hoop. David hauled the rifle, shot, sleeping robes, foodstuffs, knives and other bits required for an expedition like this.

As the day passed, the weather moderated, and the wind swung around to the south. In the late afternoon, the temperature actually climbed above freezing, and the snow became sticky and wet. David perspired heavily under his load, and he was concerned about the weather turning cold before he had a chance to dry out his inner garments. That night, they found shelter in a ravine, scooped out the snow like a grave and slept like the dead.

The weather continued mild, which made travel tedious, especially for David who hauled all the supplies. On the third night, Taopi called a halt early, having noticed David's labouring in the wet snow. Lingering over a small fire of dead willow branches, Taopi spoke to David for the first time, beyond simple commands and acknowledgements. This was an indication that David was more than a slave, more than a faithful dog brought along to pull the short sled.

'I am pleased with our pace. We shall be at the base of the hills by the close of day, two days hence.'

David nodded. He was exhausted, and tore at the dried meat like a wolf. Before them, the aurora borealis glided across the northern sky. They seemed to have a hypnotic effect on Taopi, as indeed they had had for almost sixty winters. He moved slightly, so that more of his haunches were protected by the robe, and hunkered down, his eyes sparkling in the reflected display. David paused in his eating, and looked at his companion. His face had the leanness of a hawk; the wrinkles were deep set shadows in the moonlight. His eyes had the cold glint of an enemy's knife. This was a true warrior; a defender of the people, a man whose life was expendable in their service.

Perhaps he felt David's stare. 'Many lifetimes from ours, all people will be like you,' he said.

David was startled. 'What?' he said in English, as his father would have said the word.

Taopi appeared to choose his words carefully. 'The changes which have befallen our people—the sickness, the vanishing buffalo, the reservations, even the machines such as this,' and he gestured with a tinge of scorn toward the deerskin-wrapped rifle—'all portend greater changes which will mean the elimination of all separate people. There will only be one colour for all people: they will be the colour of scorched wood, like you.' He rocked almost imperceptibly, still staring off toward the flickering boreal display. After a while, he continued:

'The grandfather of all buffalo lives under the winter fire sky,' he gestured with his head to the Northern Lights, 'where the land meets the heavens. Every year, He sheds a little more hair, and with each of His hairs, one of His sons or daughters dies. When the last hair has been shed, our life will end, for there will be no more buffalo.

'The white people with their new gods, and their possessive contempt for the land and the things it sustains, will hasten the shedding. But we will go among them, and the loss of their whiteness shall be their salvation.

'It may be that I was too critical of Wakanyanwaste and Snana, for their return to meet the demands of the whites seems inevitable.' And raising his buttock, he broke wind mightily. The stench hung in the cool air like a fog, and David wished that Taopi felt constrained by the same courtesy that governed his flatulence at home.

Taopi seemed to be making a statement, and was not looking for any reply from David. He knew not what to respond, in any event, for he did not believe Taopi's view of the future. He had experienced for himself the arrogance of the white race toward Indians and 'breeds'. There could be no more effective barrier between intermarriage than that. Only the exceptional 'breed' was accepted by white society, as far as he could see.

The other irony in this was that non-whites, such as Taopi himself, were slow to trust him, if ever. Even now, David felt more like his personal servant than his equal. The Métis thought of themselves as a nation apart, and they were hated by the Sioux, and despised by the English for their brashness, their independence, and their 'savagery'. Looking at the old man, he did not feel much kinship with him. But this might be, he conceded silently, his own feelings of inferiority and non-belonging. Both men sat consumed with their own thoughts, until the fire dwindled, and each turned without further word to his sleeping robes.

By the end of the following day, they had come to the area from which they would stage the hunt. The terrain had given way to elevated ridges and terraces, thickly covered with poplar, birch, willow and fir. In the shelter of an enormous deadfall, they built a hunting lodge.

The lodge was of poplar-pole construction, thatched over with spruce bows, and lined with the same material. Snow was banked up the sides with the snowshoes serving as shovels, and a small fire was set in a pit scooped at the centre. That evening, the men were warm and truly comfortable, and both removed their footwear.

When the dawn cast its red light which shed neither heat nor shadow across their lodge, the air had grown very cold again. This formed a thin, hard crust on top of the snow, and it was possible to move quickly without snowshoes. When the occasional misstep pierced the crusting, the men's bodies were plunged to the hips, and the only means by which escape was effected, was by rolling on their sides, away from the hole. So they wore their snowshoes slung over one shoulder, and were careful not to come down on their heels. The best pace was obtained by a sort of sliding step. As the sun came over the treetops the dazzling white carpet glistened and shone; the hunters' breath hung in the air, frosting throat mufflers and dusting over eyelashes and eyebrows.

Not more than an hour from the lodge, they came across the spoor of a large elk. The thin skin on top of the snow could not sustain the eight hundred pounds of animal, and the trail was a broken swath in the snow, easy for even a child to follow.

'He-haka!' Bull elk! exclaimed Taopi. Excitedly, he set off at a brisk pace, beside the track. David followed several dozen paces behind, carrying the heavy rifle, shot, and their rations for the day. The old man carried only his lance. They travelled all morning at a brisk pace; as the sun reached its highest point, David could see, beyond Taopi, the thrashing, lunging form of a bull elk. It was ploughing through snow up to its shoulders. A heavy coat of frost covered its shoulders, for the work of defeating the drifts in its way was making it blow powerfully; twin jets of steaming vapour pumped from its nostrils. When the beast caught wind of the hunters, it began to plunge fearfully, eyes rolling.

Up ahead of David, Taopi threw up his arms exultingly. 'He-haka!', he cried again. Holding out his arms, he began a small dance, singing a song of thanks, as his blanket slipped to the snow behind him. With his lance in one hand, and the medicine hoop in the other, seemingly oblivious to the cold, he began to slide forward for the kill.

David stood well back, for he knew that this was a sacred time. In the cold air, some of the words of the song Taopi was crooning drifted back. David did not understand their import, but he had heard it sung by the old man before. The elk was closely associated with love and sexual passion; in dances, Taopi was frequently paid to invoke the strength of he-haka by singing in the place of the lover.

> *Whoever considers themselves beautiful*
> *after seeing me*
> *has no heart*

It was a song of triumph, of passion and power. As he glided toward the winded elk, whose progress slowed with each passing moment, David thought that the old man looked magnificent. His ruined side was hidden from view. His quilled hoop was now tucked into his hair, with the white eagle breath-feather trailing down over one ear. He was naked to the waist, wearing only breech clout and leggins. There was no trace of a limp as Taopi moved forward with the trot of a startled elk. He was becoming the embodiment of the creature whose society he had served for more than forty winters. He had become Taku-shkan-shkan, the thing that moves, the essence of all magic and power. Taopi was moving forward to begin the closing of the circle of his life.

Nearing the stricken animal, Taopi raised his lance, calling out in terms David now could not make out for the distance. Lifting his lance to the fullest extension of his arm, his other arm poised for balance, he thrust in a clean, sweeping motion, casting the weapon free. The elk lunged, and the lance struck below the ribs, missing the vitals. Two twisting leaps in the snow brought the beast to a shivering halt, rolling wildly its eyes. The exaggerated movements shook the lance free, but the blow must have been causing considerable pain and fright to the animal, for it suddenly let go a steaming mess of droppings.

Taopi readied himself again, and approached more closely. Bringing his arm well back, he sank the lance deep into the lungs. Blood streamed in foaming crimson bubbles from its nostrils. Taopi pulled sharply on the lance to dislodge it. As he did so, his heel collapsed the crust of snow, pitching him sideways toward the dying beast. The bull reared up, thrashing its head in a death spasm. A prong of its great rack caught Taopi's belly, tearing it like rotted fabric. The old man's blood spilled onto the snow already shaded by the gore from his quarry. A thin blue intestine was drawn out of the gaping hole in his abdomen, for the horn had entered at his waistband, and torn up to his sternum. There was a final, sibilant whistling which could have come from either man or animal.

David could not believe his eyes. A kill so simple had suddenly gone terribly wrong. He felt some responsibility for this miserable turn of events, as he dashed to the side of the fallen hunter. He stumbled several times in the deep snow, floundering and calling to the motionless man. By the time he reached Taopi, his eyes were dull, and he was muttering incoherently. Turning in an infinitely small movement to face David, he seemed to be saying something. David inclined his ear to the old man's spittle-flecked lips.

Whoever considers themselves beautiful
after seeing me
has no heart

iv

On 19 August 1854, a visiting Dakota Sioux from Otakle's village killed a settler's cow on the Overland Trail south of the Missouri River, in the territory of the Lakota. In retaliation, federal troops from the United States Cavalry, commanded by Lieutenant John Gratton marched to the nearby Brulé village, and subjected the unsuspecting encampment to a withering barrage of cannon-fire. Many of the sleeping occupants were killed, but the warriors of the village mounted a fierce counter-attack; all thirty soldiers, including their foolish leader, were slain, scalped and, in some cases, frightfully mutilated.

Other violent confrontations followed, such as the Blue Water Creek massacre under General Harney, who was later to be made military governor of the newly created 'Sioux District'. These had a widespread and profound impact on the relations between the Indians and the streams of settlers pushing into their traditional hunting grounds. Stories of the 'atrocities' inflicted by the savages of the western plains imbedded themselves deeply in the white man's consciousness, and the way was cleared for final and, in some cases, bloody confrontation.

After Taopi had been killed, David skinned the elk, folded the hide fur side in around the corpse of the old man, and packed in some choice cuts of elk meat. Having skinned away that portion of the forehead the old man had required for a mask, he returned to the hunting lodge, with the hide frozen stiff as a plank. The following day, he started off for the village again, drawing his primitive sarcophagus behind him. There had been no thought of doing otherwise, for he had determined that his fortunes now lay with the Dakota people. Upon his return, he discovered that his act was received with the highest regard, for esteem for the dead was the greatest measure of self-respect.

But he was stunned to learn that Wakinyanwaste had departed for the Yellow Medicine, with his wife and Mahpiyatowin. It appeared that he was determined to find a new life in the ways of the white men, but he refused to accept the idea that his family should marry into their race. He had noticed the burgeoning interest of his daughter in David. Fearful that a successful hunt would lead to a proposal of marriage, and knowing his headstrong daughter was free to elope with this impoverished mixed-blood, he elected to move in David's absence. It would be a long trip, full of hardship, but the decision had been made, and the matter of timing, he explained to his family, was for him alone to decide. In truth, there were few who did not understand his true motives. This together with his intention to resettle on a reserve, diminished Wakinyanwaste's honour in the village, and no feast or dances were held in his honour, as was customary before a journey of significance.

David was devastated, and considered going after them, but he was exhausted after his long trip. He was worried as well about the tales of mounting trouble between whites and Indians. Word was that settlers would as soon shoot an Indian as hail one, and tension was high across the frontier.

Though the Dakota would not explode into open warfare with the whites until 1862, resentment and animosity were smouldering like the dung-fed campfires around which such sentiments were discussed. In each council, in every lodge, the talk was of the dwindling herds, the insatiable appetites of the whites, the wretchedness of those who had accepted the white religion, the unworthy life of a farmer, and most contemptible of all, those who had turned their backs on the beliefs of the people, the Dakota. These were the lost ones who dressed and acted according to the will of the agents and missionaries. Pretending to be white people, when the whites would have none of them in their own lodges; it was past any man's understanding!

Because of the constant pressure from new settlers, the harrying of the military, and the depredations of hide hunters whose harvesting was now on in earnest, these problems became exacerbated. The eastern Dakota eventually gave up their claims to free movement across their lands in the Minnesota territories, by the Treaty of Traverse de Sioux and the Treaty of Mendota, both of which were signed in 1851. Though these treaties were, in the minds of the Indians at least, to have erased old debts with the traders who had extended credit, sometimes on usurious terms, the traders pressed their accounts, laying claim to the purchase funds and annuities. The Indians continued to be squeezed between the thinning herds and diminished credit, even though many of those who had received the credit originally were now dead, or had fled for the plains.

David became more and more aware of these troubling affairs, as visitors came and went with fresh grievances or tales of wrongs unavenged. But soon the village had other things to concern itself with, for the supply of food had virtually run out; the spring of 1858 was yet a full moon distant.

At the end of the raccoon moon, a council was held of all the men in the village. There were twenty-two, including David. After offerings of the smoke of the sweet grass, Otakle stood up to address the assembly. He looked worn. Great dark circles cupped his eyes, and his clothing was threadbare, unbecoming a chief. Holding himself stiffly erect, for there is more in leadership than finery, he waited for the murmuring to cease.

'Friends, I need not tell you that the game has vanished. Our bellies are taut with hunger, and our children are dying. Even the white hare has disappeared, and we have nearly killed off all our dogs. Soon we will have to eat our horses, for no hunt has been successful since the return of Pahinshasha-wacekiye with the body of Taopi.

'There has been talk among some of you, that it would be better to follow the example of Wakinyanwaste, my brother, who has decided to live on the terms dictated by the whites.' There was a noticeable stir among the men, for the choice still excited controversy. 'Still others lie in their lodges, and wait for the cry of the warm-weather-returns-bird, for the buffalo cannot then be far off.

'For those who would leave for the agencies, the time is now. For those who would stay, food is needed, and here is my proposal: four pairs of hunters shall go in the sacred directions, for no more than they can travel in ten nights,' and he held up the fingers of both hands to emphasize the point. 'Then each pair moving so that the sun stays to their right, they will make a sweep back to the village in search of game. In this way, the most ground may be covered. Each pair of men will take a single horse. This will leave us sixteen ponies in camp, so that we may survive, and some, if they choose, may leave.'

There was some debate, but not the spirited kind of discourse that David had seen in the past. Hunts had been ongoing in all directions for more than two months now, and it seemed as if the earth had swallowed up all living things, except the raven, who croaked mournfully in the distance. In a short discusssion, the plan was assented to, and several men stood up for the honour of serving the village, David among them.

He was paired with a grizzled wedge of a man with flinty grey hair, and muscles on his body that looked like bunched and braided wire. His name was Su-pi-hi-ye, (his-guts-came-out), a man who was highly regarded for brave exploits which David thought qualified as reckless.

Su-pi-hi-ye got his name from a fight with a hump-backed bear, one of the last to be seen in the Dakota territories. Armed with lance and knife, he had closed with the animal and slain it, but not before it ripped a gash in his abdomen, just at the outer edge of his pubic hair. His intestines bulged out, but they were pushed back in, and the flesh was sewn tightly together by a woman whose medicine was that of the grizzly bear healer, and whose stitches were small as the track of a mouse in wind-packed snow. The killing of such a bear entitled the warrior to wear a single eagle feather in his hair, for such an adversary was equal to human foe.

When the two men set off, they were headed south. Unlike Taopi, his companion was a garrulous man, eager to learn about the Halfbreeds of Red River, and just as eager to tell of his prowess on the war path, as well as among the buffalo. At one time, he had possessed more than a dozen horses, and had three wives, each in a different lodge, so they would not quarrel over him—not that this happened frequently, for he was able to service all of them in a single night, he confessed, showing thin tracings of appropriate modesty.

David looked down from horseback, and smilingly said to him, 'Do you know what the heyoka would say to such boastings?'

Su-pi-hi-ye looked pained. 'I speak the truth, let no man defy me. Besides, it is the heyoka who has trouble responding when his own divorce is mentioned. Why, his wife put all his possessions out of their lodge, and threw him out on his ear, for he was no longer a husband to her. See how his mockery crumbles when this is mentioned. So why should I not speak the truth. Have I not proven myself? Have I not been marked by the great bear I fought in my youth, and by the many enemies who sought to take my hair back to their lodges?'

And so it went. David thought that they would never see game, for anything living would hear the incessant chatter long before the hunters came in view of it.

The prairie winds had blown most of the snow away, or piled it into drifts it into bluffs and ravines, so that the going was easy enough. But they saw nothing that moved. Su-pi-hi-ye took advantage of his turn to ride by identifying the events which went along with each scar and disfigurement. Pulling aside his breechclout, he showed David the furrowed row which marked the bear attack, and the missing toes which had been cleaved by a Cree axe-blow meant for his neck. Dismounting and running ahead, he insisted upon acting out the battle, looking quite comical as he thrashed about in the snow and frozen dirt.

But for all this, Su-pi-hi-ye was no fool. His eye picked out the smallest movement, even as he spoke of other things. The ghosting of the small white owl looking for mice, or the sly skittering of the white weasel did not escape attention. David came to see that there were two sides to the man, each showing simultaneously. Unabashedly gregarious, he was nevertheless intensely proud. He could play the buffoon but was continually in tune with his surroundings. Even when he slept, he appeared to be listening, and to be alert for altered or discordant rhythms of a world with which he was perfectly and harmoniously interconnected.

On the eighth day of their questing, seeing no game within rifleshot, they reached the rough, tumbling landscape of the Black Hills. Rounding a shaded thicket, Su-pi-hi-ye broke off his lecture on the murderous nature of the Cree, and stood motionless. 'Something large feeds ahead. Horse maybe, or big deer.'

David dropped quietly to the ground, and slipped a hobble-line around the pony's forelegs. Both men readied their weapons and moved quietly toward the scrubby growth, hope sharpening each movement into an elaborate dance step. They both burst out laughing at the same time, for there before them was a common ox. They looked about, but saw no sign of owner or habitation. The ox had discovered a wind-cleared strip of timothy grass, and was not moving for anyone or anything. Su-pi-hi-ye walked up to the animal, and slapped it on the haunches. 'We eat tonight!' he said happily.

David was not so sure. 'This is someone's draft animal,' he said cautiously, though the vision of roasting steaks set his stomach to rumbling.

'It is our draft animal now,' said the other. 'I consider that…'

Before he could finish, Su-pi-hi-ye spun around like a breath feather in a hoop. His body slammed to earth in a shapeless pile, his arms between his legs, with his buttocks sticking oddly in the air. He was dead, for his back was a gory ruin. David was frozen in numbed stupefaction; the crashing boom of a heavy calibre rifle sounded a bare moment later. Glancing sharply in the direction of the sound, David felt a stunning blow to his temple, and staggered, the pain exploding in his brain like a pinch of gunpowder thrown into a flame. Falling blindly, crying out his dismayed shock, he lost consciousness.

He awakened to the sound of a man's deep-throated, mirthless laughter, somewhere nearby. David was lying on his back in the dried, fawn-coloured grass, the space behind his eyes thrumming with each pulse of his blood. His fur skull cap had been knocked off. His hand was up by his neck, and with extreme effort he touched the side of his head. His mind reeled with disbelief, for where his ear should have been was a rag of bloody, torn skin. He moaned, distraught, uncomprehending.

The voice drew near, being addressed to a second. 'Did ya see thet shot? Clean-killed this thievin' injin from five hundred fuckin' yards! My old Poison Slinger! No wonder them fuckin' injins call it "shoot today-kill tomorrow" gun! Heh! Heh! Heh!' The laughter was dry, ugly, and evil as witchcraft. 'Whew, what a stink off the son 'fa bitch!'

The closer voice was higher, sharper, more laden with menace. 'Shadup, ya shit-stained arsehole! Ya didn't get t'other one, by the sound of it. Look, the son 'fa bitch is still drawin' breath!'

A shadow fell across David. Even squinting, David could get no clear view of his assailants. The one further back called out. 'Don't waste no more shot on him; cut the bastard!'

David heard the unmistakeable whisper of a knife being drawn from its oiled leather sheath; a long one, probably the slim-bladed type used in skinning. He tried to cry out, but the only sound which escaped his lips was a gurgle, deep in the back of his parched throat. He waited for the cool caress of the blade, wondering where it would enter, and whether it would hurt. Instead, he heard a low whistle of surprise. 'Jesus H. fuckin' Christ, boy! Ya's done shot a white man! Come an' look at this red hair. I ain't never seen no injin with red hair. An' looky here, ya done shot half his ear off; were ya tryin' fer some fancy shootin'?'

'I figured I'd get m' second shot away, afore he heard the first. If he hadn't a turned his head, he'd be well-vented now.' There was a long pause as both men tried to determine their next step. They both spoke at once, the one with the higher voice insisting his will over the other. 'Well, he's shore dressed like an injin, and his skin's near as dark as one; mebbe he's a breed. He mus' be.'

'Well, if he is, he's dogshit like the rest. We should finish him off good an' proper, an' if you've not the stomach fer it, I'll cut the fucker!'

'No. I think we should take him back to camp, an' hear what he has to say. We ain't in no shit fer killin' no injin, but if this uns a white man, we could have trouble we don't need. Let's hear his story; we can always drop him in a hole later.'

'Jesus, Sweeney,' the lower voice whined, 'this ain't good...' There was more discussion, but David was suddenly moved, as the men took him between them, and blackness took him again.

When David regained his senses, the sun was slanting low in the afternoon of the following day. The temperature had been above freezing, so that the snow was melting slowly, but as the day cooled, a hard skin of frozen snow was forming that crunched underfoot. He lay under a foul-smelling tarpaulin, which was tented against the side of a large, four-wheeled wagon. He heard steps grinding the ice crystals; no moccasins these; they had the sound of heavy, hard-leather boots. The tarp was flung aside at one corner, and a slender, pale-faced man looked in. David saw straight away that he had a shock of red hair tufted out from the brim of his greasy hat.

'He's awake!' the man called over his shoulder.

'Jesus, Sweeney,' the other man whined, 'we was just gonna have somethin' t' eat. Why don' ya leave him be, an' then we'll see to him after we's done?'

'Christ! All ya's ever think about is yer gob-hole an' yer arse-hole. Get ya self over here, an' gimme a hand. The food'll keep.'

Grumbling and cursing under his breath, the other man came over to David. Here was the opposite of Sweeney. The man was enormous. He stood easily at six and one-half feet, and had a large rounded paunch, over which he wore a filthy leather apron. He had a little round cherry of a nose, and a receding hairline on either side of his forehead, which left him with a short lick of black, greasy hair down the centre of his skull. He wore several days of growth, and was as dirty as a dung beetle. His eyes were slack and stupid in the manner of a dog beaten severely for its vicious temper. His fingers were fat and his nails blackened with dried blood and excrement, and every other variation of dirt.

For all that, Wilfred Pickett was the best shot Sven Holstrom had ever heard of, much less seen. He had decided to desert from the United States Army under General Albert Sidney Johnson, when ordered out to Utah to put down the rebel Mormon extremists under Brigham Young. Johnson was the cruel fundamentalist extremist who had ordered nearly fifteen hundred men, women and children to walk out to Great Salt Lake from the Missouri, the church having gone bankrupt, and no transport available. Hundreds died, and the army was called in. At the threat of combat, Holstrom figured to head north, maybe look for gold, or hunt for hides, now fetching as much as four dollars apiece. Damned if he was going to take on fanatic priests for a buck-fifty a day; no sir, not now, not ever.

Pickett was the man to take along, Holstrom decided, for not only was he blessed with a marksman's eye, he was also a man utterly unburdened by conscience. They had 'come by', as Holstrom liked to say, an outfit that consisted of four oxen and a 'J. Murphy wagon', a vehicle made especially for the plains traffic. Depending on the team, such a wagon could carry six thousand pounds of freight. Having given up on the gold, the two men were now looking for buffalo, which they planned to freight into St Paul, moving north, so as to lessen the chances of detection. They dragged David over to the fire, where a black iron kettle with a load of beans and corn was simmering. David thought he would faint from the wondrous smell of it. Bread was baking in an iron pan.

He was propped against a stump and Holstrom examined his ear. 'Get a look a this, Willy!'

The big man bent over and whistled. He went over to the wagon, and came back with a tin cup full of rum. Whipping out his skinning knife, he seized David's head, and turning it, slit off the ragged tendrils left by the bullet's passage. He then splashed on rum. David felt a sharp scream tear past his lips.

'Now don't yowl about it,' said Holstrom. Looking up at Pickett, then back at David, he grinned. 'Hands like th' feet of a surgeon, my Willy has, ain't he?' And he took out a faded bit of rag, and tied it around David's head.

'Honest a God, this shit-ball'd cut out ya liver, if I asked him to. They ain't nothin' that bothers him! Now tell us, how is it that a red-headed white man is runnin' around with injins, dressed like one of 'em, and stealin' other people's oxen?'

David opened his mouth to speak, but his throat was so parched, words failed him. He croaked. Holstrom handed him the cup, and David swallowed the remaining rum in a gulp. He gasped as the alcohol seared his throat, and coughed violently. The two men looked at one another, linked in a private bond of contempt for those they thought weaker than they. David had been thinking about his story, for he had overheard much of what they had said. He decided not to tell the truth, or at least, not so much of the truth as would attract their abundant animosity.

'We were not stealing your ox,' he started, the English sounding strange in his ears, coming from himself. 'I am from the English territories at Red River; I was captured while out on the chase for buffalo and enslaved by the Sioux, and the man you shot was helping me escape.'

Holstrom's glittery black eyes narrowed, and he looked closely at David. Evil has its own kinship with other evil, and Holstrom fancied his abilities to ferret out lies. 'Then why was ya headed south? Answer me that!'

David replied calmly. ' 'Cause I thought they would expect me to go north. I was making for the Missouri River.'

Both men laughed. Pickett chimed in. 'Ya's missed it by a country mile, boy!' Holstrom was suddenly interested in David in a different aspect, as his nimble brain took another turn in self-interest.

'Ya say ya was on a buffalo hunt? You know about skinnin' buffalo?'

'Yes,' said David, warily. 'Are you men out hunting for buffalo? On our ride of almost two weeks, we saw not a one.'

'Ah, it don't take no whiz-bang mountain man to find them buffalo. They's so god-damned many of 'em, that all's ya have t' do is drive in a straight line, and the beasts'll run over ya. No, what we need is someone who's done some skinnin', and we'd be mighty pleased ta have ya's on with us.'

David was astonished. These men were actually outfitted for hunting, yet had no idea about proper skinning and dressing of hides. Slit skins and peltries with an abundance of tissue left on them were worthless. The others took his silence to mean other things.

'If it's money ya's worried about, we'll split the proceeds three ways, once we get to St Paul. How about it? We'll even throw in an extra five dollars to cover the loss of ya dead friend.' Pickett started to protest, but was silenced by a murderous glare from Holstrom, cold and ominous as a smile on a hogshead snake.

David thought about this: St Paul—he could easily catch a ride back to Fort Garry with one of the many ox-cart brigades. And he could return with a few dollars in his pocket. He might wish for better companions, but out here there were few choices. 'I'll do it,' he said after a moment.

Pickett's yellow teeth gleamed dully in the firelight, in what passed for a grin. 'Good!' he exclaimed. 'Let's eat!'

Within two days they found the herds. The bitter irony was not lost on David; he and Su-pi-hi-ye would have come across the same herd, for their breath cloud hung in a shimmering apparition over the animals, marking their presence like a doomsday cloud. Pickett's aim was formidable. Not a single shot was wasted, though the barrel of his weapon got so warm, he would scoop up the brittle snow, and rub it along the barrel, making it hiss.

Pickett's rifle was a Sharps .50 calibre, breech-loading weapon, that hurled a shell with an explosion of 120 grains of powder packed in a three-and-one-half inch shell. It weighed almost fifteen pounds, and needed a rest to keep the aim steady, though in a pinch, Pickett would squeeze off a shot with the leather sling stretched over his left arm.

David showed the two men the techniques of separating hide from beast, though neither one showed much enthusiasm for the work. David was able to show the urgency of stripping off the pelt before the carcass had a chance to cool, otherwise all three men were needed to pull the hide off. They were all concerned about the arrival of Indians, or even other hunters who might wish to misappropriate their harvest, and so their work proceeded apace.

At the end of each day, the three men would tumble into their robes, exhausted. The pile of skins in the wagon slowly grew until in just over two weeks, they had secured a thousand hides, worth perhaps four thousand dollars, maybe more. Each man silently worked out his share, according to sums and divisions he alone thought appropriate. Pickett moved his lips as he counted; Holstrom wet his lips with a flickering tongue as he shaped and re-shaped his schemes. David had a faraway look as he contemplated his return to his family. Each man, as do all men according to their personality, gave clues to the inner self, for those who would but look to see them.

The hunt had not traversed more than a half-dozen miles in all, for the herd moved only as foraging was diminished. Snow was ground to a dirty paste of soil, ice and excrement, as the animals grazed off every dry blade of cover available. In places, the men feared for their team, as no fodder was left by the beasts they hunted. The oxen were hobbled in a creek valley several miles away, and the pony which David had secured just before Su-pi-hi-ye had been killed was used to ferry a man back and forth to check on them.

On one of these trips to inspect the condition of the oxen, David found himself wondering whether he should simply keep riding east. He had no kit; no bed robes to ward off the deep chill that still hung over the land, even though it was clear that spring was coming early. He had no food, no weapon and only the clothes which he had been wearing when he had been shot. These were now becoming somewhat fetid, for he had not changed them since he had started the skinning. He reached up to touch his mangled ear and grimaced. It would be necessary to wear his hair long and loose to cover the disfigurement. He cursed Pickett for his cruelty and stupidity, hissing the sharp expletives out loud, to the passing trail. The horse's ears twitched back and forth, as if in reproach, and David suddenly felt foolish, glancing around. He was suddenly and enormously homesick for his family, his home, and the simple, pleasing task of working with wood at his grandfather's side. He decided to stay with the two men, but to cut his ties with them once the hides had been sold. It would be easy to secure a place with a brigade, and get himself home.

There was another reason for his disquiet. He was becoming increasingly aware that he was a passive player in the scheme of things. His father was someone who seized life by the throat. He had died in a manner befitting a man of action; Ephraim loved the very chase which took him. Perhaps a father's stature casts a long shadow, from which a son is never entirely free. David thought that all the significant people in his life were those who had a keen appreciation of who they were and what they wanted. David did not know who he was or where he belonged. Each event in his life seemed to buffet him from one situation to another, like a leaf in a spring freshet. His decision to return to Fort Garry seemed to him a determined step, and an act of faith in himself. Cheered, he whistled until the oxen came into view.

The trip to St Paul took almost a month, for the Murphy wagon was heavily freighted, and the men had to pick their way around drifts and rivers where the ice had started to yield to moving water. From many miles out, they could see the smoke from the hearths, factories and warehouses of St Paul. David could not believe the size of the place, thinking that Fort Garry, with its thirty-five hundred inhabitants was a congested place. Soon, his astonishment was to give way to outright wonder, for reaching a rise on the outskirts of St Paul, he looked down on a river teeming with activity.

It was early April, but the navigation season had begun on 25 March, the earliest on record. The snows had rapidly vanished, and the drought of the previous few years was destined to continue. There were floating structures on the water, large as warehouses in Fort Garry, with chimneys that belched dark black smoke. They gave off loud, startling hooting noises which unsettled the horse he was on, and made David's own ears fold back against his skull. The other two chortled at his facial expressions, agog with urban sights, smells and sounds.

They drew up at the ferry, a rather rickety-looking affair slung on a thick hawser which disappeared off one end of the rough-plank deck, and emerged from the water on the other side of the river, drawn around a squat oak tree. While waiting for the ferry to be loaded with their wagon, Holstrom pointed out the fur depot of the American Fur Company. 'That's where we'll be turnin' over our hides.'

The wagon was winched aboard, but there was not sufficient room to lead aboard the stock. It was agreed by the two men that David would wait with the team and the pony while the two went on ahead to negotiate for the sale of the hides. David was excited. The prospect of cash in his pocket, and adventure on the busy streets of the first city he had ever seen, made him giddy. He did not notice the exchange of glances and the shaded smirks of the two men.

The ferry was drawn out slowly into the stream, sagging somewhat threateningly as the brisk current, engorged with winter runoff, swept around it. It was propelled by a geared winch, turned by a drooping nag whose bones could be discerned even at this distance. David watched the entire trip, saw the two men walk up the levee to the clapboard warehouse, and disappear inside. Considerable time passed, and David became restless. He went to check on the team, and strolled up the bank to look at the activity on the west side of the Mississippi River. He was getting hungry, so he went back to the landing, impatience starting to fester.

As the sun began to slant low, he approached the ferry agent who had been dozing in the small forwarding shed. When he walked to the threshold, Isaac N. Goodhue hailed him, without unfolding his arms, without even appearing to look up. 'Hold it right thaar, boy. Be darned if'n you don't smell as bad as a polecat's arsehole, boy! Whew!'

David was embarrassed. He looked down at his poor clothes. His breech clout and leggins were stained with mud and blood; he was unwashed and unkempt. His red hair was tied in a single bunch at the nape of his neck, and fell to his shoulder blades. Over all, he wore a tattered canvas shirt, open, with the tails out.

'Pardon me, sir. I know I look a fright. But when will the ferry return?'

The ferryman raised his head, a look of mild surprise coming over his features. Courtesy was a rare thing in a man who didn't dress like an eastern fop, or ranking army. 'When my brother's got 'nuther load t' come back, I suppose. They's nothin' here to be fetched.'

David felt a tickle of anxiety. 'What about me? I've got this stock to take over.'

Goodhue looked puzzled. Turning to look to the other side of the river, he sat up. 'Well, the mystery'll be over in a bit, 'cause here comes the ferryboat.'

David ran out to the end of the landing ramp. Squinting, he could make out only one figure, and it was neither of his hunting companions. He licked his lips, for his throat was suddenly dry. The realization that he had been swindled rushed upon him, striking with the slender, destructive arc of a well-aimed lance. His knees felt weak, and he sank to his haunches to await the return of the vessel. At least he had the stock, he thought, not having the slightest idea of their worth.

At length, the ferry was secured to the bank. The sole passenger, a tall, thin man, with a wispy, adolescent moustache, stalked off the dock with the assumed dignity of an undertaker. The agent came out of the shack to greet him; neither man took any notice of David, who rose to his feet, supplicative, uncertain, fearful.

' Evenin', Sam,' said the agent.

The other man nodded. 'Isaac,' he said, in a strange, high voice. 'I've just bought this team and sorry-looking pony, and I'd like to make arrangements to board them till I can sell them. I won't be long, and I'd be obliged if you would hold the ferry till I get back.'

David was thunderstruck. He protested. 'But sir! These animals are mine. You cannot sell what is mine. Where are Sweeney and Fred—they are my partners...' David trailed off, as he realized both men were staring at him in disbelief. The tall man, Sam, accountant for the American Fur Company, and a man of self-importance, turned to David.

'Look, my good fellow, I have a bill of sale for this property. Where is your proof of ownership?' Without waiting for an answer, he turned curtly away from him, and faced Goodhue.

'I think I know what's going on here. They hire this ragamuffin for a dollar to watch the animals, sell all to me, but neglect to tell me the dollar...' he snapped his glare back to David, 'or was it fifty cents?—is still outstanding. Well, it's a clear attempt to rob me, and I'm having none of it!'

Rage and fear boiled up in David, pummelling softly at his innards with their irrational, frantic, and familiar tentacles. He drew his lips back from his teeth, 'You touch my animals, and you'll have more to regret than the loss of a dollar!'

Sam Finnster, North-western representative of the American Fur Company, had seen plenty of resentful barbarians in his time at the St Paul depot, and was not perturbed by this paltry display of rude threats. His expression was that of a man who had just stepped in dog shit; he closed his eyes, and arched his brows. 'Begone with you, or I'll call Marshall Irwin to run you off.'

David clenched his fists, and took a half-step toward Finnster. Fear now started to get the better of rage in him, for there was no doubt about either the power imbalance, or the outcome of this dispute.

'That's far enough!' barked Goodhue, who had retrieved a double-barreled shotgun from his shack. 'Get along with ya!'

David looked at the two men in a state of impotency so great he could not move. Goodhue repeated his warning as he cocked the two hammers of the shotgun. David sagged visibly, defeated without contest. He had been robbed twice in a single day, and was now destitute. Sick at heart, he turned to retreat up the bank.

'Wait.' It was Finnster's voice, the tone markedly softened. David turned to face him again.

'Here's your dollar, then. Call me a fool, if you must.' He flipped the coin, spinning it toward David. It fell at his feet in the dirt. Silently, he stooped to pick it up. He straightened, and looked at Goodhue, who had put the shotgun in the crook of his elbow.

'Will this buy me passage to the other side?'

Goodhue pondered this, looked to Finnster, a little uneasily, then said to David, 'Cost ya ten cents.'

An hour later, David found himself alone at the bottom of the levee, on the east side of the Mississippi River. Finnster had gone to his warehouse without further word or backward glance. David jingled the five silver coins in his palm, then tucked them in the only pocket he had, on the front of his shirt.

The sun was gone, its blood splashed across the western horizon like an open wound. Not knowing which way to turn, David turned away from it, and walked north along the river. He came across several Indians, all of them Dakota by their dress, unloading a string of barges containing hundred-pound sacks of seed grains. He saw that all but one of the men were lounging by the wagons at the top of the levee, while the work was being done by the women. It was hard labour, for the sacks were unwieldy and heavy. Two women would lift the load onto the back of a third, and she would carry it up the bank to the waiting vehicles, aided only by a tump line passed over her forehead. He considered stopping and speaking to the men, but he could see as he approached, that most of them were under the influence of drink, probably the cask of trade whiskey they had received for the job. One raised his bloodshot eyes to David, and upon seeing his clothes, called out in a thick voice. David quickened his pace and passed on without a word. He had left the Dakota people behind. Relationships become transient, then ebb, when the purposes which brought about their formation dissolve in new circumstances. He knew he had to shift his weight to the leg which stood in the world of white men, for the world of the Indian was falling like ripened grass before the scythe.

There was more: the whites were ruthless, and he needed to discover the source of such determination. It is generally true as a comfort that assumptions are preferable to new information. But David now knew that he must discard his adopted standards, and replace them with—what? None of the teachings of his grandfather or those he had lived with among the Dakota, seemed to be of use to him now. Nothing prepared him for the way he was being pushed aside. Living as he had been, all his life at the lower rungs of the commercial ladder, he was not ready for the tyrannies of the white man's marketplace.

He thought of what his grandfather had said about gold: the easiest way to obtain it is from a fool who has it. Well, he didn't have gold, but his goods were converted to the purses of others by his own folly. What was left to believe in? David realized, as he shambled along, that he had lost faith. When this happens, there is only a condition of despair. A passage from Hebrews came faintly to mind. 'Faith is the substance of things hoped for, the evidence of things not seen.'

That was it: he had hoped to go home, money in his pocket, and none the worse for his adventures. But his mind's eye could no longer conjure up the images of a triumphant return. He knew he had been given up for dead. He was missing half an ear, and had nothing but the filthy rags on his back. The emptiness and isolation he felt as he slouched along was a dejection he had never before come close to experiencing. For a moment, a fleeting moment as sharp and slender as a dragon's tooth, he thought about ending his life. The wind whispered and rattled empty promises in his ruined ear. The absence of faith yawned like a pit of despair.

David stopped. He had come to the commercial heart of the city. Just below him was a boat landing, and the rutted roadway which led from it was lined on either side with various sorts of commercial establishments. The first building of consequence, a clapboarded three-storey structure, was the Merchant's Hotel. There were livery stables, saloons, rooming-houses, outfitting merchants and general stores, all of which teemed with activity notwithstanding the lateness of the hour. The land to the west had belonged to the Dakota, but they had relinquished their claim to it in 1851. Even prior to this, claim-jumping was going on and immigration, following the formal treaty signing, had been intense for the past seven years. In the *Pioneer*, the newspaper of the day, owned by the same men who ran the ferry, the current sentiment about the Indians was expressed:

We behold now, clearly…like an exhibition of dissolving views, the red savages, with their teepees, their horses and their famished dogs…fading, vanishing, dissolving away; and in their places a thousand farms, with their fences and white cottages, and waving wheat fields…and villages and cities crowned with spires, and railroads with trains of cars rumbling afar off.

This antipathy to Indians had not diminished in 1858, though David was slow to realize it.

Almost twenty years later, a chronicler of the times would write of the treaty of Traverse de Sioux, that '…one of the most glorious domains that nature ever created [was] signed away. [The Dakota] signed away their heritage and birthright, and were henceforth strangers and intruders on their own "ancestral acres". But sentiment is out of place in this day of progress. The resistless march of empire was doomed to sweep away the red man—it had been so for two centuries on American soil, and the Treaty of Traverse de Sioux, another chapter of the mournful epic, called forth, not sadness, but rejoicing.'

David wandered among the traffic in awe of the commotion. Though there were more than a few Indians on the street, he felt the stares of passersby. He knew his appearance must have been repelling, even by the standards of a frontier city. Most puzzling of all was the contrast between his obviously native garb and his great shock of red hair. But for all this, his passing was worth only a glance, for there was no shortage of oddities, characters and crackpot gallivants to attract the eye. David wandered about, gawking, wondering, bumping into people, and filling his senses with the sights, sounds, and smells of the city.

At length, he came to a storefront, in the window of which were arrayed all the foodstuffs David could imagine. There were biscuits and pastries, teas and spices, smoked hams and sausages. There were wax-covered cheeses and rows of bushel baskets containing dried fruits and vegetables. Arrayed on shelves were brightly coloured tins of preserves, chocolates, syrups and sweets. Jars of striped candies, licorice and sherbets beckoned. Through the open door, the odoriferous interior sent streamers of succulent smells wafting on the night air. Caught by David's nose, they reminded him how hungry he was. Digging for his coins, he stepped into the store.

Though he could read, he had difficulty determining how one calculated the cost of things, when much of the food was sold by the pound, to be scooped out with little tin shovels, and weighed in thick brown paper bags. He felt self-conscious, and he moved from item to item, to determine which selection would be the most judicious use of his funds. While he was contemplating an open tin of biscuits, his mouth watering at the sight of the rich, buttery shortbreads, he was sharply accosted:

'Just what in the name of the Almighty do you think you're doing in here?'

David looked to see who was addressing him in this tiresomely familiar way. A sturdy, bald man, with enormous handlebar moustaches, confronted him. He was wearing a full-length, canvas apron and he was angry. 'How you stink, man! You're driving out my customers! Out! Get out!' And he started to escort David to the door.

David protested. 'I have money to spend...'

'Your money's no good in here. Why don't you go across to the bath house, and clean yourself up? Get yourself a proper set of clothes? Ach! What a stink!'

David began to shove back. Getting on in the white man's world obviously required a little more assertion that he was used to. The two men scuffled, attracting attention. David tried again to explain that he had money, but he was drowned out by the larger man. 'Help! Help! Who will assist me in removing this trespasser?'

Several men responded. They seized David, and carried him out to the street. They all complained about the smell, making caustic remarks about their captive. One of them suggested an impromptu bath, and David was carried struggling and humiliated next door to the livery stables, and with laughter and hooting from the idlers who had gathered to watch, he was pitched into the horse trough.

His head came up spluttering and coughing. Both hands gripped the sides of the trough. He howled his frustration and unhappiness. 'Why is it in this cursed place a man is treated so bad? Never in all my life did I think that there could be such an inhospitable place! Are you Christians?' he demanded of the small group which had gathered to watch the fun.

'Is it not set out in the Good Book that "Thou shalt neither vex a stranger, nor oppress him?" Have the teachings of Christ not yet reached this forsaken place?' He struggled to climb out of the water, and stood dripping in the street. Clutching at his pocket, he groaned when he realized that the coins were gone. He dropped to his knees beside the trough and plunged his arm into the murky water and groped about, muttering in a babel of tongues.

He was hailed for the second time that evening. A tall, thin man was standing on the boardwalk. Even though he was in the shadows, the finery of his clothes was apparent. 'My good man, at the trough—yes, you—might I have a word with you?'

David was of a mind to ignore him, for the recovery of the money was critical. If the coins hadn't fallen out in the water, then they must have dropped out on the street, where they'd be impossible to find. The stranger persisted.

'What are you looking for? Perhaps I can help.'

David stood up. 'I've lost some money—the only money I have.'

'How much was it?' asked the stranger, stepping down from the boardwalk. 'Was it a great deal?'

David felt foolish. 'Never mind!' he said somewhat harshly. 'It's my business.'

'So it is. So it is.' The man pursed his lips, and studied David, taking in his filthy clothes, his unkempt hair, and the missing upper half of his ear. David felt uneasy under his gaze.

'What're you staring at?' he demanded.

The other replied at once. 'Look here. I would like to speak with you. Give me a few minutes of your time, and I'll make it worth your while.' Seeing the hesitation on David's face, he pressed his advantage.

'Look. I could see those roughs were unpleasant with you, but I assure you, you will be glad you took the time to speak with me.' There was something in the man's voice that suggested David should listen to him— a ring of sincerity. David had little confidence in his ability to select those worthy of his trust, but again, he had no options.

'All right. What is it you want of me?'

The stranger introduced himself as Fletcher T. (for Tinker) Norquay, Vice President of the LaCrosse and Milwaukee Railroad Company. David did not know what a 'Railroad Company' was, but he thought he'd listen. Norquay told him that he was looking to hire 'certain character types' for employ back east. The pay was good, the work not too demanding. As he spoke, they walked back along the street to a saloon, went in, and sat down at a table. Norquay called for food and drink, and continued to talk while David made short work of everything that was put in front of him. In truth, he ate like a wild animal: noisily, greedily, and with one eye on the next morsel and the other on anyone who came close to their table. Sullen and suspicious, as Norquay spoke, David listened, eyes narrowed, as terms were expressed which were unclear to him. He shivered in his wet clothes; he had the aspect of a cornered rat.

Norquay seemed not to notice, and continued to speak in his careful way, questioning David now and then, to assure himself that David was paying attention.

Seven

i

No one had come down from Gleneaglesham to see Johnathan off this time, and he was glad of it. His mother was restrained; Sir Alex formal. Elsie had not made an appearance by the time the coach came for him, and he felt a faint pang of guilt. Without emotion, he kissed his mother on the cheek, shook hands with Sir Alex and did not look back. Once at sea, he relaxed, for he had brought books with him, and had no duties until landing. His quarters were crowded and poorly ventilated in bad weather, but it was bearable compared to the stinking accommodations for the enlisted men and those wives who had won the lottery entitling them to accompany their men.

On 12 October, the *Isaac Rice* rounded up off the Bombay coast, and began the arduous task of tacking back and forth between shoals and fishing buoys marking nets, and fetching up the pilot to take them close inshore. Amidst a tangle of pattymars, dhows, junks, trade ketches and East Indiamen, the voyage came to an end. There was a palpable excitement aboard ship, for this was an exotic port of call. For more than a week, the heavy scent of cloves and ginger could be detected on the offshore breezes, especially at night, when the air drew close.

But when the novitiates of the East India Company (known as 'John Company' for nearly all of the employees bore that Christian name) stepped ashore, expectations fell like a dropped stone. The filth, noise and sheer numbers of people jostling, shouting and milling about overwhelmed the Europeans. The harbour resembled a sewer, so badly did it reek; all manner of rubbish and carrion could be seen bobbing with the ocean's ceaseless motion.

In 1855, Bombay was a centre for trade for all of Asia, including China. The principal product of commerce seemed to be opium, though Indian cotton and spices, exotic timber, tea and fruit were handled in enormous quantities. The wealth generated by commercial activity seemed not to be widely distributed, though the servants of the Company and the senior officers of the military lived in near-royal splendour. The poverty which Johnathan saw, even on the short trip by open cart to his hotel, was beyond even the slums of Liverpool or Plymouth. There were many beggars: blind, crippled and diseased, who, at the approach of a European, set up such a cacophony one could not speak at a normal level and be heard by a fellow passenger. The din of the streets did not die away until after dark.

It was a shock to Johnathan that he was expected to pay for his own accommodations; doubly so when he was shown to the small, grimy room with its single fixture, a mattress on a bamboo frame. The walls of the Hotel Victoriana were a cheap cotton stretched on frames, reaching about seven feet toward a ten-foot ceiling. Fellow officers stood on stools or footlockers to converse with each other over the walls, and neither peace nor privacy was available. The building smelled constantly of curry, save when there was a satï: a cremation. About one-half mile away, directly upwind, were the cremation grounds, and the smoke and smell of seared flesh passed directly through the three-storey building, for the windows, of necessity, remained open in all but the foulest weather. It was with considerable relief that Johnathan received his orders and posting the following week.

There was a call at the door. 'Master Snow. Are you there, sir?' The voice had a comforting, almost familiar ring to it. Johnathan was sick of drunken officers falling down and swearing in the night, and calling upon him to join in the fun. He was utterly fed up with the nasal English of the sepoys and dozens of hangers-on at the hotel. He considered all Indians to be of an inferior condition, even though he realized that they had several castes of social standing among themselves. It was therefore satisfying to hear a solid Scot's brogue, not limbered with rum, call his name.

He pulled aside the door to his room; it was nothing more than a rigid framed curtain on a rail, and there stood Sergeant Calvin Cobb, all six foot three of him, and smiling like a fox with a chicken. Calvin seized Johnathan by the shoulders. 'God! It's good to see you, Johnathan. I mean, sir!' He saluted, still grinning.

Johnathan nodded heartily. 'Indeed it is! What a surprise and a pleasure to see your civilized face in this armpit of a place! I very much suspected I'd run into you! How are you? I hope you've brought my orders.'

'Indeed I have, sir, and since the envelope came apart from the damp,

I can tell you where you're going: Lucknow.'

'And where might that be?' It sounded vaguely familiar, for Johnathan had pored over the maps and charts available on the *Isaac Rice*, but like any first-time visitor, he had no point of reference, and could not recall its location.

'It's on the other side of the country, in the Northern Provinces. We'll be travelling in stages, first by boat, to Calcutta.' Calvin paused as Johnathan unrolled a soiled map, and pressed down a dirty finger. 'Here. Here we go. Around and north along the Ganges River. You will report to Major Anderson, the Chief Engineer.'

Johnathan looked at him. 'We?'

'Aye!' Calvin seemed delighted. 'I'm to accompany you with my squad, and we are to escort a woman, Belinda Case, the wife of a Lieutenant-Colonel with the 32nd Foot—the Cornwall Regiment— stationed in Cawnpore, not far from Lucknow. He'll meet us in Lucknow. The whole trip will take us about a month, maybe more, depending upon the weather.'

Johnathan was puzzled. 'I understood that there was a metal road, the Grand Trunk Road, nearly complete from Calcutta?'

'Sure enough, but it is down for weeks at a time. White ants eat the wooden sleepers. Floods carry away bridges and embankments. And the vegetation grows so fast in some places that it clogs the tracks for miles, and has to be cut away. You're in for a treat. This is a place like no other.'

More seriously, he added, 'There's been some trouble in the north, and two English officers were shot by their own men. Shocking, but not surprising, if you don't mind me saying it. The sepoys are treated like shit around here, though we expect them to go out and die for us. Most of the men call them niggers or rag-heads and such, and though the language escapes 'em, the meaning doesn't.'

The two men chatted with that easy association that childhood friends have throughout their lives. No matter how circumstances had changed, the relationship remained the same in its central aspect. Johnathan called for some tea, and confessed that he was convinced that while abroad, he should drink nothing else. He felt that the tea was a prophylactic against cholera and all other diseases which thrived in foreign climates. And warm it was, for tropical dress had not been adopted, and most officers were uniformed as they might appear in St James's Square. In consequence tunics were invariably sweat-stained, and many of the enlisted men cut the armpits out of their uniforms and wore the collars loose.

Every European, regardless of station, had a servant for the expense was negligible. This delighted the enlisted men, some of whom shared the cost. The other officers had pointed out the value of engaging the low-caste offspring of Indians and Portuguese, known as Goans. They worked cheaply; they did not fight or make trouble, and were devoted to the last penny of their master's purse. Johnathan took on a man by the unlikely name of Chattar, which quickly became 'Chatter', for the man nattered on incessantly in a brew of Portuguese, English and Hindustani. He could speak a rudimentary form of English, most clearly an expression he had heard from European troops: 'God-Damn.' His speech was liberally peppered with these words; smiling in a show of broken, rotted teeth, he would clasp his hands before his forehead. 'God-Damn, sahib, master, God-Damn!'

All of Calvin's squad were native soldiers. This surprised Johnathan. He had heard that travelling by sea involved a loss of caste for some sepoys, and on one occasion an entire regiment was destroyed by a cannonade of grapeshot, because they refused to march to a seaport, fearing they would be required to go to sea. But Calvin had a working understanding of the language, and the men appeared to like him. It was disclosed later that these were marginal converts to Christianity. The faith as yet did not have much influence in India. But by reason of their change in belief, most likely inspired by low caste and lack of alternative prospects, they were considered by the British to be of a higher degree of loyalty. These men abhorred meat, however, and generally behaved as no other Christians Johnathan had ever met.

'You have a lot to learn about these people,' laughed Calvin. 'There are subtleties I'll never understand.'

Johnathan forced a thin smile. A lot to learn? Not bloody likely. He looked at the dark, stupid faces, and felt that there was nothing there that interested him at all. Couldn't Calvin see that they were nothing more than cannon fodder for the enemies of John Company? He looked away to sea, as their pattymar, a large, two-masted coaster, put out for the south coast. It was cooler offshore, and the sunshine flashed on the waves of the Indian Ocean. As he looked at Calvin's cheerful face on the swaying deck, he felt for a moment as he did when the two boys would ride in the water buckets carried by Calvin's father; a wave of emotion passed over him quickly, in the manner of a ghost's passing. It was peaceful, leisurely, and relaxing. Johnathan slept and ate, read, and chatted with Calvin and Mrs Case.

Now there was something to relieve the monotony. Mrs Case kept to herself. She had not followed her husband out to India when he had received his orders, for she had been pregnant and too weak to travel. The child had died of complications during delivery, and the strain had nearly finished her. Depressed for months, she became a forlorn, self-pitying recluse, until her father demanded she leave to rejoin her husband, as 'the only medicine left to try'. Johnathan had wormed this out of her, bit by bit, with no real interest in it, save that it was a game to pass time. It probably had to do with her beauty as well, for she was an intensely attractive, pale-skinned woman, with pale red hair wound under a broad-brimmed hat, and a tendency to wrap herself in filmy white gauze while under the blazing equatorial sun.

She enjoyed lazing in the sunshine, as long as not a speck of flesh showed. Her large, dark eyes glowed mysteriously from within her wrappings. She drank cold tea, and rarely ate. She was polite, but volunteered nothing beyond the barest answers to questions. She intimidated Calvin, who thought of her as a 'lovely phantom', and he left her alone. Johnathan would speak to her idly as they plodded at the rate of ninety miles a day through the steady swells.

'So, Mrs Case. You'll no doubt be pleased to be reunited with your husband,' he said tentatively.

'Yes,' she said.

'Any day now we'll be at Trivandrum, almost a third of the way there.'

Looking up from her book, there was the briefest of nods, 'Yes.'

After a moment, for the going gets difficult in a one-sided conversation. 'How have you found the country so far?'

'It's not England.' This, without taking her eyes from the page.

And so it began, siegecraft carefully employed against a walled enclave. There were matters of strategy: tunnelling, trenching and retrenching, probing steadily and persistently until the best place for the breach was discovered. Well, there was nothing but time, and the study of her was pleasant enough. Her shapely form was visible beneath the reduced layers of petticoats, and the bustle had not yet developed to the silliness it would later become, so that her natural lines were not obscured in any way. Johnathan found that he had become infatuated with her, notwithstanding that she was married. Clearly, it seemed to him, she wanted nothing to do with him or anyone on the ship.

The days passed slowly and evenly, in fair weather, as the craft leapfrogged around the coast, putting in at places with names like Negapatim, Madras, Chantapilli, and finally Calcutta, sprawled across the many mouths of the Ganges River, and the garrison at Dum-Dum.

Here the Europeans transferred to palanquins for the trip to the river. This was a sort of covered couch, from which the word derives in Sanskrit, and which was borne on poles by six or eight men. The hamals moved at a pace of eighteen kos, or units of two miles, each day. The men sang to lighten the load, one chanting some improvised verse about the weather, the load, or the countryside, and the others responding in the chorus. Lean, well-muscled men, they took pride in their work, and it showed in their expressions, for theirs was an honourable profession in India. Etiquette demanded, perhaps as much as common sense, that the passenger get out and walk when the 'palki' reached a grade.

When they stopped for the day, each man took turns walking upon the others' backs, which appeared to refresh them. This was a sight that Mrs Case found extraordinarily funny when she saw it for the first few times; these were the only occasions on the journey she had let loose with gales of laughter. It was readily apparent that the men found this offensive, and they withdrew, muttering.

When it became apparent that the hamals were becoming exceedingly resentful, Johnathan approached her before she retired to sleep on her couch. Calvin had asked him to speak to her as the senior officer.

'Mrs Case, I am advised that you must not laugh at the customs of bearers. It is a disgrace to them—a loss of stature; they may rouse to anger, or worse, leave us here.'

'I meant no offense,' she said, with no remorse softening her indifferent tone.

Johnathan felt the hairs at the nape of his neck prickle. He thought he had established some rapport with her; yet she was as indifferent at the moment as she had been the first day of their meeting.

'Look,' he said a little roughly, 'there may be other customs which you and I find bizarre, but to antagonize those upon whom we depend is most unwise. I am told that they bleed swollen veins in their legs. Will that tickle your fancy, or will you express revulsion?'

She looked at him directly, as she had not done before. 'I find the mere telling of it revolting.'

Johnathan was nonplussed; it was the intensity of her beauty revealed in a bold gaze that intimidated him, and he had no understanding of why this should be so. He stammered, and instantly cursed inwardly, 'I would thank you to keep your opinions and reactions confidential, else they may put our safety in jeopardy.' And he turned on his heel, and marched back to where Calvin was sitting, pretending not to watch.

By stages, and without other incident, the group moved from palanquin to river schooner, to cart, and thereby to Lucknow, arriving on Christmas Eve. Stiffly, and with an unease that he thought the woman shared, he bade farewell to Mrs Case. She had been cool since he had taken her to task for her behaviour with the bearers, and he was afraid that their relationship, such as it was, had been damaged.

'You must stop for a visit with my husband and me,' she said suddenly. 'Cawnpore is not far. Not more than fifty miles, they say.'

Johnathan was surprised, and he blurted out that he would come 'at once'; then corrected himself to mean that he would attend as soon as she had settled. With a touch of her slender hand that made him shiver, she turned to greet her husband, a bearded, impatient man who looked much older than he probably was. The heat was oppressive, and the introductions hurried and formal. Colonel Case was anxious to be off with his wife, for he regarded her hungrily. Johnathan turned to Calvin who sat on the small open wagon upon which they had travelled the last stretch of the journey.

Calvin gestured to the wagon bed. 'I'll drop you at the cantonment, and you can report your arrival.' Wearily, with the back of his shirt sticking to him like mud, Johnathan climbed up.

Lucknow lay sprawled and decaying for three miles between the banks of the undulating, sluggish River Gumpti and a canal which drew off the turbid water two miles downstream. Drawn close about the soft shoulders of the city was the thick green shawl of the jungle: steaming, close and impenetrable. This was the capital city of the province of Oudh, a vast, rich and fertile territory in the Ganges valley. John Company had been thirsting after the riches of the region for some time, and the following year, 1856, it was annexed by the army on the pretext of mismanagement and abuse of its citizens. Native princes were deposed and their armies disbanded, and the pensions of those so removed were reduced or cut off altogether. One of these, Nana Sahib, adopted son of the deposed Peshwa Baji Rao II, sulked in a rage until the opportunity presented for revenge. But Johnathan's immediate concerns were with his living requirements, and he looked forward with some uncertainty to meeting with his regiment.

Major Anderson was a sharp, capable man, now in poor health. He spent much of the time resting, leaving the bulk of the work to Captain Fulton, his executive engineer. Fulton had a wry sense of humour, and was quick to smile. Sometimes his sarcasm bit a little deep, and some of the men resented him. His attitude to the sepoys was marked by such mordancy, and though he did not intend to cause resentment, they did not respond to his remarks the way the European men did.

'I'm certain you're ready for a cold beer, then, Mr Snow?' said Fulton. To Johnathan's nod, he went on, 'Well, we have none, but we can supply beer that is marginally below the present temperature.' Smiling, he led the way to the cantonment. Johnathan thanked Calvin, who left for his own brigade, which was the 32nd Native Infantry under Colonel Inglis. The officers' mess was spacious and comfortable, as were Johnathan's quarters. He began at last to entertain the thought that this might be a choice posting, for there seemed to be no sign of the usual military fuss. Indeed, life for the officers seemed to revolve around favoured pastimes: shooting, riding, gambling, intriguing and 'peacocking' with other officers' wives. The incessant gossiping endemic to military bases was a main preoccupation.

In the market place beyond the Farhat Bakhsh palace, there was the red bazaar, named for the red-serged soldiers of a few years before. Here was a place that seemed to pulse with life, and was a chief attraction for men of all ranks because of the native 'wives' that were available. Attractive, lithe women with intelligent faces and small, quick hands, they were known as búbús, an English approximation of the Hindu word for lady, or wife. By 1855, the colour barrier had been sharply drawn by the Protestant Church. As well, the numbers of white women in India had increased significantly, and the mark of rank, of stature, was the presence of a white woman on one's arm. The attitude of European women toward even the high-caste daughters of India was one of condescension, even disdain, as the feeling was strong in England that coloured persons were appropriately relegated to the rank of servant or handmaiden.

The presence of clergymen of the Church of England inadvertently added to the tensions of the increasingly divided society. They condemned the easy unions with native 'wives' and preached loudly and at length of the evils of the nautch, an erotic dance by paid courtesans. This evening-long sexual pantomime performed to the accompaniment of drums, flutes and sitar, seemed to the anxious English clerics the very embodiment of Satanic temptation, and they disapproved; the nautch continued, nonetheless. The people chafed under the lash of contempt and, for the moment, took out their own bitterness on the hordes of mulatto children, who were welcome nowhere.

Most of his fellow officers, including those who were married, had taken a búbú; but these held no attraction for Johnathan, notwithstanding that there was near unanimous consensus in the officers' mess that the native women held the key to a secret inner fire of sexual desire. There were frequently told variations of the night-long possession of the body, which moved from whispers and caresses, through scratches and soft blows accompanied by gentle cries and lingering moans, to varied positions of intercourse begun and abruptly broken off, building and swelling seemingly beyond human limits of pleasure. All of this was intriguing enough, but in the half year since his arrival, Johnathan could not get out of his mind the lovely Belinda Case, and he resolved to travel to

Cawnpore to see her.

The road to Cawnpore was a poor track at the best of times, nearly impassable during the monsoon rains which came from the southwest, sometimes as early as April. Johnathan's work in the first years of his posting had to do with the survey of alternative routes which could be properly graded and drained so as to permit passage year round. This had important military objectives, but more of concern was John Company's desire to keep the commerce of the provinces, including the Punjab to the north, flowing steadily to the port at Calcutta.

One of his first tasks was to travel the length of the roadway to Cawnpore, making his own detailed observations and measurements. Upon reaching the River Ganges, it was necessary to make one's way across a floating bridge, established by a previous effort of the Company's sappers, to gain access to the town which challenged the jungle for space along the riverbank. The town was principally noted for its leatherworking, and no European left without equipping himself with all manner of boots, belts, scabbards and dress shoes at impossibly cheap prices. The buildings were well spread out, and the officers and their families occupied private dwellings scattered through the town. Of the three thousand men at arms stationed there, only about one hundred and twenty were European, as Afghan wars and the fighting in the Crimea had drawn off much of the garrison's former strength.

Johnathan had some difficulty in finding the Case residence, for the town of more than sixty thousand was laid out haphazardly like many others in the district. He was warned, as he set off with Cheater, that there was 'rather a greater strength of the dangerous classes' than elsewhere. He laughed off this caution, for he had seen little hostility other than the shadowed resentment one would expect of toiling men who were not masters in their own country.

Mrs Case's reaction to Johanathan's appeerence at the the door could not have been more surprising. She stepped forward and hugged him; her delight was spontaneous and effervescent. Startled by her forward behaviour, of which he had not seen a hint during his earlier time with her, he held his arms stiffly at his sides, and leaned slightly backwards. This was not the manner of the English ladies he had any acquaintance with. It was obvious she was alone at the moment but for the servants. Grinning, Cheater removed to the outer step, in the shade of a large veranda which surrounded the house. Johnathan took her by the shoulders.

'I fear, Mrs Case, that you will dirty yourself on my rather dusty clothing. I have not had time to clean up.' He studied her as she spoke; she was hatless and free of the wrappings she had worn on their trip. Her dress was cut very low in front, and the tops of her breasts bore a sheen of perspiration. A small brown fan fluttered in her hand like a captured thrush.

'Oh, never mind that,' she said. 'I am so glad to see you. I have been thinking a lot about you in the six months that I've been here, if you don't mind me saying. About our little talks on the boat, and through the curtains of our palkis. What took you so long to visit?' She called for tea to be prepared, and a bath to be drawn. Johnathan was mildly amused, for the 'talks' of which she spoke, he recalled as rather one-sided. What on earth had gotten into her? He rushed through his bath, attended at the end, to his mild consternation, by a native woman who surprised him in his nakedness with towels and ointments. Soon after, he rejoined his hostess, having put on a clean shirt and a pair of shoes he had Cheater bring from his kit.

As they sat down to a plate of small cheeses, fruit and bread, he asked, 'And where is Colonel Case?' He hoped that he sounded casual.

'The Colonel is on manoeuvres, and is expected tomorrow, late. For that reason, regrettably, I will have to put you up in the guest house, rather than here in the residency, which is more convenient. Unless you are planning to return to the cantonment...?'

'I wish not to impose, but if it is convenient, the guest house will be more than adequate.' He felt deliciously intimate with her, and he could tell by the way she fussed and chattered, that there was something in the air.

She apologized for her behaviour on the trip. She told him about the effect of her solitude, and the indifference of her husband after an initial 'intensity of feelings', as she put it. She found the natives insolent, lazy and reluctant to speak English; she could not speak a word of their language, which she found irritating to listen to. She realized that she had been self-indulgent after the loss of her baby, but also that she had endured enough of life in the jungle. She hated the screams from the dark bush at night. She was frightened of the strange, dark men with large hooked knives. She loathed beyond description the rainfall that tumbled out of the sky in thick sheets capable of knocking people down. The insects, the heat, the pervasive stench from the river, the dust... she looked off, staring at nothing, then back at Johnathan.

'You were so friendly to me, so solicitous. A handsome young officer showing me courtesy and friendship. And I was such a noodle-head, lost in my own world! I'm so glad to see you! I'm afraid that I've been rather lonely.' She reached out, touching him on the arm as gently as a butterfly alighting. It seemed to Johnathan that the current of the Ganges flowed through that faint contact, sweeping him away in a delirium of wanting her to continue to touch him. He remained composed, though he suspected she could see that under his tanned skin he was blushing furiously.

That night, as he lay beneath mosquito curtains, it did not surprise him when she padded into his room, slipped out of her nightclothes, and joined him under the thin cotton sheet. She folded herself around him, as fragrant and yielding as a flower. It seemed natural; almost as if she belonged to him. And that night, she did. Completely. She surprised him when she touched him in intimate places; he groaned with pleasure as she nipped and tugged at his soft parts, feeling his desire flooding beyond his capacity to control.

When they lay together, spent, she explained what she had learned in secret chats with the Hindu women in her house, and the vastly superior understanding that they seemed to possess about sexual pleasure— including that of women. These erotic sensibilities were known as the Kama Sutra, the doctrine of love, and were an ancient revelation of the physical and mental technique of sex. Colonel Case had found her interest in this 'unseemly' and 'unfit for the attentions of a wife of a senior British Army officer'.

All through the summer at the close of 1856, Johnathan found that his work took him frequently to Cawnpore, and he was a regular guest at the Case residence. He and the Colonel became friends of a sort, drinking sherry together when it could be got, and playing whist when a fourth was invited. As frequently as the opportunities presented, the lovers stole away to bed together, where their lovemaking became increasingly intense. Belinda Case liked to be taken roughly, and her cries of mock fear inflamed Johnathan's desire. He laid her across his thighs and spanked her as he had seen Schoolmaster Friar chastise Elsie; it had a powerful effect on his arousal. He knew that their relationship was getting beyond control, and that more and more people were becoming aware of it.

One morning, as he was adjusting the cinch on his saddle, preparing for a trip to Delhi to meet with the chief engineer of the province, Colonel Case hailed him. In his contrition, Johnathan imagined that the voice had a hard edge to it. He turned, anxious, 'Yes?'

'I want a word with you; stand down for a moment.' The man was striding purposefully across a patchy lawn toward him. In the trees just beyond, monkeys set up a fretful screeching. 'I told you so! I told you so!' they seemed to declaim.

'I want to thank you for spending so much time with Belinda,' he said earnestly. 'She has never really gotten over the baby, you know, and your visits really seem to have made a difference in her. She's a bit of an empty-headed girl, I know, but you humour her, and I'm grateful.'

Johnathan was dumbfounded, for he was riven with guilt mixed with relief. He stammered a farewell, muttering about the impossibility of stopping further, as he wished to make Delhi before the monsoon broke. He rode off in company with two sepoys leading the way, and his manservant not far behind. He spoke to Cheater.

'I can read your thoughts this morning, Cheater.'

'No sahib, no, God-Damn. I have no thoughts that are.'

Johnathan chuckled. 'You do not approve?'

'Oh no, sahib, no. Of the lady, I approve; God-Damn. But it is the man who may I say there is no approve. God-Damn, no.'

'Why?' asked Johnathan.

'He considers me but shit on the heel of his boot. All people, but not you, sahib. I am unworthy, but I am alive. I am unworthy, but I am a man.' Johnathan did not turn to face him, but he could hear the struggle in his servant's voice.

'When I am young, red soldiers good. They show kindness and are fine. They speak in our words. None know our words now, but they know rough ones and curse ones. Push out of way like blind beggar-boy. God-Damn. No. The Colonel has hate in his heart for me and others, but not you, sahib. No. God-Damn, no.'

Johnathan did not disagree with him, for he could see how this conclusion could easily be reached. He kept his own feelings to himself, as always, but the truth was that he shared the arrogance of the invader, and felt that this wretched nation was far better off under the guidance and beneficence of British rule. But it was critical to work with the natives, if for no other reason than their numerical superiority. Properly handled, with an appeal to vanity perhaps, or a judicious show of force when necessary, part of the richness of this land could fall into his own pockets. Nothing dishonest. The white man had a mission in these lands, that much was apparent, but he was beginning to realize that he was being side-tracked by his affair with the Colonel's wife.

This relationship had to be broken off. He could be court-martialled, disgraced, removed from all hope of influencing the course of his life and the attainment of wealth. Men who were discovered cuckolding other officers, especially their superior officers, were sent off to the worst postings in the far and unpleasant reaches of the Empire. And there were plenty of hellholes from which to choose. Yet Belinda was like a drug to him, and he did not think he could stay away, even if it meant ruin.

Men fought men, the old surgeon had told Johnathan in the Crimea, because of ideas. But more correctly, it was insistence upon the dominance of ideas that provoked conflict. When the East India Company was formed in 1600 to obtain commercial advantage in India, it immediately began to generate extravagant profits in Europe. This was done by the eviction of those plunderers who had come first—the French, the Dutch and the Portuguese; then those who preceded them, the princes and their frequently venal rule, which the British exploited by supporting one against the other. Selective bribes, crushing taxes, and the invader's artillery worked the politics of a distant tyranny, which bent the back of India. This was the cost of a civilization brought to a none-too-willing place.

It was not the crush of arms or rapacious commerce which became unbearable, however. The long shadow of the pulpit, ethnocentrism of the most exclusionary kind, and the unending procession of petty oppressions worked a stronger chemistry. In the mid-nineteenth century it was clear that the Europeans intended that their system of beliefs—their civilization—was intended to supplant that which in India had rooted deeply and continuously since the time of Mohenjo-daro, almost three thousand years before the birth of Christ.

The British had introduced the railroad, which was initially seen as a boon to a country dependent upon waterways and seasonal roads. But all castes were expected to travel together; this was an affront. The forceful exclusion from power of the native princes, and the diminishment of those who depended upon their largesse, created enemies of the conquerors, no better example of which was Nana Sahib. The 'Doctrine of Lapse', an imposed legal device which forbade the practice of the Indian nobility of naming their successor, should no natural heir exist, was employed to ensure that the lands of such rulers escheated to the East India Company.

Reform, modernization and land tenure was changed to accommodate the Company's looting of Indian wealth, without regard for custom, tradition, or religious practice. Then began the series of events which sparked the mutiny of the sepoys. Some of these were reflections of the conqueror's arrogance, as most affronts were entirely avoidable. In 1806 a new design of turban, arbitrarily introduced with a leather cockade, triggered a revolt. The Hindu thought the skin to be from the cow; the Moslem felt sure it originated with the pig. The revolt was put down with savage force, and those of influence in the affair were publicly hanged, ensuring a well-seeded future harvest of hatred whose yield was beyond measuring.

There followed the brutal execution by close-range grape shot of the 47th Regiment at Barrackpore, who feared they would be made to travel offshore, with consequent loss of caste to them. And in January of 1857, John Company introduced the new Enfield breech-loading rifle, with cartridges that required the paper powder seals to be torn away prior to loading. This was most efficiently accomplished by using the teeth, but a rumour (not without some substance) spread among the sepoys that the moisture-proofing grease was either that of the pig or the cow.

The revolt appeared to begin in Meerut, some thirty-six miles east of Delhi, and about two hundred and fifty miles north of Cawnpore. The 3rd Native Light Infantry was mustered for the purpose of allaying anxiety about the new cartridge, and that further, it could be torn with the fingers, rather than inserted into the mouth. To many present, the commanding officer's blandishments only served to confirm their fears, and eighty-five refused to comply. They were immediately court-martialled, and sentenced to ten years' imprisonment at hard labour. They were publicly stripped and hammered into irons in front of their comrades, a severe additional humiliation.

On the tenth of May the same regiment rose suddenly and violently against the Europeans. It was late afternoon, and a persistent rumour had it that the first acts of defiance were produced by a group of taunting prostitutes who questioned the manhood of those who would stand by and see their brothers disgraced for adhering to the teachings of their beliefs. The jail was broken into, residences looted, and the sepoys in revolt cut down any European, man, woman or child who happened across their path. By nightfall, they had swept off toward Delhi, intoxicated with newly discovered power that was conceived in shame and born in blood. Oddly, no pursuit was given, for the British Commander of the garrison, an old man of some fifty years of military service, dithered over his options. As a result Delhi fell, and the Indian Mutiny commenced with a shocking vengeance.

Bahadur Shah, a frail king well into his eighties, lived in virtual exile in the palace at Delhi. The British had ensured that no succession was possible, and were waiting patiently for the old man to die so that their grip on his lands could be consolidated. He was weak, given to superstitious intuitions, and spent his days writing rambling poetry and daydreaming. This was a man unfit to take charge of a revolution inspired by his people, but around whose title the fighting was to rally, and in whose name the most dreadful atrocities would be carried out against the English. Soon enough, his initially triumphant sons and subjects would be tugging at his beard, hissing, and calling him 'old man', as he tried to exert influence toward moderation and mercy.

The city of Delhi fell without much resistance. This was not Meerut, where the ratio of Europeans to native soldiers was roughly one to one; very few officers and non-commissioned officers were stationed in Delhi. These were soon overcome, and the remaining whites of all ages, and loyal sepoys who had refused to join the attackers, were killed by musket fire or hacked down with blades, their bodies thrown into the River Jumna.

Johnathan and his small retinue were making their way north along a poor road, beside which telegraph lines had been erected. They had paused to take tea, and avoid the scorching midday sun, when a party of sepoys happened upon them, excited, their uniforms in disarray, and without weapons. In bits and snatches of excited translation from Cheater, the more sordid bits of information were obtained about the revolt. These men had been loyal to the British officers, and informers had turned them in. They were now fleeing for their lives, having witnessed several massacres of both loyalists and Europeans. The two sepoys with Johnathan were so horrified at the recounting of atrocities that, with shouted apologies, they joined the others and ran off. All this took place within the span of five minutes or so, and suddenly Johnathan and his man were alone in the silent jungle, the cries of the fleeing men floating faintly in the distance.

Enough information had been obtained from them to understand that a relief force was being marshalled to march on Delhi; this would have to be under General Anson, Commander-in-Chief, Johnathan supposed. He unrolled his maps, and looked to the likely garrisons which would be drawn upon. Trouble was, there was no way to know how widely the unrest had spread. But if Delhi was taken, it was not likely just a local matter. He decided to continue north, with care, and try to meet up with one of the expeditionary forces. He looked up at the telegraph wires; there was no way to know whether the news had been flashed before they had been sabotaged, as they almost surely were. He was still almost five days away from Delhi, so he thought they had better get started. Calling to Cheater, who was looking fearful, he stood up to his mount. Cheater stood up in the manner of a scrawny stork, scratching the back of his leg with his other foot. 'God-Damn, sahib, God-Damn!'

Moving slowly, and well to the east, then north of Delhi, Johnathan was able to make his way to the road between Sialkot and Delhi. It was here that he intercepted a British force of more than four thousand infantry and cavalry and six guns, on its way to meet a rebel regiment moving to reinforce the mutineers at Delhi. The sight of East India colours was a huge relief, and he reported to the commander, Brigadier John Nicholson.

There was not a soldier in India who had not heard of Nicholson, whom the natives called 'Nikal Seyn'. He stood six foot four, had dark hair and a handlebar moustache topping a full black beard. He had wide, dark eyes, and an unchanging expression as dour as the Old Testament. He was never known to smile. His feats included hunting tigers on horseback with only a sword, and other wizardry with the heavy curved weapon he had received as a gift from Sikh tribesmen. He was known as a fierce fighter, and had a personal guard of unpaid, wild-looking fighters known as the Multani Horse.

Nicholson asked Johnathan to remain with the column, for they expected to have need of engineers. All of the European infantry were dressed in a drab, sandy-green colour. Johnathan learned that this was Nicholson's idea, to blend with the jungle. He had ordered the white uniforms, which were favoured in the hot weather, to be dyed. The colour was known as khaki, from the word khak, for 'dust'. Within a year it would become standard issue. Leaving his tent, he noticed a crew of sappers at work, and he wandered over to talk to them. They were erecting a gallows. 'What for?' asked Johnathan.

A sergeant jerked his thumb over to several bullock carts crowded with quiet men. 'For them. Mutineers. They'll dance in air as soon as the crossbeams are up, and the stages let.'

Johnathan persisted, 'There have been courts martial then?'

This brought chortles from the others. One of them, a second lieutenant with an arm in a sling said, 'When we got a telegram from headquarters for news of progress, together with a return of courts-martial, and various punishments, the Black Irishman cabled back: "The Punishment of Mutiny is Death". Heh. Heh. The road back yonder is dotted with the gallows-tree, and the corpses left dangling as a warning. It's his mark!'

Johnathan's expression must have told his disbelief, and the other man continued. 'At the first set a hangings, he spoke to us, said it might be distasteful, but the secret to winning wars is to be harder than your enemy. It's fear that's our best ally, and these rascals better get it in their woolly heads that to persist in their defiance will lead them straight to hell. Executing these buggers will help restore our influence, and show the rest we mean business.'

Johnathan nodded absently. He hoped it was true. It was a hard business, making statements in blood. But it was the most effective way surely. And it seemed necessary.

The column continued their forced march until the enemy was engaged. Johnathan was not drawn into the actual fighting, for he was assigned to the artillery, to replace those who had been killed or disabled. He had only studied the subject in theory, and knew the calibration of trajectory from books. He understood nothing of gun drill, nor the steps beyond the quantity of powder, and it was some time before he was comfortable commanding a gun crew. Nicholson had distinguished himself during the campaign in which the reserve force of rebels was driven off; principally he had chased a sepoy who was fleeing on foot, rose in his stirrups and sliced the man entirely in two with his great sword. That night at camp, the men could speak of little else, even though many fierce engagements had taken place on the battlefield, where twenty-five British were lost, compared with more than five hundred of the enemy.

On the way back to the ridge outside and above the city of Delhi, where the British forces were gathered to lay siege, Johnathan found that the lieutenant was correct. Many dozens, perhaps hundreds of gallows lined the road, and Johnathan was nauseated to discover that the corpses that hung low to the ground had their lower extremities eaten away by wild pigs. The stench of rotted flesh assailed the nostrils, and the flies were thick as a biblical plague.

Once outside Delhi, at the beginning of September, Johnathan was ordered back to the ranks of the engineers, who totalled seven hundred and twenty-two, including himself. This made for a total of just under ten thousand British soldiers and loyal native troops, with a further contingent of Kashmir cavalry of twenty-two hundred men and four guns. The British contingent was thinned by cholera and dysentery, and many of those remaining were weakened with fever. Deaths from fever easily surpassed those from battle, as had been the experience in the Crimea.

This force faced a defending army of rebels numbering more than forty thousand trained soldiers, as well as the supporting irregulars who had joined in the general uprising. And these were all behind fortified walls, topped with more than fifty heavy guns. It was known that the unrest was widespread, though not necessarily coordinated, and there was the constant worry that there might be another attack to the rear, such as the one that Nicholson's column had averted.

Starting on 11 September, and continuing until the early hours of the 14th, British artillery poured shot into the city. The cannonade was deafening and continuous, so that the screaming of the gun crews' orders was lost in the thunder and smoke; the drill was rote for the men in any event. Following the bombardment, the engineers, including Johnathan, were sent forward in teams under heavy defensive fire, to examine the breaches in the defences, and determine what further needed to be done before the positions could be stormed. It was dangerous work, and men fell on all sides of him.

The invasion commenced at three in the morning on the fourteenth day of September, a day Johnathan thought bore some kind of positive portent. This was the third anniversary of the Battle of the Alma in the Crimea where he had been instructed that the purpose of battle had something to do with 'ideas', rather than tangible gain. Shivering in the coolness, as he crouched close to the damp, musky-smelling earth, he wondered at the wisdom of these remarks. Ideas seemed inevitably to be rooted in self-interest and personal gain. Land, wealth, freedom to pursue one's inclinations, are these just ideas? Intellectual concepts seemed very far away to the soldier or citizen awaiting the call to arms. He calmed himself and took comfort in trying to recall bits of verse:

> *And near, the beat of the alarming drum*
> *Roused up the soldier ere the morning star;*
> *While thronged the citizen with terror dumb,*
> *Or whispering with white lips—*
> *"The foe! They come! They come!"*

The call came soon enough for the five attack columns to move, and the storming of Delhi began before daybreak. He thought of the Europeans inside, and wondered at their fate. Many of them were known to have been put to death in the early days of the mutiny. He thought of Belinda, and wondered whether the troubles had overwhelmed the garrison at Cawnpore. The relief expedition was headed there next.

The fight for Delhi took a terrible toll in lives. To reach the breaches torn by artillery, a huge dry moat first had to be crossed, through the use of siege-ladders. Once in the city, ground was retaken street by street under steady, withering fire from each building. Gangs of rebels would retreat under cover of groups of shouting women, upon whom the Europeans were reluctant to fire. Nicholson was mortally wounded—one among hundreds lost. But after several days of concerted, disciplined action by the British and the native troops who had remained loyal to them, the city was retaken.

The King and his three sons who had been the de facto leaders of the revolt were captured by Major William Hodson. Johnathan was present at the surrender, and the three young men were loaded into a bullock cart and drawn to the Delhi Gate. There, Hodson ordered the men to strip naked before a large crowd, as part of their humiliation and affront to their caste, and made a short speech in which he spoke evenly of the ruin they had brought upon themselves and their city. He proceeded to shoot each one, point-blank, in the chest, with a carbine. Two days later, twenty-one princes of the royal family were hanged in a public square, and the expedition turned their attentions to departing for the relief of Lucknow, for word had arrived that matters were going very poorly for the garrison there; indeed, rumour had it that Cawnpore was lost.

In fact, the besieged Europeans and handful of loyal sepoys at

Cawnpore had taken to the residency and barricaded themselves inside. The command at Cawnpore was in the main a collection of geriatric officers whose easy lifestyle in the service of John Company was sufficiently seductive to discourage retirement. Accordingly, when hostilities broke out, mistakes were made that coolness might have forestalled. The ancient commander, Major-General Sir Hugh Wheeler, turned for help to the very man who would soon lead rebels against him: the Maharajah of Bithur, Nana Sahib.

Moreover, rather than seek refuge in the heavily fortified magazine, with its weaponry, provisions and supply of water, pride induced the old general to remain in a residence, somewhat reinforced, but hardly a place of safety. When the 2nd Native Cavalry sacked the treasury, followed by two other mutinous regiments, the remaining two regiments maintained their loyalty. But Wheeler was nervous and uncertain, and he ordered his guns turned upon them, making unanimous among the sepoys what otherwise might have been saved from total revolt.

On the sixth day of June the rebels returned to Cawnpore, where Wheeler had entrenched two hundred and forty soldiers, six hundred and thirty civilians, mostly women and children, and some invalids. About one hundred and fifty Indian troops remained constant to the British. At mid-morning, the rebel guns commenced firing, and did not let up except for some hours during the night, until the twenty-fifth day of June. The heat of the tropical sun, the inadequate provisions, the daily toll of killed and shattered bodies, particularly of the children, meant that the defenders could not hold out indefinitely. A truce was negotiated, and the survivors were herded down to a small fleet of boats lying in the shallows of the Ganges. The monsoon was late, and the river level was low, so the boats were not able to be run out easily.

All at once troops hitherto hidden opened fire, and a general massacre of the passengers began. Few escaped. Most of the wounded were cut up with swords as they lay struggling with their injuries in the immobile boats. About one hundred and seventy surviving women and children, Belinda Case among them, were confined in a large house, then to a much smaller one built by an officer for his mistress, known in the cantonment as the Bíbíghur, or 'Lady's House'. Colonel Case had been shot from his horse in the initial moments of the attack ordered by Wheeler on the remaining loyal sepoys. His wife never was to discover what became of him. Wheeler died in the boats, his young daughter carried off by an Indian cavalryman before his eyes. He did not see the sabre blow from behind.

The fall of Cawnpore was doubted by the British command. Rain, cholera, and other uprisings delayed the start of a relief force until the middle of July. Though Johnathan had expressed his wish to join the column under Colonel James Neill, who expected to depart imminently from Calcutta, he was refused the necessary permission. Engineers were in short supply, and the nature of their work under enemy fire made them increasingly scarce. He was needed at Delhi, but once Dehli had fallen he would be able to rejoin his regiment in Lucknow, which was having its own troubles with a siege.

Neill's orders to his advance parties were explicit: all enemy places to be destroyed. No prisoners to be taken. Any sepoy found without papers or unable to give proper account was to be hanged immediately, and left hanging. As news of atrocities reached the British soldiers, their blood-lust was inflamed, and revenge upon anyone of dark skin became the order of the day, regardless of guilt.

By the sixteenth of July, the relief expedition had fetched up at Cawnpore with more than one thousand fighting men. Between them and the city were five thousand entrenched sepoys and artillery. The British steadily pushed them back, though with fierce fighting and heavy losses on both sides. The imminence of defeat led to the destruction of the women and children who were under arrest. Muskets were thrust through the slats of the window blinds, and repeated volleys were made upon the prisoners, who set up a fearful screaming as they rushed to the opposite side of the compound, where they were cut down savagely with sabres. So died Belinda Case, who cried for her husband, for her father, and for Johnathan. Would no one come to save her?

This massacre was the single most infamous act of the rebel sepoys, which provoked even more brutal retribution as the word spread among the British. The entire main floor of the residence was awash in gore. Most of the bodies had been removed, taken to a deep well and thrown in, without ascertaining whether life remained or not; the remainder had been cast into the river. Neill was outraged beyond restraint, and some of his officers were of the view that he would 'destroy all of black creation'. He wrote home of his 'courts-martial':

'Whenever a rebel is caught he is immediately tried and unless he can prove a defence he is sentenced to be hanged at once; but the chief rebels or ringleaders I make clean up [by licking] a certain portion of the pool of blood, still two inches deep, in the shed where the fearful murder and mutilation of women took place.

'To touch blood is most abhorrent to the high caste natives; they think that by doing so they doom their souls to perdition. Let them think so. My object is to inflict a most fearful punishment for a revolting, cowardly, barbarous deed, and to strike terror into these rebels.

'The first I caught was a subadhar, a native officer, a high caste Brahmin who tried to resist my order to clean up the very blood he had helped to shed; but I made the Provost-Marshal do his duty, and a few lashes soon made the miscreant accomplish his task. Which done, he was immediately taken out and hanged...'

Many sepoys suffered a similar fate, including the innocent. Revenge was exacted by soldiers randomly and wantonly; frequently the musket spoke before explanation was demanded. Wanton brutality became accepted behaviour: when an officer complained to a provost sergeant that the condemned men were swung up in the air from a standing position, to strangle slowly, and that the executions were cruelly carried out, the sergeant replied between clenched teeth, 'Well, I dunno, sir; I haven't heard any complaints.' A terse entry in a log read: 'Private Ladd: Hanging a native without permission—two days confined to barracks.' From these vengeful depredations, Nana Sahib escaped, and would not be heard from until 1859, when he wrote to Queen Victoria protesting his innocence.

As these stories reached Johnathan, still trapped in battle at Delhi, he mourned for Belinda, and became sick with rage at the senseless cruelty of the destruction of civilians at Cawnpore. Vicariously, he experienced the bittersweet taste of revenge as the details of Neill's retributions were told and retold. As the tale spread through the siege army, fighting was renewed with vigour and the desire to exact a similar price from the men inside the walls. Terrifying acts of futile bravery were carried out in the name of those fallen at Cawnpore, though there were plenty of examples of wasted lives all around.

The siege of Lucknow commenced on the fourteenth of May 1857, and lasted until the twenty-first day of March 1858. Johnathan was part of a small relief force of less than three thousand troops under Major-General Sir James Outran. Besieging the city was a combined force variously estimated between twenty-five and one hundred thousand men. In cutting their way through to the inner walls, almost eight hundred men had been lost, and Lucknow still was not relieved. Johnathan was immediately put to work supporting the counter-mining which had to be employed to intercept the enemy's tunnelling ventures. Not a single engineering officer of his battalion remained alive. Johnathan was field-promoted to 'Lieutenant'.

One night a group of captured sepoys was brought to Outran's quarters, though now General August Havelock had resumed command. Johnathan listened nearby as Havelock turned to his senior captain after contemplating with disgust the leader of the sepoys, who had been stripped to the waist, and forced to kneel in the dust.

'Captain, do you know how to blow a man from a gun?'

The captain, a man named Maude, replied, 'It was not part of the curriculum at Woolwich, sir, but it would be obvious, I think, to anyone, that three pounds of good powder would be pretty sure to effect the desired purpose.'

This was to form a new manner of execution. A field-piece was hauled up to an elevated spot, well in sight of the enemy, and there the condemned man was lashed to the wheels of the gun, with his midriff taut against the muzzle. A handsome fellow, he showed not a hint of fear. He looked upon his executioners with a half-smile bordering on contempt. At one point, Johnathan felt the man's direct, unswerving gaze meet his own. Johnathan looked away. The blast completely destroyed the sepoy, whose head flew into the air almost two hundred feet, coming back down near the gun again. The gathered onlookers gasped, and Johnathan cried out involuntarily, as did most of the onlookers, 'Jesus in Heaven!' Would the parade of horrors never cease?

From behind came an unmistakable voice, tired, cynical, and bitter. 'If that is truly where Christ is, then let Him stay there! He is indifferent to these monstrous deeds, or He would have intervened long ago. He has forsaken us!'

Johnathan turned to face Calvin, who looked the same as when he had left him, save for a thick layer of filth. He cried aloud, and seized Calvin by the shoulders. 'You big bastard! What a pleasure to see you still alive! There's been so much death and destruction! Jesus!' He turned back to the gun, where another prisoner was being led out. A proud man, almost haughty, he asked for the right to die unbound, but this was denied him without answer. Again the prolonged ceremony of gun drill was carried out, and again the orders called, the shouts lingering in the evening air, and the dreadful explosion tore another human being to bits.

Johnathan turned back to Calvin. 'I have had enough; let's go.' It surprised him that he was so upset. He blinked; his eyes were wet.

Calvin looked back as yet another man was being dragged to the gun muzzle. 'I hope it impresses the superstitious bastards; that's the point isn't it?' Johnathan did not reply for a bit, then he said, grim-faced, 'I think the danger is they'll visit even worse cruelties on our men, should they have the dashed luck to be taken alive. But maybe you're right. Maybe it will sap their will.'

As they walked back to the inner city, Johnathan spoke again. 'In Delhi, I waded through the remnants of smashed humanity in the tens of thousands. So much blood; it oozed into my boots like mud. I witnessed the destruction of the Light Brigade—hundreds of good men—in a single monumental act of foolishness. These were bad enough, to be sure. But the death of a single man, deliberate, for a purpose calculated to instill fear or respect, oddly has more impact than the death of a hundred, wouldn't you say?'

Calvin replied immediately, 'It's enough to keep me on the straight and narrow, mind!'

Johnathan seemed not to hear, as he completed his thought. 'At least it makes more of an impression with me.'

Calvin brought Johnathan current with the grim details of the siege: the demise of the commanding officer by shrapnel landing in his quarters, the constant deaths, fifteen or twenty a day, from sniper fire, the cholera, the heat. It was a wretched litany which Johnathan knew all too well. He was suddenly tired, and longed for the war to be over. He said as much, but Calvin was indifferent. 'It's what we do,' he said simply. 'But in various ways, the fighting can cut a man's expectations off short and sudden, I'll admit. The man you'd be reporting to ordinarily, the chief engineer, Major Anderson, is dead. Bang, like that.' He snapped his fingers, and continued.

'And how did he go? Got a case of the galloping shits, and never recovered. Not much of a passing for a soldier, but he did die with his boots on, as I recall. They were full of shit, though.'

'Who's the chief engineer now?' asked Johnathan.

'Captain Fulton. Now there's a character. A man's man. A soldier's soldier. I shall take you to him.'

'Why do you have such high regard for this chap? We have no shortage of brave fighting men of all ranks who have been stepping out to meet the enemy.'

Calvin laughed. 'It's not his exploits above ground I speak of. The man practically lives underground, and more than once has saved us all.'

Johnathan was puzzled. 'What do you mean? Come now, Calvin. Explain yourself.'

'The enemy has a number of Pasi archers who for some reason are adept at tunnelling for the placement of charges. One or two well-placed charges in these mines can bring down a wall and expose us to attack. Many attempts have been made, and one such blast knocked a hole more than thirty feet wide near the Sikh Square, which fortunately was not followed up by the black devils pressing their advantage.

'But Fulton, with a squad of Cornishmen—from the coal mines I think they are—has become a champion counter-tunneller, and by calculating angles, and digging his own mines, he or one of the squad just sits at the end and wait for the pick-axe to come through, and the startled labourer gets a charge from a pistol. Lots of skirmishes have taken place underground.'

Johnathan knew of the mining techniques, but much depended upon the condition of the soil. It was dangerous work, not for those uneasy in small, dark spaces. Being buried alive was only one of many grim possibilities waiting for the tunneller at the end of a damp, dark burrow.

It was in the aid of 'Fulton's Terriers', as the miners were known, that Johnathan was to pass the rest of the mutiny until it ended in the middle of March, 1858. He calculated angles, studied soil samples and recommended bracing accordingly. He stood 'tunnel watch', which had nothing whatsoever to do with standing, but required the sentry to lie in certain places, ear to the ground, listening for the thump of the pick-axe, the scrape of shovels, and even the muffled high voices of the miners as they called to one another. Then it was necessary to calculate where to counter-mine, whether to use an existing shaft and branch off, or whether the enemy had discovered it, and even now were waiting with cocked revolvers. It was unnerving work, and Johnathan went down only once. He had, he discovered, a fear of closed places, and was seized with an overwhelming panic once below.

The passage was so narrow, however, that he was unable to turn around, and he was compelled to crawl for a dozen yards or so in utter blackness, until an adjoining drift permitted him to turn around. As he did so, he caught the thick miasma of rotting flesh, which filled him with dread, lest he put a hand in the remains of some poor bastard who had been caught unawares in a grave of his own making. Inching his way back, he was utterly convinced that the roof was about to cave in, and he fought the ludicrous urge to stand up; his back grazed the ceiling of the passageway as he crawled on all fours, shaking bits of rubble loose over him. Once out, he avowed that not even the firing squad could make him go back in, though he was to carry an abiding sense of shame because of his fear for the remaining days of his service.

The mutiny ended with the capture, trial, and execution of the last leader of the sepoys in April of 1859. The lessons of the fighting were not lost on the British administration, and the previous year saw the transfer of the government of India from East India Company to the Crown. The Queen's Proclamation called for a greater degree of religious tolerance, and greater mobility in the institutions of government and the military. The army sponsored by the Company was transferred to the standing army of the Crown, and that September Johnathan drew his uniform as a first Lieutenant of the Royal Engineers. He returned to his cantonment at Lucknow, but the images of war remained with him. Principal among these was the fate of the lovely Belinda Case at Cawnpore. It had only been a matter of days that he had missed being trapped with her; perhaps he could have done something to change what had happened. These were vivid thoughts, impossible to banish. There was a persistent image of her white limbs, tangled and bloodied with others in the well where they had been so cruelly dumped.

For more than the following year, he was occupied with the reconstruction of the barracks, fortifications and roadways at Lucknow. There was not a single structure which had missed being damaged by the talons of war. Many were unsafe, and had to be pulled down. Bridges required rebuilding, and new roads had to be laid down. Then commercial tea plantations required additional road-building, as did the cotton exporters of the Punjab. Fortifications along the border and drainage schemes drew on his talents well into the next decade, a decade of prosperity and relative peace.

Johnathan did not realize it, but he had suffered an exhaustion of the spirit following the war. For a time, the heavy demands of work consumed his thoughts, but the suffering he had seen called for a grieving process which he would not allow himself. Even as a child, he seemed indifferent to pain; Sir Alex had called him 'emotionally flat'. At night he would wake with a start, having just felt a sensation similar to riding a swing with his eyes closed, up to the end of its arc, then slipping backwards to oblivion. Eyes open wide, he would sit up, sweating. Belinda Case and her husband were phantoms who troubled his sleep. He wondered if he were going mad.

From time to time, he would visit Calvin, though fraternization with the non-commissioned officers was frowned upon. Calvin reintroduced Johnathan to opium, and the two of them would sit silently, puffing their way into a gentle euphoria. Johnathan realized that he was not a natural comrade, preferring to keep his thoughts to himself. Calvin made no conversational or intellectual demands upon him, and this suited Johnathan well enough.

The source of their opium was a hideous-looking man with a deformed back. He and other men, whom he mysteriously referred to as his 'brothers', would occasionally sit cross-legged on the floor of Johnathan's quarters, and share in the smoke. Sometimes, at Calvin's request, women would be brought for a nautch. Johnathan's lower-caste manservant who had replaced Cheater (lost in Delhi at the hands of a maddened British cavalryman bent on revenge), would explain secrets to the two men who listened in a dreamy haze to mystic descriptions of the principal deities of Hindu worship. The king, Siva, was always represented with an enormous erection, and Sakti, the consuming, enveloping woman, symbol of supreme energy and fecundity of the universe, was his partner.

The male god was depicted passively, but in high arousal; his rest was interrupted by the female deity who took him deep within her to begin the coupling which resulted in the shudder of completion that released life forces in the universe. Such symbolism, the odd-looking rascal explained through Johnathan's servant, is powerful, and is based largely on the explicit eroticism which is forbidden to the higher castes.

On one occasion a woman was brought to the house, whose role evidently was to be that of Sakti. To the soothing accompaniment of three other chanting women, and deep draughts of opium smoke, the Sakti came to them as naked as they, and sitting on the floor in the lotus position began to massage their bodies in oils, going alternately from one to the other. She displayed her lissom body to the man opposite as she worked her magic with the one before her.

Straddling one with the help of the other women, she impaled herself slowly, deliberately upon her eager recipient. Then she would draw up, then relax; repeat several times, then disengage and move to the man opposite. So it went for an hour or more, pausing only to massage a white powder into the glans of their swollen cocks. When at last she brought the men to their completion, by powerful contractions of her thigh muscles and inner body, both men cried out sharply, gasping for air like beached fishes. This proved to be a pastime which consumed both men, and they called upon their supplier to bring a variety of women to perform the role of the Sakti. Life for Johnathan in Lucknow became dissolute, and it should not have surprised him that both he and Calvin came down with syphilis, known then as the 'French Disease'. Red-rimmed eyes, weight loss and listlessness signified both the infection and their growing dependency on opium. At the time of the initial discovery of his genital chancres, Johnathan paid no attention, for the jungle produced a myriad of diseases; one could hardly be bothered with all of them. But after a time, the rash on his body, brittleness of hair and enlarged and hardened lymph nodes, led the Chief Surgeon to pronounce his diagnosis in disapproving terms.

'Addict and fornicator! And paying a heavy price for it now, aren't we? But with the right amounts of iodine and mercury, and proper rest, ye'll be put right. But stay away from them black whores and Satan's poppy!' Calvin, with the constitution of a bear, seemed not to be troubled to the same degree.

Johnathan was ordered to Calcutta, where he was to be transferred by boat across the Arabian Sea to Abyssinia, a dry climate thought to be good for convalescence from such an infection. He bade farewell to Calvin, perhaps knowing that they would not see each other again, and reflected that Calvin was as close to a friend as he had ever experienced. Yet he expressed no emotion when they parted, though Calvin snivelled a bit, like the overgrown boy he was.

It was in August of 1866, and the rainy season commenced well before he could reach the port city. The trip was grim, and as the result of flooding it was necessary to stop over for weeks until alternative routes and passage could be obtained. It was during this journey to the coast that Johnathan came down with malaria, owing in part, he felt, to his weakened state. As a result, he was invalided out from service a second time, and shipped home to recover in England from his infections. The sea voyage was hard going for him; he rarely saw topside for the entire journey. For many nights he was delirious with fever, his body glistening with sweat. His agonies were enhanced by the forced withdrawal from the opiate grip. It was the fever which killed off the syphilis, however, and he began a slow recovery from the malaria. It was a pale shadow of the young engineer who returned to Gleneaglesham in the spring of 1867.

ii

Johnathan sat outside the office of The Honourable William McDougall, Minister of Public Works in the Canadian Government of Sir John A. Macdonald, clutching a letter of introduction from Sir Alex in his left hand. His scarred hand felt stiff, as it seemed to do each year now with the change in weather. The waiting room was comfortable, and McDougall's secretary, a man of short patience but grand manners, kept looking at him over the spectacles perched on the end of a thin nose. The clock on the panelled wall ticked off the minutes with deliberate slowness.

At last the heavy oak door swung open, and Johnathan was admitted to the Minister's chambers. Shaking hands with the man, Johnathan greeted him as warmly as he could muster.

'Good day to you, sir!' cried McDougall. He had white hands and a small, compact body, though with a slight paunch. He had a lawyer's quick, spare movements, and he fussed with papers on his desk while he spoke. 'Give me but a few moments while I attend to a small matter for the Prime Minister, and I shall be back before you know it!' Johnathan was annoyed as McDougall minced from the room; he had already kept him waiting for more than an hour. He stood up, and walked to the large windows which looked down several hundred feet to the Ottawa River below. The surface of the river sparkled in the sunlight, and the brilliant fall tapestry on the other side seemed as lush as any he had seen elsewhere on his travels. It was every bit true, as Alex Dunn had told him in the Crimea: Canada was a lovely place; at least, that which he had seen of it so far. Ottawa was very much like parts of Scotland. His thoughts drifted back to his arrival at Gleneaglesham.

It was not as if he had been unexpected. For though he did not write home frequently, he had sent enough mail to his mother to keep her apprised of his whereabouts, and his general comings and goings. He spared her the details of the fighting and the less savoury aspects of his life. Her letters numbered about five to every one that he wrote. And though he was glad enough to get them from her, he would lay the letter down for several days before he could bring himself to open it.

His mother had aged, and it shocked him. Sir Alex, who seemed the same, explained to Johnathan later that Victoria had been ill for some time, and seemed not to be getting better. It was a tumour, growing inside her ovaries, which would eventually kill her. She appeared weak and tired easily, but she was still a housemaid and was daily contributing a certain amount of work toward her keep. This angered Johnathan, for he thought there could have been more indulgence shown to his mother. He decided to confront Sir Alex on this and other things, one evening after his mother had retired for the night. He found him in the library, sitting in the same chair as he always had since Johnathan could remember. On the small round table to one side was a glass of port, and an unstoppered decanter beside it. Johnathan watched him for a moment; the lamp behind seemed to illuminate his white hair, creating a halo effect. The old man was getting on, Johnathan thought to himself. He holds the book much closer to his eye than I recall. He could make out the gold lettering on the cover: Childe Harold's Pilgrimage. Johnathan stepped forward.

'She has committed you to Byron as well, I see.'

Sir Alex's head swung up; he was momentarily startled. 'Oh. It's you. No one ever comes in here, not even your mother any more.' He looked down at the volume in his hands. 'Yes. I was rather more fond of Tennyson; always thought Byron a bit sloppy, actually; a bit insincere. But your mother's helped me to see past the immorality and skepticism, to the power and romance of his vision.'

'She has that ability,' nodded Johnathan. 'But then, I know you understand me when I say she has many talents.'

Sir Alex looked at him sharply in the low light, then nodded agreement. 'She is a special woman.'

Johnathan could not hold back any longer, and said rather more harshly than he intended. 'Then why do you continue to work her as a drudge, when she is so obviously ill?'

The other man looked almost surprised. 'It is her choice. I have offered her a pension, as well as the right to remain in the house. But she insists upon the right to earn her way. She will not be kept, she says, like some old hunting dog that's lost its teeth.'

Johnathan grimaced with confusion. 'Has she not, sir, been your mistress these many past years, and am I not your bastard son?' There. He had blurted out what had tormented him since he was a boy, and what pride had dictated he should never ask.

The old man's volume slid from his lap as he gripped the arms of his chair in surprise. He opened his mouth as a thought framed itself, then he closed it again. For a long moment he sat looking at Johnathan, then he gestured to the chair opposite. 'Sit down, my boy. Perhaps there are things I should have told you before.'

Johnathan sat. He was tense, and did not lean back. Sir Alex seemed to slump in his own seat.

'Yes. Your mother and I have been lovers. She has been a comfort to me. But somewhere along the line I offended her deeply about the possibility of marriage, though she was content to leave things as they were. I believe her decision was made because of you. By the time I realized that she would make the sort of wife I desired, regardless of her station, she refused me. And all these years, we have kept up the pretence that she is an upstairs maid, even though the whole house—and you—and the entire village for all I know—knew we shared a bed. I've been a fool I'm afraid.

'And are you my son? I wish that you were, but you are not. You came here with your mother as a very young babe, and my promise has been given to Victoria that I would say no more on the subject.'

'But why?' Johnathan felt a wave of confused emotions. Was it disappointment?

'Because, I believe, the man left you both. I don't think he even knew he was to be a father. But whatever; he left. And your mother, for all purposes, considered him dead. But truth to tell, a piece of her soul died too, and for too long I did nothing to cultivate what was left.' He seemed genuinely remorseful, and Johnathan did not press him, though his mind reeled with questions.

For a long time the two men sat in the silent room while the ghosts of literature looked on; Byron lay sprawled at the old man's feet. At last Sir Alex spoke, his voice measured and soft. 'She's dying, you know.'

'I know well enough,' said Johnathan. 'I must be away from here soon, but I will wait. It's only fitting that a son should bury his mother.' Across from him, he could see that Sir Alex's eyes were moist as he looked back at him.

'You were always so cool. Never cried, even when you got a beating. Where do you hide your misery?'

'I really do apologize.' The reedy voice intruded into Johnathan's thoughts as McDougall reentered the room. 'Prime Minister. Hates to be kept waiting, and he really does depend on me too much. Sit down! Sit down!'

The Minister had received a letter from Sir Alex a month earlier, indicating that the 'son of a very close friend, a highly competent engineer, would be coming to the new Dominion of Canada looking for work'. English nobility had considerable claim on the attentions of the Canadian bureaucracy; McDougall had spent some time in England bargaining over the lands surrounding Red River, and remained in awe of titles and peerage. And Sir Alex had influence with the Hudson's Bay Company whose claims to Rupert's Land McDougall expected to secure for Canada. Nearly one and a half million square miles would be added to the young country; this, he hoped, should bring appropriate enhancements to his own prestige and purse. Perhaps this favour could yield fruit there as well, later on. Lieutenant-Governor of the new territories! He licked his lips. It had a nice ring to it. But there were problems to overcome before he could assume the mantle of chief executive of the region.

He preferred to retain cronies and sycophants, for there had to be no question about trust and personal loyalties; patronage was the best way to ensure fidelity, he was convinced. He had an old friend, Colonel John Stoughten Dennis, in place as overall superintendent of public surveys, but he needed a man on the job location, full time, at Red River. Dennis had something of a questionable background, having been accused of incompetence and cowardice in 1866 during the first Fenian raid at Fort Erie. But McDougall was finding it difficult to hire a chief agent who happened to have the technical skills, as well as the more critical qualifications of loyalty and obligation he was after. Snow was a godsend: an invalided soldier looking for a job, connected to the Company in only a tangential way, and a qualified surveyor with experience in road-building in India. To say nothing of Sir Alexander's indebtedness to McDougall should he take Snow on. What could be better? But for additional insurance, the number two man would keep an eye on him.

'Come over here,' said McDougall, as he unrolled a map of British North America on his desk. Weighting down the corners with books and an inkwell, he pointed a stubby finger at the center of the map. 'This area bounded in blue is Rupert's Land. Soon it will belong to Canada. There are many problems associated with the transfer, but nothing insurmountable. He beamed at the map as if it were an illustration of his personal fiefdom.

'There has been a famine out there this year. All along here, the Red River.' He moved his finger up and down the thin line almost precisely at the center of the projection. 'Grasshoppers have stripped the plains, and the wild buffalo herds upon which the Métis depend during the winter have not come on their annual migration as expected.

'They are facing starvation, and we are in a position to provide relief work at prices which will be, I think, attractive to us, yet welcome to the region.'

Johnathan nodded, 'Go on; what is the nature of the task?'

'In anticipation of the imminent joining of these lands with Canada, we shall require a road to be built between here (he pointed to the junction of the Red and Assiniboine rivers), and here (he lay his finger at the west side of the body of water known as Lake of the Woods. This route has had preliminary examination about ten years ago, by a man named Simon Dawson. The land route to the head of navigation on the Great Lakes has been identified, and some parts to the east are already in use. But it is here, about ninety miles of rugged country, that we require a road. Will you take it on?'

Johnathan was surprised and delighted. The job was his. But McDougall had left out more than he had said.

'Are there sufficient funds for this project? Shall I have staff appointed, or shall I retain? Have the necessary permissions been obtained?'

McDougall pursed his lips. 'Your assistant and paymaster shall be a man by the name of Mair, Charles Mair. Others may be found locally, but I suggest that a skeleton crew of Canadians be taken out with you.'

'Is Mair a surveyor, an engineer by training, or accountant?'

'Ah, well, he is in point of fact a man of letters, ah, a poet at the moment.'

Johnathan did not know if his leg was being pulled. 'A poet?'

'I know this man personally, and can give a very good account of him. You will not be displeased I assure you.' He rushed on, as if to forestall any other discussion. 'There is sufficient funding, with a share of the surplus to come to you if you husband the government's money carefully. As for the permissions, they have not technically been obtained, but it is only a formality, and will be attended to in due course.

McDougall spoke too fast and too glibly to comfort Johnathan, but the job was his, and a major piece of work it seemed to be. He met Mair the following week and Johnathan took to him immediately. The two of them ran a short recruitment campaign for a nucleus of labourers; then the party set off on American railroads for Red River, completing the final leg by steamer. Sending Mair on to Oak Point, south of Winnipeg, Johnathan went to see the Governor of Assiniboia, William Mactavish, to request permission before commencing work. He was surprised by the fact that the Governor had never heard of the proposed project, but when he was asked for the permission of the Company to proceed with the work, the Governor agreed, though he wondered aloud to Johnathan whether he had any such authority. When Mair and the motley gang of labourers from the east arrived in Winnipeg, they descended upon Dutch George's Hotel in force. This was the roistering hangout of white teamsters, buffalo hunters, transients, tripmen, miners and outlaws, and American Army deserters. Most of the revellers and layabouts had one thing in common: they considered that Indians were vermin, and 'breeds' not much better. The Canadian survey party blended very well into the mix.

The survey of the proposed roadway began at Oak Point, which was later to become Ste Anne des Chênes; there was a small but established Métis settlement there. A log storage building was appropriated and enlarged for use as the warehouse for supplies and small equipment. Initially, the work gang was welcomed; the Métis children would come out to watch the survey crew in action, and some of the men got work clearing bush from the right-of-way. But Mair and his colleagues made no bones about their contempt for the locals, and Johnathan was true to his own character; he was aloof and kept to himself. He saw opportunity here. The grasshoppers would not last forever, and the soil was rich. A man could have as much land as he could ride around in a day, and Dennis's surveys could not have been better timed for the purchase of land. Quickly, he found that the Indians would agree to give up their claim for a couple of bottles of cheap rum, and stakes bearing survey descriptions and his own name began to sprout east of Red River.

Meanwhile, Mair had little to do, given his qualifications, and he fell under the influence of Dr John Schultz, businessman, politician, bigot and full-time meddler. Like Schultz, he envisioned a huge influx of settlers from Ontario in the near future, and saw opportunity for personal enrichment and power. So close did his association with Schultz become, that he moved from his quarters in Dutch George's Hotel to Schultz's residence. He wrote to his brother in Ontario indicating his satisfaction with Schultz, and his relief that he was able to escape the racket of Halfbreeds who had taken over the hotel, drinking, shouting and playing billiards.

Mair, who had studied at Queen's University in Ontario, had become a minor poet; some newspapers had declared him the 'Canadian poet'. The letters he wrote from Red River to his brother were published in the Toronto *Globe*—without his permission, he asserted later. Yet the letters seemed drafted for public consumption, and few outside the inner circle of Canadians at Red River believed him.

He commented on the racial tensions in the community in a way which seemed designed to increase them. He was openly condescending to the mixed-bloods, French- or English-speaking, save that he considered the English Halfbreeds marginally superior, depending upon their colour. That Halfbreed Bloode, for example, seemed reasonably intelligent; ran a business. But he had a beautiful mixed-blood wife who, it was said, was fucking everyone else in town. Didn't that prove a point? In one letter which appeared in the *Globe*, read many weeks later in Winnipeg, particular outrage was expressed by the locals.

'Many wealthy people,' he wrote, 'are married to half breed-women who, having no coat of arms but a totem to look back to, make up for the deficiency by biting at the backs of their white sisters. The white sisters fall back on their whiteness, whilst the husbands meet each other with desperate courtesies and hospitalities, with a view to filthy lucre in the background.'

As it happened, the paper arrived in the post office and was read aloud to a number of women by the wife of the postmaster, Mrs Bannatyne. Within a few minutes, in walked Mair to collect mail for the survey party. He was immediately set upon by the pack of outraged women who cornered him like hounds, tweaking him sharply by the nose and pulling his ears and hair, until dishevelled and bruised, he fled, pursued by Mrs Bannatyne who had obtained a horsewhip. Though he was to publish an apology, his return to Winnipeg was not received with any warmth by the mixed-blood population, for his presence was a reminder, as if they needed one, of the undercurrents of prejudice rife in the community. As a result, Mair spent considerably more time with the survey party than he ordinarily would have preferred. It was boring and uncomfortable in the line camps out in the bush, beautiful though it was.

The terrain between the Red River Valley and Lake of the Woods had a still, patient quality. From the thick grass-covered loam of the river plain, to the forbidding, exposed granite of the Precambrian shield, there was contrast in texture, variety in plant and animal life. Call-notes of birds ranged from the rasping croak of the solitary raven to the sweet trilling lyric of the meadow lark announcing the break of day. It was landscape alive with promise.

As the work proceeded to the east, canopied halls of birch and poplar gave way to tougher ground, thick with sentinel spruce, the advance guard of limitless stands of hardwoods and evergreens. Brooding forests of fir stood hushed as the breeze suddenly dropped. Below trunks so thick that two men could barely join hands around them, lay tangled deadfall and new growth sprouting from the musky-smelling forest floor.

It was hard going: mapping and cutting and clearing. It was work relieved only by the elongated drumlins which formed natural sandy causeways through the woods. These were the advantages for a prospective road cited by Dawson a decade earlier. Unchanged since the glacial retreat, the roadway slowly followed their contours east.

Between these natural formations lay forbidding marshes resonant with the wild music of a thousand different birds. Here, the mosquitoes made the evenings impossible for work, and men lay shrouded around the campfire like furniture in a closed house. Here, too, lay reaches of muskeg which swallowed every rock pitched into it, and occasionally a horse or wagon. Corduroy roads made of pine logs bursting with pitch were laid in, layer upon layer, until they floated solidly on the surface of the bog. Smaller logs chinked with mud made for a smoother surface that would still be bone-jarring to riders in wheeled vehicles.

Fleet deer started in the clearings, sending the men running for their guns. Moose caught unaware, knee-deep in the sloughs, threw up massive heads crowned by a glory of antlers. Plunging away, they cast off a shower of water droplets that caught and held the sunlight like prisms. Fat partridges strutted in the pine boughs, then fluttered down to where the men worked, strolling so close they could be killed with a spade. 'Fool hens', they called them, and they made good eating. With a foot on each wing, a man could wrench out the breast meat with a single tug. It was a plentiful land—spacious, open and beautiful—and Johnathan felt that his wandering had come to an end. He paused at his instruments and looked around him, taking in the deep fragrance of pine boughs.

> *There is a pleasure in the pathless woods,*
> *There is a rapture in the lonely shore,*
> *There is society where none intrudes…*

This was a place he could settle; a land where, if a man was strong and determined enough, he could get ahead and do well. Above all, it seemed an empty place, a country of lakes and forests and open plains awaiting the steady hand of the pioneer and the man of vision.

In early 1869, Johnathan found he required more help in line cutting. The survey was going well, but the road crews were not keeping up. Of the men he had hired, he had found the Métis the hardest working and most tractable, though they could not always be depended upon to show up for work. The Canadian and United States drifters were reliable, but tended to do the minimum, and spent a lot of the work day standing around leaning on shovels and axes, gabbing and complaining to one another. He hired a young, intelligent-looking fellow from Ontario by the name of Thomas Scott. Quick, polite, the man seemed promising as foreman material, but he had a cruel mouth, thin and downturned. He was sharply sarcastic, Johnathan found out later, and proved a disappoinment.

One of Scott's first enterprises was to organize the work party into a strike for better pay. Resentment had been building for some time that pay was not in cash, but in vouchers which could only be redeemed at the store in Oak Point. True, they could be sold, but prices at the store were much higher than anywhere else, and so they needed to be discounted even further. When he was confronted by his men who had declined to pick up their tools that morning, Johnathan refused to listen to their demands for more money. He was getting too rich for that. Mair had been sharing with him the funds they had been skimming, and there was no way in heaven that these shiftless thugs were going to intimidate him. His military background prompted him to order them back to work:

'Back to work immediately, now, or I shall have the lot of you laid off, and a fresh crew hired on!'

Scott snarled at him. 'Bloody limey bastard! Let's get him, boys! Into the river with the red-headed son-of-a-bitch!'

Johnathan was seized by the little mob and borne on their shoulders despite his cries insisting he be put down. They were at the edge of a small tributary of the Seine River called LaCoulee, which meandered in a westerly direction. Pausing at the bank, the man cast Johnathan in. The water was shallow and the fall stunned him. He was vaguely aware of some of the men sliding down to the water's edge. Christ! They were not done with him.

A shot sounded. Johnathan recognized the dull thump of a Brown Bess musket. On the opposite bank were two men on horseback, two Métis from Isle des Chênes named Harrison and Blondeau. At this, the work crew ran off.

'Ça va?' called Blondeau, standing in his stirrups. 'Sont-ils voleurs?'

Shakily Johnathan stood up and waved. 'Thank you, I am all right now.' And he waved them on. The two men looked at each other, and moved off slowly, several times looking back to see whether Johnathan was still standing. Johnathan stepped slowly through the mucky water to the bank, and sat down. The men were gone. He drew out his watch, Battersea's timepiece, and regarded it sadly. It had stopped, ruined by the dunking, the second such dousing by angry men in his life.

As he stared at it, he realized that it had frozen at exactly nine o'clock. He remembered the nine chimes of the village church when his mother was buried. The service at graveside was over. There were just the two of them now, silent sentinels at the edge of the torn earth. Sir Alex had stepped forward, opened a small book of poetry, cleared his throat, and read aloud:

In secret we met—
In silence I grieve
That thy heart could forget,
Thy spirit deceive.
If I should meet thee
After long years,
How should I greet thee?
With silence and tears.

Following the funeral, they had sat in the library for some time. Johnathan spoke first. 'It's not that I am ungrateful to you. I know it cost you money to send me to Woolwich; you have assisted immeasurably in getting positions for me, but I must make my own way.' And after a pause, he continued.

'I have nothing in the world now, save a rather battered volume of Byron, inscribed by my mother, and a gold watch which used to belong to a dead man.'

Sir Alex looked up at him, his expression grim. 'How can you say such a thing? Where is your mother's spark? Look…'

He took a volume, Childe Harold's Pilgrimage, from the table beside him. He flipped the pages, marked and dog-eared, with a moistened middle finger. How like his mother, Johnathan thought with a distant twinge. She would touch her tongue as she searched for a passage; this tender ritual reflected her spirit living on in this man.

'Here. Yes; listen to this, and learn something that I think your mother was hoping you'd see.' And he read aloud:

condense thy soul
To more immediate objects, and control
Thy thoughts until thy mind hath got by heart
Its eloquent proportions…
part by part…

He looked up. 'Wisdom, Byron instructs us, comes in small, incremental bits. Immediate and partial acts of perception. You must continually reformulate your understanding of the significance of what you see, especially what is in front of you. Learn this, and you will have understanding for the future, for like Harold's pilgrimage, the voyage never ends.

'You are a trained engineer, with experience in surveying and road building. You have served with honour in the British and East India Army. You have, in short, everything that a man could wish to make his way in the world. What you choose to do with your experience is up to you.'

Johnathan felt a little ashamed, and did not meet the old man's gaze. 'I have read that passage countless times. I had always thought it had to do with past blindness. I did not mean...'

Sir Alex interrupted. 'Exactly. Past and present blindness. In any event, I do not think the place for you is here. Though I think our relationship is bearable to one another, now that your mother is gone, the glue which held us together has disappeared.'

Johnathan felt his pride stiffen. 'I shall be gone in the morning.'

'Don't be a silly ass,' said Sir Alex. 'I have been following the discussions in London between the Hudson's Bay Company and the colonial government of Canada, for the acquisition of Rupert's Land and the North-west Territories. In fact, they have been seeking my advice on an informal basis. When the deal goes forward, as I think is inevitable, there will be nearly one and a half million square miles involved in the transfer, not a yard of which is surveyed. And I'm sure it has not much more than the few dozen miles of road it had when I visited the place myself.'

Johnathan was interested. 'You think, then, there are possibilities for me?'

'More than possibilities. There are not enough men trained as you. And besides, the land itself is a wonder. The biggest sky you ever saw, and yet have earth underneath your feet. A land of powerful contrasts, excesses and shortages. A land of magnificent opportunity, for I believe it sits presently at the threshold of a glorious future.' He spoke passionately, and looked off in the distance. Johnathan could tell he was seeing the place as he recalled it in his memory. He turned to look at Johnathan again.

'I shall furnish you with a ticket to Montréal, and a letter of introduction. I shall write to people of influence on your behalf. What you make of it from there is up to you.'

Johnathan stood up and placed the ruined watch in his pocket. Perhaps it could be repaired. His boots were sodden, and he would have to walk a considerable distance back to the line camp. He hoped the mutineers were not there, but he rather suspected that they would have made for Dutch George's so as to arrive before closing. He hoped they had the decency to leave at least one horse behind.

It was shortly thereafter that Johnathan was served with a summons to petty court. A complaint had been made about his dealings with the Indians, selling liquor for land. The charge was a response to a more widespread grievance. The manner of survey which Dennis was supervising was directed by McDougall in written instructions, which preceded formal closure of negotiations with the Hudson's Bay Company. McDougall wrote Colonel Dennis.

'Referring to the subject discussed at our interview yesterday, I now request you to proceed without delay to Fort Garry, Red River, for the purpose of selecting the most suitable localities for the survey of townships for immediate settlement.

'The American system of survey is that which appears the best suited to the country, except as to the area of the section. The first immigrants, and the most desirable, will probably come from Canada, and it will therefore be advisable to offer them lots of a size to which they have become accustomed. This will require you to make the section 800 acres instead of 640, as on the American plan.'

What these instructions entirely ignored, apart from formal permissions, were the existing property arrangements which were laid out on the old strip river lot system found in Québec. These parcels were for the most part held by the Métis. The proposed surveys, should they proceed as McDougall had planned, would cut across existing holdings without regard to tenure or practices such as the hay privilege. And the activities of men like Snow and Mair and those who fell into association with him, like the Halfbreed Hallett, only spread alarm through the Métis community. They were quick to jump on Johnathan when they were able to muster the evidence that he had been supplying rum to the Indians, contrary to the ordinances of the Council of Assiniboia. Indians could secure rum aplenty; it was the additional layer of venality evidenced by the signing away of title that offended. Hell, not an Indian who acted in this way could write or read. A witnessed mark was all that stood between them and a bottle of liquor that scorched the throat and addled the brain. 'You've heard of taking sweets from a baby's hand?' said Mair. 'We'll coin a new saying—easy as taking land from an Indian!'

Leaving the courtroom after paying his ten-pound fine, Johnathan was smarting. The claims were still his, he thought, and changes were coming, probably violent ones. Even Dennis was cautioning McDougall to go slow, for the mood of the locals was getting uglier by the moment. There should be nothing close to the scale of upheavals he had seen in his lifetime, though. Not enough people. He had to be a lot harder in future, and more selfish; the trick was how to best align one's strategies for the coming storm.

Eight

i

Dred Scott was a black man, the property of army surgeon John Emerson. The doctor had taken Scott from postings in Missouri, a slave state, to posts in the northern part of what would become the Minnesota Territories. While at Fort Snelling, Scott married another slave, also owned by Emerson, who gave birth to a daughter who was legally free as the result of the Missouri Compromise. When Emerson died, his widow inherited the Scotts, but white abolitionists urged Scott to bring an action for a declaration that he was a free man, on the basis of residence in free territories. He did so, unwittingly fuelling a controversy which was to tear the country apart.

The case commenced in 1846, and made its way over the next eleven years to the Supreme Court of the United States, becoming the focus of national passions aligned on either side of the slavery issue, along the way. The highest court was Southern-dominated, and the majority released a decision which was emotional, visceral, and utterly partisan: 'At the time the Constitution was adopted, Negroes had for more than a century before been regarded as beings of an inferior order...so far inferior that they had no rights which a white man was bound to respect.' Two judges who were non-Democrats from northern states objected, writing strong arguments in dissent. The decision was released in 1857, and the case polarized public opinion which in some of the territories was resulting in open bloody clashes. The North was antagonized, and there was talk of slave power conspiracies which would manifest in the new states, then assume control of the whole country. In the South, the entry of Minnesota into statehood, which would take place on 14 May 1858—only six weeks from the day upon which David had been approached by Norquay—and Oregon the following year, inflamed passions were aroused as the balance of power in Congress tipped in favour of the North.

These events stoked the arguments for disunion. For more than a decade, growth, prosperity and immigration had continued apace. Collapse of confidence in lending institutions (which came to be known as the 'Panic of '57'), among other causes, led to a depression in the autumn of 1857 and the following year. Prices fell, businesses failed, and migration west fell off. Nowhere was the financial crisis felt more acutely than in the corporate headquarters of the LaCrosse and Milwaukee Railroad, as rail lines one after the other became insolvent.

The business of railroad construction, maintenance and operations required huge sums of money. Unlike the Southern States, paid immigrant labour carried the bulk of the load in the North. Private investors provided most of the funds, and much of this came from the merchants, traders and farmers along or near the right-of-way. Only part of the money was put up, but there were guaranties for the rest; in good years the profit shares could handle the annual commitments. In lean years, many lost their businesses, farms or investments; 1858 was such a year.

Fletcher T. Norquay believed that the depression would be short-lived. He was confident that war would eventually break out between the North and South, and if ever there was a voracious consumer of both raw materials and finished goods, it was the dogs of war. Nevertheless, the immediate problem was to revive the fortunes of an over-financed railroad in the short term, and one of the schemes he had in mind was presented at the annual shareholders' meeting in Chicago, on a frigid December day in 1857.

Norquay's plan, as he proposed it to the shareholders present, rested upon three self-evident points: first, it was necessary to rekindle interest in the west and, in particular, travel and settlement. Second, information had to be disseminated about the LaCrosse and Milwaukee Railroad and its modern rolling stock and conveniences. Third, revenue needed to be raised, for though the track was barely completed, there was much additional work required, and there had been several calls on the shareholders for money to keep the project alive.

Norquay looked around the boardroom. The furnishings were opulent. The heavy velvet draperies were thrust back and secured by brass retainers; the thin winter sunshine illuminated an otherwise dark room. The walls were covered with polished buffalo leather, arranged in panels waxed and buffed to the colour of rich walnut, but with the texture of polished cork. At eye level, dark paintings by unknown sportsmen hung in overstated gilt frames. The heavy table at the front of the room was of eastern oak, massive, and showing its pronounced grain under a highly polished spar varnish. A model locomotive, passenger car and caboose sat in the centre of the table top, with the corporate name in gilt on the miniature green and black boiler. This was a confident, rich and aggressive room, but the fretful expressions which confronted Norquay seemed to have taken small comfort from their surroundings.

Norquay took up a pointer, twirling it between the thumbs and forefingers of both hands. Behind him was a curtained display board about twelve feet square. Expectant faces inclined toward him as he opened his presentation with three words: 'A frontier circus!' There was no doubt that he had their attention.

He tugged on a tassel and the covering fell away from the easel, revealing a brightly lettered marquee. Whipping and thrusting his pointer with the aplomb of a school master, he read aloud: 'LaCrosse and Milwaukee Railway Company presents—A Circus of the Frontier and Agricultural Exhibition!'

He looked around again, seeking eye contact, the consummate salesman.

'Just the thing to fire the imagination of the easterner, the appropriate potential immigrant to the golden wheat fields of the west.' He moved into the role of carnival barker with ease. 'Picture, if you will, the shimmering fields of golden wheat, recently sprung forth from the rich alluvial soils of the northwest! Golden grain, ready for harvesting, and the finest railway vehicles of the L&M Railway Company standing ready to take your surplus to market, returning with gold to line the honest farmers' pockets!'

Norquay's voice dropped, became less hectoring, more conspiratorial: 'What we need to do, gentlemen, is to intrigue people, tickle their sense of adventure, stoke their sense of greed. There's land out west, more than enough people to farm it, and we've got the means to get them there. And once there, they'll depend on us for just about everything.

'Now. How do we grab the attention of the would-be immigrant?' He looked around expectantly, though not a man in the room believed he wanted to be interrupted. 'The amusement seeker will find, in the travelling production I am proposing, a full introduction to the glorious North-west.

'He will meet the Red Indian, a noble savage whose depredations have been much overblown by the eastern press. The fear of frontier aboriginals will have to be diminished by a careful portrayal of their primitive nature.

'We will have desperadoes, who will be vanquished by the fine law enforcement officials available in the territories. There will be cavalry, farmers, marshals, coaches, buffalo and grizzly bears! And for the children, clowns, sharpshooting, trick riding, and death-defying stunts! There it is. We will be charging for admission, but the price of entry shall be very low, just enough to cover costs, and perhaps,' a smile crept out from under his thick moustache, 'a small profit. But the entire exhibition will be an exercise in propaganda, in favour, of course, of our corporation.

'There is one other thing, which I think will convince you. Attendant upon each show, there will be an agricultural exhibition. The very latest in labour-saving devices will be on display. We shall have Mr John Deere's shiny new ploughs, ready to slice through virgin prairie sod like a fish knife through butter. Delivery can be arranged through his shop in Moline, Illinois, by our corporation. Mr Cyrus Hall McCormick's newly patented reapers will be shown to advantage, as well as such critical instruments of husbandry as stoves, harness, hand tools, weaponry and the like, all the way down to the new safety matches invented last year in Sweden. Each manufacturer will pay us for the privilege of displaying his wares, and a commission shall be taken from each sale. As well, a manufacturer's discount will be offered to those who use our transportation system, which we will in turn offset against the cost of delivery of equipment.'

No one said anything for a moment. These were bankers, merchants, financiers and insurance men, most of whom had put large sums of money at risk. True, commitments had been made during the boom years, when vast, speculative fortunes were made. Hell, California gold was pumping millions each month into the economy. But those days cast thin shadows now, and the times called for caution. What was left of bank account and reputation was sacrosanct. Most men in the room had narrowly escaped the crash of '37, and all signs pointed to the same sequence of hardships. The idea of getting involved in a circus seemed remote, if not a little ridiculous.

'Who would put this together, and what would it cost?' came a dubious-sounding voice from the back of the room.

'I have done all the preliminary work,' replied Norquay. 'I have located a fairly small circus, run by Bulgarian gypsies, nearly bankrupt, to serve as the core of the project. As for the rest, I shall take a leave from my present duties, with pay and expenses of course, and do the essential planning and recruitment.'

And so it went. For each objection, Norquay had an answer. The shareholders were only to advance the seed money for the project; that was the extent of their risk. Revenues from the exhibition would, after the second show, make the circus self-supporting. The difference between a viable production and the one which presently hovered at the brink of insolvency lay in the commercial sponsorship. Norquay argued, 'Look. John Deere turned out ten ploughs in his first year of production, 1839. This year the number exceeds ten thousand. To reach the full market potential, two more things need to happen: more people have got to get out west and start breaking sod; and equipment must sell by installment. In other words, some money must be placed down, preferably the better part of the actual cost, with the rest to be paid in equal portions, perhaps following harvest, for a period of years. The advantage is, gentlemen, that by insuring these payments, we also obtain a portion of a somewhat inflated sale price. In the event of default, we may move against the homestead. Virtually no risk!'

By degrees, he won them over. He captured their imagination, made them all ringmasters. He employed the example of Phineas Barnum, who went from penniless wanderer to wealthy tycoon by the simple expedient of creating demand. In 1841 Barnum had purchased Scudder's American Museum, with no funds in advance, changed the name to 'Barnum's Museum', and by advertising and exhibiting such oddities as 'General Tom Thumb' and 'The Bearded Lady', he repaid his indebtedness within the first year. Someone sourly observed to Norquay that the great Mr Barnum was now bankrupt, this very year, having unwisely endorsed notes in excess of a million dollars. But Norquay's point was clear, and a substantial majority approved the plan.

All this, in a carefully expurgated form, Norquay related to David. He was just beginning to appreciate how vast the world really was, for he had little knowledge of most of the things Norquay talked about. David admitted as much to the financier, as he disclosed more and more of his past to him.

'The horizon looks a lot different to a squirrel in a pine tree than it does to a snake in a wagon rut, wouldn't you say?' Norquay commented. 'What I'm offering you is a chance to run up that pine tree for a while, for the rut you're in at the moment looks none too comfortable.'

He offered the part of a 'Red Indian' in the frontier show to David.

'With a little jet in your hair to cover that copper thatch, you'll pass for any Indian as stalked the plains. Best of all, you have some education, and a real facility in languages. I need someone to head up my group of Indians, all of whom I've recruited right here in St Paul. I think they're a good bunch, but not too swift. I'd prefer a white to have charge of them, someone they'll trust. You're it.'

He put two double eagles on the table. The gold gleamed dully in the lamplight. This was to be David's advance, not including a new suit of clothes appropriate for travel to Baltimore, where they would meet up with the rest of the troupe. David wiped the crumbs and beer from his lips with the back of his hand, and eyed the coins suspiciously. He had no experience with money, and his only attempt at commercial enterprise had resulted in the fruits of his labour being stolen from under his nose. Yet here was the cash, up front, where he could see it.

And so it was that David Bloode found himself sitting in a day coach, wiggling his toes in uncomfortable hard leather boots, and tugging at a high paper collar, cinched tight by a thick woollen tie. He travelled with Norquay and some of the most bizarre-looking men he had ever seen, for Norquay had the eye of a showman, and his selections were made with a view to appearance, rather than talent. Acting, he believed, was a learned talent, and with discipline even the rudest soul could act, for was it nothing more than lying convincingly? And what saleman or street urchin, lovesick swain or preacher, could not shade the truth to advantage?

There were five Indians who had taken Norquay's offer. Four were Dakota, with whom David could easily converse, though all spoke rudimentary English. The fifth was Chippewa, who only answered to the name of 'Sam'. There was tension between Sam and the others, and Sam preferred to ride at the rear of the wagon, with his back to the rest of the party. He seemed cold and indifferent. He possessed the most ferocious face David had ever seen, and his eyes were dark and hard. Sam never smiled, but took out his two gold coins and turned them over and over in his hand, examining them, tasting them, and holding them up to the sunlight. The others had various features to commend them to the theatrical life. There were tattoos, fearful scars, ugliness and regal bearing distributed among them. It was David's job to mould this motley group into a team of performers. No small feat, given that David was unsure of what to expect himself.

David watched the countryside roll by, and craned to get another look at the locomotive at each bend in the track. He had been frightened when he first saw the snorting, puffing beast sending plumes of smoke and belching steam. All six of them had bolted like deer when the fireman, seeing their curious naivety, let go a long blast from the brass whistle. Now David felt himself to be a man of the world, as he stretched out his feet, placing his hands behind his head. The other five were restricted to hard wooden benches at the back of the third-class car, but David's place was on an upholstered seat, worn though it was. Norquay rode in a car at the end of the train which was like a small house, having its own bed, table and sitting room, and even a toilet.

There was much to learn. The conductor caught him pissing between the cars, and hauled him into the toilet to give an explanation, which he ultimately accomplished by demonstration. It was apparent that he had given the same little instructional speech and accompanying pageant before, for he had flourish and drama in what otherwise was a mundane rite, carried out in private.

David watched how men boarding would touch the brim of their hats when a woman passed. He liked his new, round hat, and did not take it off for twenty miles, until he became aware that all other men placed theirs in the woven string rack, just above the seat. He thrilled at the passing countryside, and the speed with which they passed through it. The urban centres of Milwaukee and Chicago were overwhelming in their size and alien surroundings. St Paul seemed scruffy and primitive by contrast. As he sped along in this swaying, magic coach, David felt he was being transported to the future. The sheer numbers of the white men, and their dominance of the land, with their buildings and their engines, made him feel insignificant and weak. He was grateful now that he could read; he already felt superior to the Indians recruited at St Paul. He would walk back to their section, steadying himself against an embarrassing pratfall, inconsistent with his growing sense of dignity and importance. He would grandly interpret the various instructions and signs to them. His authority was starting to develop, even before his formal leadership had been asserted.

In a trip which took not much more than three days in all, David had been brought from the empty reaches of silent prairie to the bustle and filth of a major urban centre. In 1858, the population of Baltimore exceeded a quarter of a million; this compared with barely a hundred fifty thousand for the entire Minnesota Territory, including just over nine thousand for St Paul itself. He remained awestruck at the window of the car, as it rumbled its slowing beats of double couplets, tah-tah, TAH-TAH; tah-tah, TAH-TAH, into the outer reaches of Baltimore, Maryland. They had been switched to the Northern Central Line, which entered the city in the northwest, passing Druid Hill Park, where it was pointed out by Norquay that the first show was to be held some two weeks hence.

David felt a fearful thrill grip his stomach momentarily. He looked over the more than seven hundred acres which the park encompassed, with its fine gravel carriage drives, and well-kept shrubberies and lawns. Swans and ducks bobbed in the ornamental ponds and the shimmering expanse of Druid Lake, barely visible from the right-of-way. Entering the city centre, they switched to the Baltimore Belt Railway and, running parallel to North Howard Street due south into the core of the industrial section, closed on the vast car barns of Camden Station. Braking to a shuddering, squealing halt, the train was backed into the station.

All around him passengers got up, retrieved their belongings, and exited the train in impatient queues at both ends of the car. Soon, only David and his five dumbfounded companions sat in the car, unsure of their next step.

Moments later, Norquay came and laughingly retrieved them. He led them out of the station, amused by their gawking and exclaiming over small distractions that would have the five of them clustered at a shop window, or marvelling at a fire engine, bright red and gleaming, being pulled by a matched set of four, with its wailing sound echoing in the narrow streets long after it was out of sight.

They were taken to a rooming house, not more than three blocks away from the station, at the corner of Charles and East York. This was only a block away from the harbour basin, and the forest of masts and rigging could be seen from the small third-floor window of David's room. Again he and his companions were separated, the five being quartered in basement rooms, accessible by separate entrance from the laneway behind the 'Camden Arms', as their four-storey abode was known.

Norquay wasted no time in bringing his cast together. Some lived in the same rooming house as David, but most lived in a recently built but cheaply constructed clapboard hotel on West Madison, about a dozen blocks north of the Camden Arms. The assembly and preliminary rehearsals were held in a warehouse owned by the Northern Central Railway at their depot on North Street. It was a convenient location for the bulk of the troupe, but for David and those at the Camden Arms it was a forty-minute walk.

Among the group at the Camden Arms were three toughs who were chosen to play the outlaws. Their villainous appearance, David sensed, matched their personalities. Not only did they play the part of bully, they lived it. Their open contempt for the Indians, whom they referred to sneeringly as 'savages', became an instant sore spot for the group. The Indians, on the other hand, were outfitted in costumes that represented no particular tribe, being merely caricatures of tabloid illustrations of the 'wild west Indian'. The breech clout was worn over fully fitted trousers, it being felt that the exposure of male hips and buttocks was too much for the sensibilities of the age.

If the Indians were treated with little civility by some of the cast, special contempt was reserved for the one man of black and Indian parentage. He too lived in the dingy dormitory in the basement of the Camden Arms. He was a wild-looking man by the name of Alfred Okay.

His passivity in the face of the vilest provocations brought forth an invariable reply to all challenges, epithets and slurs: 'Okay.'

Alfred resembled neither race, but had characteristics of both. Once owned by a landlord, he had been freed by him upon hearing the fiery teachings of John Brown, the ardent abolitionist whose perversion of biblical teaching held that there can be no remission of sin without the spillage of blood. John Brown would be hanged the following year for the crimes his fanaticism led him to believe were justified. Alfred, troubled by the extremes of human passion the slavery issue aroused, drifted north, and was recruited by Norquay from a loading dock in Ohio. Though the North had become an industrial juggernaut by the middle of the nineteenth century, jobs for coloured men remained at the lowest and most menial levels.

His black, wiry hair hung in a thick mane down to his shoulder blades. He had skin the colour of a nut, very dark, which showed off the whiteness of his eyes. A huge, well-muscled man, he had the aspect of a warrior with his hooked nose and wide, flaring, defined nostrils. Unlike the others, however, Alfred was a passive man, quick to laugh, who did not initiate conversation. His favourite pastime was to play a banjo, an instrument David had never before seen. It was chorded like a guitar, but was plucked in a 'hammer-and-claw' style so that a torrent of ascending and plummeting notes could be arranged in a wonderfully fast-paced melody. It was a musical paradox. As foot-tapping and engaging as the tunes were, each note struck singly was the homeliest, unmelodious, plunking sound imaginable. It was the only property, beside the clothing on his back, that Alfred owned.

The three men playing the outlaws were a strange group by any standard. Greb Stader, leader of the three men, was short with intense, bulging eyes which fixed on people like searchlights. His conversations were peculiarly one-sided, for he seemed to require no actual response from anyone, beyond the apparent need to have someone listen to his rambling expatiations on an infinite variety of subjects. He smoked heavily, using his fat, saliva-sodden, hand-rolled cigarettes to underscore a point. His language was heavily laden with profanities, lurid and scatalogical. Adding to his aggressive manner was a sneering tone, which, for most people, extinguished any residual thought of responsive comment. He was ugly, nasty, and obnoxious. Never, thought David frequently, did a man's appearance so aptly fit his personality.

Stader's partners in the performance were Felix Buttman and Joshua Croat. Buttman was a tall, spare man, with close-set eyes, a nose thin as a knife blade, and a down-turned, unhappy mouth. His hair was carefully swept back in a pompadour, and he had a way of turning on a man with the look of an avenging angel. His every expression portended negative commentary. David decided that this one looked like a starving hawk, with an outlook to match.

Croat was a shorter, stockily built man, well muscled, with legs like a piano. His jaw stuck out in a pugnacious way, though David could never determine whether this was a trick of nature, or a result of Croat's looking-for-trouble attitude. His arms were always held in front, akimbo, with the hands curled into fists. He had a broken nose, and a squat, flat skull. He was an intimidating man, antagonistic in attitude, and curt and sarcastic in manner. It would have been impossible for the three of them to live together were it not for the fact that, though all three were inclined to speak their mind and hold forth at length on any and all subjects, not one of the others paid the slightest bit of attention to anything that was said.

The fact that David was to be cast in the role of Indian renegade was enough for Stader, Buttman and Croat to regard him, along with all the other Indians and coloureds, as something less than human. The result was a protest to Norquay, who was remaining in Baltimore to see that the opening show actually opened on time. 'That goddamned breed oughta be with the rest of the niggers and injins, not with decent white folk.'

It was infuriating to them that David was articulate, could read and write, and worse, he could exclude them by slipping into the Dakota language at will. Norquay waved the trio off. 'Boys, if you're not happy with the arrangements, then move on.' He had no illusions about these men. They were thugs. But they looked the part, and he felt sure they were crowd pleasers, especially when the troops finished them off in the grand finale. Besides, these were tough times, and jobs were hard to come by; they would not leave, or dare defy him.

Conditions, David found, were significantly better for the whites than they were for the others. He was glad that he could stay in accommodations which afforded a private room, even if it had only enough space for a bed, a chair, and a row of wooden pegs for his belongings. The basement dormitory had a low ceiling, was close with still air, and it was shared with the coloured help who felt somewhat threatened by this unexpected and unwelcome influx of noisy intruders. David was not prepared for the price he would pay for the privilege of living among white folk. Nothing in his short life would equip him to deal with the hatred borne of racism and bigotry. Even as a slave of the Sioux, there had been no hateful aggression or purposeful denial of esteem, or the kind of diminishment with which he was now confronted.

On the second afternoon in Baltimore, all the players were gathered in the vacant warehouse, so that the basic outline of the two-hour show could be shared with them. The choreographer, Mr Kruck, was an aging dancer whose fay step provoked snickers from some of the cast. He had a high, thin voice, and was given to shaking his finger at people in the manner of an impatient schoolmaster. Tiny round glasses, over which he continually peered, completed the image of a fussy old man. But he knew his business, and was soon to bring order to these rank amateurs under Norquay's watchful eye. 'If Mr Kruck's not satisfied, then I shall not be satisfied, and those of you who fall short will be paid off.' The threat was clear, and Kruck's eyes fairly glittered with reflected power over his troupe.

Before those present had been called to order, they had divided by natural inclination on the hard-packed dirt floor into groups of women, natives, and whites; the latter were split between the Stader group, the Bulgarian family whose circus had been pulled from the brink of extinction, and the rest. The women were three in number. One of them, Gilda Rakovski, was the fattest human being that David had ever encountered; he could not imagine anything on two legs exceeding her girth. As she walked, David thought he felt the earthen floor shake beneath them. She created the impression of an approaching prairie storm. Her face, round and pale, though with heavily rouged cheeks, shone like a moon framed by billowing black clouds of hair, ornamented by glittering paste studs. She was awful, sensual, terrifying and commanding. She was a natural comedian and a born entertainer. Gilda Rakovski was also a freak. She drew applause on the stage and in the ring, but snickers and stares in the street. It was a paucity of roles for someone as large as she which kept her in the circus ring. There was no hesitation on her part to let anyone know what she thought about the tragic injustice of one as talented as she to be trapped in a circus sideshow.

It was Gilda who first took notice of David's arrival.

'What haf' we here?' she cried. 'It's our newest redskin, is it?' She looked over David's cheap, and by now quite crumpled suit, and sniffed. 'The hair's wrong, he must be a breed. Are you?'

David felt himself flushing, though he knew not why this should be. It was true, but the manner of its being said made him feel as if he should scratch himself.

'I am indeed, madam,' he said, boldly as he could muster, 'one-half Orkney, and one...'

'Orkney!' she cried, emphasizing the first syllable in a hawking choke. 'What in the world is an Orkney?' Again, the exaggerated pretense of being unable to pronounce the word.

The others were idly drawn to this trivial bit of meanness; this was an opportunity to take the measure of the newcomer. David stood his ground, maintaining an impassive expression. He thought of the lessons of the heyoka: if we can laugh at insult, the taunt flies back to the offender.

'An Orkneyman, madam, is someone who gets stuck in the throats of ladies such as yourself.'

The crowd shouted with laughter. David was utterly unaware of the double entendre, but he was relieved when Gilda smiled. Mr Kruck clapped his hands, 'Come. Come. Let us have no more lollygagging. Let me lay out the show for you, and we'll go through it once today. Pay attention, now, everybody!'

Over the next few days the troupe settled into a steady routine, trying to get their roles established. There were almost no speaking parts, so that Kruck was free to concentrate on expression and staging. The show was arranged as a caricature of the history of the western frontier. There was a primal hunting scene, followed by a raid on a pioneer family's wagon. This involved the Indians riding in a circle around the wagon, while the family members picked them off, only to have the last marauder surrender to arriving troops.

Next, a mail shipment would be held up by desperadoes, who would first be seen drinking heavily, and planning the robbery in extravagant gestures. This attack was foiled by the arrival of the federal marshal. The grand finale brought all the players together, farmers and their families, to sing hymns of thanksgiving. The Indians were all portrayed here as subdued, heads bowed, and wrapped in blankets. The outlaws were in chains, dressed in baggy white overalls and carrying large hammers for breaking stone. Later they would be shot trying to escape.

Throughout the production there were examples of fantastic trick riding, performed by the Bulgarians on their circus ponies. Greb Stader did some sharp-shooting with rigged targets that left nothing to chance, and fat Gilda did comic cameos as the pioneer's wife and a farmer's daughter. Hiding in a wagon under attack, with her enormous, quivering bum stuck in the air, her performance reduced even the other actors to teary-eyed laughter.

The introductory scene was David's. He was expected to stalk around the ring, peering this way and that with exaggerated tip-toe steps, and holding his palm as a shade to his eyes. Feathers stuck up in his headband, and the bow and arrow he carried was ludicrous: a parody of the laminated weapons of cedar and elk horn, laid up with hoof glue and wrapped with fine sinew. The arrow was an unwieldy thing, with silly red decoration, utterly unlike the lethal missiles tipped with barbs cut from hoop iron, or hammered out of strap hinges that David had seen during his years with the Sioux. The outfit was an insult, but as the Americans were fond of saying, what the hell; it was just a show, intended for tenderfeet.

On the other side of the arena, Alfred Okay was creeping about, well suited up in the hide of a grizzly bear. He looked surprisingly authentic, with an oiled felt tongue lolling between clenched fangs. It occurred to David that the convincing performance Alfred put on was more a function of movement and subtlety; obviously Alfred had seen a bear moving somewhere before, and had studied it sufficiently well to imitate the lunging gait common to all bears. This triggered David's curiosity and respect; there was more to Alfred than met the eye.

The bear began to stalk David, and David would look this way and that, deliberately missing the animal. The idea was to work the crowd. Then the bear would set upon the hunter, and they would thrash around for a while, following which the bear would tear off David's ear. The damaged ear, of course, was hidden under long dyed hair, and a small bladder of pig's blood was tied into the hair at David's temple. With a fearsome roar designed to haunt the fears of small children, the bloodied rag would be waved about with much ursine head-swinging and snarling, and David would pull away his braid to show the gory remains of his ear. This was a guaranteed crowd-pleaser, just as Norquay predicted, once he saw David's deformity. The hunter would ultimately triumph by slaying the bear with a knife, then screaming his victory with one foot on the creature's prostrate body. The ringmaster would solemnly intone through a brass megaphone that the grizzly bear was now happily extinct on the western prairies; no more a threat to Indians or to the white settlers 'who are the vanguard of civilization'.

It was rapidly becoming apparent to David that there was a certain image of the Indian that the railroad wanted to present to those who would migrate to the frontier: the Red Man was a noble anachronism, once wild, yes, but now merely a buffoon, primitive and benign. This was made especially clear by the subdued, blanketed caricatures who drifted about the periphery of the performance during the closing finale. There was even a sideshow involving an Indian drinking, staggering and falling down, begging for drink and a white clergyman lifting him up, casting away the bottle, and pointing to the plough in an elaborate pantomime that left no doubts about the superiority of the white race and the refining influences of God and agriculture.

David talked to the Dakota about their roles in the carnival. To a man, they were indifferent. They all agreed that the props were foolish, and portrayed their people inaccurately, but shrugged it off. They received pay for what they did. That was all. White man's money was power in their world, and gold had become their god, just as it had for the white man, regardless of what he did on Sundays.

Then there was the matter of pay. Norquay knew full well that his frontier recruits could not walk around with all their money in their pockets. Hell, they would probably end up stealing from one another, especially the Indians and blacks billeted in the basement of the Camden Arms. The last thing he needed was fighting to break out, and he'd been careful to set the rules straight off: there was to be no drinking, a strict curfew, and no tardiness or no-shows for anyone. Breach of the rules meant firing, though it was a bit of a hollow threat, given that replacements were not easy to come by.

So Norquay decided he had to introduce the Indian members of his cast—the ones most likely to be liberated from their cash—to the institution of banking.

A week after their arrival in Baltimore, Norquay took all the Indians in their cheap, shiny suits to the First Savings Bank of Baltimore, a venerable institution which had first opened its doors as a voluntary association on 16 March 1818, the third such banking operation to start up in the United States. The bank, reopened in new quarters after the Georgian revival style, was at Mount Vernon Place, site of the Washington Monument. This edifice was a Doric shaft of white marble, one hundred and eighty feet high, surmounted by a sixteen-foot statue of the first president. All of them except Norquay climbed the two hundred and twenty steps inside the column to the narrow observation deck, far above the city. Once at the summit, gasping for breath, there were cries of fear and panic, but the view was awesome. Birds flitted about below them. Chesapeake Bay, some fourteen miles away down the Patapsco River, shimmered in the afternoon sun. The city harbour, head of navigation, teemed with watercraft of all descriptions. Around them the city stretched, it seemed, to the horizon. More than anything, this experience brought home to the westerners the irresistible power of the whites. The thought came crashing upon David's awareness that very soon St Paul, and even Fort Garry, further north, would soon look like this. It possessed him as he made the long descent and it continued to haunt his thoughts for many years. How men can so consequentially affect the earth, as this city demonstrated, was a question that marked David indelibly. He was not to realize its significance until much later, when his life was to hang in the balance.

The concepts of deposit, debits and credits, interest and negotiable instruments were bewildering to the Indians and to David. When the Indians were asked to put their money in the white man's grand lodge, they balked. When they were assured that the holder of these funds would not spend them, but would give them additional funds at the rate of four percent, compounded annually, they were suspicious. Why would anyone do such a thing, and what was the meaning of annual interest? And so on. Their fearfulness and mistrust was increased by the fact that this was one of the few institutions which actually welcomed them in. And it was by far the most lavish of the places they had been.

The main lobby, where the teller's wickets were arranged behind ornate bronze cages set on marble counters, was two storeys high to the ceiling. Tall fluted columns supported an open balcony which extended part way out on three sides of the cavernous room. Stained glass windows gave the place the aura of a temple. People bustled about, clutching papers, their sleeves protected against ink by black satin cuffs pulled up to the elbow. Low voices clattered and echoed as various arcane transactions were being carried out. In all, the building was intimidating, the concept alien, and the request to hand over their meagre coinage, unreasonable.

David felt that, as interpreter and as someone who had not lived all his life in a shelter made of hides, he needed to show a little more sophistication than the others. Slowly, he grasped the concept of safety deposits. The massive vault seemed undeniable proof that the money was intended to stay. The idea of interest escaped his understanding, but Norquay, whom he trusted, gave repeated assurances. Led to the counter, presided over by a skinny, long-nosed boy wearing small, round glasses, he bravely plunked down a miserable handful of mixed coins. Behind him, the others gathered in solemn but mistrustful silence to watch a fool give away his money.

The teller smiled patronizingly as he filled out ledger sheets, counted and re-counted the cash, then slid the deposit slip under the cage to David. 'If you wouldn't mind, sir, your signature.'

David stared at the slip. Four dollars and eighty-four cents. All the cash he had in the world, save one of the double eagles Norquay had given him back in St Paul. That was stashed away safely in his boot. Laboriously, he printed his name. Skill with the pen did not seem to be one of the traits for which he was going to be remembered, he thought. The teller took it from him and smiled unctuously: 'Thank you, my good sir.' And he turned his back on the rough little group, though he shot a quizzical glance at Norquay, wondering what his connection was with them. One of the Dakota shook his head, lower lip stuck out, down at the corners, 'You will not see your silver again.'

The rest agreed. They followed David out to the wide granite staircase at the front. David realized that he had no money with which to buy cigarette papers and tobacco, which he had lately taken to smoking. He had tried it when he was out on the plains with Pickett and Holstrom and had liked it, but as the supply dwindled, the two men had become increasingly stingy. The tobacco was superior to the Hudson's Bay Company's trade plugs he was used to, and vastly better than the dried calamus root which was mixed with leaves of the white ash, or shredded bark of the red willow, resorted to only as trade supplies ran out.

Now he could prove his confidence had not been misplaced; neither in Norquay, or the bank. He spun on his heel, to the surprise of the other. He marched confidently back to the wicket, but little green curtains had been drawn, and a small sign announced 'Closed' hung in front. David felt a sharp stab of mild panic. Now there was general consternation in the others, who proclaimed in their own language that David had been robbed, and they were right to have doubted the white man. The fuss, which Norquay vainly attempted to suppress, soon attracted attention from patrons and staff alike. The arrival of two armed guards very quickly resulted in the entire group being escorted, in a fashion none too solicitous, outside to the steps. David was humiliated, and Norquay was angry. 'What kind of an idiot's game were you trying to play?'

'I wanted some of my money back, but the man who took it was gone.'

'Didn't I assure you that your money was safe? Doesn't that count for something? You told me you trusted those two drifters who stole everything from you, but me, you listen to nothing I say? Look, all of you: I don't give a good gol-darn whether you lose every nickel you make. I just wanted to show you there are ways to keep your money safe.' Norquay was angrier than David had ever seen him.

His eyes were downcast for he knew Norquay was right. The lessons of life never seemed to take root in David's head. He had been taught by a number of wise people so far, but their wisdom was like unused tools in a workshop where he preferred only an axe for immediate results. Was it youth or was there some deeper-seated flaw which kept understanding at bay? He had the patience to listen, to think, but when he acted, it almost always seemed to be out of fear. He had not felt close to anyone other than his grandfather, an old man who had taken the time to share his skills with him. His mother was nurturing but distant, in the way of his people. A boy was expected to stand as a man very early among aboriginal peoples, for much depended on the men. As a slave of the Sioux, he had been cut off from all normal relationships, except those with children.

As a result, David found it difficult to form normal kinds of associations. He was lacking in experience when it came to discerning the kinds of signals all people send which attract, alarm, or simply suggest one proceed with caution.

'I'm sorry,' he said. 'I am a fool.'

The story got around, and there were a few rough jokes at David's expense. He would escape to the dormitory where Alfred Okay was billeted. He loved to hear him play the banjo while one of the house slaves played the harmonica. This business of slavery intrigued David. Until his arrival in Maryland he had never seen a black man, and the sight of Alfred Okay frightened him considerably, especially a man with such a ferocious face. But Alfred's personality was, if anything, the opposite to what he looked like. He was a very passive man, shy, and never spoke unless addressed, which was a habit formed from a lifetime of bondage. Once at the bath house behind the Camden Arms, David saw with horror the criss-cross welts, long scarred over, which disfigured Alfred's back like furrowed soil. Awed, he asked about them.

Alfred was diffident. 'I's seen some pain, yeah,' he breathed, in his deep, melodious voice. 'But it's nuffin now. I seen yo gots yo own badges.' He motioned to David's buttocks, where Wakandayamani had bitten him, years ago. His eyes flickered over the scarred-over gashes on either side of David's chest.

'A woman bit me, to mark me as her own.' Alfred looked puzzled. 'It was when I was captured by Indians,' David continued. 'I think it was supposed to be a joke, more'n anything.'

'You-uns was a slave?' David could not fail to detect the faint incredulity; this from a man whose voice was always modulated, perhaps from a habit of subservience.

'Yes, but I was treated far worse when I was in business for myself. My partners stole my share, though I had worked harder than the two put together.'

Alfred dressed silently, and appeared to muse over this statement. His fingers lightly traced over the strings of his banjo, and lowered the tempo. It was almost as if the instrument reflected his thought patterns. No other hint of what he was thinking showed on his face, or sounded in his voice, but the cadence of his instrument slowed and fell.

'I guess it all depends on who yo' massa is. My las' owner set me free. The one before that punish me somethin' awful. I think he like it, to hear me moan. Oh, how I learned to moan jus' right, s-so as when I stop, he stop. They ain't no pleasure if'n I don't yowl.'

This was horrifying to David. Limned in his brain was the image of a tormented man, adapting to the hell that was his existence. What strength Alfred must have had. What courage. After a pause, he spoke again to Alfred. 'How did you know it would end, some day?'

Alfred looked at him. 'I didn't. Oh, I could of hanged myself, an' all, 'cause I didn't have no family or nothin'. But as I see it, there's only two choices: live or die. An' if'n yo chooses to live, well then, yo's got t' make the best of it. Th' good Lord'll look after them's as looks after themselves. Things is pretty good now.'

He added quietly, 'Even the one's as set me free left me on my own, with nuffin'. Most starved t' death, till Massa Norquay take me in. Things is pretty good now.'

More of Alfred's life was revealed to David, for Alfred never refused to answer a question. David began to take instruction from Alfred in the playing of the banjo. Alfred showed him the picking style, and how to hum the tune he wanted, to match the chording arrangements. Alfred demonstrated the classic hammering and pulling on the fretless instrument, making the notes sing in rising and falling cadence, as well as the 'flyin' hard frailing', and down-picking for breakdowns and ballads he had learned upon coming north. He told David to let the nails on the thumb and first two fingers grow, and recommended that David regularly groom the circus ponies when the move was made to the park, for there was 'nuffin better'n horse sweat t' make the fingernails hard fer pickin'.'

The close association between Alfred and David was not lost on Stader, Buttman and Croat. They referred to him as 'nigger-lover'. David noticed that Alfred never made eye contact with anyone. And this was no mutual custom, as it had been with the Sioux. David supposed that, in the ordinary course of life, this mannerism blunted aggression, but it did not seem to have much sway with the three bullies. No one interceded on Alfred's behalf when they cursed him, or kicked over his tin mug of water, or otherwise preyed upon him with their paltry torments. It was simply acceptable to treat him like a dog, although Norquay had set the ground rules early on, which included no violence of any kind. He did not want the show to be without its performers for any reason; there was no budget for stand-ins and understudies. It was a matter of money, nothing more.

Someone else was taking an increasing interest in David. Each time he looked at her, Gilda Rakovski was staring at him. It was a hungry, predatory look, and David felt uncomfortable under her gaze.

Finally, the rehearsals in the warehouse were over, and the necessary bunk-wagons had been assembled with the circus out at Druid Hill Park. The entire cast was moved in two freight wagons, Indians and blacks in the second one, and all the whites in the other.

The circus tent was visible at a great distance, being an enormous canvas structure, with alternating white and red panels. As they pulled into the grounds, a brightly painted sign arched over the gravelled roadway, resplendent in gothic letters and gilt scrollwork: 'Rakovski's Frontier Circus and Agricultural Exhibition'.

As they pulled up to the main entrance, David could see that the tent was, in truth, a little seedy. What had passed for white at a distance was patched and grubby. The ring was small, not much more than the warehouse in which they had practised. They were called inside, and arranged on the plank bleachers to meet the balance of the troupe, and to have the schedule repeated to them.

The only members who had not come to the warehouse were the trapeze family: the Grueffs—the Fabulous Grueffs, as they grandly billed themselves. They performed aerial acrobatics, as well as stunts on horseback. In addition to the mother and father—short, dark-complexioned and surly of expression—there were two daughters. Both were short of stature as well, but fair-skinned, slim and athletic in appearance, pretty as a pair of pale roses. They looked almost identical, though the elder, Ilsa, was more than a year beyond her sister, Katya. Their hair was black as any Indian braid, and they wore it in a thick plait which hung down to their waists. David could not take his eyes off them, for they were the most attractive women he believed he had ever seen, all others fading distantly in his memory.

New sleeping arrangements were organized. Converted freight wagons were equipped with bunks, with the after portion given over to a small sitting space. A portable kitchen was set up in a dingy, rectangular tent. Benches and tables were planking over collapsible trestles. There were smaller, even rougher accommodations for the Indians and blacks. Some of the circus people had gaily painted wagons they called 'caravans' as their private quarters. Of these, only Gilda occupied one alone.

On the second night at Druid's Hill, David was left a message to attend at Gilda's caravan. He was puzzled by the invitation, for he felt he had little in common with such a woman. For the last two days he had been obsessed with the Grueff girls, and noticed little else. He had even suffered a few stinging remarks about his thinly veiled admiration, if that was the right word for it; many times he had been told to concentrate on his part.

After helping with the cleaning chores following dinner, David arrived at Gilda's caravan and knocked uncertainly on the door at the back. Having mounted the running board which ran the width of the vehicle, he stepped back to the ground, and scuffed the dust with his moccasined toe. The wagon lurched on its axle, as if suddenly buffeted by a gust of wind, setting the little lantern hanging at the rear asway. It lurched again, and a voice called out, high and saccharine, 'Come in, please do.' She pronounced it 'police'.

David stepped up to the door, despite some misgivings. He really wanted to be calling at the Grueff caravan. He swung the door open, and climbed the next step to the threshold. Ducking to enter, David stepped into the small compartment. It was gloomy inside; the single lamp gave off a thick, yellow light, dimly amplified by the once-polished nickel reflector on the bracket which held it to the wall.

A narrow sleeping bunk all but filled the space beyond the immediate cabin. A table, perhaps two feet by forty inches was hinged from the wall, and supported by a single folding leg. Opposite was a countered cabinet with deep drawers, some of which were open, and had various bits of clothing, brightly coloured and of indeterminate function, hanging from them. The air was close, thick with the lavender Gilda favoured, but there were other, more mysterious scents which made David's nostrils flare and work. These were the particular musks of women: intimate, urgent, and dangerous.

'Someone said that you wanted to see me?' he began shyly.

She looked at him intently for a moment, and then she said: 'I've watched you with the horses, and with the others. You're good.' She pronounced it 'gut'.

'Uh, thanks,' David mumbled, puffed by this unexpected bit of flattery.

'Yes,' she went on. 'I think you have real talent for the show. You can make people laugh, you can ride well, you can follow instructions, not like those other savages. You're not one of them anyway, I can tell, 'cause I seen you with your real hair. A glorious colour it was too.' She smoothed the folds of her enormous, lace nightdress, slowly and coquettishly. She looked up at him and smiled.

She was exotic, sensuous, and vaguely thrilling to David. He was tongue-tied. Gilda licked her lips, and shifted her weight to the edge of the bed. The wagon creaked as it coped with the adjustment.

'Have you a special girl?' she asked coyly. 'You look like someone all the girls would be chasing.'

David's cheeks flamed. He did not think of himself as someone who was attractive. The hard work he had become accustomed to had made his body lean; his muscles were sharply defined like braided ropes under leathery skin. The closest thing to a 'special girl' he had known was Mahpiyatowin and her parents had hustled her away from him at the first opportunity. To top it all off, under his lank mane, he was possessed of only half an ear. Well, he was determined to put up a bold front. He was a man of the world, after all. He had travelled extensively, had he not, and could speak at least four languages well.

'No,' he replied with a studied indifference, picking at his nails. 'Not right now, anyway. I been too busy, learnin' the show and all.'

'Is there no one at home?' she asked, smiling, her features expressive, concerned.

Home, thought David. Just where would I call home now? I have been gone so long, I can hardly remember. He closed his eyes in the gloomy chamber. In the distance he could see the fields and plains of Red River. It was said by the Scots who had come to the valley with the Hudson's Bay Company, that if a man once tastes of the Red River, he must always go back to quench his thirst. He remembered the summer afternoons on the riverbank with his grandfather, the sunshine brilliant, the sky as fiercely blue as the anemones which bloom on the prairie in the spring. The faces of his mother and sisters swam fuzzily in the pools of his recollection; they would be older now, and look much different. A hunger to return started in him, and he trembled with it, ever so faintly.

'Ah, so there is someone,' said Gilda, with just a hint of disappointment, mistaking his sentiment. 'Come over here, by me.'

David forced the images from his mind, and stepped over to the edge of the bunk, between the parted curtains which partitioned the tiny quarters. Uncomprehendingly, he stood before her and looked down at the top of her head. He was still not sure why he had been summoned. With some curiosity, he observed that she had a flower woven into her hair, a purple one which looked much like those in the beds of chrysanthemums at the entrance to Druid Hill Park. He was momentarily distracted, for why would anyone put a flower in their hair just before going to bed?

He became aware, rather than heard, that she was speaking again, but the words were not registering with him. She had unclasped his belt and flicked open his buttons, so that his trousers slid to the floor. His heart was pounding in his ears, as he realized with something akin to horror that she had taken the shrivelled worm between his legs and put it in her mouth!

She sucked at it for a moment, then took it out and examined it, rolling it between her thumb and forefinger as if it were a poorly constructed cigarette. 'It's a tiny little thing, it is for sure,' she said. 'But don't worry.' She looked up at his panic-stricken face. 'Tall oaks from little acorns grow!'

David felt humiliated. But not as mortified as he would be if he had fled, likely with the whole encampment watching, or at least hearing about it. He decided to endure the test, though he wondered with some anxiety whether she might bite his cock off.

As Gilda warmed to her task, and David realized that this was not going to be some bizarre initiation, he slowly relaxed, and let the warmth that was building there spread to his belly. He felt himself swelling, as he did when he masturbated, and he heard Gilda murmur her approval. She pulled away for a moment to examine him, but David was frantic, pulling at her head, feeling the release welling within him. He clutched her hair, conscious of crushing the flower in his grasping, and let out a cry with his completion. He thrust so hard at her, that the two of them toppled over on the bunk, his seed spilling across her face. They lay there, he gasping, awestruck.

'Well,' she said with a chuckle, as she wiped her face with some mysterious undergarment nearby. 'Enthusiasm makes up for a slow start, sure enough, I think. But have I any hair left, or teeth in my face? Gracious. You must learn to be more restrained, believe me, for it will increase your pleasure.'

David heard none of this. The intensity of his release had left behind a glorious afterglow, and he was determined to prolong the echoes of the experience. He imagined that, at the moment his seed left him, he was holding not Gilda, but the thick, dark plaits of Ilsa Grueff. Slowly, her image dissolved, and Gilda's expansive features took her place. She was nattering about the arrangements. 'You may stay as late as you like, but you must,' and she held up a finger sternly, 'you must leave before sunrise. Or we will have the whole camp to gossiping.'

And she snuggled down in her berth, moving as far to the wall as possible. This manoeuvre left a space for David to lie down, but it was a narrow shelf indeed, he thought. Nevertheless, at the prospect of another encounter, he decided to stay, and upon closing his eyes, fell asleep. Gilda seemed not to notice, and went on chattering as if she held his rapt attention.

With each passing performance, the show became more polished. Some leeway was afforded the troupe, and when it seemed appropriate, one or another of them would improvise. If it worked well, or the crowd approved, it would be incorporated. What the people seemed to want was to believe that the Indians were savage but stupid, that the outlaws were easily vanquished by the soldiers or the law, that life on the frontier was a happy one, and that with little effort, wealth and property was available for the taking. It was a comforting message, one delivered with humour and not inconsiderable showmanship, under the careful eye of Mr Kruck.

Outside the circus tent, the glittering array of agricultural implements, modern kitchen aids, government land agents, medicine pedlars and sales agents for all manner of products and services added to the excitement. The machinery and gadgets awed and fascinated David. He spent much of his free time examining the products of a modern industrial culture, learning how each thing worked, what its purpose was, and what it cost. Fletcher Norquay believed that the concourse of sideshows and hawkers was as much a draw as the show itself, and he was mightily pleased with himself. The crowds came, and the word spread, for it was, after all, a depression, and the carnival was offering—or peddling—hope. The show was held over in Baltimore for five days.

ii

The next stop for the frontier circus was about forty miles to the south, Washington, the national capital. The entire trip, which consumed the better part of the day, was taken with talk of annexation, and the increasing prospects of war between the rebellious Southern states and the North. At day's end, the troupe were informed that there had been a change of plans, and the entire group was to be rerouted to Alexandria, some seven miles to the south, lying along the harbour. No explanation was given, but it was well after midnight that the wagons were shunted off the flatcars into an open space on the outskirts of the little city.

Tempers were short, for everyone was tired. Stader and his two companions were particularly surly, so David elected to sleep elsewhere than in the whites' bunk wagon. He thought of going to see Gilda, but the fatigue she was feeling showed on her face. It had been a scorcher of a June day, and she had spent the trip sitting by an open window, fanning herself, while trying to catch the odd rag of breeze. She had not acknowledged David on either occasion when he had addressed her. He decided to leave her alone.

He wandered over to the blacks' trailer; there was still a light on. David walked up to the back door and pulled it open. No other caravan in the entourage would he think of entering without knocking, but it was simply not done with the 'coloureds'. Even the Indians, who were accommodated in tents, were hailed before a head was stuck under the flap. All the same, he called out as the door opened, 'Haloo! Alfred, are you still about?'

He heard Alfred's deep, broad chuckle. 'Get yo' white, chewed-up ass in here, afo' yo's seen!' He was tuning his banjo, and the man opposite was sounding the notes for the standard C chord tuning on his fiddle. Yet another man was holding a pair of spoons, and a fourth was tapping spit out of a harmonica. The air was musky and close in the small space, and the single lamp bathed them, perhaps a dozen in all, in a soft, eerie glow.

David scrambled over beside a chubby black man known as 'Spike', for he drove in the tent pegs, among other things. Spike nodded to David, and hefted his instrument, which was a gallon-sized ceramic jug. Blowing across the mouth made a mournful, rumbling sound, like a steamboat whistle, far off. With three taps of the spoons, they let fly a rousing rendition of 'Knockin' on the Henhouse Door', which had all of them tapping their feet and joining in the refrain. Then 'Shoo Fly', 'Chilly Winds' and 'Shady Grove'.

Alfred sang a slow ballad in his wonderfully lustrous baritone, poignant in its meaning for David, who had come to know him:

> *If I was a little bird,*
> *I'd not build my nest on the ground.*
> *I'd build my nest in the sour apple tree,*
> *Where the wild boys couldn't tear it down*

'Hey, David!' he called out. 'Show dese poor-uns what you bin larned!' And he handed over the banjo to David.

David grabbed it eagerly, did some quick chord sequences and called out 'Little Black-Eyed Susie'. Everyone laughed, for this was the only number which David had fully mastered, and the one he played when 'the boys was doin' some boogin'.' He leaned into it, mindful again how much it followed the two-part form of the Red River fiddle tunes he had grown up with at his grandfather's home. The banjo crackled out the joyous drive and syncopation of the well-worn song:

> *All I need to make me happy*
> *Is two little boys to call me Pappy;*
> *One named Sop; t'other named Davy*
> *One loves meat, an' th' other loves gravy!*

All the men joined in the chorus, stamping their feet till the bunk wagon fairly shook:

> *Hey, pretty little black-eyed Susie,*
> *Hey, pretty little black-eyed Susie, HEY!*

Each man contributed a verse; some lyrics David had never heard before, and he was sure they were made up as they went along. Then, the door was flung open with a crash, and a gunshot sounded, deafening in the close space. The music died like a drowned cat.

'You black-assed sons o' bitches! Decent folk can't get no sleep what with all this Christ-raisin' racket. Put them noise-makin'...' and Stader choked off his sentence when he saw David sitting on the floor with the banjo across his lap. 'What th' fuck...!' He was at a loss for words. Behind him, Buttman, in his long underwear, was sneering and rolling his eyes, in a parody of disgust.

'No wonder the son of a bitch stinks! He spends all his time over here wif' the niggers. Christ! Can you believe it!'

Stader pointed his long finger at David, having shoved the pistol into the pocket of his trousers. He was stripped to the waist, and his white, soft belly hung over his belt. 'Don't youse come back to our'n quarters! Youse stinkin' piece o' shit! Injun or nigger—you can't make up your mind what youse is, an' I don't give a damn! Just stay the fuck out of my way!' And he spun on his heel and stalked away, kicking over the piss pot at the foot of the short steps to the wagon. Croat, snickering, picked it up and walked back to David and upended it on his head.

'Looka this! A man with no balls in an iron hat!' And the three sauntered off, whickering at the joke.

David sat bitterly embarrassed, having flung the foul-smelling urn violently across the wagon. Iron hat. This was his spiritual name, kapi wa pickwac-totinpiw. Turned into a cruel joke by three bully-boys.

The mood had gone from buoyant to sombre in the space of a long sigh. David looked around and gathered his remaining pride. 'Sorry, boys. Those poor trash sure know how to dampen my style!' No one smiled. David handed the instrument back to Alfred, and left the wagon, depressed. Strolling over to the bunk wagon, he saw that all his belongings had been pitched out onto the ground. He gathered them up, and walked to the tents where the Indians were asleep. Calling out, he crawled in, found a corner, and fell asleep, exhausted.

As the show progressed, David noticed a curious thing. The temperament of the three men, Stader, Buttman and Croat, seemed to grow worse with each performance. No facet of the production afforded them the plaudits of the crowd, no aspect of their performance won them approval. They played villains who were either killed off or taken into custody for botched crimes against the 'settlers'. While the same was true of the Indian players, it didn't seem to bother them. The three men were by now constantly wheedling for a larger, more successful role, which would permit them to play to the crowd. It was odd. David could not imagine why they seemed to need the approval of the audience, whom they deprecated as 'rubes', 'straw-heads', and 'greenhorns'.

Kruck would have none of it. Their job was to play the parts of bungling desperadoes, and there it remained. Nothing could happen which might suggest that the frontier was actually a place of menace. The corporation which had put up the money for this venture did not want the encouragement of frontier settlement in the northwest compromised in any way. Lord knows there was enough of that in the tabloid press. Norquay's instruction was clear to Kruck: make 'em laugh, give 'em a thrill, but under no circumstances plant the thought that pioneering had any risk to it. And if that meant that Indians and outlaws were to play the fool, then so be it.

David found this to be an odd if unpleasant result of the arrested ambitions of the three men. He had rarely seen outbursts of any extreme forms of emotion among the Indians with whom he had lived, let alone such a virtually constant display of nasty disposition as was put on by Stader, Buttman and Croat. He wondered what pleasure was in it for them, and he was disgusted by their sneering and arrogance. David noted that they became servile and unctuous whenever Kruck was around, though he always took an apartment off the carnival grounds and tended to be away much of the time, now that the show was well in hand. Norquay, who elicited the same kind of response from the trio, rarely put in an appearance. He spent most of his time away trying to get new exhibitors for the show, and setting up land agencies to benefit the long-term plans of the railroad. After hours it was wise to stay clear of the three men, and David elected to remain in the Indians' tent. Worse yet, Buttman was starting to show signs of drink, which was grounds for instant dismissal.

It was a slow but obvious process: each man in his own way was becoming actively misanthropic. Stader was, true to his personality, openly aggressive with almost everyone. He was contemptuous of the black players and stage hands, insulting to the Indians, and generally ill-disposed to anyone other than those who were in authority. Everyone was afraid of him, for he carried the role of desperado with him constantly, like a mantle.

Buttman, on the other hand, showed his anger in a sort of self-effacing vindictiveness, the constant theme of which was that he was not recognized for the entertainer and crowd-pleaser that he so obviously was. He frequently compared his own talents with those of some of the other players, whose worth and ability were so clearly below his own. In conversation he was both repelling and frightening.

Croat was a menace in a still different way. He was detached, still and watching like a reptile. His disinclination to listen during conversation was even more apparent, more curt, than it had been. A more annoying theme emerged during his exchanges with Kruck, in which he attempted to generate guilt. 'Well, goddammit, not givin' us more of a role in th' show is yore decision, it's no never mind to us'n. We still gets paid th' same.' All the same, his self-effacing tone gave way in encounters with others to hints of rage: 'Ah shit! Same old crap every day. Sometimes I think I'll fire some real shots off before I clear this place!'

David felt, as did most of the cast, that serious trouble was inevitable. He wished that Norquay was still the dominant figure he had been while the show was being put together in the Baltimore warehouse. With his infrequent appearances, the troupe was becoming increasingly fragmented, for there were discrete groups within the show, each with their own sense of identity, customs, language, roles, and even skin colour. A good deal of suspicion existed between the groups, with only two factors binding them together: the show, and increasing dislike and fear of Stader and his two cronies.

Norquay, however, was increasingly concerned about the politics of the secessionist threat from the South, and the portents of economic disaster for his railroad. The Panic of '57 had hit the North hard, as it had virtually all western industrialized nations. But the South had suffered minimal impact, leading to extravagant boasts of the superiority of their system. The rhetoric of separatism became frightening. A Georgia news-paper, widely circulated, shouted: 'Free Society! We sicken at the name. What is it but a conglomeration of greasy mechanics, filthy operatives, small-fisted farmers, and moon-struck theorists, most of whom are hardly fit for association with a southern gentleman's body servant!'

This hysteria fed political partisanship. A bill was being proposed for the granting of homesteads of one hundred and sixty acres to settlers who could be encouraged to relocate in the territories and newly formed states. Minnesota and Oregon had just come into the federation. All Republicans and nearly all of the Northern Democrats were expected to support the bill, but the South was in vigorous objection. They saw it as an insidious means by which the North would fill up the frontier with Yankee farmers, and generate a dominant influence in the political affairs of the nation. Passage of the Bill was by no means assured. This worried Norquay, and most of his efforts were now directed to engaging support for the land-grant measure.

The rhetoric of sectional conflict found its way into the small world of the Rakovski Frontier Circus and Agricultural Exhibition. Stader and Croat were quick to align themselves with the uglier aspects of southern bigotry and fear. Reading from a front-page editorial, Croat called out to the loungers and workmen, 'Listen up! Listen up! Here's what I've bin sayin' all along: "Men are not born equal. It would be far nearer the truth to say that some were born with saddles on their backs, and others booted and spurred to ride them." Well. Ain't that the fuckin' truth!' And he gave a grinning snarl, separating both lips at one end to reveal yellowed canine teeth. It was his stage expression of villainy, now incorporated into his daily repertoire of expressive attitudes. It was clear his contempt was not merely reserved for blacks, but Indians and 'breeds' as well. There was a perception that even the Bulgarians were 'foreigners', and not quite able to insist upon the normal entitlements which good white folk had come to take for granted. As the country tumbled and tore itself toward Armageddon, so were the tensions and animosities replicated in microcosm among the troupe.

David was not untouched by these events. He noticed that each time he tried to draw Ilsa Grueff aside, her mother, a thin, unsmiling woman who trained the horses her daughters rode, called her away. Both girls were watched by their mother as if they were cubs, and at first David thought it was a matter of their virtue. The old women of the plains tribes watched over the maids of their village for just the same reason. But though this was a part of the woman's purpose, and though she was civil toward him, her demeanour told him that she felt he was beneath her: 'a savage', he'd caught her saying.

Then too, there was the matter of the 'niggers', as everyone called them. They did seem inferior to him in many ways. They smelled different, sure, like labourers, and not a one could read. All of them in the circus were freemen, yet none looked you in the eye, or objected to doing the most menial tasks. David had even seen one carry away horseshit in his hands after Kruck demanded its immediate removal. David became faintly conscious of a feeling of his own paternalism toward them, and it made him uncomfortable. Stader's slurs to the effect that he was 'no better than black trash', that he was 'a fuckin' breed', needled him, made him resentful of Alfred and the others. But he said nothing to either group.

Yet it was the red men and the black men who gave the least resistance to his company. Through Alfred, he learned the terrible truths of the conditions of slavery. The sale, like livestock, of men and women in the marketplace, stripped and fondled much as horses might be pried and squeezed. On the block, naked, men and women were made to spring into the air to demonstrate how lively and free from unsoundness they were, and how little flogging would be required to keep them at their tasks.

'Even our'n marriages wasn't given no protection. A man's wife could be sold away from him. De preacher changed the vows for uns, so'n it read—"Until death or distance do you-uns part". A baby, a tiny li'l chile could be taken off his mammy's tit, an' sole. An' his mammy whupped fer cryin'.'

David felt sick at these stories, and preferred that most of his time was spent at learning the intricacies of the banjo. 'Take dese songs,' Alfred had said. 'Dey diddin 'low no drawlin' songs. Lively songs only, 'cause dey thunk we'd slow down our'n work, otherwise.'

The Indians had their own stories of woe at the hands of the white men. Some escaped the wrath of the United States Cavalry, in its cyclical forays against the Indian, by fleeing west to the lands of their brothers, or coming, as these men had, to work for white masters. The alternative was death at the hands of the soldiers, directly, or in some oblique way through disease or starvation.

The show stayed in Alexandria until late summer. The plan was to keep proceeding south as the onset of winter drew near, but Norquay had some serious concerns about the way the debate over secession was going. War, it was said, was inevitable. And when it came, probably sooner rather than later, the last place a Yankee businessman wanted to be found was in the deep South. After all, apart from any safety concerns, there was the threat of confiscation by the new regime, or the possibility of incarceration as a possible spy. In the climate of 1858, every black face was a potential Nat Turner, the Virginia slave who had staged a revolt that killed fifty-five whites in 1831; every new white face was a suspected abolitionist or agent of John Brown. The alternative was to disband the show for the cold months, and given the cost and difficulty of recruiting staff, it seemed unlikely that it would start up again in the spring.

After considerable debate with his Board of Directors, the decision was made to continue south, but not so far as to prevent a strategic retreat should the country be driven to the brink of war. The tents were struck, and the wagons loaded for the overnight trip by rail to Richmond, Virginia. Upon their arrival they set up the carnival in an exhibition park on the banks of the James River.

It was during this summer of 1858 that David became acquainted with newspapers. He acquired a thirst to know about the world, which only a year ago had seemed so small. Rarely was there much in the way of substantive reference to the Canadas, but there was considerable controversy in the Southern press about the 'underground railway' which conducted escaped slaves along a route lined with abolitionists. One of the principal players in this undertaking, which it was said had brought between fifteen and twenty thousand runaway slaves to Upper Canada, was Harriet Tubman. An escaped slave, she had taken up residence in St

Catherines, the terminus of the 'underground railway', but in the summer of 1858 she had moved back to the United States. In the South, a bounty of forty thousand dollars had been placed on her head. Forty thousand dollars! I should look for her myself, thought David. They must fear her something awful to put up such a sum.

Other stories in the Colonist and the Richmond Tribune railed against the 'provocateur' John Brown, who had outlined his plans in many places, including Chatham, Upper Canada, to set up a black republic in the mountains of Virginia. His favourite Biblical passage, Hebrews 9:22— 'Without shedding of blood [there] is no remission [of sin]'—was frequently turned against him in bellicose editorials. The atmosphere of antagonism and division thus fostered by a steady flow of information, intensified in their new location. Norquay would not make another appearance at the show; indeed, David would never see him again, for all his efforts were now consumed with lobbying on behalf of the seemingly doomed Homestead Act. In opposition to it, Southern senators were intransigent.

In early January of 1859, the show had been closed for over six weeks. Everyone was waiting for instructions to move further south, but there was silence from Norquay. Stader and a number of the others started to drink openly during the evenings, but mercifully, they and others so disposed would leave the enclave and go in to Richmond to seek out whorehouses and saloons. One evening a light skiff of snow had fallen and several of the groups had gathered around burn barrels filled with scrap and driftwood from the riverbank. No one had been paid for two months and food was in short supply. The Grueffs and the Rakovski clans were talking about leaving and heading south as their circus troupe had been originally constituted, but they were having trouble convincing the black workers that it was safe for them. The Indians were silent, impassive, taking no part in the discussion, speaking in low voices among themselves. The blacks muttered to each other, falling silent even when David approached. Gilda stayed in her caravan most of the time, and since they had come to Richmond she had taken up with a tall, thin stranger in a frock coat, whom she seemed to know from a previous trip to the city. He would arrive after dark, and stay all night. She had no time for David, and once, upon approaching the door at the rear of the wagon, he could hear the unmistakable sounds of intimacy. Embarrassed and chagrined, he withdrew quickly.

So this cool winter evening, David and several of the black men were lounging about, thoughtful, downcast faces reflected in the flickering tongues of flame shooting from the barrels. Alfred sat close to the iron brazier, for he was picking at his banjo, trying almost half-heartedly to keep pace with his companion who was licking a tune out of a harmonica. Everyone started as a shot was fired; there was a deep bunging sound as a bullet struck the metal fire barrel, and sparks flew into the night air.

All heads swivelled in the direction of the gunfire. It was Stader, Buttman and Croat, with four other men, two of whom David had never seen before. They were in various stages of intoxication, and a couple of them were swigging from long-necked bottles.

'It's that fuckin' nigger music again,' said Stader. It was Croat who held the pistol. The bullets used in the show had the lead removed, and were repacked with lint wadding. But these were real projectiles. Some of the others who had been at the barrels started to melt into the shadows.

Stader laughed harshly; there was no warmth in it. 'Josh, youse miserable bastard, youse missed! Youse missed this miserable mudsill.' And he swung his red-eyed gaze back to Alfred. 'What'd I tell youse about makin' a racket again, so as decent folk can't get no sleep? Huh?' He sauntered over to Alfred, looking down at the seated man, who kept his eyes downcast, saying nothing.

'Huh?' prodded Stader, annoyed by Alfred's silence. 'Answer me!'

David felt nauseated by this bullying, struggling with an inner turmoil over whether to intervene. Always this fear created a wall between action and inaction. Nevertheless, he felt that things easily could get out of hand, and he spoke up, 'He didn't mean nothing…'

Stader looked up, his lips parted in a twitch of the raised lip, his special emblem of hostility, 'Shut youse fuckin' mouth, youse stinkin' breed, and stay out of business thet don't concern youse!' And turning back to Alfred, he slapped the banjo out of his hand. 'Stand up an' face me, youse black bastard!' The depth of his venom, even if alcohol-inspired, amazed David. Off behind him, Croat and Buttman, and one of the others, giggled like young girls. 'He's gonna teach this buck a lesson he won't ferget, hey?'

Alfred stood up slowly, but did not look at Stader.

'Look at me!' he commanded. But Alfred did not move. 'I said, look at me, you uppity nigger!' And he hit Alfred with the bottle he was holding. The cheap green glass shattered, and Alfred let out a scream as he fell back, the skin cut above his cheekbone. This seemed to enrage Stader, and he reached down and seized Alfred by his clothing, and dragged him to his feet. Alfred was whimpering.

'Stop youse stinkin' whinin'. Answer my question what I asked youse!' As he spoke, he pushed Alfred back, along the outer edge of the grounds, until they had reached the cougar's cage. At the commotion, the animal had risen on its haunches, low to the floor, watching. Its tail flicked back and forth.

Stader continued to berate Alfred, and the others jeered him on.

'This black bastard ain't disposed ta answer his betters,' said Stader. 'Well, I'm thinkin' what he's needin' is a short lesson in proper manners, which his mammy done seem t've overlooked!' And drawing back, he shoved Alfred mightily against the lion's cage.

Alfred fell heavily against the bars of the enclosure, and the starving, tortured beast sprang at him, paws outstretched, and tore at the man's back with a raging, spitting violence that made its cage shake on its gaily painted wheels. For a terrible moment Alfred's eyes bulged from their sockets, and he seemed locked against the bars, arms outspread, unable to move. Then springing forward, face down on the ground, he screamed out his agony in piercing shrieks which drove through David like frozen blades.

Alfred's jacket and shirt were torn to bloody rags. Thin ribbons of flesh hung in tatters from his ruined back. He screeched his pain to the cold earth, drumming his boots and fists in a ghastly accompaniment to his agony. Stader regarded him with a look of disdain, that almost resembled amusement: 'Is it hurtin' youse?' he asked with a sneer, his nostrils working. 'I've just the thing for it! Come on boys, I'll need help with this!' He strode forward, unbuttoning his trousers. Stopping at Alfred's head, he began to urinate on the wretched man's wounds. Chortling, the others gathered around the screaming, prostrate form of the tortured man, cursing as one man's piss splashed the boots of another.

Turning headlong, David ran blindly into the night. Coming up against a brick wall, he flung himself down, vomiting in spasms that racked his body. It was the second time in his life that he had reacted so to the disgust he felt, both for the depth of his own fear, and for the seemingly infinite capacity for cruelty and evil in the human heart. There is no God, he told himself bitterly.

Nine

i

Captain Northup touched the hunched shoulder of mate Edwin Bell, whose attention was fixed upon the innumerable mudbars and deadheads impeding progress through the shallow channel of the turbid Red River of the North. The mate flicked a glance toward Northup, who was grinning broadly for the first time on the trip; he was pointing over the breast-board of the tiny steamship's wheelhouse. Just above the tree line, Bell could make out a dark smudge.

'The cook fires of Fort Garry,' remarked Northup with evident satisfaction. 'The prize be our'n!' He slapped the other on the shoulder, as the mate spun the huge wheel to avoid yet another snag. Northup seized the whistle lanyard and drew off three thin blasts.

By the middle of the nineteenth century, serious trade links had been forged between St Paul, Minnesota, and Fort Garry in Rupert's Land. In 1857 alone, more than one thousand steamboats had off-loaded at St Paul, on the upper reaches of the Mississippi. Much of this was destined for points north, and the ox train was the only means by which this could be accomplished. The good burghers of St Paul felt that the Red River had navigational possibilities which promised a more efficient carriage of goods. In consequence, the St Paul Chamber of Commerce offered a prize of one thousand dollars to anyone who might put a steamboat on the Red, and successfully pilot her to the Red River Settlement at the forks of the Red and Assiniboine.

For a time, no one seemed interested. But after several months Anson Northup, then forty-six years of age, a hosteler and land speculator, came forward. He owned a small steamboat which had been built in Maine in 1850, called *Governor Ramsey* when it worked the Mississippi headwaters.

He had renamed it *North Star*. His plan was to take the vessel apart, and trundle the hull timbers and machinery overland to the Red River, a distance of about one hundred and fifty miles. An aggressive, ebullient man, he demanded that the reward be increased by as much again. Arguing that the cost of the venture warranted such an increase, he convinced the Chamber members after persistent debate. There was no gainsaying the man; after all, the boiler alone weighed five and one half tons. Northup set about his task over the winter of 1858-59. It was in March of 1859 that David was taken on as stoker's helper. The little vessel burned better than a cord of wood every hour; more when the current was strong. Frequent 'wooding-up' stops were necessary to keep the vessel supplied, and the cutting, sawing, loading and stoking was continuous, back-breaking work. There were few takers for the posted positions, but David was glad of the passage home, as well as the few extra dollars it would mean to his stake.

The riverboat was launched on the Red just as the spring flood had receded. There was a rush to get her boiler deck covered, and the hurricane roof (so named because of its flatness) covered with canvas and pitch-payed seams. Set atop this was the open pilot house, a small, boxy affair resting on an ungainly superstructure. Not a window or porthole graced the boat; the pilothouse sported a hinged plank which could be folded down in fair weather, and a pegged visor board moved inward to meet it overhead. In all, the *Anson Northup*, for so her vainglorious owner had renamed her, was a squat, ugly barge, only distantly related to the layer-cake, gingerbread vessels that were eventually to succeed her.

In consequence of the Northup's hasty construction, her freeboard and cabin seams were roughly joined. At dusk, when failing light forced the crew to tie up at the inner shore of a bend, legions of mosquitoes made their way inside to feast on the unhappy travellers. At the end of the second day, at least the aft portion of the after cabin, a dormitory for the passengers and crew, had been sealed off with blankets, and the more gaping seams had been payed with oakum so that some respite from the insects was possible. During the day, the heat in the cabin rivalled the misery inflicted by the humming creatures at night.

On the trip, they had seen two prairie fires. The first one, far off, cast its pall in a dark, rolling cloud northward, carried by the dry south winds. The second (or perhaps it may have been an extension of the first) bore down on the river after the wind had veered, heralding the coming of a new weather system. The breeze blew steadily from the west-northwest. David wondered about any Indian villages or hunting parties that might have been caught by the blaze. The prospect of a prairie fire invoked awe among dwellers of the plains, for there was little chance of escape from it if one were caught in the open. Horses could not outrun a blaze in the dry grass, should the wind be hard.

Initially, the hint of woodsmoke on the weather side of the steamboat told of a large fire, far off. The rivermen that Northup had recruited were set a-chatter. With luck, the fire would burn ahead of them, and there would be game for the table. The burn would drive every living creature before it into the river, where the hurricane deck of the *Anson Northup* would make a fine shooting platform.

By late afternoon it became apparent that the fire was close. The smoke was thick and ash-laden. The captain ordered the vessel tied up on the east bank, on the outer edge of a wide bend in the river. They were out of the main thrust of the smoke, though it cast a haze dense enough to hurt the eyes. The men standing on the deck had their firearms ready, and everyone was silent. David had no gun, but stood back on the lower deck with a wet burlap sack, as ordered, for they were wary of sparks. Even now he could hear them hissing in the distance, as they landed on the surface of the muddy waters.

There was a cry as four large elk broke from the screen at the river's edge opposite. Though it was a distance of several hundred paces, David could see their eyes rolling in fright. Barely had these animals plunged into the river than the woods opened up, and creatures of every kind made for the river in a panic-stricken scramble. Black bear, wolves, shedding buffalo with hides hanging in tatters, antelope, moose, raccoon, fox, lynx and a young cougar swept before the fire in a choreography of terrified haste, utterly unmindful of each other.

With whoops and hurrahs, the men above opened fire. Bullet and musket ball licked the water around the animals. As the creatures made their way to the waters forward of where the boat was moored, more shots began to strike home. Some of the animals began to bawl and shriek, as painful non-fatal wounds added to their frenzy. Many of the beasts were killed too far out in the water and the current carried them away. Some simply sank. The din was maddening, for the firing and shouting continued unabated. David thought that this was a bit foolish, for all that could be used had long ago been taken. But the killing went on as long as the parade of alarmed animals continued.

Finally the light failed. The fire burned to the water's edge about a quarter of a mile to the north and died out as night fell. A fine drizzle started as some of the trophies were butchered on the riverbank, and choice cuts were placed over cookfires near the boat. The heavy stench of wet ash and charcoal hung over the area; for the better part of the following day the vessel would pass through blackened terrain, lifeless and forlorn.

It was after dark that David was cajoled into fetching out his banjo. Many of the others had never seen or heard such an instrument, though several of the rivermen were familiar enough with it. After each rollicking song, accompanied by tapping spoons and a harmonica, his travel-weary companions would call out for more, until at last David was so exhausted that he could do nothing other than fall asleep where he sat. The vessel would require a full head of steam before the half-light, so David's day would start at four in the morning, when 'wooding-up' commenced.

On the second evening of what would be an eight-day trip, David had placed his banjo in its cardboard case, and lay wrapped in a thin blanket beside it. For a time before sleep, he thought of Alfred Okay. The others had decided that the banjo, which was Alfred's only possession of any consequence, should go to David. He had been almost too ashamed to take it; he had snatched it and run from the caravan. Not long after, he left the circus to return to Red River. The scenes of Alfred's death would not quit the fringes of his consciousness, but remained insistently, unlike any other event which had happened to him.

He was no stranger to death. He had seen several people die, some terribly. Always, the event seemed to mark a turning point in his life, but there was something ineffably dolorous about the brutal destruction of Alfred Okay. His infected wounds had carried him off within a fortnight; his torment was beyond description. David remembered the lyrics into which Alfred had so beautifully breathed life. They were as transitory and delightful as a flower, whose scent lingers long after the petals have wilted.

If I was a little bird,
I'd not build my nest on the ground.
I'd build my nest in the sour apple tree,
Where the wild boys couldn't tear it down.

David was powerfully aware that he could have been picked to suffer at the hands of those murderous bullies. It seemed only a matter of luck that there were others at a lower station whose vulnerabilities were even greater than his. He could not shake the feeling that he was only too glad he had escaped, and he was ashamed.

As the steamer churned its way past the river lots at St Norbert, David and the others could see the consternation created among the settlers who ran down to the riverbank to watch the craft go by, its single smokestack belching billowing curls of woodsmoke and ash against the cloudless blue sky. Rounding the last bend and making for the Forks, the shrill blasts of the steamboat's whistle generated an excitement onshore that verged on pandemonium. As the vessel turned into the mouth of the Assiniboine River, its paddles spanked the water with loud splashes and its whistle shrieked; horses fled, dogs barked, and children scurried back and forth crying out their fear and excitement. It seemed as if the entire community had turned out to greet the steamboat and watch as the crew, including David, made their mooring fast to a pair of 'deadmen'— nothing more than heavy iron hooks set in the riverbank for making fast a hawser or for winching over mudbars.

An American flag was hastily run up beside the Hudson's Bay Company flag fluttering limply over the gates of Fort Garry, as the *Anson Northup* drew ashore. The church bells in the twin towers of the Catholic Church began to peal, and everyone jumped as two rounds from the fort's otherwise idle cannon boomed out a late salute. Witnessing the event from his vantage point across from the Forks, Bishop Alexandre Taché wrote excitedly in his diary:

'The puffing of steam moving about on our river told the echoes of the desert, that a new era for our country was being inaugurated. Each turn of the shaft appeared to bring us nearer by so much to the civilized world.'

As David retrieved his belongings, he was paid off by the mate, who wished him luck, after his offer for work on the return passage was declined. David paused, leaning against a hull brace, and contemplated the busy, pleasantly confused scene before him on the riverbank. His anxiety was beginning to grow. Would his grandfather still be alive? What of his family? What should he do next? These thoughts delayed him for several minutes. On this machine, like those which had frightened him a few years ago as he had approached St Paul with the hide hunters, he felt at home. Now the cities of the east, and the multitudes of white people inspired no awe in him, nor did their machines of industry and commerce. The deck of this ship was as comforting and familiar to him as the skin lodges of the Dakota were in earlier years. He no longer felt, now that he had returned to the threshold of his old life, that he was welcome, or that he would fit in here.

Even his mode of dress was different. For the return he had put on his best outfit, which was the straight-legged black suit which Norquay had supplied for the trip to Baltimore. He looked every inch the frontier dandy, but now he felt acutely self-conscious. Still he lingered. The crowd around the vessel were looking at him as curiously as they regarded the still-sighing machinery. He was surprised at his own reaction to them. They seemed rude and unsophisticated. His dress and the instrument of travel which had returned him to Fort Garry, represented the mystery of the pavements he had trod, the wonders he had seen, and the grandness of a world far beyond the distant prairie horizons, where such things were commonplace. David felt a slight, unfamiliar feeling of superiority. More, he liked the sensation. It was similar to that which he had experienced as a performer. Yet different. People regarded him, quite obviously, with awe and admiration. Unlike a circus actor, he was now a man to be reckoned with, a man of substance and experience. Feigning indifference, he was loath to step down the gangplank, preferring instead to lounge near the capstan and bask in the reflected glory of modern industrial technology.

As the crowds thinned, David set off for the fort. Set well back from the river, its southern gate was at the summit of the shallow bank. The way was made somewhat easier by the rough planking laid down. With the recent rains, the boards had become as muddy and slippery as the riverbank itself, and David's hard boots slipped several times, nearly pitching him into the mire. He was having some difficulty maintaining the dignity he had so recently assumed.

The capricious prairie weather, which had parched the valley south of Pembina, had emptied a deluge upon a narrow band bordered by the Assiniboine River and the ragged delta at the foot of Lake Winnipeg. The dominant element at the foot of the gangplank and beyond was mud. Thick, black, and glutinous, it laid claim to heel and hem and everything else set down, however momentarily. Like a thing alive, it swallowed and spat, trailing up stairs and into buildings, coating hands and clothing, and rendering all pigment into some variant of grey. Most sensible men had yielded and stepped about barefoot, trousers rolled to the knee, boots or moccasins slung by laces over the shoulder.

The settlement had grown since David's departure in 1855. In that year, the total population of the settlement was just over six thousand persons; now the total stood at almost eight thousand. The wilderness, which had only grudgingly yielded to Selkirk's settlers decades before, had now been shoved back, impatiently, roughly. Nearly all the trees were gone, their forlorn stumps mute witnesses to a clamorous, frenetic swirl of activities, comings and goings. Streets had been laid out in a rectangular grid parallel to the broad, east-west, north-south cart trails which followed the two principal rivers. Along these rude boulevards hundreds of rough shanties had been set up, all but the roofing felt being constructed of local materials. Some had outbuildings and lean-to shacks added as prosperity and after-thoughts flowered. Few surfaces beyond the verandahs of the false fronts on the main street were adorned with paint.

By far the best buildings were located within the perimeter of the fort, though even here, David could see as he passed by the gate, there were signs of dilapidation and slipshod construction; these were hints that dividends paid out in London lay far greater claim than the aesthetic considerations of warehouses and dormitories in a distant outpost.

The fort had just become the administrative centre for all trade in the North-west. A stone fortress was started in 1835, succeeding the wooden forts which had preceded it. It was necessary to double its size about 1850, though the quarried limestone which the original construction had called for was considered too costly, and the new walls were created by hewn-log cribs filled with packed dirt. The outer wall originally had a coat of whitewashed plaster, intended roughly to proximate the original, but within a few years they stood as David now beheld them: patchy, crumbling, a dingy monument to the empire of the Hudson's Bay Company men in London.

Three years earlier, gold had been discovered on the Fraser River, and the path to the goldfields led through the fort at the Forks. The overland trail to the North-west made the colony at Fort Garry a convenient stopover to lay in supplies for the long trek to the Fraser River valley. Though the traffic to the western claims had diminished, a great many traders still remained, for settlement was noticeably on the increase from Canada and the decline in the fur trade had not yet made itself felt. In 1859 the settlement was growing, an adolescent really, awkward and ungainly, rough in appearance but trying to imitate its eastern elders. The contrast between rude frontiersman and titled dandy was sharp and vexing, for the inhabitants were held in some disdain by their 'betters'. All about, more in number it seemed than when he left, there were begging Indians, broken relics clutching ragged robes with one hand, and extending the other with palm uplifted, fingers opening and closing in the universal gesture of want. These wretched, shuffling creatures disgusted him. On most, the sour stench of cheap rum and vomit rankled the nostrils like old piss.

No light appeared in their eyes. David had been taught during his time with the Sioux, and in a somewhat different version from his mother, that it was the duty of all men to pass the fire of life along to the next generation. In many of these ruined faces, that fire was barely aglow; in some, it had gone out. They were ignored by men of their own people who had come to trade, or to do other business at the settlement. For these, their brethren did not exist. David turned his eyes away, and closed his ears to their muttering imprecations.

Arriving at the rutted thoroughfare which ran to the east of the fort along the Red River, David found his way blocked by a long convoy of ox carts. Normally it would be an easy matter to dodge between the slow-moving animals, but the track, some hundred and fifty feet wide, was a sea of churned mud. David sat on a low pile of freshly sawn boards. The rough lumber gave off a heavy, sweet fragrance of spruce resin, and almost immediately David felt a sliver pass through the light material of his suit into his buttock. He leapt to his feet with a half-uttered curse, digging around under his clothes for the barb. To his relief, it was substantial enough to grasp, and he plucked it out with a grunt. Nearby, he heard a deep chortle.

'Got's a sliver in th' ass, has youse?'

It was the mate of the *Anson Northup*, Edwin Bell. David had come to know him slightly, for Bell loved to sing, and he would accompany David and the others by clacking out a rhythm on two tin tablespoons between knee and cupped palm. David grinned ruefully as he lowered himself more carefully to his seat. Bell was seated cross-legged on the stack just above where David was haunched over on one side, his hand under him, trying to assess the damage to his trousers.

'Them clothes ain't fit fer this land,' said Bell. 'Won't be more'n a day till y've torn the ass right outa them. Youse need somethin' in skin or canvas.'

David looked up at Bell, nodding and squinting, for the sun was almost directly behind the mate's back. Bell was hardly the picture of sartorial splendour: he wore the wide canvas breeches favoured by rivermen, and an oversized flannel shirt which had two rows of wooden buttons so the front could be opened up entirely if the wearer wished, or conditions demanded. Around his neck was a kerchief, and slung over his shoulders by the laces were his thick leather boots. Pushed back on his head was an incongruous bowler hat, from the band of which protruded two bedraggled feathers of uncertain origin. None of these garments were free from soil. From his wiggling, mud-covered toes to his fletched hat, Bell had accumulated all manner of stains and filth, so that it was impossible to ascertain the original colour of his clothing.

'I aim to start in business,' said David. 'I thought these duds would identify me properly.' He started to pick at the clods of mud on his boots with a stick.

'Theys identify youse as an easterner, Philadelphia mebbe, or even Chicago. I knows youse not from St Paul, though I can't quite place the accent.' The tone of Bell's voice was not unkind. 'But theys identify youse as a man who's not got the sense ta—, well, take off his boots in Red River gumbo. Th' carpet-baggers an' flim-flam men'll flock ta youse like foxes ta'n stuck rabbit.' Again, the low chortle, which seemed to remove any bite his critical words may have had. As if to reinforce his good will, Bell leaned over, and offered David a small tin flask, which only a moment ago, had flashed to his lips in a brief sip. David gulped the drink, for the sun had created a powerful thirst. The rum did little to quench his parched throat; rather, it seared unexpectedly, and David fought the involuntary cough, keeping his mouth clamped shut. His body would not be denied, however, and a spasm in his lungs exploded through his nose, driving snot across his chin, and dribbles of rum from the corners of his mouth. He felt like a fool. He had expected strong drink, but not the fiery overproof he had tasted.

'On th' other hand, mebbe youse hails from Toronto. I heard them Canadians drink like that!' And his chortle gave way to gales of laughter as he rolled onto his back. 'Snot-nosed easterner!' The shift in weight toppled the loose planks, and Bell was suddenly thrown off. David continued to pick at his boots until Bell recovered and sat up. As luck would have it, he had spilled into the spot where the team which fetched the lumber had deposited their manure. It was David's turn to snicker.

'What a pair of experienced travellers! One covered in shit, and t'other covered in snot!'

They both roared at the sorry sight of each other.

'David, y' silly shit!' said Bell weakly, drawing tears away from his eyes with a dirty finger. 'This land'll eat youse alive. Mebbe youse should book return on th' *Northup* th' day after tomorra? I'm pretty sure the leaky ol' tub'll make th' trip back...'

'Look!' said David sharply. 'This is my home. I was born here, raised here. My family is here. There's been some changes, sure enough, but I know this land likely better'n you!' He was aware of Bell's astonishment, even though his features were not clear in the glare.

After a moment, Bell spoke, more subdued. 'Well, youse coulda fooled me. Youse look like youse done all right. Why come back?'

'I've come back to live here.'

Bell chortled again, but it struck a different, humourless note. 'S'like a dog circling back to eat its own vomit or lick its own shit, seems ta me. Youse leave home ta make youse own way. My home is in a little place called May's Landing in New Jersey. Soon's I could get a berth on a coaster at th' age of eleven, I wuz gone, and I ain't never been back.'

'But what about your mother...' David stopped from saying 'and your father' for even had he lived, David could not imagine having feelings for a father. '...your family?'

'My ol' man beat me ever single day I was at home,' said Bell without a trace of bitterness. 'An' my ma worked me worse than any nigger. As far as I know, they're still thrashin' them of my brothers what didn't have the sense to do what I did. No desire ta go back,' he added, almost as an afterthought.

'Found river work in Orleans,' he continued, as though somewhere within him a small dam of reserve had failed. 'Helluva lot better than coastal work, not near as hard or as dangerous—well, mebbe as hard.

'Learned my trade on the Miss which's how I ended up in St Paul, 'cause of my old boat *Maid of Ohio* catchin' fire an' burnin' to the water line. This trip looked promisin', and Northup was payin' good money fer experienced rivermen, 'specially this being somethin' of'n unknown propysition.'

'So where do you consider your home to be, then?' asked David.

'Don't ya see, David, youse home is where youse ass happens ta be at th' moment.'

'But what if you had a wife, and children, and all?'

'If'n I did, I'd bring 'em along with me, till I wuz ready ta settle, but you can be goddam sure it wouldn't be in Mays Landing! If youse life was so wunnerful here, then why did youse leave in th' first place?'

'I didn't have much of a choice. Indians ran off with me when I was a boy. Not that you could say my life here was so special.' David took off his boots to clean them properly, and elected not to put them back on. He slung them over his pack. Bell did not pry into this glimpse of David's background. He slipped down to the rack where David was, and pointed out the obvious. 'Th' last cart is passin'.'

David nodded as he stood up. 'Well, I've got to find a place to sleep tonight.'

Bell stepped off the planks. 'Let's walk along, then, 'cause I ain't sleepin' on that tub one night longer'n I hafta; the skeeters already got more a my blood than I wanna give.'

Together the two men trudged barefoot north along the muddy track. They came to a clutter of shacks and warehouses known locally as 'McDermotsville', after a pioneer trader, though some were referring to this, the area around the fort and the fort itself collectively, as 'Winnipeg', Cree for 'murky waters'—or as the old French traders interpreted it, 'stinking waters'.

Securing beds in a boarding house for the sum of eight cents apiece, they sat down to share the meal which included buffalo steak, bread and the first radishes of the season. Drinking poor beer which had the men squatting out back many times later that night, David outlined his plans.

'I've got a few dollars set aside, safe in a bank in St Paul. Plus I've the money advanced for this trip; not much considering the work, mind you.

After I contact my family, I want to start a business, bringing things here from the south; new things I've seen for the western farmer, which I'm bettin' scarce anyone even knows about here. Now that the steamer's made it to Fort Garry, I think there will be an advantage over the cart trains.'

David told Bell about the agricultural exhibition which had been attached to the circus. He had parted on good terms with the exhibitors, and felt he could still rely on the contacts he had made. He explained the installment method of payment for poor farmers which he had learned about from Fletcher Norquay.

Bell was excited. 'Sure enough, them steamers'll be bringin' tons a stuff, 'fore long. They increase capacity by haulin' barges with the current, as comin' here; they'll even push a loaded flatboat in front. Ho! There'll be more shit brought in here soon than anyone ever dreamed of!

'But youse gotta problem. The Hudson's Bay Company runs everything here. Furs, trade, law, even burials—youse gotta go through them, an' if'n they don't get some kind of profit, why, youse ain't gonna ever get anythin' afloat."

David pursed his lips, and looked skeptically at Bell. 'I know that was the case for a long time here, true enough, but things were changing even before I left. About ten years ago a Métis trader was pardoned for trading with the Americans. Guillaume Sayer, his name was. It was quite the talk of the community at the time. Since then, the Company never has tried to enforce its monopoly, and my understanding is that there are plenty of free traders in the North-west. Though of course it doesn't hurt to have the Company on your side.'

Bell's eyes narrowed, and he leaned forward conspiratorially to David. 'You know, when I first started comin' to St Paul, they was nothin' but a tumbledown collection a shanties, so humble youse'd not wanta piss in any of 'em. But between the boats and the railroads, the settlers came in droves fer all that free land. It's gonna be the same thing here.'

Reaching down, Bell picked up his boot, and showed it upended to David. "Lookit this dirt! Black an' rich as youse'll ever see. It'll grow anythin'! Shit into a gopher hole, and by the summer youse'll have a turd tree! Another ten years, an' there'll be so many settlers here, why, it'll be like St Paul all over! Youse…youse interested in takin' a partner?'

David shifted uncomfortably. 'The last time I took on a partner, I was robbed of everything but the clothes on my back.' He briefly related the story of his association with Holstrom and Pickett, the hide hunters.

Bell leaned back and whistled. 'Youse sure got fucked over, but good. Lemme tell youse somethin'. Youse can trust me. I didn't get my mate's rating 'cause I was a layabout, or shifty. I know shippin', and youse'll need someone like me fer that.

'But listen,' he continued, sensing David's interest. 'There's three things youse look fer in a man, 'specially a man youse're lookin' fer to go into business with. The first thing is honesty: does he talk straight? Does he let youse inside him so youse's knows what youse's dealing with?' Bell held up a second finger.

'The next thing is, is he growed up? Has he done enough with his life so far ta show he ain't wastin' a lot of time? And what has he made of himself, if'n he's been dealt a poor hand by a God what's cruel more often'n not?' He leaned in close to David, holding three upright fingers between them, pausing only to lick a globule of fat which was dribbling down his ring finger.

'The last thing always gives me a bit o' trouble to rightly explain it; I ain't quite got the words just so. By now youse've guessed I'm not the fanciest speaker what ever tickled youse ears. But a man's got to have a sense about him that there's enough to go around. He don't have to have it all. I've never understood these greedy ones what do. When youse got the greed in youse—it don't matter fer what—then nothin' else matters. Youse's no better'n an animal what's got to eat, fuck an' sleep, an' nothin' else.

'Come ta think of it,' he chortled, 'Sometimes that sounds like my life a lotta the time. Hor! Hor! Well, two outta three ain't so bad, I guess!'

As he was speaking, David was thinking about his own life. He'd been dealt some paltry cards over the years, but he reckoned he'd done all right. Still, he couldn't escape the nagging feeling that it was only good luck balancing the bad that pulled him out of difficult times, rather than any sense of direction. This venture was the first thing that he was embarking upon as a conscious act of will. The mark of a grown man.

He liked Bell. What he said made sense, and it occurred to David that he had always been drawn to strong people, people who could teach him something.

'...'s not as if I ain't got a brain o' my own,' Bell was saying, 'but I can see the sense in things, once th' idea's there, an' I can see it through.

'I think this'll be a rich land someday soon, as I said, so why not get rich along with it?' Bell was grinning broadly now. 'So whaddya say? I got a bit put by myself ter throw in; I'm not looking fer a handout...'

David reached out his hand; Bell clasped it firmly: 'Partners, then.'

'Partners it is, by gum!'

ii

Mary Daniel flashed her eyes at her younger sister Catherine, as the thirteen-year-old tried to remember the lines she was expected to say. But this was the grand sitting of the General Quarterly Court, December 15, 1859, and arrayed before her were some of the most important people in Red River. There at a raised table in the Court House at the Upper Fort were William Mactavish, Governor of Assiniboia; Dr Bunn, Sheriff; and Thomas Sinclair, Robert McBeath, and François Bruneau, the Chairmen of the District Courts, all stern of countenance and sombre in mood. Mary had told her that stealing would be easy, and that as long as Margaret, who was their ten-year-old sister, took the blame, nothing would happen anyway should they be caught. Well, they were caught, and nothing was going the way Mary had said it would. For Margaret had become frightened and hopelessly confused, and Catherine found it impossible to weave her own story into the nonsense which Margaret had related to the Court. Under questioning, her story largely fell apart, so she resorted to tears, the last bastion of the guilty and the innocent.

All the while, Mary Daniel, at sixteen the eldest of the three Daniel girls, watched with narrowed eyes and thinly veiled contempt for the way Catherine comported herself.

By and by it was Mary's turn to testify. It was all a terrible mistake, she said, for the first time she saw the money, six pounds of it, all in silver coin, Catherine had told her she had found it by the river. What good luck! She had given Mary two pounds and six pence of it, being sisters. Both of them had spent their money at the shop in the stone fort. Mary denied hotly that she knew it was the property of the Hudson's Bay Company. 'I stand by my plea of "not guilty", sir!'

It had been so easy. The unlocked cash drawer was next to an open window of the north wall of the shop. The first time had yielded the six pounds in a small sack; the second trip, five one-pound notes. There was a delicious irony in that the money was spent in the same store, Mary thought. If only they hadn't given any coins to Margaret; she was such a boastful child, and the display of the coins in the palm of one so young was sure to arouse suspicion, as in fact it did. Thankfully, to Mary's perception of things, the fact that she had orchestrated the whole affair did not seem to have emerged with any certainty.

Dr Bunn addressed the jury, the two accused having nothing further to say in their behalf. The jury rose from their motley collection of seats, and retired to a sorting room to consider their verdict. The gallery rose, and a low buzz of appraisals and second-guessing commenced, for the room was full of onlookers, and interest was keen in all the proceedings. Before ten minutes had passed, the door swung open with a crash, and the twelve men trooped out with their verdict: 'guilty' for Catherine, and 'not guilty' for Mary. Catherine collapsed in tears; Mary swept her head up imperiously, her lips compressed. She was a lovely woman, with dark hair and flashing, expressive black eyes. She was well aware that most of the jurors hardly took their eyes off her, even now. Some even looked hopefully at her, as if for approval. Oafs, she thought.

Dr Bunn addressed them both. 'Catherine Daniel, after a fair and impartial trial, the jury have found you guilty of felony. The offence you have committed is one of a very serious nature, and in any other country you would have, in all probability, been condemned to seven or perhaps fourteen years' confinement.' At this Catherine's sobs became noticeably louder. Mary lowered her head, showing the appropriate contrition.

'The Court, however,' Bunn continued, 'taking into consideration the fact that you are young, and hoping that you will never commit such an act again, are inclined to be merciful to you. Already you have been nearly three weeks in prison; we were disposed to have committed you for another three months. But the Governor, who has in his power to remit your term of imprisonment to any period he pleases, thinks it will be sufficient punishment to you and warning to others if he treats you with great leniency.' There was both art and bombast in the funereal speech, and Bunn paused, looking over his narrow reading glasses at Catherine.

'Therefore, the sentence of the Court is that you be imprisoned for two weeks from this day.' Catherine groaned.

Turning to Mary, his voice hardened; there was an edge to his words. 'You, Mary Daniel, are discharged. But take care.' These last three words were underscored with a tone no one in the hall mistook.

'You have had a narrow escape. There is a strong impression on the minds of everyone present that you have acted dishonestly. Avoid being brought up again; for if you come hither a second time, the evidence which has been given today will tell heavily against you. You may go.'

The old bastard, thought Mary. Here I am, acquitted, and he speaks to me as if I'm guilty. He has no such right. But she held her tongue, seeing nothing to gain by an outburst. Without a second look at her weeping sister, she grabbed Margaret by the hand, marched to the coatracks, swaddled herself and the snivelling child in hooded robes and mufflers, and stepped out into the blistering weather. It was ten days before Christmas, and as cold as a witch's tit, as the freighters said. Turning to hasten Margaret, she slipped on the packed, fresh-fallen snow, and skidded bodily down the half-dozen steps.

Her fall was broken by her collision with a passerby, whose head was down against the wind. He crashed heavily against the rough iron-clad runner of a Glengarry sleigh and lay still, face down. Mary was unhurt, and called to the two men who had followed her out, and were gawking from the landing at the top of the stair.

'Get yourselves down here, will you, and lend a hand! Can't you see this man's hurt?'

They turned him over; the side of his face was bloodied. Mary gasped. 'My God! I've torn his ear off!'

Quickly, the man was bundled up the stairs and into the rear of the hall. Proceedings which involved disputed compensation for hay, were interrupted as the body was brought in. It was David Bloode, the new trader who had come up on the *Anson Northup* this past summer. His company, Bloode & Bell, or B & B as it was advertised in the recently established newspaper, was bringing all manner of farming implements, hardware and household effects from eastern America. He had attracted considerable attention in the settlement, but as an unassuming, almost shy individual, little was known of him. This accident gave the necessary licence for those present to gather about and pass back and forth what bits of information were available for speculation. Was he drunk? What was Mary Daniels doing hovering over him like a grieving widow? Was it true his ear had come off? The man was bleeding like a stuck pig.

For the next two days Mary was a constant caller at the boarding house where David lived. She believed she had caused the loss of his ear, and the thick bandage which swaddled his head did nothing to disabuse her. She had even returned to the bloodied sleigh to find it, though to what she proposed to do with it, no thought had been given. The thought of some snarling cur scuttling away with the remnant seemed to her quite sickening. She felt some guilt lay at the bottom of this morbid quest: guilt for having caused such a terrible injury, but deeper within her innermost thoughts, guilt because she was using this fortuitous event to form an acquaintance with one of the settlement's most mysterious but promising bachelors. But no ear was to be found. A dog or a raven must have carried it off. Ugh!

David opened his eyes; squinting, he tried to focus against the brilliant wash of sunlight streaming through the small casement. His head throbbed, but it was bearable. Leaning over him was a breathtakingly beautiful woman, whose long, dark hair trailed over him as she busied herself with smoothing his covers. He sneezed suddenly, sharply. She jumped back with a startled cry, lost her balance and fell off the bed, away from David's sight. He groaned at the pounding in his head.

He tried to turn his head to look at her as she scrambled to her feet, blushing powerfully, straightening her clothes. The stiffness in his neck drove splinters into the base of his skull.

'I'm sorry,' he said, gritting his teeth. 'I must have startled you.'

'No sir, 'tis I who should be sorry,' she mumbled, her English freighted with a thick French accent.

David answered in French. 'Comme vous voulez.'

She spoke again at seeing his puzzled expression. ''Twas I who caused your injury.'

'It's strange, I remember nothing but being struck. Earlier, when I was awake for a few minutes, I thought perhaps someone had robbed me and left me to freeze to death. Did you rob me also?' he asked with a weak grin.

She looked down, her face a study in contrition. She was lovely, he thought. Why have I never seen her before? He felt intensely attracted to her. She was Métis, that he could tell from her dark skin and raven's-wing hair. He supposed that in winter dress, one woman looked much like another. There were winsome mannerisms she affected that drew him to her; there was about her a coyness, a vulnerability that charged him with desire. That her poses were practised and deliberate utterly escaped him. He was besotted, having laid eyes upon her for only a few minutes. That his earlier stirrings had prompted her to attend to his coverings like a doting nurse, thus affording her the opportunity to display face and throat to him to the best possible advantage, he would never know. That her hands had brushed the sides of his thighs, as she had smoothed the blankets, he knew well enough, for his excitement was apparent.

'How is it you came to strike me?' he asked.

She settled on the edge of the bed, seemingly unaware that her hip touched his. Looking away as if embarrassed, she replied. 'It was my fault. I slipped on the steps and fell on top of you. Our heads struck...' and here she rubbed the top of her head ruefully, '...and you fell very hard against the sleigh...I feel so terrible about your ear.'

David laughed loudly, wincing at the pain it caused him. 'My ear!' His eyes showed merriment and pain in flashes. 'My ear was cut away long ago by a murdering thief. It is a small vanity that I wear my hair in such a way as to cover the disfigurement.'

He added wryly. 'I'm sure that the fall did not enhance my appearance, but you can take no responsibility for the loss of my ear.'

She was visibly relieved. 'Thank God.' Then hastily she added, 'Oh, I mean—you should not take it that I am glad for myself; no. You are still most handsome.' She blushed as the words seemed to tumble out. 'What I mean is—I am sorry...'

David closed his eyes against his headache. 'There is no need for apologies. However, if you truly feel for your victim, you will continue to attend to him, and assist in his speedy recovery.'

He spoke again in English, opening his eyes slyly. 'Would you consider this?'

She replied in her accented tongue. 'It would give me pleasure, sir.'

No greater pleasure than mine, David thought, looking at her as she gathered her cloak and muff. 'Return soon.'

She flashed a smile at him as she swirled from the room, sweeping her long hair back with her fingers as she pulled on her tight-fitting woollen cap. She could feel his eyes fixed on her, and she smiled to herself. He was handsome, rich and captivated. She had to be careful, but played right, Monsieur Bloode was hers for the taking.

David settled back on his lumpen pillows and sighed. He was exhausted now that the excitement that this mysterious, beautiful woman had aroused in him had begun to ebb from his body. His headache made it impossible to sleep for the moment, so his thoughts moved in a tumble of images. He contemplated the state of his present existence; perhaps this knock on the head would be good for him, he thought. He had not taken a moment to relax since he had arrived in Red River.

He had been dismayed to learn that his family had perished, carried off in one of the occasional flare-ups of smallpox. His mother had not been vaccinated, though the Hudson's Bay Company had introduced the practice more than forty years before. So great were her superstitions that neither she nor her daughters had any protection against the disease. Ephraim was indifferent to David's sisters, but he insisted that David be protected. David had known full well that the Assiniboine, who only eighty years before could have presented a mounted force of forty thousand warriors, had been so ravaged by smallpox and measles that toward mid-century, total numbers were barely an eighth of what they had been. Most were left with the ugly, pitted lesions which mark the survivors of smallpox.

Yet knowing this, his mother remained obdurate, convinced of the power of prayer and the protection of the spirit world. The outside world, with all its seemingly indomitable tyrannies, had swept her and her children away. Perhaps the only defence was to experience it as David had. Perhaps a body needs to be vaccinated against cruelty and misfortune by surviving a bit of it early on, he mused. The Métis were a case in point; they were purblind to the storms of change hurtling down upon them. The attractions of the hunt and the easy draw of the tripman's life on the brigades still were preoccupations of choice. They seemed unaware that this way of existence was in jeopardy, even though events such as the arrival of the *Anson Northup*, the discovery of gold and the thickening stream of settlers portended otherwise.

Things were going reasonably well with the business. Though he had not seen Bell again, they were in regular communication through the mail packets. Bell had been busy with dealers in St Paul and beyond, managing to get at least one brigade of equipment to the hastily erected warehouse. Putting up this structure, rough as it was, had taken all of David's cash, and the first shipment was secured by Bell's savings, together with both their pledges for the balance. Most of the goods had been sold on credit, in anticipation of the following year's harvest, so that there was 'precious little in the cashbox', as Bell wrote in a note accompanying the bills of lading. All depended upon the weather, and the success of next year's planting. Perhaps some pelts would be brought in over the winter, to begin the repayments. The Company had lost its iron grip on the fur trade, so that 'free traders' were operating everywhere. There was even talk that the Company's licence to operate as a monopoly would not be renewed by the Imperial Parliament next year. This meant more competition for the same available money.

Still, a settlement boom seemed not far off. Gold had been discovered out west in the Cariboo; all kinds of rumours about it were making the rounds of the settlement. Word had it that a Chilcotin Indian had related to a local miner by the name of Peter Dunleavy that gold nuggets could be found east of Lac la Hache. Within days Dunleavy had found gold in the Horsefly River, and by all accounts, there were nuggets the size of a boy's fist sitting there for the taking.

With all the excitement, built upon stories so embroidered in the telling that the truth was beyond recognition, there was sure to be a surge in gold-seekers and hangers-on passing through the Forks, and north to Grand Rapids near the mouth of the Saskatchewan. Hearing the rumours along the waterfront in St Paul, it was Bell who had suggested that they advertise mining supplies in Western American cities. This would save would-be miners the trouble of lugging heavy goods as far north; and Bell had suggested that delivery could even be taken at Grand Rapids, the materials having been shipped there by York Boat. The *Anson Northup* had established that a trip downstream to Lake Winnipeg and back was feasible, so once regular steamer traffic got started, hopefully the following year, '...why, we'd be set!' laughed Bell.

The man's energy and creativity were boundless. He had urged that they advertise a few select items at below prices shown in St Paul. They could make up the difference by inflating the costs of other implements.

Making these arrangements consumed David's time. He had placed a commercial notice in the fledgling newspaper, the Nor'Wester, the first issue out the very day he received his thump to the head. The whole community had chuckled over the fact that editors Willie Coldwell and James Buckingham had wetted down their newsprint the night before, getting all in readiness to print, and had risen to find it frozen solid overnight.

The Nor'Wester's editorial trumpeted that 'the time had arrived when this fertile and magnificent country, thrown open to the people of all lands, needs an exponent of its opinion, its feeling, its varied yet common interests, through the medium of the Press'. David was well pleased with this statement, for it augured well for business.

At the same time, there were two ongoing expeditions exploring the frontier west of the great lakes. Both were inspired by immigration interests in the United States, Canada and Great Britain. The British party, under Captain John Palliser, would be more skeptical than the Canadian group, under Henry Hind; yet both were to report to their masters that enormous tracts of rich, fertile land were free for settlement, west of the Red River. Though Palliser was in the far west when David returned to Red River, he had met Hind briefly, as he was doing an inventory of businesses in the settlement. He had spent considerable time in the warehouse district northeast of the Upper Fort. This smattering of rough shacks and storehouses on the riverbank was moving the centre of commerce rapidly from the stone fort. From the opposite side of the river, the twin spires of the St Boniface cathedral could look down on the congested assortment of buildings, which included at least two noisy taverns: the Dutchman's, favoured drinking den of American and other transients, and the more benignly named 'Royal Hotel', and at least one 'social centre', where tired whores plied their trade.

Hind was a condescending, somewhat unctuous man, who spoke of the Indians as 'savages', and their medicine practices as the 'grossest and most debased superstitions'. His nostrils flared ever so faintly, as if the recollection filled his nose with repugnance. He eyed David's dark skin with thinly veiled suspicion, and seemed to make his speech simple in an exaggerated way for David's benefit. When he discovered that David was the owner of the enterprise, rather than the counter-man, he brightened and became more talkative. He proved to have an eye for detail and a mind for recalling it, as he related some of the anecdotes from his travels. One of them David would recall many times over:

Hind had just called at the farm of John Gowler. David knew Gowler, for he had called only weeks before to inquire about the new McCormick mower. His farm was on the banks of the Assiniboine River, only about nine miles from the Forks. After a walk through fields producing various crops—potatoes, turnips and onions, tobacco and maize—Gowler had invited Hind to come in for the midday meal. As they chatted at the entrance to the kitchen which served as a day-room, Gowler noticed that only one plate had been set at the table. Eyebrows knitted in confusion, he asked his wife. 'And where is my plate?'

His wife replied. 'Oh, John! You would not think of sitting at table with gentlemen?'

Gowler seemed a little taken aback; his children and son-in-law were watching this little drama unfold. Gesturing abruptly to Hind to be seated, he took a position opposite him. Not looking at his wife, he spoke tersely, each word bitten off a larger injustice. 'Give me a chair and a plate. Am I not a gentleman too? Is this not my house, my farm, and these my victuals?' He looked at the unmoving woman and demanded again, 'Give me a plate!'

Hind removed his spectacles and dabbed at the corner of his eyes with a handkerchief. He chuckled again. 'Can you believe it?' he said. 'There are still people here who think they should defer to their betters. How very quaint. There's precious little deference in Canada, I'll tell you certain, and none at all in America.'

The man was a welter of contradictions, but the mere fact that he was here, looking for settlement possibilities, spoke of promise for Bloode & Bell's commercial venture.

David continued to be mildly surprised at the events in his life; they seemed to drive his destiny, rather than the other way around. He felt the tug of 'gold fever', as did many of the young mixed-bloods whom he hired casually. Yet no single event beyond the failure of the business loomed to push him in another direction. Should that happen, he thought, maybe next year I'll try for the Cariboo. But he was well aware that latecomers to any venture needed more luck than anything else, and he was of a mind that Lady Luck had kept a respectful distance from him most of his life. His thoughts turned again to the dark-haired beauty he had just met. Her inscrutable features dissolved as sleep took him.

iii

About ten miles to the south, in the Parish of St Norbert, Mary stamped the snow from her moccasins on the tiny stoop to her grandmother's house. She could tell from the sleighs and snowshoes arrayed nearby that there was another rendezvous in progress. Her grandfather on her mother's side, Henri Beaulieau, was the son of a Nor'Wester who later was retained by the Hudson's Bay Company. The Company had retired him on a grant of two hundred and fifty acres, which had always been worked by Henri. His only son had married the Halfbreed daughter of an absent English clerk, sired three girls one after the other, and was killed by a falling tree before the last was born. When the combination of ill health, her husband's death, and an extraordinarily difficult delivery, rendered the three girls orphans, Henri and his wife Hélène, had taken them in.

Though they had become close to the two youngest, Mary was temperamental and difficult. She seemed to feel that the Beaulieaus were of a lesser station than she, and though this was never discussed, it was a source of quiet tension in the small homestead. Mary had no time for the incessant political discussions of the Métis. As the grip of the Hudson's Bay Company slowly loosened on the daily lives of the settlement, the question of the future government was a matter for rich and divergent controversies. The Métis loved debate more than the hunt, or even gambling on the outcome of a boxing match. Since Henri had frozen most of his toes following a late spring blizzard which had caught him unprepared while out trapping muskrat three years earlier, his friends would gather in the Beaulieau kitchen for refinement of points made on previous occasions. Besides, even if he was not competent on snowshoes anymore, Henri brewed the best beer in the settlement; after a mug or two, the least facile debater was as articulate and compelling as a parish priest, or so it seemed.

Mary had no time for such nonsense. Windbags all, she thought. There were those who believed that the Métis people should form their own nation. Others were for joining the Canadians. After all, most of the immigration was from the east. But many argued for annexation to the American states. The individualistic, freedom-loving Americans had much in common with the peoples of Red River, and trade to the south was more profitable, as were the American traders more aggressive in business. There were agitators in St Paul who felt that acquisition of the entire Northwest was only a matter of time. Fenians, organized to harry Great Britain and her colonies so as to advance the cause of Irish freedom, saw the Red River settlement as easy pickings for an attack launched from the Dakota territories; surely the Métis would join in? And so the arguments proceeded, often with more heat than light.

The men rose when she stepped in. She could feel their eyes on her as she shook her wraps and hung them on a peg near the door. There was a mumbled greeting. Her grandfather remained seated, his eyes on the drink in front of him. She flashed a smile at the men, and moved to the only other room on the main floor, as they reseated and resumed their discussions. As she was about to address her grandmother, who was dozing over needlework by a guttering lamp, she heard a soft voice behind her:

'Excusez-moi, mademoiselle...'

She knew the voice, and rolled her eyes before turning. It was Yves Sayer, frequent participant at these sessions, and an occasional lover of hers. Handsome and daring, he had captured her eye as a romantic ideal of what a man should be: clear-eyed, brave and a horseman before all else. He had taken her as a girl of thirteen in the tall grass in his father's hay privilege. The experience was dreadful. From a soft-spoken, ardent suitor, he had turned into a wild-eyed monster, snorting and huffing like one of the rutting boars in her father's pens. Her protests went unheeded, and within seconds, crying like a wounded goat, he expelled his seed. She was furious and alarmed; this was nothing more than the rape which was darkly hinted at in the Book of Judges. It was unclean, wicked. If found out, she would be condemned as a fornicator, as the native women were so commonly called. Fornication is a sin against the body, frowned the epistles of St Paul. Nothing in this experience convinced her otherwise, save that the urgency of men for connection with her gave her a certain influence with them. As for Yves, he would not let her alone, and behaved like a pup while she was about. She neither encouraged nor deterred him, but fancied that he was a toy for her amusement. With experience, he became technically adequate as a lover.

Yves was the second son of Pierre Guillame Sayer, a trapper-trader who, by a shrug of fate, had become the fulcrum for commercial tensions in the settlement. The Hudson's Bay Company had enjoyed for more than a hundred and fifty years, with some exceptions, a monopoly on trade in furs by virtue of the grant from Charles II, at the request of Prince Rupert of the Rhine. The territory which came to be known as 'Rupert's Land', was rich in furs, and as possessors of the sole right to trade, the sponsors of the 'Company of Adventurers' became very prosperous. However, as the American traders insinuated themselves further into the northwest territories, they adopted tactics which made it more attractive to conduct business; they traded in alcohol, and they paid far better for pelts. The Métis of Red River were more inclined to operate south of the border for these reasons, and the Company increased its vigilance and sabre-rattling about its jurisdiction over trade.

Matters came to a head with the arrest of Sayer, his son, and two others, who had been caught with a load of Indian furs making for a meeting with agents of John Jacob Astor's American Fur Company. Chief Factor John Ballenden demanded an indictment be brought against the smugglers. The charge incited the passions of the Métis who construed the prosecution as unjust, and plain evidence of the Company's stranglehold on their future. The trial was held in the same room where Mary herself had been tried.

Tensions in the settlement on the day of the trial were palpable even to newcomers. There was no military force to speak of, beyond a small detachment of Chelsea pensioners who had replaced the regulars the year before. The Governor, Major W.B. Caldwell, was well aware of the more egregious rumours; one held that he was seeking a pretext to fire upon the people as a show of authority. Prudence dictated that no troops be assigned to secure the courtroom, given that the Métis would in all likelihood turn out in a body for the hearing.

When the Court assembled, hundreds of armed, mounted men sat or stood beside their scraggy ponies in a silent, menacing vigil. The entire building was surrounded, the throng allowing only a narrow passage to the front steps. The docket was called in the usual way; routine and feigned indifference provided an absurd counterpoise to the implicit threat outside.

When the names of Sayer and his co-accused were called, a committe of ten stood in the back of the hall, coming forward with the respected Company agent James Sinclair as spokesman. 'There shall be no fair trial held today without the presence of French-speaking members of the jury!'

After debate, a panel of both English- and French-speaking jurors was sworn, and the trial began. The evidence was called against Sayer first. The jury retired for less than an hour, and after reassembling, the foreman, Donald Gunn, rose. Almost apologetically, he responded to the demand for a verdict: 'Though we find the prisoner "guilty", we recommend the mercy of the Court be shown.'

Almost immediately, Ballenden withdrew the balance of the counts in the indictment, announcing 'the finding of guilt by the jury stands as full answer to the indictment.' The haste with which this was carried out undoubtedly was provoked by the armed men outside, as well as the low, unhappy murmuring in the gallery which greeted the verdict.

The magistrates wasted no time in their own deliberations. Speaking in English, which was translated to Sayer and the others by Sinclair, the decision of the Court was delivered. 'Mark you, Mr Sayer. You have been found guilty by a jury of your own choosing. This is a serious matter, and one which would ordinarily call for an appropriate term of imprisonment.

However, as this is but a first offence, and it has not been established that you are otherwise than of unblemished record, you are discharged with the caution that, should you reappear before this Court, you shall not have the benefit of lenient treatment. You are free to go.'

It is not certain whether all this was accurately or entirely translated, but a large man, Louis Riel the elder, miller of the Seine, rushed forward, seized Sayer by the shoulders and steered the barely comprehending man through the jostling crowd to the front steps. Riel raised his left hand to hold back the feu de joie for a moment, and shouted: 'Le commerce est libre! Le commerce est libre! Vive la liberté!'

The resulting fusillade and shouts of joy catapulted the befuddled Pierre Guillame Sayer into the legends of the Métis nation. Though Mary was only six when this happened, everyone in the settlement could mark the time when the Company's grip began to slacken. And Guillame and Yves became unlikely heroes.

Mary looked past Yves' shoulder. The others had turned away and had resumed their disputations, noisily, and at cross-purposes. One or two, she noticed, still glanced at her furtively; enviously at Yves. Her grandmother still dozed, her head slumped on her thin chest. It was as much privacy as one could expect, and Yves meant to make the most of it.

'Not a word of greeting for me, then?'

She canted her head to one side. 'I am tired; it is all.'

'Have you been to see the American again?' he hissed. 'The whole community is talking about it!'

She laughed. 'And not a word about the false charges brought against me? They have the time to gossip about my poor gestures for someone I have hurt? And he's hardly an American; he was born here, and raised here. Why do you insist on calling him so?'

Yves looked away. 'There is a rumour that he lived with the Sioux.' He said the Indian word with obvious contempt, for the Sioux were much feared by the members of the settlement. Only eight years had passed since the last major attack on the buffalo hunters by the Sioux. Though only one man had been lost, the attack had lasted two days, and could have easily ended in disaster. As it was, when they recovered their fallen comrade, he was mutilated beyond recognition.

'Do you not remember poor René Chambert, taken away from the hunt by those murdering bastards, only three years ago? And found by my uncles, staked out by a stagnant pond. Oh, he was still alive, but black with mosquitoes, gnats and horseflies, which had been sucking at his naked body for three days. They were in such number, no one could get close to him to ease his torment. What man could live with such beasts as the Sioux, and be unaffected?'

Mary shook her head. Some men, perhaps all men, were such fools. Hate for them was like the keeping of a ledger book, into which each insult, each offence or indignity, no matter how indirect, was carefully entered. No worth was granted without assiduous resort to these terms of reference. She better understood the motives of the Hudson's Bay Company, which were reduced to one: profit. There were some collateral motives, to be sure, such as the preservation of status, but even that was linked to the possession of wealth. Why, she was sure that the Company would do business with the devil if there was a penny to be turned in the deal.

Suddenly she was tired of the petty, silly possessiveness of this boy in front of her. The story of the tortured hunter was well known, but did he have to repeat the sickening tale just now? What good did it serve, beyond keeping the hatred and fear of the Sioux fresh in everyone's mind? Did he really think that by association, she would turn away from David Bloode?

'I am tired and must attend to my grandmother,' she said abruptly, and turned away from him.

iv

The Reverend Mathew Thomas was in a very fine mood. His good humour bubbled up and over like untended milk pudding, softening his harsh aspect. His strong features gave him the appearance of stern piety and had served him well in his ambitious career in the Church of England. As he reached the top of the short hill where the Archbishop of York's manse sat, he stopped at the arched trellis that framed the footpath to the door. Ever so slightly out of breath, he plucked a purple clematis blossom from the tangle of vines, and held it to his round, somewhat overly large nose. Drawing deeply, he reflected on God's grace, and his gently bulging girth now straining at his waistcoat buttons. These were among the earthly rewards of a divinely inspired life. Ah, he thought to himself, it's good to be alive.

Matters were moving along well in his grand scheme. His immediate goal was to secure a bishopric in a comfortable, well-established see. Perhaps the glorious old cathedral at Manchester? It was a well-worn fantasy in his mind, by now. Who knows, he mused; there are no limits to what the future might offer. He allowed himself to hum as he mounted the steps, and was admitted to the dark, musty building.

In the study to which he was ushered by an ancient, shuffling butler, three robed men sat silently, solemnly; the middle member of the panel nodded slowly to Thomas's greeting, and gestured to the armless chair where he was to sit. The Archbishop was flanked by two men, only one of whom Thomas knew. It was with a twinge of annoyance that he recognized the Archbishop's coadjutor, a sour-faced Tractarianist who wielded considerable influence with the decisions of the Archbishop himself. The Archbishop tented his fingers on the writing table at which the three sat, and gently lowered his jaw to the tips of well-tended nails.

Thomas patted the fine dust from his sleeve. His travelling cloak had not protected his robes entirely, but he thought it appropriate that they should understand that he had travelled most of the day to be here.

'Your trip was uneventful?' the Prelate began indifferently.

'Your Grace, it was long, but I scarce noticed it.'

'You travel well, then?'

'Quite. It gives me time to reflect. Time away from my many duties. Time indeed, for a conference with God.' He kept his expression calm, reverential. Inwardly, he beamed. Here he was in the Archbishop's benefice, chatting as a delicious prelude to his next assignment in the work of God. He had been restrained, subtle in his approaches. His ambitions had been well disguised in the most discreet hints. Manchester was where his family was, where he had grown up. What a personal triumph it would be to return in the plumage of a Bishop of the Church of England,

'And what of the weather…'

'Wonderful, Your Grace; it couldn't have been better for a trip so long…'

'…in the north of England? Did you not find the cold and damp of the winters troublesome, as so many others have?'

Thomas fairly preened. 'Not a bit of it! Not a bit of it! Why, in the dead of winter, it was my practice to rise from my bed for a cold bath of a morning. Challenge the cold on its own terms, I say.' He permitted himself a dry laugh, as if to reflect a modesty not apparent in the little boast. These devices were carefully appropriated to the particular impression he wished to make, and were so much a part of him, his true character had long ago been submerged.

'That's excellent,' said the third man. Unknown to Thomas, he was a representative of the Church Missionary Society. There was enthusiasm in his voice. 'And what of the heat? Do you have difficulties in warmish weather?'

Warier now, Thomas shook his head. 'As God wills it…' he started tentatively.

The Archbishop nodded approvingly. 'Such a positive mind will be a great asset wherever God's work takes you; regardless which needy parish beckons.'

Ah, so there it was. It was not to be a bishopric after all.

As firmly as he could muster, he inquired, 'And where is it Your Grace has it in mind for me to go?'

The Archbishop looked at the stranger before answering. 'We are of the view that the Lord's work requires your steady hand in Rupert's Land; specifically, the parish of St John's in the Red River Colonies.'

Thomas was aghast. For a long moment in the gloom of the late afternoon, during which the long-case clock ticked off several seconds of his life, he could say nothing.

'Rupert's Land?' he echoed at last, as the dreadful thought took hold. 'Rupert's Land?'

The Archbishop nodded, as did the other two. No one smiled, for it was apparent that Reverend Thomas was not taking the news well.

'But there's very little in the way of congregation there, I understand...' he said, as he struggled to dredge up what little he knew of that distant place. 'Do we not have people there already, to minister to their needs—surrounded as they are by the popish recusants from Canada, savages, and all manner of cross-breeds in between?'

These last words were spoken with some heat as he tried to focus the anger away from the three old men in front of him, and keep his voice steady. 'Aren't most of them living in sin? Have not the primitives corrupted those who have lingered in that land? What possible contribution could I make beyond those who toil there already?'

'It is to those souls you must ultimately direct your attention, of course. It is our hope that you will be of great assistance to the Bishop of Rupert's Land...'

'And who might that be?' There was no mistaking the edge to his voice.

'David Anderson. He was sent out in 1849, so he's been there for about six years, or so. Very decent. A gentle man. But I'm afraid that his clergy need a rather more firm hand. I think, too, that our dear Bishop is heavily influenced by his spinster sister, whose generosity, shall we say, is doled out in rather meagre doses.

'Nevertheless, this will be no docile flock. This will be the Lord's struggle, for as I say, the land has a firmer grip on the souls of the mixed-bloods, than the love of God. It's civilization you represent as well, for does not civilization go hand-in-hand with Christian teaching? And you, dear colleague, are nothing if not civilized.'

Thomas could not tell if this was sarcasm or praise, judgement or observation. He let it go by, as other more insistent thoughts tossed and collided with the violent passage of his dreams.

'But purity will take generations to accomplish,' he cried, 'even if, somehow, I could stop the interbreeding like so.' Here he snapped his fingers for effect

'Your arrival will not have the grand effect of putting an end to the sins of the flesh,' said the Archbishop. 'It will be to legitimize in the eyes of God that which has been offensive to him. The moral obligation of marriage must be the parent, not the child, of civil society.'

Thomas stood in the vestry of St Paul's church, holding a dried wild rose blossom absently, lost in thought. He remembered the conversation with the Archbishop as sharply as if it had occurred yesterday. Just the thought of it set his emotions astir; the acrid taste of disappointment, of rudely blunted ambition, was still there even after all these years. Here he was, pastor of a small, fractious congregation, in a small, fractious community, and not in the more than five years had he been able to make much of an impact. If anything, his congregation had shrunk, as the mixed-bloods found his imperious manner and condescending sermons lacking in both meaning and entertainment value.

Thomas was installed at the church established by the Reverend David Jones in 1824, about twelve miles or so downstream from the Forks and the upper fort. Because of its location six miles north of St John's, the seat for the Bishopric of Rupert's Land (and the place of worship for the upper levels of Protestant Red River society), and St Andrew's, thirteen miles further north, it was known as 'Middlechurch'. It was to St Andrew's that most of Thomas's congregation gradually migrated. Founded by William Cockran in 1832, it catered to the mixed-blood sons of the fur trade. Reverend Cockran was a strong-willed evangelist, aggressive in the pursuit of God's work, tillage of the land, and sundry other occupations, including stints as a bailiff. Everything to which he turned his hand flourished under his enthusiasm, and it was he, rather than the Bishop, or Reverend Mathew Thomas, who became the dominant clergyman for those who spoke English as a first language. It was little wonder that many of the parishioners at Middlechurch were drawn to St Andrew's.

It was a stray thought about one of his flock, a woman, which prompted him to hesitate and pluck the pressed wildflower from the tangle of brambles and evergreens that had been cleverly woven into a Yuletide wreath. Women had not been a large part of Thomas's life, for he considered that a wrong choice could potentially create an impediment to his ambitions. Several had caught his eye, but he felt it wise to delay on the matter. Thomas was disciplined in all matters save the governance of his aspirations for advancement.

He had not seen Mary Daniel since her mother had died, and he had officiated at the funeral. Offering a few words of comfort to her, he was silenced when Mary had pulled away and hurried off, dragging her two sisters with her. He had put it down to grief, and resolved to follow up with further solicitations. But it had been difficult, what with her moving to St Norbert to live with her grandmother. Catholics!

Thomas could not remember with any precision when he had first noticed her. The family had already been part of the congregation, and Mary would have been, what, eleven? But sometime during her fifteenth year he found himself drawn to look at her. Mary Daniel was, in fact, the most fiercely beautiful woman he had ever laid eyes on. He fancied her dark eyes were fixed on him during the service, though if he had to be frank with himself, he could not be absolutely certain about it. She had thick black hair which was always tied up with a ribbon for church, but no sooner was she outside than she would tear the strand of colour loose, and shake her luxuriant mane, pulling out snarls with both hands. Flashing a cold smile at him, she seemed to be anxious to be away. As she started to draw his attention, he began planning his addresses with her in mind. He fancied he was speaking only to her, though he kept a practised sweep of the eye when proselytizing.

Dominating his preaching each Sunday, the woman came to hold sway over his thoughts. His calls to the Daniel residence had never once found her at home, and his off-handed questions as to her whereabouts yielded no information of comfort. When she moved away, the fifteen miles seemed an almost impossible distance. And yet, he was almost relieved. He felt he was on the verge of doing something stupid. It was lust, he told himself. He was being seduced by the savage in her; he had heard of such things happening to Europeans who went among the primitives. Surely this was the Devil's work, and the very thing he had been sent out to combat.

But his emotions swept back and forth within him like tides on a shallow shore, spilling him between reason and chaos. Thoughts of her were like a drug for him, especially at night when sleep was difficult. Today, standing in the freezing vestry, gazing at a flower which had neither life nor fragrance, he decided that he must do something to rid himself of this preoccupation. Prayers seemed not to help. He needed to confront her in some way; maybe that was the way to drive out whatever demon had made its home in his guts.

He had heard of the trial; it had been over for two months now, and he thought it would be appropriate to make a visit, perhaps to reflect together upon the unfairness of a false accusation. Possibly they could discuss larger issues of justice and equity, matters upon which he had strong views. But then again, that was unlikely, for what intellectual attainments could one expect from a person of mixed blood? She could benefit by his instruction. The more he pondered their encounter, the more attractive it seemed to him, and the more convinced he became that he should seek her out.

It was a bright day in March, and there was just a hint of thaw in the faint breeze. The sleigh pulled easily behind the woolly pony, 'whigging along', as they used to say in the north of England by the Scottish border. Thomas had few thoughts these days of home, for they were a source of torment rather than comfort. But tucked safely away in one of the vast pockets of his robes was a small box of candied sweets from England, some dipped in cocoa. It was a gift which was sure to inspire and ingratiate.

He headed south along the River Road that followed the Red River; he could drive all the way to St Paul and beyond, were he of a mind to do it. This little mission, more than anything else, made him feel connected again with the larger world. He felt grand and purposeful. But now that he was actually on his way to see her, he had more than three hours to contemplate his true motives, as well as develop an explanation for what an Anglican clergyman was doing at a Catholic homestead. He had not picked up more than a few words of French, so if Mary were not home, he could not be sure that the others would be able to understand him. He had heard that the family she was with were Métis hunters, tripmen and sometime farmers. Lord in Heaven: how did these Daniel girls slip away from him? At the first opportunity, it seemed, barbarism reclaimed its own.

And how would he reclaim her? In England, a man in his position could arrange to call on a lady; all the details were worked out in advance, so that the visitation went like a well-rehearsed waltz. Everything was understood, without anything being said. It was all so convenient, so civilized. Here it seemed, a man greeted a woman, then loosened his trousers. Thomas chuckled at the image. Not a man given to humour, he stumbled on irony the way a man out for a walk might come across a lost shilling. When it happened, the whimsy seized him entirely for a moment, and he shook with deep appreciation for his own joke. The occasional passers-by scratched at the edge of their stocking caps as Reverend Thomas's cutter skittered by, with the usually dour clergyman braying mightily, tears streaming down his cheeks.

But there were subtleties here too. Sometimes things were not obvious, like that damned sock. His thoughts drifted back to his first winter. Early in December, he had gone down to the church to inspect a shipment of hymnals, expected overland by dogsled from St Paul. The need for these was a symbol of the growing literacy and sophistication of his congregation. The cold was like nothing he had ever encountered; no amount of swaddling could protect his body from its nasty sting. Entering the log-and-post building, he approached the vestry; his breath wreathed him with each exhalation in the chilled air. He saw, with some annoyance, that someone had left an old red sock hanging on the doorknob.

Puzzled, he slipped off his mittens, allowed them to dangle by slitted bands buttoned to his cuff, and snatched the sock from the door. It was a well-worn piece of hosiery, darned many times, and by no means clean. Thomas wrinkled his nose, and reached for the ornate, metal doorknob. He realized instantly as his moist palm froze to the handle why the sock had been placed there.

He stood there for several long seconds, his hand firmly fixed. He could feel the bite of the cold metal into his flesh. A wave of panic seized him: what was there to do? Tentatively, he tried to pull his hand away, but it was clear his skin would remain fixed to the door. Horrified, he began to cry for help. During mid-wail, in walked Simon Sinclair, his lay vicar, carrying a heavy parcel of hymnals.

'What be the matter, Father?' he grunted as he laid the box on the floor.

'I seem to have stuck myself to the door,' Thomas replied sheepishly. 'What can be done? I fear that my hand may become damaged from the cold.'

Sinclair inspected the situation. Thomas did not miss his expressive glance at the sock. 'When this happens to the children, a pail of warm water usually does the trick.'

'Where on earth am I going to get warm water now?'

'Only one place I know of,' replied Sinclair, lowering his gaze to below Thomas's belt.

'Oh no. You don't mean—I mean, I can't...'

'Not to worry, Father,' said Sinclair, with an engaging grin as he moved Thomas aside and fumbled with his trouser buttons. 'I've plenty to spare.'

'No!' squealed Thomas. The thought of another person watching him urinate offended him; to be pissed on was an abomination worse than remaining fixed to the door. 'I...I'll try...I'll do it myself.'

'Well, be careful,' chuckled Sinclair. 'Don't be gettin' your biscuit stuck as well, or we'll ha' two problems 'stead a one.'

Thomas sighed and looked about. The little black sleigh slithered along well-iced ruts. To his left, the great sweep of the riverbed lay under its mantle of ice. To his right, the snow-covered land undulated in pale sugared loaves. The track was well settled by 1860, and low, dark huts alternated with more elaborate stone and clapboard homesteads of the more prosperous settlers. Thomas tugged at the frayed buffalo robe on his lap, for the breeze still had a bite to it, and pulled his fur-lined hood well down over his forehead. The reflected sunlight dazzled his eyes, and the only thing for it was to peer through the long guard hairs of the silver fox trim on his garment.

It was closing on midday when he pulled into the Beaulieau homestead, after asking directions. The pony was tired, and the sweat steaming off its back was pungent in Thomas's nostrils. He blanketed the animal, threw down a stook of hay, and marched on the house with as much authority as befitted a man of his station. He was aware that his arrival had been noticed, even if the mangy dog at the stoop had not gone into paroxysms of yelping barks as the cutter squeaked to a stop. Yet no one came out to greet him, or to ask his business. Strange.

As he raised his mitted hand to knock at the door, it opened suddenly, and Hélène Beaulieau's wizened face, brown as a dried apple, showed itself at the entrance.

'Qu'est que c'est que vous voulez?'

'I am here to see one of my parishioners, Mary Daniel,' he replied, without really comprehending the patois peculiar to Red River.

She screwed up her eyes and peered at him closely, examining his clerical collar and peering into his face. 'Elle a départé pour quelques moments.' and here she opened the door a little more, 'Vous resterez ici, jusqu'a elle a retourné'. She pointed a thin brown finger to the wall beside a row of pegs in the kitchen wall.

'Merci, madame.' Here Thomas stood in silence for almost half an hour. He kept pulling out a large pocket watch secured by a chain in the front pocket of his vest, but neither seat nor explanation was offered, nor did he attempt to converse with the old lady in his tortuous French. Although he was sweating in the close warmth of the room, he did not feel he could take off his heavy coat without some sort of bidding from his host. He began to feel faintly ridiculous.

Shifting his weight from one foot to the other, he contemplated his image in the oval bevelled mirror opposite him. At forty-two, he felt he was at the peak of his spiritual and intellectual command. But he felt he was showing his age; his hair was grey and thinning; there was a spot at the crown like a monastic tonsure. To cover it, he had taken to favouring caps which, in this forsaken world with its insects, scorching sun, and its blistering chill, were an essential part of daily dress in any event. He had a paunch which asserted itself in an unflattering way against his waistcoat, and his oval face had become heavy, almost bloated. He was trimming his side whiskers lower and lower each year, as he fancied they gave him a sternness and piety that in his earlier years youth had granted without effort. Lord in Heaven, he thought, I've become vain. It was a greater vanity that the Reverend did not realize these petty affectations were but extensions of a larger fault: a fault that permitted him to see only the image of a priest of the Anglican Church, with all of the powers and privileges appurtenant thereto, citizen of the Britannic Empire, and representative of the greatest civilization God had wrought, rather than a slightly overweight middle-aged man.

Thomas had just decided to step outside when Mary came into the house with her father. She seemed startled to see him and, for a moment, he was lost for words. She was more beautiful than his idealized fantasies had constructed. The frost had reddened her cheeks, and her teeth showed white against full lips. Her tousled hair hung across one eye, and she brushed it back in a fetching way that made him dizzy.

'Reverend Thomas,' she said, nodding her head once. 'I was not expecting…'

'Please pardon my unannounced intrusion,' he said quickly. 'I was out this way, and took the chance that you might be in. This good lady was kind enough to allow me to wait for a moment or two.'

'But what…?' She was puzzled by his presence. Hanging up her coat and shawls, she asked if he wished to sit. Visibly relieved, he slipped off his own heavy coat, and arranged it over his lap as he took the proffered chair. Surreptitiously he slipped the box of sweets from his pocket, and held them beneath the folds of his robe. The box was pliant, and he fretted that the chocolate had started to melt. But now was not the time to thrust his small tribute under her nose.

'It has been some time since the funeral,' he began, tugging at the front of his shirt where the sweat had dampened it, 'and I thought I would look in on you. I heard about the trial a short while ago, and I am very glad of the outcome for you, but quite concerned that your young sister should be locked away. It must be very difficult for you.'

'Oui,' she said. Her eyes searched his face for a clue which would explain this surprise visit. He became acutely conscious of the two old people in the other room; they were conversing in low tones, and staring with unbridled curiosity at their uninvited guest. Thomas turned away from them and spoke with apparent discomfort.

'It was my hope to speak to you privately.'

Her curiosity was even more aroused. 'Oh, never mind them. They don't speak more than a word or two of the English language. You can say what you want, for it's no different than if we were alone.'

He folded and smoothed the heavy garment on his lap. He cleared his throat, and looked away from her. The old man stoked the fire in the stove, and the flames spat and popped until he kicked the iron door shut with a tap from a moccasined foot. 'I have come to ask permission to call upon you. Ordinarily, I would request an audience with your father, but in the present circumstances,' he shot a glance at the suspicious old man who was tamping his pipe, 'I chose to come to you directly.'

Her eyes were wide; she made no sound. He took this as promising. The words tumbled out now; the Rubicon had been crossed. 'I am not without means. My allowance is guaranteed at one hundred and fifty pounds sterling, I have a small sum set aside, and good prospects for advancement in the church...' he broke off as he saw that her expression had not changed. A sudden thought seized him; he sucked in his breath with a hiss. 'Oh, I have rushed this upon you, and I have not even taken the time to ask whether or not you are committed to another?' He looked at her expectantly.

She spoke at last, though softly. 'I am not betrothed. But what would a man like you have with a woman of my station?'

He puffed ever so slightly. 'I understand that there is a vast distance between us, but with God's help...'

'You understand that I now take Communion at St Norbert from Father Maisonneuve?'

Thomas blanched. Maisonneuve was a wretched Papist Oblate! 'You have strayed from the faith of your father? Well, no matter,' he said hurriedly. 'This too can be put right.'

She looked at him for a long moment. Thomas could feel his heart thumping against his chestbone. Her eyes appeared to narrow as she sat back in her grandmother's sewing chair. 'So you would call on me, court me?'

He nodded.

'You would have marriage in mind? Or is it your intention to take me as a country wife?'

The directness of her speech scandalized him. He had never encountered such presumption in a woman. He was nonplussed. He opened his mouth twice to speak, looking for all the world like a catfish hauled out of the river and placed on a hot stone. She pre-empted him:

'It is almost more than I can stomach, the thought of a man such as you wanting union with me. Did you not think I noticed your calf's eyes upon me in church? You, a man of God? You, with your talk of "indolent savages" and "diluted blood"?' She sneered. 'You would call upon me?'

Thomas's ears burned with embarrassment. 'I meant no slight upon your people...' he faltered. 'It is the French...' and he stopped, absurdly clapping a hand to his mouth as he realized where he was. 'I meant no slight,' he finished lamely, his ears and cheeks blushing furiously.

'Perhaps you didn't,' she said. 'But you made it clear enough that we are not quite good enough. And these people,' she waved her hand to her old relatives, 'these people are no good at all, in your view.' The ancients sat up on their stools, for it was now clear that the conversation had livened up, and it included them.

'It's no good that you came so far for nothing. I would not consider your attentions welcome.' Her eyes looked him up and down with keen disapproval. 'You are a fat, pretentious snoot, with your English manners, and your little handkerchiefs. Ugh!' She stood up.

Witch! Witch! Thomas screamed to himself. Foul temptress! Outwardly, he fought to keep composed as he struggled to his feet while putting on his coat. 'Good day,' he muttered to no one in particular as he fled the house in humiliation. While he snatched the blanket from the pony's back, he heard peals of mirth from the dwelling: her low, throaty laugh and the old ones' whinnying braided together and rising like the thin smoke spiralling from the crumbling chimney. His mortification was complete with this final ignominy. Flinging the small box of sweets aside, he whipped the startled pony from the yard.

Reverend Thomas was never to marry, even as he was never to leave Rupert's Land. But his affaire de coeur was to shape his view of the world, or the world as it was narrowly bounded by the horizons of the Red River Valley. Word got around the settlement as the Métis, always quick to pass on a good story, repeated and embellished how Reverend Thomas had taken a run at a young girl, and had fallen on his commodious ass. For his part, Thomas rejected these tales as malicious nonsense, and as part of the growing body of evidence in his mind, that those 'corrupted by intercourse with the savages, and influenced by the grasping Catholic Church, could only resort to such tactics to discredit (him)'.

But the rage within him smouldered below the surface like a fire in a peat bog. It provided the passion that had been lacking in his sermons; it provided the direction that had been wanting in his life. For a time, his public pronouncements had a constant theme: the sins of the 'New Jerusalem', to which he had come to aid in deliverance. His initial sermon following his humbling at the hands of Mary Daniel generously excerpted from the Book of Ezekiel:

'Son of man, cause Jerusalem to know her abominations…thy father was an Amorite, and thy mother an Hittite.' The parallels between the marauding, nomadic Amorites, who were relentlessly hostile to Hebrews and others, and the cultured, civilized Hittites needed no elaboration, even for the slow-witted members of his flock. 'How weak is thine heart, saith the Lord God, seeing thou doest all these things, the work of an imperious, whorish woman.' The womanly image became the metaphor for all that was ill in Red River: the sexual relationships unsanctified by marriage, the illegitimate children, the neglect of baptism, indolence, the unChristian, atavistic and bloody pursuit of beasts, neglect of crops, sexual intrigues and gossip, all found their metonymy in the female image. 'As is the mother, so is the daughter…And I will judge thee, as women that break wedlock and shed blood are judged; and I will give thee blood in fury and jealousy!' Fear had its rewards for the fulminator: marriage registries began to increase in that year and subsequently. Baptisms crept up in numbers, and fewer mixed-bloods pursued the buffalo, though other reasons, including the steady diminishment of the herds, entered into it.

Thomas had his allies. Principal among them was Reverend Griffith Owen Corbett, out to Rupert's Land in 1852 under the sponsorship of Reverend William Williamson of Headingly, Leeds. He was a short, thin man, with features permanently set into a cynical scowl. His heavily lined face made him appear much older than he was. Not an articulate man, he nevertheless spoke directly at an emotional level. He was passionate, confrontational, and engaging in speech. He was thoroughly bigoted and powerfully anti-Catholic. When he wished to return to the Parish of Headingly, roughly half-way between the Forks and the Parish of St François-Xavier on the Assiniboine River, the Colonial Continental Church Society was reluctant to return such a provocative character to a settlement on the verge of change.

Perhaps because he had cultivated a relationship with the spinster sister of the ineffectual Bishop Anderson, the Bishop made a personal plea on Corbett's behalf, and so he was reinstated to Red River. Accompanying him was his wife, a withered, unhappy woman who lived entirely in the cleric's shadow. Almost immediately upon his arrival he became involved in the politics and racial tensions of the colony, fomenting dissent with the Hudson's Bay Company and becoming enmeshed in scandal. Reverend Corbett's fascination with intrigue was soon to ensnare both Mary Daniel and David Bloode.

V

Mary was pregnant almost at once. Barely four months into their relationship, she had announced that she was carrying a child. They had been married at St Norbert, and David was confirmed in the Catholic faith, a step to which he was largely indifferent, but which caused some consternation in the Anglican Church. He had been paid a visit by Bishop Anderson and Reverend Thomas. As his father was a Protestant Orkneyman, surely, they argued, it was only right and proper that David should follow in his footsteps—out of respect for his departed father, if not for the love of Christ. David was not surprised that they should try to persuade him so, for the competition for souls in the colony was keen and persistent. But he wondered how they could have known his plans. What he could not have known was that Thomas avidly followed every available detail of Mary Daniel's life, looking to discover the kind of evidence which would have tended to confirm his current opinion of her, as well as to defeat the idle rumours which continued to circulate about his visit to her step-parents' home.

David found the sleepy-eyed Bishop pleasant enough, but there was a palpable tension in the way in which his colleague Thomas spoke to him. He had never met the clergyman before, and Mary had told him nothing of his ill-fated visit. David decided, finally, that if Thomas and the plump, womanly Bishop were God's representatives from the Protestant side, he would as soon throw in his lot with the Catholics, a more robust and flexible group of God's agents. He remembered the black-frocked men who accompanied the buffalo hunters when his father had taken him along. Gentle, pragmatic, they did not insist that the Métis change their ways, as was the seemingly constant message from the Anglicans. They did not refuse the right of a non-Catholic such as Ephraim to stand bare-headed with the others in the worship of God. Perhaps they were shrewd enough to understand that conversion to a system of beliefs relied more upon the gentle persuasions of generosity, tolerance and time, rather than the ultimatums of threats, coercion and fear. To be sure, this was a form of Catholicism adapted to the realities of the frontier, born of a time when the very existence of the clergy depended upon the goodwill and charity of the indigenous people.

David's view was sealed by the intrusive questions which Thomas put to him:

'Do ye not understand that, in the matter of faith, you are not merely an Englishman with the blood of another race in his veins? Do you follow me?'

'No. My father was an Orkneyman, and the only debt he felt he ever owed to England was for the language.'

'Orkneyman then. But still of the Protestant faith, and owing secular allegiance to Her Royal Majesty, Head of the Church of England. Do you not see that you are an Englishman, a man of business? To turn your face from the faith of your father, by taking the Papist beliefs to heart, is tantamount to spitting on his grave?

'Do ye not see as well that by taking the hand of a Catholic woman of uncertain breeding...' Here Thomas paused, realizing at once that he had perhaps gone too far, for David sat back, folded his arms, and interjected, 'What is your meaning?'

Thomas shrugged. He noticed the affable Bishop looking at him, his brow furrowed. 'I simply mean that the future of this colony lies with England. I am certain that Crown Colony status is not far off, and with it will be important positions for loyal subjects of Her Britannic Majesty.'

David shook his head once. 'I have no desire to hold any position beyond what I make for myself; I cannot believe that my choice of mate would influence anyone's view of my loyalty.'

'Is it true, then, that you will be taking the woman as your wife?'

David could see more than professional interest in Thomas's eyes, almost a hunger, but he did not know what to put it down to. 'Yes,' he said simply.

'In spite of her, ah, shall we say, questionable background?'

David stood up. 'This talk is over. Good day to you both.' As the Bishop stammered attempts to smooth the moment, emotion welled up in David. He was unable to hold his tongue. Addressing Thomas, he said coldly, though with a tremor in his voice:

'You have offended me more than you know. I was prepared to endure your condescension and your lordly ways. I was prepared to ignore the fact that you took my hand, oh, ever so briefly, as if it were a dog's turd. But to attack the woman who will be my wife—I—I—' David remembered the conversation with Hind, about the settler named Gowler whose wife still clung to the view that her husband should not sit at the same table as his 'betters'.

'Am I not entitled to respect?' he shouted. 'Who are you to address me as if I were a child? I have undergone terrible hardships. I have lost my entire family. I have travelled widely. I am a man, and will not have this— this—' and he sputtered out, the rage slipping from him as quickly as it had come. When he looked up, at once concerned that he had been too intemperate with men of God, the two men were standing.

The Bishop started to speak, but Thomas spoke loudly, cutting off his superior. 'If a child receives a morsel of unpleasant taste, he spits it out. If a dog is so inclined, he may bite the hand that strokes his head. We expected more from you, for all we had intended was the good of your soul.'

The Bishop muttered a 'Good Day', and the two men left him. David felt ridiculous and angry at once. He felt that he had the high ground in this sorry encounter, and it had been snatched from him by imperious, condescending men who made him feel inferior. He lashed out impotently at a wooden butter churn, staving in its sides as it flew across the room and struck an iron stove. The two men could not have failed to hear the crash. David did not know whether he was glad they would know of his rage, or whether he should be further discomfited that they would think their point had struck home. He cursed. Even on a point of anger, I am plagued by inner thoughts of doubt, he told himself.

That was almost three years ago, and their daughter, Christine, was nearing her second birthday in January, 1862. She had arrived more than two months early, which was expected, since Mary had told David that she was pregnant within the first month that they had lain together. There was a good deal of gossip at the time of Christine's birth, since it was known that Yves Sayer had never given up hope that Mary might end up with him.

The best man at the wedding was David's partner, Edwin Bell. From the start, Edwin and Mary took a dislike to one another. David tried to mend the relationship, but could not get either side to express with any clarity the basis for their distrust. What it meant in practical terms was that Bell made fewer and fewer visits to Red River, preferring instead to coordinate buying and shipping from St Paul. The *Anson Northup* made only one trip up the Red the following year, and was crushed in the ice the next. Freighting was still done by independent agents or those hired by the Hudson's Bay Company, in trains of squealing carts, by way of the Crow Wing Trail south to St Paul.

The preferred route was by way of the Minnesota Valley, in which the Columbia Fur Company had opened four trading posts in the first half of the nineteenth century. The Crow Wing Trail was developed when a wily free trader of mixed Scottish and Cree blood was cut off in the Minnesota Territories in 1844 by the Dakota Sioux. Peter Garrioch had heard that the Sioux were harassing unwary users of the more established routes, so he elected to take his small party further to the east to avoid trouble. After two weeks of slow going through scrub and marsh, the progress measured little more than fifty miles. They were fortunate to encounter friendly Ojibway who helped them through to the open prairie. No sooner had they reached smoother paths than they were beset by an early fall blizzard. It was more than two months before they reached Pembina, nearly dead from exposure, having had several of the draught animals die of exhaustion along the way. All of the carts were cannibalized for fuel as they proceeded. But the Crow Wing Trail was open, and it became the route of choice for teamsters and traders, running at different times along the east and the west sides of the Red River south of St Norbert.

In August of 1862, trouble erupted along the Crow Wing in the Minnesota Territories. The Sioux, pushed to the limit by unscrupulous agents, an unending influx of settlers, and by arbitrary decisions of the territorial and federal governments, rose up against the authorities in a bloody spasm of resistance. The fighting lasted six weeks, and claimed the lives of nearly five hundred settlers and a considerable, though unknown, number of Sioux. The sparks that ignited the fighting were trivial enough in their inception, but they illustrated the gulf which yawned between the white and the Indian in North America.

In the first incident, a party of Dakota hunters came across a group of white travellers. Seeking to avoid them, the Indians hid in an out-building on a nearby farm. One of them stepped on a nesting hen, which sent the bird squawking across the yard. The settler's wife went out to investigate, and discovered the Indians. Angry and contemptuous, she berated them and swatted one of them with her broom, as if he were a dog. He shot and killed her over the insult.

In the second case, a warrior named 'Kill-Spirit' chastised a companion for shooting a settler's ox. The rest of the party ridiculed Kill-Spirit for cowardice, and unwarranted criticism of their brother. Kill-Spirit left with two of the party, and went to a public house called the Travellers' Inn, near Redwood. Picking a quarrel with the innkeeper, Kill-Spirit shot him, and announced to his companions that he had decided to fight. While the chiefs were in council to consider whether they would join him, a party of soldiers was seen in a boat, and the young men fell upon them, killing and scalping them all. The rage of white society was to spit back in an orgy of destruction all that summer.

The condition of Indian society in the Dakota and Minnesota Territories was no less complex than that in Red River. In addition to Indian communities, which were by this time confined to reservations, there were large numbers of Anglo-Indian and Métis settlers, traders and tripmen living in the area. But loyalties were mixed. Some joined with the uprising; some opposed it, and others tried to remain neutral. The complicated issues of pride, oppression, loyalty and the Indian's sense of fatalism played out in a way that was to be replicated in Red River a few years later. When the young men of the Dakota taunted one of the principal chiefs, Little Crow, he dashed the offender's bonnet to the ground, and made a speech which would echo in similar speeches for twenty years among the Indians and peoples of mixed blood in the American and the Canadian West:

'Ta-O-Ya-Te-Du-Ta is not a coward and he is not a fool. When did he run away from his enemies? When did he leave his braves behind him on the war path and turn back to his teepees? When he ran away from your enemies, he walked behind on your trail and covered your backs as a she-bear covers her cubs! Is Ta-O-Ya-Te-Du-Ta without scalps? Look at his war-feathers! Behold the scalp-locks of your enemies hanging there on his lodge poles.... Braves, you are like little children; you do not know what you are doing.

'You are full of the white man's rum. You are like dogs in the Hot Moon when they run mad and snap at their own shadows. We are only little herds of buffaloes left scattered; the great herds that once covered the prairies are no more. See! the white men are like the locusts when they fly so thick that the whole sky is a snowstorm. You may kill one-two-ten; yes, as many as the leaves in the forest yonder, and their brothers will not miss them. Kill one-two-ten, and ten times ten will come to kill you. Count your fingers all day long and white men with guns in their hand will come faster than you can count.

'Yes. They fight among themselves far away. Do you hear the thunder of their big guns? No. It would take you two moons to run down to where they are fighting, and all the way your path would be among white soldiers as thick as tamarack in the swamps of the Ojibways. Yes. They fight among themselves, but if you strike at them, they will all turn on you and devour you and your women and little children just as the locusts in their time fall on the trees and devour all the leaves in one day.'

Suddenly tired, Little Crow sighed and concluded: 'You are fools. You cannot see the face of your chief; your eyes are full of smoke. You cannot hear his voice; your ears are full of roaring waters. Braves, you are like little children. You will die like the rabbits when the hungry wolves hunt them in the Hard Moon. Ta-O-Ya-Te-Du-Ta is not a coward; he will die with you.'

And so the Sioux, mostly Dakota then, but some Lakota, started down a short, violent path that would see most of them herded back to even more restricted reservations, some were assembled on a public mass gallows in Mankato to be hanged simultaneously, and some fled to British North America in the fall of 1862.

David had difficulty arranging shipments from St Paul during the summer of 1862, since the Sioux had set ablaze the frontier to the south.

The International, newest riverboat on the Red and almost two and one half times bigger than the *Anson Northup*, would not travel while there was unrest. Details of the fighting came quickly enough to settlers along the northern rivers; stories of atrocities horrified and frightened many who believed that the troubles could spread to Fort Garry. Scalpings, mutilations and torture brought trade between Red River and St Paul virtually to a stop. Some teamsters would still make the run, but would demand an enormous premium, amounting to triple wages for the hazardous trip. Stories of indescribable brutality, such as entire families being lashed to their iron stoves and roasted alive, made even the most intrepid tripman think twice about making the journey.

David required a brigade to take grain and furs south before the winter to return with manufactured goods, including the new Oneida steel traps, vastly superior to the British product, which tended to crack in the extreme cold. That no one else was doing business because of the Sioux seemed to David's mind an opportunity that should not be missed. But he could not find anyone to lead the expedition. He decided to accompany the brigade personally, and offered a bonus of four pounds to anyone who would go along with him. He was anxious to meet with Edwin, as he had not seen him for the better part of a year.

Mary made no objection to his plan, which surprised him. She announced that, while he was away, she and Christine would stay with her friend, Maria Thomas, who had a fortnight's leave at least from her job as domestic to the Reverend Corbett and his wife. She did not mention even once the dangers associated with the trip, and David felt a little foolish assuring her that he would be all right when it did not seem to be of any concern to her.

And so it was that a brigade of fourteen carts squealed and squeaked their way out of Red River, to much shaking of heads and predictions of a bloody end. The cavalcade kept well east of the river. Since stealth was impossible because of the tooth-stabbing screeching of the axles, two outriders ranged several miles ahead, 'just out of sound', to keep a watchful eye for trouble. But one morning, six days out, trouble did find them.

While the brigade was at a halt so that repairs could be carried out on an axle (the first of the four or five that each cart would require on average for the trip to St Paul), David strolled to the bush lining a small, torpid creek which fed into the Red River, to relieve himself. On a whim he climbed on a stump of a white pine felled by its own weight, unbuttoned his trouser flap, and arched his stream into the water. It was a hot autumn day; the leaves had turned and had started to fall, littering the ground with orange and yellow shards rustling gently in the soft breeze.

He suddenly became aware of human presence, of being watched. Turning away from the sun which had been on his shoulder, lower now that winter approached, he froze as he saw that a small band of Indians, unmistakably Sioux, were standing, some on horseback, across the little creek, watching him. No one moved. David watched the group, still as a tableau of a Station of the Cross. Rolling his eyes down, he seemed to realize at last what it was that he had in his hands, and discreetly as possible in the circumstances he fumbled himself to a semblance of order and decency. Behind him he could hear his name being called by one of the tripmen. They were ready to move.

Without answering, David slowly turned back to the Indians. There were women and children, as well as many old people. There were perhaps seven warriors mounted. The women had bales at their sides, and there were several dogs with packs. There appeared to be no lodges. It was as if the silent group had materialized from the bowels of the earth. The other man had seen them now and, without a word, had spun on his heel and was racing back to the others. David could hear his footfalls scrunching in the leaves.

David could see that the Indians had their weapons sheathed, or held at a downward angle, though a low grumbling broke out among some of them when David's companion had run off. David realized that though his heart was pounding furiously, he had to do something; otherwise he would be a well-placed target for the crossfire that was sure to begin the moment some one spooked. Speaking in Dakota, which his crew later told him was a surprise to them, he addressed the natives. 'Friends,' he said, 'we pass in peace.'

A short, unpleasant-looking man, with a threadbare duffel coat worn open to display a round pot of a belly, raised his right hand, palm outward, demonstrating no weapon was being held, and replied.

'We are hungry, and require food.'

David answered quickly, 'Brother, we have food, and we will share it.' To his own men, he called over his shoulder, 'It's all right! They mean us no harm; they're just hungry. But be careful, just the same.'

His men needed no close supervision on the issue, for they were all edgy, and worked with one hand on their own weapons. Foodstuffs were brought to the stump where David was still standing, and they warily withdrew to the carts. Cautiously, the Sioux waded across the stream and surrounded him. He noticed that their clothing was poor, most of it well-worn European-style garments. The horses were almost as mangy as the dogs, and it was clear that they were famished. He looked down at the short, pot-bellied man with whom he had spoken. 'It is almost half of what we have; we have given you four sacks of grain. We wish to pass in peace—' He broke off, stunned.

Below him, in the circle of faces, was a face he knew well, though it was not exactly the same face he had known. 'Mahpiyatowin!' he cried. Jumping down, he made his way to her. She was holding a small, silent infant under her shawl. 'Mahpiyatowin!' he cried again. 'Do you not remember me?'

She raised her head, her eyes moist. She looked much older than he remembered her; her hair was graying, her cheekbones stood out in a thin face. There was no hint of the supple young woman who had entranced him only a few short years before.

'Pahinshashawacekiye,' she said simply, calling him by his Indian name: 'Red Haired One'.

David put his arms around her without thinking, for a man would not ordinarily touch a Sioux woman in such a way, and led her to a nearby deadfall to be seated.

'Mahpiyatowin!' he whispered softly again. 'It is hard to believe my eyes. What are you doing here?' He could see her looking at his good clothes, his strong, well-fed appearance, and he felt guilty.

She answered in a dull voice. 'We are running away. For had we remained, we all would have perished. A great force under Colonel Sibley was sent to crush our people. Though we thought that only those who chose the warpath would be punished, the soldiers make no fine distinctions. Away from their officers, they kill whomever they can find, so inflamed are they by what some of our people have done.'

'Where will you go?' asked David.

There was a faint tremor of a smile. 'Remember the old ones used to speak of us as the "Four Directions People"? We go to seek our cousins, the Wasi-ata-oyata, the north people. We have with us our medicine men, the wisest of the elders, and the chiefs of our principal societies. It is only by removing them that our brothers and sisters back on the reservations will survive, for it is our leaders they want.

'It is only by their removal to safety that our people as yet unborn will survive. Many unspeakable things have been happening, and dreadful wrongs are being committed.'

David nodded. 'We have heard terrible stories. So great is the fear where I now live, that all have arms at the ready, and nightly prayers are made for our salvation. There is a constant watch.'

David peeked under the shawl. 'And who is this?'

'It is my daughter,' she said, her voice anguished. 'She is dying.'

Questions reeled in David's mind. 'What is wrong with her? Where is her father? How can I help? Can you come with us?' he blurted out.

'My husband is dead. My daughter will soon pass from this life, and I must stay with my people. My father was wrong to take us to the reservation, but he could not know how bad it would be.

'As for you, you have already helped us.' She smiled again. A smile so faint this time, it was no more than a tremble of a cat's whisker. "I am happy now, for I have seen you in the water, just as you saw me, so long ago.'

His eyes filled with tears at the mélange of emotions that came tumbling back to him, as he recalled that spring day he had lain like a weasel in the grass, watching her bathe. But there was no time to linger, for her people were anxious to move on.

'It would be wiser to move further to the west, and go no closer to Fort Garry,' he said. 'The fear in the settlement is such that you will be attacked before anything could be said. Your enemies, the Ojibway, the Cree and the Métis, will not welcome you. More so now that frightening stories have made their way to the Fort.'

He watched her leave, head down, clutching her forlorn child. She did not look back. David was torn by his emotions, a condition over which he still had poor understanding and little control. He was profoundly upset by the encounter. What a terrible thing had happened to Mahpiyatowin! This was a woman he had loved, and might very well have taken for a wife. Would his own destiny have been linked to hers, had this been the case? Would he too now be hunted as the grey wolf was hunted: hated, feared, and valued only in death? And there was this tiny, odious, but familiar voice which wheedled inside him; he was thankful that circumstances dictated that he had not made such a choice. Shaking his head as if to clear the depressing thought, he turned back to his men. He did not see that, as the Sioux reached the rise where they would disappear, Mahpiyatowin turned to look at him. David saw nothing. At such a distance tears could not be discerned.

His men were upset and deeply suspicious that David had such apparently intimate relations with the Sioux. He could speak their language. He had given half their food away, and now sat chin in hands snivelling over some wretched squaw with a babe in her arms. What behaviour for a married man, and a recently married one at that. As relief that the encounter had not resulted in an attack gave way to anger at being surprised by the stealth of their enemy, they began to mutter among themselves. If another crowd of Indians showed up, how would they know where his loyalties lay? Would he save himself at the cost of the men hired to serve him? After all, no one knew this red-haired newcomer very well.

The most vocal of the malcontents was a man named Jack Henderson, a Scot-born tripman who would claim a brief footnote in history as the hangman who placed the noose around the neck of the Métis leader Louis Riel in 1885. Of nasty disposition, he was nevertheless useful on such trips simply because he was afraid of nothing. He would take guard duty alone at night. He would sit with unknown Indian hunters and trappers and bully them into better deals than anyone else would dare press. He would argue angrily over a half-penny wager. He respected only money. Yet other tripmen put up with him simply because he was so fiercely brave and could be depended upon unreservedly in the event of trouble.

But he had no truck with gawky sentiment, and despised David for his show of emotion and unwarranted tenderness to the 'undeserving, meurthering' Indians. All the men were Halfbreeds with not a Métis among them. There was too much hatred, too much history between the Sioux and the Métis to allow a small party to venture through the Dakota territories. The prevailing sentiment among the Métis in Fort Garry was that David Bloode was a fool for such an undertaking, with the Dakota up in arms. The Halfbreeds tended to be a little more pragmatic; the whole culture of risk and enterprise was different than that of the Métis, and each had its roots in the diverse approaches taken by the English Hudson's Bay Company, and the Montréal-based North West Company. The Bay men were conservative, and weighed the hazards of a commercial undertaking carefully.

The voyageurs from Montréal on the other hand, embraced the land and its inhabitants, forging alliances not only with indigenous people, but with their manner of living. By this year of 1862, virtually all Métis either worked for the Company, or for the nascent but emerging merchant class, entrepreneurs who crossed all race lines, who worked for, traded with, were licensed by and increasingly, were in competition with the Company. Still, issues tended to be resolved along racial, cultural and religious lines. It was confusing that David, a Protestant Halfbreed, had embraced Catholicism, and married a Métisse. Where did the man stand? It was with this issue in mind that Henderson strode over to David after the evening meal, and questioned him:

' 'Tis in my mind to have a word with ya. There's things that th' men have been troubled by.' He thrust his weather-ravaged face close to David, who was slumped against a cart shaft. Chilblains had left his nose red, swollen and cratered. His grey hair hung almost to his eyes. He sniffed. He'd be a dirty customer in a fight, it was plain.

David was depressed, and in no mood to bicker with Henderson. 'Speak,' he said shortly.

'You've not explained what happened back there; nothin'. An' it's our feelin' we've a right ta know.'

'Your meaning eludes me.' This man was as obtuse in his language, he thought, and yet as transparent as the Reverend Thomas. 'Some starving Indians requested food. We shared what we had like any Christian soul would do, and they were on their way. What could be plainer?' He shifted his weight under his robe, and made as if to retire; a dismissive gesture, clear enough. It was rooted in fear, however, borne of a reluctance to confront the bigger, nastier man. But Henderson was angered by David's curtness and his disingenuous answer, and would not be put off.

'You've not a right to play with me,' growled the tripman, gripping David by the shoulder. 'Ya owes us some explainin'. Them Indians was Sioux! They's the whole reason we got such a small brigade, and why we're so far east. So why's ya mollycoddlin' them, when they'd just as soon sneak back an' collect our scalps? Or worse yet, fall upon our neighbours, havin' been handsomely supplied by us?'

A snarl began to form on David's lips. He felt an urge to attack the man, but thought better. He needed Henderson, as he did the others, for it was certain that no crew would accompany him on the return trip without the brawling tripman while there were remnants of Dakota insurgents still active.

'Let me explain something to you, Henderson; something you may have trouble understanding. I've been robbed by men I worked with. I've seen cruelties beyond what you've heard these past few months. I've seen more shit in my life at the hands of men out for themselves than I care to see again.

'I don't know what them Indians have done, if anything at all. But they were starving, and in precious poor shape to be much of a threat to anyone. And if they'd wanted to take us by surprise, the deed've been done. Hell, I took a piss on the toes of their moccasins before I knew they were there.

'But here's my point: I shall never make a decision about a man just because I heard some idle talk that may or may not be true. You just don't know. The man you extend your hand to today could very well be the one who throws you a line tomorrow.'

'But the provisions...' began Henderson.

'They're mine to give,' snapped David. 'Tomorrow before midday, we shall reach Pembina. We'll purchase more.'

'And the woman...'

'You've no right to ask. Let me add this: I shall supply a further bonus of a one and one-half pounds to each man, for a safe and successful return. Trouble me no further, but keep a sharp lookout posted.'

Henderson hesitated, but moved back to where the others were gathered. He was not satisfied with any of the answers David had provided, but the additional bonus was an unexpected dividend. It would raise him in the estimation of the others. David turned his back to them, though he could imagine Henderson's crowing elaboration on what had transpired. The episode left a bad taste; what could he possibly explain to such a man? Tell them he'd lived with the Sioux, and they'd abandon him overnight. If he was lucky.

Worth, it seemed, was measured by these tripmen in terms of brute strength or cunning. The number of coins in a man's pocket also commanded respect and, in most circumstances, superseded the other qualities. David knew he held the upper hand for this single reason alone. But what use was it to live out one's life in no substantial way different from these oxen labouring for nothing but provender? There had to be something more to living; there had to be understanding. But how could there ever be, when there was so much unfairness, nastiness and chance? How could it ever make any sense? And wasn't a man a fool for thinking of trying?

He found these deliberations sufficient to keep thoughts of Mahpiyatowin barely beyond the troubled, flitting shadows of his memory, and he fell into a restive sleep.

vi

Mary stretched luxuriantly, and shifted her bedclothes so that she could turn and face the morning sun, now well up and luminous in the thin fall air. Beside her Yves Sayer farted loudly, and made little smacking noises before settling back into his pillow. 'M-m-mmm,' he groaned. Mary scowled. The man pleasured her more than any other man she had known, including her new husband. But he was a pig.

'Don't shit in my husband's bed,' she said. 'Oh, it is so foul. Get out!' And she thumped him with her heels. Rearing up suddenly, the coverlets slipped from his broad shoulders, and he knelt naked beside her, tumescent, his need for her urgent.

'Cover me up, idiot,' she cried. 'I am frozen!'

Seizing her by the hips, he flipped her over easily. 'Cover you I shall,' he muttered huskily. 'You shall not be frozen for long...Ah! You lie! There is heat here!' He handled her roughly, intimately.

'Be careful, fool!' she said sharply, as she started to succumb to his fondling.

He stopped his attentions abruptly, swung his legs over the bed, and began to dress.

'What are you doing, fool?' she demanded, drawing the bedclothes over her breasts. 'Get back here this moment!'

Sayer said nothing, but continued to fasten his clothes. Then he turned to her and spoke softly, 'I am heartily tired of the way in which you address me. There is no respect in your voice.'

'Respect?' she sneered. 'Respect for a man who sneaks around to have his way with another man's wife? Get back into this bed this very moment, and earn my respect in the only way you can. Don't speak to me like a fool!'

'There it is again. It is almost as if I am an amusement for you; a pastime while your husband is away dodging Sioux arrows.' He stepped toward the door as she screamed at him in response.

'You asshole of a skunk! Toad! Who do you think you are?' He turned just in time to duck the chamber pot, though stale piss sprayed over his shirt. The porcelain vessel shattered against the mullioned wall with a crash.

'Damn you, bitch. I am gone!' And he slammed the door.

It was another fight, one of perhaps hundreds they had waged, for their relationship was as tempestuous as it was ill-fated. In the next room, Christine began to cry. 'Merde!' shouted her mother.

Maria Thomas was sixteen, vivacious, charming, and scheming. She was an intimate friend of Mary Daniel; they were kindred spirits, always dreaming of the day when they would depart Red River and see the vast cities of the east. Maria was envious of Mary, who had landed a promising, handsome young businessman with prospects. In addition, David told wonderful stories of the great cities he had visited in America, which fired the girls' imagination. As a poor Halfbreed, Maria could never hope to end up as more than a freighter's wife, or the stoop-backed mate of a struggling farmer unless, by luck or artifice, she married well.

Maria was not as beautiful as Mary, though she had a lively charm that made the boys pay attention. It was Mary who showed her how to touch her lips with just a hint of vermillion paste, and to trace her eyelids with a fine dust of poplar ash. A loose chemise under a tight bodice, so that the bosom was artfully displayed, completed the picture of a lovely, seductive woman barely out of childhood, who turned heads when she was out for a stroll. Mary was pleased with her student.

It was with great excitement in the summer of 1861 that she told

Mary that the Reverend Griffith Owen Corbett had started to pay a great deal of attention to her, and though he tried to be discreet about it, people had already started to talk. They walked along the boardwalk on Main Street, Mary pushing one of the few baby carriages in Red River. A wicker basket on straps slung between two-wheeled leaf springs, it was the object of admiration and curiosity from passersby. David had imported it from a place called Pennsylvania; Mary was very proud of it, and the reactions it got.

'I don't really find him beautiful,' Maria was saying, 'he's really quite old. But he is one of the "Blues", isn't he?' 'Blues' was the term used to refer to the upper classes of society at Red River. These were mainly the retired gentlemen, their white wives, members of the senior Protestant clergy, and their wives. They affected the manners and protocol of the 'Old Country', and were patronizing and condescending to everyone else, though some classes of people were more bearable than others. The most notable of these were the emerging group of trader-merchants whose business acumen transcended their humble racial and social beginnings. The ranks of the 'Blues' were beginning to swell with the immigration of Canadians and Americans looking for land, some of whom were businessmen with money. The peoples of mixed blood were increasingly feeling at a disadvantage in their own land, more so as the buffalo dwindled and bigotry kept them from rising in status.

Mary nodded. 'He's really quite a...well, a commanding figure. He certainly understands us. Doesn't he?'

'What do you mean' asked Maria, a frown wrinkling her brow. 'I know he understands me.'

'That's not what I'm saying, silly thing. Those of us who had mothers of this country, and fathers from Britain, are British subjects they say, and citizens of a great empire. We are English, not 'Halfbreeds'. We are not dogs or cattle, as I think the Company would have it. The snots who run the Company make it plain that they think we're nothing but a step removed from savages—I all the more so because I lived with my Métis relatives...'

'There! Did you see that?' She pointed to a couple who had suddenly turned to gaze into a tinsmith's store. The two women walked by silently. 'That's exactly what I mean. That's the new Company accountant and his wife. They saw us coming, but rather than lower themselves to greet us...'

Maria looked over her shoulder. 'I didn'a really think...'

'Don't be ridiculous. It was obvious as the nose on your face.'

'But Corbett understands such things. I like what I've heard of him. And he's interested in you!' She gave Maria a playful shove. 'You lucky thing!'

Maria laughed, clapping a hand over her mouth. Mary leaned over conspiratorially. 'Has he been...familiar with you yet?'

Maria squealed with laughter. 'Oh, he's a man, if that be your meaning! Almost every night when I go out to feed the cows he's after me, grabbing me and lifting my clothes. Mrs Corbett almost caught us once, out at the byre. We was both tucking in our clothes when she happened upon us; it's never been the same between me and her since. We always got along 'fore that, but now she's quite hard on me, and they always fight about me when they think I'm not around.'

'You'd best be careful, Maria,' said Mary, her eyes narrowing as she considered this latest piece of evidence.

'Oh, we're careful. There's a loft above where he keeps his grey mare, and he always sends me up there to throw down the hay. But pretty soon he's up there too, with that look in his eye. He's even chopped a hole in the planking, so's to watch out for Mrs Corbett.'

Mary was sombre. 'I hope you're careful about other things, as I showed you.'

'Never a worry,' cried Maria. 'He's knowledgeable about these things; very much a man of the world.'

'Just be careful,' said Mary, 'that's all.' She loved to be the wiser, older mentor. Though Maria wasn't the most intelligent girl about, she was spirited and slavishly devoted to Mary. She was perhaps Mary's only friend.

The following year, Maria came to her in a panic: she was pregnant. Mary advised her to confront Corbett, and suggest to him that the only option was marriage. 'Now's your chance, girl. Give him no other choice. Make him send the old witch home to England.'

But Corbett told Maria that marriage was out of the question. He could not leave his wife. Quite impossible. What would 'England think'? This was not a real courtship, it was a…ah, a dalliance. She should marry young Chamberlain, down the way; he always had an eye peeled for young Maria Thomas. Or what about the Sayer boy? Corbett had turned the tables on her, offering either to help her with the 'condition', or to turn her out altogether. What was it to be?

Too ashamed even to go back to Mary, she submitted to Corbett's amateur doctoring. This part of her ordeal was marked by fear and pain. His attentions, on the other hand, seemed to be characterized by enthusiasm and excitement. Maria allowed herself to be probed by surgical instruments, douched with slippery elm as a demulcent, and forced to jump from an elevated stage, all to no avail, save for a terrible fever and vaginal bleeding. He finally abandoned the attempts, announcing that she had 'the constitution of a buffalo pony'.

Corbett even went to the home of her parents to examine Maria.

Maria's sister Betsy, two years younger, complained of a backache, and the Reverend agreed to examine her. In front of Maria, he made the most intimate examinations of the young girl, then instructed her to 'tie the door', while he attended to Maria. Upon hearing a piercing shriek from the room where the three were closeted, Mrs Thomas, a full-blooded Cree Indian who understood no English, nearly fainted, sagging to the floor where she was found by her husband. It was at this time that Corbett, with genuine regret in his voice, advised the parents that Maria was 'nearly three months gone with child', and that she should be married off as soon as possible.

Incredibly, he seduced her again in the woods near her home; perhaps even more incredibly, she yielded to his blandishments. Upon rearranging their clothes in the scrub by the main road, he gave her seven pounds in new paper bills and repeated his urgings that she not disclose their relationship. Once again, while he believed that he had been cautious, they were seen coming out of the ditch, and Corbett put his hands over his head in distress, crying out that he would be ruined. Abruptly he abandoned the girl, and would have nothing more to do with her. She was distraught, and turned to Mary for help.

Mary was angry with the hypocritical cleric. She related something of her experience with Reverend Thomas, embroidering the story to make it seem as if the Anglican clergy were nothing more than slavering, lusting hounds. She inflamed the simple Maria with pejorative statements which reflected Mary's own antagonisms, though, in fairness, what Corbett had done was bad enough without spiteful elaboration. She advised Maria to make a formal complaint to both the secular and ecclesiastical authorities. This action was preempted by Maria's father who, upon finally learning the details of the cause of his daughter's distraught state in a tearful confession, went before the magistrate in a rage to swear the charge himself. Corbett was indicted on a charge that he attempted to procure an abortion, and the ensuing scandal split the community.

The principal form of diversion and entertainment in Red River was gossiping. By the 1860s it had been raised to extraordinary levels of legitimacy by the way in which various groups appropriated it to their viewpoint, and the way in which the Nor'Wester printed it, or ignored it, according to its annexationist agenda for union with Canada. Gossip, of course, was nothing more than an attempt to influence the thinking and opinions of others, and had very little to do with the exchange of information. It was a power issue, usually for the most powerless. Gossip had no benign existence. Mary was well aware of the invidious nature of well-placed gossip; she had as often as not been the target of it. She began to share in the discussion of Corbett's guilt, and delighted in the fact that he was detained by the magistrate without bail, a rather extraordinary measure. David had no interest in these intrigues; for him, his business consumed both time and passion. One evening, while David sat at the table looking over accounts, she broached the subject.

'So you have no opinion on the scandalous conduct of our Reverend Corbett?'

David lifted his head and looked at her. It took his eyes a moment to focus, and he thought that it would not be long before he would be needing eyeglasses. Damn. He would look very much the accounting clerk then. 'I have not much to say about such goings-on. If he tried to abort his own bastard child, then he should go to prison. If he did not, then some punishment should be meted out to the girl for such a mischief. Is there more to it than that?'

'Piff!' she said haughtily. 'I am very close to it, as Maria is my friend, and if even half of what I know comes out, he'll be put away for a very long time. I'm told it's life imprisonment for such a crime, don't you know?'

David had lost interest, and turned back to his papers, squinting at the neat rows of entries. At his silence, Mary raised her voice, sounding petulant. 'How can you take no interest in the goings-on in this place? This is your home.'

David looked at her absently. It was as if a stranger sat across the room from him. He had married a woman he barely knew, and had an almost separate life from her. Even the ardour which had drawn him to her regularly each night had waned. She was as beautiful as ever, and their daughter was a miniature mirror-image of her, but he plain didn't like her any more. That was it. They had nothing whatsoever in common, apart from their bed, and now it seemed, not even that. All this in less than three years. Home? What did that mean?

He knew well enough how such a thing could happen. There was no good reason to bind his life to this woman, but his vanity and his masculine pride had trapped him. For a time, he was master of a most desirable mate. He was a stag bugling in the woods. For a time, he was as single-minded as a ram during the rut. He was, in short, a prisoner of his loins, but too proud to acknowledge that he did not see further than that. All he needed to do was to look at her, and she would take his breath away. What happened to that magic? How had it dissipated so quickly? They looked at each other for a long moment, thinking similar thoughts.

To be sure, theirs was not a marriage of equality, any more than other unions between men and women of the time. Men were providers; women brought to the household a utility: it was sexual or procreative; a particular form of labour or necessary support, critical on the farm or while the man was away, usually on the Company's business. Increasingly, however, it was ornamental. More and more men were taking white wives, for this was a sign of prestige, of wealth. As it was convenient, the 'country wives' were dropped in favour of this new sign of prosperity and rank. Such an appendage signalled that a man no longer had need for the kind of partnership which was as close to sexual parity as a rugged land demanded. White women from Britain were often quite useless in meeting the rigours of Rupert's Land. Their clothing usually consisted of extra layers of what they would have worn in the Old Country; they could not travel by snowshoe, nor assist with the butchering following the hunt. But no matter; her new mate had no need of these skills. Civilization was at hand.

This not-so-subtle change created enormous tensions in the colony. There were those who aspired to mix with the 'Blues'. There were those others who, by reason of skin or race or vocation, had no such chance for what others decreed as 'respectability'. This attitude became tied to political aspirations of those who would see Red River become a colony of the Crown of England; a new 'jewel of Empire'. Other groups with ties in the east preferred annexation with Canada. The Métis felt increasingly isolated and spoke of nationalism, or union with the United States. The easy relationships formed in the early days of the settlements gave way under these new tensions. The English-speaking Halfbreeds now assembled for their own buffalo hunt, even though the Anglican clergy disapproved of such savage pastimes. The Métis were suspicious and insular. During the Sioux scare of 1862 some of this fractious rivalry was forgotten, as it was realized that the Métis were the only organized armed force of any significance to repel a serious attack. The Royal Canadian Rifles, having come in 1857, had decamped in the spring of '61. There was no other force to give consequence to legal authority. Many of the English-speaking settlers were alarmed by this fact, and petitioned the Home Office for a permanent battalion of regulars to protect the colony.

There were many who moved between the communities, including David and Mary. But David was distrusted by the English-speaking community for his conversion to Catholicism, his ties to America, and his increasing wealth. Mary was simply disliked by almost everyone. She was seen as manipulative and unpleasant. She was direct in a way that all of David's acquaintances found offensive. Hurt feelings were no concern of hers; she tended to use people and discard them. It was said that her late father had been cruel to her, punishing her with frequent whippings when she was slow, or failed to complete some small task. Edwin Bell was repelled by her. David saw this one evening in St Paul.

They had retired for the day, after several hours of selecting trade samples of serge and denim clothing, of the kind favoured by American gold miners. After several drafts of beer, Bell asked off-handedly, 'So youse did not bring y' wife this time?'

David looked up. 'No.'

The relief was obvious on Bell's face; it annoyed David, for he had seen this reaction before. Bell never asked about his family, but for some time it had been apparent that Bell did not fancy Mary. Normally, he would have let the matter go, but the beer had pushed his emotions a little closer to the surface than usual.

'Why do you ask?'

'No reason; jus' wondered.'

David was determined now to have it out. 'I get the distinct impression that you're not fond of Mary. Am I wrong?' The tone was challenging, and curiously discordant; they had never had so much as a disagreement before. Both were easy-going men who preferred consensus to conquest. But here was the seed of a nettle.

'It's none a my business to comment on such things,' said Bell, clearly uncomfortable, shifting in his chair.

'But I asked,' insisted David. 'I want to know what you think of her.' And after a moment, 'You don't care for her do you?'

Bell looked at him sadly. 'There's three things a man never criticizes 'bout another man.' Ordinarily David would have smiled at this. Edwin always responded to question in several parts; he preferred options and alternatives, reasons and supporting arguments, to intuitive responses. But David's expression remained challenging, importunate. 'Three things: first, never say anythin' unpleasant about a man's taste in horses. Never say nothin' 'bout the size a his cock. An' third, most important: never, an' I mean never, say anythin' about a man's wife. No sir, nothin. No matter what.'

Bell tried a grin. 'I ain't never seen youse on a horse. I ain't never seen youse naked. An' I met your wife maybe three or four times. So how can I say anythin'?'

David felt the breadth of his rankled pride undiminished. He wanted this man's respect, his admiration and friendship, yet he felt that if Bell could not support his choice of mate, he was against him in all things. Couldn't be trusted. Even as these feral thoughts flew about, he realized the folly of his position. But emotions are no well-honed scalpel; they tear across the mind like a blunt trade axe, felling reason along with sentiment. He pressed on:

'You rarely visit Fort Garry. You're remote when you are there, and quick to return here when business is done. Some of your excuses not to come round to our new house are feeble in the extreme. Yet when I am here, all is as before. You're uncomfortable around her. Is that it? Come. Be straight with me.'

'Look, David, see here. She an' I, well, we just don't see eye t' eye, that's all.' Bell was searching for a way out. Too much beer. 'To tell the truth, I don't think she cares for me much.'

David knew this was true, though Mary had never expressed any sensible reasons for it. The plain truth of it was that Mary didn't seem to care for anyone, including her own husband. That little slut Maria Thomas excepted. David was too embarrassed, too proud to concede this to Bell. He felt that Bell might think less of him. He had moved around considerably, been alone so much of the time that he did not understand the concept of friendship, never having formed an association which he felt deserved the term. Without realizing it, David had never learned to trust.

'To hell with it.' David stood up, then blinked as the beer rushed to his head.

'Sit down, man, before youse fall down.' Bell reached out as if to steady him. 'She an' I...we just don't get along. She don't like me, an' I guess I don't like her.' There. It was out. David was flushed and upset:

'Piss on you, then!' And he lurched from the room ashamed and upset.

On the long trip home, he worried that something important had been broken in his relationship with Bell. Could he still rely on him? The following day they had not spoken of their quarrel; Bell seemed intuitively to understand that David's pain lay far beneath the petty exchange of sharp words. It had something to do with Mary, to be sure, but it was deeper. David was a troubled man who seldom spoke of himself, had no apparent friends, and seemed comfortable only when discussing business or working. So business it was, and Bell kept clear of him.

David took this to be deliberate avoidance for some spiteful reason, and the balance of his stay in St Paul was strained. He did not have the understanding to reach out. The greatest movement of the spirit occurs with the realization that even though one has the right to put oneself first in all things, one may nevertheless choose otherwise. It is the deliberate denial of self in deference to another that makes the conditions of love and friendship so grand. Such actions forge bonds far greater than those obtained by force or fear, or paid allegiance. Yet some never grow from this state of essential childhood. If there was a basic difference between the red man and the white man, it was this. Obeisance to needs of the community was pressed upon the aboriginal from birth. With the

European, homage was due to a stern and inflexible God, an authoritarian father, a hard schoolmaster and an imperious and often unforgiving state. To say nothing of regimented institutions of the day: the army, the Company, and the church.

Yet David missed it altogether, even though the men he was with, and the Métis, as well as those like himself whose bloodlines and loyalties were blurred by intermarriage, were the living embodiment of that conflict. Worse, the lessons which he struggled to understand went unlearned because of his central flaw; he could not, would not, acknowledge dependency upon others. Such a prospect made him feel weak and exposed, vulnerable. He did not belong naturally or easily to any group, standing apart from other men. The thought that he had made a poor choice in Mary gnawed at him; he was discomforted that Edwin knew this of him. But he could not acknowledge it, and resented Edwin for his insight.

His attitude toward his daughter, his lack of filial bond with her, disturbed him. But his inability to trust or accept Bell's friendship seemed inexplicable, for the man had been nothing but a sound business partner and reliable acquaintance for more than two years by now. There was the haunting thought that perhaps Mary was right about him, that she had the sharper intuition about people. He could not bring himself to rely on his own judgement in these affairs. It was all very troubling, and David was not happy. This was most puzzling of all. For if ever a man should be content, David Bloode should be that man, he told himself. But his experience was that each time he had placed his trust, it was betrayed.

Still, personal confidences were easily enough avoided, for Bell was not a prying man. There were plenty of neutral events to engage conversation. The war between North and South was going badly for the northern states. The Confederate Army was thrashing the Yankees, by all accounts from Virginia; the turnaround at Gettysburg was still almost a year away. The city was flooded with refugees from the Sioux uprising, and a fierce engagement between the Minnesota Volunteers and Little Crow's warriors at Birch Coolee saw twenty-three men killed and sixty wounded on September 2, 1862. Two of the dead, George Colter and William Russell, were men with whom David had done business, though Bell had the closer connection. They had been disinterred after the fighting and returned to the city for reburial. David and Bell attended the funeral, a gloomy affair on a rainy fall day. It seemed an omen to David to leave soon, and return home to Red River.

The railway had reached St Paul, and the first locomotive, the *William Crooks*, chuffed into the temporary station built at the end of the line.

David mused that, one day soon, the linkage between Fort Garry and the railhead at St Paul would facilitate the transfer of goods and people. The world would then be at the doorstep of the people of Red River. His thoughts drifted back to his first trip by rail to Baltimore, and how frightened and amazed he had been. Looking around, he could see much the same wonderment on the faces of children gathered around the sighing monster, with the green and gold lettering grandly announcing the future on its boiler sides: the St Paul and Pacific Railway.

These diversions, however, did not hold David for long. He had been anxious to be off before the threat of an early snow. Not two days out he was stopped by a detachment of cavalry who told him that there was great risk in proceeding, for they were still in the process of 'mopping up the renegades'. The troops were excited and boisterous, with no real intention shown to dissuade 'them northern breeds' from passing on. The Adjutant General had posted a reward of twenty-five dollars for each 'certified' Sioux scalp that was brought in. David assured them that they would travel well to the east, and was allowed to proceed, though there were many sarcastic asides from the troops, all to the effect that the brigade of carts was doomed, if not from the Sioux, then from being driven mad from the infernal shrieking of the wooden axles. A few of the troopers muttered darkly that 'no one'd know the difference 'tween a breed scalp and a Sioux'. Another was quick to point out, just as they passed from earshot, that the first man to produce a red-headed Sioux scalp should ask for a bonus. The chortles and hoots faded like the ill-boding sounds of a turtleshell medicine rattle, and David wondered what they would have thought if they had happened upon him as he appeared when he lived with the Sioux. No question about it, he'd be dead. Red hair or not. He took out his pipe and spat on the ground. Bastards. He called ahead unnecessarily to his guides to move on.

Though no incident troubled the convoy, the sky remained grey and lustreless as a clamshell. David continued to brood, alienating his men even more. His thoughts were of Mary, and how little he looked forward to seeing her. His daughter, Christine, was a pale, sickly child, with flaming red hair much as his own used to be. They were not close, and he had barely concealed his disappointment that Mary had not borne him a son. Christine cringed around her mother who paid her scant attention. She seemed not to take solace from her father, and David had no patience with her in any event. Maria Thomas visited frequently, and though David thought she was a brainless nit, she did pay a great deal of attention to Christine. There were some consolations, he considered.

He thought about having a son. He would like that, he supposed. A son was more useful; a son could inherit the business, and carry on his name. He began to fix on this goal as a real possibility, but he would have Mary to contend with. After Christine was born, and they had resumed regular intercourse, she had begun to take measures to 'protect herself'. She would insert a wad of batting secured by a strand of gut, prior to union. Following their encounter, she would draw it out, 'like cleaning a musket'. 'No more brats for me!' she'd say. David found these preliminaries repelling, and could not watch her prepare herself, even though she made no efforts to shield what she was doing. She taunted him for it: 'Come help me. Your fingers are longer than mine!'

The thought of her no longer aroused him as it had, not so long ago. She was still a beautiful woman, and the sight of her bathing or undressed still kindled a flame in his belly. But their coupling was increasingly infrequent. This still did not rule out a son, however, and he resolved to address the matter with her. For the rest of the trip, he explored the appropriateness of a name for his son.

Abruptly, he thought of his father, the man insinuating his memory into David's thoughts. He smiled to himself as he thought of his father's only possession from the Old Country: a red-stained volume of poetry. He could not read, it was obvious, but he treasured it and would recite bits of rhyme from memory while holding the book unopened on his lap. There was a fragment of verse Ephraim used to quote at table, one of the few bits of playfulness he ever exhibited with the children:

> *But man is a carniverous production,*
> *And must have meals, at least one meal a day;*
> *He cannot live, like woodcocks, upon suction,*
> *But, like the shark and tiger, must have prey;*
> *Although his anatomical construction*
> *Bears vegetables, in a grumbling way,*
> *Your labouring people think beyond all question*
> *Why, buffalo hump's better for digestion!*

David never did think that an English poet would write about buffalo meat, but he joined in on the last line with delight. It was a happy childhood memory, bright as a spark. Byron, that was the poet's name, and a lord he was, too. Byron. That was it! Byron Bloode. What a commanding name, worthy of respect and loyalty, admiration and deference!

vii

When the Reverend Griffith Owen Corbett was denied bail on the charge of procuring an abortion, many at Red River saw this as proof of Corbett's assertions that the Hudson's Bay Company was determined to suppress the rightful ambitions of the settlers. Here were the Company's servants making sure that he, an outspoken critic of the Company, learned his lesson. Corbett had no shortage of sympathetic visitors in the cramped lock-up where he was being held at the fort, and he sent each one away with this singular festering idea. All through the trial Corbett had maintained the constant theme of victimization in his defence. But prior to the trial, passions were substantially aroused in the Halfbreed community, such that one Saturday morning, December 6, 1862, a mob started to assemble at the Forks.

All that week rumours had been circulating in the settlement that there was a powerful injustice being done in the imprisonment of a man of the calibre of Reverend Corbett, and action had to be taken. Mary and Maria had heard the stories, most of which reflected negatively on Maria's credibility and reputation. This worried her, and she expressed her fears to Mary.

'The latest word is that there'll be a march on the gaol tomorrow. Can you believe it? What can they be thinking of?'

'I'll tell you what they're thinking of: they believe all the nonsense Corbett has been spouting since he got here. They don't want to believe their hero has taken advantage of a poor serving girl in his employ, so to explain all his present difficulties, they blame the Company for concocting this story.'

'All the same,' said Maria, 'I'm worried. Angry people could turn on me just as easy as not.'

'Nonsense!' snapped Mary. 'Why don't we go down to the fort tomorrow, and see for ourselves?'

'Never!' cried Maria. 'Why on God's earth would I want do do that? What if there was a riot or something? And how would it look, me skulking around the fort at such a time, like a dog 'round the dinner table?'

Mary ignored her, as she often did when an idea began to take hold in her mind. 'Yes! We'll go.' Turning to Maria, she discounted the worried frown on the younger girl's face. 'It's really quite simple. He is the prisoner; you are the one wronged. You have a perfect right to go wherever you wish. More important, I think that we need to get a better idea of what's going on. Besides, it'll be exciting if anything actually does happen—which I doubt in this sleepy, dull place.'

And so it was that the two women, heavily wrapped and muffled against the winter chill, were at the fort when more than two hundred and sixty people converged at about nine in the morning. The crowd built so fast, the only inference one could draw was that it was a carefully planned event. Though no weapons were obvious, the mood was ugly. The sun was barely up, struggling to shine through torn, grey clouds over a haggard sky. Some of those present must have travelling in the dark for some time, for there were settlers from all the parishes along the Assiniboine, and from St Andrew's and St John's as well. Converging at the Forks, the mob left their horses, sleighs and jumpers, and made their way to the south gate.

Word of their imminent arrival swept to the fort only minutes before. The new Governor, Alexander Grant Dallas, was in no mood to be interfered with. A hard, humourless man whose temperament made him an unpopular leader, but whose inflexible adherence to rules had won him promotion to Governor of Rupert's Land, Dallas sent for a force of special constables. Before they could be assembled, the crowd reached the Governor's house, and demanded to see him. There was no clear leader with whom he could negotiate, but he could see that they were angry; shouts for the release of Corbett were loud and insistent. Other, more ominous threats could be distinguished and Dallas cut short his attempts to turn back the mob by appeals to allow the wheels of justice to take their course. When it became clear that there would be a riot, he acceded to their demands that they be allowed to see Corbett, and to permit him to address them.

Corbett, grinning like a successful candidate, sprang to a bench at the door of the tiny prison. In his enthusiasm, he struck his forehead on the lintel, and collapsed heavily upon the rough floor. Undeterred, he was propped up, whereupon he gave a short speech full of references to 'justice' and 'God's will', parts of which the crowd never heard, for he was holding a rag to his brows to staunch the flow of blood. One phrase that the two hooded and scarfed women heard was a reference to a 'pale accuser, addlepated puppet of the Company…'. Maria gasped, and drew further into her wraps. No matter, the throng was moved by the image of the wounded man. David it was, against the Goliath Company.

University of Toronto educated James Ross, editor and proprietor of the Nor'Wester, aided by what appeared to be a more moderate delegation which included David Bloode, convinced Dallas that he should exercise his prerogative in favour of quashing the original detention order against Corbett, and admitting him to bail.

When word of this reached the crowd, the tension evaporated immediately, and with a great deal of self-congratulation, smiling and nodding of heads, they dispersed, taking Corbett with them. David and Ross remained on the veranda with the Governor, despite the cold. The Governor was shaking his head. 'The fools do not know what they have done to Madam Justice. She's had a black eye—nay, a bloody nose today.'

Ross laid a mitted hand on his arm. ' 'Twas the only thing you could do to avoid a gaolbreak, or even bloodshed. You had no choice.'

David nodded. 'When I saw the mob coming here, I was on my way to open my store. I feared for the safety of many people, including my wife, who was dropped off to purchase supplies earlier on. The right thing was done.'

Dallas looked at the two of them, then at David directly. 'The right thing? The right thing? What of the rule of law? Without adherence to the judicial principles of the common law, we're nothing but savages. Aye, that mob was more savage than civilized, but then, what can you expect of such people?

'I've no pride in the petty compromise made here. What happens to Corbett in the long run is quite irrelevant. The law was ousted by a mob, and I thought we'd come further than that. You may take your deviant pragmatism and smoke it in your pipe, for I shall be condemning it in my report to London!'

And with that, he went inside, slamming the door loudly behind him. With a shrug, Ross left David standing alone. When he turned about to depart, he came face to face with Mary, her face barely masking her anger. Beyond, wrapped in winter clothes, David recognized the slight form of Maria Thomas.

'I watched the whole thing. You actually demanded of the Governor that he release that swine Corbett?' she demanded, hands on hips and lips drawn back over sharp white teeth.

'I made no demands,' said David, sliding into the passive mode he employed during any sort of conflict. 'I merely pointed out that if there was to be a riot, then property and persons would suffer. And it was needless.'

'Liar!' she barked. 'I heard Ross say something to the effect of 'or you shall suffer the consequences...''

He hissed at her, mindful that Maria was drawing close to them. 'Mind your mouth, woman! You'll not speak to me in such a way, not in public!'

She laughed dryly. 'I'll speak to you any way I wish. And in this, you have permitted Corbett to sully publicly the reputation of my friend, facilitated his release, and...'

David would have no more; he slapped his wife across the cheek, harder than he later thought he had intended, and she staggered under the blow, almost falling.

'Bâtard!' she cried, turning to flee.

He made no attempt to call after her, merely watching as she fled, the whimpering Maria in tow. The few passersby who witnessed the fracas took no notice. It was commonplace for a man to discipline his wife in this way, though the 'Blues', if they were so disposed, never put on such a vulgar display in public view. There it was, he thought to himself; I'm the same as my father. How it sickened me when he abused my mother; yet here am I doing exactly the same thing. Well, she deserved it, and more.

As he walked along to his warehouse, the more he thought about the quarrel with his wife, the less he understood it. He well understood Governor Dallas's position, even though he found it rigid, unyielding, and bound for disaster without their intervention. Men like Dallas see the world in colours of black and white, with no possible variations of shade. But his wife's point of view? There was no comprehending it. Just because Maria was her friend, and Corbett was the subject of a particularly nasty allegation of hers? Why would she find David's attempt to avoid serious trouble so provocative?

During the subsequent trial, David and Mary were at pains to be civil to one another. Neither raised the slap, but a bridge had been crossed. David had no resolve that he would refrain from beating his wife if she stepped out of line again. Mary felt that he would raise his hand to her, should she provoke him in some way, and she hated him and feared him a little. She sought solace in Sayer's arms as often as she could, but submitted quietly to David when he came to bed without his nightshirt, a signal to her that he had need of her. It chafed her that he insisted that she not take her usual precautions; it became clear that he wanted another child.

'Why? When you have neither time nor affection for the one you have?'

David had neither the patience nor understanding to debate with her. He raised his hand, and she flinched, blinking, hating her fear of him. 'So, you have me cringing like a dog! Does it please you?' She was bitter that the power in the relationship had shifted because of his physical strength. Angrily she taunted him.

'Does it inflame your manhood? Then take me as a dog, so I will not have to look at you!'

And she rolled onto her stomach, tugging her sleeping gown over her buttocks. Drawing up her knees and arching her back, she opened herself to him brazenly. He fell upon her, thrusting urgently, grasping her hips as he took her, crying out as his completion drained him within minutes. As he lay panting beside her, he realized that this was the only level left at which he could communicate with her. And a forlorn, transient thing it was, too.

The conviction of Reverend Corbett was a foregone conclusion. Maria's evidence was compelling, detailed and corroborated. She was too simple to concoct such a story in any event, and be able to supply such minute descriptions. On the second day of trial, she even wore the black French merino dress Corbett had foolishly bought for her. No one on a serving girl's wages could possibly afford such a luxury. When the sentence was pronounced—six months' imprisonment without hard labour—those on both sides of the issue were aghast; six months was a lenient sentence for one who had behaved with the moral depravity described during the nine days of trial. On the other hand, the pro-Corbett faction believed he would never serve a day in gaol.

The anger at Corbett's incarceration grew. It formed the core of gossip and controversy, dominating conversation at a time when there was an increase of activity at the Forks. In addition to the Bloode & Bell warehouse, Henry McKenny had just completed the first general store in the settlement, near the junction of the Portage Trail and the Main Road which led north to the lower fort. He had bought the land from Andrew McDermot, whose trading warehouse was nearby. McKenny's structure was a huge two-storey building with a hip roof, referred to as 'Noah's Ark' by the locals who were satisfied that anyone who built on the flats near the river had more need of a vessel than an edifice, come spring.

The consequence of McKenny's strategy was to develop a commercial district away from the fort, which for so long had all other enterprises literally in its shadow. This part of Winnipeg amounted to a scrabble of frame and clapboard businesses with false fronts and raised wooden walkways bordering wide ox-trails. McKenny dreamed with the power of a frontier survivor that the future city would be laid out in the fashion of a wheel, with the spokes conjoining at the hub which, not coincidentally, lay just outside his door. McKenny was to be joined in partnership by his half-brother, Dr John Christian Schultz. Schultz had come to the settlement in the summer of 1859 to scout possibilities. Taking the populace at large for 'bumpkins', he felt there were broad opportunities for an impressive man of excellent credentials such as he possessed. David had met him while chatting with McKenney, and took an instant dislike to him. He was arrogant and loud. Little did David foresee the way in which their lives would become entangled before the next decade was out.

Large numbers of overlanders passed through Red River in the summer of 'sixty-two, on their way to look for gold in the Cariboo. Merchants were hard pressed to keep up with the demand for equipment, especially since the traffic to St Paul had been curtailed by the depredations of the Sioux.

One product that David could not keep in sufficient stock was explosives. His supply from St Paul interrupted, he brought black powder in by boat and canoe from Ontario. The Hamilton Powder Company was inspired by the success of stumping and mining endeavours, and its products were typical of the new contrivances available to settlers determined to wrest a living from the land. He was able to meet with many of the gold-seekers passing through from America and Canada, as well as those starry-eyed wanderers from Britain and Ireland who hoped to strike it rich in the gold fields.

These transients spent their money in the storehouses of Red River, and in the miserable taverns and 'sporting shops' on the Main Road. Even these strangers were regaled with the story of the Reverend Corbett, with not a great deal of care necessarily being taken with the facts. Laughing and titillated by turn, shaking heads disapprovingly over a mug of beer or rum, the injustice done to Corbett was embroidered and expanded, until it was difficult for anyone to recall with any accuracy just how the evidence had been called to establish guilt. The Company's opposition to re-routing the Portage Trail permanently to the nascent business section was further support for Corbett's thesis that the Hudson's Bay Company would continue to hold the settlement under its thumb.

In April of 1863, when the last grimy drifts of snow were melting before a cool spring sun, and the earth was as black and slippery as only Red River gumbo can be, David was in his warehouse, preparing to sell the final touches of an outfit to a straggler headed for the goldfields. A poor, thin man, accompanied by his brother and their two wives, he had laid out all of his coinage, and did not have sufficient funds to take all that he had chosen. Pinching their jaws, and worrying over the goods arranged on the floor, the two brothers debated the various merits of each piece, trying to establish the proper priority.

There was a tap at the window, and David noticed James Stewart standing on the boardwalk, holding his palms to the glass so that he could see against the glare. Crooking a finger, he beckoned to David to come out. David did so, shivering slightly in his shirtsleeves. Spring had come late and the ice was just beginning to move on the river. The breeze from it was cool.

Stewart was the Halfbreed school teacher at St James Parish School—'country-born', as he preferred to describe himself. Many of the mixed-blood, English-speaking inhabitants who aspired to more formal social pretensions were affecting this description of their heritage; David believed it was an affectation introduced by the Protestant clergy. Though David thought it was a silly bit of snootery, he didn't much prefer the expression 'Halfbreed' either. As on most other things, he did not hold strong views one way or the other. Stewart had a sheaf of papers in his hand.

'What've you got there?' asked David. He knew Stewart, but not well.

'It's a petition, laddie,' answered Stewart, who called everyone 'laddie', whether pupil or aging veteran. It had been an annoying quirk of his late father as well. 'I'm looking for your signature on it.'

'What's it all about?'

'Ah, never mind, just sign,' laughed the schoolmaster. 'Now look. It's well known that you were instrumental in having the good Reverend Corbett released during the trouble before Christmas. We're getting up a petition to have him pardoned and released, so he can get back to his work; we'd like you to sign, as a show of your support.'

David glanced back at his two customers, who were still sorting and culling. Turning back to Stewart, frowning, he said, 'But what good would that do? The Bishop appointed his Archdeacon, what's his name— Hunter—to do a separate investigation, and even he concluded that Corbett was guilty. What more is to be done? Will we ever hear the end of this affair?'

'I believe we will, laddie, if'n you'll just sign this petition to the Governor.'

David thought for a moment. What was the harm; not to sign might be bad for business, if word got around. God knows it would be, sure enough. 'There looks like a fair number of names on that thing already,' he said without enthusiasm.

'More than five hundred and twenty so far; I'll not stop until I see six hundred decent citizens put their hand to it.'

David read over the text. It used pungent language, like 'travesty', 'indecency', and 'wicked'. It seemed a lot of nonsense. The fact was that Corbett got off lightly for trying to kill the child that was now snivelling at Maria Thomas's breast. Well, what in hell. He could not afford to alienate the very people he depended upon for regular business. The gold rush was rumoured to be over, even though the hopefuls still kept coming. He sighed.

'All right. Where do you want my name?'

He went back into the building, where he was confronted with the next move in the choreography of shopping with insufficient funds. 'Will you kindly let us have these few last pieces on credit?'

David rolled his eyes and responded with all of the tact possible in the breaking of dreams.

Governor Dallas was nothing if not a consistent man. Still smarting from his capitulation to a mob in December, when approached by Stewart and his delegation he refused even to receive the petition. When he learned of its nature, he dropped it at Stewart's feet, announcing from clenched lips, and in terse language, that he would 'not interfere with the course of natural justice as displayed in this case. The man, priest or no, has naught to complain of. He had a fair trial, and he was sentenced properly. And damned leniently, if you would know my thought on it!' And he dismissed the men abruptly, without further word.

The reaction was strong. The rage which might have been defused by a more temperate response erupted six days later, when Stewart led a mob to the lockup where Corbett had been incarcerated, then liberated, before the trial. With no resistance from the token guard, Corbett was set free. Dallas was enraged, and ordered his sheriff to seize Stewart and lock him up on charges of sedition and gaol-break.

This time the Governor had anticipated some form of protest or resistance, and had deployed a force of twenty special constables armed with breech-loading military rifles, some with bayonets fixed. These men were retained on the basis that there was only to be a show of force, and no actual engagement. This confused instruction was compounded when they were issued only two bullets each.

'What will happen if we're called upon to return fire,' said one of the men to Sheriff McKenny, as he pinned on the green ribbon that identified him as an agent of the law, 'and our allotment of ammunition is expended? Can we not warn them at least that the Governor himself might fetch us a basket of dried horse turds to throw at them?'

Another man next to him snickered as he drew his length of ribbon through the buttonhole in his lapel. 'What do you want for eight shillings for a night's work? Four bullets? You've not to worry, for we've a secret weapon. If anyone shows up to prevent us from taking Stewart, we'll get the Governor out here and he can deliver a stern lecture. That'll either scare 'em or bore 'em, and while they're all standing there hanging their heads, we'll just go among 'em and collect their weapons.'

A few snorted but most remained silent, looking at the two forlorn shells in the palm of their hands.

'You're a regular horse's prick, Jack Henderson,' said someone sourly. 'Why don't you tell 'em some o' your jokes, and they'll all die laughing.'

David had been asked to serve with the 'volunteers' as Stewart termed the group, but he declined, saying it was a 'mad scheme' that had 'no careful thought, nor good reason behind it.' Stewart was angry at the response, but in too much haste to quarrel with him.

'I'll be back to see you about this,' he shouted over his shoulder. 'It's good to know where a man stands!' David watched the knot of armed men, thirty or so, move off in the direction of the fort, and shook his head. What passions were ignited in the name of God! And this affair had only to do with God's earthly agent yielding to the pleasures of the flesh, then attempting a little damage control once found out. Was it any more than that? David didn't think so. And neither did Mary, he suspected. She simply loved a fat scandal, and it was quite apparent that she had no sympathy at all for Corbett.

Stewart was incarcerated soon after Corbett's release, and without incident. The Governor had the advantage of surprise, for no one thought he would act so swiftly. Upon Stewart's confinement, Dallas decided to put together a force of irregulars to mind the prison. He was well aware of the racial tensions in the community, and he ensured that McKinney enlisted twenty-five Halfbreeds as well as twenty-five Métis. All of the Métis responded; only four of the Halfbreeds agreed to serve. Dallas made direct appeals to the English-speaking mixed bloods, but most declined even this extraordinary request from the Governor.

Dallas took his case directly to David, pressing upon him the need for law and order. If mobs were to rule, then no man was safe, let alone a man's business. Dallas looked around him, taking in the warehouse with its accumulated goods. 'Mister Bloode, I see you as one of the next generation of citizens. One who stands firmly in the future of this community.' Pursing his thin lips, and puffing florid cheeks, he lapsed into poetic verse, giving forth with a rich baritone voice. As he spoke, the Sheriff and the Governor's clerks nodded slightly, the perfect acolytes. David heard not so much the words but the direct appeal to his heart and pride: the enormity of the Governor, here for the first time in David's shop, coming almost on bended knee. David was carried away by his own exaltation. The Governor spoke, initially looking directly at David, then raising his eyes as if to invoke a higher authority than even his own grand jurisdiction.

> *There must be refuge! Men*
> *Perished in winter winds till one smote fire*
> *From flint stones coldly hiding what they held,*
> *The red spark treasured from the kindling sun;*
> *They gorged on flesh like wolves till one sowed corn,*
> *Which grew a weed, yet makes the life of man;*
> *They mowed and babbled till some tongue struck speech,*
> *And patient fingers framed the lettered sound.*
> *What good gift have my brothers, but it came*

From search and strife and loving sacrifice?
There must be refuge! Thus spake the law;
Man's noblest triumph o'er barb and blade.
There must be justice done and seen; else,
All's returned, and men perish sure as any storm.

After his speech, everyone was still. David didn't know whether to applaud or sink to his knees. He wasn't much with a weapon, but there were assurances that this was to be a show of force only, with no instructions for an engagement. He gave his agreement; he would be there the following day, as requested.

When the last man left, David heard a mocking laugh behind him. It was Mary. Holding her daughter by the hand, she laughed again. 'What a performance! Swayed by a little rhyming verse! The Governor himself! A man who would not have you at his table comes here to convince you to bear arms on behalf of a Company that competes with you, conspires in trade against you, taxes you—and you agree! Yet I suppose it's for a good cause. This is to keep the one in gaol who set that rat Corbett free.'

Christine started to sniffle, for no apparent reason, screwing up her perpetually worried face. Mary jerked her by the arm. 'I am here to tell you that I have missed my second time. I'm sure that I am to be a mother again.' There was no joy in this announcement, only resignation. 'It's what you want.'

David said nothing. He had committed to form part of a special constabulary, pitted in all likelihood against men who were his best customers. Perhaps Dallas was right, however. Without the protection of the law, no one was safe. Besides, he'd indicated that he was assembling a force of fifty 'leading' citizens, so it was likely the right side to be on for that reason alone. He turned from Mary to look for one of his trade guns. Dallas had said nothing about armaments, and David did not want to be standing guard with only a gentleman's belt-knife. Mary's announcement did not register with him. So she was with child; it had better be his son.

The following morning, April 22, David arrived at the fort as he had promised. There were only five other men whose first language was not French. All twenty-five Métis showed up, and seven others had to be sent home. There was no love lost for Corbett and his liberators in the assembly, but David and his five English-speaking cohorts were uneasy. For the larger group who kept to themselves, this seemed to be an opportunity for a scrap. They were almost in a celebratory mood.

At about ten in the morning, a small party of twenty-seven led by Hallett and James Ross called from the courtyard in front of the

Governor's house. This was not visible from the gaol, but they had not escaped attention, and David strolled anxiously over to a point where he could watch.

Dallas threw open a second-floor bedroom window, and addressed the men from there. He refused to come down to the street to speak 'face to face' as Hallett demanded, nor did Hallett seem nonplussed by Dallas's barely restrained rage. Instead, he took out a document of some sort, and holding it in front of him in the manner of a herald, he read loudly from it:

'Know all ye men by these presents: It is hereby decreed that the following matters shall obtain: first, that James Stewart, now under gubernatorial warrant, in the custody of the common gaol, shall be pardoned and set free forthwith. Second: that Sheriff Henry McKenny shall be removed from office for rank partisanship in the carrying out of his duties.

'Third: that the Reverend Griffith Owen Corbett be pardoned for any alleged misconduct, or that his sentence be remitted to time served. Fourth: that all disputations surrounding the recent trial of Reverend Corbett cease and desist forthwith.'

David could not see his expression, but Hallett lowered the paper he was reading from, and looked up at the Governor, calling loudly. 'Sir, I have here a petition in support of your signature on this document. I call upon you to sign it, so that the orderly release of Mr Stewart may be accomplished.'

Dallas looked down at them for a moment, then said, 'Send the thing up, that I may have a proper look at it.'

Hallett looked over his shoulder and flashed a smile that David could see, even though Hallett's face was thickly bearded. When it had been brought up to him, Dallas reappeared at the window, holding the document. With the same drama David had seen in his business the previous day, Dallas addressed the small group, whose reinforcements could now be seen at the outer gate, well within earshot. The Governor's melodious voice reverberated between the buildings.

'A Greek philosopher once said, "I cannot play upon any stringed instrument; but I can tell you how of a little village to make a great and glorious city". He paused, looking at the upturned faces. David thought instantly and incongruously of his banjo. 'The Little Village Where I Come' was a southern work song. He had not touched the instrument in years, it seemed. The Governor continued.

'This little village,' and here he gestured about him with his right hand extended, 'has everything it needs to become great and glorious. It has wealth in its land, its people and its future. The march of civilization will not be stopped, nor will the lawful intentions of Her Royal Majesty's pleasure, as reflected through his duly appointed servants. In consequence, we expect order, justice, and prosperity.

'Justice is a relation of congruity between two things,' he borrowed from Montesquieu, 'and that relationship is always the same, whatever being considers it, whether it be God, or an angel, or lastly a man. And you, gentlemen of Red River, may choose to set yourselves up as gods or supreme arbiters of the truth, but you do no justice. You only exert will, by force of might. And so that relationship, the one between community and citizen, is seriously impaired, and it cannot be justice.

'I see what you intend. I doubt that my words can dissuade you; perhaps these words can.' He raised his eyes as David had seen him do the previous day. The man was going to rely on poetry to divert a mob! Dallas spoke again, his voice loud, emotional, determined.

> *The days of the nations bear no trace*
> *Of all the sunshine so far foretold;*
> *The cannon speaks in the teacher's place—*

And here he paused, glaring down at schoolmaster Stewart who stood brazenly with the other petitioners, though a little shamefaced as he felt the heat of Dallas' pointed stare. Lifting his gaze again, the Governor continued, with renewed passion:

> *The age is weary with work and gold,*
> *And high hopes wither, and memories wane;*
> *On hearths and alters the fires are dead*
> *But that brave faith hath not lived in vain—*
> *And this is all our watcher said.*

He looked down at them, silent. 'The faith that hath made this settlement grow and prosper, let it not be in vain.'

There was an exquisite tension; David could feel it. He could feel it the same way that he had been swept by Dallas's considerable gifts of persuasion earlier. Others in the crowd felt it as well; he could tell, for there was that sympathetic resonance one felt in commitment to a common goal, or an idea suddenly made clear. That moment Governor Dallas rendered discordant with a single act: he tore the petition apart in a vainglorious gesture of triumph. Folding and ripping, refolding and tearing again, he cast down the bits of paper in a flutter.

It was as a match to powder. With a cry of outrage, Hallett swung about, Ross with him, and called upon the others to march upon the lockup. David sprinted back to the guards, all of whom had heard the gasp from the mob, and their sudden grumbling march on the gaol. He snatched up his gun, and turned to face the crowd. It was a bright day, and he could see their faces clearly. These were men he knew, men who had plenty of business dealings with him. He could not aim his weapon at them, but he held it at an angle across his body, as if it were a shield. Those in front raised their guns; he could hear a rattle of metallic clicking behind him as the Métis cocked their own weapons. Jesus in Heaven! Was it come to this, that he should be shot down in the mud for a cause he did not embrace, for a man he barely knew, for nothing? He was a merchant, not a guard or a soldier, or even a buffalo hunter any more. He had not a single shell in the trade rifle he was holding.

In the long pause that followed the two groups came nearly toe to toe. David thought of that long-ago moment in Baltimore, when he had looked out over the city to the harbour, from the top of the Washington monument. Surely this was what heaven was like: one would sit with the angels, looking out over the world as God had permitted man to make it. Maybe it wasn't heaven, but certainly a vision of the world as it would be. One day, Red River would be like Baltimore; it was inevitable. Yet that day seemed far away when his neighbours now seemed intent on destroying each other over an adulterous priest. He was glad that these Métis were the merchants and farmers from St Boniface. Their leader, François Bruneau, was an intelligent, careful man, who could speak passionately, yet who exercised the traditional command and discipline of the hunt—though to David's knowledge, Bruneau had never actually been on a single hunt. Thank God that there were none of the tripmen and boat crews from St Norbert and St Vital: Mary's family, Yves Sayer and his wild friends. The first shot would've been fired by now, regardless whether the Governor had promised them there would be no fighting.

McKenny lowered his weapon. Speaking loudly, though with a faint tremor, he called out. 'Take the prisoner! There will be no resistance! But lower your arms!'

Murmuring excitedly, arms still at the ready, the crowd moved forward. The cell door yielded under the crush of men, and Stewart was broken from custody to loud cheers and gunshots in the air. At the first report, David jumped, but it was clear the mood had changed from one of grim determination to one of festivity and self-congratulation.

As two men neared, David heard but could not determine who said, 'There's that bastard Bloode. I'll be damned if I'll buy another stick from him.' Hallett came to him directly, 'Turn powder and shot against your own people, will you?' He spat and turned away in disgust. It was apparent in the faces of all those who passed him; exuberance turning momentarily to disdain. David had chosen, but chosen badly yet again. That night, he fought with Mary, slapping the woman who was carrying his child hard enough that she did not get up for a time. When she crept to his bed, there was blood under her nose. He could taste it on her lip when he turned to her.

viii

At a point on the Red River, about twelve miles above the Forks, the banks were steep enough that they were overrun by the spring flood only rarely. Feeding from the east into the main current was a small tributary known as Oak Creek, so named for the scrubby thick copses of oak trees that lined the banks there. It was the site David had chosen to build a mill; it was one of the last unspoiled spots suited to such an undertaking. He had purchased it for seventy-five dollars from an old Métis who was related to his wife's family.

Once out of the scrub at the water's edge, the property opened up on open prairie on the opposite side of the river. By late May the lea was densely covered with big bluestem, switch, bunchgrass and Indian grass, high as a man's waist. Broad-leafed goldenrod, blazing stars and asters gave texture and contrast to the slender grasses. Purple prairie clover hugged the ground, sending its thick roots deep into the soil. Liatris, a delicate shade of lighter purple, added contrast to yellow sunflowers, avens and dandelions. Pale roses, breadroot, golden sneezeweed, white yarrow and panic grass contributed their fervour to the pandemonium of colour and life on the open prairie sod.

It was to this spot that Mary would escape with Yves Sayer soon after Byron was born. There was a rough-planked boat for common use, which leaked so badly that one was required to bail with a wooden scoop while the other pulled on the oars. She would leave the little red-haired boy with her relative at St Norbert, and steal away to this place of peace, now owned by her husband. It was only with Yves that she was truly happy, for her husband had become increasingly remote from her, though he was besotted with his son.

One afternoon she was out on the riverbank with Yves. They had coupled in the deep grass, and Mary luxuriated in the warmth of the sun on her bare legs and buttocks. All about her hummed and buzzed with busy insects; in the oak groves jays called, buntings trilled, and a woodpecker drummed a staccato beat against a dead limb. Closer to the water, red-winged blackbirds beyond number raised a clatter with their sharp cries. Waterfowl wheeled and returned to the turgid surface of the creek. Mary was startled as a pair of ducks on creaking wings passed low overhead.

'What's the matter,' chuckled Sayer. 'Do you think your husband has sent water birds to spy on you?'

Mary turned and fell back to the worn robe they were lying on, laid over their bed of crushed grass. She liked being with Yves; he was simple and undemanding. He had no desire to marry; he put few demands on her, was an attentive lover, and spoke only when she said something to him. She had known him since she was a child, and she felt utterly comfortable with him. She spoke, almost dreamily. 'My husband has no interest in me; he couldn't care less that I am lying with another.'

Yves was silent. She broke off a piece of meadow blazing star and chewed at the stem absently. He looked at her without moving, hands clasped behind his head. 'We give that weed to the horses to give them speed and stamina,' he snickered. 'So that is your secret!'

She made a face, gently whipping him with the purple bloom. 'No. Listen to me. For the past year, he has been striking me when he is angry. He seems angry often enough these days, though I know not why.' She added,'He has nothing to do with me, mostly.'

Sayer appeared to ponder her remarks, though she could not be sure. Finally, he uttered a short, spare sentence, as was his manner. 'He does not respect you.'

She looked at him sharply. 'You think he knows of us?'

'If he doesn't, he's the only one at Fort Garry that does not.'

She sank back again, letting the air whistle past her lips. 'What do you mean, that he doesn't respect me?' She was more than a little offended by this. A distant fear gnawed at her, but she could not identify it. Conversation with this man was not something she encouraged, for she did not believe him to be perceptive.

'You're a hard woman, Mary Bloode. I only put up with you 'cause I take no shit from you. But there's...there's not a kindness in you. I suppose we're two of the same sort. Out for ourselves.'

'Not a kindness in me?' she demanded, knowing his assessment was true. 'What do you expect of one raised as I have been?'

Sayer opened one eye. 'What has your raising to do with this?'

Mary felt sick to her stomach. She was nauseated by the thought of her father. He was a cruel man who worked his children like slaves, and beat them unmercifully. He would come to her bed after her mother became ill; it was he who showed her how to protect herself from his seed.

She loved him, and she hated him for taking away something that was beyond her comprehension to understand. She had withdrawn into herself and became hardened, her cynicism fitting snugly over her like a carapace. David's relationship with her was becoming increasingly like that she had with her father. And she was afraid.

'My father beat me,' she said simply.

He was unmoved. 'My father beat me. So what?'

'There is more to it…he was…he was…' Sayer looked up at her, surprised at this hitherto unseen show of emotion.

'He was…indecent with me.' Silent tears rolled down her cheeks. Sayer looked at her with something approaching astonishment. He had never seen her reveal her feelings in this way, let alone cry. It unnerved him. Was this like marriage?

Mary herself was bewildered. She had always kept her demons in their place; why here, and now, on this sun-splashed embankment, would the events of a sullied childhood tear down the curtains of what for her was a closed room? Sayer's remark about her lack of kindness penetrated deeply, though he did not mean it as she took it. It was true. She cared for no one but herself, and she felt it was too late for her.

Insight moves slowly, with many setbacks and false starts. The path to self-comprehension is travelled in small steps, for understanding is revealed only reluctantly by the competing traits of pride, vanity, and ambition. Though permanent insight is gained only by incremental stages, it often takes a significant event for the process to begin. For Mary, that event was nothing more than an off-hand remark by her companion, which caught her at a time when she was reflective and content. Her guard down, Mary Daniel truly regretted that she did not love, and was unloved.

Sayer was anxious to jolly her up. 'Say, did he leave marks? When he beat you, I mean. Show me. I want proof, for I have never seen any such marks!'

She looked at him, perplexed. 'You don't believe me?'

'I've known you since you were a child. I've never seen a mark on you that I remember. You've never said anything about this before. Come. Where are the marks?'

She sat up, sniffling, pulling her skirts onto her lap. 'Help me with these,' she said, as she raised her arms. He jumped to his feet and pulled her bodice and dress over her head, carrying her undershirt with them. He threw the garments carelessly to one side, and looked at her hungrily; she was completely naked before him, except for a thin chain around her neck, from which dangled a small crucifix. Bowing her head, she pulled aside her long dark hair, and bade him examine her back.

'Below my shoulder blade, this side, you'll see thin white lines, four of them. Now below, over my hips, here, there are four or five more faint stripes, almost exactly the same.

'And here.' She lifted herself to her knees. 'How you have missed these, all these years?' she pointed to a succession of pale white lines on the sides of her hips and her buttocks. 'He used a willow rod, peeled, as thick as his thumb.' She shuddered at the recollection.

Sayer ran his fingers along the indistinct scars, then kissed them. 'I did not know,' he mumbled, the excitement building in him. She had never been wholly undressed outdoors before, and it aroused him intensely. For her part, the sun felt good on her bare skin, and the eager, snuffling attentions of her lover helped ease the pain she was feeling. She succumbed to her own arousal, and as they cleaved together, she cried out to him. 'Say you care for me; speak to me of your affections for me!'

But Sayer could only groan in his urgency, as he held his face tightly against her tear-dampened cheek.

When David began to be worried about the title to his land at the forks of the Oak Creek and the Red River, he wasn't sure. Ownership of land was an issue of long standing, though it did not cause much anxiety until after the middle of the century. In 1857, the great Ojibway Chief Peguis, benefactor of the Selkirk settlers, sent a letter to the Aborigines Protection Society in London, on the issue of non-fulfillment of the treaty he and others had executed with Lord Selkirk in 1817. In the letter, Peguis complained that the land grant was made on the basis of a 'small quantity of ammunition and tobacco which in the first instance we took as preliminary to a final bargain about our lands.'

In March of 1859 Peguis dictated another letter. Part of it read: '…We never sold our lands to the said Company, nor to the Earl of Selkirk; and yet the said Company mark out and sell our lands without our permission. Is this right?' Even Hind, whose expedition to Red River was to explore the region with an eye to eventual colonization, recognized the merits of Peguis's claim to the land. In his optimistic reports to Canada, he wrote that '…it is clearly evident that the subject (of title) will require close investigation and prompt action in order to avoid troublesome disputes. It is also apparent that the calls of humanity, the interests of the new colony, and the claims of the Indians, imperatively demand that the natives should be paid for their lands…'

These commentaries, among others, excited anxious debate in the settlement, and in 1861, there was a large public meeting, at which the whole business of land ownership was discussed with passion. Many of the holdings outside the narrow strip originally obtained by Lord Selkirk were maintained solely on the basis of squatter's rights. It was the practice upon transfer to pay only for the improvements, such as clearing, tillage, and buildings. As David commenced to build his weir, and lay the foundations for his mill, he too became concerned about the security of his own tenure, should Rupert's Land be annexed to Canada, as seemed the likely outcome.

Many of the gold-seekers bound for the Cariboo had stopped permanently at Red River, settling on land which, by improvements made, they took to be their own. Americans fleeing the troubles with the Sioux, easterners, immigrants from Eastern Europe and Scandinavia— there were enough of these who saw the fertile soil of the Red River Valley as a place where their dreams could take root and their families flourish. While this was good for David's business, it raised the threat that land ownership eventually would have to be resolved, but on whose terms? And David had it in mind that he would build a house near his mill, on a grassy embankment overlooking the sweep of the river. Could he be certain that title would survive annexation?

The course of a man's life could be affected by events both immediate and remote, as David well knew from his own experience. The footsteps of a statesman, or the stumbling of a fool could be perceived from a world away sometimes as one and the same thing. Responses to occurrences which diffuse through the twin lenses of distance and self-interest, given the right sequence of circumstances, could fundamentally change perceptions, divert one's energies from a particular course. So it was with the life of a people, a community or a nation. Reactions invariably tell more about those who respond, and in the manner of it, than that which seemed to trigger events in the first place.

The future of the British North-west was far from a settled question. The Hudson's Bay Company, which had purchased back its grant to Lord Selkirk in 1836 (without prejudice to the claims of those who had taken title from the well-intentioned Earl), had enjoyed a virtual monopoly in most trade matters, since the amalgamation with the North West Company in 1821. Its corporate attempts to dissuade settlement bore no subtlety; as late as 1857, Sir George Simpson, Governor of Rupert's Land, who had spent all of his professional life in the fur trade, was called upon to defend a further extension of the Company's licence to trade exclusively in the North-Western Territory. The licence would otherwise lapse in 1859.

Sir George appeared before the Select Committee of the House of Commons set up to determine whether the northern regions which were the near-private preserve of the Company could support any other commercial or Imperial possibilities beyond the harvest of fur. The Chairman of the Committee, a dour, flushed-face septuagenarian, demanded of him whether the district at the Forks and beyond were capable of supporting a colony of the Crown. Drawing his lower lip tightly, the good knight's demeanor was the image of reluctant concession:

'A population thinly scattered along the banks might support themselves, but a dense population could not live in that country; the country would not afford the means of subsistence...' Other descriptions of the lands west of the Red River Valley left an image of an inhospitable wasteland. This report was in sharp contrast to the many laudatory depictions he had made on previous occasions. Sir George was not cross-examined from any particular knowledge base, and his dismal account stood for the time being.

The Select Committee decided that the licence should be extended, and the matter of the future of the fledgling colony at Red River and its acquisition by Canada was left unsettled, save for a well-intended but vague recommendation that the annexation should take place on equitable principles. Even less helpful was the recommendation that the boundary between Rupert's Land and Canada be 'solved by amicable adjustment'.

But the interest by Canada in the territories was evident by the keen interest of their observer at the hearings, Chief Justice William Henry Draper: 'Sweet William' as he was known, for his eloquence. When his opportunity came to address the Committee, he said, 'I hope you will not laugh at me as very visionary, but I hope to see the time, or that my children may see the time, when there is a railway going all across that country and ending at the Pacific; and so far as individual opinion goes, I entertain no doubt that the time will arrive when that will be accomplished.'

Hind's expedition in 1857, and the exploration by Captain John Palliser, fuelled more curiosity in Rupert's Land as a place of enormous potential for settlement. But there was intense American interest as well. In ten years, the Minnesota territories had gone from barely five thousand people to more than one hundred and seventy-five thousand. The Sioux uprising in 1862 dampened enthusiasm for a time, but it was recognized that pressure on the border would soon give way, particularly where the territory beyond was administered solely by a commercial interest. Already American traders and hunters, pedlars and other itinerants were moving freely through the land, with scant regard for borders. There was insufficient force to lend proper authority to the administrators at Fort Garry, let alone enforce actions far out on the plains; open ranges were transversed only by a fictional barrier raised on the forty-ninth parallel.

This was a time of expansionist rhetoric and determination in America. While the Select Committee was nattering over the future of Rupert's Land, William Seward negotiated the purchase of Alaska from Russia. The civil war brought fresh reason to seize British territory, for the British had been sympathetic to the Southern cause. Following the war, a series of suits were made against the British government, which came to be known as the 'Alabama Claims'. In sum, these demands were the result of Confederate warships which were fitted out or received and supplied in British ports, in alleged violation of principles of international law. At the time that each offending act came to light, it fostered enormous anti-British sentiment in the northern states, and there were many whose eyes turned to the limitless reaches of Rupert's Land as a means of exacting compensation.

As late as 1868, the St Paul Chamber of Commerce emphatically declared the inevitability of accretion to America of all those lands between Alaska and Minnesota, with the result that the western boundary of Canada would be fixed on the ninetieth meridian of longtitude, somewhere east of the western tip of Lake Superior. The Minnesota Pioneer carried an inflated declaration purporting to reflect prevailing sentiment at the Forks:

'Their inhabitants, largely emigrants from the United States, will never consent to be transferred by Parliamentary edict and without a popular vote to the distant and feeble Confederation of Canada.' The St Paul Daily Press, read regularly at Fort Garry, suggested that the transfer of Rupert's Land to Canada should be objected to, and that the London Cabinet should get '...a gentle hint that the course talked of over there is not at all compatible with the common understanding of good neighbourhood'. This was in large measure true. The ties between St Paul and Fort Garry were by now in fact far greater than those with Upper or Lower Canada, or with Great Britain. Linkages such as that forged between David and his American partner Edwin Bell personified the closeness of interest between the two centres. The streets of St Paul were initially comparable with those developing at Fort Garry. Commerce between the two cities was increasing, as was the flow of settlers to their respective regions. The itinerant mixed-bloods who had dominated this part of the world for nearly one hundred years were of the same stock and, indeed, were just as likely to have been born on one side of the border as the other. Notions of citizenship and boundaries that had no relationship to the land were repellant to the frontier imagination and, to the extent that civil authorities could be avoided, they were ignored.

There were other uncertainties in the future of the colony. In 1859, an organization of Irishmen in the United States formed linkages with like-minded zealots in Great Britain to take action which they hoped would lead to the independence of Ireland. They took the name first applied to a tribe of warriors known for their prowess in battle. Their greatest chieftain was Finn MacCumhail, who died in 285 AD. So great was his renown in Irish annals that these Gaelic fighting men were henceforth called 'Feinne', 'Fiana', or 'Fenians'. Their first congress met in Chicago in 1863, the order having been constituted upon republican principles, but retaining in all substantial respects the identity of the Irish Revolutionary Brotherhood formed the previous year in Dublin. By no means unanimous, there was sufficient support within the society to urge an invasion of the British provinces, to be used as a base of operations against the hated British.

On 2 June 1866, under a self-styled general by the name of John O'Neill, a force of eight hundred Fenians invaded Canada near Fort Erie. After a short engagement they withdrew, though the Canadians under Lieutenant-Colonel John Stoughton Dennis disgraced themselves. At the Colonel's urging, he was brought before a board of inquiry which concluded that there was no cowardice on his part, though dreadful misjudgement, disorganization and error was shown. Dennis was Chief Surveyor of Public Lands in Ontario, however, and his name would surface in connection with Red River and David Bloode's fortunes more directly in less than four years. Two days after the debacle at Fort Erie, an army of irregulars more than twice the size of the first invasion struck at the Eastern Townships, but after several days of looting and harassment, they retired to the United States once again. There were other threats and provocations along the border for the next several years, which kept tensions unrelieved on the Canadian side, as well as at Fort Garry.

The extreme vulnerability of the settlement at Red River was cause for concern by most citizens, including David. As a merchant and land-owner, he was anxious about the prospect of an invasion by fanatics. The stories of their plunder and destruction at Frelighsburg and St Armand quickly reached Fort Garry. It was the eastern shopowners and businessmen who took the brunt of the invading forces. What couldn't be carried off was put to the torch. Only the presence of the Métis and their Halfbreed cousins at Red River, who could be quickly mobilized, served as a deterrent for an invading force. The reputation of the mixed-bloods as fierce fighters, skilled horsemen, and formidable shots while mounted and galloping at a fast pace was well known in the North-west, and was the subject of considerable discussion in the taverns and wayside inns where Fenians gathered to plot their cause. This daunting reputation did not, however, prevent an attempted invasion which was to occur in October, 1871.

In 1867 the four British provinces were united in a federal Dominion by the British North America Act. This statute, which formed part of the Constitution of Canada, had a provision for the entry of Rupert's Land into the union. Almost immediately, resolutions were introduced in Parliament for an Address to the Imperial Crown, which would result in the transfer of the possessions of the Hudson's Bay Company to Canada, in advance of settlement of terms. Outstanding matters could then be submitted to the courts for arbitration. The Company remonstrated vigorously against such a course of action, for they had been assured that continued negotiation was a sufficient reason to ignore other overtures, especially from the Americans. After all, the territory would be just compensation for the Alabama Claims, and it was rumoured that five million dollars would be transferred to the Company's coffers by the American Treasury, in return for a relinquishment of title. Even private capitalists were putting forth proposals for North-western development, together with lucrative offers laid before the Company's directors. Strong opposition, therefore, was maintained by the Company to the proposed course of action by the Canadian government. The most vociferous objections came from the wintering partners: the old officers who held no shares, but received an annual apportionment of the profits. The Canadian approach was not accepted by the British government, though terms were eventually established by the Company. Though these in turn were rejected, the Imperial Parliament went ahead and passed an enabling statute for the transfer of Rupert's Land. The Crown Colony idea had fallen by the wayside, as desire for empire waned under the staggering burden to the taxpayer for the maintenance of far-flung outposts.

With a new British government in place in 1869, the Hudson's Bay Company was pushed into a settlement. There were not much in the way of options for them, given events in the United States and the obstinacy of the Canadian delegation. A deal was eventually struck, and the terms of surrender of territory fixed for 1 October 1869, later moved back to the first of December.

The key player in these deliberations on the Canadian side was the ambitious, visionary William McDougall, lawyer, sometime journalist, Liberal member of Parliament from North Ontario (later North Lanark), and patron of Johnathan Snow. Well-spoken but far too clever, and single-minded of purpose, he was disliked by his colleagues and by his leader in the coalition government, Sir John A. Macdonald. Once the arrangements for the annexation of Rupert's Land were finalized, it was quickly determined that the most useful function for the energetic forty-seven-year-old was the post of first Lieutenant-Governor of Rupert's Land. Stories persisted that the House was delighted to be rid of McDougall, for by all accounts he was insensitive to others, as well as abrupt and imperious in manner.

Upon his arrival at St Paul, he was seen by several tripmen from Fort Garry, all of whom had heard of the impending transfer of land to Canada, a transaction completed without their consultation or participation. McDougall made no secret of his destination and plans; he was eager to be in Fort Garry for the official date of annexation. He had celebrations to organize, and the terms of the 'Act For The Temporary Government Of Rupert's Land' were to be fulfilled by his directives. Accompanied by his Attorney-General, Chief of Police, Chief Customs Collector, and a motley array of followers and handlers, he arranged for the transfer of his goods and equipment of office to a brigade of almost sixty carts.

It was cold on the Crow-Wing trail, and though the screeching of the ox-carts was a comical novelty at first, it soon became an irritation for the Governor-designate. Added to this was the painfully tedious pace of the caravan. They were frequently passed by riders heading north, though each slowed to take in all the detail of the grand procession. He reached Pembina on 30 October 1869. By then it had started to snow, and McDougall had much to complain about to the American customs official who was indifferently reviewing documents brusquely handed to him. While he stamped his booted feet on the rough boards of the customs house, a scruffy, bearded man approached him, doffing his fur cap, and mumbling a greeting, or so it seemed. He offered McDougall a slip of paper, and stepped back to the three others who had accompanied him.

McDougall peered at the note, then exploded. 'Of all the damned presumption! Are you ragamuffins seriously suggesting that you will impede my progress at this point? I will have the names of all of you immediately, and I shall have the lot thrown behind bars! This is bloody outrageous! I won't have it!' He cast the paper upon the floor, and stamped upon it, his face red with anger.

'Go tell your bastard Halfbreed superiors that this is more than an affront to Her Majesty's lawful governance; it is damned close to treason! Tell them as well that I shall continue with my undertaking as I originally planned, your concurrence be damned!'

As the four men backed out of the tiny shack, the customs official picked up the note; soiled as it was by McDougall's boots, it was nonetheless legible:

St Norbert, Rivière Rouge,
ce 21e jour d'octobre, 1869

A Monsieur McDougall

Monsieur: Le Comité National des Métis de la Rivière Rouge intime à Monsieur McDougall l'ordre de ne pas entrer sur le Territoire du Nord-Ouest sans une permission spéciale de ce Comité.

Par ordre du président
John Bruce

Louis Riel, sécretaire

Ten

i

Had the squeaking floor awakened anyone? Louis froze, looking back at the figures lying still in the gloom of the darkened dormitory. No one moved save for the restless fidgeting of the sleeping; Louis exhaled slowly, and moved stealthily toward the window. He could feel the cool breeze caress his face as he stooped to raise the sash. Like a thief, he was over the sill and out, dropping easily to the shrubbery beds some six feet below. Confident that his exit had gone undetected, he sprinted away from the shadows of the College of the Sulpician Fathers, across the grounds and out through the unlocked gates of the heavily walled institution. The Petit Séminaire, as it was known, stood like a solemn fortress on College Street, a little to the west of McGill. From there, it was a twenty-minute brisk walk to the hotel district, Lumkin's, Prendergast's, Moore's, where the lights and music drew crowds of young men and brash, boldly dressed women to drink wine and ale and eat sweet cakes until the small hours of the morning.

The educational program at the College, French classics of the seventeenth century, Molière and LaFontaine; the ancient Greek philosophers, languages, and theology, hardly prepared graduates for anything of consequence in later life. But what such endeavours did produce was a powerful sense of cultural pride and a fierce religiosity. More, it made for passionate debaters, and hopelessly romantic poets and dreamers. The fleshpots of Montréal were not just lures for the debauched; they were the gathering places for students and lovers, immigrants and opportunists, visionaries and writers, all of whom revelled in the very worth of living.

As Louis jogged effortlessly along McGill Street, just inside the walls of the old fortified city, he fought with himself as he did each time he left the

College. To carry on in such a manner would surely be condemned by his instructors or his father's sister and her husband, John and Lucie Lee of Mile End. He felt that what he was doing was not sin in itself; it was merely an exploration of life at its shadowy edges. True, he had been engaging in prideful debates with non-Catholics. He had succumbed to the vanity of writing poetry for the purpose of public recitation, albeit to a small mob of critical fellows, well in their cups. He had even been tempted by the pleasures of the flesh, as the 'social ladies' pressed their attentions upon him. He smiled at this, for he was satisfied that his dark, brooding good looks were attractive to women, and this pleased him. Still he was not entirely comfortable with the notion of sexuality; more than anything else, his parents had pressed upon him the virtues of celibacy until marriage. What discomfited him most of all was the inherent dishonesty of stealing away in the night like a common footpad. Though no lies were necessary to be told—yet, it was perilously close to sinning by omission.

Crossing Notre Dame, and swerving to miss a cariole being driven with far too many inebriated passengers, he continued east and thought of the last time he had seen his father. With a twinge, he realized that he had not written for several months; his mother would be upset about that, and his father would express a quiet, understated disappointment. He could see the pursed lips, the frowning disapproval even now. He had to get a letter off.

It was in early June of 1858 that he and two other Métis boys, Louis Schmidt and Daniel McDougall, had been selected by Bishop Alexandre Taché to be sent from Red River to Montréal for further education. Expenses were to be borne by the College and wealthy patrons of the Church. The object in Taché's mind was to supply the vast North-west with an indigenous missionary corps. It had taken almost a month to reach St Paul by cart brigade, but quite fortuitously Louis had run into his father at the ferry on the Mississippi River. Louis Riel, Senior, briefly brought to prominence in the Sayer affair over free trade almost a decade ago, was a frustrated man. He was returning from Montréal, where he had been attempting to obtain milling equipment and financial assistance for yet another commercial venture. The outcome of his efforts was uncertain at this point, and the disconsolate father greeted his exuberant fourteen-year-old son as the paths of their lives crossed; for the last time, as it would turn out.

Schmidt and McDougall stood off at a distance, respectfully, while Louis conversed with his father. From a short distance, one could tell the difference in the two: Louis was animated, jumping up, then striding about, then sitting again. His father threw small stones down the muddy bank, making tiny splashes in the turbid water. Otherwise, he did not move, only to meet his son's eyes occasionally.

'I hope you understand, my son, that I have high hopes for your future?'

'Of course, father. I shall do everything within my power, by God's grace, to do you honour, to achieve as you have.'

'Alas,' said the elder Riel. 'I have not achieved much in my life, beyond the production of fine children.'

Louis jumped up at this. 'Oh no, father!' he cried. 'It was you who inspired the overthrow of that colossus of iniquities, the Company which ruled us! The name Louis Riel will resound in the history of the Northwest. Everyone says so.' In his heart, Louis knew that his father had never recovered from a bitter attack in the *Nor'Wester*.

The affair had to do with the obstinate clergyman Corbett. He wrote numerous letters to the paper in 1861 complaining that the Council of Assiniboia, the ruling body constituted by the Company, was recording the participation of Bishop Taché as 'Lord' Bishop, a dignity afforded only on royal prerogative. He believed all this to be part of a Papist plot to put Catholics in the ascendancy. A priest came to the defence of the Bishop by writing in turn to the editor, a fervent Protestant by the name of James Ross. The newspaper published the letter, notwithstanding that it was to have remained confidential, and pilloried the priest for a 'not very clerical stance'. Louis' father's sense of fair play was offended, and he wrote to Ross to support the priest, Father William Oram. Ross, displaying the partisan mischief for which he was known, translated the letter into stilted English. He titled the piece, 'A Cure for the Blues', observing that 'if the translation shocks the grammar of our readers, we assure them that it is at all events a great improvement on the original...which would be considered a rare curiosity in any museum.'

But these snide remarks paled beside what was written next:

'How is it that such a one comes forward as Mr Oram's champion? Is he head man among the French people? We regard as leading men the Bruneaus, the Hamlins, the Marions, the Gentons, the Ducharmes, the Fishers, the Deases, the Brélands, and Delormes, and many others too numerous to mention. These are the principal men and they are a credit to the Settlement. But as for L. Riel; pray who or what is he?'

This attack on his reputation wounded Louis' father, and by reflection, Louis himself. He would speak bravely about it, observing wryly that public opinion is only what we think other people think, but he never took another public stand. The anti-Catholic support Ross gave to Corbett was a dragon's tooth firmly planted in young Louis's outlook; the pain it caused his father scarred the son.

Louis put his hand on his father's shoulder, lightly, like a small bird coming to rest. Their fondness for one another had never been physical. 'Father, I know whereof I speak. Your name is already legend among our people.'

His father showed his teeth in a wan smile. 'My part in the pursuit of justice was a small one. But it did not contribute a single shilling toward the debt I owed—and still owe—to the Company. It will be for you to pick up the torch, and keep it alight with God's word. This is why you and your companions have been chosen to go away to study, 'to perceive the words of understanding', and 'to the young man understanding and discretion'.

'And I will hear, and will increase learning, and attain unto wise counsel!' cried Louis as he completed the next verse from Proverbs.

His father was pleased.'You know your scriptures well,' he said, standing up, for the ferry was returning and his own trip could not be further delayed. 'You must keep diligently at your studies, and write often to us.' Looking absently at the ferry as it was being drawn up and secured, he murmured, 'Your absence will be a wound to your mother, balmed only by the thought that you will return to do God's work. He has important work for you; of that we are all sure.'

Turning back to his son, his eyes misted, and he recited another verse from the same chapter. 'My son, hear the instruction of thy father, and forsake not the law of thy mother.' Bidding farewell to the other boys, he turned and was gone. Louis stood at the bank until his father had crossed and, with a wave, disappeared from view.

Louis remembered the crush of loneliness he felt for the next few days after the encounter. It was counterpoised with the enormous pressure he felt was being placed upon him. Everyone expected so much. Bishop Taché himself had told him he was a man with a mission in life, and that by adherence to God's word he would not, could not falter. Louis was very gloomy for a time after that, and neither of the other boys could cheer him up. He felt as if the excitement of the adventure they were on had been stolen from him. He loved his father deeply, but did he always have to remind him of the serious side of life?

Rounding a corner, he almost collided with a man in a new fur-trimmed coat. 'Be careful, you oaf!' he cried in English, then broke off laughing as he realized it was Robert Simoneau, a friend from the college.

'What are you doing here? I thought you had been quarantined!' Simoneau had been caught two days before trying to sneak back into the dormitory, and had been sent to the isolated room, which had no bed nor furnishings of any kind, as punishment. Yet here he was again.

'Waiting for you!' he laughed. 'We thought you'd never get here! What kept you? The Black Friar?' The night warden was not highly regarded.

Louis looked beyond him for the friend he had expected to meet, Brendan Béaloideas, adopted son of an Irish lumber pedlar, one of the few who had become extremely rich. Béaloideas's parents, fleeing the successive failures of the potato crops in Ireland, had both died of ship fever, as typhus was known, in 1847, barely days after landing in Montréal. Unknown and unnamed, they were but two of thousands of dead hauled from the twenty-two 'fever sheds' and buried in a mass grave near the entrance to Victoria Bridge. The boy remembered nothing of it, though he had been told how he had been found crawling among the corpses by the Anglican Reverend Mark Willoughby, first Rector of Trinity Anglican Church, who was working in the sheds with the heroic Grey Nuns. Willoughby would die of the plague within the month.

Whether it was this grisly story or not, Béaloideas was fascinated with death and dying; mortality formed a central theme to his discussions and debate. Louis was intrigued by Béaloideas. Though he was as committed to his religious studies as Louis, he was more ready to challenge the precepts of his faith. Simoneau regarded him with some cynicism, for 'faith was just that: faith. You either believe, or you don't. How else can God enter your heart?' For him it was simple, but he too contributed a perspective to their arguments, which grew heated as the night wore on, and the ale jar emptied.

Béaloideas grabbed Louis' arm. 'No! We're not going in there just now. I'm taking the both of you somewhere, and it'll have to remain a surprise!'

Simoneau snorted. 'What—a graveyard? Come on, I'm thirsty. I took a very great risk to get here, don't you know?'

But Béaloideas would not be put off, and he led the other two on a long walk to the eastern suburb of the city, where there was a high proportion of Irish. Threading his way between the darkened alleyways, he came by and by to a low house, and pushed his way through a small knot of people, disappearing inside. Louis and Simoneau looked at each other, and followed him in.

Just ahead, Béaloideas was shaking hands and offering small words of sympathy in a room lighted only by a small guttering lamp, and an array of candles on the mantel. Past him, the corpse of an elderly man, neatly shaved and dressed in a fine suit, was laid out on the 'hag-bed' by the fireplace. The front room of the modest home was crowded with noisy well-wishers, and the kitchen and two side rooms were filled to capacity with people. The smoke from dozens of pipes and the warm evening made the air very close, what with the sharp tang of men's sweat, boiling mutton, and the stale odour of spilled beer.

Catching up to their friend, Simoneau exclaimed in a low voice, 'What have you brought us to, man? A private funeral service? Or should I say,' he said looking around, 'a party that somehow ended up at the wrong address?' Louis was wide-eyed.

'What, good fellows, you have never been to a waking of the dead?' cried Béaloideas, much to their embarrassment. 'Come, fill your mugs with beer, and let us pay our respects to the living and the dead!'

At this point an odd-looking man squeezed in, and approached the body. His ears stuck out, and his face had the look of a simpleton. Kneeling, he recited prayers loudly in front of the deceased. Upon completion, he was about to rise, when a man called out, 'Say your prayers again, Sean, we didna hear ye!' And so he did. A call went out by another to repeat his homily, and the simple man obliged. This went on for some time, with the snickers breaking into laughter, until the whole room convulsed with merriment at the poor fellow's mindless repetitions.

More people had come by this time, and it was getting hard to move about. Revellers began to jostle one another, and compete forcefully for the few seats available. Then one man was struck on the back of the head with a potato. Turning sharply, he cried out to the throng. 'Awright! Who's the barstard wif a sense a humour?' Only to be answered by a shower of spuds, which were quickly snatched up and flung back with no particular target in mind. In the dimly lit room, it was not easy to pick out the initial culprits, nor did this seem to be a priority. Very quickly, everything that could come to hand became a missile, as the gathering degenerated with much laughter and calling out. The dead man, candlelight winking in his halo of curly white hair, remained serene, his hands clasped firmly over his bosom, even when his resting place was heavily jarred by a pair of roistering mourners.

All this seemed horrifying and disrespectful to Louis. What if this was his own father, God forbid! And here was the widow, sitting and chatting, to the extent that one could in such a setting, seemingly taking no notice of a mob that was on the verge of wrecking her home. When the singing began, it was not the hymns he would have expected; not the reverential choir one would have thought appropriate at such an event, but bawdy grog-shop tunes and sea shanties, sung at the top of the lungs, with much foot-stamping and clapping of hands. The floor was becoming awash with beer. It was time to go, in Louis's opinion. Simoneau agreed, and together they hauled Béaloideas by the arms outside to the street. As they walked back in silence, it was the better part of a mile before the sounds of revelry faded.

Louis scratched his head under his thick mop of hair. 'I find it hard to believe that people could show such disrespect for the dead.'

Béaloideas danced a few steps ahead of them, and started to sing.

> *Deal on, deal on, my merry men all,*
> *Deal on your cakes and your wine;*
> *For whatever is dealt at this funeral today,*
> *Shall be dealt tomorrow at mine!*

The other two looked at each other again: had he gone mad? Béaloideas sauntered back to them. 'Look here,' he said. 'I brought both of you here for a purpose.' He smiled condescendingly at his friends. 'What did you think?'

Simoneau frowned. 'Vulgar, disrespectful. Seemed almost happy he's gone.' Louis nodded in agreement.

Béaloideas seemed surprised. 'Vulgar? What would you have said if they'd hoisted dear old departed Jack Flanigan to the floor and danced with him, as some used to do, I'm told?' He chuckled at the thought of it, and grabbed Louis by the arms, and swung him around in a madcap tarantella. Louis shrugged him off, grinning in spite of himself.

Simoneau flipped his hat off. 'Brendan, sometimes I think you're crazy as a cockroach.'

Béaloideas was suddenly serious, walking backwards facing the others. 'Do you two believe in death as the final crisis, the end of everything?'

Simoneau replied. 'Surely we don't debate the afterlife. Are we into blasphemy now?'

'No. Of course not. Heaven is beyond doubt, as God's promise. But upon death, all life on earth ends, doesn't it? Finis. Don't we instinctively fear just that, in the same way as we normally shrink from a corpse?' Louis fought the urge to make the sign of the cross; he felt they were on uncertain ground. Béaloideas did not miss the flinch.

'Look at you, Louis!' he cried. 'You're afraid! That's what I'm talking about. Weren't you a little nauseated with being so close to old man Flanigan, even all painted up as he was? Don't deny it!

'Don't we fear death and hurting to death most of all? Because deep down inside us we have trouble with...not the afterlife so much, as the transition. Yes, that's it, the transition. Yet the dead are still among us.'

Simoneau objected, in a tone of annoyance. 'I don't have trouble with the afterlife, receiving the grace of God. So why should I fear the transition? Do not I simply commend my soul to God's gracious mercy and compassion, and leave the rest to Him?'

Béaloideas winked at Louis; Simoneau could not miss it. 'Don't be a preacher for our benefit, Father Robert. God sees your heart's intent, and is not fooled by appearances.' Simoneau glared at him, which Béaloideas deflected with an affectionate grin.

'What are you saying, the 'dead are still with us'; that there are ghosts among us?'

'Oh yes! Of course! But not the chilly vapours that float about, such as Dickens described in *A Christmas Carol,* moaning and sighing and shaking chains. But the dead govern us in a way far more tangible than that. As surely as if they had not passed on.'

The other two spoke at once. 'But how? How? What are you talking about?'

Béaloideas looked at them for a moment. 'By legacy, you frog's asses! By legacy. For good or ill, the works that men do while they are on this earth live on, and we govern ourselves accordingly. It is only when we can be selective about the legacy of the dead—we have to be able to recognize that which is worthwhile, and that which is demagoguery; only then is it that we are ready to prepare a legacy of our own. Don't you see?'

Louis nodded. 'I think that having a mission in life is part of creating that legacy. Yes,' he said excitedly, 'I see your point! A man can leave a legacy, however, with entirely the wrong idea. It may end up that he is cursed by the things he does in this life. But what has this got to do with that hooting carnival back there?' He gestured over his shoulder with his thumb.

'It's only a way of looking at death, nothing more. We're used to sobbing and wailing because someone in our life is physically no more. We've lost something. But for these folk, there's a last chance to be with the dead man, the guest of honour. The life of the party!' He snickered at his own joke.

'What's wrong,' he continued, 'with assuring the man's memory that his popularity and place among friends and family is as great now as it was before? By toasting the dead man, we are reassuring ourselves. Wakes are as much for the living as anything they have to do with the dead— though I suspect that in its primitive origins, it was very much the other way around.'

Louis appeared to mull this over as they walked along. A light rain had fallen, and the streets had a pungent, fresh smell to them.

'Well,' said Louis, 'wakes are not for me; at least, the kind we saw tonight. But I take your point about one's legacy, for I think of my own father, and the memories, instructions, and inspirations he will leave me. They will live in me and all others he has known and touched. And I in turn would walk in his steps and leave a legacy of my own, out there in Red River.

Béaloideas crept up to Louis, his arms akimbo, as if to seize him again. He whispered in mock sepulchral tones. 'Ah, but dear Louis: you are not yet dead!'

ii

André Nault was puzzled. He had taken both his cows out to the pasturage this morning, yet here were both of them pushing at the barn door. And not too much urging would be required to send the dilapidated structure toppling to the ground. They must have broken the fence at some point, yet there was plenty of grass there. It was baffling indeed. So he dropped his tools onto the perch where he was repairing his roof, slid down a rickety ladder, and set off for his 'hay privilege', the strip of land adjacent to a holding which a man could utilize for grazing or harvesting hay for the winter.

Coming upon the temporary enclosure he had set up at summer's end, a zigzag of crossed poplar poles bound by twine, he saw the opening almost immediately. But this was no breach caused by unruly stock; the poles were neatly drawn aside, and placed in a manner which would permit easy closure. Nault ran to the fence and knelt to look for the strands of cut twine. Upon hearing the muffled hum of voices, he looked up anxiously. On the other edge of his land was a small knot of men, easterners by the cut of their dress. They stood poring over some object and, looking up from time to time, they pointed off in various directions. Nault stood up suddenly. Two of the men noticed him, and turned to look at him. Nault froze. Then the men returned to their preoccupation, calmly; indifferent. Nault spun on his moccasined heel, and fled back to his homestead. He was overwhelmed with the sensation that he was being pursued, but no one followed; no shot rang out, no cry was heard. Nault heard only the swish of dry, late fall grass against his flying feet, and the roaring thump of his own heartbeat in his ears.

Passing his modest house without a shout to his wife, he slid and stumbled like an escaped felon down the riverbank where his dugout canoe was pulled up at the water's edge. The river was low, and he had to drag the cumbersome craft some distance out to launch it. Once aboard, he flailed with the paddle mightily, heading downstream toward St Vital, on the opposite side, and the home of his cousin, Louis Riel, recently returned from schooling in the East. He would know what to do.

iii

When John Schultz first began to take notice of Mary, David could not be sure. But it was apparent that the man made plenty of opportunities to be around David; it was equally clear that when Mary was around, David almost ceased to exist. Schultz was an intelligent man. He left no doubt where he stood on all issues. Handsome and splendidly dressed, physically strong and intense, he instantly commanded attention from those around him, then held it with his piercing blue eyes and compelling voice. It was easy to see why Mary was drawn to him initially. David could not but notice the quick glances and hurriedly averted eyes.

Schultz saw the North-west as on its threshold. Immigration would soon fill the vast flatlands stretching to the mountains in the west and the brooding boreal forests in the north; a man correctly positioned could profit handsomely. To assure that position, and to facilitate the advocacy of his pro-Canadian agenda, he bought out his partners in the *Nor'Wester*, so that for the years between 1865 and 1868, the newspaper was solely an instrument for Schultz to expound his own views for political union with Canada. He relinquished control over the paper only when he was assured by the new owner, Walter Brown, that he was sympathetic to Schultz's 'Canadian Party', and would continue attacks upon the Hudson's Bay Company.

During this time, Schultz became acting Grand Master of a Masonic Lodge in Pembina, where a number of American cavalry troops were stationed; several of them were Masons, and Schultz brought a number of inductees from Fort Garry to join the fraternity which became known as the 'Northern Light Lodge'. These friends who joined with him were, with one exception, 'Orangemen' from Ontario. The Orange Association of British America was a society formed in Ireland in 1795, after William of Orange (later William III), to keep alive the memory of the 'Glorious Revolution' of 1688 and the Battle of the Boyne in 1690, when the Protestant succession to the throne was secured. Its history in British North America dated from 1830, when a lodge was established at Brockville. Its fundamental purpose was the defence of Protestant Christianity, and unity of the British Empire.

But the Catholic priests were suspicious of Orangemen, and their anti-papist rhetoric. Schultz revelled in the mysteries and exclusivities of the society, and hinted at the secrets of the ancient order in the *Nor'Wester*. Because the tactics of Schultz and his cronies purported to create an upper class of citizens with access to power and influence in Canada and the United States, it made the less pretentious, established settlers feel anxious, particularly the Métis, for it was clear that the day was coming when the settlement would be turned over to Canada, if not Great Britain or the United States.

In autumn of 1868, Mary brought Christine and Byron to the warehouse to see their father. When steamboat blasts sounded from the newest vessel on the river, *Selkirk*, both children ran out of the shop to the riverbank. The *Selkirk* was a grand sight, for she was far more elaborate in her finishings than either the homely *Anson Northup*, or the utilitarian *International*. Mary watched them go, then turned to David. 'I've told them both to come back here afterwards. I've got to go over to the chemist's shop to buy some flea powder.'

David looked at her sourly. 'That's Schultz's place, isn't it?' Knowing very well the answer, he continued, 'Must you deal with him? He looks at you as if you've not a stitch on.'

'What do you care if any man looks at me so?' said Mary calmly. They had been trying to treat one another civilly since the boy was born. David wanted no upsets in his life. And Mary was somewhat afraid of triggering David's temper, but a flicker of her old fire had been started by Schultz's attentions. She knew he was married, but he was a controversial figure in the settlement which some were starting to call 'Winnipeg', rather than 'McDermotsville', or the older Fort Garry.

David straightened up from the stock-taking he was doing, and faced her. His two hired men had left for the day, and they were alone. He stepped toward her, his rage building. She took a half step backwards, but did not change her expression of belittlement.

'At least he notices me; you never see me as a woman any more, not since Byron was born.'

'Notices you!' David thundered. 'He would be on you like a rash, should I turn my back for a moment. The man thinks this settlement, and all in it, is set before him like a dinner plate. He is constantly at me for my support, being that I am an "Englishman". Asshole!'

'Perhaps his interest in me is only political,' she laughed without mirth.

David was still angry, and he felt she was demeaning him. 'Must you always act and speak like a slut?' he snarled. 'God knows that I don't believe half the gossip that goes on around here about you. But maybe I should. Maybe...'

She flared with anger at the slur. 'Slut am I? Mother of your children, and you call me slut!' She struck him on the chest; it hurt, catching him on the sternum. Without thinking, he struck her back, and she staggered backwards from the blow, falling over a chair. She sat up on the floor, holding her lip.

'Look at me! Look at me!' she cried, a thin trickle of blood showed at the corner of her mouth.

A deep voice boomed at the doorway. It was Schultz. He walked over to Mary, picked her up as if she were a child, and pulled her hand away from her mouth as he examined the cut.

'There's no harm in disciplining a woman if she deserves it, but I must say that only a coward strikes a woman with a closed fist.'

'Let go of my wife!' stammered David. He was taken by surprise at Schultz's entry. How long had he been there, and how much had he heard?

'I'm a medical doctor,' snapped Schultz, 'and this woman has a serious cut on the inside of her lip. Fetch me some cotton stuff, and be in a hurry about it.' Mary clung to him. David could not tell if she were swooning at the loss of blood, the conflict, or the nearness of the man. He scuttled away like a handmaiden to do as he was bidden, and returned moments later, to find Schultz helping Mary to recline on a broad bench. Taking the small rag as he sat beside her, Schultz shredded it, rolled it into a ball, and asked Mary to bite down on it. 'The bleeding should stop in a few minutes,' he said, taking out his large pocketwatch. 'You should be all right.' He smiled fondly, as if she were his own daughter, and smoothed away the hair from her forehead. Then he stood up. He was almost three inches taller than David, and much more solidly built.

'I have been hoping that you would have joined with me in the pressing of our aspirations for this place. As a man whose first tongue is the Queen's English, and who appears to have a nose for business, you would, I thought, be a prime candidate for induction into our Masonic lodge.

'But I was wrong. You are like the craven primitive who abuses his wife. Such a person has no worth. You have a history of not being able to make up your mind on anything. Let me leave you with something that will remind you to be clear on at least one matter: do not, under any circumstances, strike your wife again.' As he finished this statement, he struck David stiffly in the face, crushing his nose. It was unexpected, for all Schultz's menace, and David went down like a dropped sack of potatoes and did not move.

When he regained consciousness, Mary was kneeling over him, holding a damp cloth close to his forehead. Her eyes were closed, and David could see that a bruise was beginning to form at the corner of her mouth. He could see the swell of her breasts, and he was reminded of the time he had met her, almost nine years ago, in almost identical circumstances. How he had loved her then! Was it not for the way she had cared for him, and filled his eye, that he had married her? His face hurt terribly, and he moaned. She opened her eyes and looked at him. He could not see what feelings lay beneath the surface. At once he understood the pain he caused her by his physical cruelty. 'I am sorry,' he muttered.

'For what? He had no right to hit you.'

'Ah, but who has the right to strike anyone?' The image of the deeply welted back of Alfred Okay came abruptly to mind. 'I have not been a good husband, or a good father.' He could not bring himself to acknowledge that, though he had never laid a hand on Christine, his indifference to her had surely caused identical pain. With difficulty he sat up, holding onto Mary's arm. Urgently, he turned to her.

'Woman, I have been thinking about my life a great deal recently. I want for us to start again. We must make a new beginning of it, or our lives will have been spent. We must decide what we want for ourselves—and our children—and go after it. But we cannot go on tearing little pieces out of each other.'

Mary lowered her head. The tears came slowly at first, silently coursing down her cheeks, then in sobs, loud and shaking her body. David was confused and alarmed, for he thought that perhaps it was too late. Perhaps she was already of a mind to leave him; what exchange had taken place with Schultz when he had been knocked out on the floor? Fear crept into his thoughts once again, crowding, like a familiar but unwelcome visitor singing his eerie songs of doubt and anxiety.

At last, she was able to speak, though great sobs racked her body every few minutes. 'I too have not been the perfect wife. To begin with, I married you only for the hope that someday I would leave this place, and live far away, in ease.

'But this place is my home, and yet I have not done it honour. I have always thought only of my own needs, never of others. When I saw you stretched out on the floor, it came to me that Schultz might very well have killed you; he is such a big man. What would I have done then? And our children?'

They clung to one another as if shipwrecked, moving only when the children returned, laughing and calling out. Christine had come alive with Byron's arrival, for she doted on him. He in return loved her unconditionally, and she bloomed as any living creature might under the glow of such attention. Until that moment, David had not even seen the plain lesson for himself. What does it take to open one's eyes to the obvious things? he wondered. To be knocked silly?

The immediate consequence of Schultz's last visit was that David began to take a serious interest in the politics of the settlement. But not in the way that Schultz had expected, or hoped. David began to spend more time with his wife's relatives, for their anxiety about title to their land was one with which he had considerable sympathy, to say nothing of personal interest.

In addition to the business, he had the two-mile strip at Oak Creek, as well as forty acres near Silver Heights on the trail to Portage la Prairie. For both these parcels, he had paid only for improvements and, beyond the receipt, had no other guarantee of title. Schultz and his Canadian friends not only had their eyes on land, but on the political jobs that would come with the transfer; there was the real power. And what effect would it have on existing businesses? The Nor'Wester was even suggesting that the matter of franchise would not be universal. 'Are we ready at this moment for the Elective Franchise? Who are our electors?' Schultz was writing to his political connections in the east to urge that the vote not be granted until there was sufficient Canadian (by this he meant from Ontario) immigration to ensure that 'Canadian principles' would be established. He made no secret of these sentiments among the English-speaking citizens of the colony, and he soon became a symbol for all that was feared about the coming changes.

It seemed that the transfer of Rupert's Land to Canada was imminent. Members of the crews building the road from the Lake of the Woods to Red River were pacing off lots and staking them in their own names. In June of 1869 Johnathan Snow, Charles Mair and Bill Hallett had travelled south to St Norbert and pounded in stakes topped with strips of red bunting, on property whose dimensions had been measured off on horseback. They planned to have a good reserve of land claimed, ready for the new administration, whatever form it would eventually take.

These activities were cause for concern by the Métis, and several made a show of force, though no one's property had actually been pegged by the three. It was Mair, known to be an associate of John Schultz, who aroused the ill will of the established settlers in St Norbert. More than that, Mair had written open letters to the Toronto *Globe* which had slighted the morality of Métis women, and disparaged the ability and intelligence of their men. All three of the land men were run off by the armed and mounted farmer-hunters. They returned to the Beaulieu house, where they had started from, for Henri was an elder whose instruction was sound. He called for a meeting on 5 July.

When the men gathered that day, it happened that Mary and David were present, though they had not known of the meeting in advance. At that assembly were, among others, Louis Riel, John Bruce, and Jean-Baptiste Lépine. David had met Louis Riel before; the sombre, well-spoken young man with a wide, intelligent forehead had come to visit him at his warehouse, with the purpose of soliciting his support for the proposal that the transfer money to be paid by Canada to the Hudson's Bay Company, be paid instead to the original settlers.

He had made a convincing argument, setting out concerns for title guarantees, political participation, and the need for basic freedoms to be assured in the transfer documents themselves. But his view that a 'unilateral transfer' should be stopped at all costs including force, alarmed David, for he had no desire to see the sort of violence that he had witnessed in the Corbett affair. It was only luck, he felt, that no one had been killed. Like most English-speaking members of the colony, he preferred to sit and wait for developments. But Riel had been 'impressive,' he allowed him that. They were sure to hear more from him in the months ahead, David was certain.

At the Beaulieu house, the discussion centered around the possibility of land seizure, and all the threats that the coming changes presaged. David noticed that Louis was calm and did not speak first, but when he did, he spoke with a force that commanded respect. He made his points like a lawyer, arranging them in order of priority, from general to specific. If he had flaws in his manner of presentation, they were two: he tended to go on too long, and a clear argument thereby ran the risk of losing its force; and he could not brook criticism or a contrary view with much grace. This latter defect could be costly for a leader. Riel seemed to understand this failing however, for he deferred to John Bruce much of the time. That was odd, thought David, for though Bruce was older, he was in no way as articulate as Riel. Riel, educated at the College of the Sulpician Fathers in Montreal, showed among his colleagues like a rose among weeds. Though he seemed initially self-conscious about it, his false modesty quickly left him as he warmed to his purpose.

The meeting drew to a close with the group being satisfied for the moment that they needed to take action beyond the mere lodging of a complaint. Jean-Baptiste Lépine and Baptiste Tourond were assigned to set up and maintain armed patrols in south St Norbert, to assure that no 'stranger should establish himself' on lands falling within the parishes settled by the Métis. From accounts brought back to Riel and others, several men had been run off, without asking questions, or so much as a greeting called out. David viewed this as an escalation, but he saw no other choice. There was nothing more than a poplar log fence on his property at Oak Creek; in Silver Heights there was a poor hut temporarily occupied during the great flood, but nothing else. He was in the same difficulty as his Métis brethren. He decided to throw in his lot with them.

He was well aware of the fact that the English-speaking settlers of mixed blood were unhappy about the idea that the Métis should take up arms; there was even talk that they should prevent them from doing anything which would prevent an orderly transfer of the lands granted to the Hudson's Bay Company. But no citizen of prominence would act as leader, nor would the Protestant clergy act in any decisive way. Rumours abounded in the settlement that John Bruce and his followers intended to keep the new Lieutenant-Governor out of the territory until there had been full and proper consultation. The request for proper negotiation was a reasonable one in David's view, a view which was shared by most. But to reject the Queen's representative necessarily by force seemed too much like rebellion or insurrection. Torn by competing interests, the English-speaking Halfbreeds fretted indecisively, and most did nothing. David realized that, not too long ago, he would have been among their number. He knew now that he must act to protect what was his. All his life he had reacted to forces in the path of least resistance. Now he would choose to act. His home, business and his family seemed important enough to fight for, if fighting it was to be.

iv

Johnathan Snow looked at the group of men approaching him. They were on foot, and it would be the better part of a quarter hour before they reached his surveyors. Damn. More trouble from these raggity-assed aborigines, he thought. He looked back at his crew, some of whom had noticed that the group was arriving, and called out. 'We've company dropping in for tea, boys. Keep at your work, and we'll play the matter as she goes.'

His superior was Lieutenant-Colonel John Stoughton Dennis, who in turn was acting on behalf of the Minister of Public Works, William McDougall. McDougall was too impatient for the transfer of Rupert's Land to be formalized; he wanted to get on with the surveying of the lands, so that the new territories could accommodate the hordes of new settlers whom Schultz and other well-informed persons had told him were ready to pour west.

Dennis had fallen in with Schultz, who had happened to meet him en route to Fort Garry, in August of 1869. Mere association with Schultz by this time was enough to taint the intentions of the newcomer in the eyes of the Métis. For all his faults, Dennis very quickly picked up the fact that there was extreme anxiety on the question of land claims, and urged that no further work be done without the resolution of this question. McDougall would have none of it, and ordered that the work commence, on the basis of the American model of surveying. Dennis took it upon himself to concentrate on the lands beyond those contained by the strip farms favoured by the Métis, and perhaps confrontation would have been delayed had Snow's crew not strayed into Nault's 'hay privilege'.

Sixteen Métis closed upon the survey party of eight men. David was with them, for he had been at the Riel residence when Nault burst in. The Métis were unarmed, Johnathan saw at once, and was greatly relieved. Their leader, a well-built, intelligent-looking fellow, seemed to be a white man, as well as the short man who was doing most of the chattering and pointing. Perhaps he was the owner. There was another man, darker, but with a shock of red hair jutting out beneath his broad-brimmed hat; he must be white. Good God, that man looks familiar, Johnathan thought to himself.

As the men approached the survey chain, which was stretched out across the grass, they stopped. Nault fell silent as well. No weapons could be seen, though David was sure that some of the surveyors wore pistols. Perhaps they had taken them off to work in the hot weather. The tall man with the red hair, who stood slightly apart from the others, still wore a frock coat. David was sure he was wearing a holster underneath, for it showed a sinister bulge at the waist. Canadians wore their firearms on the same belt, or over their trousers belt unlike the Americans he had met, who tended to wear their weapons lower, closer to the natural fall of the hand. The man was looking at him closely, almost in recognition, but they had not met before, he was sure. But there was something about him.

The two groups faced each other. David's group was a motley collection of faces, from dark brown to sunburned pale skin. Most were dressed in a combination of skins and rough cotton working clothes; all were shod with moccasins.

The easterners seemed to exude wealth and power. They had broad felt hats, good stuff shirts, and high leather boots. Their equipment was mysterious and alien to the Métis, and they showed no fear of the scruffy men before them. Only David and Louis wore clothing which suggested that they were not humble farmers. David felt the intimidation between the men unspoken and implicit though it was.

For a very long moment the two groups continued to face one another. Not a man moved; no breeze stirred. The only sound was that of insects as they buzzed and hummed in the long grass. Riel lifted his foot, and placed his moccasined heel on one of the long metal links of the survey chain. It was the smallest of gestures, but the dynamic of the confrontation was perceptibly altered. It was as if a puff of wind had rippled a banner ever so gently. Everything was the same, yet all had changed.

'You go no farther.' said Louis quietly but firmly.

One of the crew, a red-faced, blustery Irishman, threw down his sledge hammer handle; until Riel spoke, he had been leaning on it. 'What the bloody hell,' he spluttered. 'What is this shit! We've work to do here!'

'You go no farther,' repeated Louis, simply, with no change in manner or tone, his heel still on the chain. Then, to emphasize the point, he simply folded his arms.

Johnathan saw the determination in the men opposite. Although there were no weapons, he could not know whether they had been cached some distance back, or whether mounted reinforcements were lurking in the scrub oak groves to the north. In any event, his men were badly outnumbered. He called them to gather up their tools and return to the wagon. 'Leave the chain!' he called to the Irishman, who looked as if he would tear it out from under the foot of the Métis leader.

He looked again at the strange white man who was returning his stare with the same intensity. As he gazed, the other took his hat off and mopped his brow with the forearm of his shirt. His hair was a shock of coppery red in the sunshine. A man standing next to Johnathan muttered, 'Jesus Christ man, don't he half look like you! He could be your own brother!' Johnathan turned away in disgust. The man was a bloody savage! It was only an accident of some meandering, red-haired trader that had produced this fellow. He shook his head; I've been in the bush too long, he thought.

v

McDougall was determined that a man dressed like a rag picker, who could scarcely speak the Queen's English was not going to be making a fool of him. Press on he would, and John Bruce and Louis Riel be damned. But he would remember those names for the indignity they had served up for him. Where was the open welcome that Schultz and Mair had promised? He decided to leave some of his party behind, and press on with a smaller group, which included Captain Donald Cameron, self-styled military attaché to the party, and Father Provencher, nephew of the revered first Catholic Bishop of Rupert's Land. They reached a Hudson's Bay Company post two miles north of the border, where McDougall decided to pause, and send an even smaller group ahead, just to 'test the waters'. Writing a letter to the Prime Minister that night, he betrayed his anxiety by writing. 'I am certainly not frightened, and don't believe this insurrection will last a week.'

McDougall's original plans, as he formulated them that night, were to send along young Provencher accompanied by just two men. After all, the name 'Provencher' was held in high esteem in Rupert's Land, that much was known. And Provencher was a mild sort of man, unlikely to provoke offence or otherwise alarm anyone. The disclosure of these arrangements outraged the pompous Cameron.

'Impossible! Don't you see the grievous consequences to your authority? It will be entirely undermined! There must be no delay!'

McDougall was not swayed by Cameron's flourish. 'It makes good sense to sound the waters,' he said. 'The good name of Provencher has much currency in these parts; he will fetch a reliable report to us within a few days, and we can proceed with confidence.'

'Confidence!' Cameron stamped his foot, barely able to conceal his scorn for the man opposite, who looked much too soft for this sort of work, with his florid complexion, his full lips, and his gentleman's side whiskers curled and brushed back. Altogether too foppish and unsuited for the frontier, thought Cameron angrily. As someone not officially part of the McDougall party, however, he would show this newcomer a thing or two. He announced to McDougall that he and his wife, their two servants and a wagon, as well as his own driving surrey, would advance in the morning.

McDougall's features knitted into a scowl. 'This is entirely unsatisfactory. Even though I exercise no jurisdiction over you, there is not a soul in Red River that would distinguish you from my expedition. Would that I could command it, you'd not proceed to the settlement ahead of me.'

McDougall made no secret of his displeasure; he continued heatedly. 'You may cause us considerable embarrassment by provoking some sort of a confrontation.'

Cameron gathered his belongings, and announced simply that he would see McDougall at the Fort, 'when you think it prudent to attend.' This departing remark put McDougall in a towering rage, and he dashed the correspondence he had been holding to the floor in a flurry of impotent wrath. To the departing captain he shouted that 'it will be a matter of record that I have advised against this; I assume no responsibility for your safety, or that of your party. Any mischief arising from your impetuosity shall be on your own head!'

He summoned Provencher and requested that the cleric get away before sunup, 'lest that impatient ass Cameron contaminate your arrival with his bluster'.

Though Provencher did as instructed, Cameron soon discovered the intrigue, and drove furiously to catch up with him, reaching the dust-covered priest at St Norbert. There he saw the man pleading with some roughly dressed Métis who were remonstrating with him at a barricade of felled oak, in the centre of which was a gate of poplar saplings. Alighting from his surrey, Cameron batted the dust from his topcoat, and tugged it firmly on his shoulders. Ignoring his wife's timorous bleating, and striding purposefully to the pale, he ignored Provencher and glared through his monocle at the Métis who lounged warily at the gate. Drawing himself up to his full height, he demanded imperiously. 'Remove that blasted fence!'

None of the guards comprehended English, but Cameron's meaning was plain enough. An elderly *hivernant* climbed slowly over the rails, walked to Cameron's surrey, and rapped on it with the butt of his ancient musket. This was José Ouellette, who sixteen years later would be bayoneted to death at the age of ninety-three, by a Canadian militiaman sent, like McDougall, to assume control of lands others called home. With a gesture of his head, he made it plain that Cameron should get aboard and begone. The captain began to bluster anew, but stopped when he saw that certain of his trunks were being removed from the bed of the surrey. The Métis mounted, and escorted Cameron and Provencher back to Pembina, occasionally making remarks in French which caused considerable mirth among the others. Humiliated and subdued, Cameron chafed beside his wife, and said nothing. Provencher, for his part, knew better than to translate; Cameron had done enough damage.

While this was happening, a burly Métis standing six foot three in his moccasins arrived at the Hudson's Bay post where McDougall was catching up on letter writing and sipping cognac from a tin cup in front of a crackling fire. The visitor was Ambroise Lépine, new adjutant-general of Louis Riel's incipient 'National Committee'. Backed by two dozen mounted and armed men, Lépine demanded that McDougall 'remove himself to Pembina, 'fore the sun has gone'.

In vain McDougall protested, showing his patent as Lieutenant-Governor, with its red royal seal splendidly affixed over bright crimson ribbon, and its command to all men, 'Know ye by These Presents'. Lépine barely gave it a glance.

'Who has given such an impertinent order to Her Majesty's agent?' cried McDougall, almost in tears at this humiliation.

'The government,' replied Lépine simply. 'No more talk. It is time to go.' And so McDougall and his party were led ignominiously back across the border, where they were surprised and dismayed to see the chastened

Cameron. The newspapers in St Paul went into a frenzy of glee over the foolish 'Britishers'. Though a large, comfortable house awaited the governor-designate in Silver Heights, just west of the settlement at Winnipeg, he was forced to move into a mud-chinked log hut at Pembina, and winter was drawing on. But McDougall's troubles were only beginning.

The date for transfer of Rupert's Land to Canada came and passed. Delay was occasioned because Canada could not accept the grant without an assurance of 'quiet enjoyment' and so advised the British government. McDougall was instructed to be careful to provoke no undue attention, and to be cautious and patient. But McDougall attempted all manner of devices to secure support at Red River for his assumption of power, all to no avail. He even tried to correspond with Riel, but his letter went unanswered. On 1 December 1869 he made his greatest blunder.

McDougall drafted a Proclamation in the name of the Queen, which purported to give Canada all of the North-west Territories, and to vest all governmental authority in himself. It was a fraud, but copies of it had been smuggled into Red River, principally by Dr Schultz. It caused something of a rift in the English-speaking Halfbreeds, for most knew that there no authority existed to make such a document legitimate.

The farce had two final acts to play out. Under cover of night McDougall and his small group of six companions rode across the boundary, back to the Hudson's Bay post, which had by now been abandoned for the winter. There, in the lee of a building, shivering in the intense cold, the self-proclaimed Governor read aloud his proclamation to the soughing winds. The lantern held aloft to read by was whipped suddenly by a snow-laden gust and went out. The Dominion flag, which was unfurled by a supporter, snapped and was lost in the shifting drifts. No one bothered to chase after it, for the night was getting worse. Calling his whimpering sporting dogs, McDougall and his troupe trudged wearily back to Pembina, the storm soon removing any trace that they had ever been at the post. The newspapers in St Paul crowed over the details as they became known.

The other act of McDougall's which had much graver potential for harm was the second document that he forged; this was an appointment of Colonel John Stoughton Dennis, a military man of questionable judgement, as his 'Lieutenant and Conservator of the Peace'. The document also charged Dennis with the right to raise and maintain a force to put down the insurgents by whatever means necessary. McDougall, it was well known, had three hundred military rifles in crates waiting at Fort Abercrombie.

Dennis was unable to get the support of the English Halfbreeds, but he was able to drum up the aid of a band of Cree. With their assistance, he took the Lower Fort below the St Andrews rapids, and set up his headquarters. This was a grave miscalculation, for memories of the Sioux uprising were as yet raw, what with more than six hundred settlers having died in Minnesota, some under the most horrendous circumstances. Dennis's actions touched off a firestorm of protest, and both he and McDougall were soon recalled in disgrace.

David heard of the developments with growing unease. It seemed that Canada was determined to assume control of these lands through the actions of men who were either stupid or indifferent. Others who gathered around that bastard Schultz and his 'Canadian Party' seemed that they would make good company for the likes of McDougall. The more he heard from Louis Riel, the more he was inclined to think that Riel was right. Unless they could put themselves in a position to negotiate with the Canadian government, an appointed group of functionaries would be the real authority, with people like Schultz likely to be in the pivotal roles. It just wouldn't do.

Louis meanwhile had orchestrated a Bill of Rights. In this he was heavily influenced by a strange, legless, but exceedingly competent lawyer named Enos Stutsman. Stutsman was an American with the idea that the North-west should form part of the Union, there being far more in common between Winnipeg and St Paul than with Ottawa; it was a logical consequence. Stutsman had a large hand in feeding the American newspapers information about McDougall's continuing fiasco, as well as the determination of the Métis people to secure their guarantees of freedom. It was only a matter of time before the fumbling of men like Dennis and McDougall drove the settlers of Red River to turn to the United States for assistance.

Louis had orchestrated the formation of a 'National Committee', which had convened for the purpose of developing a position to put to Ottawa. He had his work laid out for him, as the President, John Bruce— (whose name Louis had put forward)—was weak and ineffectual. Louis was eventually to take over as President, but the English-speaking Halfbreeds could not be convinced to actively take up the cause; it was too much like rebellion against the Queen. Their clergy were not supportive, and no clear leader emerged among them. Plenty of federal government money had been spread around the colony so that some of the Métis were actually against Louis. As well, there were a number of established Métis who had standing and position in the community, who did not want to risk all in a standoff with the British Crown.

Louis well understood these fears. He was minutely acquainted through his agents with the intrigues of McDougall. He had seen with his own eyes the might of the British army in Montréal. While they would be some time in the coming, once here they could not be defied—even by the full deployment of his Métis soldiers. Events in Winnipeg were soon to occupy his full attention, however. The threat from within was far greater than that which existed eighteen hundred miles distant.

vi

Both David and Mary were in the warehouse when Riel's men came in and demanded all the guns which David had stored, 'whether personal or trade weapons'. This was by order of the recently established 'Provisional Government'. McDougall's 'proclamation' had vitiated the authority of the Hudson's Bay Company, but there was no validity to the claims of the Dominion government as yet. When Dennis began his foolishness on the strength of McDougall's spurious patent, Louis shut down the aggravating *Nor'Wester*, put his men on alert, ordered a search of all shops in Winnipeg for firearms, and prepared to meet Dennis with force.

One of the men told David that Dennis had sent orders to Schultz to retire to the Lower Fort, so as to make for a stronger force. Schultz declined. 'That son-of-a-bitch Schultz is holed up in his house with about fifty of his followers; they have nailed up pickets in the windows. It looks like a little fort!'

'Why would he do such a thing?' asked David. 'It would be an easy thing for Riel to starve him out. I hope he does.' he added. Schultz had been nothing but trouble since he arrived.

'No,' said the other. 'Monsieur Schultz will not have the luxury of sitting around, while we freeze our asses in the snow. He's out, or we'll torch the place.'

'But surely he knows that. He would not resist; it would be futile. Why would a man act so foolishly?'

'He hates us,' the Métis said simply. 'We are nothing more than his dog's shit. Is it not obvious? He treats us as if we were snot on his finger, which he would flick away without thinking. No doubt he thinks we'll just leave him alone, or perhaps even run away! We'll see, soon enough!'

'What does Riel mean to do then?' asked David, fearing bloodshed. He turned to Mary who, for the first time since he had known her, showed some anxiety. What was she worried about? David turned to the departing soldier, who was cradling a dozen heavy muskets under his arm.

'Tell Monsieur Riel that if he has need of me, I shall be here.' His own words surprised him. Mary looked at him, anxiety turning to astonishment.

'Why are you getting involved in this?'

'That's just it: I'm getting involved. This is my home, and the changes that are nearly upon us threaten us all. We may lose everything I have worked hard for. I once was a circus clown; no—once I was a slave, less than nothing. Now I am a businessman, have a family. I must act to protect what I have. I think I can help.

'This Riel is headstrong, he may even be foolhardy. But he has courage, and from what I've seen, he acts in our interests. He wants nothing for himself save the honour of leading us. The list of demands is not unreasonable: language guarantees, the right to elect our own government, land for schools and roads and things. The request for a rail connection with St Paul—does this not reflect the reality of our lives?'

Mary looked at him as if he were a stranger. 'I did not know you understood—or even cared—about politics,' she said quietly.

David was slightly embarrassed. 'I do not. I am not a learned man. I only learned to write and read reasonably well when I was in America, and had regular access to newspapers and journals. But these things, the essence of what I understand politics to be about, go to the heart.

'When I was in America, it was just before the great war started between the north and the southern states. I do not pretend to comprehend what sent two great armies within the same country, some of them brothers and cousins on opposite sides, rushing against one another in bloody, vicious conflict.' He shook his head wearily.

'I do know that part of the struggle had to do with the enslavement of niggers...' Mary interrupted him, and it was necessary to explain the term to her.

'It's hard to get the head around it,' he concluded, 'but there are those who think that others—for whatever reason; skin colour, whatever—are not as good as they are. And if I were to sum it up, I'd guess that the way Schultz and his cronies treat me and others around here is close to that. And if the Canadians are like him, and I suspect they are with their stealing and haggling and reneging, I want no part of them until such time as it's been put down in writing. Like a contract.'

Mary asked hesitantly. 'Are you sure that your own dislike for this man Schultz has nothing to do with it?'

David waved her off. 'No,' he said with a sigh. 'It's true I dislike the man, and have since I met him. But it's what he represents that persuades me it is necessary to move against him.'

And so it was that David was called to the Schultz house to 'lend a hand', on 7 December 1869. He was horrified to see that the house had been surrounded, and two cannon, field pieces capable of firing eight-pound balls or clusters of canister, were drawn up and facing the planked-over door. Either one would have reduced the door and surrounding construction to a tangle of mortar and splinters with a single round. He seized Andrew Bannatyne, Orkney trader and partner of Alexander Begg, by the sleeve, and propelled him to Louis, who stood silently watching the drama unfold. Bannatyne was a good businessman, hard-headed and shrewd. He was respected, and Riel was sure to give him an audience.

'We've got to convince him to put a stop to this madness,' he urged Bannatyne. 'After the first shot is fired, there'll be no turning back.'

There were enough Métis on horseback and others bearing rifles behind hurriedly thrown-up barricades, who seemed anxious enough to begin the assault. David could see the rifle barrels bristling between the pickets nailed up as protection for the Canadians.

Louis looked at David and Bannatyne approaching in the bright sunlight; it was cold, and the sun sparkled on the snow so as to make one squint. 'So. You see what we are dealing with? See how defiant this man Schultz is? In a moment we shall take proper measure of that resistance. Ready with that fuse!' he shouted to the man standing at the cannon's breach.

'Stop, in heaven's name!' cried Bannatyne. 'They cannot win, and they surely must know it! What sense is there in smashing them like rats in a barrel?'

Riel replied coldly. 'Because they are nothing but rats in a barrel. They have caused us immense grief by turning away the English from us. Look now, as the English watch us!

'Go peacefully,' he cried to them, as he had said at the convention a few days earlier. 'Go attend to your cattle and dry the eyes of your wives, for what we do this day, we do for all of us. And if you should stand by to accept the benefit, so be it! We act only in the interests of all people who live in this fair country!'

There was some shuffling and looking to and fro among the mixed-blood settlers who had come to watch, but none stepped forward. Bannatyne saw that to argue with him was useless. He turned to David and shrugged. Riel saw the gesture, and spoke sofly. 'They shall have fifteen minutes. Then, if there is no surrender, then...it is over for them.'

David whipped out his pocket handkerchief and waved it over his head, running, calling out, to the door of the house. He thought he heard a voice—Mary's—cry out. 'Don't!'

He did not look back, but rushed to the single step, and struck the door with the palm of his hand. 'Halloo the house! You have fifteen minutes to give up your place, or it shall be torn down around you with cannonshot. Do you hear me? Do you hear me?'

There was an excited muffle of voices within. The glass had been struck from the windows, so that some of the words filtered down to David like small stones from the roof. 'Strike the bastard where he stands!' 'We have no hope!' 'Rush them!' 'Seize the traitor at the door!'

David stepped back. 'Fifteen minutes. It is quite hopeless; you must all come out!' And he retraced his steps, half expecting a shot to ring out, striking him in the back. But a quarter-hour later, as Riel snapped the cover of his watch shut and looked up, the door was kicked open suddenly, and the burly Schultz made his way out at the head of his men, hands outstretched and thunder in his eyes. Stopping before Riel, he demanded that his men's lives be spared. When this was granted, he drew heavily through his nostrils, and spat at Riel's feet. Louis was not provoked, much to David's relief, and all forty-eight prisoners were marched off to imprisonment at the fort, a cold, fifteen-minute walk away. The cries of victory and excitement from the Métis sounded sharp in the winter air.

The following day the company flag was taken down from the pole behind the south gate at Fort Garry, and the flag of the Provisional Government was drawn up. A large white banner, with a blue fleur-de-lis, it was hoisted to the sounds of gunshots, cries and shouts, punctuated by the roar of one of the Company's cannons. Bannatyne stood on the veranda of the governor's house, with David, Mary, Governor Mactavish and his wife. The sick and feeble Mactavish cackled to the others in a thin voice. 'Oh, the fools! Oh, the poor, benighted fools!'

To which David murmured. 'They have more heart than thought just now. Who among us can say they are not right?'

No one answered him, and everyone jumped a little when the cannon unexpectedly roared a second time, its blast echoing seemingly forever between the walls and buildings.

vii

Not much more than a fortnight later, Riel became President upon the resignation of John Bruce. Bruce had no stomach for the harder side of politics. Besides, Louis was de facto leader in any event, and the only one who seemed to be able to go toe-to-toe with the Canadians.

Though the conditions of their confinement were initially dreadful—all forty-eight of them crammed into three rooms under the catwalk at the fort—conditions began to improve. It was still very cold, and the men huddled together for warmth. Mercifully, the sewage in the large slop pails froze almost immediately upon deposit, so that they were spared the possibility of further unpleasantness. But cold pemmican and lukewarm tea did not make for happy prisoners, and initially their behaviour was belligerent. They made a special chorus of rude noises and obscene gestures when the flag of the Provisional Government was raised and taken down each day. But as they tired of such behaviour, particularly when their captors were in the best position to retaliate—one grinning fellow spat into the pemmican bag before handing it in to them—the prisoners became more subdued. Only one among them, surpassing even Schultz, seemed to be unrelenting in his hatred of the Métis. This was Thomas Scott.

As tensions abated—after all these were once neighbours if not friends—the prisoners were detained under more relaxed conditions. On Christmas eve, as well as the next day, dances were held, complete with rum and plum pudding, beef and sweetbreads. At certain points, even the guards joined in the jigging and square dancing. Riel required that those who were to be released were to swear upon their oath that they would respect the Provisional Government, or that they would leave Rupert's Land and not return in arms against her. Several made this pledge, and were released. But a hard core of Canadians refused to bend, and they remained antagonistic to Riel and his followers. Schultz and Scott were at the centre of these and they had their sympathizers.

Along the Assiniboine, out to Portage la Prairie, were scattered knots of pro-Canadian Protestants, who considered that Riel's actions were nothing less than treasonous banditry. These were men who were in the main opportunists, who saw their fortunes increasing with the transfer to Canada. Milner Hart and Captain Webb, Johnathan Snow and Captain Charles Arkoll Boulton were typical of those waiting for Riel to slip. Boulton had a commission in the Royal Canadian Regiment, and had served in the army for a decade. These were all members of the survey crew organized by Dennis, but Dennis had left for Canada in disgrace, along with the hapless McDougall; his last order had been to lay down arms and to 'cease from further action under the appeal' made by McDougall to move against the Provisional Government.

It was by the agency of those who conspired against Riel, as well as the slackened discipline of the guards, that small knives were smuggled into the gaol. By chewing at the window casings after dark with the short blades, enough margin was gained to wiggle the iron bars from their seats. When a diversion was created, several men escaped undetected until the morning. It was 9 January, and the cold stabbed at the flesh like a flint knife. Many were recaptured; some of them had frozen fingers and toes and were rounded up easily by the Métis on horseback, early the following morning. But Scott and Mair, two of the most virulent enemies of the Provisional Government, made their way first to Headingly, where they were taken in, warmed and fed; then to Portage la Prairie, where their welcome was even more enthusiastic. They fell to making plans immediately for the recapture of Fort Garry and the release of the other prisoners, most notably Schultz. Scott stirred the imaginations of the English-speaking settlers at Portage la Prairie and Headingly, with horrifying details of his confinement, citing starvation, humiliation, and hinting darkly of 'indignities to his person, too hideous to mention'.

But Schultz himself escaped twelve days later, using a small folding knife which his wife had secreted in her corset. Thought to be secure, the second floor of the gaol had no bars on any of the upper windows. Schultz cut his sleeping robe into a single strand, winding his blade around the skin in a spiral to the centre. As he let himself down, the hide failed where he had drawn too close to the edge, and he plummeted to the snow-covered ground, injuring his leg and back. Despite the fingers of pain clawing at his groin and hip, he made good his escape north to Kildonan, where he was kept hidden, notwithstanding a frenzied search by his erstwhile captors. Their anger and frustration were audible in their cries and signals to one another, as they criss-crossed the settlement.

Meanwhile, in Portage la Prairie Scott and his cohorts were getting up an expedition to retake the fort. Gathering support along the way, the expedition numbered about one hundred men or so, when they were forced to hold over at Headingly for two days by a storm that made travel impossible; visibility was down to a yard or two. Boulton was the only one with real military experience; yet the others took him to be irresolute and tentative in judgement. In his memoirs, he was to write that he had gone along just to keep things from getting out of hand, to lend a steadying influence.

By the middle of February, the cells were empty of all remaining prisoners; yet the threat of the approaching rag-tag band of irregulars from Portage la Prairie threatened what was so far an uneasy peace. On the fourteenth of February, the group forced its way into the home of Henri Coutu, who was known to provide shelter frequently to Riel, but, as luck would have it, Riel was not there, and the flustered Canadians muttered their apologies to Coutu and his family, and continued on.

It was their plan to meet up with Schultz, who had been active among the northern parishes, fanning anti-Riel and anti-Métis passions. On the 15 of February, Schultz set out from St Andrews at the head of almost two hundred men marching in an uneven column. The little army was divided by a team of oxen pulling two cannon taken from the Lower Fort. These were small, defensive pieces hardly suited for the assault which was planned. But spirits were high, and racial hatred imbued the brigade with a sense of omnipotent superiority. Schultz called up a song, improvising to focus upon the object of their march. The tune was that of 'Hey, Johnny Cope', the old Jacobite song:

> *Hey, Riel are ye waking yet?*
> *Or are ye're drums a-beating yet?*
> *If ye're nae waking, we'll nae wait,*
> *For we'll take the fort this morning!*
>
> *Hey, Riel, ha' ye been to hell?*
> *For we'll send ye there this morning!*

Schultz dominated the assembly of men with his physical presence and powerful voice. He brooked no dissent, shouted over those who questioned him, and Boulton, who was the nominal commandant, stood in his shadow. Though there were two separate contingents, Schultz was clearly the leader.

On the following day there occurred an incident which would ultimately see the plans of the insurgents come unravelled.

Norbert Parisien was a simple soul. His feeble mind was the product of a long and wrenching delivery, it was said, that almost killed his mother. Indians and Métis tended to be superstitious, and the mad were considered to be possessed by spirits who were more or less mischievous, or perhaps even malignant. So it was that one made the sign of the cross after crossing paths with such a person, or otherwise invoked the protection of the unworldly powers.

Not yet in his twenties, Norbert was a hard worker, if a little strange in his behaviour. Several of the English-speaking settlers in St Andrews would employ him, though for a pittance, to stack logs, split firewood, clear snow and the like. Trudging to Kildonan, on his way home, he stumbled across the little expeditionary force, still singing and calling out, brandishing their weapons. Immediately Norbert began to act in a suspicious manner, skulking behind snowdrifts to get a better look at the procession.

All at once he was seen, chased and seized. His belt axe was confiscated, and he was tied up with a strap. He was placed under arrest until it could be decided what to do with him, and what charges would be brought. He was placed in a shed, the door of which was bound by leather hinges. Using an ice saw, he was easily able to cut through the hinges and, creeping about the unguarded compound, he snatched a new rifle from its moose-skin scabbard tied to the side of a sleigh. He then fled, though the cold air carried to him the hue and cry raised by his captors, as they discovered the door hanging askew on its hasp.

Meanwhile, on the other side of the river, John Sutherland, a settler of Scots descent, had returned to his house from the Upper Fort, where he, Bannatyne and David Bloode had been pleading with Louis that the remaining prisoners should be released immediately; no further purpose could be served by their detention, Sutherland had argued successfully. Bannatyne had considerable credibility with the detainees, and eventually he was able to convince them that they should sign the requisite promise to the Provisional Government. Rumours of their liberation were becoming more persistent, and many decided that it seemed likely that Riel and his ilk were not going to be lording it over anyone very much longer. It was a good result, and Sutherland was beaming as he and David stood in the square at Fort Garry.

'I shall return home at once; it is a good thing that we have done here. I feel certain that this, if nothing else, will avert hostilities. No blood has been spilled, and the transition to Canada may yet be a peaceful one.'

David smiled, showing his relief. 'I think Riel was right to insist that the Canadians take seriously the matter of our titles, and the issues of lands for public use. I too am happy that there is no need for any further show of force.

'But I fear that the little lawyer from Pembina—that strange little man with no legs who could probably run circles around me with his clever, intriguing tongue—will still try to convince Riel that a union with America is the better option. Especially should the Canadians send more administrators like that fool McDougall.'

Sutherland smiled. 'Well, one problem at a time. When I reach home, I think I'll send my son on to the Lower Fort to speak to Boulton. He's a level-headed sort, and I shouldn't think he'll hesitate to call off this militia force he's commanding, once they know that the prisoners are all free.'

The two men parted, bidding each other a good night. Early the next morning, Sutherland sent his son, John Hugh, to carry the news to Captain Boulton, as he had planned. The fates had cast their lots so as to ensure that the paths of the young Sutherland and the boy Parisien would cross. Seeing Sutherland bearing toward him, lying low across the back of his father's chestnut mare, Parisien panicked and fired twice. The first shot passed wide, but the second struck the astonished young man below the collarbone, wrenching him from his mount, and tumbling him bloodied into the snow. Sutherland was dimly aware of the wild-eyed simpleton edging past him, then throwing away his rifle and floundering off. Parisien ran on, drawing laboured breaths like a winded hound. He turned only once, when his pursuers came upon the mortally wounded Sutherland. They let out a great cry, which all but obscured his faint plea.

'No, boys! The poor simple fellow was too frightened to know what he was doing! No…'

The Canadians caught up with Norbert not more than a quarter mile beyond, and as their footfalls padded close upon him, he turned, whimpering and covered his head with his hands. They fell upon him like wolves, the man in front striking him with a hatchet. The blow laid open the side of his head, severed his ear and dislocated his jaw. It was a frightful injury, and Norbert screamed plaintively. Several others laid on with kicks and fist, until the semi-conscious boy was bound up with his own sash. Seized under the arms by two men, Norbert, head lolling and streaming blood, was dragged at a run back to the Fort.

Captain Boulton had ridden out after the chase, and met the returning men. Appalled, he flung himself from his pony's back, and screamed at the men to untie their prisoner and attend him. Much of the heat had left them now, and they were able to see with a clearer eye what they had done, and the true nature of their quarry. Later, as the truth came out, there were still denials of culpability, though fainter as the sorry tale unfolded. A pall settled over the Canadians when within forty-eight hours Norbert Parisien died, convulsing and crying out for his mother. She sat at his bedside, weeping and clutching his unknowing hand.

As the Canadians and their supporters from the English-speaking settlements pondered the next move, and the wisdom of continuing against Riel now that all the prisoners had been released, a conciliatory note arrived from Louis. He had given considerable thought to what he should say to them; as yet he had not heard with any clarity what had transpired between Sutherland and Parisien. He entreated the Canadians and their followers to understand the terrible cost of civil war, and how Schultz would laugh if after all the settlement were to be destroyed. He reminded them that the prisoners were freed, and that they had sworn to keep the peace. 'Governor William Mactavish has asked you, for the sake of God, to form and complete the Provisional Government. Your representatives have joined us on that ground. Who will now come and destroy the Red River Settlement?'

Schultz sensed that the impetus was disintegrating, and he slipped away, determined to make his way to Ontario, where he could more effectively maintain a campaign of hatred against Riel. He would exact his revenge, but the time was not propitious.

With the disheartening events came a malaise among the men, which was exacerbated by the entreaties of the clergy, and the regular, sorrowful visits of Mrs Sutherland and her friends who had joined her in mourning. They pleaded with the men to return to their homes, and give up the challenge by force to the Provisional Government. They resorted to all sorts of histrionics: kneeling in the snow and praying, and throwing themselves at the feet of Boulton's men. Boulton, never very certain of any course of action he had chosen, was unnerved, and began to argue that all should return to their homes, after matters had 'cooled off' in a couple of days.

Soon a debate was raised afresh. What would be the manner of the retreat? To 'return singly' like coyotes slinking in and out of shadows, or, having 'come down like brave men, we should go back like brave men, in a body'. Boulton argued for discretion and caution. He suggested that they take advantage of their sympathetic hosts in Kildonan and St Andrews, then set out for home in small groups, so as not to attract attention. The majority of men sneered at this, urging him to 'be a man, and go right on'. Thus dared in the face of his little band of troops, Boulton's pride overruled his better judgement, and he agreed to lead the men in a column to their homes in Headingly, Poplar Point and Portage la Prairie. The men were satisfied that they would be able to hold their heads high; that they had not knuckled under to 'that French bastard'; that they would retain their weapons, and be it assured that they would respond to a further call to arms, should the occasion warrant.

The group moved off along the River Road to the Portage Trail. When taking a rest, Boulton pointed out that the march would take them practically under the ramparts of the Upper Fort, Scott derided him for his 'overweaning caution'.

'Come sir. Buck up your courage for this last defiance. We shall make a good show of it yet. There may be a medal in it for you, when the reports are sent back to Ontario!' Scott was sarcastic to the point of vitriol, and Boulton despised him for it. But Scott's manipulations were such that Boulton feared the scorn and low esteem of the men more than the risks which Scott was asking him to undergo. So the column proceeded, without cannons, but with rifles and musketry bristling. Their fighting song was revived, but the men soon fell silent; the aggressive language was incongruous with what was, after all, a retreat.

At Winnipeg, David was on the roof of his warehouse. The whole settlement knew that a small force of armed men was approaching, but there were conflicting reports as to their intent. Were they truly returning to their homes, or was that merely a ruse? Would they be so foolhardy as to try an assault on the fort? To be safe, David had moved his family to St Norbert; many other men had done the same with their own kin. Soldiers under Riel's command were scouring the town looking for weapons. Bannatyne told David that they had demanded all his powder. When he had refused, his storehouse had been invaded; the door smashed in, and the stock 'looted', as he had put it. David had yielded his stock of explosives, all the while wondering if there was a man among them who understood the nature of such devices, and how carefully fuses must be set and detonated. Many a farmer, through impatience or damp materials, had lost a hand, or had blown away his features or worse, in the mishandling of explosives.

Just before noon on the eighteenth of February, 1870, the column with its sleighs and horses came into view at the northern edge of town. The men were clearly bearing arms; no advance rider had made their intentions known. Boulton had made a final plea that the procession not proceed so close to the fort, and at the last minute it was agreed to pass to the west a mile to the north of the fort. But what did their actions mean? Was this a flanking action, to come at the fort on its less guarded west or south side? Was it a feint? Various opinions were formed by the onlookers atop the many buildings, and excited cries of advice and conjecture were exchanged. Lépine, in charge of the military decisions called down to Riel, who was standing with his face uplifted to the catwalks, his expression interrogatory.

'It is not clear what they do! They may intend to surround us! We cannot risk it!' He slid down a ladder, his moccasined feet curved around the sidepieces, coming heavily to ground. 'We go to meet them!'

Boulton saw the riders come out in a frenzied gallop, muskets on thigh, left hand to rein. These were the buffalo hunters in their element, and his straggling column would be cut to pieces, he was sure. Turning, he shouted to his men. 'Not a shot! Not a single shot to be fired, on any account, or we shall be destroyed where we stand!'

His men needed no reassurance on this score; the Métis horsemen assumed a chase formation, and closed upon the marchers with guns across forearms. Weapons were hurriedly thrown down, and hands raised. Scott, cursing his colleagues and hurling racial insults at the approaching riders, was the last to put down his rifle. He did so reluctantly, slamming it against the sleigh with an oath directed toward

Boulton. All were taken prisoner without a shot, and the Métis tore off their hats looking for the hated Schultz. All the sleighs were pulled apart, and their disappointment at not finding their prize was evident. The prisoners were gathered up and marched into the cold, inhospitable cells which had been vacated by their brethren but two days before. Boulton was distraught over these events; his pleas that no aggressive intent had been present were ignored. Scott was disgusted with Boulton, and made no secret of it. 'Damned coward! Why don't you ask permission to lick the froggie's asses! Have a little pride, for there must be a thimbleful of English blood in your veins!'

Boulton ignored these searing insults, for Scott was soon to turn them on his captors, needling them without letup, inventing the most obscene gestures, and reserving the foulest remarks for their clergy and their God. Though Boulton could see the intensity of the hatred that Scott was engendering in his guards, he resolved to say nothing further to the man, feeling perhaps a little smugly that he was probably going to get what he richly deserved.

However, toward the end of the day Boulton was summoned to what he was horrified to learn was a court-martial for his military misdeeds. Having been judged 'guilty' within a matter of minutes, he was led back to his cell in shock to await the deliberation on his fate. A few minutes later, Riel approached his place of confinement, and opened the unlocked door; Boulton was sitting on a bench, quite apparently in a daze.

'Major Boulton, you must prepare to die tomorrow at twelve o'clock.'

Boulton blinked. 'Very well,' was all he could muster. Riel left him, stupefied, staring at the wall.

David heard the news within the hour. Word had spread through the settlement like the plague; no one was untouched. Though death visited frequently and often terribly on the frontier, there was an inevitability to it. It was a natural consequence of risk, and risks there were aplenty. But to march a man to a wall and deliberately cut him down for a wrong not clearly established, seemed in this case disproportionate and misguided. Not even the Métis actively supported such an action, though none came forward to protest.

Others did. Andrew Bannatyne and a Halfbreed woman by the name of MacVicar attempted to dissuade Louis from the execution, but were turned away. Miss MacVicar went immediately to the Sutherland house, which was still draped in black, the occupants still in mourning for their son, to request that the Sutherlands intercede on behalf of Boulton. Mrs Sutherland agreed to come, and the emotion of her own loss caused a dramatic scene in Riel's chambers.

As she attempted to plead the case for Boulton, Louis interrupted, saying, 'No, Mrs Sutherland, Boulton must die. I hold him responsible for your son's death.'

At this, her composure gave way, and she threw herself at Louis' feet, putting her arms around his legs, and crying. 'Mercy! Mercy! Mercy!' Others in the room supported her to her feet, urging that her prayer be heeded by the only one who could show clemency. Louis balanced himself on a small table, visibly shaken by these entreaties, and bade them all leave, promising to think carefully on 'all that had been said.'

He was still unnerved the following morning by such a show of humility. And this from a white woman. When Donald Smith, the chief representative of the Hudson's Bay Company in Canada, and special envoy of the Prime Minister, called upon him, Louis displayed the appearance of a man who had not slept the entire night. His clothes were rumpled, he was ungroomed, and he paced the room like a cat. Smith was there to argue for a stay of execution, but he put the case on a somewhat different footing. He made the point that the execution was not well-conceived in the sense that such an act would deeply divide the community between English and French-speaking people. There was a fair degree of consensus already about the forthcoming negotiations with Canada, but this would be jeopardized by an act of bloodshed, which 'no civilized nation could possibly sanction'. An act of pardon would in fact have quite the opposite effect; it would generate good will, and actually speed the cause rather than impede it, as surely would transpire if the present decision were allowed to run its course.

Louis knew that what Smith was saying was true. He pressed Smith to commit to help with the negotiations, using his considerable influence with Ottawa. Though Smith was uneasy about the appearance of taking up the side of what might be construed in the east as rebellion, he felt he had no choice, and agreed. Word was sent to the prison that Boulton had been given amnesty, and the Archdeacon who was attending to Boulton rushed to give him the news. Boulton had requested a pint of brandy, 'to warm me, lest the shivering in the bitter cold be taken as fear', he had said. But in truth, he was frightened, and his greatest anxiety was that he would collapse before the moment, involuntarily piss in his pants as the rifles were raised, or give way to some other such unmanly display. He had already started in on the flask when the Archdeacon crashed into his room with the news. Boulton fainted. He was not aware, much later, when his captors came into his cell and struck off his leg irons. He had a vague recollection that Riel himself paid him a visit that night to enlist his support. But it may have been a dream.

If Thomas Scott had been contemptuous of Boulton before this, he was openly hostile to him now. He accused Boulton of 'selling himself to the enemy', and 'traitorous conduct'. These were such intense allegations that the other prisoners regarded Boulton with distrust, and they ostracized him. Scott saw himself as the leader in the absence of Schultz, particularly now with the perceived defection of Boulton who was out to save his own neck. The reversal of the execution order convinced Scott that the Métis leader had no courage; a fop, no more than a cleric with no stomach to do the necessary. This emboldened him, and he and another of the prisoners, Murdoch McLeod, set out to harass and provoke their guards afresh. Soon the world would know what cowardly bastards these creatures of polluted blood were all about.

For the next ten days, neither Scott nor McLeod lost an opportunity to inflame the temper of their captors. Their insults, especially those of Scott, were so vicious that even some of the other prisoners tried to restrain Scott's excesses. But he merely turned on them with a contemptuous sneer. 'Have you forgotten who you are? You would have me toady to these swamp-dwellers? These god-damned savages?' It was easier to sit back, even encourage the two of them, than to risk reflected wrath. Scott was a wiry, muscular man, quick to challenge, and just as quick to raise his fists.

On the twenty-eighth of February, Scott was being served his evening meal, which consisted of a slab of rye bread and a tin bowl of soup. He watched the liquid being decanted from a double-handled pan, with an expression of disgust. He looked around to his comrades with a sneer, saying, 'Isn't there a dictum somewhere that one should never eat soup prepared in a prison?' The others cackled; one of them called out. 'Watch 'e don't piss in it, now, if'n he hasn't already!' Scott turned back to the grim-faced Métis guard, who knew little English, but who got the sense of what was being said.

'Has your scabby little asshole been anywhere near this broth? For the colour of it is suspicious enough!' More snickers. He held the bowl closer to the lip of the pan, but a little splashed onto the back of his hand. Holding the bowl with the other, he raised his hand slowly, and licked the spillage away, saying as he did. 'What did you do that for, you ignorant cretin?'

Their eyes met as Scott flung the bowl of hot liquid in his face. The man shouted, more in surprise than pain, dropped the soup and tumbled over backwards.

'That'll teach you to mind your manners,' scoffed Scott.

The guard was up and on him like a wounded lynx, spitting and howling for all he could muster. This was the final insult. The two men rolled about, tipping over furniture, as other guards joined in, and the squirming body of Thomas Scott was carried outside and slung over the back of a cart. A length of board was fetched, and a muscular tripman prepared to give Scott a thrashing he would not soon forget.

Such was Scott's strength and determination that they could not keep him pinned so that his buttocks could be paddled, and before long there was a struggling clutch of men in the packed snow, shouting and cursing. This attracted the attention of a member of Louis's council, who ran over to see what the fuss was about. Tensions were subsiding with Boulton's reprieve, and Louis had left instructions that no further incidents of Métis instigation should take place. Scott was ordered to be put back in cells, where he was chained to the wall by left hand and right foot. Defiant to the last snap of his shackles, he was left with a cuff and a curse.

Louis had retired to the house of Henri Coutu, which had been ransacked by Scott and his followers in their search for him earlier that month. The stress of the insurrection against his provisional government, and in particular the agonies he had undergone in the Boulton affair, left him weak and with a powerful headache. For the four days before Scott had closely escaped his beating, Louis lay in bed with cold compresses on his forehead. A doctor had been summoned, and pronounced that the illness was 'brain fever'; he applied counter-irritants to Louis' feet and chest that only seemed to increase his discomfort. His mother was called, priests attended, and his friends and advisors gathered about. On the first day of March he seemed to improve, and he was told of the affair with Scott. It was clear that the Canadian was going to continue his abuse of the guards, and anyone associated with him. He was obnoxious, foul-mouthed, and profane. Something had to be done. Louis agreed to speak to him.

That afternoon, Louis went unaccompanied to Scott's cell; he was now detained alone and away from the others. There had been a noticeable diminishment in the ebullience of the other prisoners since Scott had been removed. The man sat sullen and unresponsive, his left hand slack in the metal ring at shoulder level. He was unshaven, and close to him, Louis could smell the fetid odor of his unwashed body. Louis pulled up a stool, and sat looking at him for a moment.

'I have been to see the guards. They are not happy with you, to say the least.' His voice was low, almost deferential. He hoped to reason with Scott. Scott did not respond, nor did he turn his head. But his eyes slid sideways, so that he could take the measure of the man for whom his hatred was so intense it clouded all other judgement.

'Boulton has been spared, as you know. It is our wish that no further trouble occur. Your...your provocations will surely lead to some harm. It almost happened yesterday, I am told.' Again, nothing from Scott. Louis spoke again, a hint of exasperation in his voice.

'Come, let us reason with one another...?'

Scott made hawking noises in his throat. 'Reason? Reason with a bloody pirate like you? I'd have better luck with a blind pig!' Louis blinked, for the rudeness and harsh tone of voice took him by surprise.

'You're nothing more than a murdering savage, what's driven out all decent folk. I'd just as soon wait for the military force from Ontario to put things right; they'll be here soon enough. And then it'll be my special privilege to watch them hang you like the criminal you are!'

Louis felt the blood rush to the base of his ears, as it always did when he was sharply contradicted; he felt the skin at the corners of his mouth want to pull back in a snarl, but he fought to keep his composure. Scott saw the inner struggle, and almost grinned. He was succeeding in upending this coarse pretender.

Louis struggled to keep calm, and said evenly. 'I ask for nothing but your co-operation. Do I have your answer...?'

Before he could quite finish the sentence, Scott hawked again deep in his throat, turned to Louis, and spat a gob of phlegm at him, striking him on the forehead.

'There's my answer!' he screamed, half rising against his restraints. 'There's my god-damned answer!' As Louis left the room, shuddering with rage, he drew his handekerchief, and wiped his face. Scott's mocking laughter and vilification followed him to the other end of the square. The insult had been witnessed by two of Louis' colleagues, and they fell to consideration of a proper response.

viii

Within two days, a consensus was reached. Had such an affront taken place on the hunt, there would have been a summary trial of the issue, and punishment meted out. The entire settlement became aware of the deliberations, and once again the passions of the citizens were aroused. David remembered an attempted assault on a hunt long ago, and how the offender was adjudged, his equipment destroyed, how he was driven off a great distance from the camp with nothing more than the clothes on his back; surely a death sentence. But with the Boulton horror safely passed, no one feared that there would be a repetition of bad judgement.

A council was struck for due consideration of the charges brought against Scott. These were insubordination and incitement of the other prisoners. Ambroise Lépine was Chief of Council. The assessors were Joseph Delorme, Elzéar Lagimodière, Janvier Richot, Elzéar Goulet, Baptiste Lépine, André Nault (the young farmer who had come across the first survey crew), and a recorder, Joseph Nolin, one of the lads chosen by Taché to go to Montréal to study with Louis, but whose parents could not bear to let him leave. This was not to be a hearing driven by the sentiments or passions of one man; yet the Métis thought as one. It was the culture of the hunt, of the plains. Survival depended upon a strict adherence to a code of conduct implicit to a marginal way of life. The council was assembled by request in some cases; others offered to serve. These were men of standing in the community who did not shrink from unpleasant duty.

The Council convened informally after the evening meal, as might have happened while out on the plains. Several witnesses were called who detailed Scott's behaviour as well as his instigations in the raising of a force against the Provisional Government. Scott was not present for this. Nolin administered the oath to each one who testified, but they were not asked questions that might test their recollection, or explore their bias. At length, Scott was brought in, shackled at wrist and ankle. He was surprised when Louis advised him in English that charges brought against him had been made out. Witnesses had been called and each had made it plain, under oath, that Scott was one of the central figures in the uprising of the Canadians and other English-speaking settlers, and that his animosity and 'criminal intentions' had continued unabated. What did he have to say in response?

Scott was nonplussed. The only person who spoke English was Riel. Scott did not understand a single word of French, and looking around the room, he could tell that this was not an audience sympathetic to him. Blustering in front of his comrades was one thing, but here, the menace was palpable. Still, Scott was not a coward. He straightened up, and addressed Louis. 'You speak of 'charges'; am I to understand that this is some sort of trial? By what authority do you exercise jurisdiction over me?'

Lépine spoke to Louis, saying that Scott should address his remarks to himself, as President of the Court. Louis translated this, though Lépine had some command of English. Next, Nolin was asked to read from his notes the gist of what had been alleged against Scott; after a hesitant beginning, Nolin turned to Louis sheepishly, and explained that his notes were inadequate. Colour rising in his cheeks, Louis summarized all that had taken place.

Scott asserted that it was not for him to make a reply to such 'fatuous allegations'. 'Where are these accusers, that I might look them in the eye?' He repeated his questions about the right of a irregular tribunal to sit in judgement of him, but no reply was made.

Then Janvier Richot stood up and announced what was apparent to all. 'There can be no doubt that what has been alleged has occurred. I propose that this man be put to death. He has offended against all rules of decency, good order and public peace. He remains a threat to the calm so important to negotiations with Canada. Last, there must be some show of determination to rule ourselves, else we will never be taken seriously.'

Many in the room nodded as Richot spoke. Nault stood up to confirm Richot's motion. And Delorme and Goulet stood as well, indicating their agreement.

Baptiste Lépine objected, arguing that this was far too severe a penalty, and his brother agreed. Lagimodière felt that banishment would accomplish all that was necessary, for even the worst kinds of offences had traditionally been resolved by sending a man out of the country, never to return on pain of being shot on sight. But each held firm to his vote, and Ambroise Lépine shrugged, and turned to look at the uncomprehending prisoner. Scott could see by the expressions of the participants that the debate was not going well for him.

In English marked with a thick French accent, Lépine addressed the surly captive. 'This Council has found that the wrongs alleged against you have been made out; it is a decision of the majority that you be put to death. That is all. Take him away.' He nodded to the guards.

Scott let out a gasp of breath. 'You would murder me? For what? Because I spat on your leader? Because I spilled soup on someone?' He craned his neck around, as if to fix them with his contempt. 'This is justice? You wretched bastards have no shame!' And he was led away, though uncharacteristically without struggle.

For a time, the room was silent. Then Lépine stood up. 'It is done,' he said simply. A low murmur started among the others. This was an awful business, the pronouncement of a man's finish. But this was the easy part. There was yet the dreadful act to see through. Lépine moved quickly, choosing a firing squad of six men. The second last man to be chosen rolled his eyes in a wordless plea to be excused, but Lépine ignored the gesture. He explained that he wanted their muskets; he would load each one, but only three have would have balls, the others powder and wadding only. He looked into their eyes, and saw that no one had taste for this work. He advised each to contemplate his duty in prayer, and each take a swig—but only one!—of rum to steady the nerves.

A Methodist preacher, Reverend George Young, was intercepted upon Riel's orders, and asked to see the prisoner, who had already been loosened somewhat from his bonds and supplied with pen and paper for any last missives he might wish to send. Scott was in a state of disbelief. 'They mean to shoot me tomorrow! For what? There must be something that can be done, is there not? I believe they are bad enough,' he told the cleric, 'but I can hardly think that they dare do it.'

Young attempted to soothe the distraught young man. 'Yes, quite so. I believe this is nothing more than a threat to silence you. Remember, Major Boulton was condemned in the same way. And in the same fashion, you shall be spared. I am sure of it. I am quite sure of it!'

Scott could not mask his true character, however, and said with the barest trace of a sneer. 'Forgive me, sir, if I express that your certainty on the matter gives me little comfort.'

Young was taken aback, but quickly put the rebuff down to the terrible tensions of the moment. He declared that he would be trying to get an audience with Riel, and would solicit other support from prominent members of the settlement. He backed out of the small, cold cell, and was gone. Scott hurled the inkwell, in which ice had already started to form, across the room where it shattered, leaving a large black stain slowly spreading down the wall.

Louis felt the agonizing fingers of doubt pressing against the back of his skull, firm as the clutch of a felon. 'It must be done,' he said to the empty room, knowing that soon he would be receiving delegations to plead clemency on Scott's behalf. He decided that all comers should be put off till the morning, so that he could get some rest, and so be able to make his position clear to everyone. The matter had passed from an issue of guilt and penalty to one of larger principle. He was President of a Provisional Government which had greater legitimacy than any other claimant to power in the settlement. No one seemed to understand this. Not Ottawa. Not London. Not Washington. Not even a foul-tempered scrabbler like Scott. Well, an example had to be set.

Death and the rituals which surrounded it sent powerful and expressive signals about a people, their culture, their system of beliefs. Louis knew this well enough. He mused over the all-night disputations he used to have with his friends in Montréal; what would they think if they could see him now? How much more difficult it was to translate the esoteric, sometimes facile, occasionally tendentious arguments to the real world. Well, if Scott had to be sacrificed on the altar of expedience to facilitate a greater good, then so be it. He, acting alone, had not condemned him. Surely he was bound to carry out the just decisions of the majority of his Council convened for that very purpose? He was no better than those who had elected him, nor those who sat with him in council.

Louis lay on the narrow cot in his shadowed room. The only light came from the pale glow cast from the next building through the thickly frosted panes. It was cool enough that he could see the disintegrating vapour of his own breath as it rose above him like a phantom. He was aware of the unusual level of activity outside, as word spread of Scott's execution scheduled for noon the following day. He could not sleep, for a contradictory torment raged within him. The influence of American frontier democrats, most notably the intellectually adroit, legless lawyer, Enos Stutsman, had pushed him toward his natural inclination of due-process, rights-oriented politics. This was reflected in his 'List of Rights' document produced on December twenty-seventh, the previous year, and of which he was very proud. This would form part of his legacy to his people; to his father.

But the clergy who had made the greatest impression upon his thinking were those who were militant in the protection of the Roman Catholic faith and the French language, and the hegemony of these two institutions over all else. But how were these beliefs to be accommodated within fundamental rights? He felt that this had been accomplished in the 'List of Rights'. Yet Scott had been condemned by a court which gave him neither his language, save his own interpretation, which could hardly be said to have the appearance of impartiality, nor due process as a British subject might understand that term. Yet his 'List of Rights' demanded that 'all customs and useages existing at the time of the transfer be respected'. Scott had been tried in the tradition of the hunt. He could not have expected any more, or any less than had he committed his offences while in company out on the plains. It was upon this slender technicality that Louis took solace.

This brought to mind Scott's expressed measure of scorn for him, President or no; the humiliation of being spat upon burned Louis' cheeks, and he raised his hand to his forehead as if the spittle was yet there. Abruptly, he swung his legs off the bed and sat up. Burying his head in his hands, he uttered a prayer in a low voice. 'Lord help me and guide me; I put my hand in thine, that thou might show me the way.'

ix

Louis shook his head. A dreadful business, this taking of a life. He could not shake the awful weight of responsibility. Perhaps to take a life was to give up a apart of one's soul. He shuddered as he snugged up the collar of his coat. Perhaps a walk would clear his head. Outside, a light dusting of snow had fallen, and the moon was edging out from behind the departing clouds. The stars stood sharply against the black velvet of the prairie sky. The air was sharp, it being well below freezing, and the snow scrunched underfoot. Louis pulled his fur hat low, and wound a long scarf around his lower face, for he needed to think, and did not wish passersby to intrude on his solitude.

Across the square in front of the fort, David and his wife Mary had come to get more information about the decision to execute Scott. Could it really be true? Would this not be the very thing to speed along the rumoured military force? Could this trigger military action from the United States? Large contingents of cavalry were now being deployed, with the conclusion of the Civil War, to the western territories, to contain the Indians. Destroy them, if the stories filtering out of Montana were anything close to accurate. And what about the Fenians? It altogether seemed to be too much of a powder keg to risk some sort of precipitous action like the killing of a Protestant Orangeman with ties to that troublemaker Schultz. At base, David was simply worried about his property, and any retribution that might befall those who either took part, or failed to intercede on the side of temperance and calm judgement. If it were possible, he would try to speak with Louis, though he had heard that the President was not admitting anyone to his chambers.

Almost as an afterthought he took Mary along with him, for her ties to the Métis side of her family were well known, and he thought this might lend additional weight to whatever he had to say. Besides, Riel was well known for his weakness for attractive women. He seemed impossibly romantic, showed almost fulsome deference, and was courtly and considerate in the company of a woman. His reaction to Mrs Sutherland's pleadings on behalf of Boulton had been common currency in the settlement's gossip.

As they hurried in the clear evening moonlight, David caught sight of a passerby, head down, walking slowly toward the arched gate. Above him, hanging listlessly from the flagpole, was the flag of the Provisional Government, startlingly white in the lunar stillness. David looked back to the stranger, narrowed his eyes, and said softly to Mary: 'That's Riel. I recognize the walk; sort of a swinging stride, with the elbows bent just so. Come on!'

Taking her by the mitted hand, he pulled her along after him. She agreed. 'Yes, that's him.' She shared her husband's fears about the future. While the demands of the Provisionals seemed reasonable enough, no one could say how they would ultimately be received. Killing an easterner, for what seemed now little more than bad manners, had the makings of folly. Even she, who took no interest in politics, could see that.

As they caught up with Louis, he was hailed by another figure who approached from the opposite direction. The French was clumsy. 'Excusez-moi, Monsieur. Attendez, s'il vous plaît!'

David was annoyed, and he squinted to see who it was. Damn. It was that surveyor, Snow. Hadn't he returned to Ontario?

Louis looked with some disfavour at all three people who had accosted him. But he understood that a certain quality of statesmanship went with the position he now held, and especially now with the English-speaking people, he wanted to be courteous, if not effusive. In English, he addressed all three. 'I see that my walk shall not proceed much further for the moment. How can I help you?' He waved off a soldier who had come down from his sentry post to check on the gathering.

Snow spoke first. 'I have heard that you will put the troublemaker Scott out of his misery at last. Is it true?'

Louis looked at him curiously; in the silver light, his dark eyes glittered with energy, but he replied calmly. 'He was found responsible for certain acts against the present regime, and a majority of the court decided in favour of execution. Yes.'

'Well,' said Johnathan, 'Good riddance to bad rubbish. The stories over at Emmerling's tavern, however, seem to have it that this is nothing more than a ploy to scare the Canadians into submission. Like Boulton. So when I saw you walking by, I thought I would find out for myself.'

David looked at this man, who had taken off his hat, and was toying with it as he spoke. The red hair, the features, the build: it was like looking in a mirror. But he tore his attention away and spoke to Riel. 'Forgive my impertinence; I am David Bloode as you may remember; this is my wife Mary Daniel Bloode—we have met on other occasions briefly. I am here to urge you to reconsider the fate of the Canadian Scott, if in fact the stories are true that he is to be dispatched tomorrow.'

Riel shook his head slowly. 'Stories? You heard what I have said to Mr Snow here. The decision has been taken; I shall not interfere.'

Snow broke in. 'The man is homicidal. On one occasion he tried to drown me, and only by the narrowest of margins did I escape. He and his ilk know nothing but a firm hand. You must be resolute, sir.'

Louis nodded. 'I heard of the incident. The man attacked me last year as well, quite unprovoked. Drunk, he was. Quite intoxicated. But on this present issue, I will not supplant my judgement for that of six others.'

David tried to make light of the matter. 'Well sir, good judgement as we all know comes from experience. And experience comes from poor judgement. In this case, is there any need to learn what we already know? That no life is worth taking for any reason save no other option exists?'

'You speak of poor judgement,' said Louis. 'Our system is not a perfect, not even a near-perfect technology of justice. Any more than the British model, grandly dressed in its wigs and robes. It is simply what it appears to be: six ordinary mortals striving to reach a result which reflects and honours their community. And preserves it,' he added after a pause.

David put his hand up, as if to signal a halt. 'But this 'community' you speak of has many dimensions. I am English-speaking, though I understand the French tongue. By all accounts, no English-speaking citizen was on the Council. How could Scott participate? Or comprehend?'

Louis was faintly annoyed, and he had the tone of a patient teacher explaining to a slow student. 'The English here, for the most part, have taken a passive stance, but for those who threw in their lot with Schultz and Scott. Would you now have it that those who stood indifferent to our struggle participate in judgement?

'Or would you perhaps nominate our enemies—those who took up arms against us—to sit in judgement of their own? I believe that destiny will prove that the actions we took were right, though it may not appear so to some, presently.'

David was not used to debate; Louis clearly was. David responded passionately. 'Even if our countrymen were to shriek with delight at Scott's demise, that cannot justify his killing. I have seen enough men killed in my lifetime. The fact is, no pressing circumstance exists here—or existed, to call for Scott to be put to death.'

Johnathan interjected before Louis could speak. He was identical in height to David, and looked him directly in the eye. Louis was slightly shorter, and as the two men faced each other, he took an imperceptible step back.

'Do you not see the need for example?' asked Johnathan. 'For a lesson to be made of someone like Scott, violent and uncouth, so that others like-minded will be deterred? So the rest of us can get on with our affairs in peace? God in heaven, there is no law here! One is unsafe on the streets or in the wilderness.'

He added almost as an afterthought, 'The lesson is important, for it instructs in the matter of power. Then we know with whom we have to deal. Yes, a lesson is necessary, even if it's a rough lesson.'

Louis gestured with his mitted hand. 'Precisely. No regime could ever be taken seriously without a clear signal that it has the determination to carry through with the decisions of its executive. No matter how distasteful the matter may be.'

Mary gasped, and the others turned to look at her. It was not a woman's place to participate in men's debate, but a woman was owed deference when she wished to speak.

'Is that what this is all about?' she cried. 'You would condemn someone just to make a political statement? I have had my own…unhappy experiences with courts, and I must say that the thought here expressed frightens me. They are capable of mistakes. Rough lesson? It won't do.'

Louis spoke softly. 'I don't know the nature of your experience, Madame, but I doubt it could have been of the cruel type evidenced by Mr Scott…'

'I am not proud of my involvement; it was a very long time ago. But I was heard, and the Court let me go. That seems to be the missing piece here: that Scott was not heard.'

Louis shrugged. 'The court which considered your matter was one constituted and paid for by the Hudson's Bay Company; yet you were fairly treated. Is it so incomprehensible to think that justice was not done in the Scott affair?'

Mary opened her mouth to speak, but her husband waved her off.

'Yes!' interjected David. 'Because the result is so plainly unfair in its result! No lives were lost save those of poor Parisien and Sutherland. And Scott cannot be held responsible for them.'

'So say you,' said Johnathan. 'Scott was part of the mob who seized Parisien and chopped him up with an axe like so much firewood! I personally have been roughly treated at his hands, and…'

'How can you assign him responsibility for those deaths?' responded David. 'To this day no one knows with certainty who laid those blows upon him. Besides, this is not what the case is about.' He turned to Louis.

'Why is this death so necessary? Is it just to show who rules here? Is there not another way?'

Louis spoke in the same measured tones he used with Mary. He seemed weary, for the moonlight made his face seem weathered and deeply seamed, as if he had aged far beyond his twenty-five years.

'It is tempting to answer you simply. The more power I have, or more correctly, my government has, the more I have to lose by actions which can be construed as suppression. The greater the inducement to use the power, the more measured should be the response. The taking of a man's life must be considered the most serious response; I concede that. But it is not so simple in Scott's case.

'At stake here is the central issue of our legitimacy. Provisional we may be, but we are still in control of our own goverment, recognized even by Mr William Mactavish himself, and supported at least to some extent by Donald Smith, the representative of the Prime Minister.'

Johnathan agreed, saying. 'You have it right, sir. The rational exercise of government is the only proper response to brute force, even if the result is ultimately the same. One is the apprentice, the other is adversary to reason.'

Mary was exasperated. 'This is just noise! We are here, Monsieur le Président, to ask you to exercise mercy. There is no good to come of this. The death of this man is not moral, and I fear we shall all lose for it.'

The cold had insinuated itself under their clothing, and they were all getting a little uncomfortable. Each rocked back and forth, or took small steps to and fro, so as to keep the blood moving. Mary was surprised at herself; she cared about very little, but in this, her husband's anxiety for the future had infected her with her own concerns for the settlement's prospects. To shoot a man down in the street seemed a poor way to begin as a territory or a province. Even she could see that, she told herself.

But this meddling man Snow irritated her. She studied his face, half silvered, half shadowed. She was struck by the resemblance to David; at a short distance, she could not tell them apart. But here, she saw a hardness to his features that was missing in David. Missing even when he had been rough with her. This was enough to banish further speculation, though she continued to steal puzzled glances at Snow's face.

David spoke at last, for the silence hung heavy and awkward when it was becoming clear that the cold would soon drive them all inside, and their debate remained unresolved. 'Isn't it so that we react to things out of self-interest? But we hardly ever admit that. So we weave a bright tapestry to cloak our true motives, taking threads of grand ideals, patriotism, religion and appeals to honour. But it all boils down to the same thing, this self-interest. It is so hard to admit it. Who will challenge motives based on patriotism? Do I not love this place as much as you? Yet, there is a self-interest for me in this execution And for you—you have as much as said so.

'Let me declare my own self-interest: I am here to plead for amnesty for Scott, for the sake of our community's future. I neither know him, nor do I have any connection with him. But like my wife, I believe that no good will come of this affair unless you relent.'

Johnathan again spoke before Louis could answer. 'Well, let me have a last word, before I lose all sensation in my toes.

'Consciousness of the moral dimension of human life is the mark, the badge of a modern society. Believe me, I have seen it very much the other way in some of the primitive societies I have visited. And moral choices are nothing more than rules about how we treat one another—and the consequences for their breach.

'In Scott's case, his violence toward recognized order has forfeited his right to live here, and he must die. It's a hard thing, perhaps, but if there's no certainty in decisions, there will be anarchy, and perhaps others will die. Who knows? One must die so that many others will have peace. That's what this all comes down to.'

Louis studied all three for a moment, then he smiled. But it was a thin, humourless smile. 'So. Two for the sentence passed; two for remission, with neither side carrying the day.

'It may well be that I will regret not interfering with this matter, but the interest of the people must be first, and it is in their interest that this decision was reached.

'And it is in their interest that I decline to reverse it. You must excuse me, Madame et Messieurs, for I have had a very long day, and I must be abed.' And with this, Louis walked quickly away, waving off another who hurried up to speak to him. Within a moment, he was gone.

Three of them looked at each other. Johnathan offered his hand, after tugging off his mitten. 'We have not formally met: Johnathan Snow, engineer and Dominion Surveyor.'

David took his hand, though without warmth. He introduced Mary, and could see the flicker of interest in Johnathan's eyes; he looked at Mary as if for the first time. She had this effect on men, he sighed to himself. Without Snow, there might have been a chance to persuade Riel. But the man had been forceful, and Riel had paid close attention to what he had said. David had put his case poorly and had not been convincing.

Johnathan spoke. 'Don't look so sorrowful, Scott has brought this upon himself.'

'I care nothing for Scott,' David snapped back. 'He has provoked men beyond reason, and stands no higher in my estimation than his co-conspirator, Schultz. It's a wonder that others have not raised their hands to him before this, including you, if I follow the story of your near-dunking correctly.

'But the shots to be fired tomorrow will echo far beyond the walls of the stone fort, I fear. Our small world will not be the same.'

'We are living in frightening times,' Mary added, moving closer to her husband's buffalo coat for warmth. 'The Company would sell us and our lands to Canada like serfs. By objecting to this, we are called 'rebels', and still others take up arms against us.

'Now to put a stop to all this, we say that someone must die. It appears as if we have invented the means of our destruction, and now seem determined to try it out, even though we know the result.

'Come,' she tugged at David's arm. 'I'm chilled, and this has been of no use. Perhaps others will approach him and persuade him not to pursue this madness.'

With a nod to Snow, they left him standing there, a man seemingly aligned with their interests, but opposed to their vision. For his part, Snow was ever more convinced that white men who allow their blood to be sullied with the lower orders were eternally unfit to govern. He had seen it time and time again. They acted with the heart, not the head; passion rather than reason. They were fools when it came to understanding the business of civilization.

Two Métis entered Scott's cell in late morning. He had begun to think that they were not going to come for him at all, that this had just been in the way of a scare tactic. But here they were, two burly men to escort him from the prison. He was permitted to make rounds of the other prisoners, to say such last words as he felt appropriate. Then his hands were tied behind his back, and he was led, silent and disbelieving, into the bright sunlight. Behind him, one of the prisoners, Jack Henderson, the pugnacious tripman who had tangled with David, called out. 'Take courage, Tom Scott! This foul deed will be avenged! This I swear on my mother's grave!'

Looking back to the pale faces of his cell mates, Scott began to splutter. 'This is unbelievable! This is horrible! This is cold-blooded murder!'

As he was brought up against a wall of the fort, he could see that large numbers of townsfolk had gathered to watch the spectacle. They were some distance off, as if no one wanted to draw close to the doomed man. This above all disconcerted Scott, for it seemed an indecent thing that they should watch the butchery, and he said so, to no one in particular.

A length of white bunting was drawn tightly around his eyes, with the uneven ends dangling like pigtails over his shoulders. He opened his mouth to speak, but only a quavering bleat sounded. His knees shook visibly to onlookers, and he cried out as his shoulders were seized and he was forced to his knees in the snow. Reverend Young began the Lord's Prayer, unevenly, for his own discomfiture showed on his face. Scott recited the verse along with him, in words that sounded somewhere between a sob and a gasp. Other members of the Protestant clergy appealed to one member after another of the official party, but the only reply they got from Louis' men was that 'it was too far gone.'

Scott's eyes strained to see through the transluscent bandage over his eyes. As the prayer proceeded, the words barely sounded in his throat. The thin warmth of the March sun beat down on the grim pageant, and birds sang in the surrounding buildings. André Nault raised his hand, in which he clutched a balled-up handkerchief; the rifle muzzles rose as one, though none too steadily. As the prayer reached its last line, the bright piece of cloth was dropped, and the muskets, all but one, crashed in an uneven sputter, sending a shattered echo from the stone walls of the fort. In the crowd several women screamed, for the front of Scott's shirt had erupted in blood, and he had catapulted backwards, stretching out in the snow. He was not dead. His moaning was grotesque and prolonged and continued until Guilmette, one of the firing squad, stepped forward with a pistol, held it against Scott's head, and pulled the trigger. There were more short, sharp screams from the crowd, and the young man in the executors' line who had not fired his weapon, cried out, flung his musket away, and fled in tears.

Immediately, the burial party organized by Lépine seized the body and stuffed it into a rough plank coffin. Several thumps were heard, but this was due to the rough handling of those eager to be done with an unpleasant task under the largely condemning glare of public scrutiny. But the sounds were enough to start the rumours, which ultimately found their way to eastern Ontario, that Scott was still alive when he was buried. Reverend Young's demand for custody of the corpse was rejected by Lépine, and affirmed by Louis. There was a real fear that the burial service might be a flashpoint for another show of resistance against the Provisional Government.

David and Mary had watched the proceedings: some obscene tableau, at once fascinating, yet repelling. The trill of finches and the five-note warble of the chickadee were strangely incongruous with this methodical destruction of a man's life. This nasty, ill-tempered labourer was put to death, not to even some cosmic scale, but as a pawn in a political struggle. He could see that; why couldn't Riel? But perhaps he could, and this, thought David, made the man a murderer, just as the Canadians and Canadian sympathizers in the audience were muttering under their breath.

David felt a hand on his shoulder; it was Johnathan Snow. The two men were bare headed, and both had thick manes of coppery red hair, streaked with grey at the temples. Their similarities were startling enough for those nearby who had recovered their composure, to comment on it.

'A man next to me has just asked if you are my brother! I replied that though I believe that we grew up worlds apart, one cannot rule out anything in this day and age.'

'I regret I am in no mood for banter,' said David. 'What I have just seen has revolted me, and saddened me. It puts all at risk, I am certain. I am distressed that Riel cannot see it.'

Johnathan shook his head. 'This is but a minor skirmish in an important struggle. As I said last night, Scott brought this on his own head; there are many who agree with me.'

David's voice was tinged with despondency. 'Scott has ceased to exist, but he'll live on for those who would have him as a symbol of oppression. Riel, of course, lives, but he is dead, as a symbol of unfairness. By one sorrowful act. And there may be a thousand such apologists as you, the quality of that act will not change.'

'Aren't you being just a little melodramatic? Isn't this overstatement?'

'Overstatement?' queried David. 'In the entire span of human activities, there is no greater wrong than the taking of a man's life where there is no justice in it; no justification. The Ten Commandments, remember: thou shalt not kill. There it is, among the first rules of God.

'That wretched corpse which they manhandle into a rough box there, moments ago was a living, breathing man who was destroyed principally so that Ottawa and London would sit up and pay attention to us.

'You can be sure they will. And it's my wager that they will be visiting upon us a much larger force, with graver consequences than we presently think.

'That's it then,' responded Johnathan. 'You're afraid. You have not the stomach to do what has to be done, to assure yourself that your own interests will be protected. That force you fear will come anyway.

'If someone were to attack your beautiful wife, here,' and he touched his hat in deference to her. 'Pardon me, Madam. You would kill him, because it is justified. Perhaps out of fear for the consequences to her. But this is something you see. It is immediate.

'What I ask of you is that you try to look beyond this poor but unlamented fellow Scott, to things that are not so clear, but just as important. Matters such as rights and protection, laws, customs, legislatures and property. Are these things not worth even a single life? Wars have been fought over less.'

David furrowed his brow in thought. 'I'm losing the thread of this discussion. All that I hear is your accusation of cowardice—'

'No!' interjected Johnathan.

'Let me finish,' demanded David. 'I don't know why this matters, that I should convince you of anything. I know nothing of you, save that you have your own interests in this—'

Mary, impatient with debate at any time, turned away from the grisly spectacle of the burial party trying to cram Scott's long legs into a space that was reluctant to receive them. 'Yes. You were seen pacing off claims for yourself, south of my father's farm. The guarantees Riel seeks would operate to protect your interests as well. Isn't this just opportunity for you, nothing more?'

'Quite so. I have no shame in that. I take, as you and your people have seized land from the aborigines who possessed it before them. It is simply a matter of being at the front of the line. But that's not the issue. What neither of you seems to apprehend is the larger view. You just cannot see past this tragic but insignificant event.'

His shoulders sagging, David let his breath hiss between his teeth. 'That's how evil has its way in this tired world. Give it legitimacy by supplying a "larger purpose"; the "larger picture". The fact is that evil can only have life in the hands of men, and its existence is always justified on the basis that it is necessary, or that it is a justifiable means to an end, or that someone of lower station has not the same entitlements. Whatever. All I know is that wrongdoing begets its own miserable consequences.'

David turned, taking Mary's arm, and walked away; Johnathan stood watching them, shaking his head slowly. Pathetic people, he thought, almost of another, gentler time. So different from me and my tribe. They will be flattened before the relentless approach of civilization. He had seen it in India; the lesson was repeating here.

x

*A*n event in Louis' life, seemingly small and inconsequential, always returned to his thoughts when he was depressed or feeling lonely. When he was a boy of eight, his father took him in one of the grand boats which plied the waterways bounded by Hudson's Bay, the Arctic, and Red River. It was only a short trip from the St Vital landing to the cathedral in St Boniface opposite the Forks. The tripmen were dressed gaily in their best clothes, with bright sashes and stocking caps. All wore the crucifix on a pendant slung around the neck. Traditional voyageur songs timed the strokes on the oars, and the unladen craft skimmed along the river, startling ducks and geese, and attracting the shouts of inhabitants along the way.

To Louis, this was a thrilling event, and one of those which profoundly bonded him to Red River. The powerful oarsmen with arms of corded sinew, the rich voices of the bowsmen and steersmen who led the refrain in deep baritone, and his beloved father who held him safely on the centre thwart, combined to engrave an image of heroic pride in Louis' mind.

But it was a soloist in the bow of the boat who captivated him. The man sang the way an angel must sound, thought Louis. The song he remembered was Petit Rocher, Little Rock, and it concluded as the brigade pulled up on the shore at St Boniface. The ride was over. The last verse captured a sweet pathos which Louis felt was the haven of the true believer.

C'est donc ici que le mond' m'abandonné!
Mais j'ai secours en vous, Sauveur des hommes!
Très-Sainte Vierge, ah! m'abandonnez pas,
Permettez-moi d'mourir entre vos bras!

Here then it is that the world me abandons,
But I seek aid in the Saviour of mankind.
Most Holy Maid! ah, do not me forsake,
Let me but die in your arms, I refuge take!

The tune echoed in his mind as steady as a hymn. He had just refused the Reverend Young the right to take the body of Thomas Scott for a 'proper Christian burial'. He had firm advice on the issue that it would offer potential for more trouble, but he was far from sure, even now as doubts gnawed at his conscience, over the still-warm body of the dead man. He saw the look of disgust on the cleric's face, and saw and heard the reactions of incredulity among those to whom he repeated his refusal to intervene. His own men were in some disarray; the firing squad had nearly disgraced themselves. Some of them had taken more than a single draft of rum, and one did not even fire his weapon, which probably necessitated the coup de grace which had so sickened onlookers. Louis had reached out to steady himself against the door frame where he was standing, when it became apparent that the volley had not dispatched the condemned man. He felt as lonely and abandoned as he had the day he received news that his father had died. The voyageur boat song reverberated ominously in his head.

Louis retreated into his room at the fort, his head pounding with a familiar tension. It was necessary, he told himself, to intimidate the conspirators. The Canadians could not be trusted. They were waiting for another chance to rise against his government. There were no options. He had to be taken seriously. He had been defeated so many times by those who would not consider him worthy. This time it would be different.

He lay on his cot, arms folded across his chest, and fought the demons of doubt. I must put aside such misgivings, such thoughts of regret; there is no going back, not even for a single heartbeat. Only a fool dwells on such things. The good or the right choice must be made sooner or later, and the only way one ever is to know is to transcend, rather than suppress doubt. Pretending doubts do not exist is different than having the courage to face them.

He rolled off the sleeping robe, and knelt with clasped hands on the frigid floor. For a long moment he tried to pray, but all that came to mind were snippets from the boat song: '...do not me forsake; in your arms I refuge take...'

In her bed, Mary awoke with a start. She had been dreaming of the shooting; she had not been able to get her mind off the events of the day. David was not beside her, and this alarmed her for a moment. Settling back on her pillow, she thought back to the early days of their marriage. It had started out as a union of convenience for her, and probably him, if she were to be candid. She had seen him as a way to leave Red River, for he represented money and opportunity. She had been disappointed when she had realized how little he had, but over the years she had come to understand that she had no desire to leave the settlement.

She had not been a faithful wife, and she had been outraged when Sayer finally did marry. It was obvious that he wasn't being faithful to her either, toward the end. Then David had begun to abuse her. She became afraid of him, disgusted by him. His disfigurations, the teeth marks on his buttock, and the torn ear, which were once objects that intrigued her, had started to sicken her. Yet there was no thought of leaving him, for reasons that were not entirely clear to her. After Schultz laid him out on the warehouse floor, he had not abused her again, and gradually they had come to a truce. It was as much the political events in the settlement as anything else that had started to change both of them. The difference now, she thought, was that they were both starting to look to the future, and the kind of life that their children might have.

She had found, she decided, what the churchgoers called 'faith'. She had discussed it with David once, and he had searched for a passage in Scripture that he thought he recalled. It was from Hebrews, he had announced with a small note of triumph.

'Yes, here it is, the first verse of Chapter Eleven.' She remembered the pleasure on his face as he recited to her.

Faith is the substance
of things hoped for;
the evidence of things
not seen.

That was it, of course. What her father had taken away from her, she could give back to her own children. What she had stolen from David, she could not give back. But she could repair. Her jealousy over the closeness of Edwin Bell's friendship, her infidelity, her anger; these things could be put right over time. And there was time left, she thought, though she worried about what the future would bring, given the tumultuous days in which they presently lived. Already she could sense that Johnathan Snow, that man who so strangely resembled David, was wrong in his intuition. The execution that day had aroused deep divisions which she feared would catch people like David and her in between.

These were new thoughts for Mary. She had started to look into herself, without really understanding why it should be so. She had never loved anyone, not even herself, and she was not certain that she could now. When she feared David, it was an emotion she knew and understood, for it was how she related to her brutal father. With the future now so clouded, she had nothing to hold onto; everything was uncertain as the result of the cruel violence she had witnessed. She was aware of the hugely increased tensions in the settlement, and while ordinarily she was indifferent to the concerns of others, this was different, and worrisome.

All that she had at present was her relationship with David, her children for whom she now had hopes for a better life, and the gradual discovery that she had no desire to leave this place. It was strange, this feeling for Red River. All at once she rose from the bed and, drawing a robe around her shoulders, went to the window to see if she could see David.

David could not sleep. The death of Scott had appalled him in a way that was imponderable to him. He had seen many men die; sudden and violent death was almost a fixed condition of life on the frontier, or a consequence of association with rough people, he thought. Frequently, these were one and the same thing, because so much was 'up for grabs' as the American traders used to put it, and it took a certain sort of man to elbow others out of the way. But he had not taken Riel for that sort of man. He was plainly a God-fearing man, careful in speech, educated and poised.

He clasped his hands at the nape of his neck, and stared at the moonlight trapped in the thick, rippled panes of glass in the dormer casement. Perhaps that was it. He had no way to recognize the face of evil any longer. He had concluded that Riel was not an evil man, yet his refusal to interfere in a case that cried out for justice was an evil act, without doubt. All the more so since it appeared he intended to use the results of this verdict and sentence for his own political purposes.

He tried to understand his own fear. Cruelty and violence had always exacted this reaction, and at his core, he was convinced that he was nothing more than a coward. He searched the tapestry of his life for some example of conduct that might be described as courageous, but nothing came to mind, and that troubled him. He decided to get up and go outside. This always served to clear his head. It would be several hours before dawn, but the moon had not yet set, and a fresh, light snow had just fallen. He rose silently, leaving Mary's inert form at one side of the bed. He could hear her measured breathing as he dressed, and envied her untroubled sleep. He stood over her, and felt a burst of unexpected and irrational fondness for her; he rationalized that the thought had to do as much with affection as it had with the fact that she would keep the bed warm for him, when he returned, chilled from his walk.

Outside, he stepped with an expert twist of his ankle into his snowshoe harnesses, and set off for the river. It was only a few minutes' jog, and he could set off unimpeded by fences or drifts. He loved it on the snow-covered ice. The snowshoes made a rhythmic whispering sound as he sped along, and the freezing air bit satisfyingly at his face. The moon illuminated the frozen river like a great, silent highway, and the treed banks were a tangle of dark shadows. It was as if David were the only human being left alive on earth. All that existed to contradict this sensation was the faint tang of woodsmoke in the air which, because of the cold, kept close to the ground.

Well over an hour headed north, he was beginning to feel the effort in his calves, and his mind was beginning to empty as the body gave its all to the run. He could feel a tingle in the cluster of scars on his buttocks, where Wakandayamani had put her mark on him, all those years ago. David always felt this peculiar sensation when he became chilled, and it reminded him of the circumstances under which the teeth marks had been put there. For a time he allowed the tides of memory to wash up vignettes, irregular and disjointed, of his childhood.

Overhead, the canopy of stars glistened sharply, and the aurora borealis shivered and crackled in the northern sky. The moon was nearly down, snared in a tangle of oak branches on the western bank just over David's left shoulder. All at once, as he rounded a broad sweep of the river, he saw a fire burning, a short distance out on the ice. There were figures passing to and from the fire. David was remote enough that he could not see how many, or what they were about, but he knew that this was approximately where a small creek joined the larger flow, and the ice was generally not the usual three or four feet thick. The men were probably ice fishing; that was it, for such a bright fire built so close to the hole attracted fish. It was odd that this activity would be carried out at such a late hour, but perhaps they had a pail of sweet tea set at the edge of the blaze, and he decided to make for the little group, and rest with them for a bit.

He kept close to the east bank, as that was where they were, but as he approached, he could see that they were not fishing. They had just completed the hole in the ice, and David could see even from a distance that it was a large one. Uneasy, David moved in close to the bank, and slowed his pace. There were five men in all, and they were engaged in removing something stiff and unwieldy from a long box-like object. He gasped. It was a coffin, and the form that they wrestled with was clearly that of a man, frozen awkwardly, but a man. They manoeuvred the corpse to the edge of the hole in the ice, and slid it in. One of the party took the coffin and upended it onto the fire. The flames shot up as the casket was consumed, brightly illuminating the grisly scene. David could hear words of admonishment being exchanged. With saplings in hand, the men surrounded the opening, working at the body. It was apparent that it was being levered under the ice so that the slow winter current would carry it further downstream before the spring flood.

David was sickened. Turning, he fled back along his path. Was Scott so feared that even in death he had to be put out of the way of exercising some phantom influence over the affairs of men at Red River? If that was the motive, thought David, there was probably no clandestine burial place that could safely harbour the body. Even in death, his mocking, sarcastic laughter would sound over the settlement.

As he moved along with these thoughts pursuing him like shadows, David thought of death. Was there indeed a life beyond, as he had been taught, as all rational men believed? What was it like, apart from some transitory pain? Maybe there wasn't any suffering at all, at the actual moment, unless of course one died as Scott had done. Maybe it was a release of the spirit to some greater happiness.

But never to hear the wind whispering her secrets to the brooding jackpines? Never to smell the earthen pungency after a fresh rain, or a summer storm pattering among the fretting poplars, always shivering and rattling? And never to see the sun again, setting like a reluctant sigh, having cast away all her glittering jewels on the roiled surface of the river? Never again to experience the glorious pageant of the seasons, that bursting forth, maturation and expiration by which one might measure one's own life? David decided he wanted to live a while yet. It was the fear of death that underlay the joy in life.

David shivered as he moved along, both from the cold and his thoughts. More from his fears, perhaps. But he decided that there was a difference between death on terms that could include such matters as timing and fulfillment, and a finish like Scott's, which had neither grace nor purpose. Bleating protests and soiling his trousers, a bully had his life snuffed out without having made very much in the living of it. He had settled no terms with life, much less his death. But the destruction of such a man told more about the executioners than it did the condemned, and David feared that by not making sufficient effort to intervene, he stood on the firing line himself. This was but one of many entries in his life's ledger he would need to balance, if he could, before his own time arrived. In a sudden flash of insight, David concluded that he had been wrong to think that it was the event—sickness, death, relationships, or accident—that brought about change; it was how one chose to react which dictated the sort of change that would occur. All possible occurrences short of one's own demise had no influence over how a man selected how he was to respond; the choice lay within oneself.

Increasing his pace at the foot of the bank where he had descended a couple of hours earlier, he swept up to the ridge, and turned south again in the direction of his home. He was surprised and pleased to see that a lamp had been lighted and placed in the small bedroom window, a softly glowing beacon in a sombre settlement filled with shadow and gloom. It occurred to him that perhaps that which he was seeking had been with him all along. And that this discovery was one which all men must make at some point in their lives before they may be truly happy.

Turning again for a moment, panting, he pondered the broad, familiar expanse of the snow-covered river, darkened now that the moon had gone. This river would flow through the settlement, indifferent to the cares of man, till the end of all time. It established not only constancy, but place. There were such places like the country through which this river passed, defined by memory and circumstance, to which the heart was always drawn. There is an ineluctable connection between all living things and the land which nurtures them, and it is in the contemplation of that bond and the experience of it that one is able to say: this is my home.

Notes and Acknowledgments

This book was inspired by the life of Isabel Gunn, who came to Red River in 1804. Sir Alex, who is fictional, speaks of her in Chapter 3. Nothing is known of her son, the first white birth in Western Canada. Victoria is fictional, though her persona is carefully patterned after Isabel Gunn. Johnathan's character is based on this event, though there is of course no established linkage between Johnathan Snow the surveyor, and Red River, before he actually came out to develop the Dawson Road in the eighteen sixties. David and Ephraim are characters who are entirely fictional, but they are composites of frontier characters whose experiences are not far removed from the daily lives of Red River.

Mary Daniel was a real person; the only known reference to her comes from the text of the Hind Expedition, and that confined only to the trial for theft where she was acquitted, as described in Chapter 9. Reverend Thomas is fictional, though most of the events described in the historical backdrop to his character actually took place. The recruiter Binscairth is a fiction. The reality was that representatives of the Hudson's Bay Company were respectable members of the Orkney community.

Nothing is known of Louis Riel's absences from school, though he was eventually expelled for them. Where Thomas Scott finally ended up is unknown, but it seems likely he was sunk under the ice of the Red River.

The details of aboriginal life are as accurate as secondary research permits. Otakle's dream of betrayal by the Europeans is found with astonishing repetition in the literature recording the culture of many native peoples. Dominance and betrayal, it seems, are persistent themes in the history of humanity, no less than they are recurrent in the story of the Red River Valley of the North.

The writing of any book represents the work of many hands. Historical fiction must depend upon the work of recorders and historians to give it the ring of truth. Though much is fictionalized, there is little in this story which may not be reasonably extrapolated from the known record, save what is set out above. The selected bibliography which follows identifies some of the many sources upon which this book relies for facts and dates. I am indebted to those scholars and observers whose efforts ensure that the events they describe will not be forgotten. I have not listed obvious primary sources, such as the *Nor'Wester*, which provided a picture of the drama that unfolded in Red River at the time this book was set. I am grateful to the helpful staff at the Provincial Archives of Manitoba, as well as the staff at the Minnesota Historical Society.

Thanks are owed to Chief Henry Skywater of the Birdtail Sioux Band, Melinda Barr, Bob Gosman, Joyce Tait, Greg Yost and Cecille Tessier. Gordon Shillingford is owed special thanks for his unstinting work on this book.

I want to acknowledge the forbearance of my children, Jennifer, Morgan, Ashleigh, Ted and Scott, who allowed me to sit, night after night, at my keyboard. I am indebted to Amy and Jennifer, the grown members of my family, for their sustaining confidence. A debt of gratitude is owed, and hereby recorded, to my wife Christie, whose cheerful support and constructive comments assisted me greatly in the final product.

Finally, I express my appreciation to a thorough, demanding and supportive editor, Helen Burgess, who without doubt made this story a cleaner, easier read. No words can sufficiently express how grateful I am for her generous warmth and enthusiasm throughout this project. I can do no better than to echo Byron once again:

> *Her heart was one of those which most enamour us*
> *Wax to receive, and marble to retain.*

Principal Sources

Anderson, G.C. and A.R. Woolworth, eds.
> *Through Dakota Eyes.*
> St. Paul: Minnesota Historical Society, 1988.

Ballantyne, R.M.
> *The Fur Traders.*
> London: Octopus, 1982.

Begg, Alexander.
> *Red River Journal.*
> Toronto: Champlain Society, 1956.

Begg, Alexander.
> *The Creation of Manitoba.*
> Toronto: Hunter Rose, 1871.

Bentley, Nicolas, ed.
> *Russell's Despatches from the Crimea.*
> London: Andre Deutch, 1966.

Charlebois, Peter.
> *The Life of Louis Riel.*
> Toronto: NC Press, 1978.

Cook, Hugh.
> *The Sikh Wars.*
> London: Leo Cooper, 1975.

Davies, Colin.
> *Louis Riel and the New Nation.*
> Agincourt: Book Society of Canada, 1980.

Edwards, Michael.
> *British India.*
> New York: Taplinger, 1967.

Flanagan, Thomas.
> *Louis 'David' Riel.*
> Toronto: University of Toronto Press, 1979.

Gosman, Robert.
> *The Riel and Lagimodière Families in Métis Society.*
> Winnipeg: Manitoba Provincial Archives,
> unpublished manuscript, 1977.

Hargrave, Joseph James.
> *Red River.*
> Montreal: John Lovell, 1871.

Hind, Henry Y.
> *Narrative of the Canadian Red River Expedition.*
> Edmonton: Charles Tuttle Co., 1971.

Howard, John K.
> *The Strange Empire of Louis Riel.*
> Toronto: Martin Robin, 1974.

Joyce, Michael.
> *Ordeal at Lucknow.*
> London: John Murray, 1938.

Kaye, John W.
> *A History of the Sepoy War.*
> London: W.H. Allan & Co., 1880.

Kingslake, Alexander W.
> *Invasion of the Crimea.*
> London: Blackwood & Sons, 1863.

Laviolette, Gontran.
> *The Dakota Sioux in Canada.*
> Winnipeg: DLM Publications, 1991.

Lussier, A.S., ed.
> *Louis Riel and the Métis.*
> Winnipeg: Pemmican Publications, 1979.

Malleson, G.
> *History of the Indian Mutiny.*
> London: W.H. Allan & Co., 1878.

McDougall, John.
> *In the Days of the Red River Rebellion.*
> Edmonton: University of the Alberta Press, 1983.

Morton, W.L.
> *Manitoba: A History.*
> Toronto: University of Toronto Press, 1967.

O'Suilleabháin, Sean.
> *Irish Wake Amusements.*
> Cork: Merger Press, 1961.

Palliser, John.
> *Exploration of Certain Portions of North America.*
> New York: Greenwood Press, 1969.

Pannekoek, Frits.
> *A Snug Little Flock.*
> Winnipeg: Watson & Dwyer, 1991.

Pemberton, W. Baring.
> *Battles of the Crimea.*
> London: B.T. Batsford, 1962.

Poole, D.C.
>   *Among the Sioux of Dakota.*
>   New York: Van Nostrand, 1881.
Ross, Alexander.
>   *Red River Settlement.*
>   London: Smith & Elder, 1856.
Stanley, George, ed.
>   *Louis Riel: The Collected Writings.*
>   Edmonton: University of Alberta Press, 1985.
Stanley, George.
>   *Louis Riel.*
>   Toronto: Ryerson Press, 1963.
Webb, R.K.
>   *Modern England.*
>   New York: Harper & Row, 1980.
Williams, J. Fletcher
>   *A History of the City of St. Paul.*
>   St. Paul: Minnesota Historical Society, 1983.